VIGILANTE KINGS

THE COMPLETE SERIES

EVA CHANCE
& HARLOW KING

Vigilante Kings: The Complete Series

First Digital Edition, 2023

Cover design: The Pretty Little Design Co.

Ebook ISBN: 978-1-998752-59-1

Hardcover ISBN: 978-1-998752-60-7

SAVAGE SECRETS

VIGILANTE KINGS #1

CHAPTER 1

Madelyn

You could say it was a midnight snack that led to my broken heart.

Normally I wasn't even the late-night-snacker type. I liked sleep too much. But I'd been working for hours getting the last of my end-of-term essays written—the last essay I'd *ever* write before my final high school exams—and I still had at least another page to go. That called for some fortification.

Both Mom and my stepdad, Holand, slept like the dead, but I slipped down the stairs quietly just in case. As I opened the fridge and let the eerie artificial glow spill over me, for just a moment I flashed back to a time more than ten years ago, when I'd woken up ravenous after a bout with the flu and Dad had snuck me downstairs to make me a PB&J sandwich.

He'd probably be making me one now to get me through this essay… if he'd still been alive to do it.

I swallowed down the pang of loss that'd faded but never

disappeared and reached for the fruit drawer. I'd just started to open it when the back door rattled.

With a hitch of my pulse, I straightened up and shut the fridge. The room fell into darkness. Only a thin haze of light seeped in from the streetlamps glowing beyond the kitchen window. From where I was standing, I couldn't see into the mudroom at the back of the house at all.

The deadbolt in the door clicked over. Whoever was there had a key. My mind scrambled for an explanation, knowing both my mom and Holand were upstairs. Unless one of them had ducked out without me noticing while I'd been grinding away at my essay? But why would they come in through the *back* door?

The fact that whoever it was seemed to have a legitimate means of entry was the only thing that kept me from jabbing 9-1-1 into my phone. I stood here stiffly, my hand creeping across the counter to the knife block. As careful footsteps padded inside, I curled my fingers around the handle of the chef's knife.

The cleaver was bigger, but I wasn't confident I could stab someone with that rectangular hunk of metal. Pointy seemed like a safer bet.

The basement stairs creaked faintly. I frowned. Who would sneak into our house just to go down there? The basement only held the laundry room, a storage room stacked with bins of nothing more valuable than dusty Christmas decorations, and the second bathroom.

After a moment, the hiss of running water reached my ears. Bathroom, then. My stance relaxed a little.

It couldn't be a homicidal psycho, right? A murderous lunatic wouldn't break into people's houses just to use the facilities.

And whoever it was hadn't actually broken in.

Still clutching the knife but lowering it to my side, I slunk across the kitchen, through the mudroom, and down the steps to the basement. The cooler underground air raised goosebumps on my arms, and I wished I hadn't already changed into the tank top and lounge pants I'd be sleeping in.

The sound of the water was loud enough to cover my approach. The possible intruder gave no sign that they'd realized they'd been noticed. The bathroom door stood an inch ajar, bright light spilling through the gap. Just as I walked up to it to peek inside, the person on the other side stepped right in front of that space.

He appeared so abruptly that a squeak of shock burst out of me even though I'd recognized the figure on the other side and knew he wasn't any threat. At least, not in the criminal sort of way.

The tap running water couldn't cover my yelp. Before I could retreat—if I'd wanted to retreat, which I hadn't had time to decide—the door flew open.

Logan Brooks, Holand's son and my stepbrother of three years, stood on the other side. He blinked at me, his forehead furrowing.

It was a nice forehead, broad and topped with tufts of dusky brown hair. Even nicer were those startled eyes, a lighter brown so bright they were almost gold. And that was without getting into the body beneath his chiseled face, tall and filled out with generous brawn across the chest and shoulders, tapering to a toned waist.

Okay, so Logan looked a hell of a lot more than just *nice*. He'd probably featured in the steamy daydreams of at least half the female student body at our high school. Seeing him sent a flush through all kinds of places on my own body.

"I—I'm sorry," I said, even as I realized that it was ridiculous to be apologizing for sneaking up on someone who'd just finished sneaking into a house where I lived and he no longer did. "I didn't know it was you."

Logan had moved out last summer, a month before he'd started college. He'd said he'd needed time to get settled into his new digs before classes started. But even though the college was only a two-hour drive away, this was the first time he'd come home—to what had used to be his home, for a couple of years anyway—since then. I hadn't seen him at all except for a brief appearance he'd made during the Christmas get-together with Holand's side of the family at his grandparents' house. One second he'd been grabbing a turkey leg, the next he'd vanished again.

It bothered his dad. I knew it did. Holand tried not to talk about parenting stuff with Mom around me, but I'd noticed the dejected slant of his shoulders when one relative or another would ask what Logan was up to these days. And now the prodigal son was finally stopping by for a visit… in the middle of the night… so he could do a little washing up?

The thought of why he was here had just started to penetrate my initial surprise when Logan tipped his head toward the chef's knife at my side with a ragged chuckle. "And whoever you figured it was, you were planning on slicing and dicing them?"

I would have shot some snarky remark back, except my brain had finally caught up enough to notice the parts of him that *weren't* all that nice at all. He'd been angling himself to the side, but his head had swiveled just enough for me to notice the bruise forming at the corner of his jaw and a small splotch of red on his light blue T-shirt.

My heart lurched, and I pushed forward, dropping the knife on the little table in the hall. Logan grabbed the door to block my way, but I caught it, already having seen as he swiveled more fully toward me that there was a heck of a lot more carnage than what I'd initially spotted.

He had a scrape running across his cheekbone. A thinner cut veered from the crook of his neck down toward the back of his shoulder with blood still beading along it. And his shirt didn't just have a small splotch of what was obviously more blood. There were several larger smears and splatters across the right side, the side he'd been trying to hide from me.

He looked like someone had already been slicing and dicing him.

"What *happened* to you?" I demanded.

Logan's jaw tightened. He pushed on the door. "Don't worry about it, Madelyn. Go back to bed."

There was something a little wild in his eyes that I hadn't noticed before either. But that and the blood weren't enough to stop a prickle of anger from racing through me.

He *used* to call me Maddie. Playfully but fondly, as though we were something like friends. But, for reasons I'd never understood, that companionable familiarity had stopped sometime not long after he and Holand had moved in.

He didn't push firmly enough to stop me from coming in. He didn't want to go too hard on me—because he didn't think I could handle it, just like he didn't think I could handle whatever had brought him here tonight. I shoved past him into the bathroom before he could make a more determined attempt at shutting me out.

As I spun toward him in the small space, he caught my arm by the elbow. His eyes flashed when they met mine, and a tingle of electricity hummed through the air between us.

That had never gone away. If anything, I'd felt it more often after I'd found myself passing him in the hallway in my pajamas or sitting across the table from him at family dinners. Sometimes it seemed like he felt it too. Other times I'd thought it was all in my head.

Right now, some kind of tension was radiating off him. I could practically taste the adrenaline in the air. I had to think it was a whole lot more to do with whatever had gotten him bloodied up than with me, though.

"What do you think you're doing?" he snapped.

"I think I've been studying first aid since I was ten, and if you came here rather than going to a hospital, *someone* had better take a look at you." My gaze dropped to his shirt. Fuck, that was a lot of blood. Oh my God. My stomach lurched. "Maybe you *should* go to the hospital. If you get an infection—"

I shouldn't have said that. I knew I shouldn't have, but the situation was so crazy the words just tumbled out.

Logan cut me off with a noise that was almost a snarl and spun away from me, back toward the sink faucet that was still spewing out water. "Most of it's not mine. You think I look bad; you should see the other guy."

I stared at him, having trouble processing those words, and not just because I had the full expanse of his well-muscled back on display just inches away from me.

Logan hadn't been the type to get into fights. When he stood up to people—to jerks who deserved it—he just shut them down with his words, his confidence, and the natural intimidation that came with his size. I'd rarely seen him lay a hand on anyone.

Because I was staring at his back, I noticed a line of red that was slowly expanding just below his shoulder blade. *Some* of the blood was his.

Logan was splashing water on his face and neck, ignoring me as if that would make me go away. I had the urge to run upstairs for the larger first aid kit we kept in the main bathroom, but I was afraid he'd take off the second I let him out of my sight. So I grabbed the smaller kit out of the cabinet under the sink, popped it open, and yanked up Logan's shirt.

I was trying to keep my mind strictly professional. It wasn't my fault that I noticed the heat of his skin and the flex of his muscles as my hand skimmed over his back.

There was absolutely nothing weird about the fact that being this close to my stepbrother got me all heated up. I'd had a crush on Logan since I was twelve, after he'd told off a bunch of junior-high bullies who'd been taunting me. That was a year before Mom and Holand had even started dating. Technically, Mom had cockblocked—pussy-blocked?—me. I should have had first dibs on the Brooks family.

Logan's head jerked around as I reached for the alcohol wipes. I caught a stutter of breath and tried not to wonder whether my touch had affected him the same way being so close to him affected me.

"What the fuck are you doing?" he growled.

"Making sure you don't end up worse off than whoever you got into it with did," I retorted. "It's going to sting. Deal with it." Then I dabbed the wipe over the narrow cut.

Logan's stance tensed with a restrained wince, but he didn't make a sound. He gripped the sides of the sink as I finished cleaning up the wound as well as I could. The bleeding seemed to be slowing—the cut didn't look that deep. But even a minor infection could be fatal given his medical history.

I smeared antiseptic cream on the spot as gently as I could manage and stuck a gauze pad overtop. The rest of his back looked unharmed, other than that cut curving over his shoulder and dipping beneath the collar of his shirt.

I frowned at it and tapped his shoulder beside the broken skin. "You're going to need to take your shirt right off for me to deal with that one properly."

"For fuck's sake." Logan whirled around to face me. His golden eyes burned into mine, and suddenly it was very hard to focus on my concern for his injuries rather than the effect his presence had on me this close up. His voice came out strained. "I can deal with the rest myself. Leave it alone."

I'd swear there was enough electricity in the room now to raise the hairs on the back of my neck with a quiver of desire. I stared right back at him, my tone firm. "You can let me help, or I'm going upstairs and telling your dad that you're bleeding all over the bathroom. It's up to you."

He glowered back at me. "Why do you always have to be so fucking stubborn, Maddie?"

The nickname gave me a giddy thrill, even though it was the most minor of victories. "Because I need to be, obviously," I said, and tugged at his shirt.

Logan yanked it out of my hands, but he peeled it off, muttering something about how he needed to rinse it off anyway. I did my best not to ogle the expanse of his sculpted chest and focused on the cut by his neck, giving it the same treatment as the one on his back.

Logan's posture remained rigid while I worked. It was a hell of a lot harder to concentrate with him gazing down at me. The musk of his skin washed over me, mixed with a salty aquatic tang as if he'd just come out of the ocean, even though the sea was hours away.

I was more than a little giddy when I stepped back—not far, since there wasn't much space in the bathroom. The whole situation was starting to feel like some kind of hazy dream, maybe because my lack of sleep was catching up with me. Had my long-time crush-slash-stepbrother really showed up in the middle of the night all battered and bruised, or was this some weird fantasy that I'd wake up from any moment now?

There didn't seem to be any other cuts on him. The pale line of his liver transplant scar veered across his abdomen by the perfect V at the low-slung waist of his jeans, and I pulled my gaze away from it.

I'd never known Logan as anything but healthy, and he didn't like the reminders of his childhood illness. Even when he'd been living here, he'd kept the medication he still needed to take in his bedroom and gotten terse with his dad if he ever mentioned it.

"All finished," I said, a little breathless. Logan was still tensed, his chest heaving more than I'd have expected, as if he wasn't done coming down from the fight—or was preparing for another one.

"Good," he said brusquely. "Let me finish washing up, and I'll get out of your hair."

He turned toward the small bathtub without another word, starting the water flowing from the showerhead. As he ducked just his head in to rinse off his own hair, another surge of frustration bubbled up inside me.

"And then you'll disappear for another year like we don't even exist?"

"What are you talking about?" Logan muttered, swiping the hand towel over his head and then sticking his shirt under the spray so streaks of blood coiled through the water spiraling down the drain. "I just saw my dad a few weeks ago."

"Right," I said. "You saw your dad for a coffee or something. You haven't come back *here* since you moved out. We were kind of family for a little while, in case you don't remember. Actually, you obviously do, or you wouldn't have thought you could just drop in and use our bathroom."

"I was halfway through high school when Dad and your mom got married. It was a little late to start picking up new family members. Shouldn't you be getting to bed?"

The words hit me like a slap. Which was probably why I spat out the last thing I'd have wanted to admit to him if I'd been thinking straight. "Did it ever occur to you that maybe *I've* missed *you*, you jerk?"

The complaint might not have been totally fair—or maybe it was way too accurate. The fact was that I'd been missing the Logan I'd fallen for back in junior high since way before he'd moved out.

From the moment he'd started distancing himself from me, leaving rooms as I entered them, not meeting my eyes during those random encounters passing in the hall…

He looked back at me now with a jerk of his head as if the question had startled him. His mouth twisted. "Maddie…"

Before he could figure out what he was going to say, I noticed the bandage I'd done my best to fix to the curve of his shoulder was coming detached. With a curse under my breath, I leapt forward to stick it back down. But Logan's efforts with the shower had left the tiled floor slick from errant spray. My socked feet slipped, and I careened over the edge of the bathtub.

The shower water splattered my hair and tank top. Logan caught me an instant before I banged into the opposite wall and yanked me upright. He spun me away from the tub, glaring down at me—and then something else flickered in his expression.

I was abruptly aware of how the wet tank top clung to my skin, particularly the curves of my breasts. I wasn't wearing a bra. My nipples stood out against the drenched fabric, and I'd swear they tingled to sharper attention as Logan's gaze raked over them.

His hands tightened where he was gripping my upper arms. He closed his eyes, and a tremor passed through his body. "I'm trying to do the right thing here."

I didn't know what he was talking about. It was hard to focus on anything except his touch and the way my body was screaming for him to press even closer. I couldn't stop myself from resting my hand on his chest. My voice tumbled out of me with an unusually husky quality. "So am I."

"*Fuck*," Logan rasped, and the next thing I knew, he was tugging up my chin so his mouth could slam into mine.

The kiss was hot and feral, and it short-circuited my brain. I didn't know how to do anything except kiss him back with all I had in me. His chest grazed mine, sending sparks through my nipples.

Logan groaned at the contact, the sound reverberating into me, and some part of me decided that this was definitely a dream. But it was a fucking fantastic one, so I'd better milk it for all it was worth.

More sparks leapt across my skin everywhere Logan touched. He swept his hands down my sides to my thighs, pausing to massage my ass while his tongue invaded my mouth with searing passion. Then he hefted me onto the edge of the sink without breaking the kiss.

My legs splayed around his hips. He was all over me, his mouth branding mine, his chest scorching, an undeniable bulge behind the fly of his jeans rubbing against my core.

A heady shudder raced through me, and my pussy clenched even as it soaked my panties. I groped at Logan, trying to somehow pull him even closer. My teeth nicked his lip, but he just kissed me harder with another groan.

His hands came up to yank up my damp top, with a strangled sound of approval as he cupped my bare breasts. I gasped against his lips at the jolt of bliss he summoned with one swivel of his palms. Clutching at his neck, I barely remembered to be careful of the bandaged spot. My back arched, pressing my pussy against his groin, and Logan's breath stuttered.

In one smooth movement, he yanked my lounge pants and panties down together without displacing me from the sink. His hand dipped between my legs and found the slickness pooled there.

"Oh, God," he muttered.

A whimper spilled out of me at the contact. God was right, because I was definitely in some kind of heaven.

I fumbled with the door of the medicine cabinet over the toilet and managed to wrench it open to grab the box of condoms stashed there. I made a point of never thinking about why exactly our parents would want to have protection available on every level of the house.

Logan snatched the box from me without a word and retrieved a packet even as he unzipped his jeans with his other hand. His mouth crashed down on mine. His lips and tongue continued their savagely divine assault as he prepared himself.

He rubbed the head of his cock over my pussy from clit to slit, and I practically came just like that. But then he paused, his mouth pulling away just an inch. He was panting, his voice even rougher than before in its plea. "Tell me you're not a virgin."

I sputtered a laugh. "Of course not."

Logan drew even farther back, his eyes abruptly darkening. "That fucker Scott Camden?"

I scowled back at him, momentarily distracted from the deliciousness of this dream. "I did date him for almost a year. I'm not a nun." Logan had always seemed irritated by Scott, though he'd never made any concrete complaints. And him getting pissed off about it now was particularly ridiculous considering— "How many girls did *you* give it up to on the first fucking date?"

Logan dropped his glower, looking briefly abashed, which confirmed enough casual hookups to send irritation flaring through *me*. But then he leaned close again, his forehead coming to rest against mine, and said in a voice so taut it tugged at my heart, "None of them were you."

I wasn't sure what to make of that either, but I did know I wanted to get this moment back on track before he had another change of heart. I gripped the side of his face and said, "It's me now." Then I yanked his mouth back to mine.

He growled against my lips, grasping my thigh, and plunged into me. He filled me so fast and well that a gasp jolted out of me.

With only a few pumps, he found just the right rhythm to send me soaring higher, faster than I'd ever thought was possible. With every roll of his hips, he drove the memory of those mildly satisfying hook-ups with my ex farther from my mind. I raked my fingers over the wet strands of his short-cropped hair, swaying to meet him as well as I could in my precarious position.

Logan kept his hand on my thigh to steady me and teased the other down my spine. His mouth traveled from my lips along my jaw and down the side of my neck, blazing a path over my skin. When I moaned, his breath stuttered.

"So fucking good," I thought I heard him mumble. "Even better than I imagined."

The possibility that he'd already imagined us doing this set me even more aflame. I trailed my fingers down his back, groped the solid planes of his ass, and moaned again when he thrust even deeper inside me.

He braced his arm against my back to curve me over and sucked the tip of my breast into his mouth. At the same time, he tucked his other hand between us. He flicked his tongue over my nipple as he pulsed his thumb against my clit and rammed into my pussy again.

I shattered. A cry that was almost a sob burst out of my throat. My head tipped back against the mirror, pleasure washing over me and wringing me out.

As the afterglow rippled through me, Logan pounded into me a few more times before following me over with one last groan. He eased to a stop, raising his head to lean it next to mine, still holding me in place on the sink. His heat wrapped around me.

I clung on to him in a daze. What happened now? Did I wake up?

Logan withdrew slowly and carefully. His jaw worked for a second. His expression had gone totally opaque, but his chest was still heaving as he recovered his breath.

He zipped up his jeans and eased me off the sink like I was a porcelain figure he was afraid of dropping, pulling my tank top back down over my chest. I reached to retrieve my pants and shimmied into them, still uncertain about where we stood.

"Thank you," he said in a tight voice. "For looking after me. I'm okay. You should really get some sleep." His tone lightened just slightly. "I don't want to be responsible for ruining your perfect attendance record."

There was enough of teasing note in that last line for me to relax a little. I touched his arm, thinking of the blood, the scrapes and cuts, the explanation he'd never really given for them. "Are you sure—"

"I'm fine, Maddie," he said firmly. "It was just—a thing. No big deal, really. I was a lot closer to the house than to my apartment, so I thought it was better to get cleaned up here. That's all. It's over."

That wasn't enough of an answer, but I didn't want to ruin whatever connection we'd just formed by badgering him more. "Okay," I said, holding his gaze.

He looked back at me and gave me a crooked smile. I thought we came to some sort of silent agreement. I thought this was the start of something different.

So I caught his hand to give it a quick squeeze and headed back upstairs, thrilled by the thought that the boy I'd loved for a third of my life wanted me too, still half expecting to wake up and find out I'd dreamed the whole thing.

But I was wrong about a couple of things. I hadn't dreamed it. And nothing was different at all.

After those last words in the basement bathroom, I didn't hear a peep from Logan Brooks for two long years.

CHAPTER 2

Two years later

Madelyn

"It's not like one night of actual fun will kill you," Keeley teased as she leaned closer to the mirror propped on her dresser. She drew her eyeliner in a fine, winged line that I knew I'd never be able to replicate on myself. Which was fine. Makeup was my roommate's thing and not so much mine, which was part of the reason she was teasing me.

I rolled my eyes playfully, throwing my cozy hoodie on over my tee and jeans, which was more about warmth than anything resembling dressing up. Even though it was technically spring now, the chill in the early April air could still be biting, especially after the sun went down.

"*I* think hearing about recent medical developments is fun," I reminded her. "The guy doing the talk is one of the top researchers at this cutting-edge facility in France. This is the first time he's come to the US—I'm lucky he's giving a presentation only an hour's drive from here."

Keeley tsked her tongue. "Or you could come to the club with me and my friends, and we'd see about getting you *really* lucky."

I laughed. "Hey, maybe I'll pick up some hot science geek at the lecture and bring him back to the dorm with me. Watch out for a warning note on the door."

Keeley glanced over at me as if evaluating whether I really had it in me to do something like that. "I'd be more than happy to crash elsewhere. You work, like, twenty-five hours a day, eight days a week. Everyone deserves a break. And hot dudes. Especially on a Friday night."

I shot her a warm smile. "Maybe next week."

My roommate let out a skeptical hum, but she didn't heckle me any further. Right now, she might have been giving the impression of a ditzy party girl more concerned about having a good time than passing her classes, but her double major in political science and psychology and the honors GPA she maintained told a different story. We just cut loose in different ways.

She swept her tight black curls back from her dark face and fixed it into a super cute updo. With a swipe of lipstick across her mouth, she straightened up and grinned at me. "Well, let's both kill it, then."

I poked her in her shoulder, taking in her shimmery club dress. "I think you'll be doing most of the killing, but that's okay."

"We really would love for you to come along with us sometime, you know," Keeley said as we headed out of the room and down the residence's staircase together. "I'm not just saying that. It's a good time. We hang out at my bestie Carmen's place for a couple of hours just chilling, and then we hit the dance floor. I know there's a wild girl under that carefully controlled exterior somewhere, just waiting to burst out."

"I promise you'll be the first to meet her."

We emerged at the edge of the parking lot. It was only late afternoon, giving me plenty of time to drive over to the conference center that was hosting the talk and grab a quick bite to eat before the seven o'clock start, but the breeze was already nippy. I zipped up my hoodie, my gaze skimming over the lengthening shadows stretching from beneath the rows of cars.

A cluster of passing students distracted me. I found myself checking each face before I jerked my eyes away, reining in my automatic curiosity. None of them had been the guy I was looking for anyway.

I'd transferred to the same university as Logan three months ago at the start of the winter semester, and our paths hadn't crossed yet. I didn't know if he even realized I'd made the transfer from my original college in our hometown. I hadn't wanted to ask around about him, which would make me feel even more stalker-y than I already did.

I hadn't *actually* stalked my stepbrother here. I'd wanted to attend the Life Sciences program at this university since before anything had happened between us. It wasn't like I'd expected anything from him anyway. He'd made it clear that he wanted nothing more to do with me when he'd blocked me all over social media as well as by phone the day after our hookup and shut me completely out of his life.

My skin tightened at the thought of the brutal rejection. It still stung a little, sure. And every time I heard a deep chuckle or saw a tall, well-built form at a distance, my pulse might have jumped before I determined it wasn't him. But the healthiest thing for me to do was to erase him from my mind as utterly as he'd erased me from his life. Apparently not just our hookup but the years of casual friendship before our parents had gotten married meant nothing to him, so why should they matter to me?

I strode along the middle row of cars as if I could outrun those thoughts. I always parked my Chevy in the same area, right over…

I stopped several cars from the end of the row, staring at those ahead of me and then sweeping my gaze back in the other direction. My mouth tensed with a frown.

I could have sworn I'd parked in this row after my last trip off campus. I'd been in such a hurry this morning that I couldn't remember if I'd noticed the car then, but I knew I'd seen the familiar green hood with its dented bumper just yesterday evening when I'd walked by on my way back from grabbing dinner.

Keeley had stopped when I had, flipping her keys in her hand. "Is something the matter?"

"My car isn't here," I muttered, confusion starting to give way to a quiver of panic. I scanned the other rows and spun around to march back the way I'd come—and jerked to a halt by an empty stall right around where I thought I'd parked.

This *was* the place where I'd left it. Last week I'd driven down a muddy lane that'd left a red clay-like dirt all over the undercarriage. It'd been flaking off in bits and pieces, and I could see a few fresh chunks of it on the asphalt now, undisturbed by yesterday's rain. The car *had* been here last night, and now it wasn't.

"What the hell!" I blurted out. "Someone stole it."

And not just my car, which I'd bought with my own savings. The flicker of panic turned into a wash of cold horror. I hadn't kept much in the vehicle, just things like lip gloss and mints and an emergency blanket in the trunk, basic objects that could be easily replaced. But there'd also been Dad's trinket box.

That wasn't anything fancy either, but the simple black lacquer box with its silver Celtic knot on the lid couldn't be replaced specifically *because* it'd been Dad's. He'd always kept it on his desk

—every time I saw it, it reminded me of our long talks when he'd listen to me babble on about my childish scientific ideas and guided me with his own knowledge.

Having it with me kept his memory close even hours from home here at college. I'd kept it in my glove compartment with my insurance documents inside. If the car was gone, I'd lost that piece of Dad too.

"Seriously?" Keeley said, knitting her brow. "Are you sure you didn't just park it somewhere different?"

"Completely. That mud came off it." I pointed to the reddish bits in the empty spot. "And it's not anywhere else in the lot. I couldn't have parked in a totally different area of campus without realizing it, right?"

My voice had started to get squeaky. I inhaled deeply to try to calm myself down. Freaking out wasn't going to solve anything.

Keeley swore under her breath. "This is getting ridiculous. I've heard of a few other people who've had their cars stolen off campus parking lots in the past couple of months. Whoever these pricks are, they're—well, they're *major* pricks."

It wasn't just me. Then maybe—

"Did the other people get their cars back?" I asked.

She bit her lip. "Honestly, I'm not sure. I only heard about the thefts, not anything getting resolved. The campus police can be kind of useless for anything where there isn't, like, video evidence."

"Video." My gaze shot to the security camera perched on a post at the edge of the lot, but the frayed wires poking from its base told me it still hadn't been replaced. I let out a groan.

"I could go to the regular police," I suggested.

"They'll just toss it back to Camp-Po. I don't know how much effort those guys will put into tracking down a car for someone whose parents aren't pouring money into the school. But it's worth a shot." Keeley paused and snapped her fingers. "Or you could try talking to the Vigil."

"The Vigil?" I said. The term sounded vaguely familiar, as if I'd heard it mentioned in passing, but I'd never paid enough attention to determine what it was.

Keeley nodded eagerly. "Yeah! They're kind of awesome—from what people say, anyway. It's this group of guys that've set themselves up like PIs on campus. At first, everyone thought they were a joke, but they've solved a bunch of issues. Everyone says if you have something stolen or someone sabotages your work or anything like that, they can usually sort it out."

"Really?" The whole situation sounded a bit weird to me. "Are you sure they could handle something as major as a stolen car?"

"I don't know for sure. This girl in one of my seminars said they tracked down her phone when it got snatched. It couldn't hurt to try, right?"

The tendrils of fear gripping me eased back a little now that I had a tentative plan. "I guess it couldn't. How do I find these guys?"

Keeley waved to the east. "They've got a sort of office in the back of the law library. They hang out there a lot during the day when they don't have class—it might not be too late to catch them now. Or if they're not in, the librarian could have contact info for them."

The longer I dawdled, the more chance I wouldn't be able to catch them until after the weekend. Who knew where my car would have ended up by then? If I couldn't find them, then I'd see if Camp-Po would prove themselves more useful than Keeley had said. But it did make a little sense that students who knew the inner workings of the school on that level might be able to trace the path of a crime and pick up clues faster than the people who just oversaw campus from a professional distance.

"Okay, I'll give it a shot," I said. "Thanks!"

"I hope they can sort it out—and fast." Keeley glanced toward her own car and hesitated. "Do you want me to come with for moral support or whatever?"

It was really sweet of her to offer, especially when she had plans and it wasn't like we were super close. I gave her a smile I hoped was reassuring. "Don't worry about it. You've got dancing to do and hot guys to snag. I can manage a walk across campus."

"Well, good luck!"

I raised my hand in farewell and hurried off along the campus paths toward the law library, which I had a vague impression lay a few buildings over, in the bottom of the Business Studies building. The brisk pace started to smooth out my jangling nerves. I became more aware of the chill outside as the breeze tugged at my long, pale hair. With a shiver, I pulled my hood up.

Thankfully, the campus was better with signage than security technology. After just a minute, I spotted a signpost that confirmed I was heading in the right direction. As the stone building loomed up ahead, my pulse sped up again.

It was no big deal. I'd go in, plead my case, and see what happened. Hell, these Vigil guys might not even be there.

I pushed past the doors into a vast, quiet room nearly as big as the first floor of the main library. At the front of the room, a checkout counter stood across from a few rows of study tables. A dozen or so long shelving units stuffed with books formed aisles along the back half of the space.

No one stood behind the counter. Was I too late to even talk to a librarian? I hustled past the tables and caught a rustling sound from farther down the aisles of shelving units.

A girl who didn't look more than a couple of years older than me was standing in the third aisle with a cart of books, tucking one into its place on the shelf. She had an official-looking tag on her cardigan, so I guessed she was one of the student workers.

She glanced over when I appeared at the end of the aisle. I must have looked a little panicked still, because her face immediately turned serious with concern. “Can I help you with something?”

“Um, yeah,” I said, plastering on my best smile. “I’m looking for the Vigil’s office? Someone told me—”

She let out a light laugh and nodded. “Yeah, that’s here.” She gestured to the wall behind me. “It’s the last door toward the back of the library, past all the study rooms. I think the guys are in.”

Her gaze lingered on me with obvious curiosity as I mumbled my thanks and hurried in the direction she’d indicated.

Doors did line the wall on that side of the space. Most of them had rectangular windows that allowed a view into the study rooms with their plain tables and chairs, but the one on the end offered no view inside. The wooden door held no sign. There was nothing to confirm anyone was inside or even what it was used for.

But the library assistant had sounded totally confident. I squared my shoulders and raised my fist to rap my knuckles against the door.

A friendly male voice filtered through the wood. “It’s open!”

Well, that guy sounded like a helpful type, at least. Slightly reassured, I grasped the handle and pulled the door wide.

There were three figures in the room on the other side, but my eyes caught on the one closest to me, who was standing just a few feet from the doorway and turning to see who’d come in. As our gazes collided, my breath snagged in my throat.

I was staring at Logan Brooks.

CHAPTER 3

Madelyn

I couldn't peel my eyes away from Logan's face. All the tightly suppressed emotions I'd worked so hard to avoid rushed to the surface with a vengeance. My hands had clenched at my sides, my heart thumping twice as fast as before, bracing warily against whatever move my stepbrother might make next.

But it wasn't just alarm clanging through my body. No, there was even more anger than I'd known I was holding in. At him over the way he'd ditched me, at my bad luck that I'd come face to face with him with zero preparation.

Logan's brawny body had gone as rigid as mine. He stared back at me, his mouth forming a flat line, his golden eyes turned hard as steel. Oh, he wasn't happy to see me either? Well, he'd just have to deal with it.

I managed to wrench my gaze away to take in the rest of the room—and the two other guys who were witnessing our stare-down. The moment I caught sight of them, everything made a little more sense.

The guy perched on the edge of the small room's central table was Slade Galvezo, Logan's best friend. When I caught his eye, he grinned with a flash of his even teeth. His wavy, dark brown locks tumbled a little farther below his ears than they had in high school, and his body filled out his button-up and jeans to more impressive effect than I remembered.

I'd seen him in the halls of our high school, he'd still looked like a boy. Now he was all man. But his playful dark brown eyes and bronze skin remained the same.

He gave me a beckoning wave, hopping down from the table. "Come on in. You don't need to be shy."

He landed with perfect balance, but his pantleg shifted on the descent, drawing my gaze to his bright red sneakers—and the vibrant blue prosthetic that briefly showed above one.

Slade could handle himself on his feet so easily you'd never know it was there, but he'd never made any effort to conceal the prosthetic, often getting a kick out of telling other students stories about how he'd lost the bottom half of his leg. I seemed to recall "hacked off by a woodchipper," "chopped in two by an ax murderer," and "eaten by a tiger when I fell into the enclosure at the zoo" being among the assortment. I had no idea what the true story was.

At Slade's beckons, I moved forward automatically, and Logan backed up just enough to let me in. Stepping through the doorway, I glanced away toward the other major pieces of furniture in the room: a long, narrow desk with a computer on it, with a matching wooden filing cabinet next to it. The third guy was sitting at that desk, peering at me much more pensively than Slade had, though his eerily bright green eyes flicked up and to the side every second or two rather than holding my gaze.

That was how Dexter Wright, Logan's other closest high school friend, had been for all of the few years I'd known him. Eye contact was not his forte. *He* still looked almost exactly like the awkward, slightly gawky boy he'd been when he graduated high school, his curly black hair a jumble atop his pale, narrow face, although the lines of his features had sharpened with maturity.

A few more chairs were strewn haphazardly around the cramped room, and closed file folders scattered the table behind Slade. Books were piled seemingly at random on the small bookcase across from the desk. A corkboard hung on the back wall, the only thing in the space that was free from clutter… because there was nothing currently pinned to it.

Easing to the side so I wasn't facing Logan quite so directly, I pulled down my hood. Slade blinked and then chuckled. "Madelyn! Long time no see."

He must not have recognized me before with my face shadowed by the hood. We'd never exactly been close, since he was a year ahead of me and my close friend circle hadn't overlapped much with Logan's.

Even though his laugh had been warm, I had the impression that he'd flinched a smidge away from me before settling back into his casual pose. That was weird. Had Logan told him something about me—something off-putting?

My head jerked back around so I could focus on my stepbrother again. Logan was watching me. His stance had relaxed a little, but his eyes were still hard and guarded.

"What are you doing here, Madelyn?" he asked curtly.

I gritted my teeth at his tone. Part of me wanted to launch into a tirade about how he'd treated me for the past two years, but I didn't really want to air our dirty laundry in front of his friends if they didn't already know. Anyway, I'd come here for a different reason, and that problem hadn't gone away just because I'd been reminded of a different one.

"This is where people come to get help with crimes on campus, right?" I said. "You're the guys who call yourself 'the Vigil'?"

"You obviously already know that, or you wouldn't have come looking," Logan replied with a thread of snark in his tone. He spoke slowly, almost patronizingly, and my jaw clenched tighter. If he was trying to make me feel as unwelcome as possible, he was doing a bang-up job of it.

It wasn't really surprising that these guys were playing detective around campus, now that I'd gotten over my initial shock. Logan had at least used to be something of a crusader, and he and his friends had been at the center of a lot of the social activity at our high school. He knew how to make connections. And he'd always liked seeking out a challenge.

I willed my own voice to stay even. "Well, good. I just found out that my car's been stolen off one of the residence lots. My roommate said the Vigil might be able to help track it down."

Logan raised his eyebrows in a way that made me want to slam my fist down his throat, and I wasn't normally a particularly aggressive person. "Did you park it somewhere new, maybe?" he asked, all nonchalance now. "It could be you just misplaced it."

I would not scream. I would not yell in his face. I would be a picture of total calm in the face of his extreme jerkishness.

"No, Logan, I didn't *misplace* my car," I said. "I always park it in the same lot, and it's not there at all, and I can see exactly where it *was* before some prick stole it."

He shrugged. "Well, we've got a lot on our plates right now. You should find out what the police can do for you."

Slade's head twitched toward Logan at that comment as if it'd startled him. Dexter's brow knit for a second. Turning down people was *not* what made these guys so popular around the campus, and

Logan was just going to send me away, knowing that I'd probably never receive justice without their help?

Dexter must have felt the need to support his friend, no matter what he thought of his answer. He spoke up, his voice quiet. "The city police are occasionally on the ball. It's worth trying them."

That statement wasn't any more reassuring than Logan's dismissal had been. Slade stayed silent, though. Clearly Logan still ruled the roost here, and his friends would fall in line.

And here he was, when I actually needed him for something not at all personal, something he'd done for who knew how many other people, and he was still pushing me away.

My frustration overflowed. "Are you kidding me?" I snapped at Logan, sharply enough that his eyes widened. "You'll help out strangers all across campus, but you'll turn away your own stepsister?"

I should have expected him to meet my frustration with his own snark. Logan wasn't the type to take blows in stride.

"I help people who need to be helped," he shot back. "Your mom's got enough money to buy you a new car without batting an eyelash, so it's hardly a big deal, is it?"

I glowered at him. "My mom works hard, but she's not *rich*, as you should know, considering you lived in her house. And I wouldn't ask her for the money she worked hard to earn anyway, not when it'd mean she couldn't do things she deserves for herself."

"Then that's your choice. You're a capable woman, aren't you? You can survive without a car."

I didn't want to admit the other aspect of the situation. Just thinking about what else I'd lost brought a burn into the back of my eyes, and showing distress in front of Logan would be *way* worse than snapping at him.

But he was stepping toward me as if to usher me out of the office, and nothing else I'd said had made a difference. It was the last card I could play. Even if he'd probably call it stupid and send me packing just the same.

I had to try. For Dad.

"It's not just the car," I said, my voice strained. "I had something that belonged to my dad in the glove compartment. I can't just buy a replacement for that."

I'd braced myself again for whatever cutting response I'd get. Instead, Logan froze. Dexter leaned forward, his gaze fixing on me for a few seconds this time before darting away, as if the admission had interested him too. Slade rubbed his jaw with a casual cock of his head, but something about his reaction niggled at me too.

Why would anything to do with my dad matter to those two, who'd never even talked to me about him the way Logan had? I wasn't sure they even knew my dad was dead and not just divorced from my mom. Of course, Logan could have mentioned it at some point.

Some of the hostility had faded from Logan's expression and voice. Now he was only grimly serious. "Something that belonged to your dad? What, exactly?"

"A black lacquer trinket box," I said, showing the size of it, about eight inches long and half as wide, with my hands. "He used to keep it on his desk. I stored my insurance papers and stuff in it. It's not worth much to anyone but me, but it's the only thing of his that I brought with me to campus."

Logan nodded slowly, and a tentative sense of relief tickled through me. He might not have been willing to give me the time of day over my stolen car, but he understood how much the loss of a parent hurt. His mom had died when he was just a couple of years older than I'd been when Dad had passed.

He hadn't really wanted to help me, though. For a second, I considered just walking away rather than having to spend another second in his presence. Did I really want to put myself through that potential agony?

But the thought of the box and of the boy I'd once considered a friend held me in place.

Maybe if we worked together on this case, I'd have the chance to figure out what the hell was up with him. Anyway, whether he liked it or not, he owed me for all the crap he'd put me through. I wasn't letting him off the hook, not when something this important to me was at stake.

When he didn't say anything, my momentary relief drained away. I folded my arms over my chest. "So, are you going to work your Vigil magic or what? If you've got some other objection, let's hear it."

His lips curved into the slightest smirk. "Someone's feisty today."

"I just want an answer. I'm not going to beg you."

"No? Not even for this oh-so-special box?"

Was he just needling me every way he could? Suddenly I felt exhausted. I wasn't going to plead, and it was starting to seem like he intended to do nothing more than drag out this encounter as long as he could to punish me for daring to ask, only to kick me aside yet again. Maybe Camp-Po or the city police department would be good enough after all.

"Fine," I said, annoyed by the roughness that'd crept into my voice. "Obviously you don't give a shit, so I'll just go."

I turned my back to the guys and reached for the door. As my fingers closed around the doorknob, Logan's voice rang out, taut with reluctance but determined all the same.

"Wait. We'll take the case. We'll find your car."

CHAPTER 4

Madelyn

Evening was falling by the time we made it back to the parking lot next to my dorm building. I wasn't sure Logan and his friends would be able to turn up much evidence with the sunlight fading, but they'd seemed determined to get started right away.

I marched straight to the still-empty spot where my car had once been and pointed. "That's where I parked."

The guys stalked over. Dexter walked right to the edge of the stall and pulled out his phone, while Logan and Slade came to a stop next to me. Logan looked at me rather than the parking spot.

"When did you see the car here last?" he asked, all briskly business, no emotion in his tone.

"Last night," I said confidently. "I was coming back from the dining hall, and I remember glancing over and thinking about how I was going to take the drive I meant to tonight. I had a lab for my first class this morning, and I was distracted planning for that when

I headed over, so I wasn't paying attention then. And when I came back to the dorm in the afternoon, I went in a different door where I couldn't have seen it anyway."

Logan nodded and turned toward Slade, effectively shutting me out of the conversation. "We're looking at about a twenty-four-hour timeframe then," he said. "During most of those hours, there are students in and out of this parking lot regularly, so it'd be difficult to get away with breaking into a car and stealing it."

"The security camera's broken too," Dexter pointed out without even looking up. He must have noticed while he'd been walking over. He snapped a couple of pictures of the empty spot with his phone and then crouched down closer to the asphalt.

"Another victory for campus security," Slade said with obvious sarcasm. He shook his head, shifting his weight from his prosthetic leg to his other leg. "Well, it doesn't take a genius to convince students that the thief locked his keys in his car or something. Anyone with decent social skills could convince bystanders that there's not a crime being committed. I've done it plenty of times."

My attention shot toward him, and Slade only gave me a wink as he pulled a small candy from his pocket and popped it into his mouth. Was he kidding me, or was that the truth? I suddenly found it easy to imagine him conning his way into a flashy sports car to zoom around town. But I hadn't thought he was quite that casual about things like the law.

"That's… good to know," I said.

Logan glanced over his shoulder at me. "Did you lock the doors to your car, Madelyn?"

Both the question and the authoritative way he said my name irked me. I rolled my eyes. "Of course I did."

"And you definitely didn't leave the key someplace a thief could grab it?"

I grimaced and fished the key out of my pocket. "It's right here.

I'm not an idiot. Do you always blame people when their property is stolen, or is that a privilege you save for me?"

He shrugged, letting the question roll right off him. "We have to cover every possibility." He focused on Slade again, giving me his back. Disregarding me so easily after his stupid questions. "With a new-ish car, chances are they managed to clone the key fob at some point, so it wouldn't have been an obvious break-in. But they couldn't have known whether someone walking by would know the car is Madelyn's. I don't think it's likely that the thief would have wanted to risk that. It'd be a lot easier to conduct a major theft under the cover of darkness."

"The three other cars that've been taken in the last couple of months went missing overnight too," Dexter put in, calmly analytical. He bent forward, still studying the ground. "There's some bits of red clay-like dirt here. I don't think that would have come from anywhere on campus."

"That's from me," I said quickly, impressed that he'd realized it was significant. Clearly his observational abilities were sharper than his social skills. "It's how I'm sure that's where I parked the car. I drove down a lane that was pretty muddy with that stuff last week, and it got plastered all over the undercarriage. It's been flaking off bit by bit."

"No way to identify the perp based on leftover mud then," Slade said with a playful tsk of his tongue. "Too bad. That would have made a good story."

"It could tell us where else the car's been once we start following the trail," Logan said, and rubbed his hands together. "Every clue matters."

Dexter was snapping more pictures, even though I wasn't sure how much he'd be able to make out in the increasingly dim light when he checked them later.

"I'd recognize the mud if I saw it again," I told him. "No pictures necessary."

He glanced back without actually meeting my eyes. "I like to keep a visual record. That way there's never any doubt. Memory is unreliable."

I guessed that was a fair point.

Slade tapped his lips. "We could still try to jog some memories. Find out who came through the lot last night and whether they noticed any suspicious characters."

"If anyone saw anything concerning, we'd already know about it," Logan said.

I raised an eyebrow at him. "How? Since when does the entire student body report to you?"

He shrugged. "We have our ways." He motioned to the other guys, and Dexter straightened up, apparently done with his visual record-taking.

I was starting to get a sense of the dynamic between this group that called themselves "the Vigil": Logan taking the lead and making major judgment calls, Slade suggesting more out-of-the-box possibilities and stopping the tone from getting too dour, Dexter keeping track of the details.

They actually did feel like a cohesive unit, each bringing their own strengths, working together in well-practiced harmony. I might have enjoyed being a part of it if it hadn't been for my stepbrother's continued jerkishness.

Which Logan decided to demonstrate yet again just as that thought passed through my mind.

"If you had a nicer car, I'd say we start with resale sites and see if anyone's offering it, but your junker isn't going to fetch a high enough price to make it worthwhile for a thief to try to put it on the market like that."

"It's not a junker," I replied automatically. I'd bought it on my own dime when I'd started my first year of college so I could get to and from campus easily while I was still living at home, and I hadn't had enough money for anything fancy. It worked, and it got decent mileage. That was all that mattered.

How would Logan even know what type of car I drove? He'd already been long gone without a backward glance when I'd gotten it.

Logan snorted. "It is by car-buyer standards. How much do you really think a 2006 Malibu is going to fetch? How much did *you* pay for it?" Before I could do more than sputter in response, he barreled onward, not waiting for an answer. "Whoever stole it would be best off selling it for parts. It's safer, and they'd get the most money that way."

Slade clapped his hands together. "Off to the chop shop, then! Darrel's our best bet." A hint of cinnamon wafted on his breath from the candy he was still rolling around his mouth.

"The chop shop?" I asked.

Logan looked at me like he'd forgotten I was here in the thirty seconds I'd stayed quiet. Like he wished I'd continued to stay quiet. But Slade gave me a wide smile.

"Chop shops are places that deal in stolen car parts behind a legit front," he said. "We know a guy who handles that kind of business out of his scrap yard."

I blinked at him. "You know a guy who's a criminal, and you just let him keep at it?"

Slade waved off my remark. "One of the first things you learn about solving crimes is that you need contacts. He isn't a bad guy. *He* doesn't steal anything. Every now and then he passes on a tip about other stuff that's going on around town, so we let him stick to his business as long as he isn't getting his nose too dirty."

"Right," Logan said brusquely, as if he resented that Slade had bothered to explain. "The scrap yard's open pretty late. We should head over there right now and get started tracking this thing down."

My spirits started to rise. At this point, there was no way I was making it to the lecture I'd wanted to attend, but maybe I'd have my car back as soon as tonight. "Great. How are we getting there?"

Logan folded his arms over his broad chest. "There is no 'we,' not that includes you, anyway. You're not coming."

I scowled at him. "Why not? It's my car."

"Madelyn, we have a job to do, and it's better if we handle it alone, since we're the ones who actually know what we're doing. You can call an Uber to go for your trip to the mall or the hair salon or whatever you were planning on doing tonight."

Anger seared through me. Sure, I went to the mall and got my hair cut on occasion like most people did, but he made it sound like those were the only things I could have needed to do. Like I was a frivolous girl with nothing in her head but appearances.

What the hell was wrong with him? Even if he'd ghosted me for two years, he'd known me a heck of a lot better than that before. Why did he have to be such a gigantic asshole?

"For your information," I said tartly, "I was *planning* on driving to an in-depth talk in medical research developments, but it's too late for me to get there on time now. Which is too bad, because maybe I'd have learned something that'd help me figure out what *your* current damage is."

Logan's face twitched and hardened, and Dexter stood there awkwardly between him and me, looking at the cars rather than us.

Slade simply guffawed. "A brainiac. I like it." He gave my shoulder a playful knuckling and then swatted Logan. "Stop heckling the girl, man. She's clearly got her priorities straight."

I couldn't totally tell if it was a compliment or a backhanded insult.

"We need to get going before Darrel leaves the yard for the

day," Dexter reminded his friends, looking down at the time on his phone.

Logan's jaw stayed clenched, and I set my hands on my hips. All kinds of other cutting remarks bubbled up in my chest, but I managed to hold them back by sheer force of will. *I need his help. I need his help.* I repeated the phrase like a mantra, hoping he wouldn't push me even farther. I wasn't sure I could stay even partly civil after much more dickishness.

"Dex is right," he said, drawing his already substantial frame even taller to glower down at me. "We have to get going. Just the three of us. Darrel knows us. He'd clam up around you anyway."

That didn't mean I couldn't ride with them so I could hear the outcome right away, but I guessed it was possible this chop-shop guy would notice me even then. I restrained a sigh and forced myself to nod.

I didn't want to ruin their chances of getting the answers I wanted. And the answers about the car *were* the most important ones, as much as I was dying to pummel Logan for an explanation of his behavior.

"Fine," I bit out. "But let me know what you find out as soon as you've talked to him." Dexter had exchanged phone numbers with me in a seemingly automatic gesture before we'd even come out here, which I guessed was standard procedure for them.

"Will do," Slade said with a jaunty salute.

The three guys strode off without a backward glance, leaving me alone in the parking lot, feeling totally useless.

CHAPTER 5

Dexter

Normally I'd have welcomed a trip to the scrap yard. Darrel often had useful information to pass on that I could fit into my broader understanding of the criminal activities in this city. But Logan's silent brooding in the driver's seat left me with an unnerving sense of uncertainty.

I didn't understand his reaction to Madelyn at all. We'd all been surprised to see her, I was sure, and given the circumstances, it'd thrown us off balance. But Logan had seemed outright hostile. I had no idea where that animosity had come from.

It was true that he'd barely talked about her in a personal way in the past few years, but he'd always seemed fond of her back when they had socialized more. I'd never heard him say anything *negative* about her that would explain him treating her like an annoyance.

I didn't know much about her in general, of course—really only what Logan had said here and there in the early years of our friendship and observing her occasionally in the halls when we were in high school. So maybe there were factors I wasn't aware of. I hadn't found her annoying, though. She'd shown real determination, and she hadn't acted offended by my quirks the way people sometimes did.

I'd have thought Logan would have appreciated those qualities too. Definitely the determination part, anyway.

But the tension remained in my friend's shoulders through the entire drive. He drummed his fingers on the steering wheel and let out a huff of breath.

I bit back the urge to ask him what was going on. From past experience, I knew that asking a direct question about a subject that clearly discomforted him wouldn't get me a straight answer. Better to just watch and glean what I could as the situation played out.

There were other things I could ask that weren't likely to get his hackles up. I frowned as I thought over everything Madelyn had told us. "Do we think that the trinket box in Madelyn's car—the one that was her father's—was significant to the theft? Was it the real objective?"

Next to Logan, Slade stretched out his legs and cocked his head as he considered his answer. "From the way she described it, it didn't sound like anything all that exciting."

"I was thinking the same thing."

Slade flashed his typical grin at me. "Then I must be right."

Logan cleared his throat. "It's impossible to know how significant or not it is until we've seen the investigation through to the end. It's important to her, anyway. It was meaningful to him. Maybe it mattered to someone else too."

"Stranger things have happened," Slade said breezily, but he shot a sideways glance at Logan. It occurred to me that he'd noticed the other guy's tension too—and was doing his best to diffuse it. Slade was much better at that sort of thing than I was. "There *has* been a pattern of car thefts on campus, though. It's not like this was out of the blue."

"No," I said in exaggerated deadpan, "I believe they were red, black, silver, and now green."

Slade snorted, and even Logan cracked a bit of a smile. Humor might not be my specialty, but I'd learned that playing up my tendency to take things too literally could often get a laugh. Out of my friends, at least, since they caught the joke rather than thinking I was just confused.

"That's a good point, though," I went on, more seriously. "When we know there are already car thieves operating at the university, it's most likely to be just a random coincidence that they happened to target Madelyn's vehicle this time. Maybe they were hanging around in a good position to clone the fob at the worst possible moment for her."

"It's about time we took those pricks to task anyway," Logan said. "Four cars in two months—that's a lot, and right under our noses in our main domain. We've got to shut the assholes down before people start to think the place is easy pickings under our watch."

"You've got to give Madelyn that much credit—she knew who to turn to." Slade shook his head. "Those other idiots taking the case to the city police, who of course just shot them back to useless Camp-Po. Their cars were probably long gone before anyone even really looked around for them. Man, I'd have given my other leg to have the chance to retrieve that red Mustang the one guy lost and take it for a little spin..."

Logan glanced at him, raising his eyebrows. "We wouldn't have been taking any stolen cars for a joyride."

"Don't tell me you wouldn't have wanted to. We both know that's utter bullshit." Slade cackled. "But I'd have been good and waited until the owner told us we could have a little fun, out of his utter gratitude. Wouldn't have been a bad thing to have a guy who can afford a Mustang owing us a favor either."

"Or whose family can afford a Mustang, at least," I said automatically.

"Yeah, yeah. Same difference."

"Well, we've already established he was an idiot," Logan said, but his voice sounded lighter now. "Favors are great, but rich idiots aren't. Anyway, we'll shut the thieves down and send them packing, and no one else will lose their precious vehicles or whatever they've stashed in them."

He spoke with a confidence I knew was justified. Ever since we'd set up shop as the Vigil once we'd arrived at the university, where we were far enough away from our families that we weren't worried about how they'd react to our unusual "hobby" like we'd been in high school, we'd handled dozens of cases. We'd pretty much always figured out the source of the problem and dealt with it.

I wasn't totally sure why the other guys were so committed to our extracurricular activities, but for me piecing together those puzzles was absolutely exhilarating. It was a hell of a lot more enthralling than working through my Chemistry and Forensic Science coursework.

That involved puzzles too, but also a lot of busy-work, and most of it theoretical. Even the actual crimes we studied were ones already solved, just for practice. It was all leading to actual practice, of course, but with the Vigil, I didn't have to wait. I got to dig my hands right in and untangle the mysteries before anyone else had.

Still, as Logan pulled into the scrap yard's parking lot, a familiar knot formed in my stomach. I'd never meant for our quest for justice to become quite as intense as it had… but it was mostly my fault that we'd tumbled this far down the rabbit hole. Even if my friends never blamed me, I wasn't going to forget that fact.

"Darrel's still in," Logan said, tipping his head toward the small building just beyond the chain-link gate. Dusk was creeping over the yard, and light was glowing through the office window. "If these jerks are trying to get a major car theft ring going, they'd need to set up a connection with someone who can disassemble and move the parts quickly. Four cars just on campus—who knows how many they've grabbed around the city and other places nearby. There's a good chance he'll know what's up."

"If he wants to tell us," Slade said as we got out. "If they're paying *him*, he might not be so eager to pass on the information."

I glanced at the barbed-wire-topped fence, making out the vague shapes of ruined cars and other metal paraphernalia through the green mesh that stopped outsiders from scanning for details. "We'll be looking for clues at the same time. The other victims might not have come to us, but I know the makes and models of all four cars."

Slade reached out his hand as if to knuckle my shoulder but stopped just shy of touching me. If it'd been anyone other than him or Logan, I'd have flinched in anticipation of the contact, but my friends knew how to adapt their friendly gestures to my comfort levels.

"Of course you do," he said with amusement. "Let's go hunting."

We found the gate unlocked, like it usually was during business hours unless Darrel had some kind of private deal going on. As we eased inside, the unpleasant smell of heated metal and grease hit me. I wrinkled my nose.

The office door opened before we'd quite reached it, and Darrel's short, sinewy frame appeared in the doorway. He smiled broadly at us, showing off his one gold tooth amid the lightly yellowed natural ones. "Boys," he said in his boisterous voice that always struck me as a little too big for his body. "I was about to lock up, but I can make a little time for you. What've you come around to talk to me about today?"

He waved us into the office. We tramped inside, my skin prickling as the door thumped shut in our wake. I never totally liked being in an enclosed space with a known criminal, even one who'd proven as friendly as Darrel. You just couldn't be sure whether you'd stay on their good side.

Darrel gave Logan's arm a firm swat and leaned against his desk, still smiling. "Well, what's on your minds?"

The office was impressively neat, really, considering the chaotic heaps of parts that filled the rest of the scrap yard. Darrel himself kept his presentation orderly as well, wearing button-ups and slacks without a hint of a wrinkle, though I knew he swapped those out for tees and jeans when he was working the machines.

I wasn't totally sure what he made of our interest in tackling the criminals who ended up on our radar. We'd ended up on *his* radar last year after he'd inadvertently pissed off a fledgling gang who'd started harassing his customers in retaliation. We'd already been investigating the small group of amateur gangsters for other reasons, and after we'd confiscated some money to cover his lost business when we sent them packing, Darrel must have realized that the quest for justice could work in his favor as well as against it.

He had a sharp mind behind his warm demeanor, and I respected that. As long as he didn't outright hurt anyone to our knowledge, keeping a mutually beneficial alliance with him served our interests much better than trying to take him down for his own crimes.

Logan smiled back, smoothly but carefully. He knew as well as I did that associating with any kind of criminal was a dangerous balance. "We're actually wondering if business has been particularly good for you in the past couple of months. Gotten any exciting new clients?"

Darrel arched an eyebrow. He wasn't just going to blurt out his latest underworld associations. "What kind of exciting?"

"There's been a rash of car thefts on the university campus. The latest belonged to a friend of ours, and we're guessing the thieves would have been looking to sell it for parts. You're obviously the guy to go to for that kind of job. Naturally we wouldn't blame you for not realizing any particular vehicle had been stolen."

Despite the assurance, I noted the slight tightening of Darrel's posture. He knew that this case was taking us onto shaky ground, since he'd be a direct participant in the crimes we were looking into.

He didn't betray any other discomfort. "What's the make and model?" he asked. "I can tell you if anyone's tried to hawk it here or if I've heard talk around town."

And maybe he'd be telling the truth, or maybe he wouldn't.

"2006 Chevy Malibu," I said automatically. I'd filed away the details the moment Logan had said them and Madelyn hadn't disputed them.

It wasn't an outright piece of junk, but Logan's assessment of the car being close to worthless was confirmed by Darrel's snort. "Not exactly a luxury vehicle, then," he said. "I'm sorry, I haven't had any Chevys at all come through here recently."

I'd been worried that he might lie to us, but I found I had no doubt that his answer was genuine now that he'd given it. He'd obviously been amused at hearing the details, and the stiffness in his stance had relaxed as he'd answered. He was relieved that he didn't have anything to do with the crime. Possibly he honestly preferred not to lie to us now that we had a decent working relationship.

"These pricks obviously didn't know what they were doing then," Slade said with a chuckle.

Darrel echoed his laugh. "Maybe not. But I'm not the only option in this area—I may be the biggest provider of that particular service, but there are plenty of smaller chop shop operations in and around the city."

"I guess we'll have to start hitting up the other ones," Logan said. "I don't suppose there are any you figure are a particularly likely bet?"

Darrel made a face. "I don't really keep track of them—they're coming and going so often. If I do hear anything about a Malibu, I'll give you a call right away. Otherwise, I can't really help."

That time he wasn't being totally truthful. He was really saying that he *wouldn't* help us more than that. No doubt he knew of at least a couple of other active chop shops nearby, but it made sense that he wouldn't want to create bad blood for his business by pointing the finger if he really had no idea who might have handled this particular car.

"Well, thank you for your time," Logan said. "We always appreciate you lending your experience to our work."

As we headed back to the car, I surreptitiously snapped a few photos of the scrap yard with my phone. I'd gotten very good at taking pictures without looking like I was taking them in the years since we'd started our lives on this course, because having a concrete visual record was so valuable. Even in the thickening dark, the yard's security lights would show enough that it was worth documenting this visit.

We slid into the car in the same seats as before. I pretty much always ceded the front seat to Slade in consideration of his prosthetic, even though he insisted he didn't need special accommodations. Extra leg room couldn't *hurt*, and I didn't suffer without it. He was taller than me anyway.

Slade sighed and leaned his head back. "Now we need a new lead."

"We go to the smaller chop shops," Logan said. "One by one."

"Yeah, but that's going to take a lot more effort. They're not going to fill us in like Darrel did. It could take ages."

"It's strange that they aren't being brought here, isn't it?" I said slowly. "It seems like an ongoing operation with cars getting stolen regularly—wouldn't it make the most sense for them to set up an arrangement with the biggest chop shop in the area? Most of the smaller places wouldn't be able to hold many vehicles or parts at a time."

Slade popped one of the cinnamon candies he was hooked on into his mouth and clicked it against his teeth. "Maybe they aren't stealing anything except those cars on campus. A small chop shop could handle two a month. Or maybe they aren't all connected after all. Madelyn's could have been separate. We didn't ask him about the other three from before."

That was true. I'd automatically assumed that if Darrel hadn't handled Madelyn's car, he hadn't gotten any of them, but I shouldn't have.

If her Malibu had been specially targeted for reasons that had nothing to do with a general thieving operation, then this could be far bigger than just a stolen car. A quiver of anticipation rippled through the air between us.

"This is all just speculation," Logan said in his laying-down-the-law tone, starting the engine. "We follow the trail and see where it leads us. The one good thing about the smaller businesses is that they'd probably need longer to get around to breaking down a car. That gives us more time to find it before it's in pieces. First thing tomorrow, we'll start working through the suspects."

I rubbed my hands together, unable to ignore a deeper thrill that shot through me, both uneasy and eager.

Most of our jobs were minor puzzles, fairly easy to connect the dots. This was shaping up to be a real challenge. I couldn't wait to dive in… but I also had no idea what dark paths the case might lead us down.

CHAPTER 6

Madelyn

I'd thought if I showed up at the law library first thing on Saturday morning, I might have a chance to poke around in the Vigil's office before any of the guys showed up—if they showed up at all. I knew from things Holand had said that Logan had an off-campus apartment he shared with his friends, and surely they had better things to do than hang out around school on the weekend.

As I tried the office door, grimacing to find it locked, my phone pinged with a text alert from my best friend and frequent co-conspirator Summer. I'd filled her in on my missing car and my interaction with the Vigil last night.

Normally, Summer would have been all for a little reconnaissance, only annoyed that she couldn't join in, since she'd ended up heading to Emerson College for its journalism program and was currently half a day's drive from me. But as soon as she'd found out Logan was involved, her tone had turned a lot more critical.

Tell me they found your car already so you can dump that jerk harder than he ditched you?

Summer had always had a strong sense of social justice, which was partly why we were such good friends. She'd been so pissed off when she'd found out how Logan had ghosted me after our hook-up that there'd been a solid three months where she never uttered his name, only referred to him as "the prick" or "the asshole" if he came up in conversation. Even these days, she mostly relied on insults.

Unfortunately, no, I wrote back. *They're still working on it.*

Well, let them do their thing and stay clear of him. I know you're curious, but he's not good for you.

I'm not going to do anything WITH him. I just want to know what's going on with him and this whole private investigator thing he's suddenly gotten into.

Unfortunately, Summer was very good at picking up on the things I wasn't saying. She sent a side-eyeing emoji with the question, *What are you doing, Maddie?*

Just trying to get into their office, I admitted. *Obviously none of them are going to tell me what all they've been doing, considering Logan hardly wanted to loop me in on the crime that affected me directly. It's totally justified snooping.*

I could almost hear her resigned sigh. *Well, I know nothing's going to get in your way once you're committed to a mission, girl. Just don't get too invested, all right? Or I'll be obligated to race on over there and rearrange his face when he hurts you again.*

I promise, I'm not giving him a chance. I learned my lesson.

Tucking my phone back into my pocket, I eyed the door. It wasn't as if I could pick the lock. How could I get my hands on a key?

It always irked me a little to play the desperate girl, but sadly being female and upset opened doors—sometimes literally—when nothing else would. I hurried over to the reception desk as if I were a little frantic and came to a stop in front of the librarian on duty, pressing my hands against the check-out counter. "I'm so sorry, but I could really use some help."

The librarian peered at me through her round glasses and offered a sympathetic smile. "I'm here to assist however I can. Is there a particular book you're looking for?"

"No," I said with an awkward wave toward the back of the room. "I just—I came to see the Vigil the other night, and I realized afterward that I left a binder in their office. I need the notes in it to study for a test on Monday, and I don't know if they're going to be back all weekend. Could you possibly let me in for just a minute so I can find it?"

It might not buy me *much* time, but at least I could take a closer look around while I pretended to search for my supposed binder.

The librarian's smile faded. "I'm sorry. I have an agreement with the boys that they have sole use of that space, and I know there are a lot of private matters that they handle for other students. I have their numbers if you need to give them a call and see if they'd let you in?"

Crap. Now I had to go along with her offer, or it'd be obvious I'd been lying. "Sure. Thank you so much."

I jotted down the numbers she gave me and walked away as if to place my call in private. Over at the back of the library where the Vigil room was, she couldn't see me anyway. I studied the solid wood door again, wondering if there was any chance I could just jiggle the lock open—ha ha ha. Maybe in my dreams.

I grasped the knob again just in case it'd only been stuck before rather than being actually locked, and just my luck, a low, teasing voice carried to my ears at the same moment.

"We tend to use the key to make it a little easier to get inside."

I whipped toward the male voice that'd come from behind me, and there, standing just a few feet away, was Slade, dangling a key from one hand while he grinned at me.

"I—" How would I explain this to him? The last thing I needed was for both Logan and Slade to believe I was a creepy stalker lady. I settled for avoiding the subject completely. "I imagine that *would* make it easier. Thank you."

Slade stepped past me to insert the key into the lock. He glanced over his shoulder at me. "I thought Dexter passed on a message to you last night that we haven't located your car yet."

"Oh, well, yeah, but he didn't say much." That was my perfect excuse right there. "I was hoping to find out more, or that you might have made some more progress since then." I splayed my hands in what I hoped looked like a cluelessly innocent gesture, although I hated playing clueless even more than I hated doing the desperate female act.

"I'm sorry, but we haven't really had time." Slade pushed open the door and stepped inside. He paused for a second before grinning at me and beckoning me to follow. "I know Logan gave you kind of a hard time. Don't take it personally. He's got a lot on his mind. If you have more questions about how we'll handle the investigation, ask away."

I hadn't wanted to get into the office while one of the Vigil members was present, but if it was going to be anyone, I guessed Slade was the one least likely to give me a hard time. Maybe I could still find something out. And I could poke around a bit without looking suspicious, just curious.

He stood to the side of the door, popping one of those candies he seemed very fond of into his mouth. As I walked in, I caught a whiff of cinnamon and the click of it against his teeth.

"What exactly happened yesterday?" I asked. "You went to that chop shop place, right?"

"Of course." Slade dropped into one of the scattered chairs and leaned back, propping his feet on the edge of the table in a way that made the leg of his khakis slide up to reveal the metal rod of his prosthetic. Just like I remembered from high school, he showed no sign of self-consciousness. He might even have been showing it off purposefully to see if I'd react to it.

"Turns out your thief wasn't a customer of that particular shop," he went on in a casual tone. "He must have taken it someplace else. Or he knew someone with a special hankering for an old Malibu. We'll figure out which. It'll just take a little time to get through all the possibilities."

"That makes sense." I'd meant to start my perusal of the office, but Slade chose that moment to tuck his hands behind his head, making the muscles in his arms and shoulders flex to impressive effect. For a second, I found it hard to drag my gaze away from his dark, twinkling eyes and well-built body.

Slade wasn't as brawny as Logan, but he had an impressive physique in his own right. And those sly eyes combined with his bright grin and his carefree personality had drawn girls to him like bees to nectar back in high school. I recalled Summer catcalling him in the halls once when he'd been showing off his nimbleness on that manufactured leg, back when we'd been measly sophomores to his superior junior status.

I wasn't here to pursue a hookup, let alone anything more than that. I didn't want to feel the twang of desire that shot through me before I finally yanked my eyes away—but I'd be lying if I said it hadn't happened.

I had more important things to focus on right now. And the last thing I needed was to get a crush on Logan's best friend.

Wandering around the table, I let my fingers trail over the surface, shifting a few of the papers lying there to an angle that made them easier for me to read. A quick glance showed nothing all that exciting: a class schedule for a student whose name I didn't recognize, a sketch that didn't look like much more than a few overlapping rectangles to me, a recent receipt for a video game. I wasn't sure whether the last was evidence or just one of the Vigil guys' personal purchases.

"Are you sure that you *will* be able to track down my car now that you're on the case?" I asked.

Slade tsked his tongue. "Don't be doubting us already. We've got a reputation to maintain here—we'll get it done."

I couldn't help raising my eyebrows at him. "You're awfully confident. How long have you guys been at this whole Vigil thing anyway?"

He shrugged. "Since pretty soon after we started classes here, so about two and a half years now."

Honest curiosity itched at me. "How did you even get started doing something like this? Most people don't suddenly decide, 'Hey, I'm going to become a crusader tackling all the crimes on campus.'"

Slade's grin stretched wider. "You should know something about being a crusader, shouldn't you, Madelyn?"

The lilt with which he said my name sounded almost flirty—enough to make me blush. Or maybe that was just residual embarrassment being reminded of my many crusades in high school.

Not that I was ashamed of the stands I'd taken… but I could definitely have tackled certain conflicts with a more polished approach.

"I asked you the question first," I retorted.

Slade laughed. "Fair. It's not that thrilling a story, as much as I'd like to wow you with grand tales of derring-do. We actually picked up a few sort-of cases back in high school. Opportunities landed in our lap, and we found that we were good at putting pieces together and figuring out the solutions to these kinds of problems. We did little investigations like the kids we were, and when we came here, we decided to make more of a commitment to getting shit done."

I blinked at him, momentarily forgetting my quest to unravel what they were up to now in my surprise about the past. "You were solving crimes back in high school?"

"Sure. We just kept it more on the down-low then. Lots of other things keeping us occupied. Remember the English teacher Miss Otterbine?"

At my nod, he continued. "Well, someone stole the mini-refrigerator she kept in her room, and she couldn't go to the school about it because technically the appliance wasn't allowed outside of the teachers' lounge. She only had it in there to keep backup lunches for students who couldn't afford them. So we decided to find out who'd taken off with it, and we did. She got her fridge back, and the culprit got a very stern talking-to." He winked at me.

I opened my mouth to ask for more details about their high-school exploits, which had gone on right under my nose, but Slade whipped his feet off the table and straightened up, fixing me with an intent look. "So, Maddie—do you mind if I call you Maddie?"

I got a weird twinge thinking of how natural it sounded from his mouth—and how natural it'd used to sound from Logan's. "Go for it," I said.

"What are *you* occupying yourself with these days? You said you were going to some medical research lecture—am I right in thinking you're pre-med?"

I was a little surprised that he'd remembered that brief part of our conversation last night—but then, he had come to my defense when Logan had been hassling me about my plans.

"You've got it," I said. "I'm majoring in biology." I paused. I knew Logan had gone into something to do with computers—his dad talked about it now and then with a note of pride, since he had enough trouble wrangling anything outside of his accounting software—but I had no idea about his friends. "What about you?"

"World languages with a specialty in linguistics."

My eyebrows rose. "World languages as in plural? Don't people usually pick just one?"

His chuckle resonated through the room. "I might look like a jock, but I *do* know languages. I got English and Spanish from home, and I taught myself a fair amount of Italian and French all on my own, enough to be fluent now."

I gaped. "You know *four* languages?"

"Don't sound so surprised, Piccolina," he said. "After you know two or three, the rest get easier. Mandarin and Russian were a more difficult challenge, since they're not under the Romance umbrella—that means based on Latin, not swoony romance, although I excel in the latter too." He shot me a smile that made me absolutely certain he was flirting with me. "Hěn gāoxìng jiàn dào nǐ? Vasha siyayushchaya ulibka voshishchayetsya dazhe nebom!"

He switched between the two languages without missing a beat, sounding totally comfortable with both. "Six languages," I muttered, hardly able to believe my ears.

"Eight if you count Tagalog and Arabic, but I'm not proficient in those yet. Those are my current projects."

Okay, clearly there was a lot going on behind that handsome face that I hadn't realized. I only knew *one* language, unless you counted the wide assortment of scientific terms I'd had to add to my vocabulary, which thankfully didn't require their own grammatical rules or anything like that.

The thought of how much I hadn't known about Slade brought my mind back to the mysteries surrounding Logan—and my main reason for being here. I pulled myself away from the table and meandered farther into the office as if aimlessly checking the place out. "And Logan's doing computer science and engineering, right?"

"You should know."

Should I? I kept my voice as even as I could manage. "A double major like that has got to be intense. Is that what's got him on edge?"

"Ah, he's a natural at that stuff, so I doubt he has any more trouble with it than you do with your biology work."

That wasn't much of a question, but there was a firmness to the words that hadn't been there before. I could tell if I tried to push further, Slade would only deflect me. His loyalty was to Logan, not me, of course. I could hardly expect him to spill his best friend's secrets.

I forced a laugh, letting my gaze skim over the computer desk. They hadn't left anything out around the computer other than a takeout menu that I suspected was for their own benefit, not an investigation. "It's been a bit of a challenge adjusting to the slightly different curriculum here, transferring in the middle of the year, but I'm getting back into the groove."

Slade cocked his head. "That's right—this is the first semester I've seen you around campus. You finally followed us here, huh? Missed being in the presence of the great Slade Galvezo that much?"

My next laugh came out more genuine. "I always wanted to come here—well, since I first started thinking about college, before any of you got accepted anywhere. But I didn't get in at first—I had to start at the community college back home."

It was Slade's turn to arch his eyebrows in shock. "You weren't accepted? A smarty-pants like you?"

I wrinkled my nose at him. "I might have been smart in certain ways, but I didn't handle school politics all that brilliantly. There was this one teacher—American History—he was always playing favorites: offering bonus assignments only to the students who'd joined the comics club he ran, giving them extra time on tests, that kind of thing. It drove me crazy. So I stood up to him, started calling him out loudly in class, and he hated me after that. Suddenly all my essays were getting Ds. I nearly failed the class, and it tanked the GPA I needed."

Slade let out a low whistle. "I do seem to remember you being a bit of a hardass back in high school. Not that there's anything wrong with that. Sometimes jerks like that need to be put in their place."

"Yeah, well, it lost me three semesters here for my trouble. I'm not saying he didn't deserve it, but I'd have gone about it a little differently if I'd thought things through more ahead of time."

"It's too bad we weren't still around to get on his case and prove he was screwing you over." Slade shook his head and tapped his prosthetic foot against the floor with an emphatic *thunk*.

The artificial limb drew my attention again. I paused, a sudden memory tickling up through my mind—but should I say anything?

Well, Slade seemed like the type to tell me off without batting an eye if I deserved it. "Would it be horribly rude if I say something about your leg?" I asked, lifting my chin toward him.

Slade waved off any concerns I'd had. "I'm curious to hear your thoughts, Dr. Maddie. Should I tell you about the awful shark attack and how I harpooned the beast that chomped it off?"

I gave him a baleful look at the obvious joke. "I was just thinking—I follow a lot of different areas of medical research, just to stay on top of new developments. There are some teams that've been making a lot of progress with new types of prosthetics with robotic elements and things like that."

"Becoming part robot? Sounds interesting."

I couldn't tell if he was making fun of the idea or honestly intrigued, but I barreled onward. "Some of the companies are looking for volunteer amputees to beta test the parts. I'm not sure if it's something that would interest you since you're so good with the prosthetic you already have. It's not like you need the help of fancy gadgets. But if you thought it'd be worth giving a shot, I can always point you in the right direction."

Slade stared at me for a long moment, his expression suddenly impossible to read. I hoped I hadn't pissed him off with the suggestion despite his reassurances, especially when my intention had been the exact opposite.

Then his lips curved with a warm smile that met his eyes. The teasing note dropped from his voice for just a moment. "That's a pretty fantastic offer. I'd be happy to become an even more spectacular cyborg. Thank you, Piccolina."

I crossed my arms over my chest. "What does that mean?"

"It means that I appreciate the gesture." He motioned me back toward him. "I'd be happy to look into it. I'll give you my number, and you can text me the deets—or, y'know, if you're ever in the mood for a booty call…"

He smirked so widely with that last remark that I couldn't help laughing. "I'm not really the booty-call type, but I'm very flattered. I can send you the info, for sure."

I passed him the phone and gave the room another scan while he fiddled with it. My gaze latched on to the filing cabinet I hadn't checked yet. I sauntered over and gave the top drawer a little tug.

It jarred without opening—locked, presumably. I tried the second drawer down with the same result. Before I could reach for the third, Slade's voice, calm but suddenly much more serious, carried across the room.

"That's where we keep case files. Gotta make sure no one else gets in there, or it'd violate our clients' confidentiality. Don't worry, we're just as careful with your info too."

Guilt heated my cheeks. "I'm sorry. I didn't realize—I wasn't really thinking."

That last part was a lie, but I didn't want him to think of me as a snoop. Somehow that seemed even more important than before I'd ended up chatting with him. I'd kind of liked our rambling conversation, I realized. I hadn't felt that relaxed simply shooting the breeze with a guy in… ages. Maybe forever. Even when Logan and I had been friendly, there'd always been my crush in the back of my mind, making me nervous. Slade had a way of putting people at ease.

Like now. His smile returned in the blink of an eye, so swiftly it was hard to believe he'd sounded so intense a moment ago.

He got up and handed my phone back to me. As I took it, he slipped his arm around me to touch the small of my back, nudging me toward the door. "It's no problem. You just never know what suspicious characters we'll need to protect our inside info from, especially when it comes to pretty girls who give away their numbers for potential booty calls."

I snorted and elbowed him playfully, but I let him usher me toward the door. It seemed like he'd decided I'd spent enough time in the Vigil's domain, and I had no excuses left to keep me there. I'd checked out everything I could with him watching over me anyway.

"Keep up those studies," he said as I stepped out into the library's main room. "We'll be in touch as soon as we find out anything about your car."

I nodded and only offered a small wave as he closed the door in my face, the lock clicking behind him. As I headed out of the building, my thoughts started to whirl in my head.

Slade had seemed perfectly content to chat casually with me until I'd touched that filing cabinet. Then suddenly he hadn't been able to get me out of the office fast enough, even if he'd still been flirting his ass off the whole time.

It wasn't as if I could have seen any of the confidential files while the drawers were locked anyway. Just what were the guys hiding in there that had prompted such a strong reaction?

CHAPTER 7

Logan

I spotted Dad's car in the parking lot as I pulled up to the diner, even though I'd arrived fifteen minutes early. How long had he been waiting inside for me already? Was he that intent on squeezing every possible second he could get out of our lunches together?

It sounded like something he would do. And I couldn't even blame him. It wasn't as if I gave him all that much of my time these days.

A pang of guilt ran through my chest, but I shook it off. The distance was necessary for his good as much as mine. Maybe even more his. If I hadn't thought it'd send him into a panic, I'd have forced myself to cut him off completely.

There was no reason that the darker side of my life should ever have to infect his.

My smartwatch vibrated on my wrist. Without even looking at it, I reached into my glove compartment where I kept one of my various stashes of pills. It was better to have them on hand wherever I happened to be, since the timing was important.

I tossed back the single pill I was down to with a gulp of water, suppressing my irritation. It sucked being chained to this routine, knowing that my survival depended on following it. The doctors had said I might be able to wean off the immunosuppressants completely one day, that there were other liver transplant recipients who'd managed it without major issues, but so far they hadn't felt confident enough at my periodic check-ups to give me the go-ahead.

I might be willing to take a lot of risks, but messing around with the extension I'd already been lucky to get on my natural expiration date wasn't one of them.

Taking the pill only took a moment, and then I could pretend to forget that anything about me was remotely broken—at least physically—until the next time that alarm went off.

I gave myself another several seconds to gather the good spirits I'd need to show Dad to make sure he didn't have a panic attack even though he *was* seeing me, and then stepped out of the car. The greasy smell of the diner's decadent burgers wafted through the parking lot as I headed for the door.

It wasn't my favorite restaurant, but Dad loved it—and it was continuing a tradition we'd established a few years after my transplant when my health had settled into a sort of equilibrium. Once a month, Dad would take me out for a "cheat meal"—something fatty or greasy or sugary that the doctors wouldn't have approved of as a regular part of my diet. Just an occasional treat, a reminder that I didn't have to give those indulgences up completely.

I'd savored those moments as a kid. These days, it didn't matter as much to me, but it made Dad happy. So I went along with it. It was one little gift I could give him. I sure as hell owed him something.

Warmth washed over me on my way into the diner. It was a small space, room for maybe thirty people around eight tables at full capacity. Retro Coca-Cola signs and records hung on the walls. It was old-school in operation too—you had to go to the counter to order, and then the server would bring the meal to your table and take care of things from there. I paused just long enough to ask for my usual and point out where I'd be sitting.

Dad was seated at our usual table at the back near one of the windows, his hands cupped around a mug of steaming coffee. I strode over, pushing my mouth into a smile, forcing my mind to empty of all the things I couldn't tell him.

We'd have long conversations—we always did—but I wouldn't mention anything about the Vigil or my recent extracurriculars. My dad would know me as a hard-working engineering student and nothing more. I could tell him about my midterms, about hanging out with Slade and Dexter when we weren't getting into trouble, and about the overall campus life. That was it.

That was how it had to be.

Dad's head came up at my approach, and he beamed at me so brightly that a sharper pang reverberated through me. He loved me so goddamn much, but he had no idea who I even was these days.

He slid out of the booth and opened his arms to me, and I allowed him to wrap me in his embrace. I hugged him back, giving myself over to the show of affection just for a moment.

I owed him this too. And part of me welcomed the gesture even if it made me uncomfortable at the same time.

Every time we hugged, I felt as if his arms had shrunk and mine expanded. I was a little taller than him now and definitely bulkier from my regular workouts. Did he even notice, or did he still feel like he was hugging the little boy I used to be?

Did he believe that he knew the man he hugged? From where I stood, he didn't. He barely knew a thing about me anymore.

"Always good to see you, bud," he said as he released me, still smiling away. "I'm glad we can still make time for these get-togethers."

"Always," I assured him. I sat down across from him, focusing all my thoughts on the subjects it was safe to talk about. "How've you been? Is the merger still working out okay?" His accounting firm had recently absorbed another smaller company, and Dad had spent some time running around getting everyone settled into the new organizational structure. I didn't think it was really part of his job, but he was the kind of guy who couldn't help making sure everyone was at ease.

"Oh, everyone seems pretty comfortable now," Dad said, sounding pleased. "Those kinds of transitions are always tough at first, but we've brought on some really great talent. And we made it through the busiest part of tax season without anyone having a nervous breakdown, so that's always a win." He winked at me to show he was joking about the breakdown thing. "Did you wrap up that big engineering project?"

I nodded. "Turned in my papers last week. Haven't gotten them back yet, but I feel good about how it came together. I used a lot of the concepts the prof's been harping on, so he should be impressed anyway."

The truth was that I didn't care all that much about my studies other than how they could help advance my other activities, but keeping the authorities at school happy meant they didn't examine those other activities too closely.

Dad chuckled. "Always smart to play to the teacher's interests. Good for you." He paused, turning the mug in his hands. "I was just telling Lindsay about the sorts of things you've been working on, and I realized I couldn't explain most of the details. She's got more of a mind for the science and tech stuff than I do. Someday you'll have to fill her in properly."

It was a subtle hint that he'd like me to stop by the house—sooner rather than later—and reconnect with more of the family. As much as I could consider the stepmother I'd gotten at sixteen years old a family member, even if Madelyn's mom was the best thing that'd happened to my dad since Mom's death years before. But Dad knew better than to push too hard, and his hints were easy to ignore as if I hadn't caught his full meaning.

"The next time I see her, I'll give her the full scoop," I said noncommittally. The next time I saw her would quite possibly not be until next Christmas, but I didn't have to clarify that.

"She'll enjoy hearing about it." Dad tapped the top of the table. "I hope you've been making time for things other than work, though. You should have the full college experience, fit some fun into that busy schedule of yours."

Oh, I did… if you could consider chatting up criminals, interrupting gang operations, and investigating thefts "fun." Sometimes it kind of was.

"Don't worry, Dad," I said. "I'm doing a lot more than just studying."

"Don't get me wrong," he said. "I'm impressed that I raised such a smart one. Your mother would have been so proud of you too, you know."

I nodded, my throat tightening a little. Dad could talk about Mom without getting emotional these days, and generally I could too. But when I thought about the two of them…

After I'd gotten sick, even after the transplant that'd ultimately saved my life, things between them had seemed increasingly strained. I couldn't help thinking the stress of my treatments had fractured their marriage. I couldn't say I was sure they'd have stayed together much longer if we hadn't lost Mom to that accident when I was ten.

"Anyway, my point is just that it's important to remember

balance." Dad reached across the table to pat my arm. "You have your studies and your friends and your health and whatever you do to relax and enjoy yourself—and of course family."

He shot me one of those warm grins, and my returning smile got stiffer. That was another hint, one even easier to ignore but that jabbed me all the same.

"That's why I'm glad we have these lunches every month," I said in my best enthusiastic tone.

"Speaking of family..." Dad paused when the waitress came over with our orders: burgers and fries, mine with pickles and raw onions, Dad's slathered in cheese and mayo. My heart had started to sink at his words, and the interruption wasn't enough to get me out of the new turn in the conversation. Dad popped a fry into his mouth, gave a happy sigh, and fixed his attention on me again. "Have you seen Maddie around campus much since she transferred over?"

I shrugged and bit into my burger to buy myself some time while I rode out the surge of emotions that came up at the mention of the girl—no, the *woman* now—who'd been way too present in my mind for the past couple of days. The meaty juices mingled with the tang of the onion and pickles, but I couldn't take much enjoyment from the meal.

"You know, we're in pretty different fields," I said. "It's a big campus. I'd never see Slade or Dexter there if I didn't arrange to meet up with them."

I knew as soon as the words came out of my mouth that I'd made a misstep. Dad waved a fry at me. "You should get in touch with her—text her or video chat or whatever you kids do instead of calling people like a normal human being these days—and offer to show her around. You've got to know the campus a lot better than she does."

I raised my eyebrows at him, pretending amusement. "Dad,

she's been at the school for what? Three months? I think she's figured out her way around by now."

"Still, I'm sure it'd be nice for you two to reconnect. You were friendly back in school before Lindsay and I ever got together, weren't you? And you always got along well after too."

"Yeah," I said quietly. Until I'd had to retreat from every part of my old life that I didn't want to put under threat.

What would he say if he knew just how thoroughly we'd "reconnected." I was handling a fucking case for her. I'd seen more of her yesterday than I had in the entire three years since I'd moved out of her mom's house. Way too much for comfort…

And also nowhere near as much as a different part of myself wished it'd been. But that was the biggest problem right there.

I couldn't act on those urges. I'd already screwed things up enough once, getting caught up in the moment and then having to cut her out again cold turkey. I could only imagine how hurt and angry she'd been… I'd seen those emotions simmering behind her eyes every time she'd looked at me when we'd been talking about nothing but her stupid car.

The memory made me wince inwardly, a sharp ache lancing through my chest. I'd hurt her badly. After she'd patched me up, touched me so tenderly, opened herself up to me…

But she could get hurt so much worse if she got tangled up in the life I had now. We'd find her car, figure out if there was anything significant about the box, and then fade right back off her radar as if she and I had never spoken.

I wouldn't bring her anything but trouble if I stuck around, which she should have figured out in spades after our last collision.

"I did give her a few tips when she first arrived," I said, just to get Dad off the subject.

It was a bald lie, but he took it as the truth without hesitation. As easily as I'd told the lie in the first place.

It was awful, wasn't it, how easy and even automatic bullshitting the man who'd raised me had become? That I'd become the kind of guy who lied to his loving dad?

But that was the trade-off I'd taken. I'd gotten a lot more of a childhood than I'd been meant to after I got sick; I'd gotten to live, period. Now I was paying back the second chance I'd been granted thanks to someone else's death by helping people in ways even the cops couldn't.

I should be grateful for as much normalcy as I'd gotten before the path I'd started down had turned dangerous. Now all that mattered was protecting the people I cared about, and if that meant keeping them as far away from me as possible, so be it.

If only doing that had stayed simpler to accomplish when it came to Madelyn.

"I'm glad to hear it," Dad said. "That girl's got one of the biggest hearts out there." As if I didn't already know that. But thankfully, he shifted to a different topic. "Hey, are you still following the Red Sox these days? Quite the game on Saturday."

"Yeah," I said, though I'd only caught the highlights, and slid back into the meaningless chatter that couldn't hurt anyone or anything. Beneath my offhand remarks, a sense of resolve had solidified in my gut.

We needed to get that car theft solved *yesterday* so I could shove Madelyn as far away from me as I could—and make sure she stayed away this time.

CHAPTER 8

Madelyn

A knock jolted me out of the zone of concentration I'd gotten into as I typed out the finishing touches to my latest Genetics assignment at my desk. When I glanced toward the door, Keeley did too, popping out her earphones that'd been buzzing the voices of her favorite podcast while she paged through a textbook. I had no idea how she managed to focus with people yammering right in her ears, but she said it actually helped her.

Her desk was a little closer, and she was the one of us much more likely to be receiving visitors anyway. She jumped up and opened the door with a curious expression that told me she hadn't been expecting anyone.

To my surprise, I caught sight of a familiar face beyond her. Dexter Wright was standing awkwardly in the residence hallway, clutching the strap of a satchel that hung from his shoulder. He blinked at Keeley and then aimed his gaze at me for a second before it darted away from both of us in typical Dexter style.

Keeley tilted her head to the side, twisting one of her curls around a finger. "Hello, there. Can I help you?"

She'd taken on a playfully flirty tone that made me reevaluate the situation—and the guy beyond the door. Keeley obviously thought he was cute. I guessed he was, if I let myself think about it. His dark curls and pale skin made his large green eyes look even more vivid in contrast, and even though he was slim, you could tell he had some lean muscle on him.

The Vigil probably had girls falling over them all across campus. What a group.

Of course, Dexter wasn't so great with the smooth charm Slade had in abundance. He made a vague motion in my direction. "I'm here to talk to Madelyn," he said, firmly and evenly.

"Oh, are you?" Keeley cooed, and peeked over her shoulder to waggle her eyebrows at me. I barely restrained myself from rolling my eyes in return, since Dexter would see and might get the wrong idea. This wasn't some kind of hookup, but I didn't want him to think I was annoyed that he'd come by. Keeley just had an overactive imagination… and a theory that I really needed to get laid sometime before the end of the semester.

Keeley stepped aside to motion Dexter into the small room and then scooted past him. "I'll leave you two alone," she informed us, flashing me another suggestive smile. "I can make myself scarce for a good long time. Total privacy. Have fun!"

Oh, God. My cheeks flared.

Dexter peered after my roommate's retreating back with a puzzled expression for the moment before the door thumped shut. Then he glanced around the room, his stance tensing as he took in the two somewhat rumpled beds that were the only furniture other than the desk I was already occupying and Keeley's.

"I'm sorry," I said, feeling as awkward as he looked. "She's very… exuberant. She's just trying to be a good friend. Is this about my car?"

Dexter nodded, catching my eyes for half a second before his gaze started traveling around the room again. "I had a few things to talk to you about, and this seemed like the most likely place to find you."

"You could have just texted me."

He shrugged. "I needed something you could only do in person. If you hadn't been here, then I would have texted."

I guess that made some sort of sense. When he glanced around again, adjusting his weight on his feet, I sprang out of my chair. Of course he'd feel weird sitting on my *bed*, for fuck's sake, especially after how Keeley had just been acting.

"Here," I said. "You can sit at my desk. What exactly did you need to go over? Have you made any progress?" It didn't seem probable that they'd accomplished much in the ten or so hours since I'd talked to Slade this morning.

I sat down on my bed, tucking my legs up so that Dexter could walk by easily. He seemed to relax a bit as he sank into my desk chair. He turned it toward me and pulled a thin pad of paper and a pencil out of his satchel. His gaze held mine again for only a second before it dropped to more like the vicinity of my mouth.

"We'd like you to draw the box that was in your car—so we'll be able to describe it accurately if we need to ask around about it."

Okay, that seemed reasonable enough. I accepted the pad and pencil and sketched out the rough rectangular shape. It wasn't a work of art, but then, I didn't think they expected it to be.

"So, I take it you haven't found the car yet," I said dryly.

Dexter didn't seem to pick up on the intended humor in my statement. "No, we haven't. But as I mentioned last night, we determined that it hasn't been taken to the largest chop shop in the area. And Logan confirmed this morning that it wasn't used in any crime that's been reported."

I blinked at him. "Used in a crime?" I repeated in confusion.

Dexter nodded, looking more at my shoulder now. "Stolen for a joyride and then abandoned, or reported as a getaway vehicle in a robbery, or anything like that."

"And how would he have confirmed that?"

Another brief moment of eye contact. "He hacked into the police department's database."

My pencil paused where I'd started to draw the Celtic knot on the top of the trinket box from memory. I gaped at Dexter. "He can do that?"

I'd known Logan was good with computers—obviously, since he was a computer science major—but I'd had no idea he'd delved into hacking. And hacking into a network I'd imagine had to be pretty secure, considering it was law enforcement. He had asked his dad for quite the elaborate computer set up back in high school, but I'd assumed he'd wanted the latest tech for gaming.

How much else had he been hiding from me and the rest of the family?

Dexter nodded as if it were no big deal. Maybe to him it wasn't. "Sure. That's one of the ways we follow the trails of clues."

Well, I guessed I had a better idea now of how the Vigil managed to solve crimes the cops couldn't. I was pretty sure the police didn't have any hackers on staff.

I directed my attention at the paper again, drawing the curves of the Celtic knot as well as I could remember them. Then I passed the sketch over to Dexter. "That's about what it looks like. Nothing too fancy, like I said."

Dexter examined the drawing and tucked it into his bag. "Thank you."

"Is that what you're going to do next?" I asked. "Start asking around?"

"With a little more direction than that," Dexter said. "We need to determine what smaller chop shops are currently active in the city, since they're hiding behind fronts, and check them all out."

"Will that take a lot of time?"

"It depends on luck, really, unfortunately. We're going to touch base with a contact or two tonight who might be able to point us in the right direction."

I immediately perked up. "I'll come along too, then. I know my car way better than any of you. I should hear what these contacts have to say."

Dexter tensed up all over again. His gaze slid to the floor, and his mouth opened and closed a few times before he seemed to find his words. "I don't think that's a good idea."

Guilt pinched my gut at how uncomfortable I'd made him, but I squared my shoulders. I'd promised myself I wouldn't back down. Logan had probably sent Dexter on this mission because he'd figured I'd be too much of a softie to put pressure on his shy friend. He wasn't putting me off that easily.

"I'm not asking," I said, standing up. "I'm insisting. You guys shut me out last night, but I want to be a part of the investigation. It's my property that got stolen, after all."

Dexter spread his hands awkwardly. "Madelyn… It's not that simple…"

"Sure it is. As long as you're not letting Logan boss you around, which I don't intend to do. You don't have to make the call. Bring me to the other guys wherever you're meeting up, and I'll make my case with them."

Dexter shook his head. "I'm not bringing you to the apartment. No one goes there except the three of us. That's the rule."

Not even casual hookups, which it'd sounded like Slade at least was keen on? Interesting. I folded my arms over my chest. "Fine. Then call them and tell them to come to campus, and I'll talk to them here."

Dexter hesitated, his posture painfully rigid. I swallowed hard, knowing he was straining his mind for a way to get out of this—a way to convince me to back off. He needed to understand that wasn't an option.

Did he have a specific problem with me, or was it just because of Logan's objections? Well, it didn't matter either way.

"Look," I said quietly, "I know there was some drama around taking my case. I realize Logan's been a jerk about it. But this is my car, my memento of my dad. It's my *life*. I won't get in anyone's way or screw things up, but I want to be as much a part of the investigation as I can be. Isn't that a reasonable request?"

Dexter's mouth twisted, and then he let out a brisk exhalation. "I'll text them. But I don't think Logan will be happy."

A sly smile curved my lips. "You don't have to tell them I'll be there. Let me handle Logan."

Dexter looked skeptical, but he tapped out a message on his phone. A moment later, an answering ping carried through the room. He glanced at the screen and then shoved the phone back in his pocket. "They'll be in the parking lot outside the main library in ten minutes."

He got up, not looking at me but not objecting when I followed him. I kept a careful distance as we walked through the hall and down the stairs, not wanting to push into his personal space.

From the brief observations I'd made of Dexter back in high school, I knew he wasn't the touchy-feeling type. I'd seen him flinch from as simple a gesture as a guy giving him a friendly clap on the shoulder. He'd always stood a little farther back from any group he was part of than the others.

He'd done me a favor, and the least I could do was keep his comfort in mind in every way I could that didn't jeopardize my own goals.

As we stepped out of the residence building, a gust of cool spring air whacked me in the face. It'd been pretty warm by daylight, but any lingering heat had died with the setting sun. Dexter strode a little ahead of me on his long legs, and I hurried to keep up as we headed along the darkened concrete paths toward the larger of the campus libraries.

Just as we came around the looming brick building to where the parking lot lay, Logan's car, a black Subaru, cruised into the space, headlights streaking through the dusk. Logan parked near us, and I could already tell from his face through the windshield that he was pissed.

He and Slade both got out, Slade leaning against the side of the car with an amused air and Logan marching a few steps toward us. "What's *she* doing here?"

"She wants to come with us," Dexter said before I needed to explain.

Logan snorted, and my hands clenched at my sides.

"I *am* coming with you," I clarified, ignoring Logan and walking over to his Subaru. "My case, my car. I'd like to see exactly what you're doing to find it."

Logan's eyes turned even icier than before. "You're going to get in our way and make a nuisance of yourself. Go back to your dorm." He motioned to Dexter as he turned back to the car. "Come on, let's get going before she wastes any more of our time."

That last comment stung. My jaw set, and without really thinking about what I was doing, I strode forward even faster. Before Logan had quite made it to the driver's side door, I'd reached the hood. Without missing a beat, I clambered right up onto it and plopped myself down in front of the windshield.

"What the hell are you doing?" Logan snapped.

I crossed my arms over my chest and glowered at him. "You're taking me with you or you're not going at all."

"You've got to be kidding me. Get off the fucking car, Madelyn!"

Dexter darted into the back seat without another word. Slade let out a low chuckle but kept out of the conversation.

I kept my gaze focused on my stepbrother, my eyes narrowing. "There's an easy way to get me to move: Say I can come, and stop acting like such a dick about this whole case. It's not like I *wanted* my car to get stolen."

"Everything after that was your choice," he muttered, glaring at me. "If this is supposed to convince me that you can handle yourself in a difficult situation, it's having the opposite effect."

"Only because that difficult situation is you," I shot back. "If you weren't being such an ass, I wouldn't have needed to resort to tactics like this. And hey, it's working, isn't it?"

"I haven't agreed to anything, and you're not going to force me to give in."

"So intent on running away from your problems." A little acid crept into my voice. *Again*, I could have added.

His own tone turned harsher. "So, you understand that you're the problem here."

I winced inwardly and braced my hands against the smooth metal I was sitting on. "I understand that *you* see me as a problem. I'm sorry it was so inconvenient for me to ask you—a campus organization with your own freaking *office* and everything—for help with something you regularly do as a job."

"None of our other clients sit on the hood of my car and insist on being a part of the investigation," he retorted with an edge that was almost a snarl.

He made a fair point, but I wouldn't let this go. I couldn't.

"Somehow I doubt you acted like you couldn't be bothered to take on those clients' cases to begin with either." Or ghosted them for two years after the last time we'd had any significant interaction. "None of them had a reason to believe you might not do your due diligence rather than brushing them off yet again."

"You…" Logan growled.

Before he could follow that up with another insult, Slade's laughter split the air. Both of our heads whipped around.

"Do you have something to say?" Logan spat at him.

Slade shrugged, a glint from the security lamps dancing in his eyes. "She's made a valid point. And she came up with a very effective strategy. I say she's proven that she can handle herself just fine. It's not like we're walking into a murder den. Let her come. The world won't end."

He spoke lightly, but I saw the tension coiled in his stance as he adjusted it. He was trying to defuse our rising tempers—especially Logan's—but he wasn't sure yet if it'd work.

"We don't take civilians on cases with us," Logan said, but his voice wasn't quite as biting as before.

I grimaced at him. "You're not a cop, Logan. You're a student just like me, and we're *both* civilians. Is it the over-inflated ego that has you acting like you're too good to take me with you, or is it something else? Please, I'd love to know."

Logan looked like the top of his head was about to explode with a blast of flame and smoke, but Slade sauntered around the car and gave him a light punch to the arm. "She's spunky. Maybe she'll even be useful at the club. Come on, man."

Club? Before I could ask about that, Logan had run his fingers through his short-cropped hair and then aimed his searing gaze at me again. He pointed his finger in my face, tempting me to slap it away.

"Fine," he said. "You can come along. But the *second* you wimp out of anything or get in the way of the investigation, you're going to back off and give us room to work."

He said it as if he assumed one or the other would happen, and sooner rather than later. Irritation prickled through me, but I raised my chin and slid off the hood without letting it show. I looked forward to proving him wrong.

"I'll take that deal. Now, what's this club we're heading to?"

CHAPTER 9

Madelyn

We stepped into the dance club on one of the main downtown streets to a staccato house beat, reddish lighting, and a pretty empty dance floor. Almost everyone around at eight pm on a Sunday night was at the bar or one of the small tables set along the walls. I'd heard Keeley mention this place a few times—it was one of the venues she and her friends circulated between for their Friday-night get-togethers—but it obviously wasn't too happening right now.

Which was probably a good thing, since I wasn't sure if the bouncer would have let me in with my basic though fitted jeans and top if there'd been more demand for access.

I came to a stop a few steps inside and glanced at the guys. "There's a chop shop run out of this place?"

Slade guffawed, but he shot me a smile warm enough to smooth over any impression that he was being anything other than good-natured in his teasing. “Right, because with all the car parts lying around, it’d be easy to get confused.”

I elbowed him lightly in the ribs as we followed Logan and Dexter toward the bar. I noticed Dexter had taken out his phone, his thumb swiping over it in a careful motion—taking more pictures? “Well, I wouldn’t expect them to leave the illegal merchandise out for the regular patrons to see. You did say the chop shops need a cover business.”

“It’s always someplace that deals more in car-type things,” Slade explained. “Mechanics, used vehicle dealers, scrap yards, etc. But we know a few people with ties to the criminal life who come by this place pretty regularly. We’ll hit them up for info if they stop by.”

Okay, that made a little more sense. I hopped onto a stool at the bar next to Dexter, Slade coming up at my other side and Logan staying on his feet a little farther down. It seemed we were going to try to blend in, since there obviously hadn’t been any reason for me *not* to come along. It wasn’t as if I was going to push myself into their interrogations. I just wanted to observe.

The woman behind the bar finished splashing and spraying the liquids from various bottles, slid a couple of glasses down the counter to a couple who looked to be in their late twenties, and turned to our group. Her gaze latched on me first. “What can I get you started with?” she asked with a professional but easygoing smile.

“Can I get a mojito with a splash of lemon juice added?” I asked. I rested my hand on my purse, prepared to pull out my fake ID, but she didn’t ask. In a college town, she probably figured anyone who looked close to old enough wouldn’t come in without supposed proof of their age. The guys were all legal drinking age anyway.

"On it, and for you three?" she asked, shifting her attention to them.

Logan didn't hesitate. "Just a Coke."

"Ginger ale for me," Dexter put in.

"I'll take a Shirley Temple," Slade said with a flirty grin.

Understanding hit me like a jab to the chest, and my cheeks flushed with shamed embarrassment.

Of course. Logan couldn't drink booze without jeopardizing his transplanted liver. The guys must always order non-alcoholic beverages in solidarity. I'd have done the same, but it hadn't really come up when we'd been living at home still in high school. We hadn't gone out to any bars together then, and he wouldn't have been ordering a beer in a restaurant in front of our parents. That factor hadn't even occurred to me in my overall nervous state.

I opened up my purse anyway, feeling the need to do something to show my own commitment to the group. The bartender nudged my drink toward me, and I pushed enough cash toward her to cover all our orders and a generous tip. "It's all on me."

Logan's head jerked toward me. "You don't have to—"

"I know I don't have to," I said firmly. "But you're helping me out. It's the least I can do."

His mouth flattened, but he didn't say anything else. I doubted he wanted to get into an argument about why we were actually here in front of the other club patrons.

I sipped my cocktail and found it tasted exactly the way I'd wanted, even though I had trouble enjoying it now as I watched the guys grab their less potent drinks. I took a longer gulp, planning to drain the contents quickly so I could switch to a club soda or something.

I couldn't chug it too quickly or the alcohol would rush straight to my head. I still needed to keep my thoughts clear, or I'd prove

Logan right about being a liability to the investigation. Taking regular but measured swallows, I studied the rest of the space.

More people were already hitting the dance floor as the night went on. A gaggle of girls bobbed to the beat of the hip hop tune now blaring over the speakers, a few couples and a couple of clusters of single guys dipping and swaying, showing off their moves and laughing together. I felt weirdly isolated sitting here with three men who'd barely wanted me along.

Logan and Dexter appeared to exchange a little conversation, but the music had gotten loud enough that it was difficult to talk. By the time I'd gotten to the bottom of my glass, none of the three had left the bar to approach any other patrons. I frowned and turned to Slade, who seemed like the safest person to ask, even though I had to lean close to avoid shouting obnoxiously over the music. "None of your contacts have shown up yet?"

He shook his head and then tipped it toward Logan, who was just getting up from his stool. My stepbrother made a vague gesture that Slade seemed to understand. When I raised my eyebrows in question, my neighbor flashed another grin. "He's going to scope out the other parts of the club to see if anyone's hiding away in a corner or something."

There was a set of stairs that led to a second floor, I realized. As Logan headed up them and Dexter took another sip of his only half-finished ginger ale, his gaze fixed on the dance floor, Slade slipped off his own stool and sidled even closer to me. "Since we've got no business to take care of yet, we might as well have some fun while we're here. Do you want to dance?"

I blinked at him in surprise before it occurred to me that the invitation was probably all part of blending in. It'd look a bit odd for a few college guys to come into a dance club and not actually do any dancing, especially when they'd brought a girl with them.

Slade confirmed that thought, leaning close enough that I

caught the whiff of cinnamon on his breath. "Standing here without dancing looks more suspicious than busting a move on the floor."

I couldn't stop the laugh that escaped me. "Busting a move? What are we, ninety?"

"I promise my dancing will woo you," he teased, extending a hand toward me. "Maybe you'll even take me up on that booty call invitation after this."

Oh, why the hell not? I didn't want to be a stick in the mud or to make us look suspicious. And if Slade wanted to have fun, why shouldn't I?

I pushed off my stool, landing steadily but with a slightly bubbly feeling in my head that told me the mojito's effects had kicked in. Slade snatched my hand and guided me onto the dance floor. As he tugged me around to face him, I started to sway with the music, getting a feel for it. I wasn't a star or anything, but I could hold my own if I needed to.

Slade jumped right into the beat, dipping this way and swiveling that way with a total confidence I couldn't help admiring. I might also have been admiring the physique that justified some of that confidence. The guy was something to look at, and not just because of his moves.

He caught me watching him and waggled his eyebrows before grasping my hand again. "I promised you a real dance. Are you ready for this?"

I bit my bottom lip, unsure of what I'd gotten myself into. "The deal for coming with you was that I didn't wimp out, so show me what you can do."

"I hope you have good balance, Piccolina."

I didn't have a second to question those words before he was sweeping me around, moving me in perfect sync with the music. I barely managed to keep up without stumbling over my own feet.

When Slade stopped, he flung my entire body backward. I felt weightless for a moment before he caught me and dipped me close to the floor. Then he lifted me back to his chest in a deft move that left my head spinning.

He slowed his movements for a minute, doing a forward and back move that I could mimic once I found the rhythm. I had to concentrate on each step and motion we made to keep up with what he seemed to be doing flawlessly. Here and there he added little extra gestures that I didn't bother trying to imitate. It looked like a mix of a more formal dance style with typical modern club moves, both coming naturally to him.

Through my awe, I realized I shouldn't be surprised. Back in high school, he'd always liked showing off with agile spins and leaps using his prosthetic leg, proving that it didn't slow him down. It really didn't at all. I mean, he was moving a hell of a lot more gracefully than I was.

He couldn't have come up with all these techniques on his own just goofing around like those teenage antics. As his pace slowed with the more languid beat of the next song, I leaned closer, catching my breath before asking, "Where did you learn to dance like that?"

Slade set his hand on the side of my waist, the contact sending heat flooding through my shirt. It only intensified when he drew me closer so he could speak into my ear. "When I was a kid, my grandfather insisted on teaching me Latin ballroom dancing. He said it would help me win over the ladies when I got older. Is it working?"

I couldn't help snorting at the wry question, giving him a playful shove to the chest, but the truth was, my whole body was getting all kinds of heated up with him this close. "It takes more than a dance to win me over," I informed him with an arch of my eyebrows, but the statement didn't feel all that true.

Slade took the declaration in stride like he did so much else. “Bummer,” he said with a wink. The hand on my waist trailed down to my hip, the brush of his fingers making my skin quiver in anticipation. He squeezed lightly, avoiding outright groping my ass, as he wrapped the other arm around the small of my back and dipped me slowly.

I allowed my head to fall back as I laughed through the maneuver. When he raised me, his breath spilled over my upper chest and neck before he pulled me completely upright just inches away from him. I couldn’t help imagining what his mouth might have felt like pressed against those sensitive planes.

The thumping beat sped up again, and Slade tugged me even closer to him. His leg eased between my thighs. Suddenly my chest was pressed against his, our bodies swaying together in a way that generated the most delicious friction. It felt incredibly dirty, but I also couldn’t bear to stop. It was still just dancing, right?

As much as I tried to convince myself of that, a flush crept over my face. Slade guided me in a rhythmic circle on the dance floor, his lips grazing my cheek. As I let my hands rise to tangle in his wavy hair, he made a sound in the back of his throat that resembled a restrained growl. He whispered a lilting phrase in my ear. “Piccolina, serías el postre perfecto para mi.”

My rudimentary Spanish from grade school in no way prepared me to interpret his comment, but it *sounded* good enough to melt me. “What does that mean?” I asked, my voice breathier than intended.

A smirk pulled at his lips as he whirled us in another direction, his leg still rubbing against that hungry spot between my legs. His arm tightened against my back, the muscles flexing. “It means that you would make a delectable dessert.”

Okay, it seemed like a simple dance was enough to win me over, after all.

Was *he* really into it, or was this all just passing the time for him? He seemed to flirt automatically, not with any significant intent. I leaned back enough to try to catch his gaze and get a read on him. My heart was pounding fast. I wasn't even sure if I wanted him to be into it. I wasn't actually looking to hook up with him or anything… Right?

The heat I found in Slade's gorgeous eyes was enough to melt any sense of resolve I'd had. A tingle raced through my body to my core. "That—that was a random thought," I murmured, and then could have smacked myself. Of all the things I could have said in response, that was the least sexy option.

Slade didn't seem to mind, though. He licked his lips. "Not as random as you'd think."

His gaze dropped to my mouth, and another rush of heat flooded me. I wanted him to lean in and close the distance between us. I was sure it was a totally horrible idea, but every part of me was aching to find out if he was as good at kissing as he was at dancing.

Oh, hell, Maddie, why not just kiss *him*? The world won't end, right?

I might have actually done it. I hadn't finished arguing with myself when a harsh voice shattered the moment between us.

"Eye-fucking the client on the dance floor—how professional."

Logan's words and his brawny frame looming over us might as well have thrown a bucket of frigid water over me. I pulled away from Slade as if I'd been caught in a crime myself, a shudder running through me.

Slade took a step back too, raising his hands, but he smiled as if he didn't think this was any big deal. "Just fitting in and making use of our time here the way people are supposed to, man."

"Well, while you were getting your rocks off"—Logan's searing gaze snapped to me—"and you were distracting him, I managed to get some information. But there's nothing we can pursue tonight.

We should get out of here before we draw any attention—or at least any more than you two might already have."

He sounded even more pissed off than before. If he'd gotten what he wanted to out of this visit, what was his problem? It wasn't like he'd asked Slade to come with him, and I hardly thought we'd made a spectacle of ourselves. Glancing around, none of the other dancers seemed to be paying any attention to us at all—other than a couple who were eyeing *Logan* as if worried he was about to start a brawl.

"The only person making a scene here is you," I informed him.

Logan grimaced at me and whipped around to march back to the bar, where Dexter was still waiting. As he motioned for the other guy to get up from his stool, Slade sauntered close to me again.

"We'll pick this up another time," my dance partner said in a voice laced with promise.

A very large part of me wished we didn't have to wait. What had he been planning on doing next?

Of course freaking Logan just *had* to interrupt at the worst possible moment—and with his continuing hostility that I didn't really understand at all. If anyone should be pissed off at anyone here, it was me at *him*.

But as much as he was acting like an ass, I needed to behave at least enough to ensure I'd get to come along on whatever the next steps of the investigation were. Dragging in a breath to even out my temper, I strode over to join the guys on the way out the door.

What exactly had Logan found out anyway?

CHAPTER 10

Beckett

The girl moved briskly through the grocery store—I lost track of her here and there in the aisles from my vantage point outside the large front windows. She wasn't particularly noticeable anyway—a typical college student with straight blond hair that hung down her back and a slim frame. Pretty, sure, but not startlingly so.

The only reason I'd noticed her in the club last night was the company she'd been keeping. Those three guys had been poking their noses into a lot of places they really didn't belong. I wasn't sure what their end game was. Often a girlfriend was the weakest link, the easiest way to get my questions answered without my actual targets having a clue.

I tapped absently at my phone, pretending I was actually texting someone on it and just casually glancing up while I waited for responses. The girl grabbed a couple of sodas off a shelf and vanished from view again. None of her purchases had been remarkable either.

I wasn't going to learn much from watching. I needed to make an approach—one that would ensure a longer interaction, endear me to her, and offer the opportunity to earn some trust upfront. How I handled it would depend on where she went next.

My phone vibrated faintly with an actual incoming text. I diverted my attention briefly to check its contents.

It was from Lana, the woman who handled a lot of the day-to-day administrative work for my family's business. *There was a bit of a squabble with a group in Atlanta over their tariff. How do you want to handle it?*

I bit back a sigh. There were always minor players trying to buck the system. It never worked out well for them.

Email me the details, I wrote back. *And let them know they have until tomorrow to make things right, or we'll right things for them.*

Understood.

Technically, she should have been asking my dad. Because technically, Dad was still in charge of our family's empire. But Lana knew as well as I did that she'd get a faster answer—and a better one—from me these days.

That was why I had to be especially wary of random upstarts interfering with any of our business ventures.

When I glanced up again, the blond girl was at the checkout counter. She slung her two bags over her arms and headed for the door. I eased off to the side, examining my phone again but tracking her from the corner of my eye.

She considered the street and walked with a peppy stride toward the coffee shop on the corner. A perfect opportunity. I started meandering after her, much more slowly, pausing for more pretend text-tapping once she'd darted inside.

Through the slightly grimy window of the mom-and-pop place

a lot of the college students favored, I followed her progress from cash register to order pick-up counter, where she grabbed a predictable iced latte, and then on toward the door again. That was my cue.

I tugged at my shirt sleeves instinctively, my fingers brushing the simple but elegant cufflinks that'd been a fourteenth birthday gift from Dad. Back when he'd paid more attention to matters of business, he'd instilled in me the belief that you should look as well put-together as you kept your affairs. That was what made people respect you before they even knew you. Not that my clothes were going to matter that much in a few seconds anyway, but I'd make the most of them all the same.

I ambled onward, angling myself so I'd pass within a foot of the coffee shop doorway. I stepped in front if it just as the girl hustled outside, juggling her bags of groceries and the cup of iced coffee that was filled to the brim.

She gave a little yelp as our arms collided. I twisted as if to try to get out of the way, but managed to ensure that some of her coffee spurted out of the lid to splash across my button-up. Then I jerked backward as if startled, staring down at the light brown blotch spreading across the ivory fabric.

"Oh, crap, crap, crap," the girl muttered, shoving herself out of the way of the entrance and setting her coffee on a nearby bench. Her voice was lower than I'd expected, serious and a little husky—not the high-pitched cheerleader squeal I'd imagined. "I'm so sorry."

I shook my head with a bemused chuckle and grabbed a tissue from my pocket to dab at the stain. "Damn. Well, it's just a shirt. And it's my fault too. I should have been watching where I was going." I shot her a smile, just a little bit of teeth, warm but not overdoing it. "I should apologize to you for stealing some of your coffee."

She blinked at me and then seemed to struggle to hold back a laugh. She failed, a soft guffaw spilling out. "Don't be silly. I'm the one who ruined *your* shirt. I can—I'll give you some money to cover the cleaning costs."

I waved her off, still smiling. "Really, don't worry about it. I'll be able to get it out in the wash." The lie slipped effortlessly from my lips. Even dry cleaning might not remove the stain; the shirt was probably a loss. But it was a minor sacrifice. "Don't worry, I'm not one of those guys who doesn't have a clue how to do his own laundry."

"Oh, I wasn't trying to imply that." She bit her lip, and it occurred to me that close up she was more appealing than I'd first given her credit for. Or maybe that was less about the details of her face and more the fact that she obviously wasn't at all ditzy. Her concern felt totally genuine. "I still feel bad. Are you sure there isn't anything I can do to make up for it?"

And so generous with that opening. I let my smile stretch a little wider and tipped my head toward her bags. "Clearly the problem is that you're carrying too much. How about you let me help you with your bags so I can ensure no one else's shirt meets the same fate mine did?"

Her eyes narrowed slightly—she was smart enough to be wary of a random stranger offering to carry her things. But I'd phrased it in such a way that it didn't sound like too much of a come-on, and it wasn't as if her snacks were all that valuable. And I could tell she was a little intrigued by me.

"That sounds like *you'd* be doing *me* a favor," she said, shifting her weight.

I shrugged. "I'd see it more as a favor to humanity in general. I'm guessing you're heading to the college campus? I have to walk that way anyway to get back to my car. You might as well be able to enjoy the rest of your coffee without having to do a juggling act."

Her eyebrow arched a smidge, but she handed over one of the bags. She paused for a moment afterward as if confirming I wasn't going to run off with it or something, but it must have been obvious this would have been a very strange scam. If that were the scam I was running.

"I am going back to campus," she said as we moved to cross the street. "Is it that obvious?"

I glanced down at her bag. "These totally look like study snacks. And this is the part of the city where most of the students come to shop. Just an educated guess. Have you been at the university for long? I haven't seen you around before."

She laughed again, a little more relaxed this time. "I don't leave the campus all that often. My roommate says I study too much. And I only transferred here a few months ago."

"I hear it's a good university," I said. Always good to lead with reasonably innocuous but friendly small talk. "I'm glad you got in. I'm Beckett, by the way."

"Madelyn," the girl said automatically, and then clamped her mouth as if she was thinking better of having given her name that freely. "I guess *you're* not a student," she ventured after a moment.

I'd already given that away with my comment about having simply heard the university was good. At twenty-three, I could have claimed to be a grad-student, but there was no point in lying about things so easily exposed.

I didn't have to be specific about the truth either, though. She might not be a typical college girl, but I doubted she'd have a high opinion of the ways I'd gotten the most important parts of my education.

"Not at the moment," I said. "My school days are behind me. What are you studying, Madelyn?"

"Biology. Maybe a second major in microbiology if the classes line up with my schedule, but I'm not sure about that yet."

She rattled off those facts so easily that I could let out an impressed whistle without needing to fake my reaction at all. She was definitely a smarter cookie than I'd have given her credit for at a glance. Not just a science major, but considering a double major? I might not have ever attended university here, but I knew the place had a reputation for its science program. She'd have needed excellent grades to get in, and it'd be a challenging program to keep up with.

Maybe she wasn't going to be the weak link I'd needed after all.

But school smarts were a very different thing from street smarts, as I should know. "You must be awfully busy," I said. "I can see why you'd need to spend a lot of time studying. It mustn't leave much room for enjoying the rest of the college experience."

"Oh, I get out enough to stop me from going bonkers. I've never been a party animal anyway."

I could easily believe that now. "Fair enough. I was just thinking, it must be hard to even socialize much—keeping up with friends, relationships."

"To be honest, I don't have a whole lot of those," Madelyn said with another laugh, this one slightly embarrassed.

I cocked an eyebrow at her. "Oh, no? Pretty girl like you?" Then I knit my brow as if I'd just remembered something. "You know, I think I have seen you in town before, from a distance, with some guy… Dark hair, maybe Latino? That's probably why I assumed. It might not have been you at all."

The guy she'd been dancing with at the club had certainly *looked* like he wanted to get a whole lot more than friendly with her. He'd been a few beats from fucking her right there on the dance floor, as far as I'd been able to tell. Maybe it'd just been a fling, but Madelyn wasn't striking me as the kind of girl who went for friends-with-benefits or one-night stands.

"Oh," she said, and her cheeks flushed a deeper pink that told me the interest between the two of them wasn't all on his side.

The sight brought an unexpected flare of annoyance into my chest. I should have wanted her to be invested in the trio so that she'd have information to share, but some part of me wanted to growl at the thought of him putting his hands on her again.

"The only guys I've gone anywhere with recently are just friends," she went on. "Well, maybe only acquaintances—I don't know how to label them exactly…" She trailed off, looking even more flustered. Interesting, even though it provoked another jab of jealousy.

"Sounds a bit complicated," I said in a gently teasing tone meant to set her back at ease, and then added more seriously, "I hope they're not jerking you around."

"Oh, no, nothing like that," she said, a bit too quickly I thought. "They just—they're helping me with a sort of project, that's all. We've only met up a couple of times."

There was more to it than she was saying, I could tell. I couldn't discern whether she was involved with them enough that she'd know anything about the activities I was curious about, though.

But maybe it didn't matter, because the more I'd talked to her, the more she'd intrigued *me*. A biology major who didn't socialize much but was perfectly gracious when I'd gotten her into a jam, who'd somehow gotten entangled with three guys who were delving into the city's criminal underworld?

I had the feeling there was so much more to her than I'd uncovered yet. But we'd just reached the edge of campus. She stopped and turned to me, and my heart sank more than I was prepared for, especially as I took in her apologetic smile that nonetheless brightened her pretty face.

"Well, this is me. Thank you for your help with the bag, and sorry again about your shirt. I promise I'm not usually that clumsy."

I doubted she was, not when she wasn't being set up. I handed the bag over to alleviate any worries she might have had that I was going to draw out the conversation by holding her belongings hostage.

Should I ask for her phone number? No, she'd probably find that too forward. I was still essentially a stranger to her, and she obviously wasn't the type to collect potential boyfriends. Anyway, I didn't want her mentioning anything about me to her friends—maybe acquaintances, maybe something more—which meant keeping this meeting low key.

"It was my pleasure," I said smoothly. "And I swear the spill was no big deal. I hope I'll see you around again, Madelyn. In the meantime, good luck with your studies."

Her shoulders relaxed when I didn't push for anything else, and I knew I'd made the right call. "Thanks, Beckett. Maybe we will run into each other again."

She gave a little wave with the hand holding her now-half-empty coffee cup and walked off toward the university buildings. I watched her for a few seconds, admiring the resoluteness in her stride that I hadn't registered before, and then strolled away.

Oh, she would be seeing me again. Before very long, too. I didn't need her phone number to ensure that. I could arrange another 'coincidental' meet-up as easy as snapping my fingers.

It was only a matter of time until I found out what I needed—and satisfied all my newfound curiosity about *her* too.

CHAPTER 11

Madelyn

"They actually brought you along?" Summer said, her thin eyebrows rising on my phone's screen. "I thought Logan was trying to keep you out of the investigation."

I bit into one of the cookies I'd gotten from the grocery store this morning as I considered my answer. Naturally my best friend had asked about my stolen car investigation not long after we'd started this video chat, and naturally I'd told her about last night's excursion, but I wasn't sure I was going to like her response to the full story.

I squirmed on my dorm-room bed and made myself look directly at the phone where it was propped on my pillow. The chewy sweetness of the oatmeal chocolate chip cookie only offset my uneasiness a little. "Well… he didn't *want* to bring me. I basically sat on the hood of his car until he gave in, and he swore that as soon as I messed up, which he assumes I'll do, he's never letting me get involved again. But he did let me come. And I didn't mess anything up. So there."

Summer lowered her fork from where she'd been bringing a bite of her lunch to her mouth. Her round face with its high cheekbones looked most natural when it was full of energy, either playful or determined. I didn't like the somberness that darkened it now.

"Maddie, he argued with you about it until you forced his hand? Just to tag along to a club that regular people go to all the time? He's still *such* an asshole."

I winced. "I know. I realize he's being an asshole. But the three of them seem to know what they're doing as far as tracking down clues. I can put up with Logan's crap for a little while if it means I get my stuff back."

Summer sighed and swept her long, smooth hair behind her ear. She'd dyed the dark strands with henna so they had a burgundy tint now. "Come on. I know you. You're not just insisting on going along because it's your car. Don't tell me you're not still hoping you'll get answers out of him."

"He didn't *use* to be an asshole," I burst out, and flushed when I realized how I'd raised my voice. "Something's going on with him," I added in a more subdued tone. "Something's been going on with him for a while. If I can find out what, then that wouldn't be a bad thing. But I'm not, like, pining over him or something, Summer. I'm *way* over that."

"I don't know. Sometimes people just change." Summer grimaced. "Look, I can admit that he wasn't a bad guy before. I remember him in high school—I know he stood up for you back in junior high. Maybe that guy is still in there underneath, but I hope you're prepared that he could simply be an asshole all the way through. Because he's had more than enough time to get his head out of his ass by now."

My shoulders slumped. I had no argument against the points she'd made. "I'm not expecting anything. Mostly I just want to find my car and my dad's box."

Summer offered me a small but warm smile that brought more of the usual glow back to her face. "I don't mean to get on your case about it. I just hated seeing what he did to you, and I don't want him hurting you again. That's all."

"Believe me," I said, "I'm not going to let him in enough that he could hurt me again. I know better than that."

"Of course you do." Summer's smile stretched into a grin. "You're Madelyn Silver, lady conqueror."

I snorted. "I haven't conquered much other than cookies and lab reports lately, but I'm working on it."

Summer's gaze flicked to the side. "Crap, I've got to get going for my next class. Talk soon?"

"Always."

After we'd ended the call, restlessness wound through my bones. I hadn't received any updates from the Vigil so far today. Had they gotten anywhere with the info Logan had pried out of whoever he'd talked to at the club—info he'd refused to share with me because he'd claimed he didn't want me going off on my own to dig into it. Like he cared about my safety and not just acting like some kind of professional detective.

I could go over to the Vigil office and find out. The guys seemed to hang out there a lot—it also made a perfect study spot while they were on campus, after all. Hopefully I'd catch one of them. If not, I'd swing by again after my afternoon class.

I hopped off the bed and grabbed my backpack and a thin hoodie in case the early spring air cooled again later in the day. When I stepped out of the building, the breeze swept over me with a subtle warmth that loosened some of the tension in my shoulders. The scent of freshly mowed grass tickled my nose, a smell that always made me feel like spring had really arrived. I sucked in a deep breath and strode forward.

Maybe some of my high school crusades had been a little over the top, but Summer was right. I could conquer anything I put my mind to.

I was just coming up on the law library, about ten feet from the front door, when a tall, brawny figure ducked through the doorway and headed along the side of the building toward a different path. Logan. He looked so lost in thought I didn't know if he'd even noticed me.

My feet stalled for a second as my pulse hiccupped. Then I pushed myself forward, hurrying after him.

Who knew when I'd have the chance to talk to him alone again? Summer was right that it was well past time that I got some answers. How ridiculous had it been when I'd been chatting with that guy Beckett this morning and I stumbled all over explaining who my stepbrother and his friends were to me?

I'd shied away from addressing the real problems between us, but that wasn't the kind of woman I was. I wasn't going to let him turn me into a cringing wimp just because he'd tossed me away like a dirty tissue two years ago.

"Logan!" I said as I closed the distance between us, holding on to the surge of boldness that'd propelled me after him.

I couldn't help noticing the way he stiffened at the sound of my voice, which he'd no doubt recognized. He wasn't happy to hear me calling after him at all. Well, tough cookies, Mr. Brooks.

I half expected him to march onward pretending he hadn't heard me, but he spun on his heel to face me, his expression hard.

I came to a stop in front of him, tucking my thumbs around the straps of my backpack as if for leverage. "We need to talk."

"I actually have somewhere to be," he said curtly.

I shrugged. “Fine. Then I’ll walk with you and we’ll talk on the way to wherever you’re going.”

Logan’s mouth flattened, which told me he didn’t really have anywhere all that urgent he needed to go. “What’s so important, Madelyn? We don’t know anything else about your car yet, but of course you could have just texted about that.”

Well, he’d just given me the perfect opening. I folded my arms over my chest. “That’d be a little hard considering you have me blocked on every form of communication I’m aware of.”

A muscle in his jaw twitched. Oh, was this topic of conversation irritating to him? Too fucking bad.

“You have the other guys’ numbers,” he said. “You don’t need mine.”

I stared him down, drawing my spine as straight as I could. “But I do need to know what the hell happened with us?”

“With us?” A hint of a sneer crept into his voice. “There’s no ‘us,’ and there never was.”

My teeth set on edge. He got under my skin way too easily.

“We were friends,” I said. “Or at least friendly. We got along in school and after our parents started dating, for years. And then all of a sudden you just put all these walls up. And then there was—two years ago—and then you *completely* shut me out like I’d done something awful to you… And you’re still treating me like that. I don’t get it. Why are you being like this? Why *have* you been like this?”

My voice was raw by the end of that tirade. I hadn’t meant to say so much all at once, but once I’d started, it’d kept spilling out. I clamped my jaw shut and held Logan’s gaze, daring him to finally give me a straight answer.

But of course that was wishful thinking.

“Not everything in the world revolves around you,” he said, his voice getting even terser. “And you don’t have the right to know everything that's going on in my life just because our parents got married."

Fury blazed through me at the brisk dismissal. "Oh, yeah? And what about what happened in the basement bathroom back home? Do I have a right to know about *that*, considering I was there and all?"

"All that happened was a stupid mistake," Logan bit out, the words hitting me like little knives. "I moved on. It's obviously time that you did too."

Something in me crumbled even as I held myself steady on the outside. *A stupid mistake.* Was that how he thought about it?

"I just don't get it," I said, quieter now. "If you have some problem with me or with something I did, you could just tell me about it. We used to talk. I thought you liked me, as a person. It seemed totally out of the blue. And then— Something must have happened, Logan."

He shook his head, his eyes flashing, his shoulders rigid. "You only see what you want to see. And you obviously can't take a hint. I'm not into you. I don't want anything to do with you. I can't wait until we find your car and we can go our separate ways again. But you *had* to follow me all the way to the same college… Do you have any idea how pathetic that is?"

I flinched as if he'd slapped me. It felt like he had. Was that really what he thought of me? That I was some clueless girl who'd transferred over a hopeless crush?

"I didn't come here because of you," I shot back, my hands clenching as they dropped to my sides. "This school has an amazing life sciences program, way better than the college back home, and—"

"And a dozen other schools in this part of the country have good programs too. If you had the grades to get in here, you could have gone anywhere else in the country too. But no, you had to come to the same school as me."

"I liked not being too far from home." My voice wobbled, my emotions fraying both in the wake of his hostility and because I knew he wasn't totally wrong. I'd come here for the science program first, but the fact that it'd meant I might see Logan again, might find out what was going on with him, had been there in the back of my mind. I hadn't really considered applying anywhere else.

Logan ignored my protest. He jabbed a finger in my direction. "You're nothing to me except a temporary client, and you can forget about becoming anything more than that. So get over yourself and find someone else to obsess over."

He whipped around and stalked off without giving me a chance to say anything else. Not that I had any idea what I could have said. My throat had constricted so tightly it ached.

I still couldn't wrap my head around how he'd gone from my defender and friend to a guy who seemed to hate me. It was *because* of him that I'd become the crusader Summer had referred to me as. I'd been so downcast after Dad's death that I'd become an increasingly easy target for the kind of kids who liked to poke fun and pull cruel pranks, and I hadn't snapped out of that haze until I'd watched Logan put those bullies in their place on my behalf.

Hearing him talk them into submission, leveraging his popularity to my advantage, had made me want to be stronger. To be able to stand up not just for myself but for other people who needed it, like Logan had for me. That was what Dad would have wanted too—not for me to end up withdrawn and eaten up by guilt.

But somewhere in the last few years, something had changed. Logan clearly wasn't interested in telling me what. Maybe there really wasn't any reason to do with me at all. Maybe he had simply changed into a total asshole.

I swallowed thickly and gave myself a shake, pulling myself together. Whatever. It didn't change anything—I'd never thought we'd actually become friends again, let alone anything more. I could live without an explanation.

But it did tell me that no way in hell did I trust him to keep me in the loop about the investigation. Had they really not made any progress, or was he lying about that so he could shut me out there too?

I walked back to the law library, gathering confidence as I left the conversation behind. Screw Logan, and screw his fucked-up attitude. He thought he could go around doing whatever and treating people however he wanted? I could take a page out of that book.

I brushed past the main desk and hustled onward to the Vigil's office at the back of the room. The doorknob turned with a twist. I peeked inside, a little surprised that it'd actually worked, and found Dexter sitting at the computer, typing away. He paused to glance over at me, his eyes catching mine for just a second before veering away. "Hi, Madelyn. Did something come up about your car?"

I guessed there really wasn't anything new if he'd ask me that instead of assuming I'd come to him for information. But a strange calm settled over me as I looked back at him. Dexter had given me straight answers so far. He didn't try to push my buttons like either of the other guys in their very different ways.

Between the three of them, he was the only member of the Vigil I trusted to treat me fairly and to put the investigation and my stake in it first.

I walked over until I was a few feet from his seat. I stopped there, biting my lip. "No news on my end. But… do you think you could do me a small favor?"

CHAPTER 12

Slade

I pushed harder through the last two reps of my workout, making my body strain to keep up, and I finished with sweat beading across my forehead and down my back. The campus gym had an expensive setup with plenty of room for students, and I took full advantage. All three of us did, even if Dexter was a little more infrequent in his visits. We knew that strength and flexibility might be the difference between life and death one day with the kind of shit we got into.

I grabbed the spray bottle and wiped down the bench and the weights that I'd been pressing, followed by a swipe of my face with the front of my muscle tee. The burn spreading through my muscles told me I'd made good use of my time.

I headed over to the rooms where the more structured fitness activities were held. Logan's kickboxing session should be just finishing up. Just as I reached the short hallway, he came around the corner, equally sweaty but looking just as grim as when we'd come in.

Damn. I'd been hoping he'd work some of that bad temper out of him. No such luck.

He nodded to me, and we walked together to the locker room.

"Good class?" I asked.

Logan grunted. "I took down everyone I was up against except one jerk who kept trying to skirt the rules."

"Hmm. I guess we're not much of anyone to complain about that approach."

Logan grimaced at me and grabbed the locker room door, holding it open so I could pass in front of him. If anyone else had done that, I might have been irritated, but I knew from him it wasn't a sign that he was catering to some assumed feebleness. He'd have done the same for Dexter, just automatically. Logan always felt like he had to do a little more of the heavy lifting.

"It was a good workout, anyway," he said as we headed toward the shower stalls. A couple of guys passing us glanced down at the bright blue prosthetic poking from beneath my shorts with widening eyes, and then hustled on by when I gave them a wave and a cheery grin. I snorted and refocused on my best friend.

He did look a little looser than when we'd come in. Maybe I could get away with some of the prying I'd been wanting to do ever since the club a couple of nights ago.

I grabbed my towel, soap, and disinfectant wipes and marched toward the shower stall at the end of the row that had a bar on the wall for extra support. Logan followed, taking the one beside mine as I bent over and unstrapped the prosthetic from the stump that served as my knee. After all that sweating, I'd take extra care to disinfect it after showering.

I propped the prosthetic on the bench outside the shower where I could still see it from the stall and hopped inside with a hand on the bar. I might prefer to make use of the same facilities as everyone else when I could match them just fine, but I could admit that in certain situations I needed a little extra help. Wet floors on one foot were a recipe for disaster. As I'd unfortunately found out back in my elementary school days in an incident I'd had to work very hard to erase from my classmates' memories with a whole lot of other antics.

I tossed my clothes onto the bench from the stall and turned on the water. After I'd given my hair a quick scrub, I angled my head out of the water enough that I could talk.

"You seem like you had a lot of stress to work off," I said casually. "Anything in particular on your mind? I'm trying to avoid thinking about the end-of-term essay that's been kicking my ass."

Logan made a dismissive sound. "It's always good to blow off some energy."

I leaned into the shower wall as I poured a generous amount of body wash in my hands and began smearing it across my body. "Does that energy have a name? Maybe Madelyn Silver?"

Logan took a long moment to reply, and my smile only grew. "It has nothing to do with her," he muttered.

I guffawed. "Yeah? I thought you were a *good* liar. So there's been something between you, huh?"

"Yeah, right. Her fucking case is frustrating as hell. Having her insert herself into the middle of it isn't any picnic either. That's all."

Why was he lying to me about it, even after I'd prodded him? *Was* he lying? Thinking back to the way he'd looked when he'd broken up our dance in the club, how pissed off he'd been, I didn't think I'd imagined the flash of jealousy in his eyes. There hadn't been any other reason for him to be pissed off. He'd gotten to talk to his contact. Nothing had gone wrong.

Of course, considering how wrapped up *I'd* gotten in Maddie's charms in that moment, maybe I'd been interpreting his reaction through that lens. He could have simply been irritated that I was getting involved with her in ways beyond the case, since he was so intent on shutting her out of our lives as quickly as possible.

"Seriously?" I wheedled. "You got to live in the same house as a girl that hot and you never even played a little tonsil hockey?"

"Get your mind out of the gutter for once, Slade. I wasn't exactly so short on options I needed to go after my own stepsister. She's a major annoyance, and that's it."

His tone firmed with the last words in a way that said, *End of conversation.*

I rinsed myself off quickly and gave my body a swift rub-down with my towel before hefting myself out of the stall to sink onto the bench. As I tugged on my clothes, Logan emerged, getting himself together with equal briskness. He didn't seem interested in continuing any kind of conversation with me at all now.

As I slipped the sock over my stump, my mind drifted back to Maddie. I'd *tried* to follow the bro code and determine his feelings for her. If he was going to insist she was nothing but an irritation to him, then what could I do but take him at face value? I'd given him every opportunity to inform me that he had a stake there or that my presumably obvious interest bothered him, and he hadn't said a word.

If he lost a chance he wouldn't even admit he wanted to take because I got there first, then it'd be his own damn fault.

Because lord, did I want to go there. I'd already been impressed by the way Maddie had stood up to Logan. Not many people were willing to challenge him as openly as she had on multiple occasions in just the past few days. And then dancing with her, feeling her rise to *that* challenge even though the steps hadn't been familiar to her, doing her best to match me…

She might not have quite kept up with the actual moves, but she'd given herself over to the rhythm rather than stiffening up.

She'd trusted me to guide her. And the feel of that sleekly curvy body against mine…

From the little I'd known of her back in high school, I'd never have expected to find her this attractive. She'd been pretty, sure, but she'd also been the studious type, only stepping into the spotlight when she was taking on one cause or another. I'd had no idea that passion permeated so many other parts of her life. What would it be like to soak it up in every possible way?

To move my hands over those curves without clothes between us. To claim those pouty lips. To hear the sounds she'd make as I unraveled her. To find out just how well *she* could unravel me.

Fuck. Just thinking about it was getting me hard, like I was a preteen who'd just caught a glimpse of a hot girl's cleavage and not a grown man who should have better self-control. She had an effect on me, all right.

And she was so much more than just a body. There was that boldness that drew me to her, but she had a caring streak a mile wide to go along with it. She barely knew me, and I was best friends with the guy who was giving her the hardest time in the history of the universe right now, but she'd still offered to use her contacts to see if I could try out one of those experimental prosthetics.

If she'd had any idea how much we weren't telling her—how much *I* wasn't telling her…

A knot of guilt twisted my stomach. I glanced over at Logan as I reattached my prosthetic. "Are we really going to keep Maddie in the dark about the bigger picture? I mean, now that she's kind of crashed our party already."

Logan's eyes hardened. "Are you kidding me? She's already pushing her way into places she doesn't belong just over her car. Nothing good would come from getting her involved in the rest."

His voice was firm, but I couldn't help pushing a little harder. "Is anything good going to come out of hiding it from her?"

Logan spun on me, his eyes flashing, and loomed with the few inches he had over me in a way I'd normally only seen him use on perps we were intimidating. "No one should say anything to Madelyn about *any* of our work other than her stolen car. Or do you have a problem with that?"

There was an understated threat in his voice. I swallowed hard, abruptly ashamed of provoking him. I knew what a sensitive subject it was, and he knew more about that area of our investigations than Dexter or I did. As much as we'd all worked on it together, it was his pet project. He should know what could get us into more danger.

"No, man, of course not," I said. "If you say that's a no go, then it's a no go. I just thought it was worth asking."

Logan held my gaze for a few seconds longer before his stance relaxed. As he turned to tuck the rest of his belongings into his bag, I adjusted the sock over my stump to make sure it wasn't creased in an uncomfortable way against the prosthetic. It'd taken me a while to adjust when I was a little kid, but for most of my life, wearing the thing had been as normal as putting on a pair of sneakers was for anyone else.

We headed out together, and I groped for another topic of conversation. Something that had nothing to do with Madelyn or anything else that might piss my best friend off. But as we stepped out of the building, Logan's phone dinged with an incoming text.

He pulled it out of his pocket and paused in mid-stride. Then he shot me a tight smile. "The guy I talked to at the club came through. We've got a new lead to check out—and we should get on it fast."

CHAPTER 13

Madelyn

I stepped out of the Uber and glanced at the concrete-walled building across the street, which had a rack of tires out front. A large neon sign above the entrance read, "Javier's Mechanic Shop," and below it, in smaller writing, was what appeared to be a list of the most common services. Contrasting with the old, yellowing color of the concrete, Logan's dark sedan was parked off to the side. All three of the Vigil members stood around it, heads bent together as if they were discussing their approach to the situation at hand.

I checked the traffic and hustled across the road before striding toward them. Slade noticed me first, confusion and then amusement flickering through his expression. Dexter's eyes pierced into mine next, revealing nothing of his thoughts before he looked back at Logan. My stepbrother finally glanced over his shoulder.

His gaze collided with mine. It didn't surprise me when his lips tightened and his expression hardened, but his reaction to my presence still stung. I could only imagine what he was thinking, remembering the way he'd blatantly told me to take a hint only to find me in front of him without his invitation.

"What are you doing here?" he demanded, turning to fully face me.

"Helping find my car." I shrugged, stopping a few feet away from them and crossing my arms. "The same thing that I told you I was going to do from the start."

Logan's jaw worked. "How did you even know we'd be here?"

Frustration flared in my chest. "Oh, you mean because you didn't fill me in, even though you said I could be part of the investigation as long as I didn't screw things up? I was really hoping that you would have kept your word, but I wasn't going to put too much stake in that, so I asked Dexter to text me if you came up with any leads."

Logan's gaze shot to Dexter, his eyes narrowing, before refocusing on me. "You went behind my back?"

My laugh came out harsh. "Only because you went behind mine. I asked him to keep me up to date on the investigation since I apparently can't trust you to do that. Dexter, at least, is good to his word."

"This isn't a part that you should be around for. That's the only reason I didn't tell you."

I snorted. "It's pretty clear you don't think I should be around for any of it, so forgive me if I'm not going to go by your word on that. At this point, I couldn't give a rat's ass how you feel. You gave me your word that I could help, so I'm going to help. It's as simple as that."

And I just wouldn't think about all the other things he'd said since then.

Logan swung around to glare at Dexter. "And you see no problem with tipping her off without my go-ahead?"

Dexter held his gaze for a moment before his focus veered elsewhere, but he stayed totally calm, no sign that he was intimidated by the bigger guy. "She hasn't interfered with anything we've been doing yet. We did agree to let her join in as long as she didn't get in the way."

Slade chuckled and popped one of his cinnamon candies into his mouth. "You never told us specifically that we *shouldn't* talk to Maddie about it, Logan. Dexter went by what you said rather than what you didn't. If you didn't want her here, you shouldn't have made the deal."

The support from the other two guys gave me the confidence to raise my chin and glower at Logan. "I'm only sticking around until I get my stuff back. Don't worry, I won't be a *pathetic* shadow once this is all over."

Something flashed in Logan's eyes, but he was the one who looked away first. His shoulders rigid, he stalked into the mechanic shop without another word. I didn't think going in there furious was going to help him handle the situation right, but who was I to tell *him* what to do? If he ruined things, he'd have no one to blame but himself.

Slade motioned to me as he and Dexter moved to follow. "Stay close to us and take a good look around. Let us know if you see any sign of your car—or parts that could have come from it. Otherwise, it's better if you focus on watching rather than talking—we've got more experience with guys like these."

He said it smoothly without a hint that he was being patronizing, which made the instructions a lot easier to swallow than if they'd come in the tone Logan usually took with me. I nodded and hustled after him. The last thing I wanted to do was make a misstep and prove my infuriating stepbrother right.

It appeared Logan had gotten his own frustrations in check quickly. I found him approaching the reception desk with a confident but unruffled air.

"I need to check on a car I brought in," he said to the man behind the desk.

The guy squinted at him and then tapped at his computer, looking a bit puzzled.

I scanned the front office quickly. It was clean enough, the linoleum floor a bit scuffed around the edges of the industrial rug. A few pictures of men standing in front of retro cars hung on the walls. Nothing appeared particularly suspicious to my inexperienced eyes or related to my missing vehicle.

"And your name is…?" the guy at the desk said to Logan, but Slade was ambling past the desk to a door across from it. He was already pushing it open when the guy gave a shout. "Hey, clients don't go in the bay!"

But Slade had sauntered right into the gloomier space I vaguely made out beyond the doorway, acting like he owned the place, and as the guy from the desk hurried over, Logan and Dexter followed. I darted after them, remembering Slade's warning to stick with them.

"Just want to make sure the work's being done right," Slade was saying breezily. He and the other guys fanned out in different directions through the large bay that held a couple of cars on jacks as well as one right on the stained cement floor. Dexter had taken out his phone, no doubt snapping pictures of everything around us, but none of the three cars looked anything like mine.

I followed him instinctively, since he was the one who'd let me tag along to begin with. The guy from the desk hesitated in the doorway as the phone rang behind him. "You need to get out of here," he snapped at the Vigil guys before dashing back to answer it.

A man in a grease-smudged undershirt and jeans scrambled out from under the car he'd been working on. He swiped his hands on his pants and started toward Logan. "What the hell are you kids doing in here? This is employees only."

How long were we going to manage to stay in this part of the shop? I forced my gaze to skim across the room, taking in all the details I could absorb.

Unfortunately, I didn't know much about cars. I could tell none of the three in front of me were mine, but what about that stack of parts in the corner? Had any of them come from my ride? Was there anything suspicious about the racks of tools along the back wall? Did chop shops use equipment a regular mechanic didn't?

Okay, so I was a little out of my depth. But I did know *my* car better than any of the guys here. That had to count for something.

Logan turned toward the advancing mechanic without any sign of concern. "We're looking for a 2006 Chevy Malibu," he said casually. "Green. Have you had one brought in recently?"

A slight edge had crept into his voice, and he folded his arms over his chest, the substantial muscles there flexing. Even I could read the understated threat that he wasn't going to be happy if the workers lied to him about it.

"You see a Malibu around here?" the mechanic demanded, waving his hand toward the rest of the bay.

"Maybe it's in bits and pieces now," Logan suggested, striding onward. The other guys moved deeper into the bay, checking out every inch of the space, so I drifted after them, my heart thumping fast.

The mechanic stomped toward them. "Get the fuck out of here!"

"Or what?" Slade drawled. "You'll call the police on us? I'm sure you *really* want the cops poking around here."

I didn't know if he'd seen something to confirm that statement or was just acting on instinct, but the mechanic stiffened a bit. His face flushed with anger. I braced myself for what he'd do next—and didn't register the rasp of footsteps behind me before it was too late.

Thick arms swung around me from behind, pinning my elbows to my sides. The smell of stale sweat washed over me as a broad body yanked me against him with a menacing guffaw. His voice came out hoarsely hostile. "Maybe they'll listen when they know their girl will get hurt if they don't."

For the first instant, my body froze up. But then years of self-defense training kicked in. The Krav Maga philosophy that we'd been reminded of nearly every class flashed through my mind: when facing a potential threat, react as quickly as possible and with all the force necessary to get yourself out of the danger.

I jerked my elbows wide, hard enough to force my attacker's grip to slide up my arms in his surprise. When he tried to tighten his hold, I jerked to the side, clenched my hand into a fist, and slammed it backward one, two, three times into his groin.

The first blow glanced off his thigh, but the second and third landed. The guy groaned and stumbled backward, and I broke from his hold, swinging around to shove him even farther away. My other hand whipped across his face, smacking into his nose just before my heel rammed into his gut.

The last move nearly screwed me over. I didn't retract my leg quite fast enough, and the big guy managed to snatch my ankle while he clutched his groin with his other hand. He yanked, and I staggered, losing my balance. I tried to catch the back of a nearby car, but my forearm just scraped across the edge of its bumper. Pain seared through my arm.

As I hit the floor ass first, my attacker sprang at me, but I wasn't cowed. I kicked out again and managed to jab the full force of my foot right between his legs where he was already tender.

"Fuck!" he shouted, crumpling with one hand pressed to his junk again and the other to his nose, which was dribbling blood from my previous blow.

I scrambled backward on the floor, vaguely aware of the Vigil guys rushing over around me. The whole scuffle had taken mere seconds. My gaze dropped to my arm, taking in the thin streak of blood running toward my wrist from the scrape beneath my elbow… and then I noticed a few chunks of dried reddish mud on the floor under the car I'd scratched myself on.

"Wow," Slade said, sounding startled but also awed. Dexter was just staring at the scene. But Logan came marching past me like a tank bearing down on the guy sprawled by the far wall.

"Put your hands on her again, and you'll face something ten times worse," he snarled, his voice vibrating with more anger than I'd ever heard from him before. He'd pulled himself even taller, looming over my attacker with his extensive brawn on full display, what I could see of his expression taut with rage. "You'll wish you were never fucking *born*."

The man sputtered and then—in a spurt of bravery or stupidity, I couldn't tell—started to pull himself to his feet, glowering up at Logan. "You'd better get out of this shop or—"

Logan pushed closer so quickly I winced in anticipation for a strike, but he didn't lay a hand on the man. He just spoke as if through clenched teeth, menace dripping from his words. "Don't even think about it. Or maybe do. I'd just love an excuse to see how much I can make you suffer. She's lying on the floor bleeding, you prick. I think a little payback is in order."

Part of me wanted to point out that technically I was sitting up, and I wasn't actually bleeding very much, and also I'd already paid the jerk back with plenty of blows of my own. Part of me stayed frozen, struggling to process what I was seeing. I'd seen Logan pissed off, sure, but never so absolutely enraged. He sounded like he might be capable of almost anything.

It was scary… and it was also, against my will, a little thrilling. He was that furious on *my* behalf, because I'd been hurt. He sounded like he was prepared to pummel this guy to oblivion to defend me. How the hell was that even possible?

How the hell could I welcome the sight?

The logical side of my brain overrode the rest. I didn't want him getting into a fistfight over me with whatever other trouble that might bring. We were here to find my car, not to do battle—and I had reason to believe we were closer than we might have realized.

"Logan," I said, loud and clear to make sure he heard me. "My car's been here. The same mud—it's on the floor where they've got this one jacked up now."

Dexter knelt down beside me—checking my arm as if to confirm the scrape wasn't that bad before turning his attention to the floor, I noticed with a twinge of gratitude. He rubbed a bit of the dried mud between his fingers. "It's definitely the same stuff."

Logan's shoulders came down a smidge. He shot one last glare at my attacker and spun around to take in the rest of the space. Without another word, he was barging past the cars to a garage-style door at the back of the bay.

"Hey," the first mechanic protested, but his voice came out so weak even I wasn't concerned about him now.

"What are you going to do about it?" Slade asked him in a jaunty tone as he walked over to help me onto my feet. "Tell us we're *not* allowed to take our rightful property back?"

He let me stand on my own, and the rest of us hurried after Logan, who'd just hit the button to open the door. The steel surface whirred upward—and revealed a small parking lot in the back of the building with four vehicles parked in a row. The one at the farthest left had a familiar green hood.

My heart leapt. I dashed over to my Malibu and ran my hand over the side as if I needed to touch it to confirm it was really there. My hard-earned ride that I'd started to think I might never see again. It looked perfectly fine, not at all damaged, no more scratches or dents than had been there before it'd been stolen. A sigh of relief rushed out of me.

"For fuck's sake," Logan growled. He spun around as if to confront the mechanics, but all I wanted to do was get out of here, not linger in the awful parts of the confrontation.

I fished my keys out of my pocket. "I've got my fob. We don't need anything else from them. Can we just get going?" I paused. "Unless we should call the police and report it."

"It won't get us very far," Dexter remarked evenly. "Since you didn't report the car stolen already, the guys can easily claim *you* parked it here just now, or that you brought it in earlier to have work done. They're probably not the people who stole it anyway."

"No," Logan said, but there was an ominous note to his voice I didn't totally like. He shot a glower into the bay and then turned back to us, suddenly all business. "Dex, ride with Madelyn back to campus so she doesn't have to go alone. Slade and I will meet you there."

Dex nodded and moved to the passenger side as I clicked the button to unlock the door. I didn't really care about getting the police involved—I had my car back, and someone else could worry about catching the assholes who'd taken it if they kept up their shady practices.

But as shaky as I still was from the fight and the sudden discovery of my car, I couldn't help lingering over Logan's last words as I sank into the driver's seat. What did it matter to Logan whether I had to make the drive alone? Shouldn't he be jumping for joy that now I'd have no excuse to seek him out again?

Or was it possible that somewhere deep down, in the same

place that rage had come from, I did still matter to him a little, no matter what he'd said to me yesterday?

And if I did, why was he working so hard at acting like I didn't?

CHAPTER 14

Madelyn

Dexter stayed quiet through the drive back, flipping through something on his phone, but I couldn't say I minded. My body was still buzzing with adrenaline after the confrontation in the mechanic shop, my mind whirling.

That guy had been so willing to use physical force to threaten me. What the hell else did they do in that place other than deal in stolen cars?

And where had the menace I'd seen from Logan come from? He'd always stood up to bullies—the fact that he'd done as much for me back in junior high was one of the main reasons I'd first developed a crush on him—but back then he'd done it with easy-going confidence and disarming words. His substantial physical presence had helped, but I'd never seen him go out of his way to be outright intimidating.

But then, I'd already realized that a lot had changed with him.

When I parked outside my residence building, a strange sense of resignation settled over me. This was it. I'd retrieved my car, and the Vigil's job was complete. No more verbal sparring with Logan, and no more heart-pounding adventures into the criminal underside of the city.

I knew it was for the best, but something tugged at my chest as I thought about going back to my comparatively mundane life with no idea what else these guys were getting into.

As Dexter pushed open the door to get out, nodding to the other guys who'd just pulled up in Logan's car across from us, I leaned over to open the glove compartment. Now that I knew how easily my car could be stolen, I'd like to put Dad's box somewhere that seemed a little less precarious. Stashed away in my dorm room seemed like a reasonable temporary solution.

The compartment swung open… and I simply stared.

There was the user's manual. There was my lip gloss and the first aid kit and mini flashlight I kept in the car for emergencies. A couple of folded papers were sitting on top of the manual, and I snatched them up.

My insurance documentation. The records that I'd been keeping inside Dad's box… which wasn't in the glove compartment at all.

I gaped at the opening for a few moments longer, as if the black lacquer box might materialize before my eyes. Then I pawed at the other items in case it'd somehow gotten obscured behind them.

There was no denying it. The box wasn't there.

I swiveled in my seat, checking under both of the front seats and then peering into the back of the car. No sign of it. I popped the trunk and hurried around to check that too. It still held my spare tire and emergency blanket, but that was it. My stomach twisted.

Slade had sauntered over with a jaunty smile. "Those were some moves you used on that prick back at the shop. Where'd you learn how to do that?"

"Martial arts classes," I said automatically, my attention still focused on finding my treasured possession. "I took them for years. Wanted to learn how to defend myself."

Partly because I'd been ashamed when I'd realized how easily Logan had stood up for me back when we were kids. I hadn't wanted to be the weak, shrinking girl I'd become after Dad's death. Discovering my physical power had been one of the steps I'd taken toward becoming as strong as the boy who'd defended me—as strong as Dad would have wanted me to be. Not that I could admit that to my stepbrother now without him laughing in my face.

"You obviously learned well." Slade chuckled, but his expression turned more serious as I shoved down the lid of the trunk and he saw my face. "What's wrong?"

"My dad's box." I spun around to look at him and the other two guys who'd joined him. "It's not in there. It's not anywhere."

The guys exchanged a glance. Logan frowned. "Are you—"

I jabbed a finger at him. "Don't you dare ask if I'm *sure*, Logan. I checked the glove compartment where I normally keep it, and all through the inside of the car, and the trunk. There's no reason for anyone to have taken it out of the glove compartment to begin with, but it isn't anywhere!"

He held up his hands. "All right, all right."

"Maybe the thieves chucked it out with a bunch of other stuff when they were preparing to pass the car on to the chop shop?" Slade suggested, rubbing his mouth.

I shook my head. "Nothing else is missing. I had a bunch of other things in the glove compartment and the trunk, and everything else is still there. They even took my insurance papers out of the box and left *those* behind." I swept my hair back from my face, my thoughts whirling. "Why would anyone take that? It didn't have anything else in it. It couldn't have been worth much money. It was only important to me because it was my dad's."

I'd rather the culprits had managed to scrap the entire car for parts but left that behind than taken the trinket box. It'd held so many memories… It'd been the one thing of Dad's I'd brought with me to college. This didn't make any sense.

Dexter knit his brow. He stepped past me to check the car over himself, brisky and efficiently—and without any of Logan's condescension, so I didn't mind that much. He straightened up with a shake of his head. "Definitely not in there. And given the other factors, it seems like whoever took it must have wanted the box specifically for some reason."

"But *why*?" I asked. "What the heck is going on here?" Had the thief already known they wanted the box before they'd stolen the car? Had I been targeted somehow? It sounded absurd, but I couldn't see why someone who didn't know me would think the box had any significance. It didn't look expensive.

But even as I sorted through those possibilities, I caught the shift of Logan's weight as he glanced at Slade and the tightening of Slade's mouth in return.

"I don't know," Logan said. "It's pretty strange."

Was it? Something about the look they'd exchanged had suggested they weren't totally surprised. I studied them. "Did something like this happen with the other cars?"

"We don't know what happened with the other cars, since we didn't work those cases." Logan's tone had turned firm. "Probably some idiot assumed the box was worth more than it looked like or that you had something valuable inside."

That didn't explain why they'd kept it after opening it and seeing what it did contain, or why they'd left all the other items behind if they'd been looking to sell off whatever they could, but maybe he was right.

I hugged myself, my nerves jittering. The loss of the car had felt bad enough, but the thought of someone going through the things inside, taking the one object that'd meant so much to me, was even more of an invasion.

"Did you talk to anyone else about that box?" Dexter asked with an analytical glint in his eyes.

"I mean, I might have mentioned it to my roommate, but it's not like it's the kind of thing that'd come up in regular conversation." My gaze slid between the three guys. "Even if I had, why would that make a difference? If someone heard me mention it, they should know it was only important for sentimental reasons."

Dexter gave an awkward shrug. Slade popped another cinnamon candy and clicked it thoughtfully against his teeth. The vibe had definitely changed between the guys. A sense of foreboding I couldn't totally explain rolled over me.

Logan squared his shoulders. "You don't have to worry about it. We'll find it for you just like we found the car. It'll probably be enough just to go back to the shop and convince the idiots there to cough it up."

Something about the way he said "convince" combined with his earlier aggressiveness sent an uneasy tingle down my back. "I'll come with you," I said. "I'm the only one who knows exactly what it looks like."

"Your sketch and description got the idea across just fine," he said, his voice hard as steel. "I don't want you setting so much as a toe in that place again after what that asshole tried to pull."

"I'm fine," I protested.

He grabbed my wrist and held up my arm, putting the scrape

below my elbow on full display. "That's not fine. And he could have done worse."

The raw skin there still stung, but the little bit of bleeding had already stopped. I motioned to the front of my car. "I'll clean it up with my first aid kit and be good as new. It's just a scratch. I did worse to the asshole who attacked me."

"Yes, indeed, you did," Slade said with amusement, his gleeful grin only faltering when Logan glared at him, dropping my wrist. I regretted the loss of his warm hand more than I liked.

My stepbrother turned his attention back to me. "You have no idea what you're getting into, Madelyn. Scuffles like that are only the start. I'm not putting you in danger like that again. And if you're with us when we go out to handle shit like this, people are going to keep targeting you because you don't look like a threat. Next time you might not be able to fight your way out so easily."

"But you'll still be in danger then." I set my hands on my hips. "You're getting into it on my behalf. The least I can do is be there to help."

"It's not the same. We've gone through this kind of stuff dozens of times. We know how to handle criminals. You don't, no matter how much big talk you spew out. One wrong step, and you could get *really* injured. What would actually help the most is if you went back to your studies and pretended nothing's wrong until we deliver your Dad's box to you. And then nothing will be wrong."

I didn't know how to argue with the unshakeable certainty in his voice. It painted a picture that made me shiver.

I *had* been attacked, and I hadn't been prepared for the assault at all. My self-defense training had kicked in, thank God, but I definitely wasn't used to getting into fights like that. Would the guys' search really put them—and me—in that much more danger?

Remembering the situation in the mechanic shop, it wasn't difficult to believe. The way Logan had reacted to the attack had shown *he* was ready for possible violence. He hadn't hesitated to step in and show the jerk just who he was messing with. And Slade and Dexter had rushed in too.

What had they been through during past investigations that'd made them so confident dealing with that kind of aggression?

For a moment, the thought of doing what Logan asked—walking up to my dorm room, opening up one of my textbooks, and acting like none of this was going on—brought a wave of relief. I didn't *want* to be grabbed by strange men growling threats; I didn't want to be used as some kind of hostage.

But before that fear could fully take hold, my stubbornness kicked in.

I'd come this far. We were only looking for a simple decorative box, not illicit drugs or a weapon or something. The people who'd have taken it couldn't be *that* dangerous, could they?

And if they could be, then I wanted to know. I wanted to be standing right there with the guys like I had at the shop, where I *had* held my own, thank you very much.

I couldn't let Logan push me away again—not this time. It wasn't about him and whatever his reasons were for holding me at a distance. This was about me and something that mattered to me more than almost anything.

I raised my chin, fixing him with my steadiest gaze. "I don't care how dangerous this gets. I'm not helpless. I took care of myself today, and I can do it again."

Logan grimaced. "If your dad were here—"

Oh no, he didn't. I cut him off before he could take that idea any farther. "My dad *isn't* here. He's dead, and this box is one of the most important things I have left of him. And you never even knew him, so you have no reason to assume that he wouldn't agree with my decisions. He believed in me."

A flash of surprise crossed Logan's face, and I realized that my voice had risen as I spoke the words.

"Damn," Slade said with a low whistle, but I ignored him as I stared down Logan with narrowed eyes.

"We made a deal, and I'm not backing out of it, so the deal still stands. I'm staying on this investigation."

CHAPTER 15

Dexter

"So, no luck with the mechanics?" Madelyn said, sinking into one of the chairs at the central table in the Vigil office.

I thought she still looked a bit annoyed that we'd finally talked her out of going back to the shop with us to ask about her memento of her dad, even though Slade and I had promised emphatically that we'd keep her in the loop and have her along on less dicey parts of the investigation. When Slade had pointed out that the guy she'd pummeled might have a grudge against her now and be less likely to talk if she was around, she'd finally backed down.

It was much better that she hadn't been with us, though. There'd been threats Logan wouldn't have wanted to make, force he wouldn't have wanted to resort to when she was watching. That part of his reaction to her I at least partly understood. I wasn't totally comfortable with the means we resorted to in order to achieve our ends either.

But who was I to complain?

"They had no idea there'd ever been a box of any kind in the car," I told her, meeting her eyes for just a second. They were kind eyes, and pretty with that deep shade of blue—at least I thought so—but holding someone's gaze for more than a moment always sent a creeping sensation over my skin. It was easier to pretend I was occupied considering other things. "Whoever stole your Malibu must have taken the trinket box out before they dropped the car off at the shop. They left it with a note saying they'd be by to pick up the cash from selling the parts in a week."

Madelyn frowned, her smooth forehead furrowing. "Is that how chop shops normally operate?"

I shook my head. "Not from what I've seen. It's definitely unusual that they wouldn't come to a direct agreement about the price and all that. The thief was being particularly secretive."

"Are you sure we can trust anything those assholes said?"

"I saw no reason to doubt them," I said evenly. After the way Logan had intimidated them while he'd asked his questions, seeing the expressions on their faces, I was sure they'd been telling us the truth. He'd made them nervous, and nervous people made mistakes, but none of their body language or comments had given any hint that they were hiding something.

"Crap." Madelyn sighed and slumped in the chair, her fine blond hair sliding across her shoulders. "What now?"

"That's why I called you in." I flicked to the notetaking app on my phone. "Anything you can tell us about this box and its significance might help us narrow down the culprits. I know it belonged to your dad and approximately what it looks like. What did your dad use it for? Did he ever say anything noteworthy about it? Why did it seem special enough to him that you wanted to hold on to it?"

Madelyn rubbed her mouth, her eyes going out of focus as she reached into her memories. I could focus on her more easily now when she wasn't looking right back at me.

"I mean, like I said before, its value was all sentimental, as far as I know. It was always a fixture on his desk—even when he reorganized or got new furniture, it kept its spot right at the corner. I liked to pick it up and run my fingers over the design when I'd go in there to visit with him while he was working."

"Did he work from home a lot?" I asked.

She nodded. "Enough that he kept that small home office. For the more intensive research, he needed to be in the hospital or the lab he had ties to, of course, but when he was reading up on a subject or compiling notes or that sort of thing, he'd often do that at home. He said he wanted to be around as much as possible to see me growing up. That's why he didn't mind me dropping in. He'd say he was always happy to have an excuse to take a quick break."

She paused with an audible swallow. I felt abruptly awkward, not knowing what to say. I knew more about this situation than she had any clue about, and yet at the same time I had no idea what the details had looked like from her perspective.

"He died when you were pretty little, didn't he?" I said in what I hoped was a gentle tone.

Madelyn sucked in a breath and gave me a wry smile. "Yeah. I was eight. Maybe it's silly that it still affects me, but it was so sudden, and— It's hard not to think about what it'd be like if he were still here. He was a really great dad, always encouraging me and there when I needed him. It was an unexpected illness, came on suddenly and hit him really hard. We barely realized we were saying actual goodbyes before he was gone. It took me a long time to get back to feeling close to normal again."

"I'd imagine that's understandable."

"It doesn't help you find the box, though." She straightened her posture with an air of determination I was starting to see came naturally to her. "I'm not totally sure why he liked the thing so much. Maybe I'd have asked him once I'd gotten older and really thought about details like that. He'd have told me—he wasn't the kind of parent who'd brush off questions or give half-hearted answers to a kid. He always gave me his full attention."

"He does sound like a great dad." I wished my own parents had been more like that.

"Yeah. I just remember he told me it was his 'box of secrets.' A place where you could hide away important things. I told him I wanted something like that, and he swore we'd pick one out, but before we got around to doing that…"

She trailed off, but my mind had latched on to her earlier words with a surge of adrenaline. A "box of secrets" for hiding important things? That *was* the sort of thing someone might want to steal, wasn't it?

"Was it some kind of puzzle box then?" I asked, restraining my eagerness. My fingers were already itching to get my hands on it and figure out the tricks.

"I… I don't think so," Madelyn said. "Like with secret compartments and stuff? It opened like a normal wooden box, and I never found any other drawers or whatever. But I could have missed something, I guess. I didn't look that hard."

This was a puzzle about a puzzle, then. Playing right to my skills… But first we had to solve the part of the puzzle that would let me get my hands on the thing. If her dad had hidden something away in the box that no one had ever found—if someone out there had reason to believe he'd done that and that whatever he'd hidden was important…

I was so wrapped up in those speculations that Madelyn must

have thought I'd totally zoned out. I barely remembered she was in front of me until she moved her hand toward my arm as if to tap it to get my attention.

The motion made me tense up before her fingers had even brushed my sleeve. Madelyn jerked her hand back with an apologetic grimace. She tucked it under the table on her lap. "I'm sorry. I know you don't really like the whole physical contact thing."

An embarrassed heat crept across my face. She must have noticed my awkwardness around touch back in high school. I didn't exactly like the idea of it having been that obvious, even though it was true. Sudden contact made my nerves jump, even if it was friendly.

I did my best to smile and make light of the situation. "I guess you must have wondered what was up with my friends getting permission before giving me even a high five and stuff like that."

Madelyn shrugged, seeming totally unfazed. "Everyone's entitled to their preferences. If Logan and Slade couldn't respect yours, they'd be crappy friends. I'll have to get into that habit of being more conscious about that stuff too."

She made it sound as if I wasn't weird at all. Which I knew wasn't true, because I'd gotten enough strange looks from other people at my reactions to a casual tap or nudge. My mom had often grumbled about how I'd stiffen up if she'd come in for a spontaneous hug.

Madelyn's acceptance was such a relief that a tickle of curiosity passed through my mind. Would I really mind it that much if she touched me? She definitely wasn't like any other woman I'd been around. Why didn't she judge me when so many other people did? She hardly knew me, and yet *she* treated me with more respect than people who'd been in my life for ages. And she wasn't just easy-going and kind—she was smart too. A whole puzzle all in herself.

Why was Logan so set on keeping her in the dark? Imagine

what she might be able to figure out alongside us if she had the full picture.

I took a deep breath and shut down those thoughts. My first loyalty was to Logan, not to the woman in front of me. He'd made himself clear when he claimed that Madelyn would be in more danger if we involved her, and I wouldn't go behind his back and do that.

"Is there anything else I can do to help right now?" she asked.

"Not at the moment," I said with forced nonchalance. "I'll let you know when we're ready to take our next real steps."

Yes, Madelyn was a puzzle, and this entire situation seemed to be full of the kinds of puzzles that I'd usually devour and solve in a matter of hours. But I couldn't let myself be distracted from what was really important. I'd have to shut down my puzzle-addicted brain before it carried me off the deep end again. I might think Madelyn had the right to participate as much as Logan would let her, but I wasn't going to pull her into a scenario where she'd get hurt.

I wouldn't make that mistake again. I'd already dragged more people down with me than I'd ever wanted to.

CHAPTER 16

Madelyn

The line at the post office had me tapping my toes impatiently. An old man with a long beard had brought in a stack of letters that looked about a foot high and was now making the lone clerk weigh each of them to make sure he had the right postage before affixing the stamps to the upper right corner with painstaking care.

I'd been here for ten minutes, and I hadn't gotten any closer to mailing my package. My talk with Dexter this morning had left me feeling nostalgic for home and thinking fond thoughts of the parent I hadn't lost. I'd decided to stop by the chocolate shop in town I'd discovered Mom loved so I could pick up some truffles to send her.

My phone chimed with an incoming text—a welcome distraction. I tucked the package with the chocolates under my arm and pulled out my phone.

What's up? Summer had written.

Not a whole lot, I typed back. *Have you ever been three people back in line behind a senior citizen who's sending letters to all their known relatives? I swear I could have gotten this package to my mom in less time if I'd driven home.*

The bubbles appeared at the bottom of the screen immediately, showing she was preparing her response. *I'll trade you. Have you ever been called a worthless waste of space for forgetting an order of fries for a table? Lunch shift is the worst.*

I winced inwardly. *There's a reason I never became a server at the diner with you.*

And there's a reason I never go to the post office. Order online and have stuff sent direct! That's the way to go.

My lips curled into a bemused smile. *Not everything can be ordered online, you know. Aren't you all about shop local?*

Only when I'm also keeping it local, she shot back with a winking emoji. Then she added, *It must be nice having your car back. No problems from the theft?*

I hadn't told her about the missing trinket box because I didn't want to worry her more. Maybe once it was found, I'd share my ongoing worries, but I didn't want to hear her tell me that I should just let it go.

I didn't *want* to let it go, and I didn't want to explain that to someone else. I'd pushed so hard the past few days with the guys, I couldn't bring myself to face convincing someone else.

Nope, I wrote. *Everything's working fine. Apparently the way they steal cars these days, with the modern models, they don't even hotwire them. So nothing got damaged.*

The old man finally handed over his stack of envelopes, and the line started moving again. The next woman briskly bought a pack of padded envelopes. *G2G*, I added to Summer, and tucked my phone away.

At the tap of footsteps behind me, I glanced over my shoulder instinctively. My heart skipped a beat just as the guy I found myself looking at raised his eyebrows at me.

"If it isn't Madelyn from the coffee shop," Beckett said with an amused glint in his gray eyes. I'd forgotten just how good-looking he was with his bright gaze and sharply regal nose beneath the artfully messy waves of his sandy-blond hair. Especially when he was giving me that subtly warm smile.

"If it isn't Beckett from the sidewalk outside the coffee shop," I replied in an attempt at being funny that sounded all wrong the second it'd come out, remembering exactly how we'd met on that sidewalk. "Did you get the stain out of your shirt?"

He held up his hand as if swearing in on a witness stand. "I promise you did no permanent damage, other than to my general focus."

"What's that supposed to mean?" I asked, already flushing a little at the teasing note in his voice.

His smile widened slightly. "I've been wondering whether I'd cross paths with you again. Didn't expect to bump into you here, though."

"Yeah, I'm just—mailing something to my mom," I said, holding up the package and abruptly wondering if that sounded weird or childish. Weren't parents supposed to be the ones sending their kids stuff at college, not the other way around? Although Mom did send me plenty. But Beckett didn't know that.

He didn't show any outward reaction, just held up an oversized envelope of his own. "Business documents to mail. It's hard to believe some people still don't use email for that kind of thing."

"I guess there's something to be said for hard copies."

The space in front of me opened up, and the clerk motioned me over. A moment later, a second clerk joined her at the second register, and it ended up that I'd finished posting my package just as Beckett had paid for his registered mail. He walked over to the door with me, easing just a little ahead so he could open it for me.

"I *am* capable of opening doors on my own, you know," I said in a lightly ribbing tone. "Or even for you."

Beckett chuckled. "Read nothing into the gesture other than that I enjoy the chance to make your life a tiny bit easier. If you want to return the favor sometime, you're more than welcome to. Where are you off to now, Madelyn?"

Something about his presence set me at ease—his upbeat calm, the steady confidence with which he'd let the implied criticism roll off him. A lot of guys would have gotten their backs up if teased like that. And his attitude couldn't have been more different from Logan's grouchy cockiness.

"You can call me Maddie," I found myself saying. "I like that better—less stuffy-sounding. And I was just going to pop into the dollar store to grab a new pack of pens. Nothing exciting."

"I'm heading that way myself," Beckett said. "Do you mind if I join you?"

I'd actually been kind of hoping he'd offer, as much as I hated to admit that. I couldn't tell whether the store was really on his way or he was just saying that so we could talk more, but it was probably better not to read too much into that comment either.

As we set off along the sidewalk, I glanced at him sideways, thinking about what he'd said in the post office. "So, what kind of work do you do? I guess you must have graduated pretty recently. I mean, assuming you don't look way younger than you actually are." I bit my lip. Why did I keep putting my foot in my mouth with this guy? "Sorry, that probably sounded awful."

Beckett laughed. "No, it's a perfectly normal question. I don't know how old—or young—I look to you, but it sounds like you judged about right. I'm twenty-three. But I've been helping out with the family business since I was in my early teens, and I basically grew up in the middle of it, so it kind of feels like I've always had this job even if I only took it on full-time recently."

Maybe that explained part of his confidence—the fact that he'd always known what he'd be doing when he grew up, unlike so many of my college peers who seemed to be kind of drifting along, still undecided about everything… often down to their majors. That kind of certainty was a privilege a lot of people didn't have, but who was I to judge when I'd spent my whole life preparing to follow in my dad's footsteps with the interests he'd encouraged in me?

I felt comfortable enough to tap Beckett playfully with my elbow. "And am I allowed to ask what the family business is?"

"Oh, we've got our fingers in all sorts of pies. My dad and my grandpa before him were always looking for ways to expand and diversify. One of our main focuses is real estate development, which is an area I enjoy quite a bit. We've also got some holdings in manufacturing and transportation."

I blinked. "Wow. Sounds like it's a pretty big business." Not some mom-and-pop-type deal. But then, looking at him in his perfectly fitted suit and shiny shoes that I had to imagine cost way more than I'd ever spent on an item of clothing, that probably shouldn't have surprised me. It was just weird to think of a guy only three years older than me being established enough to be arranging major deals or whatever.

Beckett shrugged, but his smile shifted, turning a bit softer around the edges in a way that told me the enthusiasm in his voice was genuine. "It can get a little unwieldy at times, but I generally enjoy the challenge. And seeing a development project move from an empty lot or a shell of a building into something people are actually going to use is pretty amazing."

"It's great that you enjoy it so much," I said.

Something flickered through his expression, but his voice stayed as steady and warm as before. "It's not all sunshine and roses. Some of the people I work with can be difficult, and a lot of them aren't too keen on taking orders from a 'kid.' But I know I'm proving myself."

"I admire that attitude," I told him honestly.

"You must have the same kind of determination when it comes to your career path," Beckett said, nudging me back. "Medical research isn't exactly a slacker job."

I laughed. "No, it's definitely not. But I guess it is a lot like you said. Knowing that I could work on something that's really going to make a difference to people, feeling like I'm building toward cures or treatments that could make their lives so much better or even save those lives… That makes it worth it."

"Exactly. I think I must have sensed that we had that sort of attitude in common when we first met, and that's why I wasn't willing to let you get away with just paying me off for a dry-cleaning bill. I don't run into a whole lot of people who really care about what they do and not simply getting a paycheck out of it."

I made a face. "Strangely that's not the selling point you make it sound like. Madelyn Silver: she works really hard."

Beckett grinned down at me with a fond expression that made my pulse stutter giddily. "Oh, I think there's a lot more to appreciate about you than just that, Maddie. And if I'm lucky, maybe you'll give me the chance to uncover more of it."

Okay, he was definitely flirting, right? I hadn't been totally sure with some of his earlier comments, because random guys didn't normally come up to me out of the blue and hit on me. Mom always said it was because I tended to look too serious for them to think it'd work, but she *was* my mom, so she had to make it sound like it wasn't anything actually off-putting about me.

I couldn't think of any other good reason for Beckett to not just have helped me with my groceries the other day but also be joining me on the grand adventure of popping into the dollar store, though. And that grin… It reminded me a little of Slade's, except his always felt partly joking, more playful than committed to a pursuit. Beckett made it sound like he wanted more than to just goof off a bit.

The thought of Slade drew me up short even as heat tickled across my face. Did I *want* Beckett to flirt with me—and to flirt back? My feelings for Logan were still a muddle, and I'd almost made out with Slade at the club the other night.

But was that so wrong? *Live a little, girl*—that was what Summer would have told me. Nothing was happening with Logan, and I sure as hell shouldn't put any interest I felt for another guy on the back burner because of him. And I had no idea where things were going with Slade, if anywhere.

I could play the field. It was *nice* to feel like a guy as together as Beckett saw something to admire in me. I definitely found him pretty impressive so far, inside and out.

I grinned back at him, hoping my jittering nerves didn't show in my expression. I might *want* to flirt, but that didn't mean I was any kind of expert at it.

"I think that could be arranged," I said.

"Getting my hopes up, huh? Thankfully you don't look like a heartbreaker."

I couldn't hold back a snort—or the comment that tumbled out of me. "Usually it's the other way around."

Oh, shit, why had I blurted that out? Now I sounded pathetic. I snickered as if I could pretend I'd been kidding, but Beckett's grin had faded.

"Has someone been jerking you around?" he asked, cool and even but with a firmness that suggested he thought he could do something about it if I said yes. His sudden protectiveness sent a heady shiver down my spine. "Was it one of those guys you mentioned hanging out with?"

"No, no," I said quickly, even though I'd mostly meant Logan. Damn it, why did he have to screw up even this? "It was a bad joke."

Beckett studied me for a second but then smiled again, to my relief. "Good. Because I might not know you that well yet, but I can already tell you deserve better than a broken heart."

I swallowed thickly. Funny how he could say that so easily, and Logan who'd known me so much longer hadn't batted an eye at breaking it.

The bright yellow sign of the dollar store beamed at us from the corner. I slowed as we reached the entrance, feeling abruptly shy. "Well, this is me."

Beckett turned toward me, so close with his handsome face intent on mine that a waft of heat rushed through my body. His voice dipped lower. "Then it's time for me to try my luck. Have dinner with me tomorrow evening?"

"Um." Yes, I was a straight-A student, but somehow I'd lost all my words faced with that question. "You mean like a date?"

I could have smacked myself in the forehead, but I had to clarify, just to be sure. Beckett's renewed smile showed no sign of offense.

"I'm just looking to see how much else we have in common and find out all the other fascinating things about you. And if that sparks into something more, I'm not going to argue. I'm happy to call it a date if that doesn't make you feel pressured to do anything more than enjoy some good food and conversation."

I had a hard time imagining this guy putting on the pressure like a randy high school dude. I hesitated for just a second longer with a brief thought of Logan and the Vigil guys—but I didn't owe any of them anything, especially not my jerk of a stepbrother. Why shouldn't I have some fun and see where this could go?

I beamed back at Beckett with a leap of my heart. "It's a date, then."

CHAPTER 17

Logan

I parked across the street from the mechanic shop just before closing and paused to make sure I couldn't see any customers through the grimy front window. Then I strode across the street and pushed past the door, letting all the menace I could summon rise to the surface.

It wasn't hard. These pricks had lied to us about having Madelyn's car and then tried to hold her hostage—the one asshole had left her *bleeding*. My jaw clenched just remembering the smear of blood on her arm.

Last time I'd come here, I'd only talked to them, asking them about the trinket box. But we hadn't turned up any other leads, and I was almost glad to have the excuse to beat some more answers out of them. I wasn't giving them the chance to consider lying through their teeth this time.

We were getting to the bottom of this before Maddie faced

anything worse than what these miserable lowlifes had already done to her.

One of the mechanics from before was just shutting down the computer at the reception desk. He glanced up at me with a startled expression before his eyes narrowed. "You—"

I didn't give him the chance to complain about my arrival. I lunged around the desk, caught him by the front of his shirt, and heaved him toward the door to the mechanic bay.

He was at least ten years older than me, but I was bigger and stronger. My shove propelled him right into the door, which popped open on impact. As he staggered, I stormed after him. With another abrupt push, he was stumbling onto his ass in the bay.

There was only one other mechanic still on duty this late in the evening—the big guy who'd grabbed Madelyn. "Hey!" he shouted, rounding one of the two cars currently set up there, and hesitated for just a second when he saw who the intruder was.

I smiled at him with bared teeth, the image of his thick arms swinging around Madelyn flashing behind my eyes and provoking a fresh surge of rage. Oh, I was really looking forward to this now. I hadn't really paid him back yet.

The first guy scrambled to his feet and took a swing at me. I smacked his fist to the side and clocked him in the chin. As he swayed and swore, grabbing his face, the second guy charged at me.

He was a little more of a challenge, with nearly as much muscle on him as I had. But he didn't have a raging fury driving his attack. He managed to land a punch to the side of my chest, but then I was kneeing him in the gut and tossing him into the side of the nearest car.

He glanced off it and hurtled back toward me. The first guy darted at me at the same time.

I dodged out of the way and slammed my knuckles into the smaller guy's throat. As he sputtered, I stomped my heel into his shin hard enough that the crack of breaking bone echoed off the bay's high ceilings.

You couldn't go easy on guys like these—the kind of guys who thought it was okay to beat up on an innocent woman. They needed to know just how much I meant business and just how little they'd get away with if they tried to pull anything over on me.

The guy fell with a strangled whimper. He wouldn't be getting up anytime soon. He fumbled in his pocket for a phone, but I kicked it out of his hand, snapping at least one finger in the process. The phone rattled across the floor to the other side of the room.

Now I had only one prick to deal with. A prick who was bearing down on me at this exact instant.

"Who the fuck do you think you are, kid?" the big guy snarled.

"Someone you're going to regret ever having messed with," I shot back, deflecting his swings with only a faint pain radiating through my blocking forearm.

He whipped his fist around fast enough to smack me in the side of the head. I reeled for a second, but I'd been hit worse. I bobbed and wove like I'd learned in my kickboxing sparring sessions and caught him with my knee a second time, ramming it into his side.

From the pained grunt that burst from the guy's mouth, I'd cracked at least one of his ribs, as I'd intended. He clutched at his chest but hurled his other fist toward me. But he was off-balance now.

I swept my leg into his calf and knocked him off his feet. As he sprawled on the floor, I kicked him in the back of the head for good measure, hard enough to leave him groaning.

Touch my girl again, and you won't have any breath left to groan with, you fucking jackass, I thought, biting back the words. A lingering ache spread through my skull from where he'd hit me, but it was already fading. I'd dealt it back ten times over.

"What the fuck do you want, man?" the smaller guy rasped

from where he was still crouched on the cement floor, bent awkwardly over his broken leg. "You got your car back. We told you we didn't take anything out of it."

"Maybe I don't believe you." I aimed a light kick at his leg, just enough to send another spear of agony through the limb. "You really can't remember a single thing about who brought it in? Even when I jog that memory of yours?" I turned to the bigger guy, who was starting to sit up, and brought my heel down on the ribs I'd kicked earlier. "I can keep jogging it as long as I need to," I added as he slumped onto his back again with a hiss of pain.

"There's nothing to remember," the first guy mumbled in a panicked voice that sounded genuine enough. He was afraid I wouldn't believe him, not constructing a story. I'd been through this kind of interrogation often enough to tell the difference. "It was just dropped off; none of us saw who left it. Fucking weird, but you can't blame us for that."

I snatched up a wrench off a nearby shelf of tools and flipped the heavy metal tool in my hand, glowering down at the guy who'd grabbed Maddie. *Oh please, do give me an excuse to bash your nose in and fracture every bone in your body with this thing.*

"What about you?" I demanded. "Did you notice anything?"

The guy's bravado had finally vanished, a flicker of fear passing through his eyes. He still grimaced as he spat out, "I don't know anything. You're fucking crazy, kid."

I smirked again, leaning into his claim, knowing it would unnerve him. "It doesn't seem very smart to give a crazy person a hard time, does it?" Then I whacked him in the shoulder with the wrench, not hard enough to do more than lightly bruise, just to show him I wasn't afraid to use it.

The man growled a curse word and screwed up his face. "He already told you. The car was just dropped off. No one's come around about it. I fucking wish they'd taken it someplace else."

Fair enough. I tapped the wrench against my open palm, my gaze darting between the two mechanics. "What about your regular clients, the ones you *do* know? Is there anyone who you work with regularly who's brought in other stolen cars like hers?"

"Our clients don't know shit about your car," the bigger man grumbled.

"That's not what I asked," I reminded him, aiming another kick at his ribs.

"Fuck," he sputtered, his head lolling back for a moment as he fought through the pain. "We don't have any consistent regulars on that side of the business. Different people come by—maybe some of them work for the same organization. We don't ask questions. We don't get ID."

Well, that wasn't completely surprising, even if it wasn't all that useful. "What about new people?" I asked. "Has anyone you've never dealt with before come in asking questions or sniffing around?"

"You mean like you and your shitty friends?" the big guy snarked.

I slammed the wrench into his kneecap to remind him just how shitty I could be. "Like us, or just seeming more interested than usual in your business in any way. Answer the fucking question."

"No," he grated out. "I haven't noticed anyone like that, or I'd happily send you off to hassle them instead of us, you maniac. Have you checked out the junk yard? That's the main chop shop in town. He knows a lot more people than us."

I brought down the wrench on the man's other kneecap. His shout of pain felt good as it drowned out the small cry of pain I'd heard from Maddie when she fell. Each of his sounds of discomfort warded away my memories of Maddie's a little at a time. "Right now I want to hear from you assholes, not anyone else."

"Man, we're telling you all we know," the smaller guy said raggedly.

I was becoming increasingly sure that was true, but I couldn't let this go. I needed some kind of direction, something that brought us closer to finding that box and keeping Madelyn away from thugs like these for good.

Maybe they were connected to the larger case in ways that hadn't even occurred to us before. I cast a narrow glance at both of the men. "What do you know about Southwestern Regional Memorial Hospital?"

I didn't even need a verbal response to that question as they looked amongst themselves, confusion written across both of their faces.

"Never heard of it," the big guy said. "What the hell does that have to do with anything?"

"I'm asking the questions here. Do you know anything about a man named Evan Silver?"

More visible confusion. "You're fucking insane, man," the smaller guy said. "What the hell are you going on about now?"

I couldn't help pushing one more time. "What about the Baldwin file?"

"Do we look like file clerks?" the big guy grumbled, and coughed out a grunt when I jabbed the toe of my shoe into his side. "Fucking hell. We have no idea what you're talking about."

"Sure you don't," I said. "But the car didn't drop down from heaven. *Someone* brought it around, someone picked this place. So I guess I'll just have to keep laying into you until one of you comes up with something useful."

I brought the wrench down on the shoulder I'd already hit, knowing it'd be tender, and gave the man a vicious grin. Then I turned to the smaller man, waving the tool threateningly. He outright cringed—and I saw a desperate spark light in his eyes.

"There was something a little weird!" he gasped out. "I almost forgot. I don't know if it had anything to do with that stupid car, but maybe…"

"Just spit it out," I ordered.

He winced at the threat in my tone. "I—I noticed a couple of guys scoping out the shop early one morning when I was out by the street finishing off a cigarette. It was a few weeks ago, way before the car turned up. I didn't think to connect the two. But I'd never seen them before, and I wondered why they were checking out the place."

I waggled the wrench again, a flare of hope filling my chest. This expedition might not have been for nothing after all. "Describe them."

"I didn't see them clearly… They were wearing hooded jackets and shades. Definitely guys, a couple of them. But their car—it was vintage. That was part of the reason I noticed them. They drove off in it less than a minute after I spotted them."

Now there was a lead we could use.

"What model?" I demanded, raising the wrench one more time in warning. "Tell me every detail you remember."

CHAPTER 18

Madelyn

We walked two blocks from where the Vigil guys had parked Logan's car, through a middle-class residential neighborhood that was mostly quiet in the late morning. The empty driveways and vacant lawns suggested almost everyone who lived here had gone off to work or school.

The guys hadn't told me what exactly we were doing in this part of the city, only that they'd found a potential connection to my car thief. They slowed when we reached a two-story home with neat flowerbeds out front and white wicker furniture on the small porch. Then they walked along the narrow path between it and the neighboring house to the backyard as if they belonged there.

I hurried along with them, curiosity and apprehension nibbling at me in unison. "You think the person who stole my car—or the box—lives here?" I whispered, knitting my brow as I took in the backyard with its well-maintained lawn and cedar patio furniture. Obviously you couldn't identify a thief from a glance, but I hadn't expected a criminal's house to look quite this tidy and ordinary. I could have imagined one of Mom's friends living here.

"We think this person is involved somehow," Logan said, low and terse. "Maybe not directly. But there was someone suspicious checking out the mechanic shop not long before your car was dropped off, and the car they were driving is registered to this address."

"How did you find *that* out?" I asked.

He shrugged, not meeting my eyes. "It's amazing what you can learn if you just ask around."

He obviously wasn't going to tell me more than that, but I wasn't too worried about that, only annoyed. I had trouble believing he was going to badger a stranger without a solid reason. Even so… "Will they tell us anything? They don't even know us."

Slade tapped his elbow against mine as we approached the back door. "The woman who lives here doesn't need to tell us anything. She's at work. We're just going to take a little look around." He grinned at me.

"*What?*" I clapped my hand over my mouth after the question burst out louder than I expected, my eyes darting toward the neighboring houses. The high wooden walls obscured all view of us except from one second-story window next door, and it was covered by thick curtains.

But what if someone noticed? The guys couldn't seriously be planning on—

Dexter was already kneeling by the back door, pulling a couple of slim metal tools from his pocket. I couldn't help gaping as he worked them into the lock.

"What if we get caught?" I hissed.

Logan shot me a look that felt like a dare. "It's just a little light breaking-and-entering. We're not going to hurt anyone or damage anything. We're only looking for information. You want your dad's trinket box back, don't you?"

He was probably hoping that I'd back down, turn tail and run so they could continue the investigation on their own. No doubt he wouldn't have brought me along at all if Dexter hadn't updated me as promised.

I clamped my mouth shut, my teeth on edge. My heart was thumping faster. I did want Dad's box—I wanted to know what was going on with the whole theft. I just hadn't realized we'd do something quite this illegal to get there. But the guys were acting like they'd carried out operations like this dozens of times.

What the hell *had* Logan been up to all these years since he'd pulled away from the family?

Whoever lived in this house was a criminal or had some association with one, I told myself as the lock clicked and Dexter stood with a satisfied smile. It wouldn't hurt them for us to look around. The guys seemed sure no one was home.

If I didn't trust them at least this much, what the hell was I doing here in the first place?

Dexter tugged the door open, and the guys marched inside. I followed at the back of the line, resisting the urge to hug myself. My stomach had knotted, but as we stepped into the narrow kitchen where the sweet scent of syrup hung in the air from whatever the owner had for breakfast, a little thrill shot through my chest too.

We were sneaking into someone else's life, getting a glimpse of a stranger that most people never did. Maybe we'd discover things no one else knew about her. Maybe I'd get some answers about why I'd been targeted.

We were taking control of the situation, and something about that felt right even though I knew the cops would have disagreed.

"What are we looking for?" I whispered.

"Anything suspicious," Slade said, already riffling through a stack of mail on the kitchen counter.

"The homeowner's name is Melinda Hughes," Dexter elaborated. "She's divorced and has lived alone since her kids moved out several years back, so she's the only one who's been residing in the house for a while. If you see any documents addressed to someone with a different name, we'll want to take a closer look at those. Or anything related to cars or pawn shops or that sort of thing."

Okay, I guessed that gave me a general idea. I crept deeper into the house, down a hall that led to a combined living-dining room. There were a couple of papers on the dining table, but on closer inspection I found they were only takeout menus. Maybe Melinda Hughes had ordered in dinner last night.

Dexter walked past me, snapping pictures of just about everything in sight. I got a little more into the search, easing up the sofa cushions to peek underneath, checking behind the chairs in the living room for anything that might have fallen, always careful to set things back as they'd been before. My shoes rasped softly over the thick carpet.

"If this woman isn't the thief herself, how could she be connected?" I asked.

Logan had moved to the front hall, flipping through a calendar that hung on the wall there. "So far I'm not seeing any sign of her being a criminal herself, so I'd guess that the actual perp is using her address as a cover. It's a pretty common tactic. He's probably a relative—son or nephew or cousin. Something like that."

He sounded a little less annoyed now that I'd gone along with the plan. Maybe getting down to work distracted him from how pissed off he was that I was working alongside him. I had to admit there was something satisfying about taking concrete action.

"We don't want to stay here any longer than necessary," Dexter reminded us.

Logan nodded. "Why don't you and I check the basement? Slade and Madelyn, head upstairs and split up to check the bedrooms and whatever else is up there. We'll cover more ground that way." He was all firm efficiency now, with an authoritative air that confirmed he was the unofficial leader of the group.

I slunk up the stairs, the back of my neck prickling with both anxiety and eagerness. What if I found the crucial clue? The longer we spent in the house, the less it felt like an intrusion and the more like some kind of detective game.

The first room at the top of the stairs was a bedroom. I scanned it as I heard Slade come up the stairs after me and head down the second-floor hallway. This room might have once belonged to one of the kids Dexter had mentioned, but it appeared to have been redone as a guestroom. The plain dresser and bedframe showed no signs of personality, and nothing hung on the walls with their leaf-print wallpaper.

I tugged open the drawers on the dresser and checked the closet, only confirming my suspicions. There was nothing stashed away here except for a couple of baggies of lavender potpourri. A shoe box under the bed got me briefly excited, but it only held… a pair of shoes.

The next room over must have been the master bedroom. It felt infinitely more lived in. The dark, rustic furniture set held a scattering of possessions, from a change bowl with a stick of lip balm and a couple of hair clips on the dresser to a few books stacked haphazardly on the bedside table.

I checked all of the drawers, shifting the contents as little as possible and tucking them back as I'd found them. None of the clothes or other belongings looked at all out of the ordinary for a woman who was my mom's age or older. As I finished my perusal of the last piece of furniture, an uncomfortable weight settled in my gut. I sat gingerly on the edge of the bed, grappling with it.

I'd thought we were justified in coming in here, that we'd find something that'd point to the criminal who'd invaded *my* life. But she seemed to be a totally normal woman. I couldn't shake the growing sense that we weren't accomplishing anything other than violating her privacy unnecessarily. We didn't belong in here any more than she'd belong in our homes.

Slade poked his head through the doorway. "Anything in here?"

I shook my head, my throat too tight for me to speak. Slade took in my expression and slipped into the room, a softer smile playing with his lips. "Aww, don't look depressed about it. Here, I can cheer you up."

He swung into a swift spin on his prosthetic leg, turning the movement into a brief jig of a dance and dipping into a deep bow at the end. I couldn't suppress a snort of laughter despite my dwindling spirits, but as he glanced up with a grin, my uneasiness wrapped around me again.

Slade sank down onto the bed next to me and grasped my hand. "Okay, looks like I'd better get serious. What's bothering you?"

I grimaced. "I just feel really weird having broken in here and poking around in all her stuff, and we haven't even found anything to connect her to my car or the box."

"Hey, first time jitters totally make sense." He squeezed my hand. "And sometimes leads don't take us anywhere. We have to follow them, though, because we never know which ones *will* pay off. It's a little trial and error. We haven't done any harm here, right?"

"We haven't," I had to agree. And his words made me feel better for another reason. "It's a lot like medical research that way. We have to test every possible hypothesis to make sure we get to the right—or the best—answer." Framing it that way in my head soothed my discomfort a little.

Slade chuckled. "Only a brainiac would compare breaking and entering to science." But he made the remark sound like a compliment rather than a criticism.

I couldn't resist teasing him right back. "I don't think you're in any position to be calling *me* a brainiac, Mr. 'I know a hundred languages.'"

Slade winked at me. "It's cool to know languages. It's nerdy to know science. I'm proud of not being a nerdy brainiac."

I elbowed him. "Just a cool one, huh? We'll see how cool you think I am when I come up with the cure for cancer or something."

"Oh, I already think you're very cool." He raised my hand and pressed his lips to my knuckles, his dark eyes sparkling at me. "You know, Logan and Dex are still searching around downstairs. I can think of other ways I could distract you from your guilty conscience."

A blush warmed my cheeks. "Like what?" I had to ask.

He simply smirked and tilted my hand so he could kiss my palm. His fingers tightened around mine as he brought his lips to the underside of my wrist, where the contact provoked a tingle that had me swallowing a gasp.

He charted a path up my arm, every kiss tender and deliberate, leaving plenty of opportunity for me to pull away if I wasn't into it. But with each brush of his mouth, more desire unfurled low in my belly, washing away my concerns just like he'd promised. Heat coursed up my arm and through the rest of my body.

How far was he going to take this?

But even as the giddiness of that question raced through me, something in me hesitated. My feelings about Logan were a mess. And I had a date with Beckett tonight. Should I be this into another guy touching me like this? How could my feelings be so fickle?

Slade reached my shoulder and pecked the peak. My pulse hiccupped as he scooted closer and dipped his head toward my neck, but every particle in my body was screaming to let him continue.

Why shouldn't I? I hadn't made any commitments to anyone, so I wasn't betraying anyone. And God, this felt good. Other than a couple of disastrous first dates in my first year of college, I hadn't kissed *anyone* in two years. I had some time to make up for, right?

My head tilted to the side of its own accord, offering Slade better access. He hummed approvingly and brought his lips to the side of my neck, nipping the skin lightly before pressing a more emphatic kiss there.

I bit my own lips against a whimper. Heat coiled between my legs into a deepening ache.

When Slade raised his head, I didn't hesitate again. I leaned in and met him halfway for our first real kiss.

Slade tucked his hand around the back of my neck, parting his lips just slightly as he drew me against him. My fingers clutched the front of his shirt, all the rest of me absorbed in his passionate claiming of my mouth. His tongue flicked out to tease across my bottom lip. The cinnamon flavor that laced it set me even more on fire.

His other hand dropped to my waist. At his tug, I found myself straddling him. Our bodies seared against each other, his arm sliding around my waist, our chests pressed together, and his mouth claiming mine. I had the embarrassing urge to grind right into him like I was starved for sexual contact. Although technically I was.

Slade trailed his hand down from my neck over my chest. He stroked the curve of my breast with the same caution he'd showed in his initial kisses, and then cupped it completely when I didn't recoil. His thumb swiveled over my nipple through the layers of fabric, and I let out a needy sound into his heated mouth.

He massaged my breast more eagerly, his mouth outright plundering mine, and the intensity of the moment was so overwhelming that I didn't fully register the creak of the stairs until a few seconds after the sound had first reached my ears.

I jerked back, sliding off Slade's lap. "Someone's coming up."

My gaze darted toward the door, half anticipating one of the other guys glancing in, realizing what we'd been up to from the guilty flush burned into my cheeks.

Slade nuzzled the side of my head. "I know Logan can put on a scary front, but you don't need to be afraid of him getting angry. I survived his dance-floor interruption just fine."

The amusement in his tone brought my attention back to him. "Are you only doing this to irritate Logan?"

Slade laughed. "Riling him up is a benefit, sure. Can't let him get too cocky."

All the heat fled my body in the wake of a wash of cold. I might not have made commitments to anyone, including Slade—I might have figured this could just be fun in the moment—but the admission horrified me more than I'd expected. I'd assumed Slade was at least into it because he enjoyed making out with *me*, not because of how his friends would react.

I pushed myself farther away from him on the bed, my blush all embarrassment now, my stance tensing awkwardly. "We'd better stop then, because I actually like *you*."

Slade froze, looking oddly surprised, and then caught my hand. He studied my expression with unexpected intensity. "I didn't mean I don't like you, Maddie. I was just kidding around about the Logan thing. Hell, I think you're amazing."

"Oh." I had no idea how to feel, but the sincerity in his voice set off a warm glow inside me. I couldn't help smiling, even though I was still confused. "Well… good."

He arched his eyebrows, more of his usual playfulness coming back. "I promise anything that happens between us is going to be about you and me and how awesome you are, not anyone else. And if you're actually up for more than just an occasional fun distraction…"

Before I could decide how to respond to that, Dexter's voice carried up the stairs. "Hey, guys, you'd better take a look at this."

CHAPTER 19

Beckett

It was hard to pinpoint exactly what made Maddie so attractive. When I'd first seen her, I'd pegged her as a pretty but unexceptional college student. The V-neck sweater and fitted dress pants she'd worn for our date hugged her trim curves perfectly, but that wasn't all that made the difference either.

It was her smile, I decided, smiling back at her across the restaurant table. The way a dimple formed on just one cheek, the way her dark blue eyes sparkled when she laughed, the self-deprecating note that'd crept into her voice as she related a story from her high school days, which let me know she wasn't trying to brag, just sharing a little of herself.

She took a sip of her water and continued her story. "One of the worst was the head gym teacher, who also coached a bunch of the sports teams. Every time we walked into the gym, he'd scrutinize our outfits and then dress code any student he didn't agree with. But it was only the girls. We couldn't wear T-shirts that showed any of our shoulders or had a neckline lower than an inch below our collarbone, but he'd let the guys get away with basketball jerseys and stuff like that. None of us were trying to flaunt anything. It just got hot in there, especially late in the spring."

My smile widened, sensing retribution to come. Maddie had started this line of conversation by admitting she'd been quite a crusader for justice in her teen years. "So what did you do about it?"

Maddie ducked her head briefly in apparent embarrassment, though why she'd be embarrassed about sticking up for herself and her fellow students was beyond me. I guessed girls always had people come down on them harder for speaking up and demanding attention too.

Fucking ridiculous. It'd been a couple of women who'd taught me a lot of what I knew about being a force to be reckoned with in the world, and I'd have had a lot more than harsh words for anyone who'd tried to knock them down a peg.

"One day in June it was just sweltering," Maddie said, "and I got fed up. I wore a sleeveless shirt with a neckline that was just a smidge too low, and I brought a measuring tape with me to class. Sure enough, the teacher zeroed right in on me and demanded I go to the office. So I handed him the measuring tape in front of the whole class and said I wasn't going anywhere until he measured me and the two guys from the basketball team who'd come in their jerseys and proved that my shirt was somehow less acceptable than theirs."

A chuckle burst out of me. "I bet he wasn't happy about that."

Maddie's smile turned a little softer at the memory. She might feel awkward about it, but I could tell part of her was proud of the stands she'd taken.

"Nope. Especially because the guys' jerseys were at least an inch lower cut than mine, and the straps were a little thinner, so he had no ground to stand on. He tried to get all intimidating and insist that I go anyway, but my best friend was filming the whole thing on her camera… We both went and showed the principal how he'd acted, and he got a formal reprimand. And they adjusted the dress code so girls could wear thick-strapped tank tops for gym class." She cast me a cautious glance as if checking whether I was put off by the account. "We might have threatened to take the video to the local news if they didn't."

I clapped my hands lightly in a show of applause. This woman might not have come from the gritty sort of background my former mentors had, but she had plenty of guts, no doubt about it. "Sounds like you handled it perfectly."

Maddie blushed. "I mean, that's not how everyone saw it. I was a lot to handle back then. I'm sure I stressed my mom out with all the campaigns I took up against one thing or another, clashing with teachers and all that. And it's because I was so hard-headed about this stuff that I ended up pissing one teacher off enough to screw up my grades for college admissions."

I dug my fork into my pasta. "Everyone is difficult in high school. It's the age for it, isn't it? I wasn't an easy kid—that's for sure."

I'd intended that comment to prompt a question of her own, one that would let me tease the subject I was most interested in without asking anything too pointed. It worked. Maddie popped a bit of her glazed chicken into her mouth and raised her eyebrows at me. "And how were you difficult, Beckett? I sense some juicy stories."

It was almost too easy. A pang of guilt jabbed me in the stomach over the way I was manipulating her.

It was my job. I needed to know for sure whether the guys she was associating with were any kind of threat and whether she was mixed up in that threat with them. If I didn't pursue every possible avenue toward getting that information, then I'd be letting down every man and woman working under me.

But there was no denying that I saw Maddie as a hell of a lot more than a source of information. I'd already been intrigued by her before I'd asked her out, and the more we talked, the more admiration trickled through my chest.

I'd met a lot of people in my line of work, but no one who had quite the mix of daring and sweetness that she did. She was a fighter, but a genuinely moral person at the same time.

Which meant she might not give me the time of day if she knew the full extent of my line of work, but I shoved that thought aside. That was a problem for another day, quite possibly for never. For all I knew, she might not want to entertain my advances beyond this date.

Giving her a playful smirk, I ate a mouthful of the pasta, letting the tangy rosé sauce coat my tongue as she waited. Anticipation worked wonders.

In reality, I'd spent all of a day in a public high school, and that visit had only been for the sake of learning about the son of someone my dad needed to target. I'd always been homeschooled by my dad's people and then in the thick of our kind of business, but I had enough of a gist to transpose a real story from my teens into a more appropriate setting.

"There was this bully at my high school who was terrorizing a lot of the kids," I said. "His dad worked with mine, and I knew my father wouldn't want me to intervene and potentially cause trouble at his job. But I hated seeing what he was doing to people, and I couldn't help thinking in the long run it'd be better to do something about it than not. I guess you know that feeling, like something needs to happen and you can't just stick your head in the sand?"

"Yeah," Maddie said softly, her gaze fixed on my face with an avidness that urged me on. I found I wanted to impress *her*, even if that wasn't the main reason I was telling this story.

"Well, I threw myself headfirst into the situation," I went on. "There was a group of students who'd started pushing back against the bully, but I knew some things they didn't about him that would help make him stand down. At first they didn't take me seriously, because I was a few years younger than them, but after I proved I could help, it was obvious we could accomplish a lot more working together."

I watched Maddie's expression carefully for any flicker of recognition at that kind of dynamic. Had she joined forces with that trio of guys to tackle something she saw as wrong in the city? Something to do with my and my father's business dealings, though she wouldn't have realized it was connected to me?

But her main response was to knit her brow. "How did your dad take it?"

Of course she'd worry about that. She wasn't just morally good but also compassionate.

I grappled with how to answer the question, because the basic answer was, *Not well at all.* But I didn't want to turn this into a venting session about my family issues.

"He didn't get any backlash at work," I said, sticking with a version that was brief but still somewhat accurate. "But he was frustrated that I'd gone behind his back. Things were a bit tense for a while, but I knew I'd done the right thing. And I made some lifelong friends who've still got my back if I need them."

We wouldn't get into how tense things still were at home.

If Maddie related my story to her own life, she didn't give any indication. "I'm sorry you had to go against him anyway," she said. "My mom was always supportive… I don't know what I'd have done if something I felt I needed to do conflicted with what she'd have wanted."

I shrugged. "All's well that ends well." I wished I could have left it there, but I had to give this line of inquiry every possible shot. "Are you taking up new crusades at the university?"

Maddie shook her head. "Not really. I mean, I'm sure if something really awful came up, I wouldn't be able to ignore it, but I'm not letting myself get distracted by the little things. Keeping up with my studies takes too much of my time and energy."

I cocked my head. "You don't seem like the type of woman who would let things go so easily."

Her eyes flickered around the room for a moment, and I longed to know exactly what she was thinking at that moment. "Don't get me wrong—I'm not going to stand by if something horrible goes down in front of me, but that hasn't happened so far. And I know that getting my degree means I'll be able to fix other kinds of injustices in the future, so I don't feel bad prioritizing it."

"Fair enough. There are various advocacy groups on campus, from what I've heard. I suppose you could join up with one of them if you wanted to get a little crusading out of your system."

"Good point." Maddie waved her fork at me. "Since I only transferred here a few months ago and I've been busy catching up and getting settled in, I haven't really looked into that stuff yet."

I didn't pick up on any deception in her answers. She was being perfectly straightforward with me. A sense of certainty filled my chest.

Whatever her friends—or acquaintances, or whatever they were to her—were up to, whether they were specifically interested in businesses under my family's domain or not, she wasn't involved in their investigations. She showed no sign of suspecting there were any deep-seated problems in the city that she'd consider tackling. That night when I'd seen her at the dance club must have been just a fun outing for her, not any kind of work.

Which meant that technically there wasn't any good reason for me to continue spending time with her. Not from a business perspective, anyway.

From a personal perspective… If she wasn't entangled in anything that clashed with my other interests, then there was no reason I shouldn't see her again for my own happiness, was there? I was allowed a little time off from worrying about the business now and then.

And this woman made me think that devoting the time to her would be more than worthwhile.

Maddie scooped the last of her rice into her mouth, and the server came by with the bill. I grabbed it before Maddie could and took out my wallet.

"We should split it," she protested.

I gave her an amused look. "Of course you'd say that. I'm not going to tell you that men should always pay for women, because I know you think that's bull. And it is. Some of the most capable people I've ever met are women. But my personal stance is that the person who does the inviting does the paying. Can you give me that?"

Maddie narrowed her eyes at me, but a smile touched her lips at the same time. It turned slyer before she spoke. "Then I'll just have to invite you someplace and pay for you next."

She was openly talking about us getting together again before the date was even over. I'd call that a win. The flicker of joy it sent through me was more potent than it probably should be, but what the hell.

It'd been quite a while since I'd gotten to hang out with someone who could make me smile like she did.

"I look forward to hearing your plans," I said, grinning back at her with honest enthusiasm.

After the server brought back my card, we walked out to where Maddie had parked her car. She stopped on the sidewalk by the driver's seat and turned toward me. A faint flush had colored her cheeks that only made her look more delicious.

Fuck caution. I was a man who went after what he wanted. I touched her cheek, and when she shifted toward me as if drawn by a magnet, I captured her mouth in a kiss.

She kissed me back, her lips melding with mine eagerly enough to send a wave of sparks over my skin. Her floral scent filled my lungs, and suddenly all I wanted to do was to lift her up on the hood of the car, strip the pants right off her, and show her just how good I could make her feel. But I wasn't throwing caution to the wind to the point of getting arrested for public indecency.

Besides, Maddie didn't seem like a one-night-stand kind of woman. I didn't want her to think I was only interested in getting her into bed. And she'd already talked about how important her studies were to her—as well as mentioning a project she was working on due later this week.

I eased back, stroking my fingers along her jaw. "I'll let you get back to saving the world," I said in a low voice. "But I definitely want to see you again."

As Maddie beamed at me in response, all I could think of was how much I'd meant that statement. I just hoped I didn't regret how attached I'd already become to the woman in front of me.

CHAPTER 20

Madelyn

Slade's hands ran down to my waist, hooked around the bottom of my shirt, and moved upward beneath it, his fingers stroking over my smooth skin. I arched into him, my breasts grazing his solid chest. He swept down to capture my mouth, his heat flooding me from head to toe. A needy ache was forming between my legs.

I flung my arms around his neck, and Slade gazed down at me, his dark brown eyes piercing into mine. He lowered himself so the bulge behind his pants grazed my sex, and I rocked my hips to meet him. He kissed my neck, marking a searing path along its slope. One hand slipped under my ass, pressing me tighter against him.

"Slade," I murmured like a plea, and yanked his mouth back to mine. He hugged me close against him as he parted his lips, opening the way for our tongues to tangle together. Oh, God, I wanted—I needed—

"I've got you, Maddie," a familiar voice that wasn't Slade's murmured, even and assured. My fingers slid through tufts of hair that'd turned shorter than Slade's wavy locks.

The man pinning me down wrapped his arm around my waist and flipped us over so I was straddling him, and I found myself looking down into Beckett's gorgeously chiseled features and bright gray eyes. The crisply masculine tang of his cologne filled my nose. I wanted to drink it right off his skin.

He teased his deft hands up my torso to cup my breasts, swiveling his palms over my nipples. The sparks of pleasure made me whimper. Before I knew it, I was grinding against him the way I had Slade. Somehow it all felt perfectly normal, perfectly right. I wanted him too.

I bent down to kiss him, and he growled against my lips with a wildness I didn't remember him showing before. With a powerful surge of his muscles, he hefted me up and carried me across the room to my desk. We were in my dorm, I registered vaguely. Books thumped and pens clattered to the floor as he cleared the way to place me on the desk's top. Then he was kissing me again, devouring me so thoroughly my head spun.

Beckett gripped my hips and pulled me against him. One hand delved between us to work beneath the waist of my pants. Excitement quivered through my core even though some distant part of me wondered if this was a good idea. We'd only kissed once before and now… now…

Now his fingers were gliding right over my clit, and I was crying out against his mouth, and—

The shape of the surface beneath me shifted, and so did the man in front of me. Logan's taller, brawnier form loomed as he braced me against the sink in the basement bathroom back home. His head bowed toward mine, his eyes glinting with a golden sheen full of heated longing.

"Maddie," he muttered. He'd just rolled the condom over his

shaft, the head nudging between my thighs where my pants had vanished. The ache inside me swelled, and I clamped my legs around his hips.

"Please," I said, and he plunged into me at the same moment as he claimed my mouth with his. He was all around me with his raw, musky scent, filling me and plundering me, and I wanted nothing more than to buck against him until we both—

My leg kicked to the side and hit thick cloth. Something was tangled all around me—I was on my back again, but there was only a light warmth covering me, no masculine heat.

I blinked, and reality came rushing in. I was lying in my dorm-room bed, totally alone, sweat dampening my skin. It'd been a dream. A way-too-realistic dream. My pussy was throbbing as if those three men really had brought me to the brink of release.

Oh, crap, had any of the noises I'd been making carried through to reality? My gaze shot to the bed opposite mine, and I saw with a rush of relief that Keeley had already left. It was just me in the room with my hormones racing through me on overdrive.

I sat up, rubbed my face, and gathered my clothes to take a shower. But even after several minutes under the spray, which I turned as cold as I could stand it to wash away the lingering horniness, the memory of the dream still brought a flush to my cheeks.

Back in the dorm room, I picked up my phone and typed out a text to Summer. *Had a crazy dream. You know how I told you that I've gotten kind of close with one of Logan's friends, Slade? I was making out all hot and heavy with him, and then it was Beckett I was all over, and then I was back at home that night with Logan… Am I totally insane? Who lusts after three guys in the space of five minutes?*

As I packed my bag for my morning classes, the phone chimed with Summer's answer. *Logan can GTFO, but I see no problems with getting it on with two hot guys who seem into you. Why shouldn't you enjoy both of them, in your imagination… or in reality too? ;) Let them remind you what you're worth, since that jackass doesn't have a clue.*

I shouldn't have been surprised. My mouth twitched with a smile. Maybe she was right. College was supposed to be the time for casual hookups and experimenting, even if that wasn't my typical approach. If both of the guys wanted me, and I wanted them… I'd make sure they knew I wasn't exclusive, but there wasn't anything wrong with me seeing where things could go with both of them.

It really shouldn't have been so hard for me to believe that two hot guys *could* want me. I guessed I could thank Logan for that, at least partly.

I paused after zipping up my bag and swallowed hard. Our encounter—and the way he'd ghosted me afterward—had cast a long shadow over my dating life. Somehow I'd spent more time with him in the past week than I had in years, and we'd barely touched on the one event that had altered our relationship irrevocably while also sending him running. Even when I'd tried to confront him before, I'd danced around the subject, unsure of how to address it.

We'd had something once, I knew that—even if it'd only been friendship for most of that time. A piece of my heart was still drawn to him, longing to understand him… I didn't think I could give myself over to pursuing more with any other guy until the air was totally clear between us. There'd always be a lingering "what if" in the back of my head.

He owed me a proper explanation anyway, no matter how much he'd resisted before. If it was a shitty explanation, well, that'd tell me all I needed to know and make it that much easier to move on.

I'd be seeing him tonight. We were supposed to be checking out a bar on the outskirts of downtown. Dexter had turned up an old bill at Melinda Hughes's house that'd been in a man's name, a man the Vigil guys had determined was the manager at that bar. He could be the one who owned the car Logan had heard about, using her address for that too.

But I didn't want to have a conversation like this in front of the other guys. There was no way Logan would open up with his friends within hearing. I wasn't even sure if they knew we'd hooked up.

No, this was better kept private, just between us.

In between classes, I did my readings on a bench within view of the law library entrance, enjoying the spring sunlight and the warmth it cast over me. It wasn't until the early afternoon when I spotted Logan's tall form striding toward the library.

I hadn't seen any of the other guys go in. Hopefully I'd be able to catch him alone in there. I stuffed my book into my bag, swung it over my shoulder, and hurried after him.

The door to the Vigil office hadn't completely closed, the latch just slightly ajar. I pulled it open and found Logan sitting on the edge of the computer desk, shuffling a deck of cards. That was strange enough that my eyes darted to the images on the cards, and I realized it was even odder than I'd initially thought. They weren't playing cards but tarot cards by the look of them.

"What are those for?" I blurted out as Logan's head jerked up at my entrance.

He frowned at me, his hands stilling. Nudging the cards into a straight formation, he slid them into the box that'd been sitting on the desk next to him and then shoved that into the desk's drawer. "Just a tool for inspiration. Nothing important. What are you doing here? We're not heading out until tonight, when the bar'll be open and busy."

Shit. I'd already put him on the defensive. I groped for a way to smooth over the situation and decided there really wasn't any.

Honestly, even if I hadn't asked an abrupt question, Logan seemed to take offense to just about everything I said these days.

"I needed to talk to you," I said instead, figuring it was best to get straight to the point. "Just you."

Logan's stance had already tensed when I'd come in, but now his shoulders went slightly more rigid. He narrowed his eyes at me. "About what?" he asked flatly. "I thought we were all talked out after our last private chat."

I drew myself up straighter, girding myself. I would not let him intimidate me out of this. I wouldn't let him make me feel small or pathetic. Something was going on—something *had* been going on two years ago—and I had a right to know why it'd screwed things up between us so epically.

I tugged the door all the way shut and leaned against the doorframe, crossing my arms over my chest. "I've held my own with you and the other guys through every part of this investigation so far. I think I've proven that I'm not weak anymore like I was back in junior high when you had to jump in to defend me. I can *defend* myself now. You don't have to worry about what I can or can't handle."

Logan's expression gave away nothing. His bright brown eyes, which had shone so hungrily in my dream, held only impatience. "Fine. You're a strong, independent woman. I get it. Is there a point to this or did you just want my approval?"

God, did he always have to needle me in just the right way to get under my skin? My jaw clenched, but I forced it to relax.

"I need you to tell me what happened the night we hooked up," I said, keeping my own voice as calm as possible. "I *know* something was up. I've seen the kind of things you've been doing now. Why were you all banged up? Were you investigating something all the way back in our town—something people were willing to fight you over?"

I'd thought Logan had looked obstinate before, but now his demeanor turned absolutely impenetrable. "That's none of your business."

I pushed myself off the doorframe and took a step toward him. "No, I think it is my business. I was there with you then, and I'm here now. I need to understand. You didn't want me to know what you'd been doing. And then, after— You can't tell me that you shut me out and blocked me everywhere because you assumed I'd be clingy or something. *You* were just as into it as I was. You kissed me first. And I was already giving you nothing but space up until that night. So there's got to be something else, maybe something you're keeping me out of—"

"For fuck's sake, Madelyn," Logan broke in, his tone gone harsh. "Not everything is about you. We hooked up, we both got off, and that's the end of it. It didn't mean anything, and it doesn't have anything to do with anything else in my life. I'm not interested in talking about anything to do with that night, especially the part you were involved in. Because you know what? I try not to think about it at all."

His words and the way he spat them at me hit me like a slap to the face. Shame washed over me, but with it came a surge of anger that he was making me feel ashamed for what I'd said. For letting that night have any importance at all.

Why should I even bother finding out what was going on if this was how he wanted things to be? Why was I wasting any more energy on this jerk than I already had? Nothing I'd done in the past week had made a speck of difference to him.

"You know what?" I snapped back, my patience frayed. "You should consider yourself lucky that I've cared as much about how *you* feel about things as I do. I gave you two years to get your head out of your ass and apologize for *being* such an ass, or at least give me something resembling an explanation. I've done nothing but keep out of your way until now. So forgive me for thinking you might treat me with even as much respect as you'd give some stranger you don't even know."

I spun around and shoved past the door. My feet didn't stop moving until I'd put the law library far behind me. I stalled at the edge of the path, a tremble running through my body, and rubbed my hands over my face.

I hadn't meant to lose my temper. But… we'd shared something, whether Logan wanted to admit it or not. Either that, or he'd sure as hell pretended to be affected by our hookup while it was happening. The things he'd said… He'd had no reason to lie if he'd planned on ghosting me right after.

He wasn't interested in me that way now, and that was fine, but he had no excuse for being so hostile. Unless he was hiding something. But why couldn't he trust me even a tiny bit after everything we'd been through just this week?

I glanced across the lawn toward the parking lot outside my dorm, which I'd stormed toward without really thinking about it. My gaze settled on my car—the car we'd worked together to recover. An unexpected sense of resolve rose up inside me.

I set off toward the car, my hands balling at my sides. I was going to prove to him once and for all that I was his equal, not some useless, clingy girl. And if he still didn't want to see it, at least I'd have proven it definitively to myself. He could go drown in his troubles for all I cared, but I'd look after what mattered to me for myself.

CHAPTER 21

Madelyn

I parked down the street from the bar, grateful that Dexter had mentioned its name when he'd contacted me to let me know about tonight's plans. That meant I'd been able to look up the address.

For a few minutes, I just studied the outside of the building from down the street. It was a plain if scruffy brick building, distinguished by the bright orange door and the silver lettering that stood out against the large black sign overhead. No one came in or out while I watched, but that wasn't surprising. My internet search had also told me that the place didn't open until five o'clock, a couple of hours from now.

The guys had planned on scoping the place out like regular customers, but I couldn't help thinking I'd be more likely to find evidence of illegal dealings while the clientele wasn't around. Maybe if they hadn't felt obligated to bring me along, they'd have broken in like they had the house the other day. But even the three of them going in together made it more likely they'd get caught.

I couldn't pick locks, but if I could spot something from the outside or even find my way in and dig up a clue, no one would be able to claim I couldn't hold my own alongside them. I'd have done something they hadn't managed to, all on my own.

My heart thumped at a brisk beat, but I willed my nerves to settle down. This was no big deal. Logan and the others pulled crap like this all the time. It could be just an ordinary bar—the only thing we knew about it was that the manager had used Melinda Hughes as some kind of front address. Which, okay, suggested he might not be totally on the up-and-up, but it didn't necessarily make him outright dangerous.

And there shouldn't be much of anyone around the place this long before opening anyway.

Gathering my courage, I stepped out of the car. Figuring it was better to do this with as little baggage as possible, I left my purse behind and simply stuffed my phone in my pocket in case I needed to take on Dexter's role as evidence photographer. Then I ambled down the street toward the bar at as casual a pace as I could manage.

I passed a café where patrons were chattering to each other behind the front window and a couple of shops with a few customers browsing inside. No one stirred around the bar. The front door would obviously be locked, and I'd look strange if anyone saw me trying it. I simply meandered on by the front of the building, eyeing the window surreptitiously.

The main room was cast in shadows, but I made out several square tables, all dark wood, and a wide wooden bar counter toward the back of the space. There was no one inside at the moment. Perfect.

A narrow lane on the far side of the bar led around behind the building. I ducked down it and picked up my pace, the back of my neck prickling. Thankfully, I had the foresight to set my feet quietly, because I was just a few steps down when I heard the scrape of something moving around the back.

I slowed down again and crept the rest of the way to the corner of the wall. There, I peeked around the building.

The lane connected to a wider alley that ran down the middle of the block past the backs of all the buildings. A truck was parked outside the bar, the back end open, boxes stacked inside it. Several of them had logos I recognized—they were cases of alcohol. Well, there wasn't anything particularly suspicious about a bar getting a booze delivery.

More interesting to me was the door that'd been propped open with a wedge underneath it. A guy who didn't look much older than me strode out and grabbed another case. A rhythmic hiss of music carried from the headphones he wore, which must have been blaring. He carried the case inside, leaving the door wide open.

My mouth went dry. This was my chance. I could get inside and poke around, as long as that one employee didn't catch me. I should be able to manage that, right? The guy definitely wasn't in a position to hear anything outside his headphones. As long as he didn't see me, I was golden.

I couldn't let the opportunity pass me by when luck was working in my favor.

I darted toward the back door, listening carefully for the seeping music. There was no sound in the dark hall on the other side. I slipped inside, my heart racing, and caught the sound of footsteps coming from a doorway to my right. I dashed in the opposite direction, to a door a little farther down on the left.

It was a kitchen, dim and dingy with a greasy smell lingering in the air. I didn't think this place served up fine cuisine.

Moving as quietly and quickly as I could, I slunk through the cramped space. I peeked into the cupboards and drawers, scanned the countertops and beneath the cabinets, and studied every object that came into view. I *had* to find some piece of evidence to bring back to Logan, whether it proved that the bar had nothing to do with the case or that the culprits worked here. The thought of his sneering dismissal brought a rush of anger back to the surface.

He was going to see that I wasn't some helpless kitten in need of protection, incapable of understanding whatever the hell he'd been through in the last few years. That I was just as resilient as he was, and putting me down wasn't going to stop me from getting what I wanted.

Unfortunately, the kitchen offered nothing remotely useful one way or the other. I paused with a grimace and poked my head into the hallway.

The guy was just stepping outside again. The moment he'd passed out of view, I hustled across the hall to another doorway just before the main room.

It proved to be a storage room, about the size of a janitor's closet—and true to form, it mostly held cleaning supplies. I shifted the various objects on the shelves around, finding rolls of receipt paper for the cash register, blank order slips, and a box of pens as well, but none of that was any help.

The manager must have some kind of office, right? A private area where he handled any business to do with the bar. Where was that?

I slipped out into the main bar room. The place was packed with tables, barely enough room for neighboring chairs to be pulled out at the same time. The ones near the front were all the square four-seaters I'd seen from the window; a few eight-person round tables stood closer to the back, near the bar.

The bar itself ran in an L-shape with the long end next to me along the back wall and a smaller bit jutting out at the far side, holding the cash register. Just beyond the register, I spotted another door. A tarnished brass plaque mounted on it said simply MANAGER. Bingo.

I checked the back of the bar on my way to the office, giving the shelves beneath the counter and along the wall a quick skim. Everything looked like standard bar equipment, as far as I could tell. A clipboard had been tucked away on one shelf, but all I found on the one sheet that had writing on it was a list of drink ingredients, maybe something custom a patron had asked for.

As I set it down and straightened up, my gaze caught on a folded paper left on one of the circular tables near the end of the bar. That must be something an employee had left there, right, since everything from last night's customers would have been cleaned up? I dashed over to check it out.

To my dismay, I found only a crude doodle of a guy waving his gigantic dick. Rolling my eyes, I set it down—just as a click rang through the room with the turning of the knob on the manager's office door.

My stomach lurched. I threw myself down into a crouch beneath the level of the table, squeezing between the chairs on either side of me.

Thank God I hadn't continued straight to that door and opened it myself. Three men and a woman sauntered out of the office, muttering to each other, one letting out a dark chuckle. All of them moved with obvious strength, twisted tattoos winding across one man's neck and the woman's arms, another man sporting a scar stretching across his cheek to his jaw.

The woman ran her hand through her spiky pixie cut, which was a flat black color I had to assume was dyed, and her leather jacket rode up enough for me to spot the handle of a pistol tucked in the back of her jeans. One of the men lifted his hand, and I realized he was outright holding a gun himself. My breath snagged in my throat.

Okay, these people were definitely dangerous. Shit. What the hell had I gotten myself into?

The four figures had gathered around the bar, one of them going behind to grab a bottle I couldn't make out the label on. It took several more seconds before my panic evened out enough for me to pay attention to the conversation they were having in aggressive tones that only set me more on edge.

"Pop a cap in all of them. It's the most effective way to stop their shit," the man with the bottle said in a deep, angry voice as he poured the alcohol into a couple of glasses.

The guy with the gun snatched one of the glasses and let out a sigh of frustration. "We've got to catch the pricks first. Their staff don't know shit about this."

"We can't let them get away with it," the third guy said. "A little rivalry is fine, but when they stoop to the level of vandalizing our property? Fuck that. They're all a bunch of low-life scumbags anyway. We'd be doing the city a service getting rid of the fuckers."

"No kidding," the woman said in a guttural voice, and made a grabby gesture toward the bottle. "You going to pour some of that for me?"

They were definitely criminals, but there was no reason to think that they had anything to do with my car or Dad's box from what they'd said so far. I held the rest of my body perfectly still while my head swiveled, considering possible escape routes.

The conclusion crept over me with a sinking sensation in my gut that I was screwed unless the group at the bar left before anyone came in the front where they could spot me under the table. I couldn't make a run for the front door without those four noticing me; same story with the back hall. The tables might be close together, but that only worked against me. If I tried to squeeze around them toward the hall, I'd end up brushing against a chair and drawing attention to myself.

Maybe this bunch would leave after they'd had their drink and hashed out their problem a little more? Surely they weren't going to hang out there all the way until opening time.

"Marvin's right," the first man was saying. "They attacked us, and we have to retaliate. Otherwise we're just inviting them to screw us over again."

"Can't be anything too blatant," the second guy said. "We don't want the police getting all up in our shit."

The glasses clinked, and then one of the pairs of legs moved toward my table. My hunched stance went even more rigid. I stared at the jean-clad legs and the scuffed leather boots beneath them, willing them to stop, to head somewhere else.

The man did stop, but right at the edge of the table next to mine. If he came much farther around it and looked down, he'd see me for sure. He set his glass down on the table and drummed his fingers against the surface, each tap reverberating alongside my thudding heart.

This was bad. Really bad. Every particle in my body balked against the realization rising up in me, but I couldn't deny it.

I'd gotten myself into a horrible jam, and I was going to need help if I wanted to have a decent chance of getting out of it unharmed. What was more important, my pride or ensuring these people didn't "pop a cap" in *me*?

If Logan never let me live it down, well… I guessed I'd have to back out of any further parts of the investigation. A flush that was part frustration, part shame prickled over my face, but my panic blared far louder.

I didn't want to *die*. Fighting off a single unarmed thug was one thing. Taking on four criminals, at least two of whom had guns… I wasn't a superhero. I could admit I'd gotten out of my depth.

Breathing softly and shallowly, I eased my hand over to my pocket. Ever so carefully, I slid out my phone. My hand shook, but the guy at the nearby table was focused on his companions, grumbling about trashing somebody's home. I still had a little time before I was discovered.

The name at the top of my recent text threads was Dexter. Well, he was the most reliable out of the three guys anyway. I certainly couldn't call on anyone outside the Vigil to extricate me from this ridiculous mess. The thought of trying to explain to Keeley what was going on made me shiver. And I could hardly call the police when technically *I* was the only one who'd done anything illegal here, sneaking into a building where I had no permission to be.

I set the phone on silent, typed out a shaky message as quickly as I could with my trembling fingers, hit send, and slid the device back into my pocket. Please, let them get here fast. Let them know how to create some kind of distraction so that I could get out of here.

Just let them come. They had to come, or I was the one who'd be screwed.

CHAPTER 22

Slade

"I knew we should never have let her get involved in the first place," Logan growled, his knuckles white where he was gripping the steering wheel. "Going in there on her own like that—so fucking stupid. Reckless and stupid."

The engine roared as he hurtled through the streets, cutting off other cars and speeding through stoplights that were seconds from turning red. If I hadn't been in the car with him during similar high-speed drives, I'd have been clutching the handle for dear life. As it was, my pulse thumped heavily with a combination of anxiety and my own frustration.

Still, I felt the need to defend Maddie. Logan obviously didn't have the most unbiased view of her behavior even at the best of times.

"We've done plenty of things that were even more stupid than this," I pointed out. "How many situations have we walked into that we knew for sure were dangerous?"

"We weren't even certain that this bar had any criminal affiliations at all," Dexter put in from the back seat.

"It doesn't matter," Logan snapped. "I told her everything we do could be dangerous. She's seen the kind of people we've run into investigating the theft. Does she have a death wish or something?"

I suspected the people most likely to die in this scenario were anyone who got in between Logan and Maddie, whatever we had to do to drag her out of the place. He was so worked up a vein was bulging at his temple. I wasn't sure I'd *ever* seen him this pissed off.

How much of it was because of Maddie defying him, and how much because he was worried about her safety just like I was? He could deny he had any interest in her all he wanted, but he clearly cared, one way or another.

"You kept trying to convince her that she couldn't handle running around with us at all," I said, keeping my tone light. "Apparently that only made her more determined to prove herself. Maybe that's a hint that you should change your tactics."

Logan's next growl was a wordless sound of fury. I decided I'd better drop the subject there.

Besides, my insides were so tangled up with tension that it was hard to keep the breezy tone I'd been going for. It'd already been twenty minutes since Dexter had gotten the text and alerted us. Even at the speed Logan was driving, the bar was at least another ten minutes away. What if the people Maddie had been worried about had caught her? What would they do to her if they did?

It was hard to know how worried I needed to be, but she'd mentioned they had guns. It didn't sound like they were just regular bar staff having a casual pre-opening chat.

"Have you heard anything else from her?" I couldn't help asking, glancing back at Dexter.

He shook his head, his mouth tight. Even he was worried from his intensely practical perspective. Shit.

"It's better that she doesn't do anything else that could draw attention to her presence," he said, but that fact didn't give me much comfort.

A weird twinge of what I had to admit was jealousy rippled through my panic. Maddie had my number too. I hadn't seen her talking to Dexter other than brief discussions about the case. Why had she reached out to him for help instead of me?

Maybe she hadn't figured I'd be as reliable as him? I didn't exactly present myself as Mr. Responsibility.

But I wanted to be that kind of guy for her. The more time we spent together, the more I couldn't wait to see her again. And she'd shown when we were making out in the house the other day that she saw me as more than a meaningless good time. How many girls had looked at me as more than a brief, fun fling, not caring whether I was at all invested in them?

I had to prove that I was worth that kind of consideration. Worthy of being someone she "actually liked" and didn't just want to goof around with. I should be a guy she could turn to at least as much as she could trust Dexter with that role.

But I'd never been that guy for anyone before. I wasn't totally sure how to be. Fuck.

I guessed getting her out of this jam would be a good step in the right direction, anyway. If we could pull that off.

I squinted at the road ahead. My foot tapped restlessly against the floor. I popped one of my cinnamon candies into my mouth for something to do and immediately regretted it. It reminded me of kissing Maddie… and when Logan threw the car around a corner, I almost choked on it.

"It doesn't make sense that she'd go off and do this right now, though." I frowned. "We let her be totally involved when we broke into the house. She seemed satisfied with that, and we'd already looped her in on the trip to the bar tonight. Why would she suddenly decide that she had to get in there early when nothing changed?"

Dexter hummed in the back seat. "It is strange, and not consistent with how she's acted so far. But maybe something did happen that we don't know about that made her feel the situation was more urgent?"

"Or maybe she's a clueless ditz who makes idiotic decisions," Logan snarled, but he didn't sound as emphatic about that suggestion as in his earlier complaints.

I glanced at him, one eyebrow rising as suspicion gripped me. "Did *you* talk to her earlier today? Did you get all grouchy about her being involved again? That could have set her off."

"I didn't say anything to her about the investigation," Logan shot back. "I sure as hell didn't give any impression that going into the bar early was a good idea."

I could read into what he didn't say well enough, especially with the tick of his jaw before he clenched it. "But you did talk to her. For fuck's sake. What *did* you say?"

The tires squealed as he was forced to brake at a stoplight. He turned his head to glare at me. "Nothing that's any justification for her going off like this, trying to get herself killed."

Normally I wouldn't have challenged my best friend. I trusted him, I had his back, and I knew that loyalty went both ways. But it seemed to me that part of having his back was standing up to him when he was being a prick over a woman who didn't deserve it. I could do that for Maddie even if she wasn't here to see me defend her.

I didn't want to make him more furious, though, not when we needed him thinking at least somewhat clearly to confront the assholes who had Maddie cornered. So I just gazed steadily back at him and said in an even tone, "Maybe after we get her out of that hellhole, you should think a little harder about that. Because I haven't seen her do anything so far that wasn't justified."

Logan jerked his eyes back to the road with the change of the light and hit the gas. He drove on in stormy silence that I decided it was better not to break. I tried to picture how we'd arrange to get Maddie safely out of the bar, but it was hard to come up with a plan when we hadn't scoped the place out yet—and planning wasn't exactly my specialty anyway.

We tore around another bend, and then Logan slowed. I recognized Maddie's car a block up ahead by the side of the road. "She was smart enough not to park right out front," I remarked.

Logan just snorted. He pulled in behind it, moving in brusque jerks.

"If her car's still here, then she's still inside," Dexter remarked as we got out, and then shook his head at himself with a rustle of his messy curls. "Of course, if she'd gotten out I'm sure she'd have texted us to let us know."

"Let's get going then," I said, bouncing on my feet.

Logan took a deep breath as if to steady himself. His jaw was still clenched, his hands in fists, but he still knew how to be a leader.

"We'll take a quick look around to see what we're dealing with," he said. "We could screw things up more if we go barging in unprepared. Keep your eyes peeled, and move *fast*."

We had no idea how much trouble Maddie was already in. My stomach twisted as we hustled down the street together. I picked out the bar up ahead with the glinting lettering on its otherwise black sign. Then, as we drew closer, my gaze snagged on something that made my spirits sink even farther.

I pointed to the black shape spray-painted on the dark brick at the corner of the wall. "There's a gang sign. Looks like it's been there for a while and repainted. Isn't that the sign for those assholes we tangled with last year when we were helping that kid whose mom was being shaken down."

"Shit," Logan said through clenched teeth. By now, we all knew how to tell when a gang had claimed a particular property as their own, which meant they had at least some say in the operations. If Maddie had seen armed men inside, this was probably one of their business fronts. And these lowlifes seemed to be one of the bigger gangs in town, definitely one of the most vicious. I had a scar on my bicep from when one of the assholes had come at me with a knife, even though all we'd been doing was asking a few questions.

I'd hoped we'd get to steer clear of them after that. No such luck. Their criminal affiliations made it even more likely that they were involved in the car theft and whatever had gone down with Maddie's father's box… and even more likely that she'd be in deep shit if they caught her having snuck into their hangout.

Neither of the other guys showed any indication that they were second-guessing our rescue attempt. Logan's eyes had narrowed in concentration. "We'll go in, but we need to keep it looking casual. Play it off like we're trying to help somehow, not a threat. Maybe we can stop any shots from being fired. All she needs is a distraction so she can make a run for the exit."

All she needs. As if it were that simple. I squared my shoulders and marched with the other guys the rest of the way to the bar, pasting a smile on my face but inwardly preparing to do battle.

Whatever she needed, whatever lengths we had to go to, we were getting her out of this mess.

CHAPTER 23

Madelyn

I stayed crouched beneath the table until my calves started to ache from holding so still, waiting while the four apparent gangsters hashed out how they were going to take revenge on what I was gathering were the criminals running a rival bar.

Were the Vigil guys even coming? How long would it take them to get here even if they were?

The man who'd walked closer to my table meandered around a bit, making my pulse stutter several times. Then the whole group ambled over to a table at the far side of the room from me. They sat down with their backs to me, mostly facing the front door.

My heart skipped in a different way. Maybe I could get out of this on my own after all. It was only a short distance from my hiding spot to the end of the bar where the cash register sat. If I could creep around behind the bar and make the short dash to the back hall without being spotted…

I eased out from between the chairs inch by inch and crawled around them toward the short end of the bar's L shape. I had to stop and twist to squeeze past another table, but then I was able to shuffle the last couple of steps to the shelter of the bar counter.

Slumping behind it, a breath rushed out of me. The gangsters were still talking away, their aggressive voices interspersed with harsh chuckles. They weren't at all suspicious—none of them had any clue I was in the room. Now I just had to make it to the hall.

I was just creeping around the corner of the bar when another man strode into the room from the back, the way I'd originally come. As I jerked back out of view, almost choking on my tongue, I recognized him as the guy who'd been unloading the delivery truck. His headphones were looped around his neck now.

He stopped just outside the hall. "Everything came other than they sent a replacement for the one brand of vodka you wanted—the Belvedere. The replacement stuff looks like similar quality, though."

One of the men at the table let out a huff. "They're supposed to call before making any substitutions. Fuckers."

"Do you want me to load it back in and hassle them about it?"

"Nah, it's here now. But I'll make sure they know not to pull that shit again. Hey, is that friend of yours still collecting bets on tonight's game?"

I gritted my teeth in impatient silence as their conversation dragged on. The guy was blocking my escape route. What was I supposed to do now?

I guessed while I was waiting for him to leave again, I might as well take a closer look at what was stashed under the cash register. Maybe I'd missed something.

I peered at the shelves, shifting aside the few papers I could move without making much noise. Nothing jumped out at me as particularly useful. Some receipts were tucked way at the back, but they looked totally normal—they definitely didn't have anything to do with my car or Dad's box.

A tablet was tucked away at the back of the lowest shelf. I slid it out and tried to turn it on, but naturally it asked for a passcode. I wasn't going to be able to come up with that. Making a face at it, I shoved it back into place.

My gaze lifted toward the cash register and caught on a thin rectangular shape next to it at the edge of the counter. A phone. Someone from the group must have left it there while they were getting drinks. What information might be on *that*?

I wavered, wondering if it was worth the risk of trying to grab it. If I snatched it and could get out of here, they wouldn't realize right away that it'd been stolen. They'd probably just assume it'd been misplaced, considering that as far as they knew, no one else had been in here.

Or was that just wishful thinking?

I bit my lip and was on the verge of reaching for it when a text alert chimed from the device, pealing through the room.

I clamped my mouth shut against a yelp and jerked back down. One of the men muttered a curse, and footsteps thumped toward me. My heartbeat thundered in my ears as he approached. What if he looked over the top of the bar and saw me?

There was nowhere for me to go where I wouldn't be even more easily seen. I pressed myself against the base of the bar counter as tightly as I could, holding my breath. He had no reason to check behind the bar. As long as I stayed totally still and quiet…

The footsteps stopped. I didn't even dare look up. My stomach lurched queasily.

And then the man lifted his phone off the counter with a faint rasp and walked away again without any sign of concern.

"George," he muttered to the others. "Can't that guy handle anything on his own?"

The woman snorted. "From what I've seen, nope, not at all."

Okay. I'd survived another close call. As my pulse started to even out again, I peeked around the corner of the bar toward the hall—but the guy with the headphones was still standing there, laughing at another comment one of his colleagues had made about this George person. Why wouldn't he just move?

Staring daggers at him didn't accomplish anything. Swallowing a sigh, I swiveled around—and realized that the door to the manager's office, just a few feet away from me, had been left ajar when the group had marched out into the main room.

I'd wanted to take a look in there. Maybe it wasn't worth the risk of trying to sneak right inside while there were so many employees around, but I could at least check out what I could glimpse from the doorway. It wasn't as if I had anything else to do at the moment.

If I could come out of this mess with just one useful piece of information, that would make the humiliation I was going to face when the Vigil guys got here worth it.

I crept closer, past a couple of rows of empty liquor bottles that'd been left against the wall behind the bar. I had to move a little beyond the shelter of the counter, but while I was crouched this low, the tables still hid me from everyone else in the room. I craned my neck to peer into the office.

There was a filing cabinet directly across from me with a signed baseball and a football helmet poised on it. I guessed the manager was a sports fan. Over to the side, I could make out the edge of a desk, a few papers scattered across its surface and a glass ringed with amber liquid holding a couple of them down. I leaned forward a little farther to take in more of the desk and lost my breath all over again.

It was there. A familiar black lacquer box, the glint of the silver Celtic knot just barely visible on the top, sitting off to the side of the desk at a haphazard angle as if someone had casually tossed it there.

Not only were these people connected to the theft of my car, but the manager himself must have wanted Dad's box for some reason.

Exhilaration rushed through me. I'd found it. Maybe I couldn't poke around the whole office, but could I get away with nudging the door a little farther open and slipping inside just long enough to grab it? I could have Dad's prized possession back in my grasp and prove to the Vigil guys that my expedition here hadn't been totally useless.

I edged slightly closer, running my fingers lightly along the door, testing how easy it'd be to push it. I didn't get much sense of resistance. I hadn't heard the hinges squeak when it'd opened before. The group at the table were still facing away from here. If I moved it slowly enough, smidge by smidge…

I was just about to make that first push when a chair squeaked and a figure loomed in the gap between the door and the frame. It was a man, walking past the doorway to reach for the filing cabinet. The office wasn't empty after all.

The jolt of startled panic sent me jerking a step backward—and my heel collided with one of the lined up bottles. It clicked against the others and toppled over with a *thunk* that seemed to echo through the room. My heart outright stopped.

"What the fuck was that?" one of the men at the table demanded, with a squeak of his chair's legs as he got to his feet. I froze in place, knowing it was only a matter of seconds before he and his friends with their guns descended on me.

What the hell did I do now?

CHAPTER 24

Madelyn

Multiple sets of footsteps rapped across the floor toward the bar. A shuffling sound from within the office told me the man there was turning toward the door too. With a stutter of my pulse, I pushed myself farther behind the counter even though I knew that effort was in vain.

They were going to take a closer look around this time. They were going to search for whatever had made that noise, and it would lead them straight to me. And my way to both possible escape routes was still blocked. Shit.

"Hey, is someone there?" the woman called out, sounding like she was right on the other side of the counter. I balled my hands into fists, my mind scrambling for an excuse that might get me out of this safely—

A loud banging sounded from the front of the building, someone knocking on the door hard enough that it rattled in its frame. Shoes scraped against the floor as the nearby figures must have swiveled.

"What the fuck do they want?" one of the men muttered. "The CLOSED sign is hanging right there."

Voices started to filter through the door.

"Hey! Open up."

"We've got to talk to you. This is important."

That sounded like Slade and Logan. My heart skipped a beat. They'd made it here just in time. But what kind of distraction were they making? I didn't want them getting into trouble with these gangsters because of me.

I hoped they knew what they were doing—and that it'd be enough to give me a chance to escape.

To my relief, all of the footsteps moved away from me. The guy who'd been in the office emerged, visible around the edge of the bar, but he didn't glance my way, all his attention focused on the front of the room. "What's going on?"

"Looks like some college guys making a fuss," one of the men reported from near the door. "I'll see what they're going on about."

There was the click of the door unlocking and a faint squeak of the hinges. "What the hell do you want?" he demanded.

My gaze flicked back and forth, noting that the man from the manager's office was still standing near that doorway and the guy who'd handled the delivery hadn't moved far from the back hall. I still couldn't make a dash for the back exit without being seen.

Logan's voice carried through the room, both bold and urgent. "We overheard some scummy-looking guys a few blocks away talking about how they were going to come here and smash up your bar. I don't know how soon, but they sounded serious. We couldn't just let them go ahead with it without warning you."

For the first time since I'd gotten stuck in here, a smile darted across my lips. He had no idea how perfect that story was given the concerns these gangsters already had about their property—or maybe he did. For all I knew, the Vigil guys were perfectly familiar with the kinds of criminal conflicts going on around the city. Even if they hadn't known anything about the people who owned this specific bar, it might not be hard to figure out what kind of news would get them riled up.

"Are you serious?" the man by the door demanded. "What else did they say?"

Slade spoke next. "We didn't really want to stick around to eavesdrop on guys who'd do shit like that. It sounded like they were pissed off about a deal or something? I don't know what they meant."

Both of the men I'd still been able to see stepped completely out of my view, moving toward the front door to join the conversation. From the sounds of the feet beyond the bar counter, everyone was gathering around the door to talk to the Vigil guys.

Relief flooded me. I'd just give them time to get fully engaged in the conversation, and then I could dash for the back.

"What exactly did you hear?" another of the men asked in a firm voice that suggested he had some authority over the others. "Word for word, as well as you can remember."

As Logan continued to spin his story, I glanced around again, and my gaze snagged on the now wide-open door to the manager's office. I could see Dad's lacquer box from where I was crouched. The sight of it tugged at my chest.

I squared my shoulders. I wasn't coming out of this empty-handed. They'd taken something important from me, and I was taking it right back while I had the chance.

I scrambled over to the end of the bar and peeked around the counter. The six figures were now clustered around the door, all of them focused on the Vigil guys. This was the best opportunity I was going to get. Grab the box, then get the hell out of here.

With a swift breath, I darted across the short open space and through the office doorway. My eyes swept over the contents of the office with a pang as I thought of all the other evidence that might be in here, all the answers we might be able to find about why these people had taken Dad's box in the first place, but there was no time to do a more thorough search. Even this quick maneuver was risky—and it wasn't just *my* safety on the line now.

I snatched the box off the desk, tucked it under my arm, and hustled back into the shelter of the bar beneath the level of the nearest table. As quickly as I could while ducked down, I scuttled to the opposite end of the counter near the back hall. The guys were still talking, but their voices were muffled by the thudding of my pulse.

I was just lunging into the shadows of the hall when one comment reached my ears that made my stomach flip over.

"Wait. You look kind of familiar. Weren't you and your friends making some kind of trouble for our guys downtown a while back?"

The tone got more menacing with each word. My throat tightened at the thought that the guys might be able to face some horrible consequence, but they should be able to leave now. Hopefully they'd been able to see me head this way. I pushed myself forward, my gaze fixed on the back door.

Which swung open to admit a stout burly guy I hadn't seen before.

He took one look at me, and his face twisted with anger and suspicion. "Who the hell are you, and what are you doing back here?" he bellowed.

"I—" I gasped out, and then he was charging forward, his hands already reaching to grab me.

"What the fuck is going on?" someone shouted from the room behind me, but I didn't have time to worry about that. The fury on the man's face and the muscles bulging in his arms as he threw himself at me sent my instincts honed by my martial arts classes into overdrive.

I dodged to the side and caught him in the throat with an upward swing of my elbow, slamming my knee into his gut at the same time. Despite the choked sound that sputtered from his throat, he locked his hand around my wrist. I kicked out with my leg again and managed to land a blow right between his legs.

As he doubled over, his grip on my arm loosened. I jerked backward, onto the threshold of the main room. Yells and thumps from behind me brought my head jerking around.

The Vigil guys had obviously realized I was under attack, and they'd stormed in to defend me. All of them were beating at the gangsters with vicious intensity, Logan bashing one man in the face hard enough to leave his nose bleeding, Slade cracking another man across the jaw, even quiet, unassuming Dexter kicking a third man's legs out from under him. But they were fighting off the whole group that'd been gathered by the door, outnumbered two to one, and the gangsters weren't backing down or going down easily.

And some of them had guns.

I couldn't fight properly while I was holding on to the box. I set it on the bar counter and rushed over to help.

As all three of the Vigil guys whipped out their fists and hurled their elbows and knees in the middle of the fray, the woman gangster yanked herself back from the bunch and raised her pistol. She aimed it straight at Logan's head, and he was too busy grappling with one of the bigger guys to notice.

My heart lurched into the base of my throat. I didn't hesitate for a second, just flung myself toward her as quickly as I could move. Chairs clattered and thumped in my wake.

The woman had paused to make sure she had a clear shot without her colleagues getting in the way. When she heard me coming, her head whipped around, but I was already on her by then.

I rammed straight into her and tackled her to the ground. With a smack of my hand, I sent the pistol spinning across the floor. Then I twisted around, squirming to evade her own strikes, and brought my heel down on her fingers as hard as I could.

The sound of fracturing bones sent a wave of nausea through me. The woman screeched. But even as the queasiness coiled around my stomach, a rush of triumph shot through me as well.

I'd protected Logan—saved him. I'd put all my strength into defending the guys and conquering our enemies. And it felt… kind of good.

The woman raked the fingernails of her other hand across my arm, and I pushed away from her, kicking her in the ribs. Then I caught hold of a nearby chair and yanked it down on top of her with enough force to provoke a grunt. I scrambled farther away.

A few of the men had hit the floor under the Vigil guys' assault. Slade grabbed my elbow, heaving me to my feet. "Let's get out of here!"

We raced to the back of the bar, the last two men giving chase. I snatched the box off the counter as we dashed by. The man who'd come at me in the back hall had lurched to his feet, but Logan plowed straight into him, knocking him into one of the storage rooms. We ran on by, ignoring his furious shouts and the bellows from behind us.

The door burst open in our wake. I sprinted around the side of the building and down the street toward my waiting car, aware of all three Vigil guys running alongside me. Adrenaline spiked through my veins, and a crazy laugh tumbled out of me.

We'd gotten away. We've faced down criminals and survived—and I'd gotten what I'd come for.

Logan's car was parked right in front of mine. I fumbled for the key fob in my pocket as the guys gathered around their vehicle. A couple of the men from the bar had just made it out to the sidewalk, so we couldn't stick around for long, even if they wouldn't attack us quite as vehemently in full public view.

Still, Logan felt the need to turn toward me just as I yanked my car door open, his lips pulled back in a sneer. "Was that really worth it?"

I stared back at him, still high on the wildness of our victory, and held up Dad's box where they could all clearly see it.

"Yes," I said. "I'd say it was."

CHAPTER 25

Madelyn

Somehow I wasn't surprised that the first thing Dexter did when we all ended up back in the Vigil office was ask for the box from me and then immediately start checking it over. Feeling wiped out from the stress—and, okay, the little bit of excitement—of the past couple of hours, I flopped into one of the chairs by the central table, watching him.

"Looking for secret compartments?" I asked.

"It is possible it's some kind of puzzle box, and your dad just never mentioned that specific aspect," he said. "I'm not seeing anything obvious, but if there's a hidden section, I'll find it eventually." He spoke mildly but with total confidence in his abilities. Kind of a welcome change from Logan a.k.a. Mr. Cocky.

Who'd propped himself against the computer desk and folded his arms over his chest, glowering at me with a scowl. I guessed it was only a matter of time before he decided to start berating me for my choice of actions with his words as well as his eyes. Never mind that I'd actually achieved the most important part of my goals in the end.

Never mind that I'd saved his *life*. Or maybe that was partly why he was pissed off—he didn't like that he couldn't claim I'd been completely inept.

I definitely wasn't expecting an apology for his cruel comments earlier today anytime soon.

Slade leaned against the table next to me and bumped his foot against one of the chair legs. "I knew you were kickass after the moves you showed off at the mechanic shop, but today was a totally new level. That'll teach us to underestimate you. And you found your dad's box too! You're going to put us out of a job."

I laughed a little roughly, knowing how close I'd been to potentially losing my own life. "Oh, I wouldn't go that far." But the praise felt good. It was nice to know someone here appreciated what I'd managed to accomplish, even if it hadn't been according to the Vigil's plans. "I just wanted to be an equal part in the investigation."

Logan snorted but still didn't speak. I bit back a snarky remark and focused on a question that'd started to bother me while I'd been driving back and the adrenaline rush of the fight had worn off. "There is something that doesn't make sense about this whole thing."

Dexter glanced up, still working over the box with his deft fingers even without his full attention on it. "What's that?"

I frowned. "Why did those guys at the bar have the box at all? It seemed like the manager was checking it out, since it was on his desk. And I guess they were the ones who stole my car too?"

Slade shrugged. "They're part of a pretty large gang that's active in the city—we clashed with them over a different case last year, which must be how the one guy recognized Logan. Stealing stuff is par for the course with those types. They must have grabbed the car and then taken the box with them after they dropped it off in case it was valuable."

"But it wasn't," I pointed out. "It shouldn't have taken them long to figure that out, and then they'd have chucked it. It's been a week since my car was taken. And would a gang normally be all secretive about dropping off a car at a chop shop?"

Slade spread his hands. "Who knows? Criminals don't always think the ways the rest of us would find totally logical. Maybe one of the thieves knew his boss had a thing for Celtic knots."

"It's just hard to imagine it's something that random. It's weird that they picked my car to steal in the first place when they couldn't do more with it than sell it for parts, right?"

"It's not important," Logan snapped, finally speaking up. "You have it back. That's what you wanted, isn't it?"

I narrowed my eyes at him. "I think the reason it was stolen is pretty important, because if they targeted me once over something like that, who knows whether they'll come after me in some other way again. Or if it had something to do with my dad somehow—"

Logan pushed off the desk and smacked his hands down on the edge of the table, outright glaring at me now. "There doesn't have to be a reason people do shitty things, Madelyn. It was probably just a bunch of punks being idiots to pass the time. Which we'd have found out on our own without you risking your life if you'd stuck to the plan instead of running straight into danger like you've got a death wish."

The anger I'd been suppressing flared to the surface. "I know I didn't handle it perfectly, and I'm sorry I had to drag you in to help me out of the blue. But it worked out to all our benefits in the end. If we'd stuck with *your* plan, we'd never have found the box at all or even known they had it. There's no way we'd have been sneaking into the office without being seen while the bar was open and there were employees and customers all over the place."

"If you had a problem with my plan, you should have talked to me about it and we'd have come up with a different one."

"Oh, sure, like you've listened to me so much before now."

His expression tightened. "I'd rather come up with a plan we can both agree on than have you pulling risky stunts that could get you killed."

For fuck's sake. "Right, and breaking into a stranger's house wasn't risky? Shoving your way into a mechanic shop you know is involved in illegal dealings wasn't risky? It's not like we got attacked *there*—oh, wait, we did." My hand moved to the scabbed over scratch on my arm instinctively. "None of us knew the people in that bar were going to be that dangerous—or if you did, you didn't bother to fill me in. If you can take risks, so can I."

Logan let out a scoffing sound. "*I* know how to take care of myself."

"And so do I. Or did you miss the part where I saved my ass *and* yours in the end. You'd have gotten a bullet in the head if I hadn't jumped in there."

The thought of the gang woman having gotten off her shot, of Logan dying, sent a chill through me that doused some of my anger. But Logan kept going.

"We were only in that fight because you got yourself into a mess to begin with," he growled.

"And I'd have gotten out of the mess *without* a fight if you hadn't already been hassling gangsters all over town enough to get recognized," I shot back.

Logan leaned forward, his eyes flashing. "If you really think—"

Slade pushed between us, holding out his arms. "Whoa. I think that's enough arguing. We all made it out okay, and we got what we were searching for, so I think we should call that a win and stop making a pissing contest out of it." He aimed a hard look at Logan and then reached to take my hand. "Come on, Maddie. Let's take a little walk and give this guy time to cool off and figure out where he misplaced his gratitude."

Part of me didn't want to leave without finishing the argument, but a larger part realized it would probably never be finished. Logan was never going to give an inch of ground or admit that I'd been anything other than an idiot. Fine. I could use some space from him too.

I stood up and followed Slade out of the room without a backward glance. The door thumped shut behind us.

There wasn't much of anyone around to notice our exit. It was coming up on closing hours, the sunlight dwindling beyond the library windows. Only a few students remained up at the tables near the front, across from the checkout desk where a lone librarian remained on duty. The area at the back near the Vigil office and the rows of bookshelves was totally quiet.

Slade kept walking, guiding me between two of the shelving units where the sound of distant turning pages was even more dulled and there was no one around at all. He dropped his voice low. "Don't listen to him. He's just in a mood." He stroked his thumb over the back of my hand and offered a sly smile. "I happen to think you're one of the strongest and most capable women I've ever met—and that those features are incredibly sexy."

A blush singed my cheeks. I turned to face him, suddenly lost for words. Why was it that his flirty comments and the intensity in those dark eyes could leave me tongue-tied and flushed like a preteen with the world's biggest crush?

"Is that supposed to be a pick-up line?" I said, aiming for a teasing tone and not sure whether I landed it.

Slade chuckled. "Let's just call it the truth. But I can find other ways of complimenting you if you'd prefer a little more variety. Hay una fiesta en mi corazón y tú estás invitado."

My breath caught in my throat at the poetic lilt of the Spanish words. "What does that mean?"

He waggled his eyebrows. "Isn't the mystery part of the fun?"

I raised my own eyebrows right back at him. "You could have called me worse things than Logan did and I'd never know it."

Slade placed a hand over his chest as if I wounded him. "I would never call you anything insulting."

"And how can I be so sure about that?"

He shifted closer, forcing me to lean against the books behind me. His hand reached past me to rest against the shelf next to my arm while he pinned me with his gaze. My lower belly pulsed at his proximity, the scent of cinnamon reaching my nose from his breath.

His voice was a soft murmur now. "I might say that you're deslumbrante or absolutely impresionante, but I would never call you something that didn't fit."

My whole body was flushed now. "What do those words mean?"

He leaned forward, his lips a mere centimeter from mine. "I'm saying that you're breathtakingly beautiful, Piccolina. You're a masterpiece. I want to worship and appreciate you. I want you to forget about Logan for a little while and see how much you're worth."

I couldn't think of a time in the past few weeks when Logan had been farther from my mind. It was just Slade and me, standing face to face with a chemistry I couldn't deny. I didn't need or want to think about Logan. Only Slade. Why the hell shouldn't I pursue what we both obviously wanted?

I closed the last short distance between us and pressed my lips into Slade's with an intensity that he matched immediately. As he pressed the entirety of his body against mine, pinning me against the shelves, I wrapped one arm around his neck. He captured my mouth completely, every movement of his lips stealing more of my breath, until I felt as if I were drowning in him in the best possible way.

Slade smiled into the kiss, running his tongue over the tips of my teeth. He tightened his grip in the back of my shirt and ran his other hand slowly up and down my thigh. Sparks spread across my skin, and a little gasp escaped my mouth.

"The sounds you make are delectable," he whispered, and trailed his lips down my throat. His path of kisses seared across my neck and over my shoulder to the neckline of my shirt. I arched into him automatically, an ache of need pulsing between my legs.

It'd been a long time since I'd hooked up with anyone—a long time since I'd wanted to this much. I had the urge to drag him straight back to my dorm room, but I couldn't quite bring myself to push him away in order to do that. The magic he was working with his mouth on my skin felt way too good.

He followed my shirt's neckline until his lips grazed my cleavage before claiming my mouth again with a heated passion that had my toes curling. His hands skimmed down my sides from my chest to my hips and then back up, dipping beneath the fabric of my shirt. The swipe of his thumbs over my belly provoked another soft noise from my throat.

My hips swayed toward him of their own accord and brushed against the bulge behind his slacks. My heart skipped a beat knowing how turned on he was by our collision, my panties dampening even more than they already had before. Then his hands closed over my breasts, and I had to swallow a whimper.

He worked over my curves with assured skill, tweaking my nipples until I was trembling with the jolts of bliss. My eyes slid closed, my lower lip clamped between my teeth as I struggled to hold back my sounds of encouragement. Then he dipped his fingers right beneath the cups of my bra to fondle me skin to skin, and an audible breath shuddered out of me.

"Just like that," Slade murmured, sounding a little hoarse, as if the gesture had affected him as much as it had me. As he kept caressing me with one hand, he eased the other down between us to the waistband of my pants. "Oh, Piccolina."

Everything about this—his skillful touch, the cinnamon flavor of his mouth as it devoured me whole, the sound of his voice to my ears—felt like an erotic fantasy that I'd never dared to consciously consider. The sensations swept through me, tearing me away from my physical reality and placing me only in his arms.

I quivered as his hand lowered inside my pants, sliding over my panties and rubbing a finger along the most sensitive part of me. The way his fingers worked, there might as well have been no barrier between us at all. He massaged my breast and swept his tongue across my bottom lip in tandem, and oh God, I didn't want this to end. All I wanted was to be consumed by Slade every way he would offer.

A distant thud from the other side of the library jarred me out of my blissful daze. My gaze darted to the end of the shelving unit, with a hitch of my pulse as I thought about how public this encounter was.

"Someone might see us," I murmured.

Slade gave me one of his sly grins, his eyes gleaming eagerly. He gripped my hips and spun me around so that I faced the shelves, my breasts pressing into the edge of one while I looked across the library through the narrow gap over the tops of the books. I could see one of the students standing up as she sorted through the books she'd brought to her table, another walking over to the checkout desk.

Slade traced his fingers over my thigh and delved beneath my pants again. "This makes it more fun," he said by my ear. "They have no idea what we're getting up to. But if you want to stop, just say the word."

Did I? My head was spinning with uncertainty and pleasure. The tip of his finger flicked over my clit, and I jerked in his arms with a gasp I couldn't hold back.

It felt so fucking good. And I was tired of trying to do the right thing, of trying to play by other people's rules. What we were doing wouldn't hurt anyone, and I needed everything Slade was giving me. I needed him.

I ground my ass against his erection in unspoken invitation. Slade hummed happily and tucked his hand right between my legs. "Good girl."

That comment alone had me melting in his arms, panting each of my breaths. As his hand moved back down to where I knew I'd entirely liquified, I couldn't stop the way my body jerked and writhed. Slade didn't seem to mind. He only held me there, pressing heated kisses into the side of my throat.

"You're so wet for me," he muttered into my ear. I bucked into his hand, and he began thrusting that damn finger right inside me. The sounds coming from my mouth were difficult to hold at bay, and one tumbled from my lips before I could stop it.

Slade nipped my earlobe. "Don't be too loud. We wouldn't want to get caught."

I could only nod, though I knew how hard it'd be to stay quiet if he kept up what he was doing to me right now. His fingers moved in lazy circles over the folds of my pussy, catching on that one desired spot long enough to have me stiffening and leaning my head back into his shoulder before he thrust a second long finger into me.

I clenched my teeth to avoid making any noises as he pulsed his fingers inside me, filling me until I was throbbing for more. "How do you like me now?" he rasped into my ear, and I almost couldn't suppress the moan that rushed up my throat.

The sound of footsteps came from the direction of the tables, and I froze, Slade's fingers still working inside of me. The girl I'd seen at the one table was walking toward the rows of bookshelves.

My heart stuttered for reasons that had nothing to do with my gratification. What if she walked all the way back here? Would we be able to pull ourselves together in time to hide what we'd been doing?

Slade's rhythm slowed as he picked up on the sound too. I was torn between the desire to start rearranging my clothes now and the stark resistance to the idea of ending this encounter before we'd seen it through. I was right on the verge of reluctantly pulling away from him when the footsteps stopped.

The girl turned into an aisle about five rows down. I watched over the tops of the books in front of me, my breath in my throat. She appeared to scan the titles she was facing and then grasped one of the books. Then, mercifully, she turned and walked back to the tables.

Slade let out a relieved chuckle and started stroking me again. "I think that's our sign that we shouldn't dawdle any longer while tempting fate," he said. "I don't want to finish this without you *fully* satisfied."

Before I could consider what he meant, he released my pussy just long enough to yank my pants and panties down to my knees. I bit back a gasp as he caressed my bare cheeks. "Ah, what an ass, Piccolina."

He gave one cheek a light slap with his open palm—surprising me and sending an unexpected jolt of pleasure through me. My back arched, pushing myself toward him instinctively, and I could hear the smirk in his voice. "Oh, you like that, do you? Who knew Maddie Silver was such a dirty girl behind that straight-laced exterior?"

He spanked me again, and my breath broke into panting. Then there was a rasp of a zipper as he opened his fly. With a crinkle of foil that was strangely reassuring despite the craziness of this whole encounter, he prepped himself. He must have had a condom in his pocket—did he do things like this a lot?

I didn't really care, not while he was doing it with me right now. This moment was all that mattered.

He rubbed his rigid shaft between my legs over my slick entrance, and the ache in my pussy intensified. "Don't make a noise," he reminded me in a mischievous tone, and then plunged all the way in.

He filled me so abruptly and completely that I thought I might explode just like that. A hissed swear word and a muffled groan burst from his own mouth. It took every ounce of my willpower to keep from releasing a moan as his fingers dug into my hips and he thrust into me again.

One of his hands left my hip to give me another soft spank on my ass. I couldn't help it that time—the faintest of whimpers slipped from my lips.

"You like that?" he asked, picking up the rhythm of his thrusts as he massaged the spot he'd smacked. "I can give you all the attention you need. But if you don't stay quiet, I'm going to have to make you."

I knew it was meant to be a threat, but even as I tightened my grip on the bookshelf, I couldn't suppress the needy noises that were trickling out of me. With every stroke of his cock inside me, I was seeing stars. My body was outright shaking, my self-control fragmenting. Soon there was going to be nothing left in me but bliss.

"Then make me," I whispered.

Slade plunged into me faster at the comment. "That beautiful, filthy mouth is going to get you in trouble."

Despite my best efforts, a slightly louder moan seeped up my throat. True to his promise, Slade reached forward and pressed his hand against my mouth. His palm muffled my next cry, and something about the gesture made the moment even more thrilling. The pleasure surging inside me spiraled higher, stronger by the second.

"The next time we do this," Slade panted quietly, "we're going to go someplace where I can find out just how loud you can get."

I closed my eyes as he sped up even more, filling me even more deeply. He hit the perfect spot inside me, again and again, and then my climax roared through me.

As I shattered with my release, ecstasy sweeping through me in a wave, Slade's hand clamped harder over my mouth to cover the little sounds of my release. His hips jerked, and his breath rasped as he followed me over.

I slumped against the shelves, coming down from my orgasm, and Slade released my mouth. I drew in a few ragged breaths and then glanced over my shoulder at him, taking in his exertion-flushed face and those sparkling eyes.

"Next time, I want to hear more from you too," I said.

A grin stretched across his face. "I do love it when you talk dirty, Maddie."

He was just sliding out of me when the door to the Vigil office swung open and Logan strode out right across from our aisle. He stalled in his tracks, staring straight at us.

CHAPTER 26

Madelyn

Logan froze for all of a second before he marched right into the aisle between the bookshelves, his eyes flashing with fury. As Slade hastily tucked himself back into his slacks, I fumbled to yank up my pants, a blush scorching my cheeks.

"What the fuck do the two of you think you're doing?" Logan spat out, stopping just a few feet from where we stood. He managed to keep his voice low despite its harshness, but his hands had clenched at his sides.

My first impulse was to say, "This isn't what it looks like," but it was exactly what it looked like. Why should I claim it wasn't? What Slade and I had decided to do had nothing to do with Logan. Nothing at all. He had no reason to be pissed off. If no part of his life was any of my business, then me hooking up with his friend sure as hell wasn't any of his.

So I raised my chin and glared right back at him. "I think it's pretty obvious."

"Really? Running off into a violent gang's bar wasn't enough—now you're fucking in public—in the goddamn university library? When did either of you get so stupid and reckless?"

"There wasn't anything stupid about it," I retorted, straining to keep my voice quiet too. The last thing we needed was the rest of the library's patrons noticing our argument. "We were enjoying ourselves. Sorry that's so hard for you to wrap your head around."

Logan threw his hands in the air. "Enjoying yourselves? What do you think would have happened to you if you'd gotten caught? You could have been expelled—they could have arrested you for indecent exposure." His furious whispers were becoming tauter with every sentence.

"We didn't get caught," I said. "No one came anywhere near us, and if they had, we'd have stopped. The only one who's having any problem with what we did is *you*."

Logan chuckled darkly and spun toward Slade, who'd stepped up beside me to slip his hand around my elbow. "And what were you trying to prove with this stunt, huh?"

Slade narrowed his eyes at him, tension humming through his stance. Logan might have been his best friend, but he wasn't any happier about being confronted like this than I was.

"It wasn't a stunt," he said, keeping his voice equally low. "We're into each other; she deserves someone who'll treat her right."

"Oh, and fucking her in the middle of the library is 'treating her right' now?"

Slade cocked his head, a little of his usual flippant attitude coming back into his pose. "Are you mad that we did something risky, or are you just angry because I hooked up with Maddie?"

"What the hell are you talking about?" Logan growled. "I don't give a shit what you do as long as you keep it in your pants in the middle of the goddamn university."

"Maddie's right," Slade replied. "We knew what we were

doing. The only people around who had any chance of catching us by surprise were you and Dexter, and somehow I thought someone I consider a *friend* wouldn't be pissing all over me. So it seems to me like there's something more going on. Not that you have any right to be jealous after the way you've acted around her."

"I'm not *jealous*," Logan sputtered. "For fuck's sake—"

"You're something," I interrupted. "Maybe it's just an asshole, but at this point, I don't really care. You've spent the past two years—and most of the year before that too—pretending I don't even exist. What makes you think you have the right to question what I do now? It's got nothing to do with you."

An angry flush spread across Logan's face, but it took him a moment before he could continue his tirade. "You took my best friend and convinced him to risk his entire career for a quickie."

Slade made a noise in the back of his throat and offered a small smirk. "Actually, bro, I think I did most of the convincing. Don't downplay my excellent seductive skills here."

"I thought you were a little smarter than to let your dick steer the way," Logan snapped at him.

Slade just shrugged, a gesture I could tell pissed Logan off even more. "I'd say this decision was made with both heads, above and below, and it's not one I'd take back, no matter how much you rant about it."

Logan let out an inarticulate growl and yanked his attention to me again. "And you. What happened to Madelyn Silver, devoted student with all those ambitions? Since when did you become such a slut?"

He hurled the last vicious word at me with such vehemence that I reeled back a step as if he'd punched me.

Had he really called me that? Logan Brooks, my junior-high champion against bullies, a guy who'd probably slept with more girls than he could remember the names of, was throwing a slur at me as if my worth was based on who I had sex with?

Fuck that.

My own rage bubbled up inside me too fast for me to hold it back. And maybe I didn't want to. Maybe it was time Logan got an equal dose of his own medicine. At least I could make my accusations without resorting to slander.

"Don't you *dare* call me horrible names and act like I'm some kind of evil seductress," I said, unable to stop my voice from rising regardless of the room around us. I jabbed my finger toward him. "At least I'm not going to fuck someone and then erase them from my life like they weren't worth more than a speck of dirt. At least I don't toss the people who care about me aside and then act like they're the problem when they call me on it."

Logan's jaw dropped. He looked like he was grappling for words, but I barreled onward before he could get anything out.

"You treated me like I was nothing for two years, and now that we've been forced to deal with each other, you've been insulting me and putting me down every chance you can get. Over what? The fact that we hooked up two years ago and you regret that? Guess what, you were there too. I didn't force you to do anything, and frankly, you seemed pretty fucking enthusiastic at the time. I gave you two years of space to get over whatever your issue with me is and you still act like I somehow ruined your life."

I was vaguely aware of Slade watching me with a mix of awe and shock, of my voice carrying through the library, but I couldn't bring myself to give a shit. It felt like too much of a relief to finally unleash all of this hurt and frustration.

"You talked like you were annoyed that I wanted anything from you, even just an explanation," I went on. "Like it's some awful thing that I have any feelings at all to do with you. But as soon as I'm focused on some other guy, you barge in and tear into me over that too? I obviously just can't win with you. Everything I do is wrong."

"Maddie," Slade said softly, and the tapping of footsteps reached my ears. I only pushed myself onward. I wasn't done yet.

I stepped forward, prodding my finger right against Logan's chest. "Guess what. You're getting your wish. We found everything I lost; you can shove me right back out of your life again. But you're not stopping me from seeing Slade, who I happen to like very much and who's been better to me in the past week than you've been in years. So you'll just have to get over that fact. Because the only person who's a problem right now is *you*, not me. And you're never going to convince me of the opposite again."

As my last words faded into the air, the librarian bustled into view, her eyes wide. "What on earth is going on over here?"

I dragged in a breath, jerking my gaze from Logan to her. "Nothing," I said. "Sorry for causing a commotion."

She tutted her tongue. "You can't be disturbing the other students, who are actually working here. If you need to have an argument, take it out of the building."

I dipped my head apologetically. "It's fine. I was leaving anyway. Again, I'm sorry."

The woman pursed her lips as I brushed past her, but I thought I caught a flicker of worry in her eyes. I had no idea how I looked after unloading all of my anger on Logan. I hurried to the front doors before she could ask if I was okay, before Logan could say anything that would only enrage me more.

As I pushed past the door, cool damp air washed over me. It didn't do much to douse the angry heat still pulsing through my body.

That'd been such an amazing moment with Slade. Risky, yes, but thrilling and sexy… I couldn't remember when I'd last felt that good. And now Logan had ruined it, spewed his resentment and hostility all over what should have been a giddy memory.

Why couldn't he let me have even one piece of happiness? How could he rant at me about being hung up on him and then attack me for moving on?

What had I done to make him hate me so much?

I gritted my teeth against the pang that came with that last thought. I hadn't done anything. The Logan I'd used to know had clearly changed into someone I barely recognized, someone I didn't even want to know. And that was fine.

We were done. None of that mattered. *Logan* didn't matter.

I strode on through the lengthening shadows toward my dorm building, looking forward to curling up on my bed and letting out a few final tears before I put all those churned-up emotions aside and focused on the future. Other than getting together with Slade again, I never needed to have anything to do with the Vigil guys again. I had my car back, and Dad's box—

My feet stalled in mid-step with a lurch of my heart.

The box. Dexter had been examining it in the Vigil office. I'd gotten so upset at Logan that I'd forgotten it when I'd stormed out of the library.

Shit.

I stood there for a moment, debating whether I really wanted to make the ten-minute trek across campus back to the law library immediately. Right when the other students still around would stare and Logan would glower at me and maybe have a few choice words.

But if I didn't go now, I had no idea what I'd face when I did go back. I just wanted this whole situation to be over with. Better to rip off that final bandaid than to draw things out.

Logan had gotten a little time to cool off after our argument. Maybe he'd even have headed out too, and I'd only have to deal with Slade and Dexter, who I had nothing against.

I could hope for that, but my body tensed in anticipation as I hurried along the campus paths. I would at least stay calm. No more yelling in the library. I couldn't regret what I'd said to him, but I didn't like pissing off the staff or disturbing the other students.

When I slipped back into the library, I found the main space empty. It was only fifteen minutes before closing now, and it looked like the remaining stragglers had cleared out. Even the check-out desk was abandoned, although I heard shuffling from the room behind it that suggested the librarian was sorting out some paperwork.

I hustled past, not wanting her to notice me and either send me off again or ask what was the matter. All I had to do was grab the box and get out of here again.

No one was standing around outside the Vigil office where I'd left Logan and Slade. I marched right up to the door and tried the handle. When it turned, I assumed someone was inside.

I tugged it open and found myself staring at a vacant room. No one sat at the table or the desk. They'd all cleared out.

But they'd left the door unlocked. That was strange. Maybe they'd been distracted by the argument?

Or by something else. My box was sitting on the table where Dexter must have left it. But it looked… odd. Because a tiny drawer, so shallow it couldn't have held anything much thicker than a business card, had been popped open on the side.

My pulse leapt. Dexter had discovered a secret compartment after all. It *had* been a puzzle box.

And there was something in the compartment. A slip of paper, looking like it was a corner torn off a larger sheet, with faded black pen ink scrawled across it.

I picked up the box and plucked the slip of paper out of the compartment. That was my dad's handwriting. I still had a few notes he'd written to me during my elementary school days, little messages of encouragement he'd randomly tuck inside my lunch box. I'd have recognized his arched letters anywhere.

The actual writing didn't make much sense to me. It was an address, but not one I was familiar with. No place I'd ever gone; not a street name I had any associations with.

Why had Dad written it down? Why had he felt the need to hide it away in this box in a super-secret drawer?

Did this have something to do with the reason the box had been stolen in the first place? Had those gangsters been looking for something like this inside it?

They hadn't found it… but the Vigil guys had. They'd left in a huge hurry afterward. *They* thought it was important—and they'd taken off to investigate without even letting me know.

Maybe they'd figured I wouldn't be interested in my current mood, but the knowledge still annoyed me. My jaw clenching, I tucked the paper into my pocket, hugged the box to my chest, and dashed out of the office. All my thoughts narrowed down to getting to my car so I could uncover this final mystery and how my dad factored into it before I lost my chance.

CHAPTER 27

Madelyn

Even after looking up the address on my phone's map app, I hadn't been prepared for exactly where I'd find myself when I drove out there. After getting off track a couple of times and having to stop briefly to re-orient myself, I ended up in an industrial neighborhood, cruising past old brick factories and warehouses.

Some of them were still in use—I saw smoke rising from one smokestack against the darkening sky and a delivery truck pulling out of a lot beside another—but others were obviously derelict. Broken windows gaped at me with jagged glass; others were boarded with plywood. For a couple of minutes before I arrived at the exact spot Dad had noted, there was no movement on the streets around me, no sound but the growl of my car's engine.

The fact that Dad had made special notice of a building out here made even less sense to me now. Maybe it'd had something to do with a medical research project—a public health and safety issue? But I couldn't imagine why he'd need to keep that secret. All of his work involved coordinating with other researchers and often hospital or government staff as well.

But if this didn't have anything to do with his work, what *could* it be about? Nothing about this situation fit what I'd known about my dad. Mom had certainly never hinted that there'd been anything mysterious about him or any more to him in general than I'd have noticed as a kid.

Was this something he'd hidden even from her?

As I squinted at the address numbers on the buildings, apprehension crawled over my skin. Did I really want to know what was going on here? Whatever it was, it'd ended twelve years ago when Dad had died, if not before. He *was* dead. Nothing he'd done could matter all that much, could it?

But whatever it was, the Vigil guys were already investigating it. I couldn't let *them* know more about my own father than I did. And Dad had been a guiding force for so much of my life…

If I didn't find out what was significant about the address, it was going to niggle at me forever. The truth couldn't be worse than the most horrible things I could imagine.

When I spotted Logan's car parked on the street up ahead, my resolve strengthened. They were still here. I could join up with them and insist that they shared whatever they'd already discovered. That Slade and Dexter did, anyway. I had no interest in saying anything else to Logan.

The building that matched the address from the box was one of the abandoned warehouses. Ratty cardboard had been taped over the lower windows; the hinges on the front door were rusty. It hung ajar, but there was no way of telling whether it'd been left that way or if Dexter had opened it with his lock-picking skills.

The worn red bricks held no sign indicating what company the building belonged to or anything else about it. It was totally blank.

A shiver crawled over my skin, but the guys were already inside. And the place obviously wasn't being used anymore. What could be so bad in there? We'd be lucky if we came across anything at all that might have involved my dad more than a decade ago.

I got out of the car and walked up to the warehouse. The hinges creaked as I pulled the door just wide enough to slip inside.

There was no entryway. I stepped straight into a large, dim room with a ceiling that stretched at least two floors high. A stale, slightly sour scent tickled my nose. Other than a few dusty shipping crates stacked off to the side, looking as if no one had touched them in years, the room held nothing but a cracked concrete floor, marked with smudges and stains where equipment had once stood, and silence.

Only silence for a moment. Faint voices carried from the other side of the room. There were a few doorways set in the wall there between uncovered windows that let in a little of the dwindling daylight through the grime. I hurried over, wincing inwardly at the scrape of my sneakers against the gritty floor despite my efforts at placing them quietly.

If the guys had found something, I didn't want to give them the chance to hide it from me. Who knew what Logan would decide was too risky for me to be a part of now?

I followed the voices to the doorway that was the farthest to the right. I started to distinguish words. It sounded like Slade was swearing.

"We'll figure it out," Logan muttered.

They'd figure out *what*? I marched up to the doorway—and jerked to a halt at the sight that met my eyes.

The three guys were crouched at the far end of a much smaller room that looked as if it might have been some kind of office at one point. The cardboard had fallen off the window there too, allowing the thin evening light to stream over the scene. A storage cabinet stood against one wall, and a long narrow desk filled most of the space near the guys.

But I only registered those sparse details in the first instant when I glanced through the room. What arrested me was the body lying on the floor at the Vigil guys' feet.

It was a man—I couldn't make out much more about him in the dimness from ten feet away. Other than the stream of stark red flowing down his pale shirt from the spot where a knife had been stabbed right into his chest in the area of his heart.

A knife Logan was in the middle of reaching for, his sleeve streaked with the same scarlet blood.

I gasped, and the guys whirled around. It wasn't just his sleeve—Logan had blood splashed all over the front of his shirt. More blood was pooling beneath the corpse from what was obviously an incredibly fresh wound.

A chill flooded my entire being. Oh, God. Logan had *killed* that man.

And the three of them had been standing around deciding what to do with the body.

All of the guys' expressions had frozen in startled, horrified masks. Slade managed to find his voice first, scrambling upright with a slight wobble of his normally steady prosthetic leg that revealed just how off-balance he was. "Maddie—it's not what it looks like. I swear—"

How could it not be what it looked like? My stepbrother wasn't just an asshole. He was a murderer.

One panicked thought blared through my mind: I had to get out of here.

I propelled myself backward and spun around in the same

movement, intending to race back to my car. But I slammed straight into the hulking form of a man I hadn't heard coming up behind me.

The massive stranger clamped his hands around my arms with a menacing snarl. "You're not going anywhere."

RECKLESS GAMES

CHAPTER 1

Madelyn

There hadn't been many times in my life when I'd completely frozen up, unable to act. But with the squeeze of a stranger's bulging arms around me, his vicious threat ringing in my ears, and the view before me of my stepbrother and his two best friends crouched around a bloody corpse, my brain momentarily short-circuited.

What the hell was going on? What had I gotten myself into? What had *they* gotten into?

As the Vigil guys sprang to their feet, something inside me jolted back to alertness. The attacker who'd gripped me growled menacingly, his arms pressing tighter, and my martial arts training kicked into gear.

I was not going to become another victim like the man lying slumped on the floor.

My body reacted, my heel jamming down on his toes as hard as I could slam it, my body dropping to jerk free from his grasp. I kicked back and out, managing to glance my foot off his groin and propelling a pained grunt out of him.

I spun around, scrambling on the gritty concrete floor of the abandoned warehouse. The daylight spilling through the few windows that weren't boarded up was dimming, leaving the vast room even more shadowed. The man lunged at me through the gloom. He yanked a pistol from a concealed holster at his hip, and my pulse stuttered.

I didn't let fear slow me down. I kneed him in the gut and smacked my elbow into his wrist so his fingers snapped apart.

The gun tumbled from his grasp. I had just enough wherewithal to kick it as far as I could across the room before I spun to make a run for it.

My attacker didn't want to let me go. He snatched at me again with a muttered curse. I swung out my arm and managed to crack him across the face hard enough that his nose spurted blood. As he clutched at it, I slammed my heel into his ankle with all the force I could give.

His leg buckled. I darted backward, ready to dash away—but right then the three Vigil guys rushed in.

My steps stalled as I gaped at them springing to action. Logan clocked the stranger in the temple with a swing of his fist, his substantial brawn sending the guy reeling right over on the ground. Slade jumped in, stomping on the guy's ribs and then heaving him onto his stomach. Nimble even with his prosthetic leg, he knelt on the guy's back, pinning one arm behind him. Dexter caught the other arm and pressed it to the ground, kicking away a flail of the guy's legs.

Logan's head jerked around, his chestnut hair ruffling with the movement. He spotted a dusty coil of rope lying partway across the vast warehouse room, sprinted over, and hustled back with it. With Slade's and Dexter's help, he secured the man's hands behind his back and then used the other end of the rope to tie his ankles together.

It all happened in the span of a minute. I took a few steps backward, but something held me from racing right out the door of the warehouse and never looking back.

I still didn't understand what was going on here. This place had something to do with my dad—its address had been in the secret compartment in his trinket box. Why had he been here before? And how could Logan or either of his friends have actually *killed* someone?

My gaze caught on the blood splattered on Logan's tee, and my stomach lurched.

Could there be another explanation? Maybe they'd just found the man stabbed and Logan had gotten blood on him while trying to keep him alive?

The idea sounded crazy, but I knew this was my only chance to get answers. If I walked away, the guys would never admit to what I'd seen here. They might never speak to me again. My hand dropped to my pocket where my phone was, but I didn't know yet if I was willing to bring the police into this situation either.

"What the hell is going on here?" I demanded, but my voice came out tinny to my own ears. I swallowed thickly.

The guys were too focused on the man they'd subdued to answer. Slade had gotten up now that the stranger was tied. Sweat had beaded on the bronze skin of his forehead. He brushed a few damp strands of his dark brown hair away from his eyes and prodded the man's bruising temple with the toe of his sneaker. "Who are you? What are you doing here?"

I'd never heard the playful flirt's voice so firm and fierce before. It sent a chill through me.

The man simply spat at Slade, who chuckled without any humor. "That didn't answer my question."

Logan aimed a kick at the man's side, the same place where Slade had struck his ribs earlier. "Want to rethink that answer? The faster you answer our questions, the less you're going to get hurt."

What was I watching? The man that I'd been intimate with less than two hours ago looked ready to torture a man, and the one I'd slept with two years ago was obviously on board as well. Even usually meek Dexter was stalking around the scene, snapping pictures of both the man and the room around us, his expression tightly intent.

"I'm not going to tell you idiots anything," the man growled. He squirmed against his bindings but didn't accomplish anything more than looking like a beached whale.

Slade braced the foot of his prosthetic against the man's ankle, which was lying at an uncomfortable looking angle. He applied a little weight. "I think you should reconsider. We can keep doing this all day. Who do you work for? Who owns this building, and why are you guarding it?"

"None of your fucking business."

As Logan leaned down to smack the guy across his already bloody nose, I finally managed to push more words from my throat. "What are you *doing* to him? What did you do to that guy in the other room? You have to tell me what's going on."

Slade looked at me, and his expression softened with a flicker of concern and what might have been guilt. But before he could say anything, Dexter piped up, talking to his friends rather than me in his usual matter-of-fact tone.

"We don't have much time to get him talking. More goons could show up at any time."

"I'm well aware of that," Logan muttered, not even sparing me a glance. He glowered down at the man. "Cough up something for us. A name, some explanation of what you're doing here. You'll regret it otherwise."

Did he think I'd be too shocked to force the issue? That I'd cower in the face of the violence? Well, he'd already shown time after time that he didn't really know me at all. I wasn't going to stand here and watch this man be tortured, even if he had attacked me.

I tugged my phone out of my pocket and turned it on. "I need you three to start talking to *me* right now, or you'll be answering to the police instead."

I'd hit the 9 and the 1, planning on hovering my finger over that number until I saw whether my threat would land, but before I'd even gotten that far, Logan had stormed over to me. Before I could pivot away, he yanked the phone right out of my hand.

"Hey!" I snatched after it, but he dodged and retreated, turning it off and stuffing it in his own pocket. "You can't just—give me my fucking phone back, you murderer!"

All three of the Vigil guys stiffened. Logan's jaw clenched. "I'm sorry you had to see that, Maddie. It was self-defense. He tried to murder *me*. That was his knife. I didn't mean to kill him; I was just trying to get him off me."

Slade's face fell. "We didn't get to him in time to help."

A haunted expression had crossed all of their faces. They didn't look like hardened criminals, but like men who'd been forced into an awful situation they hadn't seen any way out of. Which fit what I knew about them better than seeing them as callous killers anyway.

My stance relaxed just slightly. "Okay," I whispered. "But why was he or this guy attacking us? Why are you beating him up? Why can't we just get out of this place?"

"We don't know why they attacked us, and we need to find that out," Dexter said. "He's not going to talk if we just ask nicely." He spoke as evenly as before, but then he ran an awkward hand through his messy black curls, his gaze veering not just away from my eyes but all the way across the room with a hint of shame.

"What does it matter?" I asked, refusing to back down. "What does any of this have to do with my dad or anything else? It doesn't make any sense."

Logan sighed. For a moment, his broad shoulders slumped. The posture spoke of such defeat that my heart wrenched despite my frustration with him and my horror at the scene around me. But when he spoke, his words shocked me even more.

"If you're here, you must have figured out that your dad had this address stashed away. It must have been important to him. Which means it's important to us to figure out what goes on here and who's involved, how it's all connected. Because we've spent the last two years investigating your dad's murder."

CHAPTER 2

Madelyn

As Logan's words echoed in my head, I could only stare at him. What the hell was he talking about? My dad hadn't been *murdered.*

I remembered the sequence of events far too well because of the part I'd played in them. The summer I was eight, Mom and I had gone off to a cottage on the beach while Dad had to finish up an important work project. But while we were there in the cabin, a severe storm had struck… and I'd gotten so scared that when Dad had called to check in on us, I'd cried about how much I wished he was there with me.

He'd been so determined to comfort me that he'd dropped everything to make the drive. The roads on the way had flooded, so he'd ended up wading through the flood waters just to get to me.

And then a few days later, an illness had swept through him. In less than a week, he'd been gone, his organs failing before the doctors could figure out exactly what he'd gotten sick with. But it seemed obvious to me. He must have picked up some bacteria or a virus from the mess in the flood waters.

If I hadn't made him feel guilty about staying home, he never would have gotten sick. I'd still have him in my life.

How could it have been murder? The doctors might not have been able to identify the exact contagion quickly enough to stop its effects, but surely they'd have been able to differentiate between a natural illness and a purposeful attack.

"What the hell are you talking about?" I demanded, a flare of frustration cutting through my bewilderment. I'd talked with Logan about my dad before—we'd shared stories about the parents we'd lost. He knew how much it'd shaken me, losing him. And now he was making up crazy conspiracy stories? "My dad got sick. No one killed him."

Logan showed no sign of wavering. He looked utterly certain. "That's what the murderer wanted everyone to think. But we have proof. I can show it to you."

I flung my hand through the air. "If that's true, why are you only mentioning it now?"

His mouth tightened. "Because I was trying to keep you out of it. I was trying to keep you *safe*. When you're hunting down a murderer, you put a target on your back."

His confidence unnerved me. He'd never even met my dad. He wasn't the one who'd seen him collapse in the front hall with a sudden spell of weakness; he wasn't the one who'd clutched Dad's hand while the feverish delirium had come over him. How could he know more about Dad's death than I did?

My doubt obviously showed on my face. Logan's gaze seared

into mine. "Come back with me to the Vigil office. Then you'll understand… all of this."

I still didn't know what to think. Maybe I should have turned heel and run. But what he'd said made a lot more sense than any other theory I could have come up with about why the group had rushed out here to investigate this address and why they'd have turned to such violent methods to interrogate the man who'd attacked us here.

I didn't believe him yet, but how could I walk away now with the possibility racing around in my mind? I needed to know what he'd found.

"All right," I said, my stance tense, and motioned toward the guy tied up on the floor. "What about him?"

Logan glanced at his friends. "Keep up the interrogation. He'll break and cough up something eventually… or he'll wish he had. We'll take her car—you can take mine." He strode forward and grabbed me by the elbow to usher me out of the warehouse.

Slade caught my eyes for just an instant, his jaw clenching. Was he worried about me going off with Logan alone after the insults my stepbrother had hurled at me just a couple of hours ago? I'd rather it was him explaining all this, but Logan seemed determined to handle the situation. Slade offered us both a quick nod, and then Logan was hustling me through the doorway into the cooling evening.

Logan went to his car first, opening the trunk, tearing off his blood-smeared shirt, and pulling on a clean tee from inside—that he kept there for situations like this? As he ducked back into the warehouse to toss his fob to the other guys, I couldn't help thinking of the night two years ago when he'd come by our house, cut up and bruised.

Had he come from another fight that'd nearly led to *his* murder? Had he killed his attacker that night too?

I walked to my car in a daze. As I opened the driver's side door, Logan jogged over to get in beside me. I stared at the steering wheel for a few seconds before I got my brain in gear enough to stick the key in the ignition.

"I can drive if you're too distracted," Logan said.

I shot him a quick glare. "It's my car. I can handle it."

The engine rumbled, and I pulled away from the curb. The familiar feel of the vehicle I'd temporarily lost settled my nerves a little even with the very discomforting presence sitting next to me. The last time I'd spoke to Logan, he'd accused me of screwing up Slade's future and called me a slut.

It was easier to focus on the new subject at hand. "When did you decide my dad had been murdered?"

"It'll be easier for me to explain everything when I can show you what we have."

"Seriously? You can't even tell me how long this has been going on? How long you've been hiding it from me?"

Logan fixed his bright brown eyes on me with penetrating intensity. "I'm not going to apologize for doing what I needed to do to protect you."

Another jab of irritation shot through me. "Is that what you'd call what you've been doing? Was laying into me for hooking up with your friend and throwing around horrible names all part of 'protecting' me?"

To my surprise, Logan winced. He pulled his gaze away, studying the road moodily.

"No," he said finally. "I went over the line today. I—It's complicated. But I can say I'm sorry I came down so harshly on you. Now can you wait until we get to the office for any more questions?"

His apology and his plea sounded genuine enough that I shut

my mouth, swallowing down all the other questions niggling at me. It would be better to wait until I had his supposed evidence in front of me anyway. I couldn't evaluate his story properly until I saw all the pieces.

Silence hung over us for the rest of the drive back, gradually suffocating me. The second we pulled into the parking lot near the law library, I shoved the door open and sucked in the fresh air. Then I scrambled out and crossed my arms impatiently as I waited for Logan to follow.

The room beyond the glass doors was dark. Of course—it'd already been nearly closing time when I'd left. But Logan marched right up to it, pulling a key ring from his pocket, and opened the main door without hesitation. I hurried inside after him, my jaw dropping.

"The librarians gave you a key to the whole library?"

He shrugged with a hint of a cocky smile. "We might have done one of them a favor she was very grateful for."

I could only imagine what that favor might have been now that I'd seen what a wide range of criminal concerns the Vigil tackled. We strode through the darkened room to the Vigil's office at the back. Logan opened that door and flicked on the light switch, flooding the space with an artificial glow.

He went straight to the filing cabinet that'd caught my curiosity when I'd first poked around in here. I sank into one of the chairs at the table in the middle of the room, my heart thumping fast.

What the hell could he possibly be going to show me? What if he was *right*?

Logan came to the table with a stack of manilla files and set them down with a thud. My gaze darted to the identifying tabs—they were all labeled with the initials *E.S.*

Evan Silver—my dad. A chill trickled through my veins.

Logan opened the first folder in front of me. It was full of papers of various sizes, some of them torn, many of them crumpled. They were all marked with handwriting I recognized as my dad's.

"I came across a box of his stuff in the basement at your house before I left for college, when I was looking for some things of mine I hadn't unpacked after the move," Logan said. "I'm not sure whether your dad stashed them all away to sort through later or your mom packed them up when cleaning up his home office afterward."

I sifted through the papers, peeking at one and then another. The jotted notes were brief and full of abbreviations, some of which I didn't recognize. I could tell a few of them had to do with research projects he'd been working on—there were multiple references to the hospital back home that he'd mainly worked at, and to medications and things like that.

"This all looks like normal work notes," I said. "He was always writing things down on whatever paper he could grab—he was constantly thinking of things and wanting to make sure he didn't forget."

"Those notes are the ones we couldn't connect to anything suspicious, but we kept them just in case." Logan pushed them aside and opened a second folder. "These tell a clearer story. It was one of these that caught my eye and made me wonder what was up—that made me keep reading."

The assortment of papers looked very similar to the first pile. I knit my brow. "What's so different about these?"

Logan started pawing through the notes, pulling out one and then another and shoving them in front of me with a tap of his forefinger. "They show he was looking into something when he died that wasn't part of any of his official research. I looked through his published work and what the hospital has on file, and none of it connects. There was something called "the Baldwin file" that he seemed to think was important—we're still not sure what that is—and there are a lot of references to needing to be careful and making sure his research isn't noticed. And the ones that have dates in them are all from the last six months before he died. He was obviously onto something he thought was important—and dangerous."

I wasn't sure it was all that obvious. I had trouble wrapping my head around any of this. "I don't think that proves he was murdered."

"There's more. In both sets of notes, he mentions journals he kept at the hospital—more detailed records. Those disappeared after he died. Your mom doesn't have them, and the hospital doesn't have them either. I think they were stolen from his work office shortly after his death before anyone else could dig through them."

"Or maybe the hospital just threw them out."

Logan shook his head. "Everything else from his office, including reference books and burned CDs, was in boxes in your basement that the hospital handed over to your mom. Why would they toss out his journals?"

My stomach started to knot. "That is a little weird. But it could have been a mistake. Those things happen."

"Yeah? And how often do medical researchers who just happen to have been investigating something big that they feel they need to keep secret end up getting deathly ill with a sickness no one can identify? The doctors who tried to save him knew him as a colleague, even a friend. They'd have pulled out all the stops to help him, and they still couldn't pinpoint it?"

"What are you saying?"

He rapped his finger against the table. "It could have been poison. Some toxin designed to look like an illness."

My mind snapped back to my memories of Dad's death. "No. The doctors told us they'd checked for toxins and found nothing."

"There are poisons that are subtle and can't be picked up on the usual tests. It's impossible to cover everything in one go. And some dissipate from the body too quickly to be caught unless you know to look for it right away. Don't you think it's odd that there wasn't more of an investigation after he died when they didn't even know why he did? It's almost like it was hushed up, like someone who had the power to do so made sure no one dwelled on the incident for too long."

I shivered. "Now you sound crazy."

Logan held my gaze. "Do I? It all adds up. The mysterious death out of the blue. The lack of inquiry afterward. The missing journals. The notes that suggest he was looking into something major that he felt he had to be careful about. And now on top of that, there's that box of his. Your car randomly gets stolen, and the gang that took it swipes that one object out of it? Someone must have caught on that it was his and might contain something incriminating."

"Like that address," I murmured, my mouth going dry.

"Exactly! Why would he have hidden away the address to some warehouse off in the middle of nowhere? It must have connected to his investigation. And look at what kind of people were hanging around there for security. The one guy tried to kill me—the other attacked you. Those weren't typical security guards."

No, they hadn't been. And when my stepbrother laid it all out like that with so much vigor in his voice, it was hard to deny his claims.

I closed my eyes and pinched the bridge of my nose. All of the evidence was circumstantial, nothing definite. It didn't *really* prove anything. Which shouldn't surprise me, because if Logan had discovered a smoking gun, surely he'd have turned it over to the police.

The Vigil had been conducting their own investigation—since

right before Logan had left for college?—because they knew they didn't have enough to convince professional detectives to take on the case. But… that didn't mean Logan was wrong, either.

The idea that Dad could have been murdered—that his death could have had nothing to do with my stormy night plea—jarred in my head. I'd believed in the story I'd known for so long, I wasn't sure how to let go of it.

How much should I buy into this conspiracy theory? What if Logan was just grasping at straws? He obviously liked having a mystery to pursue. He could have convinced himself that the evidence meant more than it did just to give himself an excuse to go on this epic quest.

One totally separate factor of this situation was still gnawing at me. "You believed in this theory all this time, and you never mentioned it to me *once*. Obviously you didn't tell my mom either, or I'd know about it from her."

"I told you why I stayed quiet," Logan said roughly. "I wanted to keep you safe. If someone murdered your dad for poking around in whatever business he'd started to uncover, there's no reason they wouldn't decide to kill anyone else who poked around too. Including you. Maybe especially you, since they have no idea what else of his you might have access to that they don't know about. Why do you think I've been trying so hard to get you to stay away from us?"

Was that it? All the horrible things he'd said to me, all the times he'd acted like I meant nothing to him—it was all part of some scheme to shield me from the Vigil's other investigations? The thought set my stomach churning.

Logan had taken up the quest and turned himself into my champion all over again, at least in his mind. Defending me from enemies much more shadowy than the junior-high bullies he'd once taken down a peg on my behalf. But I hadn't asked him to act as my guardian.

"Maybe I *should* be in danger," I said. "He was my dad. It's my responsibility to figure out what happened to him. You didn't even know him. Why should you and Slade and Dexter put your lives on the line digging into this?"

Logan's face hardened. "You're not prepared for that kind of danger. We are. We already were when I stumbled on those notes and started piecing things together."

"How could you be prepared to be hunted down by a murderer?"

He shook his head. "You have no idea what we've faced since we got started with the Vigil. It didn't really begin here at the university, you know. We were taking on cases all the way back in high school, and a lot of them weren't just finding missing objects."

I studied his expression. "What do you mean? What happened to you back then?" Was that why everything had changed? It'd seemed so sudden when he'd pulled away from me, stopped talking to me, stopped even smiling at me other than occasionally and stiffly, but maybe the shift in attitude had been building up for a while and I just hadn't noticed.

Logan drew in a sharp breath. "We don't call ourselves 'the Vigil' because we watch over the university. It's short for Vigilantes. We do whatever it takes to see justice done for the people who deserve it—people who've been scammed or threatened or outright assaulted—even if that justice is bloody and violent like today."

My throat constricted. "That wasn't the first time *you've* killed someone, was it?"

Logan closed his eyes for a second. I could tell from the flex of his jaw that he wasn't unaffected by the act he'd had to commit.

"No," he said roughly. "Thankfully I've only had to go that far to defend myself once before. But I've been in plenty of situations that came close as well. And with the direction this case seems to be heading in…" He lifted his head, his gaze boring into mine. "You saw how it went down in the warehouse. You saw the lengths we need to go to. If you insist on sticking around, that's what you'd be getting into."

CHAPTER 3

Dexter

"We don't have many questions that we need you to answer," Slade snapped, rearing back and slamming his fist into the man's already bruising cheek. "Fairly simple, actually. Who you work for, what you're doing here, what happens in this place. Further questions are pending, but if you answer them, we'll go away and you can go back to your sad life."

The man's head swayed to the side where he was still sprawled on his stomach, but he kept his mouth firmly shut. We weren't experts at interrogations like this, but we'd usually been able to get at least a little cooperation once we'd shown we were willing to use force. This guy was a cut above our past opponents… which meant his employers must be too.

Slade moved around the bound form in a chaotic sort of rhythm, shifting his weight between his prosthetic and his other leg, aiming a kick here and a stomp there. The man made the mistake of trying to smack Slade's ankle with his tied hands, and Slade retaliated by snatching at his hand and twisting hard with a crunch of shattering bone. A pained grunt slipped from the man's lips.

He wasn't impervious. And we *had* to know what was going on here. How it connected to Madelyn and her father. Why it was important enough that not one but two men had attacked us for intruding.

And even though I usually disliked having to resort to violence, a little part of me might have gotten satisfaction out of his sounds of discomfort. He'd tried to do worse to Madelyn. The thought of her squirming in his arms for the seconds before she'd gotten free made my pulse stutter.

I didn't know her very well yet, but she'd held her own alongside the Vigil. She'd been brave and smart—and unfazed by our less savory methods and my own strangeness.

Of course, I had no idea how she must feel about what she'd seen just now. She'd looked horrified when she'd spotted us by the dead body in the other room. She hadn't seen us demonstrate this level of aggression before.

So let's hope we could get enough out of this asshole to ensure we didn't need to again.

The man was shaking his head at Slade's latest demand for answers. Slade glowered down at him and whacked him across the forehead with the side of his sneaker.

"Nothing? That's your go-to answer?" The man remained silent. "Fine. But don't say we didn't warn you."

I knew my cue. It always left me feeling a little queasy at first, but when I let go of my qualms and focused on just the act, the man in front of me was nothing more than a collection of body parts: perfectly ordered, easily disrupted. I pulled out my pocket knife and flipped open the blade, studying the bulky form.

Maximum pain without allowing an irrecoverable amount of blood loss—that was the trick.

As I circled the man, he watched me warily. "What the fuck are *you* doing?" he snarled.

Slade gave a dark guffaw. "My friend is *very* good at inflicting pain, but he's also quite good at stopping when he hears answers. Isn't that right, buddy?"

He was careful not to use my name in front of the thug. I nodded and knelt down by the man's feet. When the man started to thrash, Slade sat down on his thighs, holding him in place. I grabbed one of the guy's running shoes and tugged it off.

"How about you tell us who you work for, and we'll avoid bringing the chop shop to your feet?" Slade suggested as I lifted the blade. The man stilled, not willing to slice himself open with unnecessary movements.

"It doesn't matter who I work for," he spat.

I clenched my jaw and dug the tip of the knife into the arch of his foot, carving a small slice right down the center.

The man jerked, but I held on tightly. "Fuck!" he shouted.

"You know what we're looking for," I said evenly. "Cough it up and you don't have to endure any more of this."

"Fuck you."

"Wrong answer."

I dug the knife in a little higher, and his squirming intensified, but he couldn't throw off Slade or prevent my work. Then I jabbed the blade right between his toes. He sucked a breath through his teeth with a hiss, but didn't say anything else.

"Care to tell us what the warehouse is used for?" Slade asked casually.

The man only ground his teeth.

I etched another few lines into the sole of that foot before moving to the next. The image of Madelyn fighting him off popped into my head again, and I had to tense my fingers to stop myself from slicing deeper—too deep. He deserved payback, but that wasn't what we were here to deal out. Understanding this part of the mystery was far more important.

What was Madelyn making of the whole situation now that Logan must be walking her through the case? How much would he tell her? Would she be able to accept that the man she'd believed had died of an illness had actually been murdered in cold blood? I'd had years to delve into the mystery, and I'd had no preconceived notions, but for her, it would be bewildering.

Would she even want to continue working alongside the Vigil after this, or would she consider us psychopaths?

Another small part of me wasn't totally sure that we *weren't*. But at least we were on the side of justice.

Slade clicked his tongue and changed the subject. "You don't want to talk about this place. How about that bar on Steuben Avenue—McGee's Tavern. Do you hang out with the pricks who run that place at all?"

The man's expression twitched, but the flicker of emotion left me resigned rather than hopeful. He'd looked puzzled. He didn't want us narrowing down the possibilities, so he still kept his mouth shut, but I could tell he didn't understand why we'd have asked.

Which meant he had no connections to the gang who'd stolen Madelyn's car. Interesting. Was a larger force pulling the strings behind multiple groups of criminals? Or was the note directing us here only a coincidence? It'd been more than a decade since Evan Silver had died. The warehouse could have changed hands more than once in that time.

We were running out of time. Every minute that passed was another minute when his colleagues might show up and outnumber us. We needed him to spit *something* out, or this would all be for nothing.

I edged around his body and grasped his bound wrists. The tip of my knife dug into his palm, and the man groaned. But that was the only sound he made.

"Your stubbornness is only drawing this out," Slade reminded him. "You could be home with a beer by now if you were smart. Now tell us—"

The peal of a ringtone cut him off. It was coming from the man's back pocket. I exchanged a glance with Slade, who dropped down to yank out the device. The man started cursing at him, and I yanked the collar of his shirt up over his mouth so I could clamp my hand there without him biting my palm.

"Who could this be?" Slade murmured, and tapped the answer button. With his experience at picking up languages with all their varied accents and tones, he was the best of us at imitating voices. He couldn't mimic them perfectly, especially with a guy who'd talked as little as our captive, but he could work around that by keeping his answers short. And gruff, which suited this guy's apparent personality just fine.

"What?" he muttered into the phone, deepening his voice to make it more similar to our captive's. Whatever the person on the other end said, he simply responded with grunts and brief remarks like "Okay" and "Right." His eyebrows lifted slightly. Finally, with a curt "Got it," he hung up and gazed down at the bound man with a smirk.

"Looks like we got some answers without needing you to do any talking after all. That was a very interesting conversation. Kenneth was concerned about the shipment that's coming in tonight. He wanted to be sure everything will go smoothly. I'd love to hear more about that. What kind of cargo are you expecting in this shipment?"

"None of your fucking business," the man retorted in a ragged voice.

I moved back to his hands and sliced open his other palm, careful to avoid the artery that led to his thumb. But the man fell back into agonized silence. We'd learned something thanks to our efforts, but I was becoming increasingly sure that we weren't going to get anything directly from his lips.

I could justify the violence to myself as long as I believed it was going to help us fix what was wrong. Slicing up a man who wouldn't talk either way was just meaningless carnage, even if the jerk had attacked Madelyn. With a grimace, I wiped the flecks of blood off the blade onto the man's jeans and pushed myself away from him.

Slade caught my eye and followed me over to the far end of the warehouse.

"I don't think he's going to talk," I murmured to my friend. "He hasn't budged at all."

Slade sighed and raked his hand back through his dark hair. "I'm getting the same impression. It feels sadistic rather than purposeful to keep going. But what do we do with him now?"

That was the question looming over this whole situation. If we'd forced the man to talk, we might have been able to count on him being afraid enough of us and of the fact that he'd broken his employer's confidence to keep his mouth shut about our involvement. But when he *hadn't* broken, he had no motivation to do anything other than run straight to the people who'd hired him and report everything he'd seen, including our descriptions.

There was an obvious solution, the solution the man in question probably would have gone with if the tables had been turned. Dead men couldn't speak. But the thought of bringing my knife to his throat made me wince inwardly.

Before today, we'd only had to kill a couple of people in self-defense—and I didn't look back on those necessary instances with any joy. It was the worst possible outcome of a worst-case scenario.

And in both those instances and with the man in the other room, we'd been under attack, fighting for our own lives. To simply slaughter a helpless person, no matter what they'd done… The idea made me want to vomit.

Especially when it was my fault we'd ended up on as dark a path as we were already on. I couldn't shove us into even worse places.

I wished Logan were here. He might not have had a better answer, but he had a knack for taking charge of any situation. I'd have at least felt more confident in whatever decision we made if he'd been able to weigh in.

My mind worked through the possibilities, trying to see this scenario as its own sort of puzzle. "Maybe if we made it clear that we could convince his boss that he talked to us, and that he'd be in even deeper shit if he—"

Before I could work out any more of that tentative plan, a scuffing sound from across the room drew my attention. My head jerked around in time to see our captive throwing off the bonds he'd managed to wriggle loose. As my heart skipped a beat, he charged toward us.

The man threw himself at Slade with a growl of fury. "You fuckers are going to pay!"

Slade tried to dodge, but the man managed to wallop him in the chest, throwing him off balance. As he stumbled, the man aimed a brutal blow at his head.

I leapt in with a blocking arm. The impact of the man's blow reverberated through my muscles all the way to the bone. I swung at him with the knife, but he rammed his fist at me at the same moment. The weapon jolted from my grasp.

Shit.

Slade dropped to the ground and snatched up the knife. At the same moment, the man jerked a blade of his own from his front pocket. He heaved me aside and leapt down, aiming the knife right at Slade's heart—

But Slade was faster. He stabbed up with a swipe of his arm and lanced his attacker right through the throat.

Blood splattered down over him. I slammed into the man's side in time to heave him off Slade rather than leaving him to collapse onto my friend.

The body slumped with a gurgle and a few twitches. Slade scrambled away from it, but that guy wasn't going anywhere now.

We both stared down at the dead man. An ache wrapped around my gut, both horror and a sick sort of relief. Because it hadn't been me. *I* hadn't dealt out any death… not this time.

I hated that feeling, but I couldn't stop it from rising up.

"Fuck," Slade muttered, swiping his hand across his mouth and then staring down at his blood-drenched shirt. "Fucking hell."

My sense of urgency returned, twice as intense as before. If anyone found us now, we were totally screwed.

"Come on," I said, making myself yank the knife out of the man's throat. It was mine, and I didn't want anyone being able to use the murder weapon to track us down. "We've got to get out of here. You can grab one of the spare shirts from the trunk."

Slade shook his head, but he backed away, his face tightening. "Two in one day. I didn't want to."

My stomach flipped over. I reached over to squeeze his shoulder, ignoring my automatic uneasiness at the close contact. "I know." Did I ever. "You had to." I sucked in a breath. "It looks like this investigation has gotten a whole lot more dangerous."

CHAPTER 4

Madelyn

My first bite of the cookie melted in my mouth, all buttery, chocolatey goodness. I nearly moaned. "Okay, this is one hell of a cookie."

Across the patio table from me, Beckett chuckled. "That was my reaction the first time, too," he said. "I went back in and bought a dozen more for the road."

"Tempting…" I wasn't exaggerating. The chocolate chip cookie may have been one of the best I'd ever eaten. I hadn't even been aware of this small, hole-in-the-wall café at the other end of the city from the university, but now it was going on my list of local hot spots. "So how long can you stay today? When you texted me, you said this could only be a quick get-together."

He shot me one of the brightly assured smiles that always sent a flood of warmth through me. Exactly what I needed after the chaos of the past few days—and exactly why I'd taken him up on his invite.

"I wish it could have been a longer outing," he said. "Unfortunately, I've got a meeting I can't miss later this afternoon. But I'm yours for the next hour. I figured it was worth seeing if you had a little free time in your schedule."

I took a sip of my perfectly bittersweet green tea latte and admitted, "Honestly, I needed the break. I just finished writing up a lab report that required a lot of number-crunching, and that kind of stuff fries my brain after a while."

"I have to think medical science is a pretty stressful course of study in general. They don't want slackers ending up manning the hospitals."

"Oh, it's challenging, but I don't mind. I know that every assignment is getting me closer to actually being admitted into medical school and learning how to do the work that's most important to me."

And the most stressful parts of recent weeks had nothing to do with my schoolwork. But I couldn't tell Beckett about the extracurricular activities I'd unexpectedly gotten wrapped up in—especially with the murderous turn the Vigil's investigations had just taken—even though the confidence radiating from his smoothly handsome face and sharp gray eyes made me want to confide in him. I couldn't shake the feeling that he'd somehow know exactly how to fix things, as ridiculous as that sounded.

Since I'd bumped into him outside a coffee shop weeks ago, he'd been a bright spot in my life totally separate from the chaos with the Vigil. Maybe it was better being able to just relax with someone without getting into all that turmoil.

Beckett's expression softened at my comment. "You're very driven. I admire that a lot. I've met very few people who are both ambitious and have the willpower to follow through on their goals. It's a rare combination."

He'd made similar comments before, and like before, I felt abruptly awkward. It was such a huge compliment, and I wasn't sure I'd truly earned it.

"Thanks," I said, groping for words, and found myself teasing him when I couldn't come up with anything genuine that didn't sound painfully earnest. "Is that why you're so nice to me—because I'm such a rare person?"

Beckett's eyes glinted slyly in return. "I figure it's a smart move to get on the good side of a brilliant doctor-to-be. If I ever get sick or injured, I'll be totally covered." Then his voice turned more serious again. "But really, you aren't like most of the people I spend time around. *I* appreciate getting a break from my own business interests to spend with you." He arched an eyebrow, his sandy blond hair turning gold in the sunlight, and reached across the tabletop to grab my hand. "Maybe I should be asking what you get out of hanging out with *me*."

I had the sense he didn't expect an answer—that he'd have been fine with me just laughing the question off. But I was so startled that he'd even imply that I might be the bigger catch between the two of us that an honest answer tumbled out of me before I could think better of it.

"Are you kidding me? You're so—so sure of yourself, and collected, like nothing can really faze you. Being around you makes me feel… centered, I think is the best word. And safe. More than I feel around anyone else."

The second the words left my mouth, my cheeks flushed. Had I laid it on too thick, sounded like I was obsessed with him? But Beckett simply blinked at me, looking surprised though pleased.

How could he be surprised? Didn't he know how he came across?

Of course, it didn't take long for him to recover his calm. He squeezed my hand in his firm grasp.

"I'm glad I can be that for you," he said softly, leaning closer over the table. "I'd like to *continue* being that for you."

I tipped toward him instinctively, meeting the kiss he'd been offering. We'd only kissed once before, after our first date last week, but that one had left me wanting more.

This one only made me hungrier to find out everything Beckett was capable of. His hand came around the nape of my neck, his fingers weaving into the hair at the base of my head and holding it in place. His lips moved leisurely against mine, and the gentleness in his kiss unwound me in a completely different way than any other kiss had.

What the hell was I doing, though? I wanted to kiss him, yeah, but I'd just hooked up with Slade in the law library a couple of days ago. And some part of me was still drawn to Logan, even after the crap he'd put me through. How could I untangle my emotions for these three incredibly different but equally compelling men, especially when the other two were such chaotic presences in my life.

Beckett's fingers tightened in my hair for a brief moment before he pulled back with a satisfied smile. "And now I'm even more glad you could meet me today."

My cheeks heated again, but I let myself say, "Me too."

I was deciding whether I should bring up the awkward fact of my seeing other people when a ringtone sounded from Beckett's suit-jacket pocket. Knitting his brow just slightly, he pulled out his phone, glanced at the call display, and answered.

"Yes? What's this about? I'm in the middle of something."

He spoke calmly but firmly, with every indication that he assumed the person on the other end knew who they'd reached. He might like the break from his work, but seeing him get all businessman-authoritative was kind of hot.

Whatever the other person said, it must have convinced him he had to stay on the line. He gave me a gesture of apology while he offered a noncommittal hum and a "Go on" into the phone. After a minute, he exhaled with a hint of a sigh.

"All right, I'll take care of it." He hung up, tucked the phone back into his pocket, and turned to me with a pained grimace. "I'm so sorry. It looks like I need to leave even earlier than I intended. Sometimes I swear the family business would fall apart if I wasn't keeping an eye on everything."

He said the last bit with a wry tone and a shake of his head, but I'd seen enough of how he handled himself to believe it could be true.

"It's okay," I said. "Of course you have to deal with a major problem right away. We still had a great cookie." I paused, and added with more boldness, "And a great kiss."

"We agree on that." Beckett got up. "Hopefully we can do it again sometime soon. All of it. I'll drop you a line."

"I'm looking forward to it."

I watched him stride off, admiring both the toned leanness of his tall body and his overall air of assurance. He'd taken on so much responsibility at such a young age, starting from when he was way younger than I was now, but he carried himself like he was born for it.

I drank the rest of my latte more quickly now that I had less of a reason to linger over it. My mind drifted back to the question that'd plagued me almost nonstop for the past two days—the real thing I'd needed a break from.

Had my dad been murdered?

Logan's evidence might be circumstantial, but there was a lot of it. Slade and Dexter were convinced by it too. But there were so many pieces of the puzzle we still didn't have. How did that warehouse factor in? What secret project had Dad been working on in the last few months before he died?

I was just swallowing the last of my drink when my phone dinged. Summer had texted me. *Hey, girl. I haven't heard from you in a while. What's up? Is the king prick working his way up to emperor yet?*

My best friend was understandably not impressed with the way Logan had treated me two years ago, and she'd have already crowned him emperor of prick-dom if she'd known about his rant after he'd caught me with Slade.

I hadn't talked to her because I hadn't known what to say to her. What could I tell her now? Logan had hidden the Vigil's main investigation from me for my own protection because he thought that if I knew, I'd be in danger. If I revealed the secret to Summer, would her life be on the line too?

My throat constricted. The image of the bloody body in the warehouse, the knife Logan had said had been meant for *him*, flashed through my mind, and every part of me recoiled.

I couldn't take the chance. Summer couldn't get involved—telling her the truth would only put her at risk without her really being able to help anyway.

Just busy with school stuff, I wrote back. *Sorry I've been AWOL.*

No worries, Maddie. I know how hard you work.

As I lowered my phone, it occurred to me that while I didn't want to *tell* anyone else about the Vigil's suspicions, I did know someone who might be able to shed some more light on the situation without needing an explanation. Someone who'd known Dad better than anyone.

It was the weekend, so Mom wouldn't be at work. She answered my call on the second ring.

"Hey, sweetheart. I wasn't expecting to hear from you. Is everything okay?"

"Oh, yeah, I just had some free time and thought it'd been a while since we caught up. Is that new secretary still giving you issues?"

Mom let out a huff. "She's gotten a little better, but you won't believe what I had to talk to her about the other day."

We went back and forth with a few workplace and school horror stories, and Mom told me about a trip she was planning on taking with Holand. Then her tone softened. "You sound a little tense, Maddie. I wish you could get away for a little while. Maybe in the summer?"

"We'll see," I said, hoping my laugh sounded light rather than forced. "My schedule is pretty hectic. That reminds me—there was something I wanted to ask you about because of one of my classes."

It was Mom's turn to laugh. "I'm not sure how useful I'll be with the sorts of things you're studying."

"It's not exactly that. We're doing a unit on rare diseases, and I was wondering… did the hospital ever give you an answer about what exactly the sickness was that Dad died of?"

I hated bringing up the subject even though I had very good reason to. The momentary silence on the other end told me how the question had affected Mom, though her voice was steady when she spoke. "No, they never could identify what it was, as far as I was informed. Even the autopsy didn't turn up anything definitive, from what I understand."

"Did they mention any possibilities while they were trying to treat him, or specific symptoms they were particularly confused by?"

"I'm sorry, honey. I want to help, but when they started throwing around the medical terminology and Latin names for things, it went right over my head. That was your dad's area, not mine. I don't think they had any major theories, though. His condition declined so quickly they didn't have much time to run tests."

Her voice wavered a bit with that last sentence, and I swallowed thickly, wincing at the thought of the old pain I'd stirred up. I kept my own tone as light as possible. "That's totally okay, Mom. It was such a long time ago too. I just figured I should check."

"If I think of anything later, I'll let you know." Mom dragged in a breath. "You should never hesitate to ask me about him. I hope you know that. He was an important part of both our lives, and he deserves to have his memory kept alive."

"I know," I assured her. "You've always done that for me."

After I'd hung up, a fresh lump of guilt settling in my gut, I thought back to my own memories of Dad's final days. I'd visited him in the hospital. Maybe I hadn't had much medical knowledge back then, and my impressions were clouded by my childhood guilt and grief, but I might have noticed something useful.

The first visit, he'd seemed pretty okay, just a little weak as he'd sat in the hospital bed. I'd brought one of my stuffed animals to keep him company when Mom and I couldn't be there, and he'd thanked me and tucked it under his arm. He'd told me that he'd be home soon, that it'd all be okay, and I think in that moment he'd really believed it.

The second time… I didn't like remembering that.

He'd been falling into a sort of delirium, maybe from a fever. While I'd been talking to him, he'd started babbling about things that made no sense, but sounding like he was really bothered by them. Mom had left us alone together while she asked the doctor some questions, but she'd overheard his change in tone from outside the door and rushed back in to usher me away before he'd rambled on too long. But just that minute or so when he'd been totally out of sorts was burned into my memory.

He'd veered randomly from one subject to another. Somewhere in there, he'd gone on about my purple bike with the training wheels, the one he'd taught me to ride on. Then he'd sounded almost angry, talking accusingly about a fish… *Maybe it was the broken catfish—they did this.*

I assumed that he'd seen a torn up catfish in the flood waters when he'd been coming to the beach. He must have wondered if it was my fault he'd gotten sick too, even if he hadn't wanted to say that to me outright.

Except possibly he hadn't gotten sick at all. What else had there been? He'd ranted a bit about the hospital's coffee. *Tastes like charcoal mixed with chalk.* He'd claimed the picture hanging on the wall across from his bed had started moving, sliding around. It was his yell about the picture that'd brought Mom back in.

None of that connected any dots that I could think of. I definitely didn't see how anything he'd ranted about could point to what would have gotten him murdered or who would have done it.

If he had been murdered. I still wasn't sure if Logan was right. But as I got up from the café table, the knowledge gripped me like never before.

I wouldn't be able to get the possibility out of my head until I'd seen definitive proof that it was or wasn't true. I had to join the Vigil's investigation and find out what really happened. If nothing else, I owed it to Dad.

CHAPTER 5

Madelyn

It was unnerving how much the vibe had shifted in the Vigil's office. This was the first time I'd joined them since the mess at the warehouse, and it felt as if I'd never set foot in the room before.

The change wasn't all bad. Logan had nodded to me as I'd come in with a wary glance but none of his previous hostility and sounded almost friendly when he'd asked how I was doing. Slade had dragged me over to the table in the middle of the room to sit next to him, his leg resting against mine with a companionable sort of intimacy that reminded me of our library hookup without being in any way obscene. My presence seemed to be accepted and even welcomed for once instead of an intrusion.

But the atmosphere in the room had darkened as if a storm cloud hung over the space. Every look that passed between the guys and every comment they exchanged held an ominous import that I'd never been aware of before.

These guys had blood on their hands, even if it wasn't totally by choice. And they were investigating a much more horrifying sort of murder.

That was, if I was going to believe that my dad really had been murdered, which as far as I was concerned was still up in the air. There was no doubting that the three Vigil guys believed it wholeheartedly, though.

There hadn't been much talk at all since my initial welcome. Slade rustled the papers he was searching through—he'd told me he was checking the Vigil's notes on their earlier encounter with the gang that ran the bar where we'd found Dad's trinket box, seeing if there were any clues in those prior interactions.

Dexter was tapping away at the computer on the desk against the wall, his gaze intent beneath the fall of his messy curls, his mouth set in a grim line. He was searching news sites for any mention of the death at the warehouse. From his expression, he hadn't come across any yet.

Logan sat in a nearby chair with a laptop open, running a hand over the short tufts of his hair as he scowled at the screen. He'd mentioned that he was trying to connect the name Kenneth, which the other two guys had gotten during their interrogation at the warehouse, to shipping activities that might be happening at the building. He clearly wasn't having any luck either.

Before he'd gotten started on his current search, Logan had taken out the file folders of my dad's notes so that I could contribute by digging through those. If I found any mention of a Kenneth or warehouses or the street the warehouse was on, we'd take a closer look. But my stepbrother had admitted that the Vigil had already looked through them with the same purpose yesterday.

"Maybe you'll notice something we didn't, since you knew him better," he'd suggested.

I'd have been gratified that he was finally acknowledging that I could pitch in if the offer hadn't felt like busy work. I was skimming through the papers, but nothing had jumped out at me. A lot of them were just mundane notes—reminders to himself to pick up things for the house, appointment or meeting times that were part of his usual schedule. And looking at them sent regular twinges of grief through me like I hadn't felt in years.

In some ways, my memories of Dad had faded over the past twelve years. I guessed that was normal when you couldn't make any new memories with the person. But seeing his familiar handwriting with familiar phrasing and references to our lives together brought him back into sharper focus.

What would he have been doing now if he hadn't died? How would all of our lives have been different?

I set aside the last page in the pile and rubbed my eyes. What else could I do that would be remotely useful?

My gaze landed on Dexter's phone sitting on the desk next to his arm, and an idea sparked. "Dexter, you took a bunch of photos of the warehouse like you usually do when we investigate, right?"

His attention flicked to me and then back to the screen. "Of course. Not sure there's anything useful in there. The place was pretty empty."

That was true, but I had to do *something*. "Could I look through them and see if there's anything we might have missed? We did get kind of… distracted."

Slade guffawed at my phrasing and tapped his knee against my leg. "You put it so politely. I would have said all hell broke loose."

I returned the nudge with my elbow to his arm. "Same difference."

Dexter had already picked up his phone to unlock it. "Always good to get fresh eyes on the evidence," he said, passing it over. "Let us know if you notice anything at all that could be of interest."

"Thanks, I will."

He'd already opened up the first of the photos—a shot of the front of the building from across the street. The sight of its dreary brick face sent a shiver down my spine. I hoped we never had to go back there in person.

I zoomed in, scanning the worn bricks, the windows, and the door for any detail that might be significant. When I found nothing, I swiped to the next photo and repeated the process.

Slade pushed his papers away with a grimace. "I don't see anything here that would connect the gang to the warehouse or to Maddie's dad."

"That isn't surprising," Dexter said without looking up from the computer. "The guy we interrogated didn't act like he had any clue about the bar or the people who operate out of there. I think his reaction was genuine."

"You can usually tell." Slade sighed and popped one of his ever-present cinnamon candies into his mouth. "But it has to all be connected somehow, right? Both the warehouse and the box the gang stole are connected to Evan Silver. Why would the gang have wanted his trinket box if they weren't mixed up in whatever happened that made someone want to murder him?" He arched an eyebrow at me. "Somehow I don't get the impression he was the type to go making criminal enemies all over the place."

"No," I said, wrinkling my nose. "I'm surprised he made *any*."

Logan had raised his head to follow the conversation. "There could be a higher power that Maddie's dad pissed off, who controls the warehouse and also hired the gang to steal the car and grab the box. The idiots at the bar might not even know why they were supposed to get it."

Dexter hummed to himself. "It's true that whoever orchestrated

Evan Silver's death must have a lot of power and resources. They covered up the murder very thoroughly."

"Could we find out who might have hired them by going back to the gang?" I asked, even as my stomach knotted at the thought of confronting the thugs who'd attacked all of us and nearly killed Logan just a few days ago.

Logan shook his head. "The three—four—of us can't go head-to-head with a whole gang and expect to intimidate them into giving up confidential information like that. They might not know who hired them anyway, if the real power behind the situation is keeping everything on the down low. But I've asked an associate who helps us out now and then to keep an eye on their activities in case anything we'd want to look into comes up."

My own eyebrows rose. "Are there more people in the Vigil that I don't even know about?"

Slade laughed. "Nah, we've just made connections over the past couple of years. People we did favors for who don't mind returning them here and there."

Dexter pushed his chair away from the desk and spun it around to face us. "Another indication of how powerful the people we're up against must be—there've been no reports at all of dead bodies at the warehouse. Not in the local news outlets or any of the larger regional and national ones. If the owners were expecting a shipment that day, there's no way the bodies weren't found."

I froze. "Wait, bod*ies*? How many are we talking about? What happened to the guy you two were interrogating?"

"He broke out of the ropes and came at us," Slade said quickly, grabbing my hand with a reassuring squeeze. His voice became strained as he went on. "He almost killed me. I managed to stop him—not in a way I liked doing. The people guarding that place were brutal."

When I gazed into his eyes, the anguished look there made my throat clench up. These men had been through so much I couldn't comprehend. I couldn't tell him he shouldn't have done whatever it took to save his life.

And they'd gotten into all this danger to solve a mystery that didn't even involve any of them. It was only personal to me.

I wrenched my attention away from Slade and back to Dexter. "So, what does it mean that the murders weren't on the news?"

Logan answered for his friend. "It basically confirms that whatever was going down at that warehouse, it was highly illegal. The owners hate the thought of police poking around there so much they covered up the deaths of their own people to avoid an investigation. Which fits with how aggressively their guards reacted to intruders in the first place."

"Yeah." I shuddered at the memory of how the big guy had grabbed me.

"But I still have no idea what kind of illegal activities they're wrapped up in." Logan let out a growl of frustration and tossed his laptop on the table. "Just knowing the name Kenneth and the address isn't enough to narrow down what the shipment might have been. It obviously wasn't anything published publicly in any detail, and there are a gazillion Kenneths and Kens in the city, plenty of them connected to businesses that could get deliveries."

He rubbed his forehead and then wheeled his chair over to the side drawer on the desk. He pulled out a box I'd seen briefly before —the deck of Tarot cards he'd been holding one time when I'd come into the office days ago.

Logan shuffled the cards quickly with a deftness that showed he'd handled them a lot and then dealt three out onto the top of the desk.

I knit my brow, watching. "What are you doing?"

He peered down at the cards, studying them with total focus. "This was my mom's deck. She taught me the basics of the associations. Sometimes doing a quick reading helps me get out of a mental rut—suggests ideas that hadn't occurred to me on my own."

It wasn't something I'd have expected from Logan, but with the connection to his mom, it made sense. She'd died when he was ten, just a couple of years older than I'd been when I lost my dad. Our shared sense of grief was one of the reasons we'd seemed to understand each other so well when we'd first gotten to know each other in school.

I couldn't help wondering if her death factored into his obsession with uncovering my dad's supposed murder. Mrs. Brooks definitely *hadn't* been murdered—there was nothing mysterious about her death at all. A gas main had exploded in the middle of town, killing a few different people who'd been particularly close to the site and injuring several others. The kind of accident you wanted to think could never affect anyone you cared about but that happened all over the place all the time.

I yanked my attention back to the phone in my hand. I didn't think prodding Logan about his exact motivations was going to do me any good. He might be feeling less antagonistic toward me, but I couldn't imagine him reacting well to being psychoanalyzed at the best of times. Psychiatry wasn't my area of medical expertise anyway.

I flipped through a few more photos and then paused. The shot I'd stopped on showed the interior of the smaller room where the guys had fought with the first man they'd killed in self-defense. I didn't see anything in the room itself that caught my eye, but there was a shape just visible beyond the uncovered window to the left—the corner of a large, oddly shaped box of some sort, sitting in what I assumed was the shipping yard outside.

"Hey," I said. "Did you get the chance to look around out back of the warehouse?"

Dexter shook his head. "Our time became much more limited

after the guards caught us. We got in a few quick glances beforehand, though, and I don't remember anything standing out. Why?"

I handed his phone back to him, the photo enlarged to show the window. "I think that might be a shipping container you can see the edge of outside. It's kind of an unusual-looking one, not just a standard crate. Maybe there's something specific shipped in that kind of box?"

Dexter squinted at the image and then swiveled his chair back toward the computer. He tapped away for several seconds, and then a small smile crossed his lips. "I'd say that was a reefer container—the kind of box they use for shipping refrigerated goods." He glanced at Logan. "That could narrow down what kinds of items this Kenneth guy is dealing in quite a bit, if it's all the same kinds of shipments coming through the warehouse."

Logan's expression brightened. "Might as well follow that lead." He swiped up his cards, tucked them away, and grabbed his computer. "Let's see… Medications? That would fit with the Evan Silver angle."

"It has to be something illegal, right?" I said.

Slade shook his head, leaning back in his chair as he watched his friends work. "Usually illicit merch gets shipped hidden with legit stuff. Passed through a front business to avoid notice. It could also be food products. Dairy, meat, that kind of thing."

"Yeah, I'm not finding anything when it comes to medical-related businesses. Let's look into groceries." Logan's fingers darted across the keys. He might be built like a quarterback, but his main area of study was computer science, and it was easy to see how comfortable he was delving into the internet when he got into the work like this.

A flutter of relief passed through my chest. I'd accomplished something to move along the investigation after all. I *could* be an equal partner with the guys… even if I wasn't totally convinced of their theories yet.

We all waited in silent anticipation as Logan ran through his searches, his expression avid. Then he let out a triumphant laugh, and my heart leapt.

"I think I've got him," he declared, grinning at the rest of us. "There's a Kenneth Dunn who manages a seafood market downtown. It's a big place. He'll need to be bringing in a lot of fish —and who knows what else."

CHAPTER 6

Logan

As I looked at the website for the Fresh Catch Seafood Market, pride warmed my chest. We were closer than we'd ever been to unraveling the mystery around Maddie's father's death, and I'd just found the key clue that might get us some real answers. Who knew what else we might discover now that we'd put these pieces together?

Movement by the table caught my eye. Slade tapped Maddie's arm and slid his finger down to her elbow with a familiarity that turned the warmth inside me into a prickly heat. "I knew having you on the case would be worth it. Nice work."

Maddie ducked her head with a hint of a blush, but her returning gaze was nothing but avid. "Logan found the most important part. I just happened to notice that detail in the photo."

Slade scooted closer to her in his chair and leaned his forearm on the back of hers so his hand rested against her shoulder. "And those sharp eyes pointed us in the right direction. Don't sell yourself short. You're a great asset to the team, Piccolina—and not just because of that great ass."

Maddie's blush deepened, but her eyes sparkled at the same time. My hands clenched at my sides, the unwelcome memory of the two of them disheveled and flushed among the library shelves rushing to the front of my mind. He looked like he was just a few minutes away from leading her back out there and having another go—and she appeared to be totally on board.

I reined in my irritation as well as I could and pasted on a tight smile. "Tone it down, Galvezo. We've still got an investigation to carry out here."

Slade flicked his gaze my way with obvious amusement, and my gut twisted. I recognized his mischievous expression—and I knew that he hadn't been happy about my interference with his pursuit of Maddie before. He wasn't going to back down if he didn't think he should have to.

"I'm just making sure to give credit where it's due," he said in a teasing voice. "I appreciate your contributions too." Then he turned back to Maddie, running his fingers along her jaw in a way that sent a fresh flare of jealousy searing through me. "But you don't just have sharp eyes, do you?"

Maddie raised an eyebrow, but her gaze stayed locked with his. "What do you mean?"

Slade's mouth curved into a seductive grin. "You've got that sharp tongue too. Such a lovely combination. I'm looking forward to seeing what else every part of you can do… but especially that tongue."

Maddie's cheeks turned outright red. She grabbed Slade's hand to move it away from her face but kept holding on to it. "I don't think this is the best place for this conversation."

His grin grew. "I can arrange plenty of other times and places."

I just about bit my tongue off in frustration. That was enough. I couldn't stand here and watch him hang all over her while they practically fucked with their eyes in front of me. We had leads to track down. We didn't need the distraction.

If I didn't get him away from her right now, I wasn't totally sure what my fists might do next.

I motioned to him and Dexter briskly. "We should get on with following up on the new information. You two, go scope out the seafood market. Madelyn, I want to talk to you for a minute."

I couldn't help reverting back to using her full name even though I'd allowed myself more familiarity in the last couple of days. Her gaze darted to me with a tensing of her mouth that didn't make me feel all that wonderful about it.

Slade gave me a considering look, but he got up from his chair with a squeeze of Maddie's hand before letting it go. "The boss has spoken. Come on, Dex. Let's see how fishy this place is."

Dexter stood, taking on the deadpan tone of his typical jokes. "If it isn't fishy, it's not much of a seafood market."

Slade snorted and elbowed him on their way out. Maddie had stood up too, her arms crossed over her chest in a defensive stance that twisted me up for totally different reasons.

"What did you want to talk to me about?" she asked in a cool tone as the door clicked shut behind the guys. Her dark blue eyes bored into me as if piercing right through to everything I'd wanted to protect her from. Reminding me how much I'd already failed at that goal.

All my frustrations collided into a mess of emotions I couldn't hold in any longer. "Is this how you're going to be part of the investigation from now on?" I demanded, waving my hand toward where she and Slade had been sitting.

Maddie knit her brow. "What are you talking about?"

The words kept tumbling out even as I suspected I'd regret them. "Last time you were here you fucked Slade in the library. Now you're practically humping him in the office. Are you only staying on the case so you can screw him all over the city?"

Maddie winced, but her eyes narrowed at the same time. "What does it matter to you what I do with Slade as long as it doesn't interfere with the investigation, which as far as I can tell it hasn't so far? You didn't think about me for a second after *you* fucked me. At least Slade is sticking around."

Her voice broke in the middle of her retort, and the anger inside me snuffed out in an instant. She sounded so certain, and yet she was so far from the truth. Did she really believe I'd pushed her away that easily, that I hadn't given her a second thought since that night two years ago?

Somehow I'd thought we'd be past that affront—that she'd understand why I'd ghosted her now that she knew about the murder investigation. I'd told her I'd been trying to protect her.

But I hadn't really spelled out how our personal interactions factored into my decisions, had I? After the way I'd been treating her since the moment she'd walked back into my life—hell, since the moment *I'd* last walked out of hers—maybe it wasn't surprising that she couldn't set aside the past so easily.

I stared back at her, opening my mouth and then closing it again with instinctive hesitation.

"Right," Maddie said, grabbing her purse and turning to go. "Since obviously you don't have anything worthwhile to say to me—"

"Wait." I sprang forward, catching her by the elbow before she could make it to the door. As she stopped, the feel of her warmth through her sleeve set off a flicker of attraction over my skin. I dropped her arm automatically.

But I didn't have to, did I?

The revelation hit me with a jolt of exhilarated relief. I didn't have to hide *anything* from her. She knew about the investigation; she knew just how bloody and violent my life had become. I'd locked up my feelings for her to keep her safe from everything else going on around me, but she was mixed up in that now. She was already involved in the dangerous part. Staying away from her and pretending not to care didn't serve any purpose at all.

A weird sense of freedom swept through me. My throat constricted just for a second as I figured out where to start.

"Maddie, I've been thinking about you constantly since that night, no matter how hard I tried *not* to. You've always been on my mind, every single day."

Maddie blinked at me, hurt flashing across her face so blatantly that my stomach flipped over. Her voice came out taut. "Then why have you been treating me like I'm nothing? Like it was all some horrible mistake you couldn't wait to get past?"

The pain in those words tore apart my sense of relief with a gut punch of horror. Had I really hurt her that much? I'd known she'd been confused and wanting answers, but I hadn't seen—or hadn't let myself see—just how much the situation was killing her.

She'd become so impervious in high school, taking on everyone and everything that was wrong with the place. I'd assumed she'd handle my asshole behavior with the same unshakable strength, that I couldn't have meant that much to her. But she was shaking now, literally—a tremor running through her body as she waited for my response—and all I wanted to do was wrap her up in my arms as if that could heal the wounds I'd inadvertently dealt.

She wouldn't want me touching her, though. Not after everything. And I couldn't fix this mess with a simple embrace anyway.

I ran my hand over my face, my insides in turmoil. "Maddie… You're *everything* to me. That's why I stayed away, even though all I wanted was to be with you. It terrified me that you could become a target of whoever went after your dad… and maybe it was partly selfish too, because I didn't know how you'd react if you found out all the things I've gotten involved in."

Maddie stared back at me, the skepticism on her face like a knife to my chest. "You didn't just stay away. You've been horrible to me."

I swallowed thickly. How the hell did I make this up to her? "I know. It was the only way I could stop myself from showing you how I really felt. Because as soon as I let down my guard, I knew I wouldn't be able to keep you out of any of this. So I pushed you away as hard as I could… but I never wanted to hurt you. Fuck, I was trying to *stop* you from getting hurt."

Maddie's mouth tightened. "I'd rather have had some stranger trying to murder me than be iced out by someone I used to think I could trust. Someone I cared about. I don't even know how much to believe you now. How can I know you're not saying all of this as part of some other plan to get what you want?"

I flinched inwardly, because I couldn't deny that she had a point. As I groped for an answer, her words echoed in my head. *Someone I used to think I could trust. Someone I cared about.*

We'd had something back then, before I'd started pushing her away. That night in the basement bathroom, she'd wanted me as much as I'd wanted her. So maybe I could show her just how much she'd mattered to me without her thinking I was crazy.

Or maybe she would think I was crazy, but at least she'd know. She'd know everything.

"Actually, I can prove it to you," I said, and held out my hand to her. "I can show you just how much you've been in my mind the past few years. Would you come with me?"

CHAPTER 7

Madelyn

The low-rise concrete apartment building Logan parked outside wasn't anything spectacular, but as I got out of his car and looked up at it, the occasion felt momentous. I'd known he and the other Vigil guys shared an apartment off-campus, but I hadn't known where it was, let alone seen it before. And he was going to take me right into their home.

His confession in the Vigil office had left my stomach wobbly. As I followed him to the lobby door, I still felt off-balance. What was I supposed to make of his claims and the intensity with which he'd delivered them after the way he'd chided and berated me through so much of the last couple of weeks? Even right before he'd told me how much I meant to him, he'd been accusing me of only caring about sleeping with Slade.

It was hard to imagine what he could show me that would convince me to trust him.

Logan led the way through the lobby to the elevator wordlessly. Our feet thudded across the cracked linoleum floor. The elevator took us up to the top—third—floor with a little lurch that set me off-balance in a much more literal way. I grabbed the railing along the back wall.

"It's not the fanciest place, but everything generally works," Logan said. "In almost two years, we've only gotten stuck in here once."

I just had to hope that this wasn't my unlucky day, then. Right now, I couldn't think of anything much worse than being stuck with my stepbrother in a tiny elevator car for hours.

To my relief, the elevator door opened on cue, and Logan stepped to the apartment just down the hall, pulling a key ring from his pocket. He unlocked the door and pushed it wide for me to go in ahead of him.

The main living space didn't offer much sense of the guys' personalities, other than they'd all obviously preferred to stick with practicality and comfort over anything flashy. The sofa looked a bit worn but was long and covered with plump cushions. The basic TV stand across from it held a mid-sized flat-screen and a couple of game systems underneath. A four-person table of scuffed maple stood near the open-concept kitchen, where a surprising array of shiny pots and pans hung from a ceiling-mounted rack.

I nodded to them. "Are those just for show, or do you guys actually cook?"

Logan smiled crookedly. "Mostly just Dexter. He uses them a lot, but he takes such meticulous care of them you can hardly tell. When he's got free time, he likes to experiment in the kitchen—throwing together new recipes like he's some kind of mad scientist.

But hey, most of the time the food turns out great, and Slade and I get to reap the benefits."

The affection in his voice as he spoke about his friend eased my nerves a little. Logan might have been a jerk to me, and he'd been kind of a jerk to Slade too about our hookup, but he *did* still have a caring side to him.

"My room's over here," he said, beckoning me to one of the four doors that branched off from the main room—a bathroom and the guys' bedrooms, I assumed. "What I need to show you—it's on my computer."

I eased into the room after him, peering around me cautiously. The first thing that hit me was the scent, musky and masculine, so familiar from the brief time we'd lived together. It sent a weird pang of homesickness through my chest.

His bedcovers were rumpled—Logan moved to them quickly and jerked them straight with a hint of embarrassment. The extensive computer setup that'd traveled with him from home took up most of the desk across from the bed. The bookcase next to it was the only other furniture in the room, half of it stuffed with texts on programming languages and tech developments, the other with the legal thrillers and horror novels he'd always enjoyed reading.

I found myself drawn to a cluster of photos tacked to the wall next to the desk. After the way Logan had distanced himself from the entire family, the sight of them surprised me.

The central photo was of his dad, mother, and Logan when he was a young child, squinting in the sunlight in a park. Then there was a picture of Logan and Holand at a beach when he was a preteen, around the age he'd been when I first met him. On the other side was one of him and his dad on a family ski trip, a few other teens who were either cousins or friends around them, all bundled up in winter coats but smiling widely.

And then there was the fourth photo, the one that surprised me the most. This one was of our parents' wedding. Mom and Holand stood with their arms around each other while Logan and I looked at them from either side, beaming at the love they'd found with each other. I remembered that moment so well. I'd had no idea things would sour between the two of us so much afterward.

I'd had no idea that it'd meant enough to Logan that he'd want to look at it every day.

Logan must have noticed my interest, but he didn't comment on the photos. He sat down at his desk and wiggled his mouse to bring the desktop computer to life.

I shifted my weight from foot to foot and twisted my hands in front of me, unsure of what to do. There wasn't another chair, and I didn't want to awkwardly stand looking over his shoulder, so I stepped back and sat tentatively on the very edge of his newly made bed. I tried very hard not to think about Logan lying in that bed or the way the smell of him intensified once I'd sat down.

What did he have on his computer that he figured would prove his case anyway?

"Where are you going with this?" I asked. "If you think you can just wave away the last couple of weeks—"

"No," Logan said quickly, glancing back at me. Had his voice gone a little hoarse? "I—the only way I can justify that at all is to tell you… I thought I had to choose between putting your life in danger and having you hate me. And given the choice, I'd rather that you hate me than see something horrible happen to you."

His words tugged at my heart, but I folded my arms over my chest. "And how did calling me a slut and accusing me of wanting to fuck Slade all over town help anything?"

Logan winced. "Okay, maybe some jealousy crept in there too." He rubbed his hand over his face. "It's been killing me seeing you with him when I felt like I couldn't let myself go there—when I know... Anyway, I definitely said some shitty things. You didn't deserve that."

"Slade didn't either," I had to point out.

"Let me sort that out with him." He sucked in a breath and turned back to the computer. "What I can prove to you now is that I have been thinking about you all this time. Wanting you to be okay. Wanting to know you're happy. And wanting to keep you safe. Ever since I started suspecting your dad was murdered, I've been worried they'd target you too. So I hacked into your social media accounts to keep an eye on any private messages you got, just in case anything concerning came up."

It took a second for that last remark to sink in. I stiffened on the bed. "Wait, you *what*?"

Logan motioned to the computer. "It was only to keep an eye on the situation," he said adamantly. "I never interfered with your conversations or posts. I just... watched from afar."

I stared at him, hardly able to believe what I was hearing. I didn't think the flare of anger that'd shot up inside me was the response he'd wanted to provoke. "What the fuck, Logan! They're called *private* messages for a reason. Who gave you the right to muck around in my life like that?"

He held up his hands, but he didn't look all that repentant. "You've seen the kind of people we run into. The thought of anyone like that weaseling into your life... I realize it was a violation, but Maddie, I was afraid someone would *kill* you."

My fingers curled around the edge of his blanket. "You could have just asked me what was going on in my life, like a normal human being. We used to talk. You were the one who made it difficult."

"I know." His head drooped for a moment. Then he lifted his gaze to pin me with it. "It killed me doing that too. Maddie, I've been falling for you since you showed up at high school ready to take on the world. I mean, I liked you even in junior high, but by your freshman year you were really something. You still are. I would have gone for it except our parents were dating and I wasn't sure how you felt, and then when they started talking marriage it seemed even more awkward."

I swallowed thickly, unwilling to tell him that I'd had a crush on him even longer. Could he really mean what he was saying?

"I don't think our parents would figure it's that weird," I said. "It's not like we were raised as siblings. We lived together for less than two years."

"Maybe. I was going to wait and see how things went once we were settled in at the house… but then everything else got more complicated."

"Complicated how? You said you found the stuff that made you think my dad had been murdered when you were packing for college, and you started getting standoffish with me way before then."

Logan grimaced. "Slade, Dexter, and I started getting into our investigations years before that, and all of a sudden that pastime turned… intense. We were dealing with established criminals, not just petty thefts at school. We all felt like we had to keep at it, like we were doing something good making sure justice was served, but it was dangerous. Anyone we cared about could become a target if someone went looking for revenge."

I cocked my head. "So you're saying that part was to protect me too."

"Basically. And maybe, with all the shit going down, I wasn't sure I even deserved you. I thought I'd drag you down… or that you'd be horrified if you found out the lengths we were going to…" He let out a ragged sigh. "And then the stuff with your dad came up and made the situation even more precarious."

I guessed that made a sort of sense. But that didn't explain everything. "How did hooking up with me in the bathroom fit in with any of that?"

"I didn't mean to lose control. I was hyped up from the fight I'd gotten into, and you were right there, and I wanted you so badly." He closed his eyes for a second. "I'm so sorry, Maddie. I swear the only part of that night that I regret is that I had to push you away again afterward. But I've never been able to bring myself to totally ignore you."

He pushed his chair over so I could see the computer screen and clicked open a file in a folder. I found myself gaping at a screenshot of an article from our town's local news blog—about me winning the science fair in my senior year of high school. There was a photo of me, with a kind of dorky smile, amid the text.

I hadn't known Logan had even realized I'd entered the science fair, let alone that I'd won it. He'd certainly never congratulated me.

Logan flipped through more images, one after another, giving me just enough time to take in each one before moving to the next. Some of them were public information, like the award I'd won last year at my old college and a special research project I'd contributed to there that'd gotten written up online. Others were from my private accounts: emails where I shared smaller victories and joys with Mom or Summer, posts he could only have seen because he'd hacked into my account since he'd blocked me on his own.

Every little moment of happiness and success in the past few years of my life, Logan had documented. It was like he'd made a digital scrapbook devoted to me. And I realized from glancing at the file names that I could see the dates when he'd taken the screenshots—and he'd been doing it consistently across those years. This wasn't something he'd pulled together only recently.

I wasn't totally sure how to feel about the invasion of privacy, but the sight sent a giddy sort of wobble through my chest anyway.

He'd been a total ass to me… but he'd also clearly cared. More than I'd ever let myself hope he could.

Logan was watching my expression. "I'd look through this stuff when the Vigil was struggling with a case or when I was feeling particularly crappy about pushing you away. It seemed like it was the only way I could be with you at all. But you know now. If there's danger coming, you're already in its path. So I don't have to hide how I feel anymore."

As I gazed back at him, my resolve wavered. For so much of my life, there'd been few things I'd wanted more than Logan Brooks's adoration, and now he was offering that up to me on a platter. But still…

"You've been a *huge* jerk," I had to say.

"I have," he agreed without hesitation. He scooted the chair over so his knees pressed against mine and grasped my hands, holding my gaze even more intently than before. "I'm so sorry for how awful I've been since you showed up asking for help with your car, Maddie. The rest of it too, but especially that. I just hope you can understand that it seemed like the lesser of two evils. It'd have been even more awful if you'd gotten hurt."

A burn of tears formed at the back of my eyes. "It wouldn't have been your fault if I had, Logan. It's not your job to protect me. If we're going to have *any* kind of relationship, it has to be as equals, not you being all white knight to my supposed damsel in distress."

"I get that," he said dryly, but then his attention dipped briefly to my lips. He slid forward in his chair, tucking his legs right around mine and raising one hand to touch my cheek. My heart hiccupped at his nearness, tingles racing over my skin. "I'm just overjoyed to hear you still think we could have some kind of relationship."

He leaned in, and my brain short-circuited. I didn't know how to do anything but bend forward to meet his kiss.

There was something bittersweet about the meeting of our lips. Logan's mouth molded against mine, demanding and yet coaxing, making me lose my breath, but the knowledge of all our history hung over me. I couldn't quite lose myself in the heat of the moment, as much as my heart fluttered giddily.

He kissed me harder, teasing his other hand up my arm, and part of me wanted to pull him even closer. I wanted to find out what it could be like with him when he wasn't fighting our connection the entire time. The hunger seared through me to find out what those hands would feel like all over my body, not just in a hasty hook-up on a bathroom sink.

But he wasn't the only guy I felt a connection with now. I might have had a crush on Logan forever, but Slade had stolen his way into my heart. And I hadn't been able to stop thinking about Beckett either. *They'd* both treated me like someone worthwhile, someone special, from the start.

I forced myself to pull back. The molten heat in Logan's eyes nearly did me in. But I held myself in place and forced myself to speak instead of crushing my mouth back against his.

He'd changed his tune on me before. I had to be sure it wouldn't happen again. And I didn't even know if I would pick him if I had to choose between the three men who'd captured my interest.

"I don't know if I'm ready to do this with you," I said. "Not again. Not after everything. And not just because of that. I like Slade, a lot, and I'm not ditching him just because you finally pulled your head out of your ass. I've been getting to know someone else too… I'm not ready to settle down with anyone yet, and I'm definitely not jumping straight into something serious with you."

Logan's jaw clenched. He dropped his hands, his fingers curling into fists, but with a deep breath, he managed to relax his stance. "I get it. It's my own fault for not showing you how much you mattered to me sooner. Slade… Slade's a good guy."

I raised my eyebrows, unable to hold back my sarcasm. "You sound so sincere."

"I mean it," Logan said. "That doesn't mean that I'm going to *like* the idea of you being with him instead of me. But…" He motioned to the computer. "What's mattered the most to me is seeing you happy. If he makes you happy, I shouldn't get in the way of it. I just hope you'll give me a chance to keep making up for the past. Since you're not settling down just yet." A hint of mischief lit in his eyes.

I couldn't stop my lips from twitching into a smile. "I guess that's fair."

"Good." He took my hand again, squeezing it gently. "We can take it slow and see how everything works out. And I can promise you this: no matter what happens, I'm never letting you feel like you're nothing again."

CHAPTER 8

Madelyn

I wasn't totally sure what to make of the fact that *Logan* called me up to ask if I wanted to come check out the seafood market with the Vigil. He didn't even sound grudging about it when I immediately jumped at the chance. He smiled when I came down to meet the guys at his car, and that smile only tightened a little when Slade slung his arm around my shoulders in a quick embrace before the two of us got into the back seat.

"From the terrific trio to the quintessential quartet," Slade announced as the other guys got in too, and Logan didn't argue.

"So, what exactly are we doing at the market?" I asked. "I thought you and Dexter already scoped it out."

"We stuck to the outside," Slade said without hesitation. It seemed that Logan had loosened everyone's lips when it came to the Vigil's activities.

Dexter nodded. "It's always best to get the lay of the land before going in for a more intensive mission."

"You said the security wasn't anything to be worried about, right?" Logan asked.

"I can pick the lock on the back door no problem," Dexter said. "And they had a logo up for a security system, but I didn't see any sign that it was actually installed." He glanced back at me. "Sometimes people put up the logo stickers as a deterrent without actually having the system."

"Not like there'd be much to steal in a fish market anyway," Slade said.

I shivered. "We don't know what else they might be stashing there."

"They wouldn't want to go overboard with the security and make people wonder what they're protecting," Logan said. "It's possible they don't keep anything illegal on the premises anyway, just use the business as a front for shipments they redirect elsewhere."

He gave the explanation in a tone that was outright warm, as if he *enjoyed* filling me in on how criminal operations work. I was having a little trouble wrapping my head around this new, more companionable dynamic… but I couldn't say I minded it.

Slade stretched out his legs and took my hand, running his thumb over my knuckles. "Even if the alarm system is in place, Logan's found the codes for disabling most of those."

Logan had been doing a lot of digging into all kinds of things I wouldn't have imagined a few weeks ago.

Dexter swiveled in his seat more fully and held a thermos and a spoon out to me. When I accepted them with a questioning glance, his vivid green gaze flicked away from me with his usual discomfort at sustained eye contact.

"I made a lamb and vegetable curry," he said. "I thought you might like some."

As if on cue, my stomach gurgled. "Oh," I said, startled but remembering Logan's comment about the pots in the guys' apartment. "You didn't have to."

His gaze flitted around the car before returning to meet mine briefly. "It's easy to end up skipping meals when you're wrapped up in a case—or at least, I find that happens with me. I haven't noticed you eating when you're with us at all, so I figured I'd make sure you have some fuel, just in case."

An unexpected flush warmed my cheeks at the sweetness of that gesture. Dexter didn't show much emotion, but he was trying to take care of me in his own way. And getting the awkward gesture of affection made it hard to ignore the striking face of the guy who'd made it. My pulse skipped a beat despite myself.

Like you don't have enough guys on your mind already, Maddie, I chided myself, and opened up the thermos. The hearty, spicy scent wafted into my nose, making my mouth water. I hadn't actually eaten since lunch, and it was now late in the evening, an hour after the market had closed.

I took a bite and almost swooned. The meat was perfectly tender, and the sauce was rich and flavorful without being too biting. "This is amazing!" I said before shoveling more into my mouth.

Slade chuckled, looking nothing but pleased that I was enjoying the fruits of his friend's labor. "Dex is quite the star in the kitchen."

"I'll have you know I have nothing in common with gaseous giants," Dexter replied in a deadpan tone, which made both of his friends crack up. It took me a second to realize he'd meant the comment as a joke, not a real misunderstanding, and then I giggled too.

I was just finishing the curry when Logan cruised past the Fresh

Catch Seafood Market. I took in the sign with its lobster logo and the darkened windows. Definitely closed.

Logan parked down the street, and we all got out. Slade motioned for us to follow him. "The best route to the back door is down the alley."

He loped along in front, his strides so perfectly even you'd never have known about his prosthetic if the swish of his pantleg hadn't revealed occasional glimpses of the brightly colored metal. I remembered how well he'd danced on those legs, and then I was getting heated up for a totally different reason.

Nope. Not going to get caught up in those thoughts. It was time to focus on this case.

Something in this building might lead us to answers about Dad's death—or at least whatever he'd been interested in at the warehouse to have written down its address.

The alley, unsurprisingly, smelled strongly of fish. I suspected the nearby dumpster was full of discards from the day. In the shadowy space, Dexter knelt down, pulled out the thin metal rods he used, and made short work of the two locks on the door.

He eased it open carefully to a rhythmic beeping that had him beckoning Logan over. "They do have a system, just inside. You'd better deal with it."

Logan ducked past him, peered at the alarm systems control panel, and quickly typed in a code. The beeping stopped at once. He flashed a grin at me. "Every system has technician codes that allow access. They're supposed to be closely guarded secrets."

"Not closely guarded enough to keep them out of our computer expert's hands," Slade murmured jovially, and we tramped inside.

Logan and Slade both stuck close to me as we slunk around a storage room and out into the main market. "Don't wander off too far," Logan ordered me.

I bumped him lightly with my elbow. "It's an empty store. The biggest threat is death by fish stink."

The merchandise had been cleared from the racks, but a cacophony of fishy scents saturated the air even in their absence. The only light in the place was the streaks from the streetlamps outside the front windows. My heart thumped faster as we peered through the empty space.

We weren't meant to be in here, and I couldn't help tensing at the thought that a security guard might leap out of nowhere. But at the same time, I couldn't deny the thrill of it. We were searching for answers, carving a path where no one had wanted us to look. And I was in it right beside the Vigil guys.

We made a quick circuit of the main market space, Logan glancing over his shoulder continuously to make sure I was nearby and Slade guiding me here and there with a light touch on the small of my back. I felt weirdly cocooned between their combined protectiveness. It wasn't exactly a bad feeling.

"We need to find where they keep the records," Dexter muttered.

Logan nodded and pointed to a door on the far side of the store area. Dexter snapped photos the whole way there.

The first room we found beyond the door was clearly where the butchering happened. The huge stainless steel table had been wiped clean, but the smell of fish filled the air even thicker there. The drawers held knives of all kinds of sizes and styles, many of which I'd never seen before.

We pushed open the next door, and Slade let out a low whistle. "Jackpot."

A long narrow desk ran along one wall, scattered with papers. Binders were stacked on a shelving unit opposite it, and more papers poked from the drawers of a filing cabinet nearby. Whoever worked out of this room clearly wasn't the most organized person ever.

The guys immediately spread out. After closing the door, Slade flicked on the light so we could make out the writing on the papers. Dexter snapped photos of everything, Logan flipped through the binders, and Slade moved to the filing cabinet. I started sifting through the papers on the desk, hoping that whatever I should be searching for would jump out at me.

After a few minutes, I frowned. "Nothing here looks out of place. Payroll and receipts and that sort of thing. There are some shipping records, but it all sounds like fish, nothing that you wouldn't expect to be delivered here."

Dexter came up beside me. "I'll keep track of those anyway. The dates might be useful later."

"I'm not finding anything suspicious either," Slade reported. "Employee applications, profit margins—boring."

"Same." Logan pushed away from the shelves and scanned the room again with a frown. Then he cocked his head. Bending down, he fished out a paper that'd been wedged way at the back of the desk behind one of its legs. He uncrumpled it avidly but then shook his head with a self-deprecating laugh. "Well, that's not getting us anywhere. I can see why they changed the logo, though."

He turned the torn paper around for us to see, and I realized that it was an old, dirt-smudged flyer for the Fresh Catch Seafood Market. Who knew how many years it'd been stuck behind the desk. But like Logan had said, it didn't have the lobster logo I'd seen on the front of the store. Instead, it showed a fish that looked as if it'd just been chopped in half, separating the head end from the tail.

My gaze snagged on that image, and my pulse stuttered. For a second I just stood there frozen.

Logan's laugh faded as he took in my reaction. "What is it, Maddie?"

I pointed at the flyer. "That—that isn't just any fish, right? It's got that rounded head and the whisker things... That's a catfish."

Slade took a closer look. "I'm no marine biologist, but I think you're right."

Dexter inclined his head. "Definitely. Maybe not the best idea to use a cute fish in a gruesome position. I can see why they switched to the lobster." But he shot me a curious glance, probably suspecting that wasn't why I'd asked.

My throat had constricted. I took the flyer from Logan's hand and ran my fingers over the wrinkled paper. The guys waited while I groped for words.

The only words I could think for the first several seconds were Dad's—some of the last he'd ever said to me while he'd been in the delirium of his sickness.

"My dad," I said in little more than a whisper. "When he was sick, he got pretty out of it and started babbling about a bunch of stuff. A lot of it didn't make any sense, at least at the time. One of the things he said was about a broken catfish. That maybe they 'did this.'"

The guys stiffened as well, clearly catching the significance just as I had. I'd assumed Dad had been talking about the fish in the flood he'd waded through to get to the beach rental. But now... now I had to think it hadn't been that at all. Here was a broken catfish right in front of me.

Right at the place the address in his trinket box had led us toward.

Had he realized he wasn't just sick—that someone might have made him ill on purpose, with poison or some other means? Had the same investigation that'd brought his attention to the warehouse led him here just as it had us, and he'd suspected the people who worked out of the market had something to do with his mysterious condition?

What other conclusions could I draw? This old logo pulled the pieces together in a way that made so much more sense than him talking about dead fish he'd seen in a current of water… that had probably had nothing to do with his sickness anyway.

Certainty gripped my gut. I looked up and met each of the guy's eyes in turn.

"He really was murdered. And he thought the people here had something to do with it. We have to find out why."

And then we could see justice served for the man those villains had murdered after it'd been such a long time coming.

CHAPTER 9

Slade

"Stand right in the doorway," Dexter ordered me.

I struck a pose on the threshold of the seafood market's back door, balancing on my whole leg while jutting out my prosthetic as if at the end of a dramatic dance. Even my practical friend's lips twitched with a hint of a smile, but when I glanced at Maddie, she was gazing off into the shadows down the alley, her expression not just serious but haunted.

I held my position while Dexter checked the feeds from the three tiny cameras we'd concealed around the back end of the market so we could keep track of the deliveries the place wanted to keep out of the public eye. "Good," he said, and I moved to join Maddie, but the expression on her face made me hesitate.

What could I say to her? She didn't look like she wanted to goof around. Tonight's expedition had obviously bothered her, and I didn't know what to say that would encourage her to open up or make her feel better.

Logan was still focused on the surveillance we'd put in place. "As long as no one notices the cameras, we'll get a good sense of the regular activities around the market. Whatever shady shit they're into, we'll figure it out."

He glanced at Maddie too, maybe hoping to lift her spirits with the declaration. She shot him a small tight smile that wasn't particularly convincing. My stomach knotted, watching.

"Let's get out of here before anyone notices *us*," I said. Getting some distance from this place might take her mind off whatever was gnawing at her.

We hustled back to Logan's car and slid inside. Maddie stayed quiet the whole drive back to campus, staring alternatively out the window and down at her hands. I grappled with my words. I knew how to speak in more than half a dozen languages, but I still had no clue what the right thing to say to this woman would be.

I had to show her I was good for more than just flirting and risky hookups. She was something special, and I had to be impressive enough to keep her. And she definitely wasn't the type to be too impressed by a little suaveness. This was a woman who needed substance in a guy.

I had a little of that in me someplace, didn't I?

Logan pulled into the parking lot near the law library, but as Maddie got out, somehow her expression seemed even more shellshocked than before. I took a gamble, grabbing her hand and tossing out the suggestion before I could second-guess it. "Hey, why don't the two of us go for a walk while Logan and Dex sort out what we found? You look like you could use the chance to clear your head."

Logan's jaw flexed as his gaze flicked between us, but for once, he kept his mouth shut about our relationship. Something had shifted between him and Maddie recently—he'd seemed gentler with her and in how he approached everything to do with her. I couldn't say I disliked the change, but it did make me wonder what was up with him—and what he planned to do next.

"Don't take too long," he said after a moment. "I want to get everyone's observations down so we don't miss anything."

I gave him a playful salute. "We'll be back soon to deliver a full report."

Maddie exhaled in a long stream and squeezed my hand. "Yeah. I think a walk would be good right now."

We meandered down the path that led away from the law library, the intermittent lamp posts providing occasional breaks in the thickening darkness. A small group of freshmen hustled past us, chattering and laughing with each other. Maddie drew a little closer to me.

Well, maybe starting with basics was the way to go. "How are you feeling?"

She rubbed her forehead. "Just… overwhelmed. Until tonight, I still found it hard to believe that my dad could really have been *murdered*. But seeing that logo, remembering the things he said… With that on top of everything else, suddenly it's hard to deny."

"I guess that's shocking," I said. "But you already knew it was a possibility. At least now we're getting closer to finding the evidence we need to figure out who and why."

"Yeah." She stuffed her free hand in her pocket, hunching her shoulders against a chilly gust of breeze. "It means something really horrible happened all those years ago, something I had no clue about. But it also means… You know, for a long time I thought it was *my* fault that he died."

I blinked at her, unable to hide my surprise. "Why would you think *that*?"

She grimaced. "He got sick just a few days after we had a family trip to a beach house my parents rented. He was going to come a day later than my mom and me because he had some work to finish up. But there was a huge storm, and when I talked to him on the phone that night, I told him how much I wished he was there with us. He drove through the storm and then waded right through the spot where the road had flooded just to get to me."

Her voice wobbled, but the main thing I heard was how much her dad had loved her. He'd gone to those lengths to try to comfort her. That was how a good parent acted.

"I figured he got exposed to something in the flood waters," Maddie went on. "I mean, with the timing, and how quickly the sickness hit him… Maybe it didn't totally make sense, but nothing else made *more* sense."

I tucked my arm right around hers, searching for the best way to reassure her. "At least you know now that it isn't true. You had nothing to do with what happened to him. The dip he took didn't hurt him."

"It seems that way." She knit her brow. "I don't know why I'm having so much trouble letting that idea sink in. I've spent so long connecting his illness to the flood, and now there's this other totally different, totally crazy story… My head's a total muddle."

"That's understandable," I said. But I had to manage better than that. I sucked in a breath and added, "The three of us in the Vigil have had years to get used to the idea, and he wasn't a parent to any of us. Don't feel bad about needing time to process everything."

"I know." She stopped at the edge of the path by a looming tree and gave me a smile that was still small but brighter than before. "Thank you."

I guessed I'd done something right. I knew exactly what I

wanted to do next. I stepped toward her and slipped both my arms around her, holding her close.

Maddie let out a ragged breath and let her head sink against my shoulder. The feel of her relaxing into my embrace melted something in my chest. I stroked my hand over her hair.

"We're going to get it all figured out—the four of us, together. We've gotten so much farther since you joined up with us. You were obviously the missing ingredient."

Maddie let out a soft snort and pulled back to meet my eyes. "I'm going to do my best to keep up with the rest of you, even if you've all been through a lot more of this kind of thing than I have. My dad deserves justice for what was done to him. My mom deserves to know what really happened."

I touched her cheek. "You deserve closure too, Maddie."

She gazed back at me, her eyes darkening with concern. "How are *you* doing? What you had to do in the warehouse—the way this investigation has been going—you don't deserve to have to fight for your life against criminals who've killed who knows how many people."

The fact that she could worry about me even while she was dealing with so much of her own trauma made my heart swell with affection, but my stomach lurched at the same time. Whenever the memories flickered up of the moment when I'd had to stab that thug before he could off me, I felt like vomiting.

We had good reasons for doing what we did. Ultimately, we were doing what we could to set things right in the world. But that didn't mean I always enjoyed the shit we ended up immersed in.

"I'll be okay," I told Maddie. "We've seen… a lot, over the years. When you're dealing with people that tough, you learn to toughen up too." At least when you were staring them down face to face. Not always when you were alone in the privacy of your own bedroom, but I didn't need to mention that. "It'll be worth it if we can finally find out what happened to your dad."

"That shouldn't be your responsibility."

I stroked my thumb over her cheek, my discomfort vanishing as I took in her gorgeous face and the compassion shining in her eyes. "I'm happy to take it up. Especially when I know how much it means to you."

Her lips pursed for a second, and I couldn't resist them once my attention had been drawn there. I leaned in, and she tipped her head to meet me.

Our mouths brushed against each other, a ghost of a kiss turning into something deeper. This part, I knew how to do right. I tangled my fingers in her hair and hummed encouragingly when she gripped the front of my shirt.

But after another kiss that left my heart racing, she eased back, her stance tensing a little. "I— You should probably know, Logan and I have started to work things out between us. I'm not sure how that's going to go, but I can't say it's going *nowhere*…"

Ah, that explained a few things, mostly about my best friend's change in attitude. I arched my eyebrows at her. "You already told me you were still playing the field. I don't mind if you're into both of us. Have all the fun you want."

The words had only left my mouth when I realized how *I* felt about it might not be the problem at all. Logan had obviously taken issue with my interest in Maddie from the start. He'd backed off on the jealous rages, but he still didn't seem happy about it. If he was trying to make a move on her, he probably minded very much that she was still involved with me.

And what if she wanted him more than she wanted me? It wouldn't be so surprising, would it?

I backed up a step, an embarrassed heat filling my chest. "Of course, if *he'd* have a problem with it—if you want to focus on seeing where things could go with him… I'm not going to pitch a fit about it. I know he was in your life first."

Maddie's brow furrowed. "What are you saying? You figure he would get first dibs because I knew him before I knew you?"

I rubbed the back of my neck. "I mean, basically? I don't want to mess anything up for you if—"

"Slade," Maddie cut in, with an edge of irritation in her voice, "please don't tell me you buy into that kind of chauvinistic bullshit. Nobody gets to *reserve* me for later dating. I'm not an object available first come, first serve."

Okay, when she put it that way, it did sound like some kind of bullshit. I had the urge to bite my tongue off. "I was just trying to say… I want you to be happy. I'm not going to get in the way of *that*. If you'd be happier with him."

She glowered at me, but her shoulders had come down a little. "That wasn't what I was trying to say. I still want *you*. We've had a lot of fun together already, and he's been a jerk about a lot of this. You've made me happy while he was acting like an asshole. I'm just in a muddle about that too, trying to figure out where I stand and how this whole playing the field thing is going to work. I'm trying to be upfront with you about the situation."

A different sort of embarrassment flashed through me alongside my relief. I'd come up with this whole scenario where she picked Logan over me out of thin air. Or maybe because it wouldn't be the first time someone I'd assumed cared about me walked the other way.

I'd been bracing myself to get abandoned all over again, because it'd mattered to me that she might. This woman had gotten under my skin even more than I'd realized.

But gazing into her determined eyes, I couldn't say I had a problem with that.

"I appreciate that," I said. "And I'm sorry for jumping to

conclusions. You'd better believe I want *you*, Piccolina, as long as you're on board."

I grasped her hand again, a smile returning to my face. "You know what, I think we probably *all* need to take a break and burn off some steam. To have fun without worrying about where it'll lead. Let's go grab the others and head to that club downtown. I can't wait to see what else we can do on that dance floor."

CHAPTER 10

Madelyn

The Vigil guys so often shared Logan's car that I hadn't realized Slade had one of his own until tonight. As he pulled the low-key but sporty blue Subaru up to the curb outside the club, his phone chimed with an incoming text. He pulled up the parking brake and checked the message. "Logan and Dexter are on their way. Not without a little grumbling from the boss about the reports we were supposed to deliver." He flashed a grin at me. "He'll get over it."

"I don't think I'm going to forget what I saw anytime soon," I said, pushing open the passenger door. "But I wouldn't mind getting distracted from it for an hour or two."

"I'll make that my new mission, then." Slade swooped around the car, incredibly nimble as always despite his prosthetic, and grasped my hand as he closed the door for me. "Would you like a drink first or to head right onto the dance floor, Piccolina?"

I glanced at the face of the club—the same place where we'd danced a couple of weeks ago while the Vigil had been meeting up with contacts trying to track down my stolen car. Thumping bass emanated through the wall, making me want to sway on my feet. I remembered far too clearly my jolt of embarrassment last time when I'd ordered a cocktail and then realized the rest of the guys were sticking to soft drinks in solidarity with Logan, who wasn't supposed to drink given his transplanted liver and the medication he was on.

They automatically avoided excluding each other—that was real friendship. Slade hadn't hesitated for a second about inviting the other guys to join us here, even though he could have had me all to himself and I'd just admitted that something might be sparking between me and Logan.

Maybe playing the field didn't have to be so hard after all. I just wouldn't look ahead to the point when I might have to choose between the various guys who'd appealed to my heart.

"Let's dance," I said. "My nerves are still jumping. I need to burn off some of that energy."

"Dancing it is!"

He practically dragged me through the door with an enthusiasm that had me laughing. Slade grinned back at me and swept me onto the dance floor amid the many other patrons who'd poured into the club this late in the evening. He spun me around and then pulled me to him, still holding my hand while he set his other on my waist. When he kept the steps to a simple shuffle, I had no trouble at all keeping up.

We moved with the beat, Slade turning us here and tossing me into a little dip there, because of course he couldn't resist showing off. The brief bursts of exhilaration kept the smile on my lips and washed away the worst of my inner turmoil over the discovery we'd made tonight.

Whatever had happened to Dad, it'd happened twelve years ago. Taking a moment to let the new knowledge sink in wasn't going to hurt anything. It was a relief to let go and just have fun with Slade, knowing that nothing too intense could happen here in the middle of a crowded dance floor. There was no pressure, no expectations other than that we enjoy ourselves.

Slade's dark eyes glinted slyly as he spun me around again. He brought me back to his chest in time with the music and slid his hand down to my hip to guide my movements to match his. We swayed together, closer than before, but before the heat kindling between us could overwhelm me, he stepped wide and showed off a more complicated series of footwork.

I hesitated, afraid of tripping over my own feet. "I don't think I can keep up with that."

Slade leaned closer and murmured in my ear. "Sure you can, Piccolina. Just follow my lead. I'll make sure you don't stumble too badly."

I wished he could make that promise carry all the way through the rest of my life. But I wasn't letting myself think about that right now. I just nodded and matched his moves as well as I could.

He slowed down a little so I could see exactly how he was setting his feet and swiveling his hips. As I caught on to the pattern and settled into the rhythm, he gradually picked up the pace again. When I wobbled, he covered for me with a sudden dip or flourish, one time whirling both of us around until I was giggling breathlessly.

When we fell back into the regular steps and he shot me a broad smile, a rush of affection filled my chest. He was doing everything he could to help me through this crazy situation, even if there wasn't anything more in it for him than a dance. There was so much more to him than the flirty jokester he presented himself as. How could he have thought I'd throw what we'd found together away just because Logan had decided to stop being such an asshole?

I squeezed his hand, letting myself sway closer to him for a moment. "Thank you for suggesting this. It was exactly what I needed."

Something softened in his eyes, showing so much fondness that my heart skipped a beat. "You have no idea how glad I am to hear that."

He teased his hand up and down my side, and suddenly I thought we might get up to a little more than just dancing, crowded club or not. But then his gaze jerked away from my face, looking at someone behind me just as fingers tapped on my shoulder.

I felt Logan's looming presence before I turned to see him, a wisp of his scent washing over me. "Mind if I cut in?" he asked, his gaze fixed on me.

I glanced back at Slade, not sure how he'd respond to his friend stealing me away, but the other guy just leaned in and gave me a quick peck on the cheek. "It wouldn't be any fair if I invited him along and didn't share you," he said in a teasing tone, and twirled me toward Logan.

My stepbrother caught me with both hands on my waist. I couldn't find anywhere to put my own hands that didn't feel totally awkward other than resting them on his shoulders. My chest brushed against the solid planes of muscle in front of me, and all at once I didn't know where to look either.

Logan peered down at me as we fell into a basic two-step in time with the beat, his expression unreadable. "How are you doing?"

I grimaced, knowing he was referring to the discovery at the seafood market. "No shop talk here at the club. Ask me tomorrow."

"I guess I can hang up my detective cap for one night, just for you." He turned us in a slow circle, much less flamboyant than Slade's preferred style but no less seductive. One hand eased down to my hip, tugging me a little closer, and I had to resist the urge to melt right into his brawny frame. "We don't need to talk at all."

His thumb moved in rhythmic circles over my hip as his fingers trailed down to my thigh. His other hand slipped around me to hold me by the small of my back. His head bowed next to mine, hot breath spilling down the side of my neck. A giddy shiver rippled through my body.

I couldn't help thinking back to the only other night we'd gotten as close as this—and closer still. To how good it'd felt being wrapped in his embrace, consumed by his passion. A pulsing ache woke up low in my belly, urging me toward him.

As if he sensed my growing desire, Logan nudged me even closer up against him. He eased one leg between mine so we were interlocked as we swayed and shuffled together on the dance floor. His hand stroked right over my ass, and I had to swallow a gasp. His head dipped lower, his lips brushing the crook of my jaw.

Oh, God, I was going to unravel right here in the middle of all these strangers. I was practically a puddle of longing already. My body was outright throbbing to press right into him, to rub up against him in the dirtiest of dances. There were other couples around us doing the same thing. We wouldn't even stand out.

But was I really ready for where that kind of dance would lead next? I'd only just started accepting Logan back into my life as someone I could count on. The last thing I wanted was to rush headlong into another hookup.

At least, that was the last thing my brain wanted. The rest of me was undeniably on board. Even the smallest caresses of his fingers electrified me, making my breath catch. I glanced up at him and was pinned by his eyes, searing with intensity. My skin crackled with the heat.

My lungs clenched up. This wasn't what I'd come here for. I'd wanted a momentary escape, not to feel trapped by urges I could hardly contain. I didn't totally like how out of control I felt after just a couple of songs in Logan's arms.

When the music shifted to a new track, I yanked myself away from him. "I—I need to take a breather," I said, hoping my voice sounded reasonably normal.

Disappointment flickered across my stepbrother's face and then vanished with his nod. "I'll be right here if you want to pick up where we left off," he said, and there was no denying the promise in those words.

I walked away from him on wobbly legs and made my way over to the bar. As I emerged from the crowd, I spotted Dexter perched on one of the stools on his own. He was leaning back against the counter with a soda by his propped elbow, scanning the crowd with a casually thoughtful air. When he noticed me coming over, he dipped his head to me with a slight creasing of his forehead that suggested he was concerned.

Guilt pinched my stomach. Had he really come along expecting to just sit on the sidelines while his friends danced with me? He'd always been there when I'd needed him, watching over me along with the others in his more subdued but no less dedicated way.

And even though his green eyes veered away from me after the first moment, even though I knew he'd have tensed up if I'd so much as touched his arm, I couldn't deny the spark of attraction that flared in me seeing his glossy dark curls and his pale face lit up by the shifting club lights. He might not have been as buff as Logan or Slade, but the lean muscles that flexed in his forearms beneath the rolled-up sleeves of his shirt showed he wasn't any slouch either.

He fought alongside his friends. He took on all the same bad guys. He'd stood up for me and defended me, even to Logan.

I didn't like seeing him left on his own as if he wasn't as important as them.

Without letting myself reconsider the impulse, I walked right up to him and rested my hand next to his arm without touching it. "It's your turn."

Dexter blinked, his eyes darting back to meet mine. "What?"

"To dance." I motioned him toward the dance floor. "Come on. I'm sure you can manage at least a few moves."

His mouth slanted crookedly. "I'm not really much of a dancer."

I gave him a reassuring smile. "Hey, neither am I, so I won't be judging. But we might as well make full use of the club while we're here, right?"

He held my gaze for a few beats longer than usual, as if trying to read my intentions through my eyes. Something shifted in his expression, and for a second I thought he was going to refuse me. Then he put on a determined face and pushed himself to his feet.

"Yeah. Sure. I can do that."

He sounded like he was psyching himself up as much as agreeing with me, but he did walk with me into the crowd. I stopped in a fairly open patch of floor and shimmied with the music as Dexter joined me. He positioned himself across from me and bobbed with the music, shifting his weight from one foot to the other and swaying his arms to the beat.

I resisted the urge to give him a playful swat, knowing he probably wouldn't appreciate the physical contact. "Look at you. You've got this. As soon as you're warmed up, you'll be putting me to shame."

He caught my gaze just for an instant. "I saw you with Slade. I don't think anyone would be criticizing your abilities. I'll just stick to the basic school-dance shuffle."

I raised my eyebrows at him. "I don't remember seeing you at the dances back in high school."

"I stayed near the back," he said, his tone even but dry. "One of the biggest puzzles I've ever encountered is why anyone wants to go to those things."

A laugh tumbled out of me. "I guess we were all pretty awkward back then. But if you've got awkward people all around you, then it doesn't matter so much." On the other hand, it must have been particularly uncomfortable for a guy who didn't like being touched having his classmates bumping into him all over the place in the crowded gymnasium.

Maybe I shouldn't have dragged him over here. I opened my mouth, about to thank him for humoring me and tell him he could go back to the bar if he wanted, but Dexter cocked his head, glancing at something beyond me.

"It could be the biggest mystery is why drinking and dancing go together so often when the former seems to make the latter a lot more difficult."

I followed his gaze to see a gaggle of college girls stumbling and colliding with each other as they tried to keep up a rhythm while clutching their mostly empty glasses. He did have a point.

"I guess it's about finding the right balance where you're relaxed enough to be less nervous without outright losing your balance," I suggested.

Dexter's mouth twitched with a quiet smile. His gaze veered in another direction, toward a couple who were groping each other more than they were doing anything that could be called dancing. His voice came out totally deadpan. "Although it does seem like in some cases, ending up tipped over is the goal."

I couldn't hold back a snort of amusement even as my cheeks flushed at his insinuation. Somehow I hadn't really thought that Dexter would pay much attention to people's sexual exploits, but it wasn't as if that couple was difficult to notice. And just because he was awkward didn't mean he had no inclinations of his own. I hadn't realized he could be this much fun just to talk with either.

Were there any circumstances when he didn't mind physical contact? What would it be like to kiss that smart mouth and feel him respond not by recoiling but with equal desire?

Unexpected heat rushed through my veins at the thought. I wanted to discover the answer to that question more than I'd have imagined.

A second later, I could have smacked myself. What was going on with me that I was fantasizing about yet another guy, as if three potential boyfriends wasn't enough? I couldn't even blame it on a dry spell, considering I'd gotten it on with Slade in epic fashion less than a week ago.

I'd hoped that letting loose here at the club would help me get away from my problems, and instead I was just making new ones for myself.

I would have felt like a jerk ditching Dexter out of the blue after encouraging him to join me, but to my relief, the song was just winding down. I shot him another smile, hoping he couldn't read the more salacious thoughts that'd been passing through my mind on my face. "Thanks for keeping me company. I think I'm going to go out front just for a minute to get some fresh air."

Slade or Logan might have insisted on following me out, but Dexter simply nodded, giving me the space I was looking for. We wove through the crowd back to the bar, and I felt him watching me as I made my way along the edge of the dance floor to the front door. He might not have felt the need to directly stand guard, but he was still equally determined to catch any potential threats.

As I stepped outside, the cool night air washed over me, putting a damper on my mess of desires. It was tainted with a chemical smell from the cigarettes of the patrons who'd ducked outside for a quick smoke. Wrinkling my nose, I wandered a little farther down the street away from them to where I could fill my lungs without the unpleasant prickling.

I stopped outside a shop that was closed for the night and leaned against its wall, taking several slow breaths. As my pulse evened out, movement on the other side of the road caught my eye.

A few storefronts down, a couple of figures were standing on the sidewalk next to the cars parked there. One of them I didn't recognize, but the other I knew in an instant even though he had his back to me.

I'd recognize Beckett's sandy blond hair and confident stance anywhere. He'd leaned toward the man he was talking to, something about his posture more intimidating than I'd ever seen it around me. His voice was so low I didn't catch any of the words. But if I'd had any doubt about it being Beckett, he turned his head briefly to glance down the street, giving me a clear view of his profile with its sharply regal nose. His frown drove home that whatever was going on, he was taking it seriously.

He made a brusque gesture, and the man nodded swiftly, his jaw twitching nervously. Beckett clapped him on the shoulder in a motion that looked more imperious than friendly and walked around the nearest car to get into the driver's seat. The engine thrummed. He pulled smoothly away from the curb and drove off while the guy he'd been talking to hustled away on foot.

A frown of my own crossed my lips as I tried to fit what I'd just seen with the things I knew about Beckett. What kind of real estate developer did deals with random men on the street in the middle of the night?

And if it hadn't been business, what in the world had that encounter been about?

CHAPTER 11

Madelyn

As Logan drove toward the seafood market, I peered at the screenshot Dexter had sent all of us, taken from the video footage through the cameras the guys had set up in the back alley. The man in the image was standing next to a plain black sedan in the late afternoon sunlight. He'd have been easy to pick out in a crowd with his red hair and full beard.

"How often has he been coming by the market?" I asked.

"Every other day over the past week," Dexter said automatically. "Always around the same time. He parks by the back door, the manager comes to the doorway, they talk for five minutes or so, and then he leaves again."

"But we have no idea what they're talking about."

"You can't get much from a camera small enough to hide it

properly," Logan said from the driver's seat. "Based on their body language, I don't think they want anyone overhearing anyway."

Slade hummed to himself. "It definitely doesn't look like any kind of official store business. He never brings anything or takes anything away. And I'd say the manager looks a little scared of him."

Dexter nodded. "I get that impression too."

I dragged in a breath. "And you have no idea who he is?"

"Nope," Logan said, a hint of frustration coming into his voice. "The car is registered to a woman's name, so that's obviously not the guy dropping by. I haven't been able to match his image to any records involving the store."

"Which makes it even more likely that he's part of something unofficial," Slade put in, clicking his cinnamon candy against his teeth. A whiff of its scent drifted over to me. "So we see where he goes from here and what we can find out from that."

He made it sound so simple, but I had to hold myself back from squirming on the firm seat. The man we were planning to tail might be wrapped up in Dad's murder. For all we knew, he was responsible for that murder. A mix of fear and impatience squeezed around my gut.

Now that I was sure Dad really had been killed in cold blood, I desperately wanted to understand why. But I couldn't help being nervous about where getting those answers might lead us after seeing how violent our last encounter with people connected to the case had gotten.

My phone let out a ping, and I pulled it from my pocket to find a message from Summer. *Daily check in. I'm off work, about to exfoliate, shave, and do a face mask. Maybe light a candle for dramatic effect. How are you treating yourself today?*

I smiled at her optimistic way of recovering after a hard week. Maybe I needed to look into some self-care tips to ease my stress. *I think tonight's going to be all about writing up assignments, unfortunately.*

Her response came immediately. *Boring. Wyd now?*

I hated lying to her, but I couldn't exactly give her the full truth. I could only imagine how she'd react if she found out what I'd gotten into and what I believed about my dad now. That wasn't the kind of revelation you dropped on someone in a text conversation.

But as much as I dreaded her response, I didn't want to completely fabricate my answer. I hesitated and then typed out, *Hanging out with the guys rn.*

When the next response took a longer time coming, I could far too easily picture Summer scowling at her phone.

The guys? As in Logan and his friends? I thought you already found your car.

I groped for an explanation I could give her that might divert a little of the criticism she'd make. *We did. But I'm helping them out with some other things. It's given me something to do other than study. And I found out some things about Logan that prove he's not a total jerk after all.*

Oh, yeah? Do tell.

The next time we see each other in person, I'll spill. I promise.

I could almost hear my best friend's huff of disappointment. *I'm going to hold you to that. No fair leaving a girl hanging. You watch yourself around him, all right?*

I'm being careful.

You'd better be. If that asshole hurts you again, I'm going to have to come down there with a baseball bat and lay down the law.

I might have laughed if the idea of someone beating Logan up hadn't felt far too close for comfort after the things I'd learned about his recent pastimes. *Don't worry*, I assured her. *It won't come to that. I won't let it.*

I hoped that much, at least, was true.

As I put away my phone, Logan pulled the car up to the sidewalk just before we reached the market. He parked, and we settled in to wait. We'd timed it well. It was only a few minutes before the black sedan cruised past us and turned into the alley.

Logan leaned over to look at the feed he'd set up on the laptop Slade was holding. "Looks like he's doing his typical routine. Just a little chat with the manager. Hopefully he'll make this stop quick."

"Have you seen any signs that he's associated with the gang that stole my car and the trinket box?" I asked.

He shook his head. "I checked that out too, but nothing I could dig up connects them."

Slade glanced back at me with a swift smile. "We'll figure out his deal, Maddie. We haven't met a challenge we couldn't tackle yet." His gaze darted back to the screen. "I think they're wrapping things up."

A minute later, the red-haired man had gotten back into his car. As we waited for it to emerge from the alley, Logan started the engine. The moment he spotted the sedan, he eased into traffic, letting a couple of cars get between us and our target so it wasn't too obvious we were following him.

We drove onward through the lengthening shadows cast by the sinking sun. The sedan took a few turns, and Logan followed at a leisurely pace, letting the guy pull a little farther ahead of us. The rest of us sat braced on our seats, watching closely for what our target might do next.

Finally, the sedan pulled into a plaza with a simple but tidy strip mall along one end. As our target parked outside one of the businesses, Logan pulled into a parking spot at the far end of the lot as if we'd come to do some other shopping.

The red-haired man got out and strode straight into a building that held a sign saying *Hartshorn & Associates Accounting*. My forehead furrowed. "He's going… to get his taxes done?"

"It's a little late for that," Logan said, and I guessed he'd know, considering how caught up his dad got in tax season at his job. "Any business can be a front for criminal activities. The more innocuous the better, really."

It was difficult to picture hardened criminals hanging out in an accountant's office. I shifted on my seat, studying the white-washed front of the building and its darkened window. Logan grabbed the laptop from Slade and started typing, presumably searching for more information on the business.

"Hey," Slade said. "He's coming back out."

Our target had stepped through the doorway, a couple of other men joining him. As they stood in a cluster on the walkway outside the office, my attention landed on the bulge at the back of the nearest guy's jeans, partly hidden by his shirt. I stiffened. "Does that guy have…?"

I didn't want to finish the sentence, but Dexter did it for me. "That's a gun," he confirmed matter-of-factly.

Slade guffawed. "Somehow I don't think *that* dude's any kind of accountant."

My fingers curled over the edge of the seat, my heart thudding painfully fast. "We need to know what they're talking about. It's got to be something to do with whatever criminal stuff he's involved in, which could be the same stuff the market is involved in too." And therefore tied to the reasons for Dad's murder.

"I can't drive right over there," Logan said. "It'd be too obvious."

But with every passing second, we were losing our chance to hear critical information. I hesitated and then blurted out, "I'll walk over there and listen in. I won't get too close."

As I reached for the door handle, Logan jerked around. "Absolutely fucking not," he barked.

Slade's expression had tightened. "Maddie, I don't think that's a good idea."

Only Dexter looked at me calmly, waiting for me to make my argument.

I stared back at the other two. "I'm the best person to do it. You three have been running around hassling criminals all over town for more than two years now, right? You could get recognized again. But no one has any reason to notice me. Just a clueless college girl doing a little window shopping." I raised my chin toward the clothing shop next to the accounting office.

"I can't let you do this alone," Logan growled, but I cut off any further argument.

"You can, and you will," I said firmly. "Now shut up or you'll blow my cover." Then I pushed the door open so he couldn't protest any more without risking our targets hearing him.

My stepbrother glowered at me as I strolled away from the car, but he didn't chase me down, so he couldn't think I was in *that* much danger. He had to know I was right. I was the best possible option to run this maneuver.

Even if I was just as terrified as I was exhilarated to be doing it.

A few other people ambled along the walkway, checking out the shops, going in and coming out again. I matched their pace, doing my best not to give away how eager I was to get close enough to eavesdrop.

I was really doing this. I was a full member of the Vigil now, a key component in the investigation that would bring Dad's murderer to justice if we could see it through. The knowledge sent a little thrill through me despite my nerves.

When I reached the shops, I peered through each of the windows in turn, drawing closer and closer to the three men. They were speaking in lowered voices, quieting down completely whenever anyone walked right by them. I stopped at the clothing store, tipping my head to the side as if contemplating the summer dress on the mannequin in the window.

"...doesn't want us hanging around in there anymore," the guy with the gun was saying in a gruff voice.

"It doesn't matter," the redhead replied. "The deal's already done."

"Not until the payout arrives. They're taking their sweet time."

"Oh, it'll come, or they'll regret it."

They dropped their voices even lower, and I couldn't make out their next words. I sidled even closer, still gazing at the window, but studying their reflections rather than the clothes on the other side. My mouth had gone dry.

Before I could get close enough to hear them again, the third guy muttered something with a hint of a snarl—and jerked his finger across his neck in a brief but unmistakable throat-slitting gesture.

My skin went cold. They were talking about killing someone else.

The next thing I knew, the three men broke apart. One of them went back into the accounting office, another strode toward the far end of the strip mall, and the redhead got back into his sedan. My pulse stuttered at the thought that we should be following him again, but there was no way I could sprint back to Logan's car in time without drawing way too much attention to myself.

I meandered back in the direction I'd come, only picking up my pace after the car had pulled out of the plaza. Then I hurried the rest of the way to the car, my thoughts whirling in my head.

I had no idea what deal the men had been discussing, but I was sure of one thing. Whatever business the three of them were wrapped up in, it was both serious and deadly.

CHAPTER 12

Beckett

"Everything about the transaction went smoothly?" I checked, leaning back in my leather office chair with my phone to my ear.

Lana, my family's main administrative contact for the less savory parts of our business, made a noise of agreement. "In spite of the initial squabbling, when push came to shove, they coughed up what they needed to without a fight. I think the earlier pressure you put on them did the trick. If they get out of line again, you'll be the first to know."

"Perfect, thank you. I'll let my dad know—I'm sure he'll be pleased too."

I hung up and glanced at the door to my small office in the family home—the one I'd been using since I'd returned to the fold four years ago ready to take a real place in the business. The truth was, I didn't know exactly what response I'd get from Dad, if much at all. But he was still the Storm while I was just the heir to the metaphorical throne, and I'd never want him to feel I was shutting him out of the day-to-day happenings of our work. Even if it wasn't clear how much he really cared about those happenings anymore.

That was the last situation I'd needed to resolve today before I could take some sort of break, although really the job was 24-7 if anything urgent came up. I pushed to my feet and headed down the hall to our expansive house's real office area, three times larger than the room I'd claimed for myself.

I knocked on the door in my usual gesture of respect and opened it at Dad's bland, "Come in."

I found him sitting behind his huge maple desk, leaning his broad body back with his laptop poised on his thighs. He tapped a few more keys before setting it on his desk and focusing his gaze on me.

"I thought you'd want to know that the problem with the appliance store was sorted out without any hitches," I said quickly. "We got everything they owed us, and they didn't make any more fuss about it. Lana thinks they'll be okay from here on."

Dad hummed with an approving nod, but his expression didn't shift from its mildly weary expression. His gaze drifted away from me as if my news didn't interest him all that much. "I'm glad to hear it. You handled that conflict well."

The praise would have warmed me more if he hadn't sounded so mechanical about it. My chest tightened even as I put on a smile—the business smile I used with clients, not the kind of smile I'd have liked to be able to aim at my father.

Nothing had really been the same since I'd come back four years ago… and I knew that was mostly my fault. Three years before that, I'd made a decision that'd shaken his faith in me and the business.

I couldn't regret what I'd done. After the catastrophe we'd

already gotten into in Paradise Bend, the actions I'd taken had been the only way I'd seen to get us out of the mess while protecting Dad from the worst possible fallout. Given how things had gone afterward, it seemed like I'd been right, even with the limited experience I'd had at sixteen years old.

But Dad was never going to forget that I'd turned to the people he'd seen as targets at best and enemies at worst. That I'd spent three years as their theoretical hostage before I'd come back to him. He couldn't have understood that the leaders of the gangs I'd ended up allying with had been better friends to me than anyone I'd been able to associate with under his roof and that they'd treated me like a respected apprentice, not a foe.

It was Dad's teachings that had given me the foundations I used to run much of our empire now, but I had to give a lot of credit for everything I'd built on those foundations to the people back in Paradise Bend.

I just wished my approach hadn't taken such a toll on Dad. His typical suits and loafers gave him the same professional appearance as always, but I could see how the strain had affected him in the thinning of his gray hair and the stress lines sunk into his increasingly jowly face. Yeah, he was getting older like anyone did, but he looked like he'd aged twenty years in the last seven.

I had no idea how to rekindle his enthusiasm for the job or for whatever familial relationship we had left.

"Everything else I had on my plate has been taken care of too," I went on. "If there's anything you feel needs extra care—"

Dad waved his hand dismissively. "No, no, I'm sure it's all fine. I've passed a few things on to Lana that she might bring to you for confirmation if my schedule gets too full."

"Of course. Well… I'll see you later."

He inclined his head, looking at me again only briefly, and I ducked out of his office. We rarely even ate together despite living in the same house. I probably wouldn't see him again other than a brief passing in the hall until the next time I gave him an update.

I closed my eyes for a moment and shook off the lingering tension in my gut. It was what it was. I'd rather have preserved our family legacy and Dad's life than acted as an obedient lapdog going on with his increasingly crazy scheme for expansion. We'd found plenty of other ways to grow the business since then that hadn't involved psychopaths or large-scale bloodshed. I'd just added a new nightclub in Chicago to our holdings last week.

The thought of the club reminded me of the place we owned right here in our home city. I'd popped in there the other night and immediately spotted Maddie on the dance floor, getting close with one and then another of those guys she'd been hanging out with. The guys who'd been poking around more than I liked into the city's black market activities.

The guys who'd all looked so eager to get their hands on her that it made my teeth grit to remember it.

Walking down the hall and away from my uncomfortable feelings about Dad, I decided it was time to focus on other relationships I wanted to establish. I needed to see Maddie again. I needed to make a real claim on her affection before any of those men horned their way in. And just this morning, I'd come across the perfect opportunity.

I paused on the second floor landing, pulling out my phone and tapping her number in my contacts.

Do you have plans tonight? I asked, licking my bottom lip. *Because I found something that I think you'd enjoy.*

I had no idea what she was up to right now, but she replied just a minute later. *Give me a time and place, and I'll be there.*

A smile crossed my face, this one not at all forced. Whatever she felt about those other guys, she wanted me at least as much. I just had to make sure it stayed that way, because the more time I spent around Madelyn Silver, the more I wanted to see even more of her.

Maddie was totally absorbed by the displays around us—and *I* was totally absorbed by her reaction. Her eyes widened and her lips parted as she took in the special exhibit's installations about new advances in human life sciences: fresh discoveries about aging and the functioning of the brain, records broken involving strength and endurance, and, as I was sure excited her the most, revolutionary medical treatments that'd been recently developed. She was so caught up, it was a wonder she managed not to walk into any of the other visitors.

"I had no idea this was going on," she said, breathless in a way that sent a jolt of attraction straight to my groin. "I'm so glad you heard about it."

I grinned at her. "I saw a poster and immediately knew it'd be up your alley."

She tore her gaze away from the explanation for the interactive display in front of us long enough to raise her eyebrows at me. "And you figured you'd impress me by bringing me, huh?"

Her tone was so teasing it didn't rankle me at all. I kept smiling, trailing my fingers down her spine to the small of her back and feeling a flicker of triumph when she stepped closer to me to welcome the touch. "Mostly I just love seeing you in your element. But if I *have* managed to impress you, then that's an excellent side benefit."

She laughed and moved on to the next fixture, gazing avidly at it. The sparkle in her eyes and the eager flush in her cheeks made me want to drag her off into a corner and devour her in all the best ways, but that would defeat the purpose of this part of the date.

Hopefully we could get to the devouring part later, somewhere I could show her just how much I appreciated *all* of her assets.

There was something to be said for a woman who had just as much to admire in her mind as her body. It'd been obvious to me from the start that Maddie wasn't any slouch when it came to smarts, but the ease with which she'd filled me in on some of the more complex implications of the exhibit's offerings had raised my estimations even more. No doubt she'd be graduating at the top of her class once she got to medical school.

And now she knew just how much I supported that side of her.

When we reached the last display, she let out a satisfied sigh. I took her hand, and she twined her fingers with mine automatically.

"If there's anything you want a second look at, we can always double back," I said.

She considered and then shook her head. "No, I think I caught everything on the first pass. It is getting kind of late."

"I'm happy to stay as long as you're enjoying yourself."

She beamed at me. "Thank you. But I did want to check out the statues in the museum's front courtyard too."

I tugged her toward the entrance. "As the doctor-to-be desires."

She laughed again and stepped even closer to me as I slid my arm right around her waist. We walked down the front steps into a paved courtyard that stretched half a block from the museum's doors, holding several looming modern art sculptures made of metal and concrete. I peered up at them, not totally understanding what impression the artists had been going for, but appreciating the effort that'd gone into them all the same.

A damp breeze washed over us through the night, and the clouds hazed by the glow of the city lights rumbled overhead. Madelyn's gaze flicked upward. "That sounded ominous."

"Do you want to hurry back to my car?" I asked. The exhibition had been popular enough that I'd had to park a few blocks away.

As Maddie hesitated, more thunder boomed, and a couple of fat droplets hit my forehead. Maddie only had time to let out a yelp before it seemed as if the entire sky opened up to pour its contents down on us.

There was no time to sprint all the way to the car. I glanced around and yanked Maddie with me under the shelter of a statue that arched over like a broad, rippled rainbow.

In even that short time, the deluge drenched me. As the rain cascaded down in a sheet on either side of the arch, I swiped my dripping hair back from my eyes and caught Maddie's gaze. Only the thinnest glow from the nearby security lamps seeped through the downpour, just enough to show the glint in her blue eyes and the way her own hair was slicked to the sides of her head.

She glanced down at her soaked dress, plastered to her curves, and snickered. "This isn't how I saw this evening ending. How are we going to get to the car?"

"Usually a storm like this doesn't last too long. We can try waiting it out under here."

A shiver ran through her body, and I moved closer, slipping my arm around her again. She glanced up at me through her damp eyelashes. Her voice came out lower with a slight sultry note that made me totally forget my own chill. "Are you going to keep me warm?"

"It would be my pleasure," I murmured, bringing my other hand to her jaw, and leaned in for a kiss.

This wasn't just pleasure—this was paradise. She kissed me back with the same passion that was burning in me, her soft lips sliding against mine, her arms looping around my neck. I tipped my head to deepen the kiss and teased my tongue across the seam of her lips to coax them apart. The moment she welcomed me in, I delved inside her mouth to tangle my tongue with hers.

The little sound that worked from her throat disintegrated my last shred of self-control. I nudged her up against the side of the arch, pressing my body against hers, and she clutched me tighter. The rain still cascading over both sides of the statue might as well have formed walls cutting us off from the rest of the world in our own private room.

No one could see us. We could get up to whatever we wanted in this pocket of solitude. And I knew exactly what I wanted from this woman.

My dick was already throbbing in my pants. I stroked my hand over Maddie's breast, and she whimpered against my mouth. I drank in the sound and then charted a path across her cheek to the crook of her jaw before nibbling my way down her neck. At her gasp, I nipped a little harder.

Her hips swayed against mine. With a growl I couldn't contain, I dropped my hand to her thigh and molded her against me. At the press of my groin against hers, her breath stuttered even though there were still several layers of fabric between us.

Way too many layers. A fire lit in me to have her right here, right now. That would be a first time to remember, wouldn't it? Just imagining plunging into her liquid heat sent a tremor of molten desire through my veins.

"Fuck, Maddie," I murmured by her ear. "I want you so damn bad."

I had a condom in my back pocket. I'd thought we might make use of it elsewhere, but if she was game…

I trailed my fingers down her leg to the hem of her dress and tucked them beneath it. As I caressed her thigh skin to skin, she yanked my mouth back to hers. Her body swayed against mine with every sign of being just as eager.

But when my hand reached the waist of her panties, ready to hook over it and drag them down, a sudden tension stiffened her body. I paused, pulling back far enough to meet her eyes again in the dimness. I wasn't going to push her past the point of comfort. Her desires mattered just as much as mine did, no matter how much I was aching for her.

"I'm sorry," she whispered.

"There's nothing to apologize for," I said. "If we're moving too fast—"

"It's not exactly that. I want you too." She hesitated, worrying at her lower lip. Her expression firmed with resolve. "I just want to be honest with you. I—I'm not just seeing you. I've been… dating, or something, at least one other guy. Which maybe you don't care about, I don't know, but *I'm* not used to the whole multiple partners, playing the field kind of thing. I'm still figuring out how I want to handle it."

I found myself immediately calculating which of the three men she'd been hanging around with might have staked enough of a claim to be considered a *partner* already and then tamped down my instinctive jealousy. She considered *me* a partner too, apparently. That was the most important thing.

If the other guys were worthy of her, then she deserved them too. I wouldn't fight about it. If they weren't… Well, we'd have a fight on our hands then, but I'd deal with them myself.

"*At least* one?" I repeated, torn between curiosity and possessiveness.

"Definitely one," she admitted. "And another where something might happen but hasn't exactly yet. At least not recently." She let out a huff of frustration and hung her head. "Sorry. Apparently my romantic life is a total mess right now."

Had I made her feel embarrassed by her situation? A flash of concern seared away my lingering jealousy.

"Hey," I said, cupping her cheek to lift her gaze back to mine. "I don't think there's anything strange about what you just told me or about being into more than one guy. I actually—some of my best friends are in a very committed joint relationship. One woman and four men, and they make it work. I've seen how happy they are. They've even done an unofficial marriage ceremony, and now they've got a couple of kids."

Maddie blinked at me. "Wow. I never even thought—to take it that far…"

I shrugged. "Why not, if that's what your heart wants? My point is, I'm not going to judge you. I'd even support you." The corner of my mouth quirked upward. "Don't get me wrong—I'd love to have you all for myself. But if you aren't willing to let these other guys go, that's not a dealbreaker. I'd rather share you than lose you, no question about it."

"Oh," she said, the breathlessness coming back into her voice. The excitement lighting in her eyes now had nothing to do with intellectual curiosity. I'd just opened up possibilities to her that she'd clearly never imagined before. "I'm not sure what *they* would think about the whole thing."

I'd certainly like to find that out for myself. I smiled at her, stroking my thumb over her cheek. "Since I'm the one the most familiar with those kinds of relationships, I could always come around and talk with them to clear the air and figure out where we all stand." And whether they did actually deserve a real place in this woman's life.

Maddie's brow knit, but only for a moment. "That might actually be good. I have no idea how they'd react, but I guess I have to find out sometime."

"Exactly," I said, anticipation tickling through me. "Better to get it all out in the open and let the chips fall as they may."

CHAPTER 13

Madelyn

The building didn't look particularly ominous or important from the outside, just a four-story concrete office building, its pale gray walls gone dingy with age. As Logan parked his car down the street from it, I glanced at him from the back seat. "Are you sure it's worth checking out this place?"

He nodded, his eyes fixed on the building. "It took a lot of digging, but I finally found a connection between the seafood market and that accounting office. There's a very low-profile corporation that appears to own both of them, with a couple of steps in between to obscure that fact. And the people behind it wouldn't be going to those kinds of measures to hide the connection if they weren't up to something nefarious."

I could see his logic, even if I didn't totally understand how he'd unearthed that information with his computer skills. My heart thumped a little faster as I readied myself for the task ahead, the now-familiar mix of excitement and apprehension rushing through my chest. "How do we handle it from here?"

"It's got a lot of offices, some of which take regular clients," he said. "We should be able to walk in without anyone thinking it's strange. Once we're at the office for this corporation on the third floor, Dex will get us in there and we'll see what we've got."

Dexter swiveled in the front passenger seat to briefly catch my eye. "I brought a few of those small cameras so we can keep an eye on the business going forward too, just like we did with the seafood market."

"Okay. Sounds like a plan." I exhaled slowly in an attempt to ease my nerves and couldn't help wishing that Slade had joined us to lighten the mood with his playful attitude. But he had a major presentation this afternoon that the other guys didn't want to distract him from, and Logan had said it was better if we didn't bring too large a group anyway.

We'd arrived just after usual business hours, when some of the offices—including, we hoped, our target—would be closed for the day, but early enough that some of those that kept extended hours were still admitting clients. A woman pushed into the building ahead of us and walked past one of the doors on the first floor. We continued on to a stairwell that appeared to be the only way up in the old building and tramped up the steps to the third floor.

The guys set a swift pace without any sign of discomfort, but I was breathing a bit hard by the time we reached our destination. We peered through the window in the stairwell door and found the hall on the other side empty. Logan waited until Dexter had snapped a few photos with his phone and motioned for us to get moving.

The door of the office in question held no company sign or any other indication of what the business located there did. Logan rapped his knuckles against it, paused with his head cocked toward the door, and then nodded to Dexter when there was no sign of anyone on the other side.

With a nonchalant air that still impressed me, Dexter crouched down with the picks already in his hand and wiggled them into the lock so quickly and efficiently that the bolt clicked over just a few seconds later. He shot us a swift smile that lit up his green eyes and nudged the door open.

I tensed as we eased inside, but nothing horrifying or murderous met us beyond the threshold. If anything, the small room we stepped into was depressingly bare. It held a metal desk and a matching shelving unit, but no papers or books lay on either surface. No electronics either. Not so much as a pen or pencil. The walls were blank. It was hard to believe anyone had ever worked here, let alone recently.

"What the hell?" I murmured as the door tapped shut behind us. I walked to the desk and opened one of the drawers, but it was as empty as the rest of the space.

Dexter had his phone out recording our discovery, his expression unperturbed. "This is typical of large-scale organized crime," he said. "They create various layers of corporate fronts to disguise who's really responsible for their business activities. This office probably only exists so they have a real address to associate with a corporation that doesn't really do anything except shield the true players."

A shiver ran over my skin. "So we haven't really found out anything, then."

Logan scanned the shelves and peeked behind them in case anything had been left behind. "I wouldn't look at it that way. We have confirmation that something about this corporation is shady. I'll just have to dig deeper. And someone will come by every now and then to check on things like any mail arriving, since they won't want evidence that the place is vacant to pile up. If we can catch that person on camera, we'll have another lead."

Dexter frowned as he considered the sparseness of the room's furnishings. "I don't think there's anywhere I could hide one of our cameras in here without it getting noticed. There's just not enough… anything."

Logan grimaced. "No kidding. Why don't you check where the mailboxes are and see if there's any mail for the corporation in there right now? Maybe there'll be a good spot to place a camera around there or in the hall outside."

"I'll try both," Dexter said, and bobbed his head to us before ducking out of the room again.

Logan moved to the desk, checking each of the drawers and prodding their interiors, I guessed to test for hidden compartments. It hadn't even occurred to me to do that. But then, I was still very much a newbie to this world of vigilantism that the guys had settled into years ago.

That knowledge still gnawed at me. Tension prickled over my skin standing there next to Logan, alone together like we hadn't been since he'd brought me to his apartment several days ago. I couldn't just stand here silently.

"Have you done a lot of this already?" I asked, keeping my voice low so no one from the neighboring offices could hear. "Chasing down leads related to my dad?"

Logan sighed and propped himself against the edge of the desk, where he hadn't turned up anything. "Not much actual chasing. We spent a lot of time combing through his notes and trying to connect bits of information there to anything in the outside world that might explain what he was looking into and who he might have pissed off, but we didn't get very far with any of that. Or with what I was able to scrape from the hospital records during his time working there. His trinket box getting stolen along with your car was the first major development in a while."

I folded my arms over my chest with a fresh jab of frustration. "You didn't even know I had that box of his. You didn't talk to me about *any* of this, or we could have been figuring out the mystery years sooner."

Logan's jaw twitched, and he clenched it. "We've already talked about this. You know why I didn't want to drag you into this mess. I'm still not totally happy about having you involved *now*, I just know there's no way we could keep you out after what you've seen."

"Well, I'm glad you figured out at least that much," I muttered. "You wanted to keep me safe. You were afraid I'd be in danger. Right. But *you've* been putting yourself in so much danger without even having all the information you could have had if you'd talked to me."

"I was already prepared for the danger," Logan said. "I told you. We'd been getting deep into fixing problems for people before I ever stumbled on your dad's notes."

"You were prepared to deal with *murderers* back in high school?"

He paused and lowered his gaze before meeting my eyes again. "The first time we had to kill someone in self-defense—because they were trying to kill *us*—was around the middle of our junior year. There was a freshman whose family was getting hassled by people with gang connections, and we stepped in to resolve the situation… and it turned bloody. Dexter had to…" He trailed off, the anguish plain on his face.

My throat tightened. "I'm sorry."

"It is what it is," Logan said. "We'd already been getting into some scary stuff, so I'd already started keeping my distance from you, but that was when I knew there was no way I could pursue any kind of relationship with you. Or anyone else. Hell, I've barely maintained any kind of relationship with my *dad* since things got serious for the Vigil. I know how much it bugs him that I've shut him out so much, but I don't want him getting hurt either—and can you even imagine how he'd react if he knew what I've been doing?"

His head drooped, and every particle in my body cried out to go to him, to put my arms around him. He hadn't let himself turn to anyone except the two friends in the same mess with him for years now.

But I held myself still. "Maybe he'd understand. You've never tried, have you? You never tried with me until you didn't have a choice. But this was about *my* dad. I had a right to know—to decide how much danger I wanted to get into."

"You wouldn't have understood how dark it could get. Not if I just told you."

"You don't know that," I retorted. "And what about you? Getting into fights and all that—it's even worse for you than it would be for me because of the transplant. If you took a bad blow to the wrong place, that could trigger a rejection, couldn't it?"

I hadn't meant to bring up his liver transplant. Logan's hand fell to his abdomen where I knew the surgery scar marked his skin, and his expression hardened even more than before. He'd always hated anyone bringing up his possible weaknesses, even before he'd gotten into the hazardous activities he'd taken up with the Vigil.

"That doesn't matter," he snapped.

"How can you say that?" I demanded. "It matters to me—it matters to your dad. I'm sure it matters to Slade and Dexter too. It *should* matter to you."

Logan fixed me with a firm stare, but his gaze had gone more haunted than angry. "It matters, but not like that. I—I could have died back when I got sick. If someone else hadn't died at the right time for me to get that transplant, I *would* have died when I was seven years old. I've gotten fourteen more years on top of that already. I don't know why I got those years and someone else didn't. But I'm doing my best to make something good out of them, to help people who need it—to make sure that second chance means something."

His words wrenched at me. I'd had no idea he saw his recovery that way—as if he needed to prove something to justify the transplant he'd received.

I couldn't hold myself back any longer. I stepped toward him, and Logan caught me in his arms. Before I could decide whether I actually wanted to go this far, he'd captured my mouth with his.

His sharply masculine scent washed over me. We melded together as if we'd never been meant to do anything other than this. A twinge ran through my gut at the memory of how close I'd gotten to hooking up with Beckett just a couple of nights ago, but I'd been honest with both him and Logan about where I stood. And kissing Logan right now felt nothing but right, like coming home after a long journey away.

It could have been like this all along. But after the things he'd said, I found that the last bits of resentment in me had faded away. He'd been carrying this huge burden, so much more than I'd had any clue about, and he hadn't wanted to turn to *anyone*. It wasn't about me but about his fear of anyone he cared about getting hurt because of the decisions he'd made. I didn't know how to stay angry with him about that.

Logan drew back just far enough to rest his forehead against mine, his head bowed over me. He raised his hand to my cheek. "I feel so guilty," he murmured hoarsely. "I've tried to protect you for so long, and now you're in so deep I don't know if I can… but part of me is *happy* that you're in this mess with me. I'm so fucking sorry, Maddie."

I wasn't sure exactly what he was apologizing for, but I hugged him tightly all the same. "We're here now, whatever happened before—and I'm happy I understand now too. I'll be standing right beside you, no matter what we find out."

He let out a strangled sound, and his lips crashed into mine again. I clutched his shirt for dear life, caught up in the maelstrom of sensation—broken by the chime of Logan's phone.

He pulled away with a ragged inhalation and fumbled his phone out of his pocket. At the sight of the text on the screen, his eyes widened.

"Dex says someone's just headed up the stairs," he whispered. "He doesn't know what floor she's going to, but she could be coming here. We've got to get out before she makes it to this floor, just in case."

My pulse skittered. My gaze darted around the room, but we hadn't left any sign of our presence.

Logan pushed open the door and set it to lock once it closed again. We hustled out into the hallway. As we set off toward the stairwell, he grasped my hand. "Just act like we had a totally legitimate reason to be up here."

I slowed my pace to a stroll despite my impulse to race to the stairwell. That would definitely look suspicious. We ambled along, forcing smiles onto our faces that I hoped passed as reasonably relaxed.

We were just ten feet from the stairwell when the door opened and a woman in a trim business suit strode out, her heels tapping on the tile floor. Her gaze drifted over us without stopping, and she brushed by without a word.

It took every ounce of my willpower not to glance back after her and see which office she was heading toward. We walked on into the stairwell, my heart thumping twice as hard as before.

We hadn't gotten caught, but I had no idea whether the woman we'd just passed was a threat or not. Anyone in this city could be tied to Dad's murder, and I'd never know it.

CHAPTER 14

Madelyn

I tried to lounge in my chair in the Vigil office with the sort of casual air Slade had perfected, but I couldn't stop myself from fidgeting.

Any minute now, Beckett was going to arrive. I'd convinced the Vigil guys to meet up with him so the three guys I'd been seeing would know who each other was and maybe feel a little more at ease about the fact that I was dating all of them, but part of me wasn't sure it was such a good idea.

Well, if any of them freaked out about the situation, I guessed that would be useful information too.

Logan and Slade had wanted to have the meeting here in the office, presumably because they felt more comfortable on their home turf. I couldn't imagine them wanting to invite a guy who was a stranger to them into their apartment when even *I* had only been granted access once. But the same tension I felt hummed through the air between them too.

Slade had just popped a cinnamon candy and was clicking it between his teeth as he studied the book he had open on his lap. His pose might be casual, but I didn't think he'd turned a page in at least five minutes. Dexter wasn't quite as affected as the others, but his gaze had gotten twitchier since we'd settled in to wait.

And Logan was scowling at the laptop where theoretically he was working on an assignment for one of his classes.

He shut it with an abrupt thump and spun his chair toward me. "What do you know about this Beckett guy anyway?"

It was kind of a relief to talk about it instead of stewing in silence. "He's twenty-three and he works in his family's business, which involves real estate among other things. It seems like it's a pretty big and well-established company. He cares a lot about his work, and he likes that I'm passionate about my studies too. He's a good guy—he's always been considerate with me, and he appreciates my interests."

Logan's mouth tightened momentarily, maybe as he recalled that until recently *he* hadn't been all that considerate of my feelings. "What else?"

I held myself back from rolling my eyes. I didn't think he wanted a recap of how it felt to kiss Beckett or how tailored his suits appeared to be. "I've only gone out with him a few times. I don't have a detailed file of his life history. Anyway, some of that would be up to him to tell you, not me."

"You've gotten to know him well enough to have mentioned us to him," Slade pointed out.

"Yeah, because I'm trying to be honest with *everyone* about the fact that I'm not settling down with just one guy at the moment. You're important to me, and he's becoming important to me too, and I want to make sure that isn't going to be a problem."

Logan still looked skeptical. "And it was his idea to meet us?"

"Yes," I said firmly. "Beckett doesn't think there's anything wrong with me seeing him and you at the same time, and he thought you two might feel better about the situation if you got to know him a bit. Like I said, he's a good guy."

Logan made a noncommittal sound and exchanged a cryptic glance with Slade. Dexter appeared to be pretending none of this was even happening, peering at his phone as if it were the most fascinating item on the planet.

I narrowed my eyes at my stepbrother. "You need to at least be civil with him. If you decide you don't like him, I don't want to hear about it until after he's gone."

I didn't get to find out what Logan would have said in response to that demand, because just then a knock sounded on the door.

"It's open," Slade hollered automatically. "Come on in."

I tensed in my chair, but I should have known Beckett could take care of himself. He stepped inside, his gray eyes meeting mine for just a moment. As he shut the door behind him, he took in the room's other inhabitants. He was wearing a typical dress shirt and slacks that looked more expensive than anything I had in my college student wardrobe, his sandy hair neatly combed back, his stance loose but authoritative.

He nodded to the guys with a small but relaxed smile. "Hey. I'm glad you agreed to meet up with me. As I'm sure Maddie's already told you, I'm Beckett."

He stepped forward easily, extending his hand to Logan first as if he sensed who was the most domineering out of the three. Logan's gaze hardened, but he got to his feet and accepted the handshake. "Logan."

Slade raised his hand in a little wave from the chair he hadn't left. "Slade. And the quiet one in the back is Dexter."

Dexter studied Beckett for a moment with a shift of his phone that made me wonder if he'd taken a picture of the other guy. It'd figure.

I'd scrambled to my feet at Beckett's entrance. I went over to stand next to him, hesitating and then daring to bob up and give him a quick peck on the cheek. When I turned back to face the other guys, Logan's gaze was so searing you'd have thought he was trying to incinerate Beckett by sheer force of will.

"I'm still not totally sure why you wanted to see us so much," Logan said in a voice that wasn't outright hostile but definitely curt.

I glowered at him. "Logan."

Slade laughed. "No, I want to hear this guy's explanation too. If Beckett figures he can handle you, I'm sure talking to us will be a breeze."

Beckett arched an amused eyebrow at the implicit if teasing challenge. "I don't find Maddie all that difficult to handle. And if you appreciate her as much as I do, then I'm sure you can understand why I'd want to confirm that we're all on the same page."

A sharper glint came into Slade's eyes, his smirk stretching wider. "So you're here to ask permission to get it on with her?"

I turned my glower on him, my cheeks flushing, but Beckett simply chuckled. "I don't think I need your permission for that. I'm pretty sure Maddie can make her own decisions there. But I care a lot about her, so it makes me feel better to get a sense of who she's hanging out with when I'm not around. I figured that'd go both ways."

"And we're supposed to trust that you're good for her just because you stopped by to chat us up?" Logan asked.

Beckett cocked his head. "I'd think that'd be a better sign than if I wanted to lurk in the shadows, don't you? We're all interested in Maddie, and she's interested in all of us. As long as that's the case, I think it's good if we're comfortable with each other."

Slade leaned back in his chair. "Are we supposed to believe that you don't mind the competition at all?"

"I don't see it as a competition," Beckett said smoothly. "I think Maddie deserves every bit of devotion she can get. If you make her happy, of course I wouldn't want to take that away from her. Why wouldn't you want her to be as content as possible, even if that means she's seeing more than one man?"

Logan fixed him with a hard stare. "That would mean assuming you *are* going to make her happy. I don't think showing up here and giving a little speech about it proves anything."

A sigh tumbled out of me. But before I could chide Logan for not giving this meeting more of a shot, Beckett kept going without a hint of offense. "That's understandable. I guess we could find out."

My gaze flicked back to him with a flash of confusion.

Slade's eyebrows drew together, echoing my response. "What do you mean?"

Beckett gave me a measured glance, setting his hand on my back with a reassuring stroke of his thumb as if to tell me he'd defer to any interruption I made. Then he shifted his attention back to the guys. "Maybe we can't determine right away who'll make her happy in the long run… but we could see how well we can satisfy her in thc moment."

The lilt of his voice made his implications clear. My cheeks outright flared. "Um…"

Logan had already shifted forward on his feet. "You think we can't 'satisfy' her? What makes you such a hot shot?"

Beckett raised his hands. "I'm not assuming anything. I'm just saying that we could discover now whether she'll find the two of you so superior to me that I can't offer her anything more. You'd even have the advantage of being able to work together to please her when I'll only have myself to rely on. As long as Maddie's on board with putting our skills to the test."

He looked at me again with a twinkle in his eyes, slyer than I'd ever seen before but not at all unappealing. My mouth opened and closed again like I was a fish tossed onto a dock. I had no idea what to say.

He couldn't really mean… Hooking up with each of them right here in the Vigil office? With the others watching? That was crazy.

So why was the idea sending a burning ache of need down through my chest to collect between my legs? A thrill shivered through me. I was abruptly giddy at the thought of being the center of all that attention, of having not one but three men intent on getting me off in every possible way.

Maybe *I* was crazy. But I wasn't sure that was a problem. Was this scenario any less crazy than sneaking into a gang-owned bar or tracking down a murderer? At least no one would be in any danger… Well, as long as Logan didn't perfect that whole incineration by sight thing he was working on.

Slade wet his lips and pushed to his feet, looking at me like he wanted to set me on fire in a totally different way. When he glanced at Logan, the other guy hesitated and turned his gaze on me. I could tell they were startled but ready to rise to the challenge. Another rush of heat through my body had my panties dampening.

Yes, I'd done a lot of crazy things lately. So why shouldn't I go wild in a way that was about nothing but enjoying ourselves? I bet if I texted Summer for advice, she'd tell me to go for it in a heartbeat. No one was holding me back but myself.

"Okay," I blurted out, my voice steady but a little breathless. "I'm in."

The temperature in the room seemed to rise by at least five degrees with that one statement. Beckett stepped back from me, nodding to the other two guys. "You're welcome to go first." His gaze slid to Dexter, who was now watching the proceedings with a slightly bewildered expression from the far end of the room. "Since you're not directly involved, you can observe and evaluate who actually gives her a better time."

I thought my cheeks would burn right off, but Dexter didn't argue, only sat up straighter as if taking this duty very seriously. Logan and Slade walked up to me on either side. Logan's gaze didn't leave mine as he made a brusque gesture toward Beckett. "Lock the door."

The command had me tingling with anticipation. My nipples tightened against my bra.

Slade slipped his arm behind my back and nuzzled my hair. "Are you sure about this, Piccolina?"

When he touched me like that, I was even more sure than before. I felt like I'd explode if both of these guys didn't have their hands all over me in the next few seconds. I dragged in a breath. "Yeah."

It was like the word set off a chain reaction of motion. Logan moved in front of me, hooking his thumb under my chin and tugging my mouth to his.

Heat rushed from his mouth all across my skin. I kissed him back, swaying toward him, a small sound carrying up my throat as his tongue prodded at the crease of my mouth. As my lips parted, he swept inside, his familiar taste meeting me. Our tongues tangled together, sending more sparks racing through my veins.

And not just from Logan. Slade eased my hair to the side and kissed the back of my neck. I tipped my head to give him better access, trembling when he teased his fingers around my waist. I raised one hand to grasp Logan's neck and the other to grip Slade's shirt, holding them both to me in this mass of rising passion.

Beckett was watching us quietly from one end of the room and Dexter from the other, but I found I didn't care. There was nothing shameful about what we were doing. I wanted these two men and they wanted me, and we were going to embrace that fact in the most concrete possible way.

Logan gave up any hint of restraint and tangled his fingers in my hair, pulling me as close to him as I could get, his lips ravenous against mine. As he consumed me, Slade maneuvered his hands up under my shirt and cupped my breasts through my bra. At the heady rush of pleasure that came with his caresses, I gasped against Logan's mouth.

I pulled away from my stepbrother to glance over my shoulder, and Slade leaned in to claim my mouth in turn without hesitation. His tongue flicked across my lower lip, and I shivered eagerly. Everything beyond our circle of heat was fading from my mind, burned away by the desire driving us onward.

Just as a strain crept up my neck, Slade clutched my waist and spun me to face him. He devoured my mouth again and then charted a blazing path along the edge of my jaw, nipping my earlobe, continuing on down my neck. As I whimpered at the incredible sensations he was stirring up, Logan pressed in behind me, completely encompassing me between the two of them.

Logan's hands traveled up over the terrain Slade had already explored and stroked over my breasts tentatively and then with more force. He tweaked my nipples through my bra until I moaned into Slade's mouth. Then there was a click behind me, and the material fell away.

Logan yanked up my shirt to expose my bare breasts, and Slade couldn't resist. "Stunning," he whispered, cupping my curves to form a makeshift bra between us and then lowering his mouth to suck one peak into his mouth.

Logan's lips branded the crook of my shoulder at the same time. His hands trailed down my belly and flicked open the fly of my jeans. As the bulge of his erection brushed my ass, he slipped his fingers down over my panties.

Slade had held me in almost this position just a couple of weeks ago. Logan's touch felt different, firmer and more determined, but no less thrilling. His fingertips slid over the thin fabric, grazing my clit, and I jerked in the guys' combined hold. Slade's lips formed a smile before he tested his teeth against my nipple.

Pleasure quivered all through my body. I swayed with Logan's administrations, clutching Slade's mussed hair at the same time.

As Slade turned his attentions to my other breast and Logan delved his hand right beneath my panties, my eyelids fluttered. I found myself looking past them to Beckett standing near the door. The lust that blazed in the other man's normally thoughtful eyes made me gush against Logan's pulsing fingers.

My gaze darted in the other direction and found Dexter, who was watching just as intently but with an unreadable expression. A faint flush had crept up his pale neck, but otherwise he seemed to be studying us like I had the displays at the science exhibition Beckett had taken me to.

Logan's fingers curled right inside me, Slade lapped his tongue to draw my nipple to a harder peak, and I tipped my head back against my stepbrother's chest. I couldn't stop myself from arching my back slightly, letting out another moan, giving Beckett more of a show as Logan tugged down my jeans and panties to crumple at my feet. The feel of his gaze on me was like yet another touch adding to the tantalizing mix of sensations.

Logan bit down on my shoulder, and a little cry burst from my throat. He groaned in response, rocking against me, his erection nudging my ass. "God, Maddie, I've wanted you so bad for so long."

"Me too," I mumbled, and groped backward toward the waist of his pants. "So, have me."

With a growl, he jerked me around so I could plant my hands on the table for balance. Slade leaned against the edge next to me, stroking me with his hand now while Logan unzipped himself. At the crinkle of a condom packet, my breath caught in my throat.

As Logan lined himself up, teasing his shaft over my folds from behind, Slade stole one more kiss. At my whimper, he grinned. "I told you I'd hear those gorgeous sounds again. Maybe next time we can make them even louder."

I could only nod and gasp my agreement as Logan pushed into me. He swore under his breath, bending over me, gripping my thigh hard. He slid into me inch by inch with the most delicious burn, and I trembled for more.

"I'm never leaving you again," he muttered. "Never giving this up again. I never should have in the first place."

I choked up for just a second before he thrust the rest of the way in with a swift, brutal motion that had my breath stuttering. I wasn't sure I'd ever felt so full, even when we'd fucked on the bathroom sink those two years ago.

He pounded into my pussy, sending me spiraling higher, faster than I could have believed possible. Bliss crackled through my nerves. My fingers curled against the tabletop, and then Slade was kneeling down next to me, easing into the space between my hips and the table.

As Logan picked up his pace even more, Slade trailed his fingers over my thighs. He kissed the sides of my knees, nibbled my hip just below where Logan's hands were clamped. Then his mouth closed over my clit, catching it as Logan's thrusts propelled me forward.

"Oh, fuck," I rasped as Slade's tongue swiveled over my clit in time with his best friend's strokes inside me. It was a miracle my arms were holding me up. I felt as if I were melting into a puddle of pleasure, every particle of my body singing out with joy.

Logan held me tight against him with an arm looping around my waist, slamming into me again and again. Each thrust jolting me farther into the wave of ecstasy. Slade sucked me hard, and Logan's next stroke hit just the right spot inside me, and I shattered apart with a cry that had Logan clapping his hand over my mouth to muffle it.

I shuddered and whimpered between the two men, my legs wobbling beneath me. Pleasure radiated through my limbs. It was all I could do to stay standing as the impact of my orgasm rocked me.

Logan swore as his hips jerked with his own climax. He buried his face in my hair at the back of my head, and I felt in the hitch of his breath how much this moment had meant to him.

Slade eased away and straightened up, licking his lips with a pleased expression. "Now that's what I call satisfying our woman."

I caught his hand and squeezed it, needing to feel connected to both of them in the moment. I'd never felt anywhere near that good before. I'd never known anyone *could* feel that good.

And the two men hadn't shied away from taking care of me together, despite Logan's earlier reluctance to accept even Slade's role in my life.

As Logan slid out of me, Slade's gaze veered from me toward the other man involved in this sharing situation. Beckett's eyes seared into me, but his mouth had formed a careful smile. He glanced from Slade to Logan. "I take it you're finished."

Slade rotated me with a hand on my side and kissed my cheek. "I think *she* is."

I should have felt embarrassingly exposed, standing before Beckett with my pants around my ankles and my shirt wrenched up. But all that raced through me under his warmly assessing gaze was more hunger.

"I don't think you're right about that," Beckett said in a voice full of promise. "What do you think, Maddie?"

Quivering in anticipation, I held my hand out to him. "All

three of you was the deal, wasn't it?"

Slade guffawed at my declaration, and Logan let out a hint of a snarl at my other side. But neither of them moved to stop Beckett as he walked up very deliberately between them. As he set his hand on my waist, gazing down at me, the other two men pulled farther away.

I swallowed thickly, tasting the tension in the air but too caught up in my desire to spend much time worrying about it. This was what I'd gotten into when I'd insisted I wasn't ready to choose between the men who'd captured my attention. This was what *they* needed to understand they were getting into if they stayed with me. I didn't belong to any one of them.

Beckett's attention stayed focused on my face. He caressed my cheek, holding my gaze. "We don't have to do anything you're not comfortable with. I don't need to prove anything to them."

The statement only made me want him more. I didn't know how to answer him with words, so I simply grasped the collar of his shirt and yanked his mouth to mine.

There was no hesitation in his kiss. After how much I'd felt with Logan and Slade, I hadn't been sure how much more bliss I was capable of experiencing, but at the slide of Beckett's lips against mine, all kinds of renewed longing woke up in my body. My cunt throbbed in anticipation as if it hadn't been filled just minutes ago.

Without breaking the kiss, Beckett scooped me up and set me on the edge of the table, my legs splayed around his hips. He kissed me again and again, lingering when a gasp or a whimper tumbled from my lips. His hands stroked over my sides and my chest until he seemed to have teased out every sensitive spot that could make me shiver with delight. The knot of need low in my belly expanded with every caress.

Beckett dappled more kisses down the side of my neck, murmuring between them. "I haven't stopped thinking about you since the other night. Those lips. These hands." He teased his teeth over my skin, and a breathless giggle tumbled out of me. "That laugh."

I fumbled with the buttons of his shirt, wanting to bring my hands to the toned planes of muscle I'd felt beneath it. Beckett hummed encouragingly and massaged my breasts with his deft hands.

He gave special attention to the peaks, rolling my nipples beneath his thumbs gently and then more firmly as if he were studying my reactions. Figuring out what got me off the best. His mouth lingered over a particularly giddy spot just beneath my ear, and I started to squirm at the jolts of pleasure he was setting off with his tongue and teeth.

Then he moved his hands farther down, stroking over my abdomen and slicking a finger across the folds now swollen with friction and need between my thighs. I bucked into his touch.

Beckett seemed to know I was too sensitive there for a heavy-handed approach. He claimed my mouth again and stroked my pussy carefully until I could take a firmer touch. Until there was nothing but pleasure burning between us.

I rolled my hips into his hand as he held me in place, prodding with small, quick circles that had my pleasure building and eddying. This was going so fast, and if he made me come this soon…

It didn't matter, I told myself. I only sank into what he offered and allowed my climax to swell with each swivel of his fingers. So close—so close—

He pulled his hand away, dragging it down my inner thigh and then back up my stomach. I couldn't restrain a groan of frustration. I was throbbing for release, and he'd jerked me right back from the edge.

"Don't worry, Maddie," Beckett whispered. "We're nowhere

near finished."

I gasped as his lips worked down my chest, his tongue flicking across one of my nipples as he went. I wasn't sated—not even close. Logan and Slade had done their job well, but Beckett drew every ounce of possible bliss from me.

As his mouth worked downward, I leaned back on the table, only holding myself up with my elbows. His breath washed over the place he'd been stroking moments ago, and then he started up the same swift, meticulous circles with that damn tongue of his. This time, his finger wound up my inner thigh before dipping into me. I threw my head back, a moan leaving my lips.

"Delicious," he growled, pushing two fingers into me in rhythmic pulses. I panted as he allowed my pleasure to rise without reaching the breaking point. He changed the motions of his tongue, starting the process of building pleasure over and over again.

"Beckett," I pleaded when another climax was ripped away, leaving me panting for what I needed. "Please."

He pulled away slightly, looking up at me through his lashes. "Did I just hear a please?" he asked, and damn him, he sounded far too satisfied with himself.

I only nodded.

"Good."

Beckett stood, unfastening his belt and allowing his pants to drop. He showed no sign of self-consciousness about revealing the rigid erection that jutted from between his thighs. My mouth watered at the sight of it.

He'd grabbed a condom from his pocket. He ripped it open with his teeth, a gesture I'd never considered might be so erotic, holding my gaze the entire time. As he rolled it over himself, he stepped forward to meet me. He grasped my hips, positioned himself between them, and yanked me forward to impale me on him in one swift thrust.

I saw stars.

I'd already been filled by Logan, so the hasty penetration came with no discomfort. Beckett hit the exact spot deep within me that had been yearning for him. He looped one arm behind my back to hold me close, his mouth descending on mine, and tucked his other hand between us to fondle my clit.

After being denied my release so many times, the sudden flood of pleasure came over me with a roar. A mewling sound shuddered out of me. I hooked my legs around him to urge him onward.

Beckett's breath was turning ragged as he pounded into me. His lips jerked from mine.

"Tell me how much you want me," he said raggedly by my ear.

My voice shook. "God. So much."

He chuckled. "Tell me *how* you want me."

"Just like this. Right now. Please, Beckett." Tears of need tickled at the back of my eyes as the craving for this final release spread through me. "Please."

"That's my girl," he whispered, thrusting into me so hard my head bowed back.

I didn't totally understand why he'd drawn this moment out so long, why he'd denied me over and over, until I soared up to the pinnacle at last. Beckett bucked into me, his thumb strumming my clit to a perfect crescendo, and finally allowed my orgasm to crash over me.

I sobbed with the force of it, arching up to meet him. Beckett's persistent waiting and teasing had built to this moment—this incredible, unfathomable climax that rocked me so hard that I didn't hear any noises I made. I couldn't focus on a single thing other than the ecstasy hurtling through me and sending me flying. Not even the release I'd gotten with Logan and Slade's combined efforts had thrown me quite this high.

CHAPTER 15

Madelyn

My legs were still wobbly as I reassembled my clothes. A weird mix of exhilaration and disbelief coursed through my body. Had I really hooked up with three guys in the space of half an hour like I was totally wanton?

But they'd gone along with it. All three of them had wanted it just as much as I had.

I glanced around at the men as I fastened the fly on my jeans, unsure of what I'd see on their faces. Tension still hummed through the air, but it had a heated flavor that made it less unnerving. Beckett had stepped off to the side as he'd tidied himself up, and Slade and Logan leaned against the desk near the computer, Logan's eyes smoldering with more emotion than I could identify.

And then, of course, there was the fourth man in the room, the one who'd been only a spectator—and our assigned judge.

Dexter cleared his throat. His gaze darted between all of us, his shoulders slightly hunched, and then he announced in a rush, "I think that was a tie."

Beckett let out a low laugh. "I'll take that as a win, considering you should be biased toward your friends."

Slade's eyebrows shot up. "Now wait a second there," he said, waggling his finger at Beckett with a sly glint in his eyes. "We made sure Maddie got to enjoy herself all the way through, none of the jerking her around and making her beg for it."

Beckett grinned right back at him. "I didn't get the impression she minded the begging—especially by the end. The grand finale is what makes it all worthwhile."

Logan snorted, his scowl suggesting he was taking the supposed competition a lot more seriously than the other two men. "A tie? That's bullshit, and we all know it. I felt how hard she came."

Beckett simply gave him an amused look. "And so did I. Which I accomplished all on my own, no assistance required."

"It was *your* idea that Slade and I work together," Logan snapped. "Don't go turning it around on us now."

Slade considered his friend with a bit of concern before turning back to Beckett. "I personally think teaming up made us the dream team."

Beckett's gaze slid to me where I was standing awkwardly, my cheeks about to burn off all over again. "I suppose only Maddie can tell us whether she thinks any of us provided a superior experience."

His easy-going tone told me that he didn't expect me to crown a winner anyway, but a prickle of irritation ran through me at their bickering all the same. I folded my arms over my chest. "I thought the point of this get-together was to confirm that you *all* have something to offer. I wasn't disappointed by any of you, so if it's up to me, I'm keeping all of you. No winners or losers required."

Slade chuckled and tapped my arm with his knuckles. "Spoken

like a woman who knows her own mind. As long as I'm still in the mix, I'll take it."

"I thought we were going to settle something here," Logan groused, his expression still stormy.

I stepped closer to him and prodded him in the chest, feeling a surge of power at the way heat flared in his eyes at that brief touch. I'd just taken three enticing men, and I'd affected them just as much as they'd affected me.

"We're settling that I'm happier having all of you than having to choose, at least for the moment," I said. "Don't make me regret including you in that 'all.'"

Logan's mouth snapped shut. He glowered at me, but he couldn't find any comments to back up his annoyance.

I turned away from him and realized that Dexter's chair was empty now. A glance around the office told me that he'd vanished. "Where did Dexter go?" I demanded.

The guys looked around, Logan tensing and Slade's face falling.

"He must have left while we were having our little debate," Slade said with a guilty grimace.

Guilt of my own twisted my gut. I'd been so high on desire and the three guys' attentions that I hadn't really thought about how Dexter would feel in the middle of that whole scene. We'd probably made him horribly uncomfortable. He couldn't have known the meeting was going to take that wild turn when even I hadn't.

I should have considered his feelings more before going ahead with it.

"I'll find him," I said, turning toward the door. "The rest of you can continue your dick-measuring contest if you're so committed to it. Just try not to start an actual brawl."

"I think we'll survive," Beckett said, but he looked a bit concerned too. I didn't think he'd have wanted to alienate any of my friends, regardless of my exact relationship with them.

I stepped out into the main room of the library, where the lights were dim and the atmosphere quiet. We'd invited Beckett over right before closing time so that we didn't have to worry about any disturbances, and everyone else had left. The librarians trusted the Vigil guys to lock up after they headed out for the evening.

I didn't see Dexter amid the shelves. I hurried through the library, sweeping my gaze down the aisles and over the tables up ahead. He hadn't totally left the building, had he? If so, I'd have to send Logan and Slade after him, since he'd probably gone back to their apartment. I wouldn't be able to apologize to him myself. That possibility gnawed at my gut.

Just as I reached the seating area, an odd noise reached my ears. It was muffled, but it sounded like a sharply drawn breath.

Spinning around, I saw I'd come up beside the library's single-stall bathroom. The noise had come from in there. Dexter had ducked into the restroom?

I stepped closer, opening my mouth to call his name—and froze. The sounds that filtered through the door when I stood right next to it painted a very different picture from what I'd have assumed.

There was another rough breath, and a rhythmic rustling with the friction of flesh on flesh that my instincts recognized as a guy jerking off. Even as the understanding sank in, that guy—Dexter—let out a soft grunt and a mumbled name: "Madelyn."

With those three syllables, every inch of my skin electrified. Holy shit.

He hadn't left because he'd been upset at being roped into that scenario—he'd been *turned on* by watching me with the other guys. In spite of how thoroughly I'd already been satisfied by all three of those other men, a tingle raced straight to my sex.

I'd been attracted to Dexter more with every day I'd spent in his presence. It'd just never occurred to me that he'd be interested in me that way. He'd never come on to me or flirted… but then, it was hard to picture the reserved, socially awkward guy doing that with anyone.

It shouldn't have mattered. I *did* already have three guys I was totally into who were into me. But the thought of what could spark with Dexter too had my hand rising toward the door.

I'd already done something crazy. Why shouldn't I see how far it could go? Dexter was a part of the group I'd found myself mixed up in even more than Beckett was. How did it make sense to push him aside from this part of our complicated relationship if I wanted him and he wanted me?

I had to know where he stood.

My knuckles tapped against the door. "Dexter?"

The rhythmic noises stopped, followed by a different sort of rustling that I assumed was him getting himself back into his pants. "Yeah?" he said, sounding unusually hoarse.

I wet my lips. I could do this. "Um, could—would you mind if I joined you? I think we should talk."

There was a momentary silence. Then the lock clicked over. "You can come in."

I eased into the stall tentatively. Dexter was standing by the sink, his stance tensed, the stark lighting turning his face even paler than usual beneath his messy curls other than the pink blotches where his cheeks had flushed. I stepped back to the other side of the stall to give him a little distance in case he wanted that.

"I noticed you'd left without saying anything," I said, unsure of where to start. "I was worried that whole situation made you uncomfortable. I'm really sorry we didn't check and make sure you were totally okay with it to begin with. But… now I'm thinking maybe you didn't mind so much after all?"

The flush expanded across Dexter's face. His gaze met mine for a typical brief instant before veering away. He rubbed the back of his neck.

"I didn't mind," he admitted haltingly. "I just—it was a little too much. I needed to… get my own feelings out of my system."

That was one way of putting it. And I'd interrupted his attempt at release. My lungs squeezed with a different sort of guilt—but maybe if I pushed this conversation in the right direction, he'd get something that would fulfill his urges even better.

"Feelings for me?" I clarified.

Another darting gaze. "I don't expect anything. I don't know what I'm doing the way the other guys do. I have no idea how to be all suave or whatever. So you don't need to—"

"Dexter." I took a step toward him, wishing I could touch him and know he'd receive it well. "I'm not here because I need to be. I think you're just as incredible as the other guys—and just as attractive. I didn't think *you'd* be into me that way."

For the first time, those bright green eyes lifted to catch mine and held there for several beats. The full force of Dexter's gaze was enough to take my breath away.

"I don't normally feel this way," he said. "I'm not even sure how to talk about it. But something about you draws me in. I've felt it since you first started working with us. I've wondered what it'd be like to touch you, to have you touch me… Watching you with the other guys… you have no idea. I kept wondering what it'd be like to be with you the same way."

My heart thumped faster, an eager flutter passing through my chest. Dexter wasn't anything like the other guys, but that made his confession thrilling in a totally different way. I didn't know what to expect from him or where this could go, but a huge part of me was dying to unravel that mystery.

"I'd like to find that out too," I said quietly. "I'm here now. What would you like to do with me, Dex?"

At the implied familiarity of the nickname, his eyes flickered. He took a step toward me, closing most of the remaining distance. His gaze skimmed down my body and back to my face. Then he lifted his hand and let his fingertips come to rest against my cheek.

That delicate touch woke up every nerve in my body. I knew how much Dexter normally avoided physical contact—I knew how special it was for him to initiate it, to want this closeness with me.

"Can I kiss you?" he asked, matter-of-fact as always but with an intensity beyond anything I was used to from him.

My heart just about leapt out of my chest with excitement. "Please."

He bowed his head and carefully brought his lips to mine. The second our mouths met, a sizzle of heat shot over my skin. I had to hold myself back from grabbing him and pulling him even closer.

Instead, I let Dexter take the lead. His hand slid from my cheek into my hair, his fingers curling to grip the long strands with a tug against my scalp that made my pulse skip. He leaned closer to deepen the kiss bit by bit. When he tipped his head, seeking out the best possible angle, I couldn't hold back a gasp of delight.

The sound seemed to spur him onward. He nudged me against the wall next to the hand dryer, bringing his other hand to my face, and kissed me so hard pleasure trembled down to my toes. I tentatively grasped the front of his shirt, and his breath stuttered against my mouth.

He drew back no more than an inch, an eager shiver passing through his own body. "This is good. Really good. I—there are so many ways I'd like to touch you. But not in a place like this. You should have better than this."

The library bathroom was pretty clean as public restrooms went, but I had to agree it wasn't the best site for a first sexual encounter with a guy who was pretty cautious about the entire experience. Just the fact that he *wanted* more than this had me soaking my panties.

I could wait. The challenge in the Vigil office had been about me. I could make this moment about him instead.

Monitoring his reaction for any sign of discomfort, I trailed my fingers down his chest to the waist of his slacks. "Maybe for now I could just help you finish what you already started?"

Dexter's eyes widened, but with a spark of hunger. "Yes," he rasped. "Yes, if you want to—"

"I do," I assured him quickly, and he dove in to claim my mouth with even more enthusiasm than before.

I fumbled with his fly and then delved my hand inside his pants. My fingers closed around the silky skin of his rigid cock. He was a little slimmer there than the other guys, like the rest of his body was, but just as hard and twitching against my palm when I gripped him.

A choked sound burst from Dexter's throat. He kissed me hard enough to bruise, one of his hands dropping to cup my breast through my shirt. His hips bucked with the jerk of my fingers over his shaft, and I swallowed a moan at the thought of what it'd be like to have him inside me. What this intense, pensive, unusual man might be able to bring to the bedroom that'd be totally unlike anyone I'd shared that kind of intimacy with before.

I increased the pressure, stroking him faster until he was groaning against my lips. Dexter thrust into my hand with increasing desperation, his kisses turning wilder but still searing. I swept my thumb over the head of his cock and smeared the precum beading there down his length, and his fingers pulled tighter on my hair.

His lips crashed into mine. His breath had gone ragged.

"Madelyn," he mumbled against my mouth as I pumped him toward his release. "I'm going to— *Fuck.*"

The curse sent a shiver of pleasure over my skin in the same moment as his body stiffened against me. Warm fluid spurted over my palm and wrist, and then Dexter sagged over me with a shaky sigh.

"We should clean that up," he murmured, but he couldn't seem to resist stealing one more kiss before he reached for the paper towels. His gaze caught mine, hopeful but nervous until I'd wiped the cum from my arm and drew him in for a final kiss.

"Next time we'll find a place where we can get more comfortable," I suggested, and a rare, shy grin stretched across Dexter's face.

"You have no idea how much I'm looking forward to that."

His smile set off a renewed flood of heat through my veins. "Oh, I think I have a bit of a clue."

When we'd completely cleaned up, I grasped his hand, and we headed back to the Vigil office together. My pulse kicked up a notch imagining the other guys' reaction to the statement I intended to make, but if they had a problem with this development, they'd just have to get over themselves.

The guys were still standing in a loose cluster, Slade and Beckett next to each other and Logan keeping more distance. Their voices fell away as Dexter and I stepped into the room. I felt as much as saw their attention shoot to our clasped hands.

"Are you done bickering?" I asked, giving them all a pointed look.

Slade smirked at me. "Are you ready to pick a winner—either of you?"

I set my free hand on my hip. "In case I didn't make it clear enough before, I'm not doing any picking at all. I want to keep seeing all of you—and that includes Dexter."

I gave his hand a light squeeze, and he shot his friends a hesitant smile.

As Slade's jaw dropped, Beckett let out a low whistle. "You do know how to go after what you want, don't you, Maddie?" he said with both amusement and admiration sparkling in his eyes. "I won't stand in your way."

"Wait, Dexter—holy shit." Slade laughed, his expression shifting with what might have been pride. "Good for you, letting yourself go for it, man."

Logan didn't look anywhere near as happy about the situation. "When the hell did *that* happen?" he demanded.

I fixed him with a firm glare. "Just now. But we can always reduce the number of men I'm dating to three if you have so much of a problem with it you want to take yourself out of the picture."

His jaw flexed, but his posture straightened at the challenge. "There's nothing in heaven or hell that could make me give you up again, Maddie."

Something in me released. I hadn't been totally sure I really could have all of them for however long this lasted until I'd gotten that final confirmation.

"Good," I said. "Then we all know where we stand."

"And that's right beside Maddie, because where else would any sane person want to be?" Slade teased.

A ripple of laughter spread through the room as some of the lingering tension dissipated.

In the middle of the moment, my phone pinged with an incoming text. I grabbed it out of the purse I'd left on the table, assuming it was Summer. How the hell was I going to explain to her what I'd gotten myself into now?

Only it wasn't from Summer or any of my other regular contacts. I didn't recognize the number at all. And what the hell was this message supposed to mean?

Next time it might be fatal.

I knit my brow, staring at it as if the words might make more sense if I peered at them long enough. Could it be a wrong number? But what kind of message was that to send to anyone? It sounded like some sort of threat.

I was about to show it to the guys when the phone rang with a call, so abruptly after the strange text that I nearly jumped out of my skin.

This time a familiar name popped up on the screen. It was Holand—Logan's dad, my stepdad. Why would *he* be calling me right now? I didn't usually chat with him on the phone the way I did with my mom.

Logan must have noticed my odd reaction. "What is it?" he asked, shifting toward me.

"I don't know," I said, hitting the answer button and lifting the phone to my ear. There was only one way to find out. "Hey, Holand. What's up?"

"Maddie, I'm so glad I caught you," Holand said with a faint crackle of static on the line, his tone serious and grave. My body tensed at the sound. He dragged in a breath and went on. "Your mom's been in an accident."

CHAPTER 16

Madelyn

By the time I'd lowered the phone from my ear, my mind was spinning with everything Holand had told me. I barely saw the room in front of me.

"Maddie," Logan said urgently, grasping my upper arm. "What's going on? What happened?"

My mouth opened and closed a few times before I managed to propel sound out of it. "That was your dad. My mom—she was in a car accident. Bad enough that they rushed her to the hospital. She's having some kind of surgery right now. She's alive, but they don't know what condition she'll be in when they stabilize her."

The last words came out in a croak. Beckett grabbed my other hand and squeezed, his eyes full of concern. "I'm so sorry, Maddie. Does she live nearby? Can you go see her?"

All of the guys had gathered around me. Slade was nodding.

"Even if you have to miss classes tomorrow, the professors will totally understand."

Through the blur of shock and worry in my head, a memory flickered up. My gaze dropped to my phone again, my fingers clenching around it.

Next time it might be fatal. Could they have meant…?

"I think—someone *warned* me," I said, my chest constricting even tighter. "Warned me that this isn't as bad as it could get. As if *they* had something to do with the accident."

Dexter's forehead furrowed. "What do you mean?"

I fumbled with the phone. "I got a text right before the phone call. It didn't make any sense on its own, and it was from a number I didn't recognize. 'Next time it might be fatal,' they said. They must have meant the accident. The timing was way too close to be a coincidence."

"What the hell?" The menacing note I'd only heard in Logan's voice a few times before—when I'd been attacked—rippled through the question. He leaned over to peer down at the screen. "Give me the number, and I'll track the maniac down. We'll find out who meets a fatal end then."

My gaze flicked toward Beckett, hoping he took Logan's statement as rage-fueled hyperbole rather than a literal plan of action, and then darted to my phone again. My trembling fingers managed to open my Messages app.

The first contact at the top was Summer. Then a text I'd sent to my lab partner earlier this afternoon. Then one from Dexter giving me an update on the guys' observations of the footage from the cameras we'd planted. Slade, Mom, another lab partner, a tutorial leader who liked to communicate through text… I scrolled back two weeks and then up to the top again.

"It's *gone*," I sputtered. "I swear it was there. I couldn't have made it up out of thin air."

Logan frowned and held out his hand for the phone. "There are ways to time texts so they're temporary," he said as he double-checked my messages. "Most people don't know how to do that, though."

Slade's expression had darkened too. "You got it right before the phone call about your mom?"

As I nodded, Beckett rubbed my back in an obvious attempt at comfort. "Maybe it was a prank from someone who found out about the crash before you. Some people are assholes and take jokes way too far."

Even in my dazed state, I noticed the look the Vigil guys exchanged. A chill wrapped around my gut.

"I don't think I know anyone who'd do something like that," I said weakly. But I did know a very good reason why someone might have wanted to target me and my family. Logan had been afraid of this all along—that if I got involved in the investigation, I'd become a target for the people who'd murdered my dad.

I'd been willing to take that risk. It hadn't occurred to me that I'd be risking other people I cared about too, people who had no idea they'd been drawn into the line of fire.

"Someone realized," I started, and cut myself off when Dexter's attention shot toward Beckett. *He* didn't know about that—about anything the Vigil had gotten into. How the hell could I explain it to him?

"Damn it," Logan snarled under his breath as he handed the phone back to me. "We should have been more careful."

"We will be," Slade said, but his mouth twisted as if he were queasy.

Beckett took us all in, his brow knitting with confusion. "What are you talking about? Did something happen that would have put Maddie and her family in danger?"

Logan stepped toward him with a glower. "Nothing's happening to Maddie on my watch. But I think it's time you left. We have family business to take care of."

Beckett's eyebrows rose. "I care about her just as much as you do. If she needs help—"

"I'm her stepbrother," Logan snapped. "It's my stepmom in the hospital. We'll handle it."

I didn't like the way he was talking to Beckett, but I couldn't focus on anything other than the thought of Mom lying in some hospital bed while doctors cut pieces of the wreckage out of her and stitched her up. Because of me. Because I'd dug too far into business no one wanted me to know about.

The words tumbled out. "I need to see her. I should go, now."

Logan caught my shoulder. "You're not driving like this. You're too upset. I can take you. I'd want to be there for your mom and my dad anyway."

I caught Beckett's gaze and grasped his hand again. "I'm sorry. I just—it's too much. I'll call you as soon as I know what's going on back home."

Worry was written all over his handsome face, but he dipped his head in acknowledgment. "Take as much time as you need. Your mom's health is way more important than me."

Before either of us could say anything else, Logan was ushering me out of the office. I glanced up at him, tugging my elbow away from his grip. "I *can* drive myself."

"I don't think that's a good idea," Logan said with iron firmness. "And like I said, I'd want to be there anyway. So I'm not giving you a choice."

Any other time, I might have kept fighting. But right now it was a struggle just to keep walking while my stomach felt like it was about to plummet right out of my body. Maybe he had a point. I could barely remember where I kept my key, let alone how to maneuver a car on a freeway.

Home was two hours away. What else might happen to Mom before I got there?

Logan directed me to his car and opened the door for me. As I sank into the passenger seat, he hesitated just for a second. "Do you need to stop by your dorm and grab anything?"

I shook my head. "I just want to get to her."

"I'll get you there."

He dove into the driver's seat and gunned the engine. We roared off campus through the deepening evening. I pulled my legs onto the seat in front of me and hugged my knees.

The problem with a two-hour drive was that there wasn't much to do other than stew in my anxious thoughts for mile after mile. How would Mom be when I saw her? Should I have said something more to her the last time we talked? What if it had been the *very* last time? Oh, God, I didn't want to think like that.

I rubbed my forehead and stared out the window at the lights along the freeway, trying to think of nothing at all.

Logan cleared his throat. "I could put on the radio if you want."

Somehow the thought of hearing music made me tense up. "No, I'd rather not."

Silence hung between us for a few minutes longer. His hands flexed against the wheel. "If you don't want to talk about this yet, I totally understand. I just—are you okay with everything that happened back at the library?"

I'd hardly even thought about our crazy interlude from the moment I'd gotten the call. It rushed back into my mind, a not entirely unwelcome distraction but far too overwhelming for me to really wrap my head around right now.

"I—I haven't really had time to process it completely," I said. "But I think I am. I was feeling pretty good about it up until your dad called." I paused. "In a weird way, it feels kind of right that I'm with all of you instead of trying to pick between you." My gaze slid toward his brawny form, his grim gaze aimed at the road ahead. "Are *you* going to be okay with it?"

Logan's jaw worked. "I didn't like watching you with that Beckett guy," he admitted, his voice rough. "Even with Slade…" He let out a huff of breath. "But I could tell how much *you* liked it. I've put you through too much shit to tell you to give up anything that makes you happy now, Maddie. Beckett was right about that part, anyway."

I swallowed thickly. "If you can't handle it…" I didn't know how I'd react if he said he was walking away now that we'd finally reconnected after all this time, but I had to know if he planned to.

Logan glanced at me for just a moment, but his eyes were so intense my skin tingled under his gaze. "I've wanted you for years, Maddie. To have you *any* way is better than not at all. I meant what I said—I'm never pushing you away again. No matter how many guys you decide to date."

The corner of my lip quirked upward despite my horrible mood. "I'm pretty sure four is more than enough. You don't need to worry about me adding anyone else to the mix."

Logan let out a dry chuckle. "I guess that's a small relief."

With the air cleared between us, the silence that followed didn't weigh on me with the same discomfort. A little of the tension released from my chest. Logan and I were rushing back to take care of our family, as family—and whatever else we were now too.

Night had totally fallen by the time we reached our home town. Logan drove around the outskirts to the big hospital that served both our town and a couple others in the same region—the place where Dad had worked.

My lungs contracted all over again as he parked in the familiar lot off to the side of the building. Had someone in there been involved in Dad's death—and in what had happened to my mom?

There was no way of knowing yet.

Holand had given me the room number. It blazed up through my memory as I hustled toward the doors. "328. If she's out of surgery, that's what room she'll be in."

We strode through the doors, and Logan had to catch me to stop me from bursting right into the ward before he'd explained to the nurse on duty who we were and what we were doing there. She motioned for us to go on. Unwilling to wait for an elevator, I dashed up two flights of stairs and shoved out into the third floor.

Logan had started tapping on his phone. I realized he'd been texting his dad, informing him of our arrival, when Holand stepped out of a room up ahead, glancing around for us. He looked exhausted, but his face brightened a little at the sight of me and his son.

He wouldn't be able to look like that if Mom wasn't at least mostly okay, right?

I almost sprinted the rest of the way to him. He grabbed me in a hug and then offered Logan a quick one as well, his eyes going abruptly watery.

"Mom," I said hurriedly. "Is she—"

"She just got out of surgery an hour ago," Holand said. "It was touch and go for a bit, but she pulled through, and they think she'll make a full recovery. She's awake for the moment but pretty groggy with the pain medication, and she's awfully banged up. I'm sure she'd like to see you if you're up for it, though."

Relief and horror collided inside me. Mom was all right—but she almost hadn't been. It almost *had* been fatal.

Because of some sicko who was trying to send *me* a warning.

I shivered at the thought and shoved it away. I needed to be here for Mom now. I could figure out the rest later.

"I'll go right in," I said.

As I eased open the hospital room door, Logan and Holand took up a hushed conversation behind me. But that and everything else fell away at the sight of my mother's form sprawled in the bed in front of me.

A bruise mottled her forehead where it poked from beneath a large bandage that swathed most of her upper head. A cut with fresh stitches veered along her jaw. Her left arm was propped up in a cast, and there was a faint rattle to her breath as she inhaled deeply at my entrance.

Tears welled up in my eyes. Oh my God. It'd been even worse than I'd let myself picture. Seeing my mother like this, the woman who'd supported and protected me for my entire life, felt utterly wrong.

I pushed myself to the side of the bed. "Hey, Mom. I got here as fast as I could. How are you doing?"

"Maddie," Mom mumbled in a faint voice. "My little girl." She reached up to finger the strands of my hair as they fell across my shoulders. "It's good to see you."

"It's good to see you too, Mom," I managed to say around the lump in my throat, and took her hand in mine. I wanted to lean in and throw my arms around her, but I was afraid of hurting her more.

I settled for pulling over a chair and tipping my upper body next to hers, resting one arm gingerly around her waist. Mom hummed as if she was totally content, and my heart wrenched.

She had no idea that this might be my fault. *Had* the accident been a threat—a warning that my involvement in the Vigil's investigations had been noted and would be punished further if I continued?

Would the same person—or people—who'd stolen Dad from me rip another parent out of my life too?

The thought just about broke me. I closed my eyes against the tears that'd started to trickle down my cheeks and just lay there next to Mom as her breaths evened out with a sleep I hoped would be healing.

I couldn't do this anymore. I couldn't lose Mom too. It was too much—too hard—too terrifying.

I lay still for more minutes than I could count, an ache spreading through my chest and my eyes burning. Part of me wanted to crawl under the bed and never come out. But that feeling was so familiar it dredged up other memories of much longer ago.

There'd been all those years right after Dad's death when I'd become a mere fragment of my usual self. I'd barely talked to friends, sleep-walked through my schoolwork, cringed at bullies' taunts rather than standing up to them. My world had felt like it was cast in shadow, and I'd let those shadows consume me.

A tendril of resolve rose up in my abdomen, winding through me. I couldn't let myself falter like that again. I couldn't shrink away and leave it to other people to stand up for me and fight my battles for me. I'd taught myself how to be strong after those years of weakness, and I had to hold on to that strength.

If someone was attacking my family again, they needed to be stopped. I couldn't back down. Dad deserved justice, and everyone else I cared about should be able to live without a threat hanging over them. I wouldn't let them get away with hurting Mom like this.

If our enemies thought this move would scare me off the case, they were sorely mistaken. The Vigil would just have to work smarter so the people responsible for this wouldn't know we were still on the case. And then we'd crush them like *they* deserved.

CHAPTER 17

Logan

The freeway was nearly empty as I drove back to campus, occasionally jarred by another set of headlights out so late. It was past one in the morning now, and the buzz of the cup of hospital coffee I'd chugged was wearing off.

Dad had tried to convince Maddie to stay the night at the house, but then Lindsay had woken up enough to get concerned about Maddie missing tomorrow's classes. As soon as Maddie had seen her mom upset, she'd been frantic to reassure her. So when the doctors had come to kick us out for the night, I'd promised to get Maddie back to campus. No doubt she'd make the drive back again on the weekend and be glued to her phone in between for updates, as would I.

I was glad I'd insisted on driving her. She'd been so exhausted that she'd drifted off in the passenger seat within a half hour of us leaving the hospital. I glanced over at her now, her head cushioned by her bent arm against the window, her pale hair drifting across her face that was momentarily relaxed with sleep. A shiver ran through her body as if even unconscious some part of her was still dealing with her panic over her mom, and my chest clenched up.

The urge to pull over and gather her in my arms gripped me with an ache that ran all the way through to my bones. But I knew that getting her back to her dorm where she could sleep properly mattered more than any comfort I could offer. How much comfort *could* she even take from me right now, when I'd been acting like such an ass toward her until recently?

That thought sharpened the ache so it dug into my gut with an edge of guilt. I loved this woman so much. The emotion flooded me so fully it was difficult to breathe.

How the hell was I ever going to make up for all the ways I'd hurt her? I'd convinced myself I was protecting her, that it was better for her in the long run, but those efforts had failed, and now she was in the thick of it right along with the rest of us. All I'd accomplished was putting her through years of anguish.

My hands tightened around the steering wheel. Never again. Never again was I going to watch that kind of agony cross her face because of me. Even if I couldn't fix everything I'd broken before, I'd damn well make sure I was everything she could possibly need from here on out.

I had no idea what she might be going through now. We'd both experienced losing a parent as kids, but even that had been more traumatic for Maddie than for me, since she'd had to watch her dad slip away without any idea why it was happening. The thought of Mom's death still sent a jab of loss through my heart, but I could recognize with the benefit of time that it'd been mercifully quick and simple. One moment she'd been walking to work, the next she'd been gone, the victim of an explosion that'd claimed three other lives at the same time.

Dad had campaigned to ensure better safety testing from the gas company, and we'd buried the hand that was the only whole piece they'd recovered of Mom's body. And then it'd been over, no lingering questions other than the basic, *Why did it have to be her bad luck and not someone else's?*

And now Maddie might lose her other parent if we couldn't figure this out. Lose her to villains lurking in the shadows, knowing that her attempts to help us uncover her dad's murderer might have provoked them.

I couldn't wrap my head around that idea either. It'd been bad enough seeing how wrung out Dad looked over Lindsay's "accident" without wondering how I'd feel if he'd been harmed too.

We had to find the assholes responsible and shut them down, whatever it took. I wasn't going to let Maddie endure that kind of loss all over again.

As I pulled off the freeway and slowed for the drive through the city streets toward the campus, Maddie stirred in her seat. She raised her head, swiping at her eyes and then her mouth, and blinked blearily at the lights glowing in the darkness outside.

"We're just about there," I said.

"Sorry. I didn't mean to pass out."

My gaze flicked toward her. "You've got nothing to apologize for. I'm glad you got some rest. But I'm sure you'll be a lot more comfortable in your bed."

"Yeah," she said, and that single syllable contained so much uncertainty and worry it just about tore me apart.

I parked as close to the entrance of her dorm building as I could and got out to walk her upstairs. She clutched her purse a little shakily, but she managed to stay steady on her feet as we tramped up the stairs. Another pang ran through my heart at the resilience she could still show, the determination in the set of her chin. She was shaken, sure, but Madelyn Silver didn't let anything break her.

She paused at the door to her floor and glanced at me, her eyes flashing with momentary alertness. "We need to go after the assholes who did this. We have to *stop* them before they hurt anyone else."

Even more affection swelled in my chest. I grasped her arms, gazing down at her, willing her to feel how much I meant this. “We will. They're not getting away with anything. We'll regroup in the morning and figure out our next steps. For now, you need to get some proper sleep so you can think clearly.”

Her head drooped a bit, but she nodded with the same determination. “You should get some rest too. Thank you for driving me.”

“I was happy to.” One tiny gesture I could offer toward making up for all the crap before.

Maddie had texted her roommate to tell her she'd be getting in late. She raised her keycard to open the door, but at the faint beep, it flew open to reveal the slim, curly haired woman who'd obviously waited up. Her eyes widened as she took in Maddie's rumpled, weary state.

“Get in here,” she said, ushering Maddie inside. “You're exhausted. I grabbed a snack for you from the dining hall in case you didn't eat at the hospital, but you look like you really just need to crash.”

She glanced at me with a dismissive nod, and I backed up. Maddie shot me one last look over her shoulder with a tired but apologetic smile. I gave her a little wave that felt ridiculous even as I did it, and then the door was shutting between us.

I turned to stalk back down the hall, my own resolve wrapping around me like armor.

I was tired too, sure, but I wasn't going to sleep just yet. There was something more important I couldn't wait one more minute to get started on.

I'd thought I was going to be working alone, but when I eased past the apartment door, I found the living room lights still on. Slade leapt to his feet from where he'd been sitting on the sofa—Dexter glanced up at the other end, his stance tensing.

"Is she okay?" Slade demanded with a forceful energy that I'd rarely seen in my friend. "You dropped her off at her dorm?"

I nodded, a thread of uneasy emotion winding around my stomach. The concern on both of my best friends' faces brought me back to the interlude in the Vigil office just hours ago—to watching Maddie respond to Slade's touch just as enthusiastically as my own, to seeing her hand wrapped around Dex's and both their cheeks flushed when they'd come back into the room after doing who knew what.

My hands balled at my sides before I caught my reaction. I forced them to open, inhaling slowly and deeply before expelling my jealousy in a rush.

These two men were like brothers to me. We'd had each other's backs for every important part of our lives. I wasn't going to let my feelings for Maddie—or theirs—destroy that bond.

"She's upset, of course, but not quite so panicked now that we know her mom got through okay," I said. "Mostly she needed to get some sleep after everything."

"Of course," Dexter said, even but quiet. "Were there any signs of who was responsible for the threatening text she got or the accident?"

I shook my head. "If it wasn't for the text, which only Maddie saw, there'd be no reason to think it was anything other than an accident. Her mom got T-boned by a car that made a sudden left turn and cut it too close. The driver of the other car is in a coma—I'll look him up in the morning, but somehow I don't think we're going to find anything there."

"Can't leave any stone unturned," Slade put in.

"We can't," I agreed. "Which is why there's someone else I'd like to investigate first." I looked from him to Dexter, folding my arms over my chest. "Just the three of us, without Maddie."

Slade's expression tensed. "You know how she felt about us hiding the stuff about her dad from her. We can't keep her in the dark."

"This doesn't have to do with her dad. Hopefully it won't lead anywhere at all. But I want to look up this Beckett guy. Make sure *he's* not some kind of threat."

I braced myself for an argument, but obviously it wasn't just my jealousy driving my decision there. Both of my friends tipped their head in agreement, Dexter looking thoughtful.

"There is something a little off about him," he said. "And he didn't tell us much about himself."

"To be fair, we didn't tell him much about us," Slade pointed out. "But he is awfully smooth for a guy who's just out of college. We don't run into many people around our age who've got that much confidence."

"Exactly," I said. "We need to know who we—and Maddie—are actually dealing with. If *he's* hiding anything, it's better that we find it out sooner rather than later."

Slade rubbed his hands together, not showing any sign of fatigue despite the late hour. "Let's get started then. We never got a last name, did we?"

"No. But Beckett isn't that common a first name. Between that and knowing he's got a significant family business that involves real estate, I should be able to track some stuff down."

I grabbed my laptop and dropped onto the sofa between my friends. Slade sat down to watch my search while Dexter pulled out his phone. "I snapped a few photos of him. I'll see if there are any distinctive details I didn't notice in person that we should follow up on."

It only took a couple of minutes for me to find the first reference to a Beckett I assumed was the one we'd met this afternoon. His last name was apparently Alderman. With that additional information, I quickly dug up a couple of social media profiles. The blond guy with the slick smile who'd walked into the Vigil office like he owned the place gazed back at me from the profile photo.

"Jackpot!" Slade said. "What's he been up to?"

We both peered at the screen as I scrolled down through the profiles, but they were sparse, nothing but a few photos of Beckett around the city and innocuous posts about a café or a restaurant he liked. The business information I uncovered connected the company he appeared to work for to some real estate acquisitions, like Maddie had said, but when I looked up those buildings, I couldn't see anything unusual about them. The only unusual thing was that this guy had his life so together at twenty-three, and maybe that was a different kind of jealousy talking.

"He's got a strangely small internet footprint in general, doesn't he?" Slade said, though I could hear his enthusiasm for the search was dwindling. "Usually you'd find all kinds of photos and references for an ordinary guy."

I sighed. "He's not totally ordinary, though. Maddie said he's in a family business, so he's probably been coached to keep a low public profile so that nothing he gets into on his personal time can interfere with his professional life. It makes our job harder, but there's nothing all that odd about it in general."

"His clothes appear to be expensive brands, but I'm not getting much else from the pictures." Dexter flicked through to more of his albums, but at this point checking any other photos he'd taken seemed like grasping at straws. "I wonder how he and Maddie happened to meet?"

Slade cocked his head. "She said they just bumped into each other downtown, didn't she?"

"Yeah, that's right." My teeth gritted all over again at the memory of that guy with his hands all over her. Making her moan. Urging her to beg him for release.

My frustration must have shown on my face. Dexter glanced up from his phone and hesitated. "Maybe there isn't any reason to be worried about him. But… you've been into Maddie for a long time. Are you really okay with *any* of the rest of us being involved with her?"

The tentativeness with which he asked the question made me flinch inwardly. He sounded almost… afraid of how I'd respond to him, as if he thought I might be angry with him.

I should never have made him feel like he had to even ask that question, like I might try to bully him out of pursuing Maddie if she was interested in him too. Dexter had barely even dated before—why shouldn't he have just as much of a shot as anyone?

Hell, both he and Slade had treated Maddie way better than I had in the past month. If anything, they both deserved a chance with her more than I did, no matter how long she'd been on my mind.

"It's up to Maddie who she dates, not me," I said. "You know she'd have my head if she thought I was trying to lay claim on her. She *doesn't* belong to me. I'm totally aware of that fact." Even if part of me wished that she did. I took a deep breath. "We'll just see how it goes. And if she ends up wanting just one of us in the end and it's not me, it'll be my own damn fault. I won't resent either of you, no matter what happens. I swear it."

When it came to Beckett, I couldn't make the same promise, but I didn't really care how he felt about any of this anyway.

A faint smile touched Dexter's lips that both reassured me that I'd said the right thing and sent another jab of guilt through me that he'd needed my confirmation.

I threw myself back into looking for an excuse to drive off the one guy I didn't have any loyalty to, which I could admit at least to myself was what this continuing search amounted to now. With the late hour and the emotional strain I'd already gone through tonight, the lines of text on the screen were starting to blur before my eyes.

I shook myself back into alertness and got to work hacking into one of Beckett's social media profiles in case he had private photos or messages that might tell a different story. But when I cracked in, it turned out there was nothing I hadn't seen already. It didn't appear that he used the messaging function there to communicate with anyone. He hadn't posted anything that wasn't publicly viewable.

As I scowled at the screen, Dexter let out a startled sound. "Look at this." He shoved his phone toward Slade and me.

It took me a moment to figure out what I was seeing. The photo on the phone was from the club where we'd gone with Maddie a few times. I could see her with Slade at the edge of the image—Dexter had been taking his usual surveillance photos for future reference, not focusing on any specific part of the club, just documenting all of it.

"What about it?" Slade asked, looking equally puzzled.

Dexter took the phone back for just a second to zoom in on the opposite side of the image. When he showed us again, my pulse stuttered in my veins.

Beckett was standing off to the side of the bar, far enough away that his face was slightly pixelated, but still recognizable. He was talking to someone I couldn't make out between the mottled club lighting and the crowd around them.

"This was the first night we were there with Maddie?" I clarified, based on the clothes I'd seen her wearing. "Weeks ago?"

Dexter nodded. "I'm not sure if she'd even met him yet at that point. He definitely didn't come over to talk to any of us while we were there."

"It could be just a coincidence," Slade said. "It's one of the most popular dance clubs in the city. No reason why he couldn't have been there for his own sake on the same night." But his tone was doubtful.

My mouth set in a tight line. "Maybe it's just a coincidence, but we don't see a lot of those, do we? The other possibility is that he's been following her… and if that's true, we need to find out why."

Why would a pulled-together, successful businessman like Beckett stalk a college girl like Maddie from the sidelines rather than approaching her directly the way he'd ended up doing anyway? Was it just romantic interest, or was there something more to his presence that we hadn't stumbled on yet?

CHAPTER 18

Madelyn

I sighed and sank deeper into the chair I'd taken in the Vigil office. "We *have* to keep investigating. We can't let assholes who'd do something like this get away with it. But how can we do that without them realizing that we're still poking around? I don't want them punishing me through my mom—or anyone else I care about."

Logan shot me a concerned glance, his expression full of the kind of affection I still couldn't totally believe he was willing to offer me after everything that'd gone down in the past few years. He pushed his chair closer to mine so that he could rest a hand on my shoulder. "We won't let anything like that happen again."

"But how can you be sure? We don't even know how they found out I was looking into their activities. Was it because of the warehouse, or the seafood market, or the office building—or even the accounting place? I was hanging around those guys outside it for a few minutes."

Slade let out a harumph where he'd perched on the table at my other side and gave a strand of my hair a playful tug. "The one good thing that came out of this awful situation is we know we're definitely on the right trail. These people are up to no good, and they felt threatened enough to show a little of their hand."

"I know," I said. "It feels like we're so close." The thought of getting justice for Dad, of uncovering the criminals who'd murdered him and destroyed my family, sent a quiver of anticipation through my nerves too. But now the thrill of the investigation was dampened not just by the anxiety about the lengths we'd gone to but dread as well.

Who might get hurt next if I kept pursuing these people? How far would they go if I didn't back down? The text message had said that the next time might be fatal.

Logan looked down at the computer he had open on his lap. "They can't trace anything I look into over the internet—I can make sure of that. Maybe I'll find another solid connection while I'm digging through the other companies that connect to that shell corporation."

Dexter turned to face us where he'd been sitting at the computer on the office's desk, scanning more footage from the various cameras the Vigil had set up around the businesses we'd checked out. They were all still running, which implied that no one had discovered them yet, or we might have been able to use that fact to narrow down where I'd been spotted.

His gaze caught mine and held it for a beat longer than I was used to, sending a flicker of warmth through me. It was a strange sensation having been so close with all three of these guys, knowing that they cared about me and I cared about them far beyond the boundaries of the case we were investigating together. Strange, but… I definitely liked it.

"The problem is getting bigger and more dangerous faster than we were prepared for," Dexter said. "The attack on Madelyn's mother proves it. I think we should recognize that we may not be able to see this all the way through on our own."

Logan frowned at him. "What do you mean?"

Dexter's mouth formed a tense smile. "I mean we need to get the police on the case. They're equipped to deal with criminals on this level—at least, they've got more manpower and better equipment than we do."

I knit my brow. "I thought you all had already decided that there was no point in bringing my dad's case to the police."

"We had," Slade said slowly, studying his friend. "But that was when we only had scraps of evidence, a lot of it circumstantial. Now we're much closer to getting at the real dirt."

Dexter nodded. "We're not all the way there yet. We'll need to do at least a little more work to come up with concrete proof of some kind of criminal activity so that the cops will take notice. But if we can hand that over, then they'll start investigating too. Either they'll find the connections and be able to prosecute the people responsible for all their crimes, or they'll put those people on the defensive, distract them so we have more of a chance to carry out our own investigations without backlash."

Logan let out a rough sound. "The cops can be so useless."

Dexter's suggestion had given me a little hope—a way to avenge Dad without putting more lives on the line. "They aren't always, though, right? I mean, they do catch a decent number of criminals. And this is bigger than any crime you've tackled before, isn't it?"

He gave a grudging scowl. Slade bumped his knee against my

arm. "He doesn't want to admit it, but this is a rabbit hole way deeper than any we've jumped down before. I think Dexter has a point. We don't want these pricks going after anyone else who matters to us. We don't really know anything about them yet, and they know too much about us."

"Not all of us," Logan pointed out. "They haven't gone after the three of us so far, which suggests they didn't realize we were on their trail. They went straight for Maddie. They'd recognize her as a threat because of her connection to her dad."

I wrinkled my nose at him. "That's not exactly comforting."

He ran his thumb over the peak of my shoulder, sending tingles dancing over my skin. "I know. But it does give us more room to maneuver. I'll accept that Dexter could be right and maybe we need to hand this off to the professionals, but we *do* still need more to hand over to them if we want them to actually get involved and not just laugh us off as conspiracy theorists. Especially when the main case is twelve years old. If we could find something more recent that these people have done…"

"Step one is to find enough evidence to entice the cops," Slade said, holding up a finger. "Step two is to punt the investigation to the police for appearance's sake. And step three is to monitor their progress and keep looking into it discreetly if they don't come up with enough on their own."

"Emphasis on discreetly," I said, but my heart had lifted now that we had a more definite goal in mind.

My phone pinged with a text. I checked it and had a jab of guilt, realizing I'd rushed right over to the Vigil office without updating the other man who'd been looking out for me.

Just wanted to check in after what happened last night, Beckett had written. *How are you? Is your mom all right?*

I glanced up to find all three of the Vigil guys watching me. "It's Beckett," I said, though I had the sense they'd already guessed that.

"He's asking how I'm doing. Do you think I could tell him at least a little about what we've been doing? I don't like hiding things from him. It would help him understand how we all reacted last night. We don't have to mention the, er, illegal bits."

I wasn't sure how Beckett would react to finding out I'd been a party to not one but multiple breaking and enterings. I could ease into explaining that part, right? Or maybe it wouldn't need to come up at all if we could sic the police on the bad guys sooner rather than later.

Logan was already shaking his head. "I don't think you should mention anything about our investigation into your dad's death or even what we do in general. We don't know him that well. You've only been seeing him for a few weeks, haven't you?"

I raised my eyebrows at him. "I know he's not a jerk. I think he proved yesterday that he's pretty open-minded. He was a lot more welcoming to you all than you were to him."

"You can't know how he'd react to information like this," Logan said. "*You* thought it was crazy at first, and it's your dad we're talking about. And even if he's okay with it, how much do you know about his family? His friends? You can't guarantee there's no one in his vicinity who could tip off the wrong person, even inadvertently. Is not hiding things important enough to put your mom even more at risk?"

He knew exactly the right button to push. I winced and looked down at my phone, grappling with two opposing forces of guilt now.

Slade teased his fingers over my hair. "I think Beckett presented himself pretty well yesterday, Piccolina. I don't have any vendetta. But I also think Logan makes a good point—at least for now, until we have a better idea of who we're dealing with."

I sighed. "All right. But if I keep seeing him, I'm not keeping him in the dark forever."

"Of course not," Dexter said mildly, but his expression twitched as if he'd suppressed some emotion. Was *he* jealous?

I pushed that question aside and brought my thumbs to the phone's keypad. *Sorry I didn't update you earlier! My mom made it through and is in stable condition now, thank God. I'm doing okay now that I know she'll pull through. I wish I hadn't needed to rush off on you yesterday.*

He replied almost instantly. *I completely understand. It made sense for you to go to her—she's family. You haven't gotten any more of those strange texts, have you?*

Oh, hell, what should I tell him about that? I wavered and then typed, *No, nothing else like that. I'm starting to wonder if I did just imagine it. It all happened so close together.*

As I sent that message, Dexter made a wordless exclamation and motioned to his computer screen. "Someone's just left something at the shell corporation's office."

I leapt off my chair alongside the other guys. We all gathered around Dexter's chair, staring at the computer screen.

He'd managed to mount a camera in the hall, in a position that captured the office door at an angle. Even with the awkward view, I could see a large manilla envelope taped to the door.

"When did that happen?" Logan demanded.

"The person who dropped it off came by just a couple of minutes ago, while we were talking," Dexter said. He rewound through the footage to show a figure wearing a baggy jacket, the hood pulled up so we couldn't make out the person's face. They stopped at the door just long enough to stick the envelope there and then spun around and hurried off again.

My pulse skipped a beat. "We need to know what's in that thing. Could we go grab it before anyone from the office shows up?" I paused, and my stomach sank. "But they might be keeping an eye out for us—or at least me—there. We don't know if that's the place where they noticed me."

"You shouldn't go in," Logan said firmly.

Dexter tipped his head toward Logan. "We probably shouldn't either. If they saw Maddie there, then they probably know we were with her. Even if they're not sure who we are, they'll recognize us if we turn up again."

"What about Beckett?" I had to say. "I know you didn't want to tell him anything, but he'd do this as a favor for me. I know he would. And he hasn't been at all involved in our investigations before, so him coming around the building wouldn't tip anyone off." And then they'd see that they could trust him too. Or I'd find out that we couldn't after all, but without revealing anything really risky.

"Maddie," Logan started with an edge in his voice.

Slade's hand shot into the air as if he were eagerly answering a question in class. "Simpler solution," he said with a grin. "I wasn't with the rest of you that day. I can waltz on in there and no one should be the wiser. These quick fingers will grab the prize, and I'll be out in a blink."

My mouth twitched with a smile despite myself. Okay, that probably was a better solution. I'd forgotten Slade hadn't been with us the other day.

Dexter reached out and wrapped his fingers around mine so tentatively that I didn't startle even though the gesture surprised me. "It's still a risk," he said. "Everything we do involving these people is a risk now. Your mom is the one who got hurt. I think you should make the final call on whether we do anything."

My throat constricted. I gripped his hand in return, recognizing that from him the gesture was as momentous as a full-body embrace. Slade and Logan waited for my reply.

I dragged in a breath. "We can't do nothing," I said. "And as far as we know, the criminals have no idea *any* of us came to the office, since they haven't looked around carefully enough to find the cameras. Slade going takes out even more of the risk. So I say we do it." I tore my gaze from Dexter's face to Slade's. "Just don't get caught."

He saluted me. "You can count on me. Now I'd better get going while it's still there."

CHAPTER 19

Slade

The office building wasn't exactly a busy place, but enough people were drifting in and out through the front doors in the late hours of the afternoon that I could saunter in as if I had every right to be there. Which technically I did. There weren't any laws against walking through the hallways.

What I planned to do next was another story.

I held my phone in my hand, ducking my head as I passed the legit security camera in the front foyer so it wouldn't get a good look at my face, pretending to be checking a text. I brushed past the door to the stairwell and performed the same trick at the sound of footsteps thudding toward me. A middle-aged man in a cheap suit hustled by without giving me a second glance. He'd see just another client or employee of one of the businesses in the building, glued to his phone.

I didn't want anyone to remember me after I left.

After peeking through the window on the third floor landing to make sure the hall was clear, I strode out of the stairwell and down the hall as if I had urgent business. The shoe around my prosthetic foot hit the carpeting with a slightly different sound from my regular foot, but I put a conscious effort into walking perfectly, not showing any sign of the one particularly unique thing about me.

The envelope was still hanging from its piece of tape on the door of the office in question. I veered a little closer as I walked by and tugged it off without breaking my stride. As I dropped it into the canvas shoulder bag that normally held my course books, I ambled a few steps further, peered at a door farther down as if confused, and then turned on my heel and marched back to the stairs.

If anyone other than the Vigil had caught me on camera, hopefully they hadn't seen anything especially odd.

I didn't linger. I headed down to the first floor at a steady but swift pace, walked out of the building while staring at my phone, and kept going until I reached my car parked a couple of blocks away. Even after I got in, I simply tossed my bag onto the passenger seat and started the engine. I didn't want to be anywhere near the office building when I let myself get distracted by my find.

I drove downtown and pulled into the parking lot next to the grocery store where we did a lot of our essential shopping. There, I called up Logan on speaker phone and fished the envelope out of my bag.

"Hey," Logan answered. "Did you get it?"

"Yep. It was a breeze." So far, anyway. I worked my finger under the flap and tore the envelope open. It didn't feel like there was much inside. "Just checking out the contents now."

I pulled out a thin sheaf of papers. A quick shuffle through them showed there were four pages, stapled on one corner. They looked photocopied, a slightly grainy logo printed at the top of the page over a list of figures.

"It's from some company called Roadway Express Trucking," I reported. "Did that business name come up in any of your searches?"

I could hear Logan's frown in his voice. "No, that doesn't sound familiar at all. But I'll look into it as soon as I get out of the class I'm heading to. What's it showing about them?"

"Nothing that makes a whole lot of sense to me." I squinted at the data. "One column is dates, but the others are in some kind of code I don't know. If it's a trucking company, maybe it's a list of shipments—what they contain, where they're being picked up and dropped off?"

"That sounds like a reasonable guess. We know there were shipments going out of that warehouse. Does any of the code look like it could match that address?"

I made a face. "I don't know, man. Seriously, it's all random letters as far as I can tell. But Dex can probably break it, being the brainiac he is. He's got that exam starting soon, though, doesn't he?"

"Yeah, so just bring it to the apartment and we'll go over it later tonight." Logan's voice tightened. "Hopefully this will point us toward the evidence we need. I don't like knowing these assholes are walking around scot-free."

"I hear you. We'll get them." The thought of Maddie's distraught face when she'd heard about her mom's accident made my hands clench around the papers. But we had to play it safe specifically so something like that didn't happen again. If these people went after my dad or anyone else in my family… My teeth set on edge.

"We will," Logan said firmly. "I've got to go. I'll see you in a few hours. Good work."

I stuffed the papers back into the envelope and the envelope into my bag and stretched my arms. My gaze drifted down the street toward the club where we sometimes met our contacts.

The club where I'd danced so enjoyably with Maddie the other night.

The club where Beckett had been hanging around in the background, up to who knew what.

I couldn't say I disliked the guy based on first impressions. Yes, the memory of him all over Maddie, making her gasp and shudder, sent a flare of jealousy through me. But I'd made my peace with the fact that she was an impressive enough woman that she'd caught the attention of not just me and him but my friends as well, and if I'd forced her to pick… well, I didn't think I'd necessarily come out on top.

Anyway, it was kind of wonderful seeing her taken over by so much passion, more than I could have generated on my own. How could I try to steal that away from her?

Otherwise, Beckett had seemed cool and easy-going, the kind of guy I'd have happily shot the breeze with if I *had* run into him someplace like the dance club. I hadn't noticed any warning signs in his behavior toward Maddie. He'd seemed just as enamored with her as I was.

That wasn't a guarantee that he was above board, though. The fact that he'd been skulking around the club the same night we'd been there and never mentioned it was a little concerning. And Logan had a point that we didn't know much of anything about him. He was awfully pulled together for a regular guy our age, which meant he might not be all that regular.

I had time to kill before the other guys would be back at the apartment. It'd be nice to stretch my legs and have a little fun regardless.

I walked over from the lot to get those legs warmed up and

headed right past the bouncer, since there wasn't any kind of line this early in the evening. The music was already thumping and lights streaking over the dance floor. I cracked my knuckles and decided that if I showed I was game and busted a few moves before hitting anyone up for info, I was more likely to get a friendly response.

With only a dozen other people around me in a few casual clusters, I didn't break out anything too fancy. I just moved with the beat with a little spin here and a flourish there, loving the way my body fell into the rhythm so easily. I'd often complained about the lessons my grandfather had insisted on when I was a kid, but now I could only send up a silent thank you to him. Dios guarde su alma.

As I jived around the floor, my pantleg must have shown flashes of my brightly colored prosthetic. A woman who was bobbing with the music next to a couple of friends pointed toward it. "You can really move even with that thing," she said over the music.

I flashed a grin and performed a little swift footwork to show off. Hey, I'd never claim I was modest. "Lots of practice. I've had it for a long time."

Her face fell a little, like often happened when I said something like that. "I'm sorry."

I shrugged. "No big deal. The Great White could have taken a lot more. I consider myself lucky."

Her eyes widened. "Wow."

As she turned away to murmur to her friends, I had to suppress a laugh. The real story of my leg—that I'd been born missing the lower half—was so mundane that I'd started making up tall tales about it when I was little. Crocodiles, woodchippers, ax murderers—they all got a turn in the spotlight. It was amazing what people would believe if you delivered the story without any sign of pretense.

I wasn't here to spin fables, though. When the current song

wound down, I decided it was time to try my hand at getting answers.

I strolled over to the bar and hopped onto one of the stools. The bartender handed a drink to a guy a few seats down and came over. "What can I get for you?"

Since Logan wasn't here, I didn't feel the need to avoid alcohol. "I'll take a Tom Collins, if you don't mind."

She dipped her head. "Coming right up."

She mixed the drink with deft movements and slid the glass across the counter to me. I took a gulp and raised the glass in a gesture of appreciation. "Nice! Hey, can I ask you a question about the clientele here?"

Her head tipped to the side. "What about them?"

"Just wondered if you recognize this guy—whether he's a regular. Maybe you even know his name."

I pulled up the zoomed-in image Dexter had sent to Logan and me that showed Beckett in the club and turned my phone so the screen faced her. "I was here on the weekend and ended up bumping into him, and a paper fell out of his pocket. But by the time I'd picked it up for him, he'd walked off and I couldn't find him again. I don't know if it's important or not, but I realized he was in a photo I took so I figured I might as well ask in case I can get it back to him."

The woman's eyebrows rose. She definitely recognized Beckett. But even with that reaction, I wasn't at all prepared for what she said next.

She raised her chin toward the photo. "Yeah, I know him. He *owns* this place."

I blinked at her, so startled a stupid question dropped from my mouth before I could catch it. "Are you sure?"

She laughed. "Of course. He came around my first day on the job and introduced himself. Beckett. He usually drops by a couple of times a month to check up on things. If you've got that paper, I can make sure it gets back to him."

I had the wherewithal to pat my pockets and then shake my head at myself. "Crap, I wasn't expecting something like that. I think I left it back in my dorm."

The bartender smiled. "Well, bring it around another time, and it'll be easy enough to pass it on."

"Thank you," I said, and sipped my drink as she walked away, my mind spinning.

Beckett didn't just have a role in a family business that involved real estate. He outright owned one of the most happening clubs in the city.

Was he aware of the criminal element that liked to make use of the place for covert meetups? Could he be tangled up in *that* side of the business that went on here?

And if so… what else might he have been getting up to that he hadn't mentioned to Maddie?

CHAPTER 20

Madelyn

I spent a couple of days going to all my lectures, doing the lab work, and working on a long research paper, but I couldn't say I was paying as much attention to any of it as I should. As soon as the weekend came, I drove back home to see Mom.

She was still in the hospital, but I knew from our last call that she was supposed to be released on Sunday. I arrived around noon on Saturday, walked through the same halls as last time, and found her alone in the room, watching something on TV.

I rapped my knuckles lightly against the door before stepping inside so that I didn't startle her. "Hey, Mom."

When she turned her face toward me, I had to restrain a flinch. The fresh bruises I'd seen there before had turned a nasty shade of purplish brown, mottling more skin than I remembered. The cut on her forehead was no longer bandaged, stitched up but still uncomfortably stark against the unbroken flesh around it. She looked like she'd gotten into a fight with a Mac truck, which I guessed wasn't that far from the truth.

I'd never wanted to see my mom like this.

And I never would have if I hadn't gone poking around where certain dangerous figures didn't want me to go.

"Honey," she said with a bright smile that offset the worst of the damage, and held out her hand to me.

I leaned over the rail of her bed, receiving her one-armed hug and allowing her to squeeze me as tightly as she wanted. Despite the injuries, the embrace was like a death grip.

"Where's Holand?" I asked when I finally straightened up. I knew he wouldn't leave her side unless it became essential, so it surprised me to see her alone.

She rolled her eyes. "He refused to leave for three days, but that man smelled worse than me. I told him that I needed my robe from the house, and I asked him to shower while he was there. I'm sure he'll be back soon."

I had no doubt he would. "How are you feeling? Do you think you'll be ready to be discharged tomorrow?"

"I was ready to be discharged as soon as I woke up. Do you know how much sleep I get in this place? None. There are nurses in here every hour on the hour, and the second I manage to doze off, I'm woken up again to be poked and prodded and who knows what else." She took a deep breath. "So yes, I'm more than ready. I've had enough of hospitals."

"I can understand that. I bet you'll be a lot more comfortable at home if they're sure there's nothing else that needs strict monitoring."

"Absolutely. And I'm so happy you could come home again. Are you sure it isn't interfering with your schoolwork?"

"Mom," I said, making a face at her. "It's better for my schoolwork if I can see you for a while and reassure myself that you're okay. I was pretty freaked out the other night. The rest can wait—and I'll be able to concentrate better when I go back to it."

Not that I didn't have a dozen other things to distract me, not least of which the case that'd gotten us into this mess to begin with, but I wasn't going to bring that up.

I half-expected her to argue, but she seemed to relax into the pillow, which told me how glad she was to have me here. "In that case, it's wonderful to see you. But you don't need to worry. I'm made of strong stuff."

"I know you are." I squeezed her hand, trying not to look at the cast her other arm was in.

Mom's forehead furrowed. "I'm sure it must be hard for you, Maddie. You can't have good memories when it comes to this place."

Because of Dad, she meant. I sucked in a breath, both grateful and discomforted that she'd given me such an easy opening. Because as much as I'd wanted to see her for her own sake, that wasn't the only thing I'd hoped to get out of this visit.

We needed to track down Dad's killer soon, not just for his sake but to make sure Mom wasn't in any more danger.

"I've actually been thinking about Dad a lot recently," I said, easing into the subject as gently as I could. "Not just since coming here."

Mom's gaze softened. "Is there any specific reason?"

Not one that I could tell her. I bit my lip. "I guess it's just with all the medical studies I'm looking into for school, it's gotten me thinking about how little I got to know him and his work, since I was so little. I'm sure there are all kinds of things he didn't think I could understand yet that he was researching. Did he tell you about what he was focused on around the time right before he died?"

Mom frowned, her eyes going distant as she thought back. "I think his current project with the hospital had to do with skin and bone grafts. I remember him talking about it a few times. But he didn't like to let his job creep into our family time all that much, and it's not really my area, so I couldn't discuss it very well anyway."

Whatever he'd been working on that'd gotten him into trouble probably hadn't been part of his official job anyway. "Did he ever take up projects just for himself?" I asked, doing my best to sound as if I were just following a random thread of curiosity. "For his own personal interest, not just for work?"

"Oh, he was always reading. You must remember how many books he kept in his office. But it isn't as if he had a whole lab in the house or anything. I think the work with the hospital and the periodic outside contracts he took on filled most of that well for him."

But not all of it. I groped for another angle to come at it from. "I thought it might be interesting to read through some of his notes and things from that time. It'd make me feel a little closer to him now that I'm more familiar with the subject. Did he have many files at the house that you've kept around?"

Mom knit her brow. "There are a couple of boxes in the basement, but he didn't have much at home. I think he mostly kept his paperwork at the hospital, especially since some of it was confidential—patient information and that sort of thing."

The boxes in the basement were the ones Logan had already looked through. I couldn't say that to her, though. Instead, I plastered on a smile. "I'll check those out sometime, then."

Mom's attention lingered on me, her expression shadowed with concern. "Has this been bothering you a lot, honey? I think you knew your father better than maybe you realize. He was always trying to let you in on his interests and help teach you about the world. And he'd definitely be proud of what you're doing with your life."

My chest constricted. "I know. It's not a big deal. I guess being in the hospital got me thinking more about it—that's all."

"Are you sure?" Mom scooted a little more upright. "If you're struggling at all, you know you can always arrange an appointment with Mr. Yanicho. I'm sure he'd be able to fit you in for a session."

Oh, crap, now she was really worried about me. She was suggesting I might need to see my old therapist who'd talked me through the worst of my grief as a kid.

I grasped her hand again and gave it a reassuring tug. "If I think I need that, I'll totally do that, but I promise you I'm fine, Mom. I didn't mean to hassle you with all those questions. I was only curious."

"If you're sure," she said, studying me so intently that guilt prickled through my gut. I definitely couldn't pry anymore about Dad now, or she'd be convinced I was having some kind of episode of delayed trauma.

To my relief, Holand strode back into the room before I had to figure out what to say next. His hair was still slightly damp from the shower, and he carried a velour robe over his arm.

Thank God.

"Maddie!" he said with a welcoming smile. "It's good to know Lindsay had company while I was gone."

"I had to check in on her," I said. "But why don't I let you two have some time together, and I'll be back in a bit. I need to grab some lunch from the dining hall."

"Oh, yes, don't go hungry on my behalf," Mom said, waving me off.

I wasn't actually hungry, but there was something else I wanted to check while I was here. It'd been twelve years since Dad's last projects with the hospital, so my chances of finding out anything were slim. But I had to take whatever opportunities I could.

I rode the elevator to the fourth floor, where half of the wing was devoted to research offices. I'd visited Dad there several times as a kid, although of course even if I'd remembered exactly which room he'd used, his office would have been cleaned out ages ago. But maybe they stashed old job materials in a storage room somewhere. I just needed to talk to someone who'd be able to point me in the right direction.

I passed a couple of staff who looked to be in their late twenties, too young to have worked here at the same time as Dad. Then a woman with curly auburn hair walked out of one of the rooms, and recognition lit up in my head. Her face looked more worn and she'd put on a little weight, but she was a doctor who'd collaborated with Dad on some of his assignments.

She hesitated and took me in too, but it was probably harder for her to place me when I'd grown from a little kid to an adult in the same time.

"Rebecca?" I said, hoping I wasn't totally mistaken.

Her eyes widened a bit. "Is that Madelyn Silver? It's been such a long time."

I couldn't help grinning even as a pang ran through my gut at the memories stirred up. If Dad had still been alive, he'd have still been working here alongside her. "That's me. It's good to see you."

Sadness tensed her expression. "I heard your mother was admitted a few days ago. You must have come by to visit her. Is she still doing all right?"

I nodded. "She's being released tomorrow, and she can't wait. Everyone's taken good care of her here, though." I paused. "While I was here, I was actually hoping to ask something about my dad too. So I'm glad I ran into you."

"Of course. What can I help you with?"

I motioned vaguely to the rooms around me. "I realize it's a long shot, but I know Dad must have had a bunch of work papers and stuff in his office when he died, since it was so sudden. I wondered if the hospital would have hung on to any of that—if it's in storage somewhere, and if I could take a look through it."

She cocked her head, considering. "I helped them clean out his office since I was fairly familiar with his work. There actually wasn't all that much. I remember thinking it was a bit odd that the room was so empty—I assumed he'd taken a bunch of things home to work on after hours. Your mom should be able to tell you more about that."

My stomach sank. Logan had told me that one of the reasons he assumed Dad's death wasn't natural was missing journals that had disappeared—probably stolen—from the hospital. It looked like he'd been right, since whatever documents Rebecca had expected to find in his office definitely hadn't ended up at home.

Someone had gotten here first and cleaned out everything they'd thought might point back to them. Crap.

It was too much to drag Rebecca into this whole mess. I forced a light laugh. "I'll have to ask her. Thanks anyway."

"Of course. It was good to see you. You've come a long way from that little girl who was always skipping through the halls."

She had no idea. Another pang of loss hit me, and my smile wavered. "It was great seeing you too."

I turned and hurried back to the elevator before the heat behind my eyes could condense into tears.

After the elevator doors closed, I took several deep breaths to get a hold of myself. I probably should go down to the cafeteria and grab some food. I'd need lunch eventually, and then I wouldn't have to lie to Mom and Holand when I went back to her room.

I got off on the first floor and headed for the cafeteria. I'd just stepped inside the white-walls space with its rows of rectangular tables when a familiar but unexpected voice rang out from across the room.

"There you are, Madds!"

I'd have known that energetic tone anywhere, but somehow my brain couldn't quite believe it until I turned and found Summer jogging over to meet me.

My thoughts jarred, the world I'd been silently immersed in where I was investigating Dad's murder colliding with the everyday life I'd been trying to maintain with everyone I was close to outside of the Vigil. For a second, I didn't know what to say to my best friend, even though I should have been excited to fit in an impromptu visit.

"Summer," I said, knowing my shock showed in my tone. The happiness in her expression faded slightly, and I fumbled for a smile as I opened my arms to offer a hug. "What the heck are you doing here? I had no idea you'd be coming."

"Hey, what good is a bestie if I'm not around to have your back when you really need it?" Summer squeezed me tight. Then she pulled back to study my face with narrowed eyes. "You've gotten so quiet lately. Always vague about what you're up to. I've been worried about you. When I heard about your mom, I figured you'd be dropping by as soon as you were done with classes for the week. I wanted to see you in person and make sure you're okay. I just talked to your mom—she said you'd be down here."

"Yeah," I said, abruptly aware that I was going to sound really vague all over again. I wasn't going to tell her where I'd gone before coming to the cafeteria. "It's awesome to see you. I'm sorry, I've just been so busy with school stuff, the end of term coming up, you know how it is."

It was a weak excuse. Frankly, I'd been kind of a shitty friend in the last couple of weeks. There was so much I hadn't told her, and in avoiding those conversations, I hadn't been there for her either.

But anything I said to her would put her at risk just as much as Mom was. My mouth went dry.

Summer obviously wasn't buying my excuse either. "You've never clammed up like this before, Maddie. Is it because you've been hanging around Logan? You can't let that asshole mess with your head again."

Of course she'd assume it was Logan's fault. And it was, but not at all in the way she assumed.

Suddenly I felt exhausted. She'd come all the way home to see me, but I didn't want to have to navigate this conversation. I didn't know how to talk to her and keep her safe at the same time.

"He hasn't," I said with all the assurance I could muster. "I promise I'm fine, Summer. Things have just been crazy." I motioned to the hospital around us.

But Summer knew that I'd gotten cagey ages before Mom's accident. She shook her head. "I don't think so. Something's up with you. Why are you shutting me out, Madds? You know you can tell me anything."

Not if I wanted to be sure *she* wouldn't end up having an unfortunate accident too. *Next time it might be fatal.*

Guilt speared through my gut, but I knew it was nothing compared to how I'd feel if I was visiting her hospital room—or her grave—next.

"If there was anything to tell, I would," I said with forced cheer, and backpedaled toward the doorway. "I actually just remembered something I need to pick up for Mom, though. And one of my professors asked me to look into a few things around town while I'm here that relate to our current unit. I wish I had more time to talk!"

No, I didn't. I wished I hadn't needed to talk at all. As I hustled away, feeling Summer's stare burning into my back, my throat closed up.

I was being a *really* shitty friend now, but I didn't know how to be a better one, not with all the danger hanging over me. I guessed now I had some idea how Logan had felt every day for the past few years.

I just had to hope that Summer would forgive me when I finally could let her in on the horror show my life had become.

CHAPTER 21

Madelyn

Keeley eyed my chosen date outfit skeptically.

"What?" I said, looking down at the short-sleeved top that displayed just a little cleavage and the jeans I thought showed what curves I had below to their best effect. "We're just going to grab an ice cream in the park."

My roommate clucked her tongue. "It's cute, but not cute enough for a date with someone who's at least a nine on the hotness scale."

I glowered at her playfully. "I never should have showed you Beckett's picture."

"Oh, you just saved me badgering you endlessly until you gave in anyway." She flashed me a smile. "But you know what, it looks perfectly Madelyn, and he's obviously crazy about you, so don't mind me. I'm just itching to get you into something really eye-catching."

"One of these days," I promised her, grabbing my light jacket, and headed out.

The spring afternoon was chilly enough that I tugged on the jacket as soon as I'd stepped outside. As I headed down the path toward the campus entrance, I spotted a familiar figure heading my way.

Slade slowed his graceful lope when our gazes met, a grin stretching across his face. "My favorite person. How lucky am I?"

"Where are you off to?" I asked, unable to stop myself from grinning like a maniac in return. It was a little odd to see him on campus on a weekend.

"I'm meeting Logan at the gym in a few. These muscles don't build themselves." He flexed his arm and winked at me. "How about you? Don't tell me they've got you in classes even on a Sunday."

My cheeks warmed. "No, ah, I'm actually getting picked up by Beckett for a date."

Slade raised his eyebrows, still playful but with a twitch of some emotion in his expression that I couldn't read. Maybe it was only a momentary jealousy that he'd quickly snuffed out, but something about it niggled at me.

"Beckett, huh?" he said. "You know, while you're hanging out with him, you should ask him some more about that job of his. Hit him up for some details on what-all that family business does."

I frowned. "Why are you so interested in his work all of a sudden?" I knew enough to satisfy me for the moment. The dedication and passion Beckett had shown for his career mattered more to me than what exactly it involved.

Slade shrugged casually, but another prickle of apprehension raced over my skin, as if some part of me could tell the subject mattered more to him than he was letting on. "The dude's an enigma. He's definitely got his shit together—maybe he has connections that would help our investigations after all. If you can find that out, Logan will have to loop him in more, right?"

That explanation did make sense, but it didn't totally satisfy me. Would Slade really care that much about whether we could bring Beckett on board?

Before I could push for more answers, he stepped closer to tug a strand of my hair. "I've got to get going. Don't forget your other boyfriends while you're having fun out there."

He followed up the teasing comment with a kiss, brief but emphatic enough to make my heart thump faster. Then he was striding on toward the gym with a quick smile over his shoulder at me.

Well, I definitely wasn't forgetting *him* anytime soon.

Just moments after I reached the main road outside campus, a black BMW cruised into view. It was sleek but not showy, the kind of car you wouldn't glance twice at if it drove past but that if you took a closer look you could tell hadn't come cheap. A far cry from my poor Malibu.

The windows were tinted, so I didn't realize it was Beckett's until it drew up next to the sidewalk and the window rolled down to reveal him smiling in the driver's seat. "Come on in."

I opened the passenger door and hopped in to a piney scent mingled with a hint of Beckett's freshly aquatic cologne. Buttery leather welcomed my thighs. I had to restrain a sigh, sending a silent apology to my trusty vehicle.

"Hey," I said as I relaxed into the seat. "Thanks for picking me up."

"I was happy to." Beckett studied me for a second as he pulled away from the curb. "How are you doing?"

The question brought a pang of stress and grief to the base of my throat. I reminded myself of all the reasons I had not to be worried right now. "Not too bad. My mom went home this morning no problem. She really just needs time for her arm and the bruises to heal up. I'm looking forward to taking my mind off it and school and all that for a little while."

His gray eyes flicked toward me again with obvious concern. "And there hasn't been any more weirdness like that text message?"

I shook my head, the pang sinking to my gut at the thought of what I was hiding from him. But I could honestly answer, "Nothing at all. Who knows what was going on with that? The shock of hearing the news and everything..." I waved my hand vaguely in the air.

To my relief, Beckett seemed to accept my explanation. He offered me one of his small but warm smiles. "I'm just glad you're all right. And your mom too, of course. It's no wonder you were shaken up. But I can definitely do my best to take your mind off it for a bit. If you've never tried the ice cream shop in the middle of the park, you've been missing out."

"Hey," I said with a little laugh. "I moved here at the beginning of January. It hasn't exactly been ice cream *or* park weather for very long."

Beckett chuckled in return. "Fair enough. I'm happy to be the one who gets to broaden your horizons."

"Well, it'd better be good now after the way you've talked it up."

"Oh, I have no fear that you'll be disappointed." He shot me a sly look. "What flavor do you typically go for, Maddie? Somehow I'm guessing you're not a vanilla girl."

The mild but unmistakable insinuation in the remark brought a flush up my neck. "I think I'll have to see what they have and make up my mind then."

"Spoken like a true adventurer."

It was only a fifteen minute drive to the largest of the city parks.

The weather was cool enough that the place wasn't swarmed, only a few other cars in the parking lot Beckett turned into. He parked at the far end away from the others that were clustered near the paths and got out fast enough to offer his hand as I emerged.

The sun beamed over us with enough heat to offset the chill in the air. We ambled along the main path between beds of flowers and trees just spreading their leaves to a courtyard around a small building painted in vivid pastel colors. I studied the wooden sign and decided that chocolate cherry sounded fantastic. Beckett asked for butterscotch ripple. As soon as we had our cones in hand, we wandered on through the park, which stretched for a few acres through this end of the city.

I wouldn't have necessarily picked ice cream for a snack this early in the spring, but after the first few swipes of my tongue, I was in heaven. I nibbled a cherry from the creamy frozen mass and grinned at Beckett. "You were right. This is the best ice cream I've ever tasted."

He tipped his head toward the shop we'd left behind. "It's a mom and pop place, been in the family for a couple of generations from what I hear. People who love what they do tend to make the best stuff."

"I'll say." I couldn't help noticing that his comment gave me the perfect opportunity to follow Slade's encouragement and ask Beckett more about his own work. I wasn't going to interrogate him or anything, but it would actually be useful to get a sense of whether he was involved in any areas that might be useful to us. And I was just generally curious. "Kind of like your company, then? All in the family?"

Beckett smiled back at me. "I hope so. Although we've had to bring on a lot more people than the ice cream shop would to handle everything we're juggling."

"It does seem like it keeps you pretty busy. You mentioned real estate—what exactly do you do with the properties you work with?"

"Mostly management," Beckett said easily enough. "We pick up properties that we think have good potential, renovate them to bring them up to snuff, and then rent out the space to clients who are looking. Occasionally we invest in new constructions, but I find breathing new life into older buildings more fun." He bit off a chunk of his ice cream and looked over at me as we took a turn on the winding path. "That reminds me of something I wanted to ask *you.*"

"Go right ahead," I said, wondering how the subject could possibly connect to me.

"My company recently acquired a new building here in the city. A retail-slash-office space, pretty flexible in the exact use. We'll be bringing in some shops and that sort of thing, but I'd like to include an aspect that'll give back to the community as well. I was thinking maybe a pro bono medical clinic if I can get that working. Your expertise might be useful in figuring out how to approach the project."

A flutter passed through my chest, both at the thought of his generosity and the possibility that I could help bring it to life. "That would be amazing. There've got to be so many people who could use that."

Beckett nodded eagerly. "What demographics do you think we'd want to focus on targeting? I'd like to make sure we have staff who'll cater to their needs as well as possible."

A little anxiety tangled with my excitement. "I hope I'm not the only person you're consulting. I'm not an expert."

He nudged me lightly with his elbow. "You're on your way to becoming one. And I know that you'll answer totally based on what's good for the community, not your own self interests. Don't worry—I won't leap without doing more research. Your feedback is just a starting point."

Well, in that case… A thrill passed through me at the thought of all the people who'd benefit from the kind of endeavor he was proposing.

"I don't know the city that well yet," I said. "But in general, you'd want to target low-income neighborhoods. And the elderly—they can end up in a bad spot once they've retired, especially if they had pre-existing conditions. But if you're looking to get sponsorships to help fund the clinic, focusing on how it'll help children in need is a great angle too. They're often overlooked if their parents are afraid of the medical expenses, since they can't advocate for themselves."

"That gives me a few different avenues to focus on," Beckett said. "Perfect. This is exactly why I wanted to get your opinion. It definitely sounds like it'd be a worthwhile project with a lot of people who could benefit from it."

"Yes, absolutely." As I polished off the last of my ice cream, I looked at him with affection swelling in my chest. He really was a great guy, not just to me but with good intentions in general. How many businessmen would go out of their way to set up something that would spend their money rather than earning more, just because it'd help people?

A jab of guilt cut through my admiration. He was sharing his plans so freely, asking me for my input, and I hadn't told him about such a huge factor in my life. Hell, I hadn't even told Summer when she'd been right in front of me begging for answers. If Beckett had any idea what kind of secret I was keeping from him, I suspected he'd be just as upset.

But keeping my mouth shut protected him and Summer way more than it did me. I couldn't let my guilty conscience convince me that it was better to confess than to keep them out of the line of fire.

A gust of wind swept over me, more intense than before. It

seemed to cut right through my jacket. I tugged it tighter around me, but my teeth momentarily chattered anyway.

As we walked on, the breeze settled for a minute and then picked up again. When it blasted me with a frigid smack, tossing my hair and seeming to sink right into my skin, I couldn't hold back a shudder.

Beckett tugged me to him. "It's getting colder. Are you all right? You look chilled."

"I'll be okay," I said, but the wind kept whipping around us, washing the chill deeper into my limbs. I tucked myself closer to Beckett instinctively.

He slipped his arm around my shoulders. "Let's get back to the car. I didn't expect the weather to take this sharp a turn."

I stuffed my increasingly icy hands into my pockets and let myself absorb as much heat from his body as I could as we hustled back to the parking lot. The bottom of Beckett's suit jacket flapped with the rising wind, but it appeared to be thick enough that the cold wasn't bothering him as much as it was me.

I managed a giggle. "This might win the world record for shortest stroll around a park."

"Hey, at least we got some delicious ice cream in before everything else cooled off." Beckett gave my shoulder a comforting squeeze.

When we made it to the lot, the other cars had gone. The wind and the chill had cleared out anyone who'd thought it might be a nice day for a walk. As Beckett ushered me over to the car, shivers started to wrack my body.

To my surprise, he guided me to the back seat. When I got in, he slid in after me. He hit a button on his key fob to start the motor running and send heat wafting from the vents, and then pulled me right to him. He lifted my legs over his lap and wrapped both of his arms around me in a tight embrace.

"I can get you warm faster this way," he murmured with a tickle of breath against the side of my face.

Oh, I was getting warmed up all right, and from the inside as well as the outside. Especially as his hands stroked up and down over my arm, my side, and my back. The numbing parts of my body thawed, and a tingle of anticipation spread through every inch of me, remembering what had happened the last time I'd been anywhere near this close to the man holding me.

Apparently our position had stirred up similar thoughts in Beckett. He raised one hand to my cheek and traced his thumb along my cheekbone, his gaze seeking out mine. This close, the mix of fondness and desire in his eyes made my heart skip a beat.

"We haven't talked about what happened the last time we were together," he said quietly. "Before you got that awful phone call."

"We haven't," I agreed, wetting my lips. "But the other stuff definitely wasn't awful."

His mouth curved into a pleased smile. "You're not having any second thoughts about the whole multiple boyfriend thing, then?"

I couldn't help smirking back at him. "My second and third and all additional thoughts on the subject have been that it's an incredibly good deal for me." My attention dropped to his mouth with its assured smile, and a surge of confidence raced through me. "Also, I'd really like to finish what we started before that, when we were on our own the other night."

From the arch of Beckett's eyebrows, I could tell he knew I was talking about when we'd made out under the statue outside the science exhibition. "What exactly would that be?"

I snorted. "I could refresh your memory." With a twist of my body, I shifted one leg over so I was straddling him, chest to chest. "If you're up for it, that is."

Beckett didn't bother to answer me with words. He just gripped the sides of my face and pulled my mouth to his.

I groaned into his lips, tightening my fists in the fabric of his shirt as I pressed the full front of my body into him. The scent of him, sharper now that we were so close, made me giddy. He deepened the kiss, claiming my mouth so thoroughly my hips rocked instinctively against his.

There would be no stopping this time. And now it was just us —no competition, no watching eyes, nothing but our breaths and bodies colliding.

I wanted this. I needed it. Maybe I couldn't tell him everything that was on my mind, but I had no reason to fear sharing my body with him. I could be with him completely that way if nothing else.

I grabbed his shoulders and pulled away slightly, maneuvering around so I could push him down on the backseat with me overtop. Beckett chuckled as he sank down. I glanced at the windows, but remembering the tint on them and the empty parking lot around me eased my momentary uncertainty. I leaned over and recaptured his mouth with mine.

Beckett's fingers tangled in my hair with a gentle tug that sent sparks over my scalp. When I slid one hand up under his dress shirt, dislodging it from his slacks, he let out an encouraging hum. The grinding of my hips into the growing hardness behind his fly provoked a groan.

The sense of control exhilarated me, but I couldn't shake the feeling that it was entirely at his whim. If he'd wanted to take charge, I could lose my position in an instant.

So I'd better make the most of it while I was here. When we'd come together the first time, he'd teased me so much, driving me to the edge of release and stealing it back. We'd see how he liked it when the tables were turned.

A wicked smile crossed my lips. I could be Madelyn Silver, the studious student and general do-gooder, but I'd discovered a darker side in the past few weeks. I'd developed a taste for making my own rules.

"You look like you're making devious plans," Beckett said with amusement.

"Just you wait and see."

As I kissed him again, he pulled my shirt up over my bra and stroked my breasts through the thin fabric. The swipe of his thumbs over my pebbling nipples had me whimpering, pleasure pulsing through my chest.

I couldn't let him distract me from my intentions. I dropped one hand to the waist of his slacks and undid the fly. When I delved my fingers beneath to circle his rigid shaft through his boxers, another groan tumbled from his mouth into mine. "Fuck, Maddie," he muttered. "I've never wanted anyone the way I want you."

A different sort of thrill rippled through me. I ran my hand up and down his cock, loving the way it twitched against my palm, and devoured his mouth. When he squeezed my nipples, my hips bucked against him.

It wasn't enough. I was aching down below—aching to have him fill me just as thoroughly as he had the other day in the Vigil office.

I jerked his slacks further down and his boxers in turn. "Condom?" I murmured raggedly against his lips as I pumped him skin to skin.

Even unfazable Beckett's breath was coming rougher now, a touch of pink coloring his pale face. "Glove compartment."

I pushed away from him just long enough to fumble open the compartment and grab one of the few packets tucked in a corner there—not looking as if they'd needed to be ready for other recent use, I was relieved to see. Not that Beckett had given me a reason to think he'd been pursuing any women other than me.

I tore the packet open and rolled the contents over him. Beckett tucked his hand between my legs to fondle me through my jeans, setting off a sharper flare of need in my pussy. I ground into his hand with a little growl.

"I think I like you ferocious like this," he said with a glint of humor in his eyes.

He popped open the top button for me, and I squirmed out of my jeans as quickly as I could. His fingers pressed against my naked cunt, slick with my arousal, and we both groaned.

Holding his gaze, I dipped my own hand between my legs, drenching them in my wetness and then wrapping my fingers around his shaft. Beckett's eyes blazed with lust as I worked him up and down. He flicked his thumb over my clit, and I swallowed a gasp. Then I scooted just a couple of inches forward so I could lower myself over him.

He thrust up to meet me, filling me so swiftly and fully that a moan reverberated out of me. Beckett matched it with a hungry sound of his own. Bliss resonated through my whole body from where we'd joined.

I bent over to claim his mouth. As we kissed, sloppier now with our ragged breaths, I rocked up and down over his cock. Beckett matched my rhythm, arching to meet me, hitting a point even deeper inside that had me gasping for release.

But I didn't intend to end this quickly. I bucked faster until I caught the sharper hitch of his breath, and then I slowed right down, ignoring the impulse inside me screaming to careen over my own edge. Beckett's eyes darted up to catch mine.

"What's the matter?" I teased. "It's more fun if you don't get there too fast, isn't it?"

A rumble that was both amusement and frustration sounded in his chest. He gripped my hips, urging me onward. I let myself get lost in the rhythm and the pleasure racing through my veins, lifting me higher and higher—and then I eased off again, coasting on the exquisite denial.

Beckett swore through a laugh. Then a look of determination came over his face.

Before I knew what was happening, he gave a heave and managed to flip us around. My back hit the buttery leather seat, and then his cock slammed into me all the way to the hilt.

He pinned my wrists over my head and grinned down at me, his eyes alight with a passion so fierce it seared me to the bone, but only in the best possible way.

"You had your turn," he announced. "Now I'm the one who'll do the fucking."

His mouth crashed down on mine with so much hunger I nearly came just like that. I tugged at my wrists, but he refused to release them. A few seconds later, as he thrust into me again, I was seeing so many stars I didn't even care.

A chorus of needy sounds spilled from my lips. I pushed my hips up to meet him frantically, and he met my desperation for release by slamming into me harder, faster. It was an aggression I hadn't gotten from him the other day in the Vigil office, but I knew that the instant I made any indication that I was in discomfort, he'd stop. He watched my face avidly, speeding up his thrusts to match the gasps and whimpers flowing out of me with the rush of bliss.

"I won't make you wait any longer," he said raggedly. "We've had enough teasing." His other hand slipped between us, fingering my clit as he bucked into me even harder. "Come for me, Maddie."

The pressure of his fingertips and the heat in his voice sent me careening over the edge with a cry. Ecstasy crackled through me as if I were a firework. It burst from my core all through my limbs, leaving me shuddering with glee.

Beckett tipped his head back with a few more brutal thrusts. He tensed with a shudder of his own and then bowed over me as he slowed to a stop. He caught my mouth with one last, sweet kiss before releasing my wrists.

"Wow," I whispered, not even bothering to lower my arms from where he'd pinned them. He eased more of his weight onto me, blanketing me in his heat but bracing himself on his elbows so he didn't squash me.

Beckett beamed at me, the merciless lover falling away, leaving only that handsome, adoring face with a gleam of almost boyish delight in his eyes. "I'd say that worked out well for both of us in the end."

I laughed. "No kidding. You've definitely given me a stroll to remember."

With a guffaw, he rolled us so we were both on our sides and pulled me in to snuggle close to him. I relaxed into his solid frame, letting his warmth and the afterglow of the sex wash away any lingering worries for a little longer.

As much as I'd enjoyed the ice cream, this workout had clearly burned most of it off. My stomach let out a faint, embarrassing gurgle. My cheeks flared, and I ducked my head next to Beckett's. "I don't suppose you'd like to go grab some dinner?"

His body tensed just slightly. He tipped his head to check the car's clock and sighed. "I wish I could, but I can't squeeze it in. I've got an important business meeting that I'll need to head off to in less than an hour. I'll have to drop you off soon, but we can stay here like this for a little bit longer."

"Oh, okay," I said, tamping down on my disappointment. It wasn't as if he'd offered dinner when he'd asked me out. "I figured I'd ask."

"We'll do dinner later this week," he promised, kissing my forehead. But even as I nestled against him again, I couldn't help wondering what kind of business meeting a major business owner would have to attend on a Sunday evening.

CHAPTER 22

Beckett

I straightened the lapels on my jacket as I strode up the front steps of the upscale hotel. Two doormen opened the glass doors simultaneously. My shoulders straightened a little more with my first steps into the lobby, which was full of marble tiles and gold accents on the furniture.

Now more than any other time, I needed to present myself as totally impervious.

My loafers tapped against the polished tiles as I walked right through the lobby, already having received directions to the hotel's boardroom in advance. For meetings like this, we dealt with the local staff as little as possible. They'd have been instructed by the member organizing this meeting not to interfere with specific guests on their arrival.

As usual, it was a space with maximum privacy, tucked away at the back of the fifth floor with a door so sound-proofed not a hint of sound penetrated it until I'd pushed into the room.

A crystal chandelier hung above the long mahogany table, casting splotches of light across the vast room's walls. Floor-to-ceiling satin curtains covered what I assumed was a long stretch of windows, which would only have shown darkness beyond them anyway, other than the globe of the moon.

The Devil's Dozen always met at night, always when the moon was at its fullest. I didn't know when the tradition had started, and when I'd asked Dad as a kid he hadn't been able to tell me, so I didn't think he had a clue either. Probably no one in this room did. But we kept to those long-held customs all the same.

Thirteen chairs surrounded the majestic table with plenty of space in between: six on one side, six on the other, and one at the head for this month's meeting leader. We each got that spot once a year.

Most of the seats were already filled. Several cool gazes had turned my way at my entrance. I offered a mild but unaffected smile, knowing I was facing down the heads of the biggest and most secretive criminal empires in the world. They were the most powerful people currently living, and they knew it.

And I was one of them—almost.

I ignored the skepticism I could feel in their gazes and marched to one of the vacant chairs without hesitation. Not the one next to the Long Night, whose skeptical gaze was more a glower, though he didn't say anything. I'd rather not deal too directly with him.

In his sixties now, the older man's hair was almost entirely white, but there was nothing frail about his broad frame or the sharpness of his eyes. And he had a good reason to offer a less than warm welcome. I was here representing the Storm in my father's place, and as the Storm, my father had staged a hostile takeover of some of the Long Night's territory in Paradise Bend several years back.

The man glowering at me had no idea that it was *my* intervention that'd saved him the trouble of having to fight to get that territory back. I kept my family's internal conflicts as private as I could.

It would have been nice if Dad hadn't gotten it into his head to make a power grab like that to begin with. I'd rather not have been starting my theoretical reign with enemies within the inner circle of the Devil's Dozen. But I had to work with the hand I'd been dealt.

I noted that the Red Shark, the other party in the Paradise Bend fiasco, had placed himself a few seats away from the Long Night too. He didn't meet my eyes at all, fiddling with a pen he periodically clicked against the table as if he were bored by the proceedings. Just more posturing.

Before I'd quite reached the chair I was aiming for, another member strolled over. My teeth set on edge as I forced a smile at the fifty-something man in the sleek violet suit. He was grinning at me, but there was no warmth in his expression.

"The old man couldn't be bothered to make an appearance, hmm?" Doom's Seed said, pulling a cigar from his suit pocket. His thick tie was banded with silver stripes so shiny they were almost blinding. The guy always wore the flashiest clothing out of all of us, sauntering around the place like he was the sauvest man in the world. I was pretty sure *that* wasn't true.

He'd asked the question mildly, but behind the sparkle in his eyes, his penetrating gaze told me that he'd meant to rankle me. He was poking for weak spots. It wasn't unusual—it was what we all did. The most powerful people in the world couldn't help evaluating each other's power at every turn.

I kept my voice perfectly even. "I'm starting to transition into the role of the Storm myself. My father and I have decided it's best if I attend some of the meetings so that I can become fully immersed in the work. I assure you that I can speak for him and that any decisions I make are the Storm's."

Attending the meetings of the Devil's Dozen when the baton hadn't officially been passed on was unusual, but I knew it wasn't unheard of. Doom's Seed couldn't accuse me of any kind of misconduct. He tapped the end of his cigar against his lips with a soft huff. "He has a lot of faith in youth then, does he?"

Another attempted jab, but easily ignored. "He's very satisfied with how I've handled our business so far."

Doom's Seed shrugged. "With the way of the world these days, I would have thought your father would be interested in hearing about any new threats and opportunities first hand, that's all."

"He trusts that I'll tell him whatever he needs to know," I said calmly. "And it's better that I'm prepared for when we make the full transition."

"I know I don't plan on giving up *my* position any time soon," the other man said with a lightly scoffing tone.

I couldn't resist getting in a subtle jab of my own. "I suppose we don't always get a choice about it. I doubt the Blood Hunter planned to give up his seat when he did."

Your time may be limited, was the unspoken message. *You're not untouchable.*

Both our gazes slid to the young woman sitting at the other end of the table, the current Blood Hunter who'd taken over the position two years ago after some kind of hostile takeover that I wasn't clear on the details of. She was the only person in the room under forty other than me, probably only a few years older than my twenty-three, but her pose emanated strength and quiet confidence, her dark eyes alertly assessing beneath the fall of her black hair as she scanned the room.

Doom's Seed appeared to feel he'd gotten everything he could out of the conversation, which wasn't much, and ambled back to the chair he'd taken. I settled into my own, holding back the urge to clench my hands.

He had no idea how close to home his comments had hit. I wasn't here because of Dad's investment in my learning the ropes but because Dad had become so *un*invested in so much of our business in general. I had no idea how much the true Storm even cared about keeping the business afloat these days. He might even have preferred to see it slip through his fingers so he could walk away.

But I would keep the family legacy together. I would set the Storm's empire on a new path, and I wasn't going to let any of the people around me catch one hint of our current weakness.

Especially Doom's Seed. No doubt one of the reasons he liked to test me, if not the main reason, was the fact that some of his territory bordered the Storm's. Maybe he thought he might stage a little takeover of his own if he got the sense that he could get away with it without consequences.

All of these people were circling me as if I were the bait in a tank of sharks, and one misstep would ruin everything. But as long as they never realized how precarious my position was, Dad and I would be just fine.

I took in the rest of the table from my new vantage point, reflecting as I had the few times I'd attended meetings before on how same-y this group was. Of the thirteen of us, ten were men, and ten were white. All but me and the Blood Hunter were middle-aged or above. Yet another committee of sorts run mostly by old white dudes. But then, that was where the ultimate influence tended to land even in this day and age. It was impressive to have a few who didn't fit the mold among us.

One of those was this meeting's leader, the only member of the Devil's Dozen who broke the mold in not onc but two ways. The

Deadly Rose was sitting at the head of the table, glancing over notes on her tablet with occasional flicks of her gaze around the room to confirm who'd arrived.

I could tell at a glance that this woman could live up to the "Deadly" part of her name if required. She looked to be in her early fifties, but her slim brown arms were defined with toned muscles. She held herself with an air of authority that more than matched the men around her. Her trim white pantsuit contrasted with the dark complexion that came with her obvious Latina heritage—and highlighted the vicious flash of her teeth before she pushed herself to her feet as the last of our number reached the table.

When she cleared her throat, the few conversations that'd started around the table ended in an instant. Her gaze traveled around the table, holding each of ours for a second, her expression carefully neutral.

"All right," she said, drawing herself up even straighter with a tone that was strictly professional. "Lets get down to the business of being the people who actually rule this world."

CHAPTER 23

Madelyn

I strode into the law library with a travel mug of coffee in hand, holding on to optimism that the trucking company Slade had grabbed documents for might get us somewhere with our investigation. The last I'd heard, Dexter was working on the code and Logan was digging up whatever he could find on the company online.

I'd arrived a little early like I preferred to, since being late always made me feel guilty, so I slowed as I walked past the tables and the shelving units beyond, anticipating that I'd need to wait for one of the guys to show up to unlock the door. My mind was so wrapped up in the possibilities ahead of us that I'd almost reached the Vigil office before I registered the smoky scent in the air.

My legs stiffened beneath me. My gaze flicked around the room and snagged on a thin waft of smoke seeping from beneath the office door. I backed up a step, a startled yelp bursting out of me.

Even as I watched, more smoke curled up from under the door and wisped into the air. A prickling sensation formed in my throat. Why hadn't any alarms gone off?

"Help!" I shouted, backing up more. "Someone call 911! I think there's a fire back here."

As I spun to make sure my warning had been heard, my gaze caught on a smoke detector on the ceiling not far at all from the Vigil office. But the round contraption was strangely dented. Had it been broken somehow?

Someone had set a fire purposefully and made sure it wouldn't be detected quickly. If I hadn't gone to the back of the room ten minutes before our meeting, who knew how far it'd have spread by then?

Footsteps thumped behind me. One of the librarians caught sight of the thickening smoke and gasped. A hint of orange flickered in the tiny gap at the threshold—flames licking at the door.

As the librarian whirled and hustled back the way she'd come, hollering for all the students to vacate the building, I hurried after her. Enough smoke had filled my throat to leave me coughing hard enough that I nearly spilled what remained of my coffee. I took a gulp of it to try to wash away the irritation.

Students and staff were all grabbing their belongings and rushing out the doors, a few of them with phones raised to their ears. Just as I came outside, one of the smoke alarms toward the front of the room finally let out its frantic wail. The whole room behind me was hazing with smoke.

Sirens pealed in the distance. I pushed into the crowd that'd gathered outside the building, not just the people from the law library but several classes of students and professors from the upper floors of the building. Everyone was murmuring in confusion and concern.

God, I hoped the firemen were quick enough to stop the whole place from burning up. All those books!

And all the stuff in the Vigil's office. My throat tightened. That room had obviously been the main target—it was where the fire had started. I wasn't sure I'd have believed this could be an accident, a mere coincidence, even if I hadn't noticed the damaged smoke detector.

Just as the first firetruck roared into view, a figure burst from the front of the crowd and ran at the doors. The frantic motion was so unlike the guy I knew that it took me a moment to realize those were Dexter's black curls bouncing wildly as he reached for the library entrance.

One of the professors caught him and hauled him back, saying something I couldn't make out. Dexter turned, and I saw his face, even paler than usual and tight with panic.

"My—my girlfriend could be in there," he protested, his normally subdued voice taut with worry. "I haven't seen her—she was supposed to meet us at the library. She's never late."

My heart stuttered. I squeezed through the crowd to reach him, a sudden swell of emotion filling my chest—the urgent need to calm his panic, but also a rush of affection at hearing him call me his girlfriend and the fact that he knew my habits so well.

"No one can go in there," the professor was saying as I approached, ushering Dexter away. "The fire department is here—they'll get anyone who's stuck inside to safety."

"But what if—"

Several firefighters were already jogging over, shouting for the crowd to move farther back. I grabbed Dexter's arm, and he spun to face me with a flinch.

In my hurry to get his attention, I'd forgotten his usual aversion to touch. I jerked my hand back automatically, but as the panic in his eyes faded into relief, he snatched my fingers to hold on to them.

"There you are," he said, his voice still a little shaky. "I saw the smoke—I couldn't see you in the crowd—"

"It's okay," I said. "I'm fine. I was actually the one who spotted the smoke first and sounded the alarm. Not a scratch or a burn on me."

I held out my other arm as if to display myself. Dexter sucked in a ragged breath and then grinned at me, squeezing my hand tight. I wanted to hug him, but I wasn't sure if he'd want that in his current keyed-up state.

I hadn't known he could get that emotional about anyone. I gripped his hand in return, wishing I knew how to express how much it meant to me.

"Hey, Piccolina!" Slade came up next to me with a gentle bump of my shoulder.

I'd been so focused on Dexter that I hadn't realized the other Vigil guys had arrived. Logan joined us at my other side and motioned for us to step farther away from both the building and the rest of the crowd.

I glanced over my shoulder. The firefighters had yanked open the library doors and ventured inside, the hiss of water from their hoses and the sizzle of doused flames carrying through the air. More smoke billowed through the doorway.

We stopped on the other side of a nearby path under the slim branches of a sapling. Logan's mouth had set in a tense line. "How the hell does a library end up catching fire?"

He didn't know—of course, he couldn't know yet.

"I think it was on purpose," I said, still clinging to Dexter's hand. "There was smoke coming from under the door of your office, but the alarm hadn't gone off. The nearest smoke detector looked busted."

Slade's eyes widened, and my stepbrother's shoulder's went rigid.

"Fuck," Logan spat out. "They're trying to ruin the whole investigation now."

A different sort of fear rippled through me. "The fire *won't* ruin it, will it? I mean, you have everything backed up outside the office, don't you?" I couldn't imagine a guy as computer savvy as Logan failing to make backups.

"Of course," he said, his gaze still fixed on the building. "The digital files are stored in the cloud, and we took photos and scans of most of the paper records… but those won't count as proper evidence if the actual objects are destroyed. It's too easy to doctor digital images. Your dad's notes… the flyer from the seafood market… Hell, even the shipping records from the trucking company." He glanced at Dexter. "You left those in the filing cabinet and just took a photo to go over at home, right?"

Dexter nodded with a grimace. "I thought the original would be safer here than in the apartment."

Slade let out a rough laugh. "So much for campus security. This is why they need us. Except now we *are* the case."

"Why *now*?" I had to ask. "Is it because Slade picked up that envelope?"

Logan frowned. "It could be, but he was pretty careful not to show anything identifiable. I wouldn't have known who it was from our own footage if I hadn't been in on the plan."

"If that's the case, then there must be something *really* important in those records," Dexter put in.

My gaze shot to him. "You haven't broken the code yet?"

"No, unfortunately. I'm not sure I can. With closer inspection, I'm pretty sure it's based on an external key. Which means it's very simple to break the code when you *have* the key, but nearly impossible if you don't."

"Shit." I rubbed my mouth, and another possibility occurred to me with an icy jolt. "Or it could be my fault."

Logan aimed his frown at me. "What are you talking about, Maddie?"

I waved vaguely in the direction of our hometown. "When I went back to visit Mom on the weekend—I asked her a few questions about Dad's things. And I talked to one of his former colleagues briefly to see if there were any old notes of his in storage or something at the hospital. I didn't see anyone else around, but it's possible someone overheard me—or that her room was bugged—I have no idea." I groaned and dropped my face into my hands. "I shouldn't have risked it."

I half expected Logan to chide me for my carelessness, but he'd locked the asshole side of him firmly away. He squeezed my shoulder instead, his expression only concerned. "You were just trying to help. And it could have been the envelope we stole and not anything you did. Hell, it could be they have no idea we're still on the case and this is just a follow-up to the attack on your mom that they'd have done anyway. Did you find out anything useful at the hospital?"

"Nothing that helps us figure out who murdered him, but I confirmed that a bunch of his things went missing from the office right after he died. His colleague assumed he'd brought some stuff home, even though we know it isn't there."

The corner of his mouth curved upward in the slightest of smiles. "I guess I'll take that as a tiny bit of progress, since it means there's even less chance of you deciding I'm just paranoid after all."

I wrinkled my nose at him and looked back toward the building. Logan followed my gaze. The firefighters were tramping out, a little sooty but not looking particularly worse for wear. They dragged their hoses out with them.

"We need to see if there's anything left in the office that can be salvaged," Logan said.

"They probably won't let us back in for a while," I pointed out.

Slade smiled mysteriously. "We have our ways. But it'll be a bit before they've totally secured the scene. Let's grab some lunch and see what we can find when we get back."

I tagged along with the guys, but my head was in such a daze that I barely tasted the burger I ended up buying. All four of us stayed mostly silent as we ate, pensive expressions all around. I had no idea how much stuff the guys might have lost to the fire, how much they'd had stashed in the office for safe-keeping, but the setback was clearly weighing on them.

We came back to the law library around the side of the building. The crowd had wandered off, and the firetrucks were gone, but caution tape was stretched across the main entrance.

While the three of us blocked him from view, Dexter made short work of a side door's lock. We slunk inside through a maintenance hall and emerged into the library through a doorway next to the staff offices.

The space was dark and empty, the carpet squelching beneath our feet, still saturated with the sprayed water. The smell of smoke lingered in the air. The bookshelves at the back near the Vigil office and the floor in front of its doorway were charred black.

I couldn't help holding my breath in dread and anticipation as we reached the door, which had been bashed in to allow the firefighters entrance without unlocking it.

Logan and Slade flicked on the flashlights on their phones. As we stepped inside, the thin beams sweeping over the room, my heart sank.

The only items in the room I could still identify were the table, the desk, and the filing cabinet, although even those were warped and scorched. The computer had melted into a featureless blob. Every paper and book in the place was nothing but ashes. My sneakers squished into the waterlogged cinders on the floor.

Slade went to the filing cabinet and yanked at the drawers. They creaked and rattled open just enough for him to peek inside.

"It's all garbage," he said with a sigh. "Everything burned up."

Logan tugged open the drawer on the desk, the edges of which were blackened. He stared at the charred contents inside for several seconds without speaking, his posture slumping. When I came up beside him, I made out the corner of a thin cardboard box mixed in with the ashen contents.

His mom's tarot cards. They'd been destroyed too. My heart wrenched, and I slung my arm around his back as if my embrace could make that loss any less painful.

"It's okay," he said, but in a voice that sounded more like a snarl. "It just means these bastards have one more thing to pay for."

I shivered at his words, because they stirred up another question I didn't want to consider. Our enemies clearly wanted to make *us* pay in as many ways as possible.

Were they finished now? And if they weren't, how would they strike out at us next?

CHAPTER 24

Dexter

With each new revelation, the puzzle that this case had become only expanded, all the pieces reshuffling in my grasp before I could place them and categorize them. I needed some level of structure—something to allow me to confidently connect at least two of the chaotic fragments, but the information we accumulated seemed to become more varied rather than less with each new development. It was getting harder to believe those fragments would ever fit together.

And now the concrete manifestation of an awful lot of those fragments had been destroyed in a burst of fire.

I stared at the room full of blackened furniture and ash, my mind spinning in a way that felt uncomfortably aimless. The sodden remains of our office stared back at me without giving a single answer. On autopilot, I forced myself to raise my hand and snap some pictures. I captured every corner and crevice of the darkened room, scanning it over with my eyes and camera simultaneously while looking for any clues.

Since we'd formed the Vigil, I'd always been confident in my ability to connect the dots and find the bigger picture even if the other guys couldn't. Now… now I wasn't sure how I'd manage it. This case might have pushed me beyond my abilities.

Madelyn eased over to me through the wreckage and shot me a small smile. "Always documenting everything."

I shrugged. "It can't hurt. We've found new details looking back through the photos before."

"That's true—we have. I won't stop you. I just know this has got to be hard for all of you. You've been working out of this place for a while."

She let out a breath that was shaky enough to tell me that she was awfully unsettled by what had happened even if she'd used this space much less than the rest of us. Then she raised her hand as if to rub my arm the way she'd touched Logan reassuringly earlier, but hesitated before her fingers reached me. Unsurprising, given the way I normally reacted to physical contact. The way I'd reacted just a couple of hours ago when she'd first come up to me outside the library.

"It's okay," I said. "I don't mind with you. As long as I know it's you."

Her smile softened a little, and she let her hand rest on my arm.

It was strange how much sensation flowed from that one small touch. Warmth bloomed over my skin all the way to my chest, making my heart skip a beat. A tingle raced through my nerves alongside it.

The emotions this woman stirred up in me were a puzzle too, but one I didn't mind anywhere near as much. I wasn't sure how to navigate the new territory I'd uncovered with her, but at least it seemed to be leading someplace good.

I'd never felt this comfortable with any other woman. Never been this drawn to anyone, this curious to discover how much I could make *her* feel. I'd had a couple of brief encounters during my first year at college, classmates who'd found me intriguing, but it'd been obvious they just got off on the idea of hooking up with someone unusual and didn't care all that much about me personally beyond that.

Madelyn treated me like my reactions were no less normal than anyone else's. Like she saw all of *me,* not as a puzzle but as a person worth caring about. A person whose company she actually enjoyed. Which was good, because the more time I spent with her, the more of her company I wanted to keep. She held her own with us so well in spite of being new to this kind of situation, but there was a sweetness to her at the same time that appealed to me in a *very* different way from my appreciation for either of my friends.

The pull toward her was exhilarating but also unnerving. I had no idea where it would lead me. But most of me was dying to find out.

Across from us, Slade shook his head and kicked at some of the mess with the toe of his shoe. "Well, this office is a steaming pile of horse shit if I'd ever seen one."

Logan stepped out into the main library room and squinted toward the ceiling. "The security camera aimed this way might still have been functioning," he said tersely. "We should see about getting access to the footage. It's a long shot given how careful these people have been so far, but there's a chance we'll spot something useful."

Madelyn squared her shoulders as if preparing for battle, but I couldn't help noticing how tight her jaw had gotten. She was holding herself together, but this was another attack on her as well as us, and one that she was worried she'd instigated with her questions. Though none of us had been prepared to face this kind of pushback, she had been least of all.

"Why don't you two look into that, and I'll take Madelyn back to our apartment," I said before I could second-guess the impulse. "We can re-group there."

Logan's forehead furrowed for a second before his gaze settled on Madelyn. He must have noticed the same signs that I had, because he nodded.

Madelyn raised her chin with visible effort. "I'm fine. If there's some way I can help—"

"There isn't," Logan said, firmly but kindly. "It'll be up to me to get in and I only need one person as lookout. All the rest of our materials related to the case are back at the apartment, so that's the best place for us to go over what we still have later."

She hesitated but then dipped her head in acceptance. I brushed my fingers against her elbow to guide her out of the room.

We were just stepping out from the maintenance door when one minor problem occurred to me. "I don't have a car. But we could—"

"It's fine," Madelyn said easily. "I'll drive. You'll just have to give me directions. I've only been there once, and I was kind of distracted at the time."

"Of course."

There was something strange about getting into the passenger seat of the car we'd found for her. Maybe because so often when I'd been heading anywhere in the past few weeks, it'd been with Logan in the driver's seat.

Would he have insisted on driving Madelyn to accommodate her emotional turmoil? I didn't know whether demanding the keys would be a caring act or a patronizing one. If there was anything I knew about this woman, it was that she didn't like being told what she couldn't do. She was already starting the ignition and pulling out of the parking lot.

I wanted to be that kind of guy for her—the kind of guy who'd look out for her and do anything in his power to keep her safe. Logan had been so devoted to protecting her that he'd damaged his relationship with her for a long time.

Or to do what Slade could, crack a few jokes and have her laughing freely with that sparkle of joy in her eyes. Make her forget about the worries weighing her down for a little while. But looking around the car, I couldn't see anything I had a good idea to spin off of.

I might not be as good for her as either of them. But I'd give it my all. As I glanced over at her while she concentrated on the traffic ahead of us, a tiny line forming on her brow, determination flooded me alongside the clang of concern and desire and all sorts of other feelings I hadn't totally identified.

I was going to be as good for her as I possibly could be, in every conceivable way.

I directed her through the streets to the apartment building, and I could tell from the way she repeated my instructions under her breath that she was committing the route to memory. She obviously expected she'd be coming here again. That knowledge sent an unexpected thrill through me.

The afternoon sun glared down at us from overhead as we crossed the parking lot. We escaped into the shadows of the lobby, and the elevator whirred us upward. When I opened the door to the apartment, a whiff of the lasagna I'd made last night tickled my nose.

Madelyn perked up. "It smells good in here. Have you been cooking again?"

"It's a pretty regular thing," I said, enjoying the eagerness in her tone. "I know we had lunch not too long ago, but if you want some of the leftovers, there are plenty."

She licked her lips, a motion that sent a quiver of sensation straight to my groin. "I wouldn't mind a bit. Just to give it a try."

I had to smile. "My pleasure."

And it really was. *This* was something I could offer that was all my own. I got the casserole dish out of the fridge and cut out a half-sized portion before popping the plate into the microwave. Madelyn settled into a chair at the table like she belonged here, which pleased me in a wholy different way.

"I made it with sausage and beef, and the tomato sauce is totally from scratch," I said with pride I couldn't restrain. Not all of my culinary experiments turned out well, but I could tell when they had—and Logan and Slade had made it clear they agreed last night.

"Sounds fantastic. And smells fantastic. I feel like I need a little sustenance to get me steady again after seeing the office."

"Perfect." I set the plate in front of her and passed her a fork. I couldn't help studying her response as she slipped the first bite into her mouth.

A gleeful smile crossed her lips, her shoulders coming down an inch from their previous tensed position. "You make lasagna as well as you make curry," she told me, digging in with even more gusto. "Which means really, really well."

I couldn't say whether her enthusiasm for the food or the fact that it'd clearly helped soothe her nerves made me happier. A smile played across my own lips as I watched her finish.

A momentary boldness took over me. "If there are any favorite dishes you'd ever like me to try out, I'd love to see what I can do with them."

Madelyn's eyes lit up even more. She waved her fork at me. "I'm pretty sure I'm going to take you up on that offer, so you'd better mean it."

"One hundred percent."

After she'd set her plate and fork in the sink with a quick rinse, she turned, her gaze skimming through the apartment. Then she shot me a glance with her eyebrows slightly arched. "I haven't seen your room yet. Or is that off-limits?"

My own nerves twanged with a weird combination of anxiety and excitement. "Do you want to see it that badly?"

She shrugged, looking abruptly awkward. "I mean, I think you can tell a lot about a person from their private space. And I'd like to get to know you even better. But it is private. You don't have to invite me in just because I'm nosy."

"You're not nosy," I said automatically. She wanted to understand me even better than she already did. I had no idea how to tell her what that meant to me.

Instead of speaking, I beckoned her over. "There's nothing particularly secret in there. And I suppose it's only fair when I saw your dorm room ages ago."

"Good point," Madelyn said, amusement lacing her tone. "Thank you for making such a solid argument on my behalf."

I found myself grinning back at her. "Anytime." I nudged the door open and stepped back so she could walk in ahead of me.

Madelyn eased past me and stopped in the middle of the room, turning slowly so she could take in the whole space. I was abruptly grateful that I had a thing about always leaving my bedcovers tucked neatly and keeping my clothes either hung up or in my hamper. There was no mess to put her off.

She focused on the bookcase, which I'd admit had the most interesting collection of items in the room. Reaching out, she skimmed her fingertips down over the spines of the forensic science and chemistry texts, my assorted cookbooks that had been my jumping off point but that I rarely consulted these days, and the shelves holding various puzzle boxes and other tricky contraptions I'd collected over the years.

A lot of them were from before my college days, but I hadn't wanted to leave them at home. I wasn't totally sure my younger siblings wouldn't snatch them up and do who knew what with them if they proved too difficult.

"This all fits the Dexter I know," Madelyn said. "No wonder you were able to crack the secret of my dad's trinket box. You obviously have lots of experience."

"Honestly, I find those relaxing," I told her. "There's always one solution, one that seems very simple once you figure it out. Not much else in life is like that."

"After what we've tackled in the past few weeks, I can understand the appeal." She straightened up, and her gaze veered to my desk. As usual, it was mostly bare, only my computer and a notebook sitting on it—and a single framed photo at the back. A picture of me with my parents and my brother and sister on a family camping trip several years back.

Madelyn paused over it with a pensive expression. "This is your family?"

I nodded. "They're very into the outdoors."

She glanced over at me. "You say 'they' rather than 'we.' Not so much your thing? You do look a little separate from them somehow. You're kind of standing off to the side rather than right there with them."

I hadn't thought of it before, but when she pointed it out, I could see exactly what she meant. Mom and Dad were poised under the huge oak tree we'd found by the river, Mom's hand resting on Jack's shoulder and Ella gripping Dad's arm as she grinned eagerly at the camera. I stood next to Dad and Ella, but with enough space between us that we weren't anywhere near touching. Both my smile and my posture were a bit stiff to my eyes, but I wouldn't have expected anyone else to notice that.

"I've never really felt like I totally connected with the rest of them in general," I admitted with a twinge through my stomach. "They're all athletic and social, and I'd rather be in my room reading or figuring out some new puzzle. I think my parents were kind of relieved when my younger siblings turned out to be more like them than I was."

Madelyn's mouth twisted. "I'm sorry."

"It's okay. I'm used to it. Now that I'm not living at home, I don't feel the same pressure to try to fit in with them. And it's not like they were mean about it or anything. They just didn't really get me."

I paused and decided to share more than that. Madelyn wanted to know me, and I could let her see my weaknesses as well as my strengths. "They didn't know how to handle the bullying I got when I was younger—it wasn't something they'd ever had to deal with… I'm lucky that I met Logan and Slade and found people I could belong with instead of always being off to the side."

"That is lucky," Madelyn said softly. She turned toward me, and the affection in her eyes made my pulse stutter.

I kept talking, not letting myself chicken out of the confession. "Those two guys are the only people who really took the time to get to know me and understand what matters to me… until you. So now I'm even luckier."

Madelyn beamed at me so warmly that her expression melted any nervousness I'd felt. Like a moth compelled by a flame, I couldn't stop myself from stepping closer to her. Running my fingers over her hair and then letting my palm come to rest against her cheek.

Her lips parted, and I knew she wanted me with the same longing that was coursing through my own body. That one fact seemed perfectly clear—so clear that nothing at all seemed to stand in the way of my lowering my mouth to hers.

Madelyn kissed me back with obvious enthusiasm but also a sense of restraint, as if she were checking to make sure I was into it rather than diving right in. And maybe that was a good thing, because every nerve in my body seemed to be crackling like a sparkler, nearly overwhelming me with giddiness at the soft heat of her lips pressing against mine.

How could another human being make me feel so much? So alive? But she did. And even though it scared me a little, I reveled in the sensation.

One kiss merged into another and another, each one getting deeper and more intense. Madelyn dared to flick her tongue across my bottom lip, and I did the same in return. At the rough sound in her throat, I delved it farther into her mouth to tangle with her tongue. I was drowning in her and consuming her all at the same time.

I eased up on the kissing enough to focus on what the rest of me was doing. My hands trailed down the sides of her body, eager to touch every part of her. All the places I hadn't gotten the chance to explore in our hasty interlude in the library bathroom.

Which parts of her would make her gasp or whimper? How could I provoke the same giddiness in her that she was in me? She was a puzzle herself, one I intended to find every special trick to that would leave her satisfied.

I slid my fingers up the curves of her hips and stopped at the hem of her shirt. Madelyn stroked her hands down my chest in turn, and I found the confidence to tug at her blouse. She raised her arms immediately, giving me free access to peel the shirt off her.

I tossed it aside and found myself staring down at her modest but gorgeous curves, boosted by her simple bra. Tracing my thumb over the peak of one, I watched her nipple pebble against the fabric and absorbed the hitch of her breath. That terrain deserved plenty of my attention.

But there were other areas I hadn't tested yet. As I caressed her breasts through her bra, I brought my mouth to the edge of her jaw, then the side of her neck, peppering kisses all the way to her shoulder. Making note of the spots where she trembled or let out a sound to return to later.

One of her hands clutched my shirt. The other wound into my hair with a fierceness that heated me up even more. As she started fumbling with the buttons on my shirt to reveal my own chest, I reached behind her to unclasp her bra.

She was even more beautiful now that I could see all of her. The graceful arc of her natural curves, the pert nipples that called to be fondled, the taut line of her belly below, which I knew held as much strength as softness.

I must have held there, staring, for a few moments too long. Madelyn's hands stilled with my shirt still on though completely unbuttoned. The fingers that'd twined with my curls glided down to touch my cheek.

"We don't have to do more than this," she murmured. "I won't put any pressure on you. I want you to be enjoying this just as much as I am."

A raw chuckle tumbled from my mouth. "If you think I'm not looking forward to enjoying *everything* we can do together, then I'm going to have to give a better demonstration."

Any remaining tension left her body as she bobbed up to catch my lips with another kiss. I kissed her back harder than before, walking her backward at the same time. I knew my room well enough to mark the exact moment when the backs of her legs would hit the side of my bed.

I grasped her hips and eased her down on the covers, then tugged at her jeans. As Madelyn wriggled out of them and peeled off my shirt, I dipped my head to her breasts. When I lapped my tongue over one nipple experimentally, the twitch of her body and the moan that escaped her told me I'd done well.

I worked over one breast and then the other with my lips, tongue, and teeth, finding every gesture and point of contact that could turn Madelyn's breaths into something closer to panting. With every passing second, my confidence grew. There was no mistaking the hungry noises slipping from her mouth or the almost frantic way she clutched at my hair and my shoulders.

"Oh, Dexter," she mumbled. "Feels so good."

Her hips had started to cant upward as if seeking friction. A fresh wave of heat rushed through my body with that observation. I slid down her body, placing a kiss here and there, stroking her thighs as I eased down her panties, marking even more territory I'd want to return to again and again whenever I had the chance.

Then I reached her pussy, and at first I could only stare again. Taking in the delicate folds and the slick arousal that'd already gathered there. Inhaling the heady scent of her desire.

Now this was more than just a puzzle to unravel. This part of her deserved worship.

It felt completely natural to lower my mouth to her sex. To slide my tongue over those folds and up to the sensitive button with a flick that earned me another moan.

The wild, musky flavor of her took me from half-hard to achingly erect in an instant. Madelyn bucked to meet my mouth, and I suckled her pussy more avidly, rocking with the motions of her hips. Her fingers snagged in my hair again, little cries spilling out of her.

I could have kept going, could have brought her all the way to her release with just my mouth. I could tell I'd be able to take her there like this. But I wanted more than that this time. With every throb of my cock, I longed to join with her fully, to move inside her as well as against her.

"Dexter," she gasped. "Please."

I didn't need more of an invitation than that. Abruptly grateful for the few condoms Slade had insisted I take to stash in my bedside table's drawer—"Because I don't want you having to knock on my door for them when you finally do find yourself a girlfriend who deserves you," he'd said with a grin—I lifted myself up, licking the taste of Madelyn from my lips, and fished a packet out.

Madelyn smiled up at me as I ripped open the foil. She reached down to massage my balls while I rolled the condom over my shaft, and my brain just about short-circuited from the zing of pleasure. With a groan I couldn't restrain, I pushed her back down on the bed and lined myself up.

I couldn't go slow, but I didn't think she wanted me to. As I plowed into her, she raised her hips to welcome me. A rough sound escaped her, and she dragged my mouth back to hers.

There was no word for the next sensation that swept through me other than pure and utter bliss. Our mouths collided again and again as I thrust into her.

"So lucky," I murmured against her lips, thinking back to our earlier conversation. "So fucking lucky."

"Mmm. Me too. Me too, having you."

It'd never occurred to me that any woman would consider me a lucky catch. An unexpected laugh tumbled out of me, turning into a groan as she teased her fingernails down my back.

I bucked into her harder, faster. Madelyn writhed beneath me, but I wasn't sure it'd be enough. I shifted my weight onto one arm so I could trail the other hand down over her breast, rolling her nipple, and down to where we were joined to stroke her clit. She'd liked it when Beckett had done that, I'd noticed.

"Oh, fuck," Madelyn rasped, a shudder running through her. I picked up my pace just a little more, and she clenched around me with a cry that was the most delicious sound I'd ever heard. Her head bowed back into the pillow.

The clenching of her cunt around me yanked me over the edge with her. I came with a sharp burst of heat, groaning into the crook of her neck.

Madelyn hummed happily and wrapped her arms around my shoulders. I eased down partly on top of her, partly beside her, still enjoying the warmth generated where our bodies touched. Taking in her smile, I couldn't restrain a wide one of my own.

I might not be the perfect man, but I'd given her everything she needed in this specific moment. And I would do it again, as many times as I could.

CHAPTER 25

Madelyn

I sat with my feet propped on the coffee table as Dexter played some kind of war game on his gaming console. He'd done the chivalrous thing and offered me a controller, but I'd declined. Based on the way he flew through the game with effortless ease, barely even focusing his scope on an opponent before pulling the trigger, I knew that if I'd taken him up on his offer to play, I would have either been in the way or obliterated in seconds by the opposing team.

Anyway, I had something much more important to worry about. I couldn't get Summer off my mind, especially when we'd gone longer without talking than we ever had. She'd texted me once after I'd blown her off at the hospital, and I hadn't figured out how to reply yet. But the longer I waited, the worse it got.

And my best friend had done nothing to deserve my silence.

Only one thing could really solve this mess: the truth. Unfortunately, the truth was the last thing I could give to her when the situation was so precarious and anyone connected to us might be at risk. If Summer found out what I'd discovered, there was no way she wouldn't insist on getting involved.

I couldn't let that happen.

I could only hope that our friendship was strong enough to handle this.

I tapped out a message carefully, trying to keep it simple. Short, but sincere.

I'm so sorry, Summer. There's a lot that I need to tell you, and I'm going to explain it all to you as soon as I can. I promise. I'll let you know if there's any way you can help, but for now, I'm okay and it's stuff I can only really handle on my own. I hope you understand. I miss talking to you every day. :(

I knew that it didn't explain anything, but I sincerely hoped she would recognize how much I meant the apology.

Thankfully, I was distracted from staring at my phone waiting for a response by the opening of the door. Logan and Slade strode inside.

Dexter immediately turned off the game and set the controller aside. As Slade came over to the sofa, I scooted over to make room, and Dexter's hand caught mine. That casual contact lit me up from the inside out, waking up the memories of all the other ways he'd touched me just an hour ago.

Slade took in our joined hands with a slight raise of his eyebrows, but he didn't comment on it, just flopped onto the cushions next to me and claimed my other hand. Logan paced the room with a grim expression.

"I take it you didn't find anything useful from the security footage," I said.

"No. No surprises there. Whoever came by blocked the view of the only camera in range when they must have set things up this morning." Logan halted abruptly and spun toward the rest of us. "Which means we need to talk next steps."

He paused, taking in my pose with his friends on either side of me. A shadow passed through his eyes, but it disappeared before I could say for sure what it'd been. If he was jealous, he kept any snarky comments to himself.

"Obviously we need to dig into this trucking company more," Slade put in. "When we checked it out yesterday, there were a lot of tough-looking guys around, and a few of them were armed in a way that I don't think the average trucker usually is."

Dexter frowned. "That isn't concrete evidence of anything. We need hard proof if we want the police to get involved."

Slade grinned at him. "So we go back and poke around until we find something hard."

I shot him a nervous look. "The three of you are going to go cozy up to a bunch of tough-guy truckers, some of whom have guns? Are you sure that's a good idea? What happened to keeping a low profile?"

"It's not like we're going to go in throwing around accusations," Logan said. "We'll just ask a few questions like we're potential customers as an excuse to look around. Get some ideas for possibly breaking in and taking an even closer look after closing hours. They only had one security camera around; we can avoid getting caught on that."

I guessed the only alternative was to stop investigating altogether, but my stomach had knotted. I worried at my lower lip. "Didn't you find a few other companies connected to that shell corporation? We know they seem to have something to do with it all too."

Logan nodded. "There's the seafood market, which we already checked out, and the accounting office, which has tighter security and is more likely to get us noticed if we try to go in. I've done some digging there, and I think it's pretty peripheral to any criminal operations—all the data I turned up on their network looked legit. Then there's a restaurant that closed down a few years ago, and a women's only spa downtown. Obviously *we're* not going in there."

Slade nudged me. "That'll be your job. You can treat yourself and snoop around a bit for evidence while you're at it."

I narrowed my eyes at him. "Is that your way of suggesting that I couldn't hold my own against the trucker guys?"

"I know you could," he said with an admiring smile that melted most of my annoyance. "But the truckers will see you as a target like the mechanics did before. And you'll be more memorable there. There's nothing so odd about you going for a spa day. It could be a total coincidence that it's owned by the same company."

"And none of us can investigate it," Dexter pointed out.

They had a point. Still, I folded my arms over my chest. "I feel like this is just an excuse to make me go chill out and pamper myself. I'm not going to relax all that much knowing my dad's murderers could be lurking in the background, you know."

A hint of a smirk touched Logan's lips, which told me I wasn't entirely wrong. "You'll just have to try your best then."

I glowered at him half-heartedly, unable to come up with a good argument to turn the tables on him. "Fine. But I'm going to dig up at least as much dirt as you do."

The spa I found myself in the next morning definitely didn't *look* like a front for violent criminal activities. The chair I sat in was all creamy leather like the others spaced around the waiting room. Potted flowers let off a sweet scent from the marble reception counter. Gentle strains of new age music filtered through the air. But who knew what lay behind the posh front?

I'd been able to book a couple of basic services as a walk-in customer, settling on a facial and a pedicure. The cheerful woman behind the counter had assured me it'd only be fifteen minutes before my pedicure would start. I intended to make maximum use of those minutes.

First, I took out my phone, pretending I was texting a friend. Instead, I snapped several pictures of the waiting room, channeling Dexter's commitment to visual records.

I kept my ears pricked for any conversations around me, but when the receptionist murmured into her phone, it was only to book appointments, and the middle-aged woman sitting across from me appeared to be immersed in her book. Most of the staff worked beyond the doors at the other end of the waiting room. Hopefully I'd find out more once I got back there.

Hopefully this really *was* connected to that shell corporation and the guys hadn't simply tricked me into a pampering session.

A young woman peeked past the door and called to the other inhabitant of the waiting room. As the avid reader left the room, I resisted the urge to squirm in my seat. There was nothing I could examine here without looking very strange to the receptionist, who showed no signs of leaving her post.

The outer door swung open with a soft chime. A woman who appeared to be in her thirties, with a trim dress suit and her hair in a loose bun, strode up to the counter as if she'd been here dozens of times before and knew exactly what she wanted.

"I'm here to get the Eve's Special," she said in a low voice, as if she didn't like the idea of being overheard.

The Eve's Special? I didn't remember seeing anything with that name when I'd scanned the list of treatments. I picked up the brochure the receptionist had handed me and paged through it more carefully, but there was no mention of it there.

"Of course," the receptionist said smoothly. "I'm sure we can fit you in."

Did her voice sound a little stiffer than before? She motioned the woman to one of the chairs without giving her a time estimate or mentioning payment. That was definitely weird, right?

Gathering my boldness, I got up and approached the counter again. "Hey," I said, aiming for a casual but confident tone. "That special she asked for—what does that involve? I didn't see it on the list."

I thought the receptionist's smile looked stiffer than the one she'd offered me before too. "Unfortunately we only offer that treatment to regular clients of a particular standing. If you make a habit of enjoying our services, one of our staff will let you know when you qualify."

How very exclusive.

"Okay," I said with a returning smile as if I wasn't fazed, and went back to my seat. But my pulse had sped up a couple notches.

What kind of treatment would they keep off the regular menu and only offer to a few clients? Could it be code for something less than savory?

My instincts were twanging with an undeniable sense of alarm. If there was something suspicious about the setup here, I'd better make sure to figure it out before my time was up.

CHAPTER 26

Madelyn

I wouldn't have thought pedicures would really be my thing, but there was something awfully relaxing about the gentle foot massage that accompanied the nail cleaning and painting, even with the tension inside me about my real mission here. I let myself sink into the padded chair, my eyes scanning the room surreptitiously as the woman attending to me did her work.

Unfortunately, there wasn't much to see. The private treatment room was about the size of a walk-in closet with just a couple of the padded chairs, a cabinet and shiny metal cart that held various supplies, and a small sink in the corner. Everything looked polished and clean. The scent of fresh lavender hung in the air. Nothing about this space suggested criminal activity any more than the waiting room did.

The woman finished her work, surveyed my toes with a look of satisfaction, and stood up to put away her supplies and wash her hands. "All right, ma'am. Hailey should be by in about ten minutes to do your facial. She's finishing up with another client now. There's always a bit of a wait for walk-ins."

"That's totally fine," I said with a skip of my pulse. It would give me time to do a little more poking around unsupervised.

I waited until she'd slipped out past the gauzy curtain that hung over the doorway and then got to my feet. It felt strange padding across the tiled floor with my bare soles, but I didn't want to waste time putting my shoes back on. Ten minutes wasn't much to work with.

Beyond the curtain, identical doorways lined the bright hallway with its baby blue walls. Soft voices carried from a couple of the rooms, but the hall itself was empty. I hesitated and then pushed myself forward. If anyone caught me wandering around, I'd claim that I needed the restroom. That would sound like a legitimate excuse, right?

I pulled my phone from my pocket and snapped a few photos while holding it as if simply carrying it, slipping down the hallway. At the far end, it branched into a T. I peeked out into the intersecting hall with my breath held.

A woman was just ducking into one of the rooms to the right, but her back was to me so she didn't notice my presence. To my left, a figure I recognized stood by a doorway that held an actual door, half ajar.

It was the woman who'd asked for the Eve's Special. I drew back, wondering why she was just hanging around in the hall. After a moment's debate about how to watch without being caught, I switched my phone's camera to selfie mode, pressed my back against the wall on the left side of my hallway, and eased my phone a couple of inches around the corner so that the camera would capture the view down there without anything more than a small rectangle being visible if someone glanced over.

As I studied my screen, another woman appeared in the doorway. She glanced up and down the hall, making me doubly glad for my precautions, and quickly held up a plastic baggie of what looked like white powder. At the client's nod, she dropped it into a paper bag and handed it over. The woman pressed a few rolled bills to her in return.

What was *that*? It didn't look like she was selling some regular spa product—the waiting room had a cabinet holding those up front. And surely they'd want to record any legitimate purchase with receipts and all that.

Apprehension prickled through me. Were they dealing some kind of drugs to a certain segment of their clientele through the spa? I'd definitely heard of middle class and even upper class women getting hooked on illicit substances—and they weren't the types to want to hit up a scruffy dealer on a street corner for a hit.

I tipped my phone slightly to make sure the recording caught the spa logo painted on the wall just beyond the two women. At the same moment, they both turned toward me, their transaction complete.

My heart hitched. I yanked my phone back and hustled back to my treatment room, nearly stumbling into the wrong one on my way there but catching a whisper of a voice on the other side of the curtain just in time. Nerves jangling, I darted into the next room and spotted my shoes on the floor, confirmation that I'd made it back to the right place.

I dropped into the chair and tried to steady my breath. Less than a minute later, another woman breezed into the room. To my relief, she didn't give any sign that she saw anything unusual about my appearance.

"Hey there, I'm Hailey," she said in a chipper voice. "I'll be doing your facial today. First I'll ask you a few questions about your skin, all right?"

"Sure," I said, managing a smile that wasn't even all that shaky. Once I'd filled her in on the state of my face, I leaned back into the chair and let myself fully give over to the experience, even closing my eyes.

I'd already found one huge piece of evidence. It wasn't likely there were *more* criminal activities going on here at the same time, and even if there were, I couldn't go seeking them out when Hailey was smearing a cool gel over my forehead.

Why not enjoy the rest of my time here? After what I'd already accomplished, I was pretty sure I deserved it. Just a few moments without worrying about the investigation or the lab report due next week or anything at all.

The gels solidified on my face and tugged gently at it as the woman peeled the layer off, leaving my skin feeling pleasantly tingly. If I'd had money to burn, maybe I could have gotten used to being a regular spa-goer.

"We're all done here," Hailey said. "No huge rush getting your things together, but we'll need the room in about five minutes."

"Thank you," I said. I pulled on my shoes, grabbed my purse, and was out of there with plenty of time to spare.

As I reached the door to the waiting room, my gaze lifted to its small window, and I froze with my fingers clamped around the handle.

A woman was standing near the counter, one hand on her hip, her head cocked to the side. Nothing about that was particularly strange, except I *knew* that woman—and not from pleasant circumstances. There was no mistaking her spiky black pixie cut or her arrogant demeanor.

She was part of the gang that'd run the bar where I'd found

Dad's trinket box. The gang the Vigil guys and I had gotten into a tussle with. I'd tackled her to stop her from shooting Logan.

It seemed like a little too much to hope that *she* wouldn't recognize *me*.

Logan hadn't found any connection between the bar and the shell company that owned this spa, but that didn't mean there wasn't one buried even deeper. She might be here to take a day off, or she might have official business. And she'd definitely be suspicious of why I'd happened to show up here after sneaking into her bar.

One of the spa staff had come up behind me with a soft clearing of her throat. I jerked away from the door, my mind spinning as I scrambled for an excuse. "I—I think I left a bag in my treatment room," I mumbled, and hurried back over to duck behind the curtain.

There, I inhaled and exhaled, getting a grip on myself. If I just waited, the woman would be escorted to her own treatment room, and I could leave without her noticing me. But if she waited more than a few minutes, another client would be coming to use this room. I couldn't wander the halls aimlessly for who knew how long.

"Shit," I muttered under my breath. I needed something to distract her in the waiting room so that I could hustle by without her noticing me. But I couldn't arrange that on my own. I couldn't call on the Vigil guys for help—even if they could easily leave whatever they were currently doing, she'd recognize them too.

We couldn't let the criminals we were up against realize just how immersed we still were in our investigation. My mom's *life* might be on the line.

There was one other person I trusted to lend a hand who might be nearby enough, though. My stomach twisted as I considered it, knowing how Logan would react, but surely it'd be even worse if the woman from the gang caught me?

I pulled out my phone and shot a hasty text to Beckett. *This is going to sound crazy, but can you come to the Lotus Blossom Spa on Trinity Avenue and create some kind of distraction in the waiting room? I just need people's attention to be somewhere else for, like, thirty seconds. I've ended up in a tight spot.*

I hoped that was enough of an explanation to avoid a big discussion upfront. And it appeared that Beckett trusted me too. His answering text, just seconds later, asked no questions at all.

On my way. Six minutes out. You hang tight.

Six minutes. I could delay that long. There was a single-stall restroom down the hall—I'd make a quick pit stop to stretch out the time before anyone insisted I leave. Surely they wouldn't mind if I occupied it for just a few minutes.

Those thoughts whirled through my mind, but as my initial panic faded, a surge of annoyance rose up in its wake. I looked down at my phone and grimaced.

I should be able to get myself out of situations like this on my own. How many times had I insisted to the guys that I was just as capable as them? And now as soon as I faced a little trouble, I freaked out and went calling for help.

I bit my lip, sensing the seconds ticking down before someone asked me to leave. It'd be better if there wasn't any commotion in the waiting room at all, nothing to make this visit memorable for the woman from the bar. If I could just get past her…

My gaze darted through the room, searching for inspiration, and snagged on the tray of creams and gels Hailey had brought out for my facial.

Not giving myself a chance to chicken out, I twisted open one of the lids, dug my fingers into the opaque, rose-petal-pink substance inside, and smeared it in a thin layer all across my face. Then I grabbed a handful of wet wipes from a nearby container, balled them in my hand, and rushed out of the room.

I slowed my pace a little as I reached the door to the waiting room. With a firm shove of the door, I strode past it and right through the middle of the waiting room. A couple of women sitting on the chairs glanced at me with curious expressions, but the woman from the gang was still chatting with the receptionist. Her gaze veered toward me and slid on by without a hint of recognition.

Thank God.

I didn't stop walking after I reached the sidewalk outside until I was halfway down the block. Then I paused and swiped at my face with the wet wipes.

I'd done it. I'd saved myself without anyone's help. Now I'd have to clean up the other mess I'd inadvertently made.

I'd just cleaned the last few blobs of cream from my skin when Beckett's usual car whipped around a corner down the street. I raised my hand to wave to him, and he pulled up at the curb next to me.

He rolled down the passenger side window and leaned over, his expression tight with concern. "Are you okay? I thought you needed me to go inside. What happened?"

"I'm sorry," I said with a wince. "I spotted someone who was a jerk to me back in high school and had a moment of panic about facing her. But then I realized I was being silly and just walked right by, and she didn't pay attention to me anyway. I shouldn't have made you come out here."

"No, it's totally okay," Beckett said, frowning. "I'd happily get you out of a conversation with a bully any time. Are you sure that's it?" He glanced from me to the spa farther down. "Why were you going to that place anyway?"

I shrugged, hating that I was lying to him, knowing I'd be betraying the other guys I cared about if I didn't. At least these lies couldn't hurt him. "I heard good things about it from someone in one of my classes. And it was a pretty enjoyable experience up until the blast from the past part."

Beckett studied me for a moment longer as if he wasn't totally convinced by my story. The determined heat in his eyes, all protective fury, sent a tingle down my spine. If someone *had* hurt me, I suddenly had no doubt at all that they'd have met a horrible fate at his hands.

"Let me give you a drive wherever you're going next anyway," he said after a moment, relaxing just a little. "Now that I'm here and all."

That seemed only fair. And I didn't really want to hang around waiting for an Uber. I'd taken one here so there was no chance of my license plate giving me away. Who knew how the people we were up against might be monitoring me?

"Thank you so much," I said, getting into the car. "I'm just going back to campus. I'm supposed to be meeting with the other guys to grab lunch."

Beckett chuckled. "Maybe I'll join in for that too."

Not if the guys had anything to say about it, since we were actually meeting to go over what we'd learned. I rested my hand on my phone in my pocket, thinking of the video I'd managed to take.

"That would be nice," I said, figuring we'd deal with the rest when we got there. We *could* always get lunch together and then discuss the rest afterward when Beckett left.

He glanced over at me as he stopped at a red light, that intensity coming back into his eyes.

"I want you to know if you're ever in *any* kind of trouble, you can always call me," he said. "All right, Maddie? It'll never be a problem. I'd want to have your back."

He spoke so emphatically my throat tightened. If he'd had any idea the dangerous situations I'd already gotten into…

But he didn't. He was just being his caring, devoted self, and I was a lying liar who lied.

"I know," I said quietly. "You have no idea how much I appreciate that."

CHAPTER 27

Logan

Slade, Dexter, and I sauntered into the front office for Roadway Express Trucking as if we had total confidence about our visit. As if they should be the ones catering to us. A plan like this worked better if we gave off the right vibe to begin with, and right now we were playing newly successful entrepreneurs and potential clients.

Most of the men we'd seen around the place when we'd scoped it out from more of a distance had worn jeans and casual tees, but the middle-aged guy behind the front desk had gone for a polo shirt and khakis. Trying to look a little more professional than the employees doing the grunt work, I guessed. He looked us over with an air that suggested he was not impressed. "Can I help you?"

I stopped in front of the counter and glanced around as if assessing the place. The main truck bay was off to the side of the office, accessible through the big garage doors out front and the door set in the wall there. We could have strolled right into that section from outside, but I knew the workers would have been escorting us right back out in a matter of seconds.

"My colleagues and I have recently gotten a much higher demand for a product we invented," I said. "We've got the manufacturing side covered, but we need help transporting it to distribution centers around the country. We're checking out trucking companies in the area to decide which one to go with. Would it be a problem if we took a quick look around at your vehicles and asked some questions?"

The man straightened up at the prospect of new business, though he still looked a bit wary. "We can accommodate you." He got up and led us over to the door into the loading bay. "We always pick reliable models and replace the trucks when there are any signs of continuing performance decline. They're inspected and tuned up regularly. What else did you want to know?"

"A price sheet would obviously be handy," I said. "And are there any types of products you have a policy against handling?"

"I'll be able to email you the sheet. We don't transport restricted substances or objects because of the complications when you're crossing state lines. Otherwise we can handle just about anything."

Including outright illegal goods that they kept on the down low? Maybe we'd see some clues about that inside.

We stepped into the wide, high-ceilinged space, my nose wrinkling at the smell of engine oil that hung in the air. The bay was about half full with several trucks currently on the premises, ranging from a couple of small delivery trucks to a few sixteen wheelers. Some were being loaded at the moment, others simply waiting for the next job.

The guy from the reception area stuck close to us as we made our way from truck to truck, watching us like a hawk. The workers who were handling the loading shot a few glances our way, with expressions that sent apprehension tickling through my nerves. It definitely wasn't a friendly vibe. I didn't think they liked strangers poking around at all, as essential as it was for them to maintain a legitimate business—whether that business was a front or not.

Dexter had taken out his phone, but I doubted he was getting many useful pictures while we were under such close surveillance. He'd be doing his best, anyway.

At the trucks being loaded, I ambled close enough to glance surreptitiously at the clipboards left here or there with the shipping documentation. One was heading across the country with a bunch of furniture. Another was carrying electronics to a discount store on the other side of the state. Both of those sounded like totally legit businesses, but then, they wouldn't have advertised anything unsavory they were doing where a passerby could spot it.

"Watch where you're standing," one of the truckers growled at me, motioning for us to get out of the way. We hustled to the side, and he heaved a stack of boxes into the back of the truck we'd been checking out. Now the faces around us had become even less welcoming.

I strode onward to the smallest of the trucks, curious about what they were handling locally. As I approached, the worker there snatched up the inventory before I could get a close look at it, but I did manage to make out the name of the delivery location.

It was the club downtown—the one we often chatted up contacts at. The one Slade had recently discovered was owned by the mysterious Beckett.

I froze, momentarily thrown off my game, and the man at the truck shooed us away from the crates awaiting loading. "Every bottle of booze in those is worth more than your fancy sneakers. Steer clear."

I glanced at my friends, but I couldn't tell them what I'd seen and show it'd mattered to me while the reception guy was still hovering nearby.

He seemed to have had enough of us anyway. "You've had the full tour," he said, getting brusque again. "Did you have more questions? We can go over anything else back in the office."

I debated arguing that we wanted to take a closer look, but that might sound odd, and we were supposed to be avoiding suspicion. We didn't have any proof that this place was at all involved in the attacks on Maddie's family or the Vigil's office. If we found some… then it'd be a different story.

"I think we're good," I said. "Let me just give you my email for that price sheet, and we'll be back in touch if we decide to use your services."

Back at the reception desk, I rattled off an email I used specifically when I didn't want any chance of the recipient using it to track down other private info on me. Then we headed out.

I kept my mouth shut until we'd reached the corner a few buildings away from the trucking company. There, I turned toward the others.

"What did you see?" Slade asked immediately. He knew me well enough to have picked up on the momentary change in my demeanor.

"That last truck," I said. "The one with the fancy booze. It was going to Beckett's club."

Slade's expression darkened. "Beckett has some kind of connection to this place? To a place that's also connected to the assholes we're investigating?"

"It doesn't necessarily indicate that he's up to no good," Dexter pointed out. "There were other legitimate businesses using their services. The club could be just another of those, totally unrelated to whatever illegal jobs they're carrying out secretly."

I shook my head. "I don't like it. It feels like too much of a coincidence."

Dexter smiled tightly. "I agree. I'm just making sure we don't jump to conclusions too quickly."

"We don't even know for sure that this company is taking any illegal jobs at all," Slade added. "Although the whole armed truckers thing and the atmosphere in that place definitely doesn't give the impression of sunshine and roses."

I rubbed my jaw. "We could stake out the club—wherever they'd bring in deliveries. See if there's anything handed over other than the crates of alcohol. Maybe get a chance to peek in those crates and make sure it *is* just alcohol."

"Or we keep an eye on who else comes into the trucking company. They're the ones—" Slade cut himself off at the sound of footsteps.

A guy who only looked a few years older than us had ducked out from the alley beside the trucking company building and was hustling toward us. He was dressed in a tee and jeans like the truckers, but he didn't hold the same air of menace. The opposite, really. His gaze flitted from side to side as he approached as if he were afraid of being seen.

He came to a halt a few feet away from us, his stance tensed and his eyes still twitchy. We all turned to face him. He swallowed audibly before he spoke in a hushed, ragged voice. "Are you looking into the death of Evan Silver?"

My eyebrows just about shot right off my head as my pulse hiccupped. It took me a second to respond. "What do you know about that?"

The guy's mouth tightened, his shoulders hunching defensively. But he seemed to take my response as a confirmation. "I've heard things… I've seen you other places and now here… It's not the kind of thing I think should be kept quiet."

"Who are you?" Slade demanded, glowering at the guy.

The guy winced at Slade's sharp tone and glanced around anxiously again. "I—I work for a man named Beckett Alderman. He's all mixed up in that murder—his family, from way before—and he's been working to cover it up since he noticed people were poking around."

My breath stopped in my throat. "Do you have any proof?" I asked, fighting to stop my voice from rising.

The guy shook his head with a jerk. "I'm sorry. It's been hard enough just telling you this. I'm putting my neck on the line. But if I don't say something, I don't know how far he'll go next… or how many more people might die to cover up his family's crimes."

CHAPTER 28

Madelyn

As Beckett drove me toward the campus, my panic completely subsided, and a growing sense of victory emerged in its wake. The Vigil needed solid evidence of criminal dealings to get the police involved, and if the video I'd taken wasn't enough, it had to at least get us partway there. I quickly brought it up on my phone and made sure it was backed up on my cloud service so it couldn't be accidentally—or purposefully—deleted.

With that done, a smile stretched across my face. The guys had thought they were going to send me off to be pampered, but I might have discovered even more than they had with their own investigations.

Beckett drove right onto campus at my directions and pulled into the parking lot near the café where the Vigil guys and I were supposed to meet. As he put the car into park, he glanced over at me.

"Maddie, are you sure everything's all right? Your text sounded frantic, but now you look like you're really happy about something. I feel like there's got to be something more going on than you've told me. If it's personal or whatever, you don't have to get into it. I just want to know that you're okay."

"I promise you, I'm fine now," I told him. "You really don't need to worry about me."

He tipped his head to one side. "The other guys aren't putting any pressure on you about the whole multiple boyfriends thing?"

That question was so unrelated to what was on my mind that I laughed. "No, they seem to be coming around pretty well. They don't hate the idea, anyway."

"So they'll get over the fact that I swooped in on 'their' girl?"

I shot him an amused look, although my good humor dwindled when I remembered how Slade had questioned me about Beckett's work the other day. "Technically I started dating you before any of them. And they'll warm up to you, I'm sure. They've been best friends for years, and adding someone new to the group will be difficult for them."

"They added you."

I shrugged. "I'm not exactly new to them. We went to high school together. And obviously that's different. We'll have to get all five of us together more often so you can get to know each other better."

I pushed open the door and stepped out. I hadn't had the chance to close it again before my name reached my ears.

"Maddie!"

My head jerked around at the strangely urgent shout. The three Vigil guys were marching toward us, all of their expressions stormy.

My heart skipped a beat. Had something gone wrong? Had the people we'd been investigating struck out at us again?

"Hey," Beckett said in greeting, raising a tentative hand. The hostile vibe the other guys were giving off couldn't have been lost on him.

Logan ignored him, striding right up to me and grabbing my arm. As he pulled me away from Beckett's car, Slade and Dexter stepped between us and Beckett.

"What's going on?" I sputtered as Logan dragged me right to the edge of the parking lot.

"Take your hands off her," Beckett said in a terse voice, coming around the car. "You can't push her around like—"

"You shut up," Logan snapped, his tone so vicious that my whole body went rigid.

"Stay the hell away from her," Slade said in an equally ominous voice, the muscles in his shoulders flexing.

"Will someone please tell me what you've gone crazy about?" I said, raising my voice. "Or I'm going to start screaming for help, and you're going to have to explain it to a lot more people than just me."

Dexter glanced back at me, the worry in his eyes making me even more frightened. Then Logan spoke, low and fierce.

"We've found out why we're having so much trouble looking into your dad's death. Beckett's family is behind it, and he's been covering their tracks all along."

WICKED LOVE

CHAPTER 1

Madelyn

Silence seemed to have settled over the campus. Other students were chatting and laughing as they walked along the paths, but they might as well have been miles away from where I stood with my stepbrother's hand clamped around my arm, his best friends flanking us, and all three of them glaring accusingly at the other guy I was falling for.

Logan's words echoed in my mind, sounding no less ridiculous than when I'd first heard them. *We've found out why we're having so much trouble looking into your dad's murder. Beckett's family is behind it, and he's been covering their tracks all along.*

Beckett was blinking at Logan, his forehead furrowing. "What the hell are you talking about? I thought Maddie's father died from a sudden disease."

Of course he did. Because that was what I'd told him, back when I'd believed that story was true too.

How could he or his family have anything to do with Dad's death? I wasn't *that* bad a judge of character, was I? Beckett had never seemed anything other than considerate and protective toward me.

Heck, he'd just raced to my rescue over an anxious text message I'd sent him. I hadn't seen the slightest sign that he meant me any harm. If he was mixed up in the murder in any way, wouldn't he be trying to get rid of me, not keep me safe?

Logan scoffed, his brown eyes glinting harshly beneath the rumpled tufts of his chestnut hair. "You can't fool us with that innocent act. We know just how many lies you've been peddling."

"This doesn't make any sense," I burst out, spinning to face the Vigil guys. "I know you weren't totally sure about Beckett, but you can't just go around making up crazy stories—"

"It's not crazy, and it's not just a made-up story," Dexter said in his usual matter-of-fact tone, folding his arms over his lean chest and fixing his bright green gaze on Beckett. "We have photographic evidence that he's been hiding things."

Slade looped one of his well-muscled arms around mine—the one Logan didn't still have in a death-grip. An angry flush darkened his bronze skin. "Don't worry, Piccolina. We'll make sure he gets what he deserves—and that he doesn't set foot anywhere near *you* again."

Beckett ran a hand over the smooth strands of his sandy blond hair, his gray eyes stormy with what still looked like genuine confusion to me, along with a fair bit of frustration. "I have no idea what you three are ranting about. How could I be covering up a murder I didn't even know about? Why would anyone have murdered Maddie's father anyway? What the fuck is going on?"

Logan finally let go of me to march toward Beckett, his massive frame looming over the other guy, who was half a foot shorter. "If one more lie comes out of that mouth—"

I leapt forward and snatched the back of Logan's shirt, yanking him to a halt. "Enough with the threats and the accusations. I want to know what the hell is going on too! Whatever it is you think you know, tell us." I couldn't decide whether it was remotely reasonable or if my other boyfriends had gone insane until I had some idea what had gotten them so riled up.

Slade's hand had slid down my arm to grasp my fingers when I'd lunged after Logan. "He owns that night club in town," he said tightly. "He was there at least one of the nights when we went dancing, before you ever talked to him. I bet he never told you that. He was stalking you."

"Preparing for your 'chance' meeting," Logan added, his voice dripping with derision.

Beckett raised his hands, his mouth tightening. "Yes, my *family* owns a club downtown. It's part of the family business. I swing by to check up on things periodically. I don't see how it's lying that I didn't tell you that when you never asked me about it. How was I supposed to realize you'd find it so suspicious? Do you need a full list of all my family's assets?"

"That would be a good start," Dexter piped up as if he hadn't realized it was a rhetorical question. I couldn't tell whether he was joking or serious.

My mind was reeling. It wasn't totally bizarre that Beckett might own the club and simply not mentioned it, but he definitely hadn't mentioned seeing me there. It *had* been just an accident that I'd bumped into him the one day outside the coffee shop… and the second time another day in the post office… hadn't it? Or had that been more than a welcome coincidence?

I caught his gaze. "Had you already seen me at the club before the first time we talked?"

Beckett looked back at me without a flicker of hesitation. "What does it matter? Would it really change anything if I had?"

He hadn't actually answered the question. A little chill quivered down my spine. "It might—if that means you went out of your way to make sure we'd end up talking as if it was a random meeting, when really you'd planned it all along."

Logan's lips had drawn back from his teeth in a silent growl. "He's got connections to the trucking company too. When we went to investigate it, we saw a truck with a shipment for his club, ordered in his name. We're supposed to believe it's just random chance that he's associated with a company that's got ties to all those other businesses in the trail we've followed—a company that probably also ships illegal merchandise?"

My stomach plummeted. Too many coincidences adding up tended to mean they weren't coincidental after all.

Beckett *had* turned up right after my car had gotten stolen—right after someone in town had realized I might have information to do with my dad.

I took a step back, tugging Logan with me. Beckett's eyes widened.

"Maddie," he said, "you can't really be buying into this bullshit. Clubs need to get shipments of alcohol. Someone's got to deliver them. There's nothing nefarious about it."

Slade snorted. "There is when you had so many other options and you just happened to pick the company that's mixed up in this case. And—" He cut himself off, his mouth setting in a grim line that wasn't like the joking, flirty guy I was used to at all. "We're not telling you everything we found out. You'll just use the information to make excuses and hurt even more people."

Beckett rubbed the bridge of his nose as if he had a headache. "I think I'm starting to get an inkling of what must have happened. Did someone you talked to today give you the impression that I was involved in whatever happened to Maddie's father? Whatever exactly happened, *they* were lying to you, probably to mess with this 'case' of yours. I didn't know anything about Maddie or her family until a month ago."

"You really expect us to believe that?" Logan said with a bark of dark laughter.

"There's an easy way to confirm it one way or the other," Beckett said. His usual air of confidence was coming back, his bewilderment smoothing away so easily.

Before, I'd admired his sense of calm. Now I couldn't help thinking it was incredibly strange that he could keep his cool in a situation like this. It made me wonder how many hostile people he'd had to face before, under what circumstances. This standoff wasn't anything like a standard business meeting.

Dexter cocked his head, his expression still tense. "What's that?"

"Tell me who spoke to you, where, and exactly what they said," Beckett replied. "I know a lot of people in this city. It shouldn't take long for me to determine who's behind the false accusation—and whoever that is, they're most likely the ones you should be yelling at. Why would they point you in the wrong direction if they weren't trying to protect themselves?"

"Right," Slade said skeptically. "And it's not at all that *you* want to point us in the wrong direction now."

Beckett ignored him and focused on me, his gaze unwavering. "Maddie, you know I'd never hurt you. I swear I had no idea about this investigation or anything to do with your dad—and if anyone working for my family was involved, I'd know about it. Someone is trying to screw me over and using you to do it. Let me help you figure this out."

"We're not accepting 'help,'"—Logan made air quotes around the word, his voice dripping with hostile sarcasm—"from a person who has been in the middle of the situation all along without ever saying anything."

I opened my mouth and closed it again. I wanted to believe Beckett. He sounded so sure—but that was part of the reason I hesitated. He had an explanation for everything. He was barely even fazed by the guys accusing him of being tangled up in a murder.

He'd obviously hidden some small things from me. What if he'd hidden bigger things as well? The Vigil guys wouldn't be this worked up without plenty of reason, would they?

I grimaced, my throat tightening. "I think you should go," I said to Beckett. "I need some time to figure out what to think."

"Maddie, you can't really believe—"

I shook my head. "I don't know what to believe, Beckett. Please, just leave. I can't think while we're arguing like this."

He opened his mouth to speak again but closed it before any words escaped. With a stiff nod, he stepped back. "Can I call you?"

I shook my head. "I'd rather you didn't. I'll call *you* when I'm ready."

If I'm ever ready, I didn't bother saying. Or would the next call I made involving Beckett be to the police?

"Then I'll respect that request." Beckett's voice stayed even, but his hands were balled at his sides as he walked back to his car. I watched him get in and drive away, my spirits seeming to sink farther as he vanished from view.

Then I whirled toward the Vigil guys. "What exactly happened? Do you have more proof tying him to my dad's case than what you just said? Something we could bring to the cops?"

Logan scowled, which answered my last question all on its own. "No. Nothing concrete. But we talked to a guy who works for Beckett, who saw us scoping out the trucking company. He was scared to talk to us but made himself do it—he told us outright that Beckett's family is behind the murder of Evan Silver and that

Beckett has been taking steps to cover it up. How would he know about any of that?"

He could if Beckett was right and someone who was really involved in the crimes was trying to frame Beckett. But why would anyone want to do that?

I swallowed a groan of frustration. "Do you think that guy would go to the police and tell them his story?"

Slade shook his head dejectedly. "He seemed panicky enough about telling us. I can't imagine him talking to the cops. If we could even find him again to ask him to. He wouldn't give us his name."

"He seemed like he was scared for his life," Dexter put in.

My stomach knotted. "What about leaving some kind of anonymous tip with the police so they'll investigate the same things we have, and we see what they turn up?"

Logan shook his head. "We can't leave a tip about a murder they don't have any record of happening, especially one that's twelve years cold. They'd think it was some crazy person and write it off." He squeezed my shoulder, his stance turning from threatening to protective in an instant. "But we'll figure it out. We've put a little fear into Beckett. Maybe he'll make a careless move that'll reveal more of his hand. We'll have to keep a close eye on the trucking company."

"And on Maddie," Dexter said quietly.

I knit my brow at him. "What are you talking about?"

Slade's smile came back for the first time, if muted. "Dex is trying to say that he's worried about you. We all are. When we saw you with that guy…" His fingers tightened around mine.

"You should come back to our apartment rather than staying in your dorm," Logan said in a definitive tone. "We can make sure you're safe."

"Safe?" I repeated. "You don't really think…"

My stepbrother's expression turned even more somber. "If

Beckett has been covering up the murder, then he's behind your mom's accident and the fire in our office. Now that we've got him on the defensive, there's no telling what he might do next. If we could have gotten you away from him without revealing anything… but who knows what he was already planning…" He sighed. "He's dangerous. And next time, he might come after you."

CHAPTER 2

Beckett

"I need an idea of what they could have found here," I told the owner of Roadway Express Trucking, standing in the doorway to his office.

My jaw had been clenched tight since turning my back on Maddie and walking away, and I'd come straight here for information. If the other guys had come here in their amateur investigation and uncovered information that tied me to a murder, I needed to know how that had happened.

It *shouldn't* have happened, because I didn't know about any crimes involving Maddie's father, and the people under me wouldn't have been carrying out random hits.

The trucking company owner was scowling as he skimmed through the security camera footage that showed some of the main bay. "They claimed they were here as potential clients. Justin said it seemed like they were sniffing around for more than that, so he was careful about what he said, but you know the boys would never have shared anything it wasn't their business to either way."

"I certainly hope not," I said, firmly but calmly. "There'd be major consequences if it turned out someone under your employment was sabotaging my family's reputation."

The tensing of the man's stance told me he knew just how severe those consequences could be. He raised his chin. "I'm careful about who I hire, and I oversee them closely. There aren't any snitches or backstabbers around here."

He paused the footage and pointed to Maddie's three guys standing by one of the smaller trucks. "That's the only way they could have associated you with the company. That truck was being loaded with the latest shipment for your club. But you can see we were quick to make sure they couldn't examine the manifest or anything like that. Right afterward, the manager sent them off."

"No one talked to them except him?"

The owner shook his head. "And he said they didn't ask much other than basic business questions. None of them mentioned you or any concerns about the activities we're involved in."

I rubbed my forehead. I could see for myself that the workers in the bay had barely acknowledged the three guys besides some wary glances. No one had really talked to them in view of the camera other than to tell them to clear out.

Most of the employees weren't even aware of the shadier side of this company's operations. And making up a story about the murder of a man from twelve years ago in a town two hours from here would have been pretty bizarre.

"All right," I said, restraining a sigh. "Thank you for your help. Tell your people not to admit those three into the building again if they come around to badger you more."

The owner nodded with a swift jerk of his head. "I was already planning on that."

I stalked out of the office and glanced up and down the street as I headed to my car. Nothing about the neighborhood offered any clues either. Had the guys gotten suspicious simply because of a couple of random connections that as far as I could see had nothing to do with Maddie and her family at all? It didn't make any sense.

There were obviously pieces of the puzzle I was missing, and they hadn't wanted to tell me about those key factors. I supposed if they saw me as a murderer, that wasn't surprising, but it was pretty fucking frustrating all the same.

As I slid into the driver's seat, I pulled out my phone. If anything had changed in the day-to-day operations of the Storm's holdings, the woman Dad had turned to as a general manager for the past fifteen years should know about it.

Lana picked up on the second ring, her tone briskly efficient. "Beckett, what can I do for you today?"

"Hey, Lana," I said, willing the frustration out of my voice. "I've encountered a bit of a… situation involving our business, and I was hoping you might be able to shed some light on it. Are you aware of any unusual behavior from groups our people might have clashed with in the past or signs that another organization might be on the attack, even if it's only in subtle ways?"

She paused, with a few clicks on the other end as she must have glanced through whatever data she had available on her computer, double-checking. "No. If anything like that had come to my attention, I'd have notified you and your father right away, naturally."

"I know. But even if it was so small you didn't think it was worth worrying about yet—"

There was a rustle as she must have shaken her head. "I can't think of anything that would fit your question. Why are you asking? What's the specific concern?"

My jaw clenched even tighter, an ache running through my gums. I forced it to relax and closed my eyes for a second. The ache seemed to travel down into my chest.

I didn't want to explain the specific circumstances to her. It was too personal. She wouldn't understand what Maddie meant to me—and if she hadn't seen anything unusual at all, she definitely didn't know about someone framing my family for murder.

"I think it's better I handle this on my own for now," I said. "It may end up being a completely personal matter. I just wanted to confirm that nothing related had come up on your end." I paused. There was one person who could have carried out a murder and a cover-up without feeling the need to inform me. "My father hasn't given you any orders recently that you haven't kept me in the loop on, has he?"

"I always make sure to coordinate between the two of you," she said, which was a diplomatic answer. I suspected she hadn't heard anything from Dad in a week if not longer. We both knew that I handled almost all of the Storm's operations these days.

"I know you do. Again, just wanted to confirm. I appreciate you humoring me."

"Any time, Beckett. And if something does come to my attention that seems at all concerning, I'll notify you at once."

The drive home didn't do anything to soothe my nerves, no matter how many slow, steady breaths I made myself take. In the back of my head, I kept seeing Logan yanking Maddie away from me. The three guys glaring at me like *I'd* ripped her father from her life. Maddie's expression shifting as she realized that I hadn't been completely above board with her on the subject of my business dealings—and how I'd first noticed her.

I couldn't let my emotions cloud my judgment. I needed to

consider every possibility until I'd gotten answers. Whoever had gotten to the guys had it in for my family, and stopping them before they did more damage of any kind had to be my first priority.

There was a small chance that Dad had done something in the past that I wasn't aware of and that it was so long ago Lana wouldn't have thought of the incident. After all, I'd have been only eleven when Maddie's father had died. Faking illnesses wasn't a technique I'd ever heard of our people using, but I couldn't assume I knew everything.

I passed through the electric gate and parked in the five-car garage. Our big suburban house on the outskirts of the city was where I'd spent the majority of my life when we weren't on the move handling business transactions and overseeing activities elsewhere. It was home, but it often didn't feel like one these days. Because the moment I walked through the door into the expansive front hall, I sensed the gloom that had fallen over the place.

That, and the faint voices from a distant TV. I followed them to the family room and found Dad sitting back in his recliner, the remote on the arm next to his hand. Evening was falling outside, the sunlight dwindling, but he hadn't bothered to turn on the lights. The TV's glow cut starkly into the room. His gaze flicked to me and then back to the screen without so much as a hello, his expression slack.

I studied him for a moment, trying to imagine this shell of a man launching an attack on Maddie and her other boyfriends. It was hard to picture him summoning enough conviction to bother. Lately, he'd only given the most cursory attention to our basic dealings. Why would he go out of his way to stir up more trouble over a long-cold murder?

But I couldn't ignore the possibility completely, not when everything about this scenario seemed ridiculous.

"Hey, Dad," I said. "Any thoughts on dinner?"

His gaze returned to me, but I felt like he wasn't totally seeing me. He waved his hand dismissively. "I'm sure whatever Emilio whips up will be fine."

Fair enough. I inhaled deeply, steadying myself. "True. I'm looking forward to it. By the way, a name came up today as someone who might have interfered with our operations at some point—Evan Silver? Does that ring any bells?"

Dad frowned, but he looked more annoyed that I was making him think than concerned about a possible business problem. "I can't think of anyone by that name. Did he work with one of the other families?"

The Devil's Dozen families, he meant. I shook my head. "Not as far as I know. He was a doctor. A researcher at Southwestern Regional Memorial Hospital." I'd looked up the one hospital in the area of Maddie's hometown, based on what she'd told me before about her father's work.

The air of confusion lingered around my dad. I could tell he had no idea what I was talking about, which relieved me even as his lack of investment niggled at me.

"None of that sounds at all familiar," he said definitively. "If you find out he damaged our holdings in some way, I'm sure you know how to deal with that." His attention slid back to the TV.

"I do. No need to worry about it." Not that he looked like he was particularly worried anyway.

I stepped out of the room and hesitated in the hallway. The ache in my chest tightened.

Years ago, I'd have been able to turn to Dad for guidance. I could have laid the situation out, and he'd have considered it from every angle alongside me, suggesting strategies and avenues of inquiry. But even if I tried to tell him I needed help, he wouldn't be able to offer much these days. He just didn't care enough. He'd probably tell me I should be proving myself, not leaning on him.

All because of the choices I'd made trying to prove myself and protect the family before, which had shattered his faith in both me and himself in the process.

I swallowed hard and headed upstairs, but my own worries chased at my heels. Yes, someone clearly had it in for me and the Storm, but I'd handled vengeful assholes before. I wasn't afraid of that.

I *was* afraid for Maddie. It didn't matter what kind of hotshots her other guys believed they were. They couldn't be prepared to tangle with the sorts of criminals who ran in my family's circle, the few who were even aware of our level of society. Whoever *was* behind the cover up and the murder was obviously dangerous. The threat the guys had decided I represented was still out there, unknown, maybe already planning another attack.

My hands closed into fists at my sides. I couldn't stand back and watch someone hurt her. I needed to know what they'd uncovered so I could deal with it *my* way.

But the guys were never going to be on board with that, not now. Our confrontation this afternoon had made that painfully clear. They'd never really trusted me in the first place, and whatever they'd heard had only confirmed their suspicions.

I had to get through to Maddie. I had to make her understand why I'd told the lies I had and that they had nothing to do with the threats she was facing now. That I could protect her from those threats. I didn't want to lose another person because they didn't understand why I'd done the things I'd done or how much they mattered to me.

But what the hell could I say to her that would convince her while the three of them had her ear and I'd been pushed aside?

I paced in my bedroom for several minutes before sitting down on the edge of the bed and getting out my phone again. If I couldn't talk to my dad, there were other people who'd been a guiding force for me after he'd pulled away. Everyone in Paradise Bend had my back, but Rowan had taken me under his wing more than anyone from the start.

I hit his name in my contacts and tipped backward on the bed.

The phone had almost gone to voicemail when Rowan picked up, his familiar easygoing tenor sounding a little harried. "Beckett?"

A childish voice was chattering in the background on a rant about jellybeans. The corners of my mouth twitched upward. "Sorry if I'm interrupting something. Busy with the kids?"

He chuckled. "Always." He paused and muttered something off the line, and a lower rumble of a voice I recognized as Kaige's carried from farther away. The little girl squealed with laughter as he must have swooped in.

Rowan came back, a little more relaxed now. "The baby went down a few minutes ago, but Josey'll do anything to delay bedtime. That's four-year-olds for you. What's up?"

I could tell he could actually talk now. "I just wondered how you're all doing."

Rowan hummed, probably able to tell it was more than that but playing along while I worked up to my real question. "About as well as we can with the new baby keeping us up at all hours. At least we've got plenty of us to spread the sleeplessness around! Mercy's already back on the job, laying down the law with her people and telling off anyone who thinks a mom can't keep them in line."

I snorted. "They'll regret that mistake fast." Mercy was just about the toughest person I knew, man or woman.

"Oh, believe me, they do."

He paused, and I could feel him leaving an opening for me to get to the real point. I stared up at the ceiling for a moment before saying, "How do you handle it when she's in danger? Like before, when Xavier was terrorizing her, and all the other stuff that goes on around her… How do you keep your cool and figure out the best way to help her rather than going batshit trying to protect her?"

Rowan's voice softened. "Sounds like someone speaking from new experience. Congrats if you've found a woman who means enough to you that you'd go batshit for her."

I glowered at the ceiling. "That doesn't really help."

He gave a light laugh. "I know. I guess…" His tone turned more serious. "I just decided I'd do whatever it took to make sure she got through okay. Even if *I* got hurt instead. Even if I put my whole life on the line. No holds barred. I love her, and I wouldn't feel right standing back if there was anything at all I could do. Knowing I'm that committed, that I'll take whatever action I need to, makes it easier for me to simmer down long enough to figure out what the best action would be. If that makes sense?"

The sentiments he'd expressed about how far he'd go rang completely true. "Yeah," I said. "It does."

"So you do have someone like that now?"

I thought of Maddie—of her smile, of the passion that came over her face when she talked about her future plans, of the mix of affection and determination in her kiss. My fingers tightened around the phone.

"Yeah. And I would do anything for her, so you're right. I've just got to figure out what the right thing is, the thing that'll protect her the most."

CHAPTER 3

Madelyn

I used my chopsticks to pick at the small carton of rice that had been drowned in the sweet and sour chicken from a local Chinese restaurant. The Vigil guys were all digging into their own cartons around their apartment's living room, though Dexter had opted to use a fork, looking as if he wasn't totally pleased that he hadn't had time to cook while we tried to work out what Beckett's full connection to their investigation might be.

He popped a mouthful of lo mein into his mouth while peering intently at the shipping records with the trucking company logo that Slade had grabbed several days ago. The records had been in an envelope tacked to the door of a shell corporation we'd tied to two other businesses it was clear Dad had been looking into, but we hadn't figured out how the trucking company fit in.

From Dexter's expression, he wasn't getting any closer. He

flipped to the second page and sighed. "There's definitely no way I can break the code on this without the key. And no way to figure out what that key is."

"I bet Beckett knows," Logan muttered darkly as he scanned through our surveillance camera footage on his laptop.

"We still haven't found any evidence that proves his family has anything to do with my dad's death," I reminded him. "Nothing connecting him to the warehouse Dad had the address to or the seafood market that was receiving deliveries from them—that had the logo he mentioned when he was sick. You're trying your best to pin this on him, and it's still not sticking."

Logan looked up to briefly glower at me. "He's a crook. He lied to us, and one of his employees was so wracked with guilt the guy spilled the beans. Don't defend him."

I guessed I should be glad Logan didn't say anything harsher considering how close I'd gotten to our supposed enemy. But I still couldn't shake the sense that nothing about this felt totally right.

There was definitely more going on with Beckett than I'd realized, but he'd never asked me anything about my dad other than a couple of typical questions when I'd brought up his death. I hadn't gotten the slightest sense that he was checking whether I knew about the murder or had evidence he might need to destroy.

"What about your tour of the spa?" Slade asked, waving his chopsticks at me. "We've barely had time to go over that. Maybe something you saw there will connect the dots."

I tipped my head back, letting my vision go vague as I reached into my memories. I'd stopped by a spa that was another business under the same shell corporation as the warehouse and the seafood market earlier today, hoping to get a better idea of what the overall organization was involved with.

"I did see some sketchy stuff," I said. "It looked like they might be selling drugs to some of their clientele, pretending it's a special service. I caught a hand-off of the drugs on video—that might work as evidence. But it's got nothing to do with Beckett."

When he'd picked me up, he hadn't seemed at all concerned that I might have learned something incriminating about him there. Although he had acted pretty protective in general... maybe like he had some reason to believe the place might be dangerous beyond my urgent appeal for help.

But if he'd been worried about crimes he was involved in being exposed, I'd have expected a much different reaction. He'd only seemed concerned about my well-being.

How could that guy have been responsible for causing my mom's car accident? How could he have set fire to the Vigil office knowing I might be in there?

A different part of the memory clicked in my head. "I did see the woman who was at the bar the day I snuck in and got my dad's trinket box back. The one who was part of the gang running the place." The one who'd nearly shot Logan when the guys had charged in to help me escape.

Slade perked up. "Then there is a common thread between all of them."

"All of the places where we've found evidence related to my dad," I said. "Those documents we can't even read are the only things that tie Beckett to any of the rest, and even that evidence is shaky. He was getting a delivery from the trucking company. He might not be any more involved in the business than that."

Logan grunted abruptly. I thought he was making a wordless objection to my point until I glanced over and saw his attention was completely focused on his laptop screen.

"The camera's down," he said.

All of us immediately gathered around the armchair where he was sitting. The window open on the screen was totally blank other than the small words *NO SIGNAL* in the middle.

"Which one's that?" Slade asked.

Logan opened a different window, which showed the same thing. "This is at the office building where the shell corporation was located. Both of the feeds are down—the one in the hall outside and the one by the front entrance. That's got to mean someone found them and purposefully disabled them, not that one got bumped by accident or something."

Dexter considered the screen as avidly as he had the trucking company documents. "When did they cut out? Do you think Beckett went looking after we confronted him?"

"Let me see…" Logan skimmed back through the recorded footage and found the last section where there was actual video showing. The time and date stamp in the bottom corner was just after eight last night. One feed went black, and then the other followed a minute later. It definitely looked like someone had gone and found both.

"The cameras at the seafood market are still running," Logan said. "No one's discovered those yet."

A sinking feeling pulled at my stomach. "This *really* doesn't make sense. They were disabled before you accused Beckett. And if he's at the center of this conspiracy and someone found those cameras pointed at a key site last night, wouldn't they have reported it to him? Shouldn't he have realized we were on to him?"

Slade cocked his head. "Maybe he did. He must have already known we were poking around, or he wouldn't have gone after your mom or our office to try to threaten us into backing off."

I threw my hands in the air. "But he seemed totally confused when you guys confronted him this afternoon. Like he had no idea what you were talking about."

"Maybe he's just a good actor," Logan muttered.

"Then wouldn't he have come up with a better story? He wasn't prepared at all for the accusations you threw at him or the questions I asked. We didn't shove any real proof at him. It shouldn't have been hard for him to come up with a fake explanation that would make it all seem reasonable if he'd known in advance that the subject might come up."

Logan snapped his computer shut, his expression stormy. "Or he just wanted you to think that. You can't let your emotions get tangled up in this, Maddie."

I folded my arms over my chest. "Like your emotions aren't? I'm sure you've been champing at the bit for an excuse to hate Beckett from the first second I mentioned he existed."

He scowled at me, but he didn't deny it.

Dexter cleared his throat and rested a tentative hand on my shoulder—just for a second, but his touch was rare enough to send a heated shiver through me before he withdrew it.

"The only solid connection we do have between Beckett and Maddie's dad is the employee who told us about it," he said. "We're not getting anywhere with the records we have here. We should see what else we can find out about that guy. Maybe if we track him down, we can convince him to go to the police with what he knows or hand some real evidence over to us after all."

Okay, that was a plan I could at least partly get behind. I nodded, shooting Dexter a grateful smile. "How would we do that?"

Slade tapped his lips. "The only place we saw him was by the trucking company."

Logan sprang out of his chair, aggressive energy radiating off his brawny frame. "Let's head back there then, and see if there's anything we can make use of in the area."

We tramped down to the parking lot and piled into Logan's car, Slade sliding into the backseat next to me. He reached across the seat to twine his fingers with mine, but tension hummed through the air. All of us were on edge as we waited to find out if this course of action would finally get us somewhere.

Logan drove swiftly along the darkened roads. "It's just up here," he said as we approached the trucking company. He leaned forward to squint at the storefronts nearby, lit up by the yellowed glow of the streetlamps.

"There," Dexter said, pointing at something beyond the windshield. "That convenience store has a security cam out front at an angle that probably caught the other side of the street."

"Perfect." Logan pulled over to the sidewalk just down the street. "Let's check it out."

I'd been around the Vigil guys enough that I didn't bother to question *how* we were going to manage that. Their methods weren't always what you could call legit. Or legal. But they did get the job done, and right now, we needed answers.

Dexter had already pulled out his lock picks before we'd made it around the side of the convenience store to its back door. He made quick work of the lock and nudged the door open. The interior of the store was dark and silent, no one around this late at night.

"No other security system," Dexter murmured. "They probably can't afford anything much."

"Makes it easier for us." Slade slunk down the hall and paused at a room just before the larger area up ahead where I could see shelves lined with merchandise. "I think this is the manager's office. There's a computer."

Logan flexed his hands. "My turn to do the breaking and entering."

He stepped ahead of Slade into the small office room and dropped into the chair at the metal desk. As his fingers whipped across the keyboard, sending the monitor flickering to life, the rest of us gathered behind him.

I couldn't tell what he was doing exactly, but after a couple of minutes of clicking and tapping, the password request window vanished, and the regular desktop full of icons appeared before us. Logan grinned tightly and sent the cursor veering across the screen. "Ah ha. Looks like the footage is stored here. Usually these kind of systems are set up to delete after no less than twenty-four hours, so this morning's footage should definitely still be there."

He opened up the folder and skimmed through the file names, which seemed to be labeled by the day and hour. Then he clicked one open. It showed a view of the sidewalk outside the shop—and the road and the trucking company building on the other side just ahead, as Dexter had predicted.

Slade let out an approving whistle and gave his friend a thumbs up. "Now we're talking."

Logan played the footage at three times the normal speed, racing through various people coming and going from the trucking company door and its bay off to the side. I guessed none of the guys spotted the man who'd approached them, because none of them said a word. Then Logan clicked the mouse to bring the video feed back to regular playback, just as I saw the three guys currently around me walking up to the building.

They stepped in through the front door, and Slade let out an urgent sound next to me. He pointed at the screen.

The second after the Vigil guys had entered the building, a gangly man with slicked-back hair had strode into view from the same direction they'd arrived from. He walked briskly but confidently toward the trucking company.

Dexter knit his brow. "That's him, but he doesn't look nervous at all. The opposite, really. He seemed so anxious when he approached us."

Slade frowned. "Where's he going now?"

The man had veered down the alley next to the trucking company instead of continuing on to the door. He stopped there, standing where he was only just visible in the shadows near the mouth of the alley, braced as if waiting for something.

"It looks like he followed you there and then hung out until you left," I said. "I thought you said it seemed like he only noticed you after you showed up?"

"Maybe he'd spotted us somewhere we were investigating earlier and…" Logan paused, clearly not sure how to explain how the man would have tracked him down again. "Or he could have just seen us from farther down the street when we pulled up."

I guessed that was possible.

The man stayed in place until the Vigil guys emerged several minutes later. They continued down the street, clustered close together in conversation. As they passed out of view of the camera, the man in the alley edged closer, clearly having noticed their presence. He waited for several beats and then slipped out onto the sidewalk.

As he headed after the guys, his posture slumped, his head ducking and his shoulders hunching. His head jerked with nervous twitches as he scanned the street. Then he vanished from the frame too.

Logan stopped the playback, staring grimly at the screen. I knew he had to have noticed how strange this was too.

"It's like he planned out how he'd talk to you," I said. "He only acted nervous when he knew you were about to see him. It *was* an act."

"Or maybe he started out confident and then got freaked out as the possible consequences of blabbing on his boss sank in?" Slade said, but he couldn't put a lot of conviction into the suggestion.

I hugged myself. "I don't know what's going on here, but I don't like it at all. Too much doesn't add up."

"It doesn't add up because we don't have all the pieces yet,"

Logan said stubbornly, but he was obviously just as uncertain as the rest of us.

I didn't know if he was letting himself think this far yet, but I couldn't help it. What if Beckett's confusion had been completely real? What if he really had been set up?

What if we were focusing all this energy on blaming him when the real villain was still lurking behind the scenes, ready to strike again?

CHAPTER 4

Slade

I groaned as I came into consciousness, stretching my legs out to relieve the stiffness in my back. The couch was comfortable to lounge on while watching TV, but not the greatest for a full night's sleep. My joints cracked as I sat upright with a brief yawn. The scent of last night's Chinese food still hung in the air, provoking a gurgle in my stomach.

Logan was just stuffing a couple of textbooks into his bag near the front door. He glanced over at me when I moved and offered an apologetic grimace, keeping his voice low. "I hope I didn't wake you up."

I shook my head. "Happened all on its own."

He slung his backpack over his shoulder with a huff of frustration. "Have to get to class. It seems stupid even *having* classes while all this shit is going down."

"At least they're teaching you skills that'll make you an even better hacker," I said with a half-hearted grin. "Whether they meant to do that or not."

"One can only hope."

"We won't do too much work without you. Gotta make sure you're still carrying your weight."

Logan snorted and gave me the middle finger as he walked out of the apartment. As the deadbolt clicked into place behind him, I grabbed my prosthetic from where I'd left it on the armchair, fixed it onto my stump, and ambled over to my bedroom.

The hinges squeaked faintly when I eased the door slightly open. Maddie didn't stir from where she'd sprawled amid my bedsheets. I sent up a silent offering of gratitude that I'd washed them recently.

When we'd gotten back from our investigations last night, we'd all been too wiped to do anything other than crash. Logan had tried to nobly offer *his* bed to Maddie while he took the couch, but I'd had to point out that he was way too tall to get any sleep that way. He'd barely fit on the thing. So he'd grudgingly allowed me to make the gesture and take the minor discomfort.

Did I regret it? Not at all.

Did the crick in my neck have me wincing as I turned my head? Yes, absolutely.

But seeing the way she lay there so peacefully made every bit of discomfort worth it. I'd give up a hundred restful nights to see her sleep like this. She'd been under so much pressure over the past few weeks—first because of the situation with Logan and her stolen car, and then with her dad's murder.

I wished I could do more to help her through this mess, but offering my bed seemed to be the most I could manage. Aside from jokes and fun, I wasn't much good at anything else. Showing off my language skills wasn't going to fix anything. Even if we found the people responsible for this murder, it wouldn't be because of me. Dexter and Logan were the brains and strategists behind this investigation.

I was just… here. Providing moral support and an extra set of eyes and hands—that was about it.

Dexter emerged from his bedroom on the other side of the living room, his dark curls even more rumpled than usual and the boxers and tee he'd worn to sleep in a similar state. He padded across the floor to join me and peeked past me at our sleeping girlfriend.

"She was really tired, huh?" he murmured.

"We went through a lot yesterday."

"No kidding." A fond smile touched his lips, a glow of affection lighting in his eyes that I didn't think I'd ever seen from my typically anti-social friend before. "But she's taking it all in and keeping up with the rest of us, even though she's not used to situations like this. She really is something."

"I've never met a woman like her," I agreed.

Dexter paused and swiped his hand across his mouth with a hint of his usual awkwardness. His voice dipped even quieter. "I don't know if I'm going to be enough for her."

My head jerked around so I could stare at him. "What are you talking about?"

He shrugged. "I just—obviously she's got you and Logan too. It's not like I'm in this alone. But I want her to be happy that she's with me too. I don't have any real experience with relationships—romance, sex, any of it. I have no idea what I'm doing, not like the two of you. And… it's not exactly a secret that I'm what most people would call weird."

I aimed a playful punch at his shoulder, not quite making contact since he wasn't much of one for physical touch. "Your weirdness is your best quality. You'll be good for her in totally different ways from the two of us. Maybe she'll even decide she likes you best."

Dexter's expression remained doubtful. Looking from him to our dozing woman, inspiration sparked in my head. A small smile curled my lips. Maybe I couldn't offer a whole lot, but I could certainly deliver more of the stuff I was good at.

"Hey," I said, tipping my head toward Dexter. "You know, Logan and I were able to, ah, work well together when it came to giving her a good time. I don't see any reason you and I couldn't do the same. Why don't we start off this morning by giving her something fantastic to remember amid all the awfulness that's been going on?"

Dexter's gaze flicked to me, desire flaring in his eyes alongside the affection I'd seen earlier. "You think she'd like that?"

"Oh, I bet we could make sure she likes it an awful lot. And I could give you some tips from my vast expertise." I grinned at him. "Totally up to you if you're comfortable with it."

He wet his lips, looking at Maddie again. "Yeah," he said softly. "That could be good. Just to make sure I'm not missing anything. And so she gets as much out of it as possible."

From the way he'd been observing her since she'd joined our investigations, I didn't think it was likely there was much he hadn't figured out or couldn't if the right moment arose. He probably knew more about Maddie's little quirks than I did. But by collaborating, we could give her more than either of us could on our own. And she deserved every bit of pleasure she could get while we had a chance to bestow it on her.

As if she'd sensed our discussion, Maddie rolled over on the bed. She rubbed her eyes and spotted us in the doorway.

"Good morning?" she mumbled questioningly, squinting at us. "Did I sleep in?"

"Not too much." I stepped into the room. "How are you feeling?"

"Other than completely confused by this mystery we can't seem to unravel, pretty good." She raised her eyebrows at me and Dexter following behind me. "So, you were just watching me sleep? Some people would consider that strange."

"Or romantic. What do you think, Dex?"

"It was a little strange," he said, and I narrowed my eyes at him.

Maddie cracked a laugh and sat up in bed, allowing the sheets to fall to her waist. "I can always count on Dexter to have my back."

She'd slept in the tank top she'd had on under her sweater but taken off her bra, her nipples lightly pebbled against the thin fabric. My dick twitched to attention at the sight.

"Hmph," I said in mock-annoyance, and sat down on the bed to grab one of her feet. "But I have your foot."

I dug my thumbs into the arch in a firm massage, and Maddie relaxed back on her hands, flexing her ankle. "Feel free to keep having it if that's what you're going to do with it. I hope the couch wasn't too uncomfortable."

"It was fine," I said, and teased my thumb over her toes. "Of course, I'd have enjoyed sharing this bed with you even more, but I don't think we'd have gotten much sleep that way."

Amusement warmed Maddie's expression. "Is that so?"

"Oh, definitely. So I made that immense sacrifice for the sake of our health. But of course now that we *have* gotten some sleep…"

I let my hands slide over her ankle to her calf. She'd taken off her jeans to sleep, and my fingers kneaded silky skin. She mustn't have anything on beneath the sheet other than her panties. My cock got even harder just picturing her.

Maddie hummed happily. "I'm so curious to see what you have in mind." Her eyelids had lowered, but she lifted them again to glance at Dexter, who was still standing by the corner of the bed, his hands at his sides. "And did you have big plans too?"

Her tone immediately gentled when she spoke to him, and a rush of affection swept through me. It was obvious she understood how uncertain he was about this kind of intimacy. She didn't want to force anything on him too quickly.

She got him in a way so many other women hadn't—she appreciated what made him such an amazing guy, weird or not. How could *I* not love that about her?

Dexter's tongue flicked over his lips again, his gaze glued to her. "Absolutely. If you'd like both of us."

A brilliant smile stretched across her face. "Both sounds pretty amazing. Come here?"

It was definitely a question, not a demand, but Dexter moved as if pulled toward her. He knelt on the bed, his eyes never leaving her face. I half expected him to freeze up, for me or Maddie to have to encourage him onward, but he had more confidence than he'd given himself credit for. He raised his hand to stroke her cheek and then lowered his head to claim her mouth.

His kiss gave Maddie all the encouragement she must have needed to wind her arm around the back of his neck. As she kissed him back, I tugged the sheet off her legs and bent down to press my mouth to her shin.

My hands traveled farther, over her knee and partway up her thigh, massaging the whole way. Maddie let out her first small groan of pleasure against Dexter's lips. He made a strained sound of his own and kissed her harder.

Oh, it looked like my friend was a fast learner, all right.

He moved his mouth from her lips to her jaw and then down her neck as Maddie tipped her head back to give him better access. A sly smirk crossed my face.

"Use your teeth too," I suggested. "Just a little nip here and there. She likes that." As I well knew from the fun I'd had with her before.

Dexter must have taken my advice, because Maddie's next breath came out stuttered. "That's playing dirty."

I chuckled. "That's *exactly* what it is. But you'll reap all the benefits."

I slid my hands even higher, caressing the skin just below the apex of her thighs. Maddie squirmed at my touch, and I thought I could see a patch of dampness already forming on her peach-pink panties. My mouth watered at the thought of tasting her there like I had before. But I didn't want to take over the encounter too much, not while Dexter was still getting used to the idea of us sharing her.

Instead, I simply grazed the tips of my fingers over her pussy through the fabric. Maddie whimpered and dug her fingers into Dexter's curls. He didn't object when she yanked his mouth back to hers.

I fondled her lightly through her panties as their kisses turned more passionate. Dexter pulled away, but with no sign of being overwhelmed. He was keeping up better than I'd expected after his earlier doubts.

He worked both his hands under her tank top across her toned stomach and tugged the fabric up. Maddie raised her arms and let him peel the shirt off of her. Both he and I paused, taking in the expanse of pale skin he'd bared. Her breasts bounced slightly as she adjusted her position next to him, her rosy nipples perked.

Dexter cupped his hand around one breast and swiveled his thumb over the nipple to draw it to a stiffer peak. Maddie let out an eager murmur, a flush spreading up her neck and across her cheeks.

I wanted to be up there with her too, sucking those little noises into my mouth with a kiss, tasting those soft mounds, but somehow it was even more electrifying to watch Dexter work her over.

"Use your mouth too," I said raggedly. He could pleasure her on my behalf too.

When he dropped his head to suck the peak of her other breast between his lips, I resumed my delicate caresses between Maddie's legs. As her grip on Dexter's hair tightened, her eyes rolled upward with a moan. I couldn't help grinning even while my erection strained against my boxers.

God, I wanted her. She was absolutely fucking perfect.

"Ease back a bit," I murmured to Dexter, stroking a little more firmly. Maddie's hips lifted to meet my touch. "Blow on her nipple and then lick it."

He followed my instructions, and Maddie shivered with bliss. The sight had me aching twice as hard as before. I couldn't stop myself from delving my other hand into my boxers, sliding them down my hips so I could grip my rigid cock.

"Good," I muttered, pumping myself hard while I watched.

Dexter nipped and licked and ghosted his breath over one breast and then the other, and Maddie writhed between us with those lovely sounds of pleasure. Then her gaze caught mine. Her eyes dipped lower to how I was occupying my other hand, and a glint of delight lit in them.

She tugged Dexter's head up to capture his mouth with one more kiss. Then she eased onto all fours, turning toward me as my fingers fell away from her panties.

"We should all be having fun," she said, running her tongue across her bottom lip.

"Oh, I am, Piccolina."

"But you could have even more."

She lowered her head to my lap and took the head of my cock into her mouth without hesitation. Fuck me. Her tongue swirled around my shaft, and a jolt of pure bliss shot through my dick, radiating through the rest of my body.

"Hell, yes, you bet I can," I rasped, but I couldn't let our woman stay unattended. "Dex, get those panties off her. Stroke her pussy until she's even wetter."

Dexter crawled closer and dipped his fingers between her legs from behind. Maddie gasped around my cock. She sucked me harder, and a groan reverberated from my chest.

I wasn't going to last very long like this.

But Maddie wasn't above a little teasing herself. She swiveled her tongue around me once more and then raised herself up to turn toward Dexter again. He didn't show a hint of resistance as she nudged his chest, pushing him down on his back so she could climb atop him. She rocked on his lap, her pussy brushing against the bulge of his erection behind his boxers. Dexter let out a guttural sound and arched to meet her.

Maddie grasped the waistband of his boxers and dragged them down before glancing around. "Condom?" she asked breathlessly.

I practically lunged for the bedside table where I kept my stash. I tore open the foil with my teeth before passing the packet to her.

Maddie flashed me a smile of lustful thanks before rolling the condom down Dexter's length. His chest heaved with anticipation, his eyes almost feverishly bright.

He didn't wait for her to initiate the final step. He grasped her hips and positioned her over him. They groaned together as she sank down and he bucked up, penetrating those slick folds in one go.

Heat flooded my body, and a need I couldn't deny gripped my chest. I scooted across the mattress toward the pillows and tangled my fingers in the hair at the back of Maddie's head.

She glanced down at my straining erection and smiled dreamily. At my pull, she eased down while she kept rocking over Dexter and took me into her mouth again.

The choked sound that escaped me at the press of her lips was totally primal. I didn't hold myself back, tightening my grip on her hair and swaying my hips to fuck her mouth. Maddie took me down with eager swipes of her tongue and squeezes of her lips, still bucking with Dexter at the same time.

She sucked hard and flicked the flat of her tongue against the underside of my cock at the same time, and I came so fast I didn't have time to even grunt a warning. Pleasure raced through me, and I exploded in her mouth.

Maddie didn't so much as wince, swallowing down my cum as if it was the best drink she'd ever tasted. The pleasure lingered on as she slid her lips off of me.

Dexter reached up to fondle both of her breasts. Maddie sighed and rocked faster, their bodies smacking together as they chased their own release. I pinched her ass, gazing up at her passion-filled face.

"Let it all out, Piccolina. I want to hear it all. Every goddamned sound."

She obliged, opening her mouth to emit a deeper moan. "Fuck," Dexter muttered, his hips jerking faster. Every whimper and gasp that spilled from our woman's lips set me on fire all over again until her muscles clenched with her release.

Maddie tipped her head back, a shudder running through her torso. Dexter groaned and rammed into her even harder, his breath shattering when he followed.

They rocked to a stop, and Maddie sank down to sprawl between us. I nestled close to her, slipping my arm around her waist. Dexter rolled onto his side with a content expression and rested a careful hand on her hip.

"That's what you sound like when you're allowed to make noises," I mused, the thought of it bringing a grin to my face. "We need a replay."

Maddie giggled breathlessly. "Right now?"

"I need a few minutes if we're going to do anything like this again," Dexter admitted.

Maddie and I both laughed, and I nodded. "Me too, Dex. Maybe we'll wait for another day."

We all lay there and caught our breaths, but I couldn't tear my gaze from Maddie. Joy brightened her face. We were all sated and pleased with ourselves—and fully pleasured.

But as we relaxed in silence together, her eyes started to cloud with worries again. I could see the strain of them creeping across her expression.

No matter how hard I tried to make her happy, I hadn't gotten rid of the source of her stress. And I had no idea how I could.

CHAPTER 5

Madelyn

As I stepped out of my last class of the afternoon, I let out my breath in a sigh and rolled my shoulders. The genetics seminar went over a lot of material I found fascinating, but it was getting harder to absorb all the information when my head felt so full of theories and possible evidence related to Dad's murder and Beckett's potential role in it.

I meandered a short distance down the hallway and resigned myself to plopping down on a bench by the wall, pulling out my phone to occupy myself. The Vigil guys all had classes during this time period that ended later than mine. Logan's had the closest timeframe, and he'd insisted that I should wait in the building by the lecture hall for the twenty minutes it'd take for his class to let out and him to hustle across the campus.

It seemed a little ridiculous that I'd need protection just to walk anywhere on campus, but Slade and Dexter had agreed with Logan. I hadn't felt like getting into a big argument with all of them. It wasn't as if I had anything urgent to do right this minute anyway, so I might as well humor them.

I scrolled through a couple of social media feeds, and then a text from Keeley popped up. My roommate sounded typically energetic even in text form.

Hey Maddie! You should swing by our room as soon as you can. The RA dropped off something for you—it looks pretty cool!

I knit my brow as I re-read the message. What would the RA have brought for me? I'd barely talked with the senior who oversaw our floor. But it could be that a package from home had come in and been misdirected, and she'd needed to bring it to me by hand. That would be just like Mom, only out of the hospital for a few days and sending something to cheer *me* up.

Hesitating, I glanced around the hallway. It looked the same as always, the students for the next class already filing into the seminar room, a few more lingering around chatting with each other. My dorm building was just a couple of minutes away, and Logan wasn't due for another fifteen. Why the hell shouldn't I quickly pop over and find out what "cool" thing I'd gotten?

Sure, I'll be right over, I texted back. *Thanks for letting me know!*

I set a brisk pace along the campus paths, not stopping to enjoy the warmth of the spring day. I'd prefer to get back to my waiting spot before Logan showed up so I could avoid whatever lecture he'd give me. In no time at all, I was climbing up the stairs in the dorm building and pushing into the hall.

I already had my keycard in hand when I reached the door to our room. I swiped it and headed inside, expecting to see Keeley waiting eagerly for me to discover my surprise.

She wasn't there. I stalled a couple of steps into the room, frowning as I took in our beds with their rumpled covers, my neat desk and hers with its chaos of binders and make-up, and the thin rug on the floor. I didn't see anything inside that hadn't been here the last time I'd been in the room either—no special deliveries. What the heck was going on?

My surprise had just given way to a jolt of apprehension when footsteps thudded behind me. I spun around just as Beckett strode into the room.

My pulse stuttered. A startled yelp burst from my throat, lost to the hall in the thump as Beckett shut the door behind him. I backed up to my desk and gripped my chair, wondering if I should scream for help.

Before I'd made a decision, Beckett raised his hands in a gesture of surrender. His mouth twisted at a pained angle, and he stayed at the opposite end of the room, giving me as much space as he could. His dark gray eyes pierced into mine. "I'm not going to hurt you. I'd *never* hurt you. I just want you to hear my side of the story—properly, without the other guys interrupting with accusations every few seconds."

My shoulders came down a tad, but I remained braced for a fight. "How am I supposed to trust you when you snuck up on me like this? How did you even get in here—what happened to Keeley?"

"I didn't hurt her either," Beckett said, slowly and calmly. "All I did was tell her I wanted to surprise you by showing up unexpectedly and ask her to send you a text to get you to come over. She was more than happy to support my romantic gesture." His voice turned a bit wry with the last few words, but he kept his hands in their submissive position.

Damn it. Keeley would have recognized Beckett from the photo I'd shown her of him—which she'd highly approved of—and it'd never occurred to me to tell her that I'd discovered he might be dangerous. I hadn't even seen her since I'd found that out myself.

"I would never hurt anyone you care about, and that includes your family," Beckett went on into my silence. "I swear to you that I had no idea your dad was murdered until yesterday. And I've never lied to you about how I feel about you. I just… wasn't completely upfront about everything *my* family is involved in, as far as our business goes. Will you please hear me out?"

My stomach churned as I sorted through my emotions. He'd scared me by making this impromptu visit—but only because of the fears the Vigil guys had planted in my head. Two days ago, his arrival would have been a pleasant surprise. Until yesterday, I'd never seen any reason to think Beckett had malicious intentions toward me or my family.

And none of the investigating we'd done had given us any proof. If anything, what we'd seen on the surveillance camera last night had only cast doubt on whether the story the guys had heard from Beckett's supposed employee was true.

I wanted to know what was really going on, and the man in front of me might know more than anyone.

"All right," I said carefully. "But you stay over there. And talk quickly." I turned my chair around so I could sit down on it.

Beckett didn't move from his position by the door. He ran his hand through his sandy hair, looking briefly uncertain—more uncertain than I'd ever seen from this confident man. Then he squared his shoulders and met my eyes again.

"The only things I kept from you didn't have anything to do with you or your family anyway," he said. "They aren't the kind of things I'd tell *anyone*, because of the trouble it could make for us. I do work for a business that's been in my family for generations. We do deal in real estate among various other things. But not all of those business dealings are strictly legal… Actually, quite a few of them aren't."

My chest tightened at that admission. I felt the need to say the words out loud, to put a clear label on what he'd just confessed to. "So, you're a criminal, then?"

Beckett gave me a small, crooked smile. "That's one way of putting it."

He hadn't even tried to deny it. I swallowed thickly. "And I'm supposed to believe that even though you're involved in all this illegal stuff, you had nothing to do with the crimes the other guys and I have been investigating?"

"Just because I'm a criminal, that doesn't mean I'm out to attack you—or that I go around hurting innocent people in general. I've always tried to limit the collateral damage from our activities as much as possible and to focus on victimless crimes."

My eyebrows shot up. An edge crept into my voice as I spoke. "And are you sure there really are crimes with no victims at all?"

Beckett inclined his head. "Okay, so possibly someone is always taking a minor hit. But there are plenty of victims from all sorts of technically legal business practices too, a lot of them way worse off and less deserving of their trouble than anyone affected by my actions."

"And I'm just supposed to take your word for it?"

He gazed back at me with the unflappable composure I'd always admired in him. "You know who I am, Maddie. I didn't tell you the details, but I didn't pretend to be someone I'm not either. Everything you already believed about the kind of man you knew is still true. Maybe you don't like the new details you've learned, but consider that my work also puts me in a position to do plenty of good for the people around me too. Like setting up that pro bono medical clinic, which is still in the works. I wasn't lying about that either."

My stomach knotted. He sounded so sincere—but how could I trust a guy who'd just admitted that most of his dealings were illegal?

"I'll understand if you can't accept this side of my life," Beckett went on. "I knew it was going to come out eventually, so maybe it was wrong of me to put off the confession. You don't have to decide whether we could continue our relationship right now, as much as I'd like to. But no matter how you feel about the kind of work I do, the more important subject right now is your father's murder. And I promise you—I swear on the entire family business and my life—no one connected with me had anything to do with that."

My mouth pulled into a grimace. "That's easy to say but not so easy to prove."

"It's always difficult, if not impossible, to prove a negative. I'm sure you know that from your studies." A fond note warmed his voice just for a second and sent a tingle over my skin that I didn't know what to do with. "Like I told you, I had no idea he even was murdered until yesterday. I've spent the past day verifying that my family wasn't involved. The 'proof' the other guys offered revealed my ties to some of the businesses you didn't know about, but none of those businesses actually factored into your dad's death, did they?"

They didn't. We hadn't been able to find any connection between Beckett and the places we actually knew Dad had been mixed up with. I sucked my lip under my teeth to worry at it.

"You did see me at the club before we met," I pushed, watching his reaction.

Beckett sighed, and for the first time a twinge of regret passed through his expression. "The first time I saw you, you were at the club with the other guys. I'd been keeping an eye on *them* for a few months because they'd been sticking their noses into the underworld of this city, and I didn't know what their end goal was. I wanted to make sure they didn't know anything about my operations that could harm my family."

A prickle ran down my back. "So you set yourself up to bump into me—so that you could find out more about them?"

"At first," Beckett said quietly. "But it became clear very quickly that if they were wrapped up in anything on my level, you didn't know about it... and also that you were more than worth pursuing simply for who *you* are. I didn't really *need* to talk to you again after that first conversation. I simply wanted to. I wanted to get to know you, and then I wanted to keep seeing you, only because of how much you brighten my life. You're something special, Maddie. And if someone's been threatening you, then I'll do everything in my power to stop them. I'm sure I can do a hell of a lot more than that trio of college boys."

He'd continued speaking softly the whole way through, but a thread of menace wound through his tone with the last couple of sentences. His back drew a little straighter, his expression hardening.

I was dealing with not just a criminal but a leader among criminals, and he was willing to put all his influence and power into defending me. It should have scared me, and it did a little, but at the same time I couldn't deny the thrill that shot through me at his intensity.

It took me a moment to find my tongue. I wasn't going to let him win me over that easily. "I still don't know that it isn't someone under *your* orders who was making those threats. It isn't just the club and the trucking company. The guys have direct reason to believe you're involved." I wasn't going to betray them by giving away what they'd heard and from who, not until we were sure it was safe to tell Beckett.

Beckett frowned. "Then they must have been misinformed by someone with a separate agenda—most likely, to cover their own tracks. I have to assume that whoever was responsible for your father's murder, it was another criminal who's aware of my family's dealings and saw us as an easy target to frame so they could divert your investigation." His eyes flashed. "Unfortunately for them, with my underworld connections, I can help you track them down. And see justice done however you'd like it served."

The dark promise in his words provoked another tingle that raced straight to my core. I glanced away, grappling with my feelings.

Everything Beckett had said made sense. It was a much more reasonable story than anything the Vigil guys had been able to cobble together with the vague evidence and hearsay they'd had to rely on.

If Beckett was telling the truth, he could be the key to finding out what had really happened to Dad—and who had done it. How could I throw that chance away because of a sketchy stranger's words?

I had no idea how to wrap my head around everything he'd told me about his life. I'd been falling for him, hard, but the idea of dating a guy who was a consummate career criminal… I winced inwardly at the thought.

But then, was that reaction really fair? Beckett did illegal things, but how many times had I watched the Vigil guys break into buildings they weren't supposed to have access to and resort to violence to get their way?

They did it in the name of justice. Beckett's family used crime to make money. So maybe the ends justified the means in the Vigil's case. But I couldn't even say that Beckett's ends were all that bad if he used the profits from activities he claimed didn't hurt anyone innocent to set up places like that pro bono clinic.

I rubbed my forehead with the heel of my hand. He'd said I didn't need to decide how I felt about him personally or our relationship right away. That the most important thing was figuring out the crime that'd now affected all of our lives. And no matter how conflicted my emotions were about the things he'd admitted, I couldn't say I thought he was lying.

Between his story and the way the evidence added up—or didn't—I couldn't see how he could be involved in Dad's death or the cover-up. It was much easier to believe that the guy who'd pointed the finger at him had been purposefully misleading us for their own gain. The stranger had put on an act to convince the Vigil guys, and they'd fallen for it because they'd already been uneasy about Beckett's presence in my life. He really had been a perfect target.

I dragged in a breath. "Okay. I'm not saying anything about what'll happen between you and me until I've had more time to process all this and see what happens next. But if you're ready to—"

Before I could finish accepting his offer of help, my dorm-room door burst open, slamming into Beckett's back. As he stumbled forward, Logan hurtled into the room with Slade and Dexter at his heels, all of them tensed with protective fury.

CHAPTER 6

Madelyn

Logan threw himself straight at Beckett. He slammed the other man's body into the wall behind the door with the full force of his massive frame and whipped a dark object out from the waist of his jeans. As he pushed the thing against Beckett's throat, the bottom of my stomach dropped out.

It was a gun. Logan was holding a pistol to the underside of Beckett's jaw, glowering at him with so much brutal fury my pulse stuttered at the thought that he might use it.

"Logan!" I burst out. "What the hell are you doing?" Where had he even gotten the gun? I'd never seen him or any of the other Vigil guys packing anything like that before.

Slade and Dexter had stepped close around me as if to shield me, Slade touching the small of my back protectively and Dexter looking me over as if checking for injuries. Logan's attention stayed focused completely on Beckett.

Beckett stared back at him, his jaw tight in the uncomfortable position but his expression cool. His voice came out shockingly steady. "I can tell you don't have much experience with that pistol. If I wanted to, I could take it from you and you'd be the one with a gun to your throat. But I don't want this to be a fight."

"Too late for that," Logan snarled. "What the fuck are you doing here? Maddie told you to leave her alone. We're not letting you mess with her head any more."

"So, what? You're going to kill me here in her dorm room?"

Logan gave him another shove, his hand clenched around the front of Beckett's shirt and the other holding the gun in place. "Fuck you. I *should* kill you after all the shit you've pulled, and now this."

"If we can't trust you to stay away from Maddie, how can we trust you about anything else?" Slade demanded.

Beckett's gaze slid to me and then the man at my side. I couldn't imagine how he was staying so unfazed, but then, who knew how many times he'd had guns pointed at him before?

"She needed to know the truth," he said evenly. "She needed to know that I can help her figure out what really happened to her father."

"Bullshit!" Logan snapped. "You're trying to turn this around so you don't take the blame, when you're a lying piece of shit who—"

My nerves were jangling with apprehension, but I'd had enough. I pushed past Slade and Dexter and grabbed Logan's arm by the elbow. He flinched at the sudden contact, and my heart lurched at the thought of him squeezing the trigger.

"Stop, Logan," I said, unable to keep my voice from shaking even as I spoke as firmly as possible. "Put the gun down."

"I'm not dropping the only thing that will have this motherfucker thinking twice before touching you."

I grimaced at my stepbrother. "He wasn't touching me before either. He really did just come to talk. And after everything we've seen and what he said, I believe him that he wasn't involved in covering up my dad's murder. I don't think he wants to hurt me—he honestly wants to help."

Finally, Logan let his eyes meet mine. His voice came out only slightly softer than when he'd been talking to Beckett. "Did you invite him in here, or did he sneak in like a weasel and—?"

"It doesn't matter," I broke in. "I understand why he came. He knows more about the kind of people we're dealing with than any of us, including you. If we're going to find out who *has* been targeting my family, we need everything he can offer. Isn't that what really matters?"

Logan's gaze flicked between me and Beckett, his expression hard. "He's been playing you. You can't believe anything he says. He's fucking dangerous, and I don't want him anywhere near you."

I dug my fingers into my stepbrother's arm, wishing I could wrench his hand away from Beckett with a yank. "I'm not saying I totally trust him. I'm not saying I forgive him either. I'm just saying he's on our side when it comes to this investigation, and we could really use his help if he's going to give it."

"After everything he's done—"

My temper frayed. "Oh, please. You're in no position to rant about hiding things from me or treating me badly. Do I need to remind you how the last two years went down? And you're the one holding a gun on an unarmed man—a gun I'm going to guess you didn't get by any legal method? You're the only one who looks dangerous right now."

Logan's jaw twitched. "That's not the same. I'm *protecting* you."

"And so is he. Maybe he screwed up along the way, but so did you. I know Beckett—I know him a hell of a lot better than the rest of you, and you should know you can trust my judgment by now. His family wasn't involved in the murder, and Beckett has nothing to do with the cover-up. Whatever else he might be guilty of, those things aren't part of it. He's been framed, and we need to figure out by who, because they're our real enemy."

Logan growled and turned back to Beckett, prodding his neck with the gun. "I don't know what you said to her to pull the wool over her eyes, but—"

Dexter cut in with a clearing of his throat. "Actually… it's obvious he didn't hurt Maddie in any way when he came here. They must have been talking for a while for him to have convinced her, but he was still at the opposite end of the room from her when we came in. And we all know that the logistics don't add up as far as Beckett being responsible for the recent threats. We saw that last night."

Logan's head jerked around with a flash of betrayal on his face. "*You* think we should trust this prick?"

Dexter raised his hands, holding Logan's eyes for a second before his gaze darted away. "I don't think it would hurt to hear him out. I doubt Madelyn would have believed him if he didn't have a good explanation. If we can poke holes in his story, we will."

"Yeah," Slade said, glancing between us uneasily. "Maybe this has gotten a little out of hand. You are okay, aren't you, Maddie?"

"I'm perfectly fine," I said sharply. "Thank you for finally checking instead of assuming I'm a damsel in distress." Then I let out my breath in a huff and gave Logan's arm another tug. "You don't have to trust him. Just hear him out."

"He broke into your dorm. He forced this confrontation. He doesn't deserve to take another fucking breath."

For fuck's sake. I let go of Logan to fold my own arms over my chest, glaring at him. "I don't remember inviting the three of you over either, but you seemed to think it was fine to come barging in. I've had enough of this alpha bullshit. If you don't lower the gun right *now*, I'm going to call Campo and tell them you're threatening someone with a weapon. How do you think that report is going to look on your academic record?"

An incident like this would probably get him kicked right out of the school. Logan stared back at me, but I refused to budge. When he didn't answer in the first few seconds, I pulled out my phone.

"Fucking hell," Logan barked. He pushed away from Beckett and lowered his gun hand, keeping the pistol out but at his side. I could tell his muscles were tensed to whip the weapon up again if Beckett made one wrong move, but the other man stayed where he was by the wall, tensed but utterly composed at the same time.

"Thank you," Beckett said quietly. "I understand why you felt that approach was necessary. I'd want to do the same thing if I thought someone was going to hurt Maddie. But I promise you, I only came here to clear the air and set things right."

Logan snorted in disbelief, but he seemed to have run through the worst of his rage. I jumped into the moment of silence before he could start shooting off his mouth again.

"We need to work with Beckett to keep this investigation going—and to see it through before anyone *else* gets hurt," I said. "We clearly don't have enough connections to put together the pieces on our own, and it must be someone on Beckett's radar, or they wouldn't have targeted him as a scapegoat. Although we're lucky he still wants to help out after the way you just attacked him."

Beckett tipped his head to me, his mouth twisting for just a second. "It's all right. I *have* screwed up; I'm not blaming anyone for being angry or having trouble trusting me."

Logan glowered at him. "All that smooth talk with nothing to show for it yet."

"Shut up," I told him without much real rancor. "You haven't given him a chance to show anything."

Dexter rubbed his chin. "No matter who we're getting information from, we have to continue the investigation with a lot of care. When these people have found out that we were getting too close, they've lashed out: first Madelyn's mom, then the Vigil office. I don't think we'd want them to realize that we're working with Beckett—or that we're continuing to investigate at all."

"My people know how to keep a low profile," Beckett assured him. "Now that we know what kind of a situation we're in, we won't let anyone see anything we don't want them to."

"Your people?" Slade repeated with a skeptical air. "What are you, the leader of the CIA now?"

Of course the Vigil guys didn't understand just how well Beckett and his people could handle themselves in the criminal underworld. For all they knew, Beckett's family was simply involved in a few dirty local businesses and that was the end of it.

I swallowed thickly and squared my shoulders, bracing for the less-than-positive reactions I anticipated to come. "Beckett, I think you'd better tell them the whole story like you did with me. About who you are and what you're involved with. They're not going to understand until they've got the full picture."

For the first time since the guys had burst in, I caught a flicker of uncertainty in Beckett's gray eyes. He didn't like the idea of exposing his darker dealings with the guys. But he only hesitated for a few seconds before exhaling in a rush.

"You've uncovered a small portion of my family's business dealings. We have a long history in this area and throughout other parts of the country—and quite a lot of our activities are not entirely legal. And along the way, we've naturally made some enemies."

CHAPTER 7

Madelyn

"I don't think my family has ever done business in this town," Beckett mused as he drove toward the hospital in Logan's and my hometown. "I've never even been here before."

"Then bringing you was a useful decision," Logan said with a sarcastic edge.

I kicked the back of his seat. "Whoever has it in for Beckett *and* my family targeted my mom here. Beckett knows who his people have clashed with. He'll be able to recognize signs that could point to the culprit that we wouldn't notice." Then I glanced at Beckett. "We'll be at the hospital in a minute. If you want to drive around while we're inside, you can go and see if anything in this area gives you some ideas."

"You're just going to let him leave us high and dry without a ride?" Logan muttered.

I kicked his seat again. "Can you stop being an asshole for two seconds so we can make some progress here? He's trying to help us. It's his car."

Beckett held up one hand in a pacifying gesture. "I'll wait nearby just in case you two need to make a quick exit. I'd like to get the data sent off to my friend as quickly as possible anyway."

Logan scowled. "Your criminal friend who knows so much more than a doctor would."

"Doctors already looked over Maddie's dad's symptoms and test results, and they couldn't put the pieces together," Beckett said mildly. "My friend has a lot of experience with toxins and the ways they can affect the body, especially those that can be used to create the appearance of a natural illness. If there's any progress we can make from having a better idea what killed him, she's the one who'll get us there."

"Assuming we can get his records without a hitch," Logan grumbled.

Only with Beckett would my stepbrother downplay his own computer prowess for the sake of taking a dig at the other guy. I rolled my eyes at him even though he couldn't see me where I sat behind him. "I'm surprised you hadn't already grabbed his file when you hacked into the hospital system before."

"I looked at it," Logan admitted, "but it was obvious none of us in the Vigil could have made any sense of the data. We don't have any medical training. And at the time I didn't have the skills to rip the files right out of the network without setting off red flags in the system."

"Well, this should be easy enough, grabbing them right from the source." I rubbed my hands together, hoping my confidence wasn't misguided. My heart was already beating a little faster at the thought of the deception I was going to be a part of.

Beckett drove past the hospital parking lot and pulled over to the curb a couple of blocks away. He wasn't coming in with us because we didn't want any of the security cameras catching us together. He'd picked us up away from campus too, in case we were being monitored there.

We didn't want our common enemy realizing that their gambit to frame Beckett had failed and we were now combining our efforts.

He glanced back at me as he turned off the engine, and I gave him a nod I intended to be reassuring. I still wasn't sure how to relate to him after the secrets he'd revealed. Keeping my mind on the mystery of Dad's murder was easier than figuring out what would become of the relationship we'd been building.

I picked up the manila folder I'd brought as part of my cover story and got out of the car. Logan hopped out to join me, and we hurried back toward the hospital.

"I guess we'll see if this friend of his is half as good as he claims," Logan said under his breath.

I elbowed him. "You don't have to be such an ass to him. He didn't have to help us at all, especially after how you went after him. His connections *are* better than what we had access to on our own."

"If he's telling the truth about them," Logan said, and frowned. "And don't think I don't realize why he's really helping us."

"What's that supposed to mean?"

"He's still after you."

I shook my head. "You can't be pissed off at him for supposedly using me for his own ends *and* for really wanting to date me. It's either one or the other. And you shouldn't really be pissed off at him about the whole dating thing anyway. Last time I checked, that wasn't a crime."

My stepbrother settled for an inarticulate growl in response to that point, which was fine, because we'd reached the side entrance to the hospital.

As I reached for the door, Logan caught my hand. He pulled me to a halt and forced me to meet his eyes. "Be careful, okay?"

"All I'm doing is chatting up an old friend of my father's," I reminded him. "You're the one doing the risky part. *You* be careful. Don't bother with anything other than getting the record and getting out of there."

"Yes, ma'am," he said in a lightly teasing voice, and bent down to give me a quick but sweet peck on the lips. We couldn't afford to indulge in more than that.

This entrance was the closest to the research area of the hospital. We tramped up the stairs to the second floor, and then I went on ahead. Logan would be keeping watch to see when I'd cleared the way for him.

I walked along the row of offices, sharply aware of the door to the one that had used to be my dad's as I passed it. The name on the plaque was different now, of course, but I'd visited him here enough times as a kid to remember.

Rebecca's office was just a couple of doors down. She'd worked with Dad when he'd been alive and taken a few minutes out of her day to talk to me the last time I was here. I was counting on her being willing to pitch in on my behalf again. That way we'd know one office was definitely empty so Logan could get into the computer network from there—and I'd keep her busy until I was sure he'd retrieved the file we needed.

The knowledge of the deception left me queasy, but I ignored the sensation as I knocked on Rebecca's door. She opened it a moment later, and a smile spread across her face as she looked at me over her glasses. "Madelyn! It's lovely to see you again. Was there something I could help you with?"

She was so genuinely pleased that the smile I'd thought I'd need to force came naturally. "I'm in town to visit my mom, and I was really hoping you'd have some free time as well. I'd love to pick your brain about a research project I've been working on in school. I'm sorry I didn't call ahead—I wasn't sure how to contact you. I don't suppose you have time today? Maybe we could chat on your lunch break?"

I'd purposefully shown up around noon to make that offer as easy to accept as possible. Rebecca paused for a second to consider and then nodded with another bright smile. "I think it should only take me another minute or two to wrap up what I was in the middle of, and then I was just about ready for a break anyway. If you don't mind the cafeteria food, we can talk down there."

I sighed in totally unfeigned relief. "That would be perfect. Thank you so much."

In no time at all, we were walking over to the elevator to travel down to the cafeteria. "Tell me about this project," Rebecca said as the car whirred downward.

I forced myself to focus on the project I really was working on for school, one her expertise could be of some use for, and not what Logan might be encountering upstairs while I kept her distracted. Or my guilt over causing that distraction.

"I'm looking at inherited diseases and how they can interact with contagious illnesses to exacerbate existing conditions," I said. "Chronic health conditions are one of your main areas of research, right? I was hoping I could bounce some ideas off you about which interactions would give me the most material to investigate—where there's the most data and that sort of thing."

Rebecca's eyes lit up with scholarly interest. She hummed to herself as we stepped off the elevator and headed into the cafeteria, where a rich savory smell told me that pasta with marinara sauce was the day's special. "I can definitely point you in some good directions. That's a fascinating subject! Complex, but I'm sure you're up to the task. You're your father's daughter, all right."

She flashed a smile at me, and I smiled back while tamping down another flare of guilt.

"I try," I said, grabbing a premade salad from a display to keep up appearances even though I wasn't really hungry. "I figured getting your advice would help me hone my research."

I didn't want to talk about Dad. Ideally I'd like to avoid having him come up again in the entire conversation. If anyone listened in on our chat, they shouldn't get the slightest impression that this was anything other than an academic endeavor. No investigating happening here.

Please, let Logan find what he was looking for without getting caught.

Rebecca got the pasta, and we sat down at a table in a quiet corner to dig in. In between bites, she mentioned a few different conditions and the illnesses they often coincided with, and I tapped many hasty notes into my phone.

Getting her thoughts really was giving me a lot of ideas about the direction I'd want to take. I just wished I wasn't pulling one over on her at the same time. Every bite of salad stuck in my throat.

If Logan *did* get caught, she'd realize I'd been manipulating her. The thought of how she'd look at me then, the way her smile would crumple, sent a jab through my chest. I wrenched my mind back to the comment she was in the middle of making, plastering a renewed smile of my own onto my face.

I was almost finished with my salad and Rebecca was halfway through her pasta when a text alert popped up on my phone. It was Logan, simply saying, "See you soon!" An innocuous message designed to let me know he'd finished the job in a way that no one else would recognize meant more.

My shoulders relaxed, a little of the tension in my gut unwinding. I dismissed the text and gulped down the rest of my salad, not wanting to take up too much more of Rebecca's time after she'd already given so much.

"Thank you," I said when she finished her current line of thought. "This has been so helpful. I'm definitely going to incorporate some of your suggestions into the project. I'm excited to get started on it now."

Rebecca beamed at me. "I'd love to see the finished report when you have it all written up."

We said our goodbyes, and I headed out, trying not to feel as if I had a mark of shame branded on my back. No one had any idea that I'd come here with nefarious intentions. And they weren't really nefarious when it was all in the name of finding Dad's killer, right?

As I hustled through the halls to the side entrance and out into the early afternoon sunlight, my stomach knotted with the thought of another person I hadn't really done right by—someone who deserved honesty from me way more than even Dad's former colleague did. Looking around at the streets I'd walked and driven along with my best friend beside me, I couldn't shake the sense of uneasy resolve that gripped my heart.

Logan was already in the car when I got there, back in the front passenger seat. He rolled the window down a little as I came around beside it. Beckett peered at me from behind the wheel, examining my expression.

"It all went smoothly?" I asked Logan.

"Simple as anything," he said, sounding a little more at ease than he had when we'd arrived. "I've saved the file to a couple of different backup servers and also passed it on to Beckett for his 'friend' to look over."

Despite the slight edge he gave to the word "friend," the two guys didn't appear to be in imminent danger of murdering each other. My hand dropped to my phone in my pocket. "Good.

There's one more thing I want to take care of quickly before we leave. Give me a few minutes."

At their nods, I ambled a little farther down the street. I didn't want to have this conversation in the car with them listening in, and I knew by the time we got back to campus, I'd end up wrapped up in the mystery again. I couldn't give Summer the explanation I'd promised her just yet, but I had to at least make sure she knew how careful she had to be.

To my relief, she picked up on the second ring, though her voice was rough. "Maddie. I was wondering how long you'd leave me hanging this time."

I winced. "Hey. I'm so sorry. There's just been so much going on—"

"I know, I know. But what kind of stuff? What the hell is going on with you, Madds? This isn't like you at all. You've got to fill me in."

I swallowed hard. "I want to. I swear it. And I'm going to when *I* know the whole explanation, okay? I'm still working on that."

My bestie let out a huff. "Is Logan messing with your head again? You can't cover for him, you know."

"It's nothing like that," I insisted. "I just—I've seen some things that've made me worried. I want you to be careful, all right?"

"Careful? What are you talking about, Mads?"

"Like—don't go out with anyone you don't know, and try not to be on your own when you do go out. Keep an eye on your surroundings, and get out of any situation that feels at all off."

I could practically hear Summer's eyebrows arching. "Okay, you're kind of freaking me out now. What have you seen? You're not on drugs or something, are you?"

I sputtered a laugh. "No. No drugs. I can't really get into it. I just—" I scrambled for a reason that would make sense. "I've been a little paranoid after my mom's accident. It was just a freak thing, and I feel like it could happen to anyone, you know? I'll just feel better if I know you're being careful."

"Sure, Maddie. I don't want to end up in a car accident or anything like that either. You know I'm not exactly a wild child anyway."

No, but Summer wasn't a wallflower either. She enjoyed being bold and assertive. Hopefully my warning would sink in enough to make sure she recognized it if there was a moment when running away was the better option.

"I know, I know. It just makes me feel better to talk to you about it. And I should be able to fill you in on the rest soon. You take care of yourself."

"Maddie—" Summer started, and my throat constricted. I didn't know what else to say to her.

"I've got to go. Talk soon!"

I hung up, feeling twice as shitty as before. Had I done enough to protect her? How could I possibly know that?

All I could do was hope to hell that my warning hadn't even been necessary.

CHAPTER 8

Dexter

The hotel on the outskirts of town didn't look like much, the dingy, white-washed bricks in need of a fresh paint job and a lone employee in the small lobby who gave me a bored look. She said nothing as I strode down the hall as if I belonged here, following the directions Beckett had given me.

Our theoretical ally had said this was a neutral location, and Logan hadn't dug up any sign of a personal connection to the place. We'd arrived separately and discreetly to ensure it wouldn't be obvious we were meeting. All the subterfuge had me feeling like I'd stepped into a spy flick, which was both unnerving and a little exhilarating, if I was being honest. None of our work as the Vigil had ever gotten quite this complex.

My role was to fill Beckett in on the pieces of the puzzle we'd put together so far. It was easier not to be noticed going alone, and we'd agreed that I had the clearest grasp of all the moving parts in the conspiracy we'd gradually been uncovering. Besides, if Logan had come, he'd probably have been throwing Beckett against another wall within a few minutes. I wasn't sure Slade was feeling that much friendlier toward the guy.

I couldn't say I was totally on Beckett's side, but I could keep a clear head. I'd ask my questions, make my observations, and come to a conclusion about how he'd factor into our lives based on evidence rather than emotion. It was evidence that mattered more than anything right now, after all.

A plain sign saying MEETING ROOM 1 labeled the door I was looking for at the end of the hall. I pushed inside without hesitation and found Beckett already sitting at the eight-seater table inside.

He looked out of place amid the worn furnishings and the air that smelled like stale coffee someone must have spilled on the floor weeks ago. I'd always noticed he took care with his appearance, but maybe because today he was here in a business capacity, he'd donned a full suit, perfectly fitted, and combed his hair neatly back. He stood smoothly with an air of total professionalism.

"Dexter," he said in greeting, and started to extend his arm. But before I could indicate that I wasn't much for handshakes, he caught himself and switched to simply lifting his hand in an informal wave.

So, he'd noticed that I wasn't much for physical contact, just from our brief previous interactions. He was a sharp guy—I'd give him that.

I dipped my head in return and took a seat across from him. "I've brought everything useful from our files. But first I have some questions."

Beckett offered an easy smile as he sank back into his chair. "Straight to the point. I appreciate that. Just a second—a quick precaution." He tapped on the screen of his phone, which was sitting on the table, and it started playing a white noise track. To muffle our voices if anyone tried to record us, I realized. Probably unnecessary, but a simple protective measure.

Or maybe he was wary that *I* might be recording him for the Vigil's purposes.

If he distrusted me, he didn't show it. Beckett leaned back in his chair and spoke just loud enough for me to hear him over the hiss of static. "Ask away."

I rested my hands against the edge of the table, gathering my thoughts. I knew what I wanted to ask, but really all those questions were beating around the bush, trying to get at the one thing I couldn't ask directly.

The Vigil had already ended up veering down such a dark path—and I'd been the one who'd set us on that course. I couldn't let Beckett and his criminal dealings drag us even farther down. If I got the chance to save us from ending up in a worse place, I had to take it.

My friends deserved better.

The impression of calm authority that Beckett maintained did relax me a little. Whatever he was involved in, he clearly wasn't erratic or unhinged about it. But that didn't mean it wasn't dangerous.

"You told us a little about your family's activities," I said. "I'd like to know exactly what sorts of business you're involved in. As many as you're willing to say."

"Sure." Beckett folded his arms loosely over his chest. "I think I mentioned that one of our main focuses is real estate flipping and property management. That's all legitimate. We also have a stake in several casinos and our fingers in the stock market."

I lifted my eyebrows slightly. "And your not-so-legitimate businesses?"

"Those we maintain at least a degree of separation from, if not more. Any gangs or other organizations operating in our territory kick a portion of their earnings back to us. We don't exert much control over what they do, but if we find out they're involved in any areas we disagree with, like human trafficking and specific drugs, we intervene."

"And you don't participate in any illegal activities directly?" I said, not bothering to hide my skepticism.

Beckett chuckled. "I shouldn't make it sound like that. We always have front men, but we take a direct interest in some revenue streams from gambling, stolen and counterfeit goods, and extortion. Higher level targets, of course. People who can afford to lose."

I supposed those people had more to give up in profits anyway. None of this sounded particularly horrifying, if I could believe him. It *was* pretty hard to imagine the man across from me sending people off on murder sprees or anything like that.

"You have some connection to that trucking company," I prodded.

"Yes. They're one of the businesses within our domain, answering to us, paying our tithe, and occasionally providing services."

"Are they involved in the criminal side of things?"

"Some of their clients have them ship illegal goods," Beckett admitted. "We've occasionally gotten rare alcohols that need to be smuggled in for the club through their connections, for example."

I pulled out the document with the trucking company logo on it and slid it across the table to him. "We picked up this report—I'm guessing now that it was planted as part of the effort to frame you. Most of the data is in a code I couldn't crack. Do you have the key to it?"

Beckett took a moment to study the papers and then tapped on his phone again, writing out a text. "I can get it. What's your number?"

I blinked, startled, and then rattled it off. In less than a minute, my phone pinged with an incoming text. The image that came with it was a page from the Bible, of all things, with one of the line numbers circled.

Instantly, my puzzle-honed brain latched on and started unraveling the code from there. I held out my hand, and Beckett passed the document back to me.

The previously nonsensical strings of letters formed words in my head as I scanned the paper now. It was simply a list of dates, all of them from a few weeks ago, and locations that shipments had been dropped off at. Nothing unsettling there. They didn't even mark which deliveries might have been of stolen or otherwise illegal goods and which were legit.

"Thank you," I said after I'd finished my inspection. My nerves had settled some more, but there was one final gnawing question at the back of my mind. I forced myself to hold Beckett's gaze for a beat longer than I generally found comfortable before letting my attention shift to his forehead and then his cheek, where I could still judge his reaction. "If we find the person responsible for murdering Evan Silver, what are you going to do about it?"

"*When* we find him," Beckett said without hesitation, "I'll take care of it."

"Meaning?"

"Meaning you don't even need to worry about what I mean. I'll make sure they're never in a position to harm anyone else again. I'm not going to drag you, your friends, or Madelyn into that mess. You won't have to be involved, and you won't face any potential consequences. I'm the one best equipped to deal with the situation, and I know it isn't the kind of thing you'd want to be mixed up in."

He spoke coolly and firmly, and I found I didn't doubt his

honesty for an instant. It mattered to him, seeing this brand of justice done… not so different from the kind we dealt out as the Vigil. And he wanted to protect us and Madelyn from it.

How could I see him as a threat after that?

I leaned forward, my doubts satisfied, and took my laptop out of my shoulder bag. "I want to make sure it really is a 'when' and not an 'if,' so I've brought all the information we've gathered. It hasn't gotten us far enough, but maybe combined with your resources, we'll get some real answers."

I talked him through the full timeline, starting with Logan's realization that there was something questionable about Madelyn's father's death three years ago and our early investigations, then getting into the theft of Madelyn's car and the new directions that event had pointed us in. As I spoke, I brought up photos I'd taken and video footage from our surveillance cameras on the computer screen. I mentioned the bar where we'd found the trinket box, the old warehouse where we'd been attacked by security guards, and the seafood market that seemed connected to it.

Beckett took it all in silently other than occasional hums of acknowledgment. He studied the images I brought up on the screen with total focus, his mouth gradually curving into a frown. Now and then, he typed notes into his phone. As I got into the finer details, he started asking questions to clarify.

"What's this Baldwin file that comes up a few places?"

"We don't know," I admitted. "It seems to have been meaningful to Mr. Silver, but we haven't been able to locate it or to figure out who the name refers to."

"And this flyer from the seafood market is relevant because…?"

I could starkly remember the horror that'd gripped Madelyn's face when she'd seen it. "Madelyn says her father was babbling while he was sick—he sounded delusional. He said something about how a broken catfish had 'done this'—as in made him sick.

Madelyn thought he was referring to an actual fish during a flood that'd happened a little while before, but when she saw the market's logo, she realized it was probably that instead."

Beckett's gaze darkened. "He'd made it that far through the chain of connections, then."

"Presumably. We don't know what he found out there or what the shipments passing through the market might involve." I watched him as he peered at the screen for a little longer and then added to his notes. His whole expression was shadowed now with a sense of gloom I couldn't remember seeing from him before. "Can you make anything of this that I haven't mentioned? Do you know who might have framed you?"

Beckett sucked in an audible breath. "I have some possibilities I need to look into, but nothing definite. I don't want to put ideas in your head until I've had time to confirm them. Thank you for going over all of this with me. I can tell you've been very thorough." He paused and turned his penetrating gaze on me. "Is Madelyn going to continue staying in your apartment for the time being?"

My hackles immediately came up. "She's a lot safer with us than in her dorm building—as *you* proved just a couple of days ago. We're not doing it to keep her away from you."

He held up his hands in a pacifying gesture. "Don't get me wrong! I'm not complaining about it. I *want* her to stay with you—I'm concerned about her safety too. And the three of you have shown that you take that very seriously." A bit of a smile came back, curling his mouth at a wry angle.

"We do," I confirmed, eyeing him for any sign that he was only faking his acceptance.

"And protecting her matters a lot more than who's spending the most time with her. Not that she's all that enthusiastic about one-on-one time with me at the moment anyway." Beckett shook his head ruefully. "I have a few trusted employees patrolling the campus surreptitiously when she'll be there for classes, but I can't cover everywhere she could possibly go. I'm glad she has the three of you watching over her as well."

I couldn't detect the slightest hint of a lie in his tone or his words. My stance relaxed. I didn't know if Madelyn would ever fully trust him or how I felt about him becoming part of our joint relationship again, but any doubts I'd had about how much he cared about her had vanished.

He understood how important she was. And if he was going to put his criminal affiliations to use defending her, then I wasn't going to argue with that.

"We appreciate any steps you're taking to keep her safe too," I allowed, though I wasn't sure that "we" really included Logan. It was hard to say he appreciated anything about Beckett right now, even if I was starting to believe he probably should.

"She doesn't deserve to be stuck in this mess," Beckett said, standing up. "I'm going to do everything I can to get her out of it as quickly as possible. I'll be in touch as soon as I have any definite answers."

His face had gone tight again. He gave me a tip of his head and then marched out of the room as if in a hurry to start up his own investigations right now. Not quite the same coolly collected professional he'd been when I'd first come into the room.

Dread wound around my gut. What could this long-time criminal have noticed in the evidence I'd shared that would have made even *him* visibly worried?

CHAPTER 9

Madelyn

The smell of herbal incense drifted through the new age shop. I eased past shelves packed with crystals, essential oils, and other objects I'd never have come browsing through for myself. This wasn't my typical scene, but the place had seemed like my best bet in the city for finding what I was searching for.

"Hi there," the cashier called brightly from behind the counter. "Can I help you with anything?"

I paused, scanning the room, which was so packed with its narrow wooden shelves that it was hard to make out anything that wasn't directly in front of me. "I'm guessing you carry tarot cards—where would I find those?"

"We have a wide selection of decks on the back wall. Let me show you."

She led me over to the far corner of the shop. There had to be at least a couple dozen decks on display, but as I scanned the boxes, I didn't spot the one I wanted.

"There's a specific deck I was hoping to pick up," I said. "I don't see it here. Do you ever order things in specially?"

"Sure, as long as we can get it through one of our suppliers. What's the name of the deck?"

I grimaced. "I'm actually not sure. But I've seen the image on the box—the same as on the back of the cards. If I could look through an online catalog or something, I might be able to identify it."

The cashier gave me a kindly smile. "I'm pretty familiar with the options out there. If you describe it to me, I could probably figure it out without too much trouble."

As I followed her over to the counter, I dug through my memories of seeing Logan working with the deck. "The box was kind of a silky black. The top had a silhouette of a woman with her hands raised and her hair flowing out on either side—just line art, silver and not very detailed. The same image was on the backs of the cards but not shiny there, more of a pale gray."

"Oh!" The delight in the cashier's voice gave me a jolt of hope. "That's a more obscure deck, but I've always liked that one. I'm sure our main supplier carries it. Let me just see how long it'd take to get them in. And I'll let you take a look to make sure it's the right one."

"Thank you," I said with a rush of relief.

The woman tapped away at her computer and then swiveled it so I could check the image on the screen. A smile stretched across my face with a lifting of my spirits. "Yes, that's exactly it. I can get them?"

"Definitely. It should only take a few days before they arrive. You can leave your phone number, and we'll send you a text when they're in."

"Perfect. Thank you so much."

The cashier beamed at me. "It was my pleasure. Thank you for stopping by!"

I walked out of the store with the sense of a small weight lifted from my shoulders. It wasn't a lot, but at least I'd made progress on one of the many problems that'd been nagging at me lately.

My victory gave me a boost of confidence. I had other problems to tackle—and I might as well get on with doing that now. It was only a phone call, but my stomach knotted up every time I thought about it.

I was going to have to lie to my mom again so that I didn't have to tell her the real reason I was asking questions about her and dad's old life together.

I dropped into the driver's seat of my car and leaned back, willing myself to relax. Then I pulled out my phone and dialed Mom's number.

"Hey, hun," she answered in a breezy tone that set me even more at ease. I couldn't hear any hint of lingering pain still coloring her voice. She really had set the car accident behind her. "Is everything all right?"

I let myself give a soft laugh. "That's what I was going to ask you. I just wanted to check in and see how you're doing." Lie number one.

"Oh, you shouldn't be worrying about me. I'm doing great. You've got enough on your plate with school and the rest."

She had no idea how large "the rest" actually was. I swallowed thickly. "It's easier to concentrate when I know for sure you're recovering well. Anyway, this has been a bit of a slow week for school." Lie number two. I didn't want to keep counting.

"Have you been working on anything particularly interesting these days?" Mom asked with a rustle that told me she was moving around the room as we talked. Maybe doing chores, maybe assembling pieces for one of her scrapbook projects.

"I have a new project on interactions between chronic diseases and contagious ones," I said, remembering my conversation with Rebecca. "It's bringing up a lot of information I didn't know before. And genetics is always fascinating—how much gets decided before we're even born."

"I find it so hard to wrap my head around any of that. I'm glad you have more of a mind for science."

"Yeah." Not that my mind had been all that focused on it lately. I thought of the lab reports I'd dashed off and the lectures I'd only half listened to and winced. *Mom* would be the worried one if she knew how distracted I'd gotten.

I jerked my mind back to the subject I'd really wanted to talk about. "Have you been keeping busy while you're healing? Lots of friends dropping by to check in on you?"

"Oh, yes, I've had a few visits and offers to help. One of the benefits of small-town life." She chuckled. "Not that there's anything wrong with living in a bigger city, but I do like that close-knit feeling."

I strained my mind to dredge up the names of family friends we'd seen fairly regularly when I was a kid. We had no reason to believe that whoever had targeted my dad had known him personally, but we didn't know it *hadn't* been someone close to the family either. They'd figured out what he was up to somehow. If any of Mom and Dad's friends had faded away shortly after his death, that would be worth looking into.

"Do you still see the Brylers these days?" I asked. "Joanne and… I don't remember her husband's name?"

"Oh, dear, I haven't thought about them in quite a while. They moved out to Connecticut a few years ago. Or maybe it was

Colorado." Mom paused. "Somewhere starting with a C. I doubt they even heard about the accident. But Maureen and Joe stopped by with a casserole, if you remember them. Their daughter's just finishing her first year of high school."

I vaguely recalled a plump woman with curly red hair and a little girl I'd had to barricade from my room for fear she'd tear into my toys. I guessed that wasn't something anyone needed to worry about these days.

"That's great." I groped for another name. "There was that couple down the street you and Dad used to get together with now and then too, wasn't there? Stacy and Kyle?"

"Yes, of course. I'm impressed that you remember. They were always fun to spend time with."

My ears perked. "Were? You don't see them anymore?"

"No, not in years."

"Was there any particular reason? Did you have a fight or something?"

I could hear the frown in Mom's voice. "Well, no. I can't even think of what it was. Sometimes people just drift apart, you know."

It felt too pointed to specifically ask if it'd happened right after Dad's death. "I can't remember the last time we saw them…" I said, attempting to prompt her.

"Neither can I. Oh, but I remember they came by with a cupcake for you when you graduated from elementary school. That was so sweet of them."

My interest deflated. I'd graduated elementary school a couple of years after Dad's passing. It didn't sound like that couple had pulled back specifically around that time. But if they'd already started to fade, it could be related, I supposed.

Mom's voice took on a puzzled tone. "Why are you so curious about them? Is there something else on your mind?"

I clenched my jaw for a second before pushing out another lie. "No, I guess I just got caught up in thinking about that close-knit neighborhood we had. Everyone is a lot more distant here in the city."

That line of questioning had pretty much been a dead end. Thankfully Mom gave me an out all on her own. "I hope you're not getting lonely out there. You know you can call me whenever you like, but make sure you're going out to the college social events and that sort of thing too. It can take some time adapting to a transition. I should let you go so you can get on with that."

My mouth twisted into a bittersweet smile. "I'll do that. It was good talking with you, Mom."

After I'd hung up, I sent a quick text to Beckett. That one couple probably had nothing to do with Dad's death, but they'd slipped out of Mom's life soon enough afterward that it couldn't hurt to alert him. I had to feel like I'd accomplished *something*.

I want to hear all the details straight from your mouth, he wrote back. *I have some news too, and it's better not to have much of this written down anyway. Meet me at the park where we grabbed ice cream the other day?*

I hesitated, but the truth was, I didn't feel at all worried about my safety around Beckett, no matter what shady business activities he was involved in. He might be a criminal, but I knew he didn't want to hurt me.

I just wasn't sure how far I could trust him outside of pursuing this investigation together.

When I reached the park, I spotted Beckett waiting in the shade of a tree a short distance down the path that led to the ice cream shop. He tipped his head to me, the wind ruffling the leaves and his sandy blond hair, and a pang shot through my chest.

Just a week ago, I'd have stepped right into his arms and enjoyed a kiss. Would we be able to get back to that easy intimacy?

Would I *want* to?

To his credit, Beckett didn't push for anything more than a conversation. He walked a little ahead of me on the path and turned off it into a secluded clearing where I found a bench surrounded by enough trees that it wouldn't be visible to anyone passing by on the path. He sat down at one end, leaving plenty of room between us when I sank down at the other side.

"You think these family friends could have been involved?" he asked, pulling out his phone.

I shook my head. "It's a long shot. I just want to cover every possibility. They were pretty good friends with my parents, and they drifted out of my mom's life not too long after he died. Probably just normal life changes, but there's a tiny chance guilt played a part."

"Names?"

"Stacy and Kyle. I don't remember the last name, but they lived on the same street as my parents' house for several years—they may still be there. Hopefully that's enough for you to trace them?"

"Absolutely." He shot me a mild but warm smile and tapped the information into his phone. When he looked at me again, the intensity in his gaze brought to mind his passionate touch when we'd run back to his car out of the wind the last time we were here. A flush crept over my skin despite my best efforts.

"You said you have some news on your end too?" I asked quickly as a diversion—and because I did want to know.

Beckett's mouth twisted, so I knew it wasn't anything all that good. "I heard back from my poison-expert friend. Anthea's pored over your dad's medical records, and she's found a few hints that suggest foul play. But there's nothing overt enough for her to even be sure of exactly what toxin was used. Whoever was responsible, they covered their tracks very thoroughly."

My heart sank. "So there's no evidence we could use to prove the case in those reports, then."

"Not with just the hospital records. They may help us connect the dots to other proof we turn up. And it tells us we're dealing with someone who's both skilled and meticulous."

"Wonderful," I grumbled. "Anything else from the other things you were looking into?"

Beckett hesitated, his gaze lingering on my face. "I've made a little progress, but I'm still sorting through all the information."

"Is there any way I could help with that?"

"Maybe," he admitted. "But, Maddie, I don't want to put you in any more danger than you already are."

Hearing him use my nickname with all the familiarity of our past relationship tugged at my heartstrings, but the rest of what he said sent a prickle of irritation through my nerves.

"It's my dad we're investigating. I want to be involved as much as I can." I narrowed my eyes at him. "Logan tried very hard to push me out when my car got stolen, and that didn't go his way. I don't recommend you take the same tactic."

One corner of Beckett's mouth quirked upward. "You have always struck me as a woman who goes after what she wants—and generally gets it."

"Well, there you go."

He spread his hands. "It isn't just you, though, is it? The more you're involved, the more chance there is that the people we're working against will realize and strike out not just at you but the people you care about again."

My thoughts slipped back to my conversation with Mom, and my chest tightened. "I don't want that. Isn't there anything I can do from behind the scenes, things that aren't likely to get noticed? The sooner we crack this case, the sooner we'll all *really* be safe."

"You do have a point there." He tipped his head to the side in contemplation and then met my eyes again. "I can think of one thing you can do that shouldn't put any spotlight on you. It's a small help, but it could lead me straight to the person who tried to frame me."

I sat up straighter with a jolt of eagerness. "What? Let's do it."

Beckett let out a soft laugh. "I'll have to get a few things set up first, but we should be able to give it a try tomorrow." His hand twitched as if he'd considered reaching toward me and then thought better of it. "I really do admire how dedicated you are—to this cause and everything else you're doing with your life. And that bravery, being more than ready to jump right into action no matter what we might face. I never lied about how much I liked that side of you either."

A lump rose in my throat. My gaze dropped to my hands as I fumbled for the right response while his praise tingled through my veins.

It was so easy for him to talk like that. Just like he'd made himself seem like the perfect Prince Charming when we'd first met. But there was so much more going on behind that polished front.

But he'd given me what I needed in the ways that mattered most too. I lifted my gaze to meet his again. "I appreciate that you're letting me be an equal part in this situation instead of shunting me off to the side for my supposed protection. It means a lot."

The gleam in his eyes sent off a fresh flare of heat through my body. "I've always seen you as an equal, Maddie. I know you're more than capable of holding your own. If I *can* protect you and the people you're close to from the worst parts of my life, I'm going to do that, but I'll be upfront about it the whole way through. You can count on that."

When he said it that way, I believed him. I restrained a giddy shiver. "You said we can do this thing tomorrow?"

He nodded. "Let me know what time in the morning works best for you working around your classes, and we'll meet up then. I'll pick you up behind the theater downtown—and we'll see if we can catch at least one rat."

CHAPTER 10

Madelyn

The van had looked old from the outside, with smudges of dirt and patches of rust, but the interior proved that was just a disguise. I sat in the back on a bench padded with smooth leather while thin but soft carpeting rested beneath my feet. But the comfortable furnishings didn't stop me from squirming on the bench as the vehicle swayed around a corner with a rumble of the engine.

A moment later, the driver parked. We must have reached the seafood market. He glanced back at Beckett, who was poised on the bench across from me.

Beckett gave him a quick nod. With no further prompting, the guy adjusted the collar of his polo shirt uniform, grabbed a clipboard that was part of *his* disguise, and stepped out of the van.

We watched through the grimy windows as he headed over to a

neighboring building and put on a show of theoretically inspecting the vents protruding from the brick wall. When I turned back to Beckett, he was watching me.

"Are you ready?"

I dragged in a breath. "Yes. Let's get it over with."

He handed me a burner phone and a slip of paper with a single phone number scrawled on it. The phone number that would give me a direct line to the store manager at the Fresh Catch Seafood Market.

"Do everything as we discussed," Beckett said. He'd gone over the plan with me the moment he'd picked me up behind the theater. The market was just opening for the day. The manager was definitely in, but he shouldn't be too busy yet.

There was nothing to worry about. Other than that we were pulling a con on someone who was probably connected to my dad's murderer.

The people involved in the crime would undoubtedly know my face. That severely limited how much I could help with any hands-on investigations. But this maneuver wouldn't be caught on any cameras, and the manager wouldn't know my voice. Beckett had come through with a way I could be a part of our mission to take our enemies down, just as he'd promised.

I tapped in the number and willed myself to breathe slowly and evenly as the line on the other end rang. The words I was supposed to say whirled in my mind. I focused all my attention on the first sentence.

One thing after the other. It was no big deal, really. But the reaction we might provoke mattered a lot, in ways I didn't fully understand but Beckett was clearly equipped to deal with.

My pulse jolted at the click of the answered call. "Carl here, Fresh Catch Seafood."

My mouth moved automatically, the words I'd rehearsed

spilling out. “Your next special delivery has been moved up by three days,” I said, keeping my voice monotonous but firm.

The statement sounded strange coming from my mouth, but the manager inhaled sharply. “No, that can’t be right.”

“We expect the market to be ready,” I went on, as if he hadn’t spoken. As he started to sputter something about usual timelines, I simply hung up.

A tremor ran through my body as I sagged back against the side of the van. Beckett tipped his head to me approvingly. “You were perfect. I’d love to see how he’s freaking out right now.”

“*If* he’s freaking out.” But the guy definitely hadn’t sounded happy. “And now…?”

Beckett was already setting a small metal box on his lap. Two cables connected it to a laptop that was open on the bench beside him. He flicked a switch and scooted even closer to his side of the van, which had been parked just inches away from the back wall of the market. Studying the data that trickled across the laptop’s screen, he adjusted one dial and another before appearing satisfied.

“Now we wait for him to follow the bait.”

“I didn’t know you were a techie too,” I said, raising my eyebrows.

He laughed. “I wouldn’t know how to use this gadget without help. I got it from one of my friends back in Paradise Bend—a county I’ve spend a bunch of time in. *He’s* the real techie, a tech genius really. He’s brilliant at this stuff.” Beckett paused and glanced over at me. “I’d bet in a few years, Logan could get to where Gideon is if he keeps working at it.”

What would Logan have made of that compliment from the guy he’d been so hostile to? The lack of respect must have only gone one way. “You really think so?”

One corner of Beckett’s mouth quirked up into a crooked smile.

"I might not appreciate his attitude toward me, but I can recognize talent when I see it."

He checked the screen again and fiddled with the controls a little more. "This should pick up nearby cell signals, but I don't want the range to be too broad, or we'll catch people all the way over on the street... We just need to cover the market building, and maybe only the back. That's where the manager's office is. I don't think he'd make this call where the regular employees can hear—"

He cut himself off at an emphatic *beep!* from the machine. "Here we go," Beckett said, and tapped a couple of keys on the laptop's keyboard.

As I leaned forward, my heart thumping in anticipation, a voice I recognized as the manager's burst from the speakers with a faint hum of static. "—got a call about the special deliveries. I don't know how they even had my number! Aren't you supposed to deal with this stuff, Sharply?"

The voice that answered sounded much more collected, low and cool. "When did they call? What exactly did they say?"

"It was just a few minutes ago. They said... something about the delivery being moved up. That the market should be prepared for it. I don't remember exactly. I was thrown off by the whole thing."

"It would have been helpful if you'd paid more attention. Did you recognize the voice?"

"Of course not! I've never talked to them before. It was a woman—that's all I know about it. She didn't give a name, obviously." The manager let out a huff.

The other man's voice turned even flatter. "You don't seem to have very much information to go on."

"That's because this isn't my thing, Sharply," the manager snapped. "You're supposed to handle all this shit. You need to talk with them and sort it out. And tell them you're the one they deal with, not me. I've got a business to run here."

"So do we. But I'll look into it. Go back to your spreadsheets and order forms, and you'll hear if anything needs to change on your end."

The other man sounded almost bored by the exchange, but the manager was so flustered I knew it was a big deal. These 'special deliveries' couldn't be legal, right?

The call cut off with a crackle, but Beckett was grinning. His fingers clattered over the keyboard before he clapped his hands together in satisfaction. "I got the number for the outgoing call. We're going to track this bastard down—Sharply, it sounds like his name is."

A fitting name for someone who killed people. But who knew if this was the kingpin or one more step up a long ladder. The people we were up against seemed to deal in all kinds of layers of subterfuge.

It got us closer to answers, though. "Sharply isn't a common name," I pointed out, my spirits lifting a little. "That should make it easier to narrow down who it was."

"Let's hope so. It could be an alias—but even that will be useful with my connections." Beckett pulled out his phone. "I'll pass the information on to my own tech team to see where it takes them. We should be able to follow this thread to whoever's in charge."

He didn't think the Sharply guy was, then. I guessed it wouldn't make much sense for a criminal mastermind to be the contact person for store managers at their front operations.

But the farther we worked our way up the chain of operations, the closer we'd get to the people who were truly responsible for destroying my family—and attempting to destroy Beckett as well.

He must have sent a text to our driver too, because a moment later, the man in the false uniform returned to the driver's seat.

Without a word, he started the engine and pulled out of the alley behind the market.

I rested my hands on the warm leather on either side of me. "Where are we going now? I have the whole morning—are there other ways we can prod information out of these people?"

"I think we've covered all the ground we can for the moment," Beckett said, and hesitated, holding my gaze. "But I was hoping we didn't have to end things for today like this. There's something I'd like to show you."

I tensed automatically, but there was nothing about the suggestion to provoke any concern. Beckett's expression remained mild if hopeful. He'd stayed on the other side of the van the entire time.

I bit my bottom lip. "What would you be showing me?"

"I'd rather it was a surprise. I don't think it'll mean much until you're seeing it. But if you're uncomfortable, I can drop you back off by the theater instead. It's up to you. I realize you might not fully trust me still."

He wasn't pressuring me. He'd been giving me plenty of space all along. And he'd kept his word in everything he'd said he'd do so far, including letting me have a hand in tracking down Dad's killer today.

If I didn't give Beckett the chance to show whether he was worthy of more trust, how would I ever know whether we could rebuild what we'd once had?

I wavered for a second longer and then said, "I trust you enough to come along for the ride. Let's see this thing."

CHAPTER 11

Madelyn

The van pulled to a stop outside a large building that was all gleaming glass and steel. Beckett opened one of the back doors and offered his hand to me to help me step out.

When he shut the door with a thump, the engine thrummed and the driver set off again. I wondered what instructions Beckett had given him.

Through the broad front windows, I could see that the rooms at the front of the building were empty, no furniture or decoration. As Beckett motioned for me to follow him up the front walk, I glanced over at him. "What is this place?"

"Part of my family business. I wanted to show you around."

He fit a key into the double doors and tugged the door open. I hesitated for a second before walking inside.

Light streamed down all through the entrance way from skylights high in the arched ceiling. A set of escalators that weren't yet running led up to the second floor, while a plaza with marble tiles and sleek columns stretched out beyond them, with windowed commercial spaces on both sides. A few already had signs mounted over their entrances.

Beckett strolled through the plaza at a relaxed pace. "I told you we'd bought a new office complex. This is it. We have plenty of legitimate business endeavors, and places like this are a big part of that side of our work. This is only our most recent purchase. Every company that sets up shop inside will be one hundred percent above board."

His pride in the acquisition rang through his voice. Then he stopped and pointed to one of the office spaces that filled one corner at the back of the plaza. The sign over top read, SMITHSON MEDICAL CLINIC.

"I'm still planning on setting up the pro bono clinic we talked about," he said. "That wasn't any kind of gambit—no matter what you think about me or how our relationship ends up, I really do want to give back to the communities we operate in. It shouldn't be all take. We've got a major sponsor on board, so the wheels are in motion."

My heart lifted, taking in the space. That office already had some furnishings set up: a row of padded chairs in the front waiting area and a broad front counter that would serve as a reception desk. I could easily imagine people in need settling into those chairs, filled with relief that they could get their problems looked at by a proper doctor without having to worry about going bankrupt.

"I don't think most criminals worry about how much they're taking," I couldn't help pointing out.

"We aren't most criminals. I'm not out to ruin people's lives. This community has helped support us in ways they don't even realize, and I think we have a responsibility to return the favor when we can."

Those were pretty words, but as I studied his eager expression, I couldn't ignore the twist of my gut. He couldn't present himself as a champion for good, not with the other things I knew about him now.

"If you feel that way, why do you get involved in anything on the criminal side at all?" I had to ask. "Why not go completely straight?"

A shadow crossed Beckett's face. He swiped his hand over his jaw, which had tensed as if he wasn't sure he wanted to answer that question.

Something tensed inside me too. I might have walked away right then if he hadn't started talking.

"I didn't exactly tell you the full story when I made my confession," he admitted. "I mean, everything I did tell you was true, I just didn't get into the full scope..."

I gave him a pointed look. "I think you'd better do that now."

He dipped his head in acknowledgment. "What I'm part of, it's a family legacy going back generations. We aren't a normal criminal organization. We're one of a small number of crime lord families who control essentially all organized illegal activity around the world. The businesses we have a direct stake in are vastly outnumbered by the operations we oversee and monitor all across the globe."

I blinked at him, my voice failing me in the wake of that revelation. "All around the *world*?" I managed. Just who was this guy I'd thought I'd known?

But when Beckett turned his pensive gaze on me, I still saw that guy—assured, thoughtful, calm, and still with that glint of pride in his eyes.

"It's my heritage," he said. "I can admit that it's a challenging one, and not one I'm always happy about, but I feel like I've gotten pretty damn good at what I do. There aren't many CEOs or presidents out there juggling as many responsibilities as I need to on a daily basis."

"But… so much of it *must* be hurting people. If you're involved in that much of the crime around the world—if you've got that much power—why don't you *stop* it instead of keeping it going?"

Beckett's mouth slanted into a crooked smile. "It doesn't work like that, Madelyn. There are a set number of families who divide up the territory between them. If I pulled out or started trying to shut down all the operations in our domain, the others would find someone else to take our place. By participating, I *am* stopping some of the worst aspects of our legacy from continuing. I can moderate a certain amount of the criminal activity in this world to my own standards. If I backed away, who knows who'd fill that gap—what their priorities would be?"

I stared at him. It was impossible to wrap my head around dealing with those kinds of expectations and pressures. But Beckett had been born into it.

Had he ever really had much of a choice?

"It isn't fair," I said, my voice coming out quiet. "Just because you're part of one specific family, you have to take on this burden—"

He shook his head. "It's fine. It's *good.* I'm glad I'm part of it so that I can do what I need to. I've been in a position to prevent violence that would have happened otherwise, to save thousands of lives—I've made sure innocent people were protected when other forces meant to destroy them. I've gone against my own father…"

His words cut off as if his throat had closed up. He swallowed audibly, and I couldn't believe he was faking the flash of anguish that showed on his face before he regained his usual calm.

My own throat tightened. "That must have been hard."

"Yeah." Beckett ran his hand back through his hair. "There are power struggles sometimes, conflicts over turf. Dad jumped into one I didn't agree with, and things got bad, and… I wasn't going to just stand by and let the maniac working for him destroy a bunch of people who'd done nothing wrong, even if they were strangers. That's what I stand for."

There was no denying the conviction in his voice. It wrenched at my heart. I didn't understand what it must have been like growing up the way he had, with the expectations that'd been placed on him his entire life, the principles that'd been drilled into him that were so different from my own. I was judging him from my safe, peaceful, middle-class life, when I'd had no idea criminal organizations on the scale he was talking about even existed.

Would I really rather someone else was in his place? Someone who'd probably have less of a conscience than Beckett had shown he had in spades? I'd known plenty of people who were more selfish and vicious than he was who weren't even criminals.

I hugged myself for a moment, rubbing my arms up and down, and then let my hands fall to my sides. "I know you're not a bad person. I just—it's been a lot to take in."

"I get that." Beckett held my gaze for a moment, his eyes searching mine. Then he held out his hand to me, not looking like he expected me to grasp it but more as a symbolic gesture. "Come with me a little farther? I have one more thing here to show you."

I had no idea what to expect next. I trailed behind him, still absorbing everything he'd just told me, and he led me across the plaza to another office that appeared to be unclaimed. There was no sign up top, anyway.

Someone had been making use of the space, though. Stepping inside after him, I found a small table with two chairs, the table draped with a white tablecloth and set with glasses, plates, and napkins.

Beckett bent down by a bar-sized fridge that was plugged in nearby and got out a few different trays of food: one a charcuterie board with sliced meats and cheeses, another with a rainbow spread of different fruits, and a third with three different types of sushi rolls. He laid them out on the table between the plates and poured sparkling lemonade into the glasses.

The tang of the beverage tickled my nose as I stared at the spread, my mouth watering and my mind whirling. "Is this some kind of picnic?"

He chuckled. "You could put it that way. I was hoping you'd have lunch with me."

He'd gone to an awful lot of preparation to set things up. A pang of affection reverberated through my chest. I cocked my head, unable to keep my curiosity in check. "What would you have done if I hadn't agreed to come with you after the phone call at the market?"

One corner of Beckett's mouth curved upward. "I'd have eaten on my own. Wouldn't want good food to go to waste. It was a gamble worth taking. But I'd rather eat with you, if you'll stay."

He pulled out the chair on his side of the table, and I rested my hands on the back of the one for me. Some distant part of my mind suggested that I should still be cautious, that I shouldn't let myself be convinced, but I couldn't summon even a particle of real fear about the man standing across from me.

He had a difficult life that he'd made the best of—that he was trying to do good things with. I could respect that. And knowing how much pressure rested on his shoulders, how much power he wielded not just in this city but around the world, made it all the more incredible that he was stepping away from those duties even momentarily to have this moment with me.

It was incredible that he *wanted* me. Who knew how many women he'd met in his line of work who were tougher and more experienced and more accepting of his career than I was? But I was the one he'd come back to.

Maybe he wanted me *because* I wasn't like the people he normally associated with. He'd said something like that before, hadn't he?

I slid into the chair, my heart thumping faster. I didn't know exactly what we were doing, but this felt an awful lot like a date. And maybe I was okay with that now.

"Sushi and charcuterie are an interesting combination," I couldn't help teasing as I helped myself to a few pieces of both.

Beckett grinned, looking more at ease now that I'd officially joined him. "I happen to be a big fan of both, and I see no issue with indulging in them together. Also, you mentioned to me on one of our dates that you haven't had fresh sushi in ages and you didn't care for the grocery store stuff much. This was prepared just a couple of hours ago by my family chef, who spent a few years training in Japan among other places."

I blinked at him and quickly raised one of the tuna rolls to my mouth to try it. The raw fish melted like butter as I sank my teeth into it, the rice breaking apart but not crumbling, faintly sweet. I gulped it down, my eyes widening. "Wow, that is good. Family chef, huh? One of the perks of your line of work?"

Beckett shrugged, his expression both amused and pleased. "I'll admit I'm not very handy in the kitchen, and neither is my dad. Having someone like that on staff ensures we stay fed. It's not an indulgence I'm particularly proud of… other than when I can use it to make a pretty girl happy."

I raised my eyebrows at the flirty remark. "And how many pretty girls have you had your chef preparing picnics for?"

Beckett's eyes smoldered. "You're the first. If I have my way, you'll be the only."

A quiver of heat raced over my skin, pooling low in my belly. I had to pop another roll into my mouth to stop myself from drooling—and not only over the food.

"What time is your first afternoon class?" Beckett asked.

I was about to rib him about whether he had even more plans for our time together when a generic ringtone pealed out… from my pocket.

My head jerked down. I stared at my hip for a second, trying to figure out why my phone would be making that unfamiliar sound, and then it clicked.

"It's the burner," I said with a hitch of my heart. "The one I used to call the manager at the seafood market."

Beckett had tensed in his seat. "It'll be someone involved in this mess," he said in an urgent tone. "Answer it on speaker phone and see what they have to say."

I yanked the phone out of my pocket and hit the speaker button as I set the device down on the table between us. "Hello?"

My voice wavered just slightly. I inhaled deep to try to steady myself.

A baritone voice growled from the other end of the line. "I'd like to know who I'm speaking to and what business you had with the Fresh Catch Seafood Market."

Beckett's expression tightened even more with a twitch of his jaw. He made a cycling motion with his fingers, indicating that I should talk—and keep this man talking with me.

I groped for the right thing to say that sounded suitably criminal-ish for someone who'd have been making deals and arranging top-secret deliveries. "I could ask the same thing. Who are *you*?"

"I asked first, and I don't like people who play games. Identify yourself."

I gathered all the false bravado I could. "I don't see why I should have to. And I can do business with whatever stores I want. It has nothing to do with you."

The voice on the end crackled through the speaker, getting even harsher. "It has every fucking thing to do with me, and I think you know that. Cough up some answers, or you're going to regret it as soon as I get my hands on you."

Somehow I had the feeling I'd regret it even more if I did tell him who I was. I folded my arms over my chest, and Beckett waggled his phone at me. He'd typed out a sentence in his notes app for me to say, since he couldn't speak without giving away that he was here.

I read the line and quickly recited it, even though I wasn't totally sure what he thought it would accomplish. "I think we might even expand our association with the market. There's plenty to gain out of grabbing customer credit card information."

The man sputtered with apparent fury. "You can't be serious. Only an imbecile would bother with that kind of petty fraud." He let out a huff. "You're wasting my time. I don't know what you're up to, but I'll figure it out. And then you'd better believe I'll deal with you."

He hung up with a sharp click.

I let out my breath with a shudder, all my nerves jittering, and glanced across the table at Beckett. He was frowning at the phone, his expression gone ominously dark.

"Do you know who that was?" I ventured.

He grimaced. "I think I might." He shoved back his chair and stood up, contemplating our half-finished meal with regret. Then he pulled out his own phone. "I hate to abandon our lunch, but I should check a few things right away—things I can't look into from here."

My stomach knotted, but not because of the meal cut short. I pushed to my feet. "I get it. This is way more important. Are you sure you'll be okay?"

Beckett nodded briskly, typing out a text as we hustled toward the complex's front doors. "I know how to deal with people like this." His gaze slid back to me, and his voice softened. "Before I get going, I'll have the van swing by and drop you off closer to the university."

I was dying to badger him with questions, but I knew Beckett well enough by now to realize that he'd tell me what was going on when he was ready. "All right. If the driver could let me out near the new age shop downtown, that would be perfect."

"I'll tell him that." Just a few steps from the doors, Beckett paused and touched my arm. "I'll be back in touch soon. Stay inside until the van comes around, and then walk straight to it."

"Okay." I wasn't going to argue when he was speaking so somberly.

He nodded to me and hesitated again, leaning toward me just a tad as if he were about to go in for a kiss. Then he squeezed my arm and yanked himself away.

I watched him stride down the front walkway, my spirits sinking. What could he have heard in the call that'd disturbed the most implacable guy I'd ever met so much?

CHAPTER 12

Logan

The damn code *wouldn't* run.

I'd gone through it well over ten times, trying to find the character that made the entire sequence invalid. It had to be a typo somewhere—something small and nearly impossible to find in the dozens of pages of code. My frustration had been progressively rising as I searched for the error, and after my twelfth—thirteenth?—time going through it, I still found nothing.

I knew why I couldn't find it, of course. Each time, I'd make it through a handful of lines of code, fully focusing, and then once I reached the end of the page, I'd realize that my mind had been elsewhere. On Maddie, mostly.

The project was important, and I had to turn it in by the end of the weekend, but nothing could top the danger she was facing. That was all I could think about, and it consumed every corner of my mind. What was a stupid computer science project worth when some murderous psychopath had Maddie in his sights?

What was any of the work I'd put in here at college worth when I couldn't guarantee I could keep her safe? What was the point in getting a degree, in setting myself up for a good job—what was the point in any of this if I lost her?

Finally, I pushed myself off the sofa and stalked around the apartment's living room as if I could outpace my worries. My hand automatically reached for the pistol I'd stuffed in the back of my jeans. The feel of it in my hands—the warmed metal, the solid weight of it—settled my nerves just a fraction. It was something concrete I could put to use if Maddie was threatened.

At least, until I remembered the panicked expression on Maddie's face when she'd seen me pull it out and aim it at Beckett. She hadn't been prepared for that. *I* hadn't expected to ever handle an illegal firearm… but after her mom's accident and the fire in the Vigil office and then finding out Beckett had been lying to our faces, I'd felt worse *not* having a weapon that could match the kind any of those criminals could pull out.

Thank God for our own criminal connections. I'd been able to arrange to get this through Darrel with just a couple of brief visits to his chop shop, and he hadn't even asked any questions. I didn't trust the guy farther than I could throw him, but he was reliable in very specific ways.

And as long as Maddie was okay, I wouldn't *need* to use it anyway. I simply had it just in case.

As I meandered through the living room again, running my fingers over the barrel, Slade strolled out of his bedroom with his backpack. He dropped it onto one of the kitchen stools and gave me an unusually contemplative look that raised my hackles before he turned toward the fridge and grabbed a bottle of water.

He opened it as he swiveled back toward me and chugged a few gulps. As he lowered the bottle, he tipped his head to me. "We'll get this whole thing sorted out, man. It's going to be okay."

A rough laugh burst from my throat. Of course he'd say that.

"Nothing about this is okay," I snapped before I could rein in my temper. "We have no idea what could come at us—or at Maddie—next. So don't pretend you know shit about it."

The second the words had burst from my mouth, shame prickled under my skin. My best friend hadn't deserved my anger. *He* hadn't done anything wrong.

But Slade wasn't easily fazed. Maybe he could tell I hadn't really meant the criticism. "I don't know shit about what's coming," he agreed easily. "But I know us. I know we won't back down until we've figured everything out and destroyed the threat. It's as simple as that."

He slung his backpack over his shoulder and headed out of the apartment. I watched him go, my stomach knotting. I couldn't get my assignments done, I couldn't talk to my friends like an actual friend… I had to get a grip, or I'd become a liability rather than any kind of hero.

I shoved the gun back into my jeans and flopped down on the sofa. I couldn't do anything about the assholes we were up against right now, so I might as well at least get this assignment off my plate. Surely I could locate one little error.

I'd barely had a chance to try when the doorknob clicked over. Maddie eased inside and shot me a warm smile as she closed the door behind her.

Relief flooded me at the sight of her. Her blond hair and sweater-and-jeans combo were unrumpled, her face bright. She'd gone off to do some kind of reconnaissance with Beckett against my muttered objections, but she hadn't come back any worse for it. If anything, she was in a better mood than she'd been in when she left.

Which probably shouldn't have irritated me as much as it did.

"Did you have a good time with the mob boss?" I couldn't help asking, even as I winced inwardly at the snark in my tone.

Maddie simply rolled her eyes at me, which was about what I deserved. "The point wasn't to have a good time. I think we made some progress. He acted like he had a lead, but he didn't want to tell me about it until he'd confirmed his suspicions." She paused, her gaze going momentarily distant with a crease in her brow, and then smiled again. "And I got to do an errand I've been looking forward to. I have something for you."

I blinked at her, thrown off course enough that I forgot my annoyance over Beckett. "For me? You didn't need to get me anything." A small pang resonated through my chest at the thought of her going out of her way to do something for me when she had so much else weighing on her.

"I know I didn't *need* to. I wanted to." She reached into her purse and pulled out a purple plastic bag. "I realize it can't make up for what you lost, not completely, but at least you can use them the same way."

She held out the bag to me. I took it and dipped my hand inside, registering the shape and size of the object with a tingle of recognition before I pulled it out. Then I just stared.

It was a deck of cards—of tarot cards. And not just any deck, but the exact same design I'd gazed at a thousand times on the back of Mom's old deck. The one that'd burned up in the library office fire.

My throat constricted. Maddie had been right, of course. They couldn't totally replace that old, familiar deck. They didn't have the worn corners where Mom's fingers and then mine had moved over them or the shiny star sticker on the bottom of the box that she'd let me stick there when I'd been a little kid. But they brought back so many of the same memories. It was almost as good.

The pang in my heart expanded into an ache that spread from

the base of my throat to my gut. The sensation was bittersweet. There was grief at the thought of all the time I hadn't gotten with my mom and the connection to her I'd lost with the original deck, but also a swell of gratitude and affection toward the girl who'd gone out of her way to try to mend that loss the only way she could think of.

And it'd been a pretty great attempt. No one could have done better. Maddie had wanted to do this for me—had considered my pain that thoroughly despite everything she was dealing with.

I got to my feet and wrapped my arms around her, tugging her into the tightest of hugs. The floral scent of her shampoo filled my nose as I bowed my head next to hers. "Thank you. So much. You have no idea how much this means to me."

Maddie squeezed me back. "I can imagine. I just—I don't want to let them win. I don't want them to take anything more from us."

How the hell had I ever let myself push this amazing woman away? But as I held her close, an image rose up in the back of my mind of her leaning into *Beckett's* embrace instead—welcoming his touch, offering him affection. My body tensed up before I realized what was happening.

I pulled back, peering into her eyes. My voice came out taut. "How can someone who's as good a person as you be okay with what Beckett's admitted to? How can you even stand to be around him?"

A shadow crossed Maddie's face. She took a step away from me, the corners of her mouth pulling down. "Are you serious right now?"

I grimaced. "What? It's true. He's a fucking career criminal, and you—"

"Stop it!" Maddie interrupted, jabbing her finger at me. "Just stop it. All I wanted was to do something nice for you, and you had to turn that into another excuse to rant about Beckett? Do you hear yourself?"

I flinched. I'd just told myself I'd never push her away again, and then I'd turned around and done exactly that, if inadvertently.

"I just don't get it," I said stubbornly.

Maddie let out a huff, narrowing her eyes at me. "I'm still with you even though I've watched you break into buildings, hack into private databases to steal information—hell, you were even responsible for a murder that you covered up rather than going to the police about it! You know you did all those things—and who knows how much else that I don't have a clue about—and you're still a worthwhile human being. Why can't you accept that Beckett could be too?"

I gaped at her for a second, unspoken words clogging my throat. The ones that spilled out of me weren't anything I'd have wanted to say if I hadn't felt as if she'd socked them right out of me.

"I *don't* think I'm a worthy human being."

The second the admission was out, I longed to take it back. Maddie froze, staring at me.

"What do you mean?" she asked in a quiet voice.

A sense of hopelessness swept over me. It was out now. I couldn't pretend I hadn't said it.

I sank down onto the sofa and rubbed my hand over my face. My gaze focused vaguely on the wall across from me.

"I hardly think I deserve to be *alive*," I said hoarsely. "I got this second chance thanks to the liver transplant—because someone else, some other kid, died instead of me. I sure as hell didn't earn that. And my illness, even after the transplant, totally messed up my family. My parents were arguing a lot after I got sick and while I was recovering… They weren't really on good terms even when my mom died."

Maddie lowered herself onto the sofa next to me and clasped my hand. I let her, but I couldn't bear to look at her.

She twined her fingers with mine. "You have to know none of that was your fault. You were sick. You didn't have any choice in the matter. The kid whose liver you got would have died whether you needed the liver or not. And if the situation put that much of a strain on your parents, then their marriage wasn't that strong to begin with. That's not on you."

"I just don't see why I should have gotten to live and not someone else." My head drooped. "I've tried to convince myself that I've earned it by helping people as much as I can—finding things for them and getting justice when they needed it. But doing *that* has led me into all kinds of dark territory I can't say I'm really happy about… Why do you think I've worked so hard to shield you and everyone else I care about from who I've become?"

"Logan—"

I shook my head to cut her off. "It's fine if I end up getting hurt while I'm protecting people—helping people—the best ways I can. I've already gotten so many more years than I was originally supposed to. But I've got to draw the line somewhere. I don't want to see anyone getting caught in the crossfire."

With those last words, I sagged into the sofa cushions. My entire abdomen felt hollow, as if I'd been wrung out by my confession—all the things I'd never admitted to anyone out loud before.

What the hell could I say now? What could Maddie say to me? Now she knew just how fucked up I was.

But she didn't shy away. She scooted closer on the sofa and wrapped her arms around me, resting her head against my shoulder.

"Don't you know how many good things you've already done?" she said softly. "If you hadn't gotten a second chance, you wouldn't have been there in junior high to stand up to the kids who were bullying me. You made me feel that *I* was worthy of more, of being treated better—of demanding better for myself and everyone else."

I turned my head toward her for the first time, her words wrenching at me. "Of course you deserved better."

She touched my cheek, holding my gaze with her gorgeous blue eyes. "You say that so easily for me but not for yourself. But—you think I'm so amazing? It was *your* confidence that inspired me to take more stands myself. I wouldn't be who I am without you in my life. And the darkness you've gotten mixed up in could be the reason we finally find justice for my dad. I can't believe there's anything wrong with that."

I couldn't argue away the conviction or the admiration in her words. It was hard to wrap my head around the picture of me she was painting, but there was no denying that Maddie believed it. And if she believed it, with that keen mind of hers and her unshakeable moral code, then who was I to debate the subject?

I pulled her closer to me, tucking her legs over my lap and nestling her head under my chin. She relaxed into my embrace, her body melding against mine as if there was no place else she was meant to ever be.

But that wasn't totally the case. There *were* other places she belonged—other guys she belonged with.

And maybe, if I absorbed some of her compassion and generosity, I could admit that it was possible Beckett was one of those guys.

He hadn't done a single thing to hurt Maddie, which was more than I could say for myself. If I looked over all our interactions and what Dexter had reported back after their meeting, it'd appeared he was doing everything in his power to protect her.

Maybe I'd been too hard on him because of how hard I was on myself, not because of anything definitively horrible that he'd actually done.

It was going to take time before I'd fully accept what Maddie had said, but my spirits lightened as I held her close. The space inside me no longer felt so empty.

If I could have cuddled there with her for the rest of my days, I thought I'd have been perfectly happy with that as my life.

But of course, I was never going to get *that* lucky. We'd been tucked together for maybe ten minutes when Maddie's phone pinged with a text alert.

She eased back just enough to retrieve it from her pocket. The screen cast a starker glow across her face.

"It's Beckett," she said, and tensed slightly as if in anticipation of another caustic remark from me.

A twinge of hostility rippled through me, but I let it pass. "What's he got to say?" I asked, keeping my tone even.

Maddie shot me a gentle smile that made my effort worthwhile before her gaze flicked back to the screen. Her forehead furrowed. "He says he needs to talk to all of us about something important. He wants to know if he can come over—he'll be discreet."

She glanced at me again, waiting for my answer. I dragged in a breath and acknowledged to myself what I'd been fighting so hard to avoid.

We needed Beckett and his resources. And maybe, just maybe, the woman in my arms needed him too.

"Sure," I said. "I'll call in Slade and Dexter. Let him know we should all be here within the hour to hear his big news."

CHAPTER 13

Madelyn

"Are we sure Beckett's coming?" Slade asked impatiently, tossing one of his cinnamon candies to the ceiling and allowing it to fall back into his hand as he lay sprawled across the sofa. "Maybe he's blowing us off."

I shook my head and snatched the candy midair when he tossed it again. I dropped it on the coffee table in front of me.

"I second that question," Logan added from the chair across from me.

"He said that he'd wait until everyone arrived so that we could get started right away," I reminded them. "He should be here any time."

Slade let out a huff that was half-heartedly impatient. "He didn't tell you anything about this big news of his?"

I shook my head. "I'm guessing it's the kind of thing he wouldn't want to bring up on the phone."

Logan grimaced. It looked as if it took particular effort for him to say, "That does make sense."

My eyebrows just about shot right off my head. Logan caught my gaze and held it for a moment, and the memory of how we'd embraced on the sofa just an hour ago tugged at my heart. He'd wrapped his arms around me as if I were an anchor in a storm, the only thing keeping him from spiraling into disaster.

But he seemed settled now. I thought the things I'd said had dissolved the worst of his fears about himself and what he deserved. How could he think he wasn't even worthy of being *alive*?

Dexter shifted on his feet where he'd been standing by the window, leaning forward to peer between the blinds. "He's here."

I was too restless to stay sitting after that announcement. I pushed myself to my feet and hurried to the window in time to see Beckett closing the back door of the car he'd just gotten out of. It was a modest Kia, not the kind of car I'd ever seen him in before, but he had wanted to stay anonymous. I'd bet it was an Uber.

He'd taken other obvious steps to stay under the radar. Rather than his usual tailored business clothes, he'd donned a baseball cap and sunglasses, his leanly toned frame hidden beneath a baggy sweatshirt and jeans.

It only took a few seconds for him to stride to the building's front door and disappear from our view.

Dexter moved to the apartment door automatically, hitting a button when the entry buzzer sounded. I forced myself to sink back into my chair. There wasn't any point in all of us jumping on the guy the second he came inside.

At a firm knock, Dexter pulled the door wide. Beckett stepped over the threshold, his sunglasses in his hand now. He considered Dexter and the three of us around the living room in the space of a heartbeat, as coolly collected as always, and walked over to stand by the entertainment system where he could face all of us.

As Dexter joined Slade on the sofa, Beckett gave us all another assessing glance. He held himself with an air of such authority even dressed so casually that there was no mistaking the power he could wield.

How could I ever have failed to realize that he had to be a major leader, someone who pulled the strings behind innumerable operations? His dominance was etched in every particle of his being.

"What's this all about?" Logan demanded, brusque but to my relief not overtly hostile.

Beckett folded his hands together in front of him. "We have a lot to discuss. I'm sorry for the urgent meeting, but I didn't feel it was right to leave you all in the dark now that I know what we're dealing with. Or rather, who."

Slade had straightened up while the other guy spoke. He cocked his head, curious but also wary. "And who is that?"

Beckett took a deep breath. "To explain that, I have to tell you more about who *I* am and how I factor into the criminal underground. What I tell you today should not leave this room, or people who are much more vicious than me may see you as a threat to be destroyed simply for knowing."

Dexter studied him for a second with narrowing eyes before his gaze dropped. "That doesn't sound like a typical underground organization."

"That's because it's not. There's a group of thirteen families who call themselves the Devil's Dozen, and between them, they have influence over all the significant criminal activity that goes on throughout the world. My family is one of those. My father is the current head who generally meets with the other leaders, but I'm his heir, and I've already begun the process of taking over from him."

There was a moment of silence. The other guys simply stared at him. Then Slade let out a low whistle. "Fucking hell. You're some kind of black-market royalty—is that what you're saying?"

Logan's expression was more disbelieving. "All the crime in the entire *world*? That's not possible."

Beckett shrugged. "You can believe me or not. I've seen our empire in action. All that's important is you believe that I'm operating on a stage with only a handful of other major players who hold incredible sway, and one of those other players is directly involved in Evan Silver's murder."

My stomach lurched. "What? Why would any huge criminal king pin have it in for my dad?"

Beckett's gaze slid to me with obvious sympathy in his eyes. "I don't know that part yet. But this city is divided between territory belonging to my family, the Storm, and some that's part of a different family's empire: a man who goes by Doom's Seed."

"That doesn't sound ominous at all," Slade muttered wryly.

Beckett's mouth twitched with a hint of a smile. "He is a little over the top. But that doesn't stop him from being just as dangerous as his name sounds."

"What does he have to do with my dad?" I broke in.

"I'm trying to figure that out," Beckett said. "I only just confirmed that he's even involved. When I first found out that someone had been framing me and that Mr. Silver's death was connected to specific businesses in the city, I wasn't sure whether those were under Doom's Seed's control or part of some upstart criminal enterprise that was so new none of the Devil's Dozen had exerted authority over it yet."

My mouth had gone dry. "What we did at the seafood market this morning—was that to help you answer that question?"

Beckett nodded. "A man who has a definite interest in the shady transactions happening there is one of Doom's Seed's top lieutenants, Clarence Lindell. He's the one who called you up and tried to browbeat you. I was pretty sure I recognized his voice—and his attitudes about certain types of crime. A little digging confirmed his connection to the deliveries passing through the market."

I couldn't restrain a shiver, remembering the harsh voice that had threatened me.

Logan had tensed where he was leaning forward in his chair. "So, he's tied up in whatever illegal business the seafood market is handling. How does that tie him to Maddie's dad?"

Beckett aimed a baleful look at my stepbrother. "We know that Mr. Silver stumbled on something that made him a target. We know that whatever it was, it brought him to the seafood market and the warehouse that's also part of their delivery chain. We also know that someone with a lot of resources was able to set up Maddie's mother's accident and the fire at your office, as well as arranging evidence to frame me. It doesn't really make sense for it to have been anyone else."

I groped for my words. "Then we're assuming that this Doom's Seed guy had my dad murdered to protect his business. Whatever he found, it was part of this guy's dealings?"

"I'd imagine it's something like that," Beckett said, his voice softening. "It might not have even been Doom's Seed himself but his underlings handling operations for him that they don't think are important enough to run by him. Or that they don't think he'll approve of. I have trouble imagining them thinking coming at me was a good idea unless he'd either approved of it or they'd decided they didn't care what he wants."

"Maybe they've gone rogue," Dexter suggested.

"That's a possibility. Whatever the case, I'm going to confront the man in charge and tackle the problem head on."

Logan frowned. "And where do we come in?"

Beckett's jaw tightened. "You don't. The one thing we do know for sure is that Doom's Seed and his lackeys are incredibly dangerous on a level far beyond anything you've needed to deal with before. They have a thousand times more resources than four college students do, and it'd be much too easy for them to arrange a few more 'accidents' to dispose of you if they feel you're causing too much trouble again."

"They haven't come at us directly so far," I pointed out, though my heart was thumping faster.

"I think that's only because you've appeared to stop investigating," Beckett said. "And they'd only take measures that extreme if they believed they had no other choice, because it *would* look suspicious if something happened to all of you. But I don't know how long they'll hold off, especially if it becomes clear that you're still on the case."

He paused and swallowed audibly, the first outward sign of distress he'd shown since arriving. "I don't think I can fully protect you. I'm not even sure I can protect myself."

Those words punched a hole in my gut. I could hear how much Beckett hated admitting it—how much he hated this whole situation.

"It isn't your fault," I had to say.

"It's not," he agreed. "But I'm tangled up in it now, and I'm *glad* that I am. I know how to handle these people—I've got by far the best chance of getting us all out of this situation alive and well, with justice served."

"What does that mean, exactly?" Dexter asked.

"I'm going to handle the entire investigation from here with my own people. The four of you should stay out of it—as far out of it as you can. Go completely back to your regular lives, whatever you'd have been doing if you didn't believe a murder had happened. That's the only way to ensure you won't become targets. I'll find out why Maddie's father was targeted and keep you all in the loop about everything I uncover. I promise you that."

Slade snorted. "You're going to take all this on your shoulders by yourself? Are you kidding me?"

Beckett's mouth curved into a tight smile. "I won't be alone. I'll have plenty of help—from my people, who've trained for this, who've dealt with Doom's Seed before."

"No fucking way." Logan shoved himself to his feet, his muscles flexing. "If you think you're going to steal our case out from under us after—"

"I'm not trying to steal anything," Beckett interrupted sharply. "I'm trying to keep you all *alive.* It's the only thing I know I *can* do."

Logan hesitated. Silence fell over the room again as the full impact of Beckett's stand sank in.

He was willing to take on all of the danger and the responsibility himself to avoid putting us at any risk. He'd rather go it alone than take the chance of backlash against us. Even though Logan had been tearing into him at every opportunity over the past several days; even though the other guys had viewed him with suspicion.

He'd told me he had a code of ethics, lines he wouldn't cross. That he tried to protect innocent people as much as possible. He couldn't have given a more concrete display of those principles than he was right now.

Maybe I didn't totally understand his way of life and how he justified it to himself, but any flickers of doubt I'd still had snuffed out. He might not be a good guy in all the typical ways, but he was more than good enough for me.

The same startled awe was crossing the other guys' faces. Logan opened his mouth, but I leapt in before he could say anything.

"No. You're not shutting us out."

Beckett gave me a pained glance. "Maddie, it's not like that."

I stood up like Logan had and set my hands on my hips. "However you want to put it, it's not happening. You want to protect all of us? Well, I want to protect *you* just as much. It's my dad. None of this would have happened if we hadn't been trying to unravel his murder. I'll be careful, but I'm not going to step back now and let you take all the heat. I'm standing with you, pitching in every way I can."

To my surprise, Slade got to his feet next, his expression tense but his eyes sparkling with determination. "I'm in this until the end too. It's our fight as much as it is yours. We'd be real cabrones if we let you march into battle alone."

Dexter sprang up too, his stance rigidly defiant. "I'm in. We stand together, all of us."

That left only Logan, standing there with his jaw working and turmoil in his dark gaze. He stared at Beckett for a long moment.

"I appreciate what you're trying to do," he said finally, his voice rough but genuine enough that relief washed through me. "You could have walked away from this whole mess and left us to deal with it, but instead you're doing the opposite. You insisted on pushing into our lives—well, now we're insisting on being part of yours. As far as we have to go, as long as it takes, no matter what hell we have to go through."

A tingle raced over my skin at the conviction in his words—and the knowledge that there really might be some kind of hell ahead of us.

Beckett gazed at all of us as if hoping we might change our minds. Then he sighed and rubbed his face. "Somehow I feel like arguing isn't going to get me anywhere."

I moved toward him and grasped his hand. "It isn't. Because we're in this together, all the way to the end."

CHAPTER 14

Beckett

I watched the clock above the door as it continued ticking. Seconds turned into minutes as noon came and went, leaving me pacing the hardwood of the office floor.

He was late.

I'd requested a meeting with Doom's Seed at his earliest convenience, and today at noon was the agreed upon time. It wasn't in person, of course. Though I would have preferred that, he had denied the in-person invitation and countered with a video chat.

That was fair. Being a part of the Devil's Dozen awarded most people a level of anonymity. Nobody knew where he held a residence. He could have been in this country or halfway across the world.

Our jobs made it possible to live virtually anywhere.

Our jobs *didn't* make it impossible to join a damn video chat that'd been scheduled in advance on time.

I understood the game he was playing. It was the same sort of game that my father had played for years before his authority had dwindled. It was the same sort of game that I'd watched Mercy play so expertly in my time in Paradise Bend. Doom's Seed was intent on showing who held the power in this meeting, in this case by making me wait.

So far, he was nine minutes later than expected.

I hated playing into his desire for power and control. I had half a mind to disconnect from the video chat before he joined, walk off, and not be here when he finally got around to signing in. If it'd been any less pressing a situation, that's exactly what I'd do.

But if it were any less pressing a situation, I wouldn't have requested the meeting in the first place, and Doom's Seed probably realized that. If I wanted to keep Maddie safe, I needed to assess his involvement in the recent schemes I'd stumbled on. I couldn't turn back for the sake of my pride.

The clock hit precisely 12:10, and an alert pinged on my computer signaling that the other party had joined the video chat. I turned toward my desk and settled stiffly into my chair. As I put on a mild but firm expression for the camera, I approved his icon.

The man I knew only as Doom's Seed appeared on the screen. The plain beige background gave away nothing about his location, contrasting starkly with his typical flashy clothing.

In his usual garish fashion, he wore a vibrant gold-and-purple plaid vest over a shiny black button up with a tie that might have had actual gold thread woven into it in a paisley pattern. I restrained myself from rolling my eyes.

"Storm's heir," he said in greeting, with a sardonic tone that managed to make it sound as if he didn't think the title was earned.

Not that he knew all that much about me. "My apologies for the delay. I had something important come up."

He didn't *sound* the slightest bit apologetic, which no doubt was purposeful. All the same, I treated the apology as if he'd meant it, not allowing the implied insult to affect me. It was better if I pretended I hadn't even noticed his subtle rudeness, though I kept my own tone brisk rather than placating. "I understand. Things come up. Thank you for coming."

I'd thought long and hard about how I'd structure this conversation. I had to be so careful with my words. Every conversation within the Devil's Dozen was a struggle for control, a fragile balance between maintaining authority and bargaining for what you wanted.

If I seemed weak, he'd consider it pointless to entertain my questions. If I outright challenged or insulted him, he might withhold the information I needed out of pride.

It was a precarious path with innumerable unpredictable obstacles.

Before I could begin, Doom's Seed cleared his throat. "Reaching out to a fellow member between official meetings over unestablished business is highly irregular. I trust you have a good reason for breaching typical protocol?"

"Of course," I said evenly. "Unfortunately, a matter has come up that couldn't wait. I recently discovered that one of your people has taken hostile action against me and therefore the Storm's empire as a whole. If you or one of your people are aiming to start a war on our territory, I don't plan on sitting back for weeks until the moon is right."

As I spoke, I studied his expression on the screen. His eyebrows rose slightly at my comment about war, but otherwise his face remained neutral. I willed my jaw not to clench.

If we'd been able to meet in person, I'd have had so much more body language to go by when evaluating his intentions. Communicating through a computer was an inadequate substitute. But it was all I had.

"I'm disturbed to hear that," Doom's Seed said as if he hadn't known already. He furrowed his forehead. "I was unaware that anyone who answers to me had acted against the Storm, and I'd certainly have wanted to know. What exactly happened?"

He was acting startled and confused, but not exactly upset. No one made it to the level of the Devil's Dozen without being good at subterfuge. Was his surprise an act, or had his lackey really gone rogue?

Not for the first time since I'd come back home, I wished I had Rowan here with me. Rowan was a master at reading people. He'd have picked up on more from the man across from me than I could.

But he wasn't here, and I needed to be able to make those judgments on my own.

I kept my gaze trained on Doom's Seed as I spoke. "I've been monitoring a group of college students who've gotten a taste for vigilantism. They've been investigating local criminal activities, recently some that appear to fall within your domain. One of your people tried to deflect those amateur detectives by claiming I was responsible instead. I'm sure you can recognize that the consequences of framing me, especially to civilians who might turn to the police, could be severe."

Doom's Seed rubbed his chin, looking thoughtful but still not particularly concerned. I hadn't mentioned anything about the ties I'd formed with the students in question or about the connection to Evan Silver, not wanting to show too much of my hand.

I'd hoped my adversary might give away some telling detail, but it was becoming increasingly obvious that he had an unshakeable poker face. My hands balled under the desk in frustration as I waited for his response.

He hummed to himself and gave me a look that felt irritatingly patronizing. "While I keep an iron fist with most of my people and operations, I give a certain amount of leeway for them to defend me as they see fit without informing me of every detail. It makes my underlings feel more comfortable in their positions. Less like I'll kill them for small indiscretions." His lips spread in a smirk. "It boosts morale."

I couldn't imagine anyone feeling all that happy working under the flamboyant brute on my screen no matter how much morale-boosting he did, but there was no accounting for taste.

"I would have hoped you wouldn't give them enough leeway to launch a turf war with one of your own," I said, letting an edge creep into my voice.

Doom's Seed gave a careless wave of his hand that only raised my hackles more. Whether he'd initiated the move against me or was only hearing about it now, he clearly didn't *mind* that his people had attempted to sabotage my family's business.

"It's possible whoever acted against you didn't even realize they were turning on a fellow member of the Dozen," he said.

I swallowed a snort. That was unlikely. I'd dealt with this specific lieutenant before—Lindell was perfectly aware of who I was and my familial connections. But harping on the issue would only make me look too easily shaken.

I raised my eyebrows at the man across from me. "Whatever the case, I trust you'll sort out the problem quickly and thoroughly, taking all appropriate measures to ensure it won't happen again? Or should we be prepared to deal out proper sanctions ourselves?"

Doom's Seed shrugged. "I'll tell my people to back off on anything directly to do with the Storm. But they aren't going to sit back and allow some kids to screw with my operations. If those 'vigilantes' impose on my dealings again, they'll face appropriate consequences too."

Was that meant as a threat toward me? *Did* he know that I was interested in that group of students from more than just the standpoint of caution?

I held my expression as implacable as his own. He might be testing me, checking to see whether I was invested in their fate. And if he knew that I was, I could turn them into even more of a target in the game he seemed to be playing.

"The students don't appear to be an issue anymore. Your men did a thorough job scaring them off. But of course you'll handle that matter however you see fit—as long as it doesn't impinge on the Storm's work."

"Naturally," Doom's Seed said, rolling the word off his tongue far too casually for me to believe he meant it. "Was that all you called on me for?"

I shaped my next question with even more care than the ones before. "Actually, there was one more matter I wanted to address while we're already speaking. A name has come up that seems to have some significance. Do you remember anything about a death about fifteen years ago—a man named Evan Silver?"

I didn't expect Doom's Seed to admit it even if he did. I only wanted to see his reaction to my tossing the name out there without warning.

But I was dealing with a tough customer. Doom's Seed didn't show any sign of emotion other than disdain with the purse of his lips. "Do you know how many deaths I've heard mentioned in the time I've been doing this job, Storm's heir? Most of them are barely memorable. I don't recall even a fraction of the names. That one means nothing to me."

"I understand," I said. "I simply wanted to check."

His gaze veered to something beyond the camera, and his eyes narrowed. His attention flicked back to me. "You've gotten your time and presented your complaints. This conversation is over."

He didn't waste time for farewells before dismissing the video chat. I was left staring at a blank window.

I let out my breath with a brief growl. How much had I even learned from the attempt? I didn't think he cared what happened to me or my family's business, but he hadn't given away enough to convince me that he'd purposefully undermined us either. I still had no idea whether Doom's Seed had intended to move against us or if it'd really been only a lieutenant taking initiative he shouldn't have.

One thing was clear: Doom's Seed was no friend to the Storm, to the guys who called themselves the Vigil, or to Madelyn Silver. I'd have to keep an even closer eye on his people's operations in this city and their surveillance of the college. Things could take a much more dangerous turn so quickly.

As much as I admired Maddie's resolve and determination to find answers, I couldn't help worrying that we were all in over our heads—and we wouldn't find out just how much until the next unexpected strike.

CHAPTER 15

Madelyn

There was something warmer about our next meeting with Beckett despite the main circumstances that brought us together. We were perched on stools around the kitchen island, only Dexter standing as he moved between the island and the stove, where he'd cooked jasmine rice and a couple of different curries to fortify us for the conversation ahead.

I already knew to expect great things from Dexter's culinary efforts. Beckett hadn't sampled them before. As my first bite of the tofu and yellow peppers in ruddy sauce melted on my tongue, he brought his fork to his mouth. He chewed carefully, and his eyes widened.

"This is fucking good," he said to Dexter.

A broad grin stretched across Dexter's normally subdued face. I had a feeling Beckett had just won a few points with the other two guys as well. There was no denying he meant the compliment, and the fact that I'd rarely heard him swear only emphasized his enthusiasm.

Slade stretched out his legs to the side of the island and scooped up another forkful of his own. "Yep, we're pretty spoiled around here. Dex has his place in the Vigil assured for all time as long as he can work a stove."

He winked at his friend, but something about his tone sounded a bit off to me. I couldn't put my finger on it, and my stomach twisted despite the delicious food.

It'd been too long since we'd really been able to relax and have a proper conversation with each other that didn't revolve around murderous criminals. I had no idea what other things might be on Slade's mind.

A small smile had touched Logan's lips, but he got down to business, waving his fork at Beckett. "This isn't a dinner party. What have you found out in the past few days? You said you were going to talk to that guy you think is behind this—Doom's Sprout or whatever."

"Doom's Seed," Beckett corrected him with a hint of dry amusement, but any sign of humor quickly faded from his expression. "I did speak to him. Unsurprisingly, he didn't launch into a full confession of wrongdoing or an overt declaration of war."

I frowned. "Did you get anything out of him?"

"Not directly." Beckett offered an apologetic grimace. "But it was a necessary step to make sure he knows he can't expect to hide his involvement. If he *doesn't* want a war, then he has to ensure his men stand down, at least when it comes to anything that interferes with my business."

"Wonderful for you," Logan muttered, and I aimed a kick at his shin.

Beckett appeared unfazed. "I do think I found out something else useful. I mentioned Evan Silver in passing at the end of the conversation. Doom's Seed didn't let himself react in front of me, but there's been a telling shift in behavior among his people since then."

Hope shivered through me. I leaned toward him with my elbows on the island. "What do you mean?"

"I've had my employees monitoring all of the companies the four of you connected to the theft of Madelyn's car, Mr. Silver's past investigations, and his death. Business was proceeding as usual at all of them until my conversation with Doom's Seed. It's been the same since at the chop shop, the bar, and the spa, but my comments must have spurred some changes at the warehouse and the seafood market."

Slade stopped chewing, his dark eyes lighting up with curiosity. "What kind of changes are we talking about?"

Beckett took another bite of curry before answering, as if he didn't realize the rest of us were hanging on his next words. Or maybe he did, and this was his way of heckling Logan right back.

"The warehouse from the address in the trinket box is now for sale through back channels. It looks like they're trying to offload it so it's no longer part of Doom's Seed's holdings. And the man you had footage of regularly coming by the seafood market hasn't been back since then. Neither has the guy named Sharply who used to work there every other weekday."

Dexter came over to stand between Logan and Slade with his own plate. He set it down, his expression pensive. "What do you make of those changes? Do they point to anything we should be concerned about?"

"Not immediately," Beckett said. "But those two businesses were the ones already tied the most directly to Mr. Silver's death from the evidence we had. The fact that they're the only two where

Doom's Seed has adjusted his operations confirms that they're a key factor, while the other businesses must not be all that involved. He doesn't want there to be any chance of you finding more proof of what happened back then."

My pulse stuttered. "Then this Doom's Seed guy is definitely behind my dad's murder?"

Beckett gazed back at me evenly. "It's too early to be sure. But either he knows the details, or he mentioned my comment to that lieutenant of his who could be making the changes independently. Either way, someone high up in the organization is moving to protect themselves."

"Then we need to dig deeper into those places," Logan said. "Especially the seafood market. It seems to have been some kind of hub for whatever they were moving around."

"The secret is in the fish," Slade said with a light laugh.

Dexter knit his brow. "It was the freezer container that led us to the seafood market in the first place. The thug who attacked Maddie was overseeing deliveries for them. We still haven't figured out what they're shipping."

"What would need to be kept cold over long distances?" I asked, tapping my fork against my mouth. "I guess it could be something edible—some kind of illegal food. Or—" The idea hit me with a jolt as I thought of the labs in the biology department where I spent so much of my class-time. "What if they're transporting bacteria or viruses for some kind of biological warfare? Or organic materials that contain toxins? Something like that is what killed my dad."

Beckett nodded slowly. "Something along those lines wouldn't surprise me at all. And it would definitely fit with the method of your dad's murder."

"Who the hell are they waging biological warfare on around here?" Logan demanded.

Beckett cut his gaze toward the other guy. "It can be on a small scale. Infect a small group that's in your way here or there. Or this is only the first step to transporting them overseas where there are plenty of wars being fought that you're barely aware of here in the States."

A chill ran through me with the knowledge that he was right. We could barely wrap our minds around the potential depths of this man's villainy.

This was the kind of person Beckett was standing in the way of when he kept his spot in the Devil's Dozen. If he backed away, there might be no one working against the worst of the criminals—and another psychopath like this Doom's Seed psycho could take his place.

Suddenly it was hard to have any qualms at all about what he did, given the alternative.

Dexter hummed to himself. "That could explain how Maddie's father got involved in the first place too. They could be stealing samples from hospitals or other laboratories he did work for. Or he might have heard about a mysterious death that got him started on the trail. If he noticed something suspicious and then discovered the shipments, the criminals involved could have seen him as a threat."

"But why wouldn't he have told anyone?" Logan said with a little growl of frustration. "If he even suspected—he should have sounded the alarm, not gone digging all on his own."

When I gave him a pointed look, he made a face at me. "At least the three of us had each other for backup."

I guessed he had a point. But I could easily imagine why Dad would have kept quiet. "You should be able to understand his point of view, given how you've acted the entire time you knew. He must have realized he was onto something dangerous, and he was trying to protect me and my mom until he had something concrete he could bring to the police."

Logan hesitated. "I guess that does make sense. And it's hard to think of how he could have stumbled on any illegal materials these people are shipping that wouldn't be related to his work in the hospital. If we assume they're transporting biological samples or toxic substances, what would we need to look for next to prove that?"

In the moment of silence that followed, Slade pushed back his stool with a rasp of the feet against the floor. I realized with a start that he hadn't said anything in a while, just sitting there watching the rest of us hash out the possibilities. Like he was pulling back from the group.

"As much as my brilliant insights are solving both world hunger and global warfare, I've got to get to my study group," he said in a typically joking voice before I could ask if he was okay. "We've got an exam next week, and they'll all be lost without me. It'd look strange if I didn't show up."

We all nodded, but an ache formed in my chest as I watched him stride away. Something wasn't quite right with him, no matter how much he tried to pretend he was his usual jovial self. I didn't know how I could force him to talk about it, though. The next time I had him to myself, I'd have to bring it up.

As the door shut behind him, I yanked my thoughts back to the problem right in front of us. "I should try to get into more records at the hospital back home. I could look for any mysterious deaths or illnesses that came up there in the last few months before my dad died. Whenever he started writing those notes that you found about the investigation." I glanced at Logan. "If we figure out what tipped him off, that'd be a huge step forward."

"You don't need to be the one to do that," Beckett said. "I have people who can handle it."

I narrowed my eyes at him, understanding his protectiveness but unwilling to give in. "I have easy access to the hospital because my mom's still going back for check-ups after her accident. There'd be no reason for anyone to think it was strange for me to go back to visit."

"Doom's Seed might have people watching the hospital at this point. I don't like you putting yourself in unnecessary danger."

"It isn't unnecessary," I insisted. "I won't let anyone see me doing anything that'd be strange for a daughter helping out her mom. He'll be keeping an eye on you now too, won't he? Do any of your 'people' have a good excuse to stop by?"

Beckett's jaw tightened, but I could tell he didn't have a good argument for that. "We could get at it using a more roundabout approach."

"Which would take more time."

"Hey." Logan set his hand on my arm and, to my immense shock, tipped his head to Beckett. "He's making a reasonable point. *None* of us wants you in danger."

Because being overprotective was something that Logan could always relate to. I wanted to roll my eyes at the suffocating masculine energy in the room. "Of all the things you guys could have agreed on, could you pick something else?"

They both gave me a similar look that said, *Absolutely not.*

I glowered at each of them in turn. "Well, I don't want any of you in danger either, and I'm the one who'd be in the least. So I'm the obvious option." I paused. "Of course, there is the small problem that I don't know how to hack into the hospital network once I'm in the building."

The guys appeared to stew on that for a moment, Dexter shooting me a sympathetic glance. Then Beckett squared his shoulders. "Fine. I might know a way to help with that."

He looked at Logan, who hesitated before letting out a resigned sigh.

No more arguments. We were doing this.

We would make this work. With Logan and Beckett finally allied, there was nothing that could come between us and the truth.

CHAPTER 16

Madelyn

"Everything is healing well, Lindsay," the doctor said with an approving smile. "You've obviously been looking after yourself and keeping up with your physio."

Relief rushed through me. Mom kept her expression calm as she smiled back, but she squeezed my hand a little tighter where I'd grabbed hers while we waited for the doctor's assessment.

We both knew how bad her injuries from the car accident had been. She'd needed emergency surgery and been kept under observation for days. But now that she'd been home for a little while and was gradually getting back into her usual routines, it seemed she was recovering quickly. She had to be at least as reassured by that as I was.

"I've been doing my best not to be impatient about getting back to normal," she said with a light laugh.

The doctor nodded as he closed Mom's file. "Remember, strive for a *new* normal. Some of those injuries will likely be finicky for years to come. You want to continue being patient with yourself, and recognize that sometimes you may need to adapt rather than push through. There's no shame in that. But I think you'll get awfully close to that old normal eventually, if not all the way there."

"Of course. I'll keep that in mind."

He said his good-byes and left the exam room, and Mom sighed before getting to her feet and grasping her purse strap. The dejected sound made me leap up. "Are you okay?"

She swatted at me. "Yes. You heard the man! I just wish I healed as fast as a person half my age still."

"It hasn't been very long."

"No, not at all." She bumped her shoulder against mine affectionately. "You know, honey, you really didn't need to come. I'm used to attending appointments by myself."

"Not appointments like this," I said. "I'm glad I could be here when Holand couldn't this time. And before you say anything about concentrating on my schoolwork, it'll be easier for me to concentrate now that I've heard for myself that you're doing well."

Mom let out a teasing huff. "You know, usually it's mothers who attend doctor's appointments with their children, not the other way around." She paused as she slung her purse over her shoulder and gave me a more penetrating look. "You don't talk to me about school all that much anymore. You used to tell me about interesting lectures and projects you were working on all the time."

I feigned a laugh of my own. I hadn't had much to report because my mind had been so wrapped up in other things, and I'd been afraid that if I tried to fake enthusiasm where my heart wasn't in it, Mom would sense that something was wrong. It seemed like saying less might have given her that impression anyway.

We headed out the door and down the hall past bustling nurses and the beeping of machines from open doorways. "Oh, well, it's getting down to crunch time," I said. "My first semester at the new college, and final exams are looming. It's less exciting when you're scrambling to make sure you're stuffing your head full of every possible fact."

And worrying about your dad's murderer who nearly murdered your mom too, I didn't say.

Mom knit her brow. "Is that how you feel—like you're scrambling to keep up? I've never heard you talk about college that way before. You always seemed energized by the work rather than stressed."

"Oh, no, it's not that bad," I said, scrambling now to cover up the way I'd misspoken. I couldn't seem to remove my foot from my mouth with her today. "I'm exaggerating. But I am really busy, in a good way. You don't need to worry, I promise."

She patted my shoulder. "I want to make sure you're okay, just like you do with me." She peered at me again in a way that sent an apprehensive prickle over my skin. "You know that if you ever start to feel too stressed or uncertain about anything—school or otherwise—you can always talk do me, don't you? I'm here for you no matter what. I *want* to be here for you."

My stomach knotted. Where was this pep talk coming from? Had I been that bad at hiding all the stress that really was weighing on me?

I couldn't tell her the truth. Not when I had no proof yet. Not when the people I was trying to bring to justice had already left her with these injuries she might never fully recover from. She needed to stay as much out of this mess as I could keep her until it was all over.

"I promise that I'll come to you if I need your help. Pinky promise." I offered her a pinky.

A chuckle tumbled out of her as she grabbed my pinky and shook it.

"You never broke a pinky promise when you were little," she said, narrowing her eyes. "I expect the same now."

I gasped and placed my hand over my chest as if her words wounded me. "Have some trust. A pinky promise is permanent."

But I'd only promised to go to her if I needed *her* help, and this situation wasn't anything she could help with anyway.

Mom grinned, looking as if her momentary bout of worry had faded away. Which was good, because I had a trick to pull before we left the hospital, and the front doors were fast approaching.

We were just a few steps away when I stopped in my tracks and patted my pockets. "Shoot," I muttered, making sure to look at Mom and feel my pockets a second time as if double-checking. "I took my phone out back in the room to make some notes—I think I must have set it down and forgotten it. I'd better go grab it before someone else finds it. You go ahead. I'll meet you in the car in a minute."

"Oh, that sort of thing happens to me all the time. Good thing you realized before we left."

She waved me off, and I kept my game face on until I'd turned away. Even then, I restrained a grimace at my lie, far too aware of the hospital staff, patients, and visitors milling around the lobby.

I headed back the way we'd come as if I really were going back to the exam room, but I quickly turned down a different hallway—one with fewer patient rooms and more admin offices. It was almost lunchtime, which I hoped would work in my favor. I brushed my hand across the USB drive in my pocket, reassuring myself that it was still there, as if I hadn't felt it moments before.

I knew nothing special about computers and nothing at all about hacking, but I knew how to insert a flash drive. It would be hard to screw *that* up.

All I needed was to find an unmonitored computer accessible enough for me to insert the drive. Beckett had said that the way his techie colleague had programmed it, the app on it would run automatically and insert the necessary code for our purposes in less than a minute.

I had to walk confidently and briskly as if I belonged here to avoid getting questioned by the staff, since there weren't many visitors wandering around in this section of the hospital. I picked up my pace when I spotted a nurse's station with a few computers up ahead, the chairs currently empty. My heart thumped faster.

Jackpot.

But just as I stopped on the opposite side of one of the desks from the computer, dipping my hand into my pocket and glancing around to see if I could lean over the counter to plug it in, a man in scrubs hustled into the station. "Can I help you?"

Shit. "No," I said, pasting on a smile. "I almost forgot the room number I needed, but it came to me the second I decided I had to ask. Isn't that always the way? Sorry to bother you."

"No bother at all," he assured me, but I hurried off with a false sense of purpose in case he watched me go.

Farther down the hallway, a woman strode out of a room, leaving the door ajar. Did that mean it was empty now? I slowed down just enough so that she'd pass me well before I got to the room and approached it cautiously.

I could see a computer on a long desktop just beyond the door. Was there anyone else in the room?

I rested my hand on the door—and a voice spoke from right behind me. "Were you looking for Beth?"

It took all my effort not to jump out of my skin. I turned with as much self-control as I could summon and smiled at the man who'd approached me.

What was a decent excuse? "I was just going to see if she wanted a coffee," I said brightly. "It looks like she's stepped out, though. I guess maybe she went to get her own."

The guy dipped his head. "Probably. I'm sure she'd have appreciated the thought, though."

I forced myself to walk onward and turned into the next stairwell, since I'd almost reached the end of the hall.

Plug in a USB drive. It'd *sounded* easy, but locating a computer where no one would see me pull off the maneuver was proving next to impossible. I wasn't some magician who could flick it in there while talking to the person at the keyboard. Although right now I really wished I was.

Mom was waiting for me at the car. I could expand my lie, make up a reason it'd taken me so long, but with every passing minute, that lie would become harder to make convincing. Maybe I should have taken Logan up on his offer to come along and create some kind of distraction, but that'd seemed so irresponsible in a hospital where lives were on the line.

That thought had barely finished passing through my head as I strode down the new hall I'd come out into when the PA system crackled to life.

"Code blue," a voice announced. "Second floor, corridor three, outside room two-seven."

The woman who'd been poised behind the nurse's station up ahead sprang into action, rushing away from the desks toward the emergency. The two other staff I could see farther down vanished into a side hallway.

The nurse's station was totally empty.

Guilt jabbed through my gut at taking advantage of someone's potentially fatal event, but I didn't have time to weigh the morality of my choice. This could be my only chance.

I darted forward and leaned over the counter toward one of the computers, fumbling for the drive at the same time. It didn't have a lid on it, thank God. Where was the port? There.

I shoved the drive into place, wiggled it to make sure it was all the way in and steady, and tugged the computer just a smidge to the side so that it was less likely anyone would notice the new accessory. I couldn't risk sticking around while the program did its work. When someone did find it, it was apparently programmed to look totally empty unless you knew how to crack its secrets. It'd be dismissed and thrown away with no one the wiser.

My pulse racing, I pushed away from the counter and spun around. I half expected a staff person to be charging toward me with an accusing yell, but there was no one around except for a nurse who was just backing out of a room several doors down. She hadn't seen anything.

I dragged in a breath and marched back to the stairwell, already formulating my excuses to Mom in my head. At the same time, I pulled out my phone from my purse, where I'd actually left it.

Everything's in place, I texted Logan. *Ready for the next phase of the plan.*

CHAPTER 17

Madelyn

"Have you found anything?" I asked, glancing from the apartment's sofa over to Logan where he was perched at the kitchen island. He was in the middle of making a face at his laptop's screen. He'd been poring over the extensive collection of records he could now access from the hospital all day.

He tore his gaze from the screen to look at me with a frustrated shake of his head. "Not much. I've looked at everything from the first few months before your dad's death so far, and no unexplained illnesses or outright poisonings are coming up. But we don't know exactly when his suspicions were raised or how old *that* case was when he stumbled on it. And he might have noticed some detail that I wouldn't."

"Well, if you see anything that you think *could* be strange, let me know. I might be able to tell." I wasn't totally confident in that offer, since Dad had accumulated a lot more medical expertise than I had by that point in his life, but it'd be worth trying.

"Of course." He paused, and his attention shifted to Beckett, who was sitting at the other end of the sofa. The mafia heir had stuck around even after Slade and Dexter had needed to leave for afternoon classes, waiting to see what we might dig up. "And if Maddie can't tell, maybe that friend of yours, the toxins expert, could?"

A small smile crossed Beckett's lips. I suspected he was pleased that Logan had suggested his connections might be useful instead of snarking about them like he had so often before. "I'm sure she'd be happy to help. What about that name you mentioned from Mr. Silver's notes—the Baldwin file, I think it was?"

Logan nodded. "I already searched for that back when we first came across the mention, as well as I could at the time. But I went looking for any Baldwins again now that I have better access, and I didn't turn up any patients with that last name across all of the records that've been digitized."

My stomach knotted. "Maybe Doom's Seed or whichever of his underlings were involved realized it'd be key evidence and erased it."

Gloom crossed Logan's face. "That's definitely possible." He dipped his head and pinched the bridge of his nose with a grimace. "I'm going to keep searching, but my eyeballs feel like they're going to fall out of my head from all this staring at the screen. I think I should take a quick break."

"Don't wear yourself too thin," I said quickly, with a rush of a different kind of concern. He put too much pressure on himself as it was.

"Don't worry about me." He got up and walked to the fridge. "Anyone else want a soda?"

"I'm good," Beckett said.

I waved away the offer, my mind veering back toward the

problem at hand. A rough sigh escaped me. "I wish I could do more to unravel all these threads. I hate not knowing what's really going on—now or back then. And it seems like the mystery just keeps getting bigger and more complicated."

"You've been so focused on trying to figure it out. Maybe you need a break too." Beckett scooted closer and lifted one of my socked feet onto his lap. He ran his thumbs over the arch with just the right pressure to send a tingle of released tension racing through me. "This is about your dad. I can only imagine how stressed out you are over it. But it'll be easier for you to put the pieces together if you can relax enough to give your thoughts some space."

I raised my eyebrows at him. "Are you a psychotherapist now too?"

He laughed. "I'm just speaking from personal experience, as someone who ends up in a lot of stressful conflicts."

"Hmm." I couldn't help pushing my foot into his massaging fingers as he worked the muscles over. It did feel incredibly good. "I think I like your theory as long as this is the solution to it."

Beckett aimed a slow smile at me that sent a much more heated tingle to other parts of my body. It occurred to me abruptly that this was the first time I'd let him touch me at all intimately since I'd found out the truth about him.

I didn't want him to stop. I wanted him to touch me a whole lot more while looking at me with all that affection and desire in his gaze. My own hunger unfurled from low in my belly.

"You know," I said quietly, "I'm glad that you stuck around through everything—I'm glad that you insisted on helping. And not just because of what it means for the investigation."

Beckett paused for a second, obviously recognizing the significance of the statement. His smile widened and softened at the same time, and he reached for my other foot. "I'm glad too."

I became abruptly aware of Logan standing at the edge of my

vision. He'd come around the island, standing a few feet away from the back of the sofa, studying me and Beckett. Watching Beckett's deft fingers run over my foot in a way that had my eyes rolling back and my lips clamping against a groan of approval that I didn't think would reduce the tension still in the room.

My stepbrother didn't say anything. He barely moved, standing perfectly still, his fingers clamped around the bottle of craft soda he'd grabbed without raising it to his lips.

I started to tense up again, wondering what he'd do when he snapped out of his frozen state. Would he yell at Beckett for touching me? Try to bully him out of the apartment? Or maybe snap at me for allowing the massage in the first place?

Then Logan spoke, his voice low but steady. "There are ways we could help you unwind that are a lot more effective than just a foot massage, you know."

My pulse hiccupped as his implication sank in. It obviously wasn't lost on Beckett either. The other guy's fingers paused against my foot, and he glanced over at Logan assessingly. "We?"

Logan's stance remained taut, but the corner of his mouth curled into a hint of a smirk. "If you're up for that."

"You're serious?"

I couldn't blame Beckett for feeling the need to double-check after the way Logan had responded to him before. Even after what he'd just said, it was still a shock to see my stepbrother lift his shoulders in a casual shrug. His voice stayed firm.

"It's become incredibly clear that you care about Maddie just as much as I do. And I'm not really in a position to criticize any other part of your life, considering what I've gotten myself into." Logan's gaze slid to me, both heated and tender. "I want to see Maddie happy. If that means having you on board, I can deal with it. I've been responsible for too much of her *un*happiness already."

"Logan," I said softly. "I've already forgiven you for that." And I understood why he'd done it, even if I wished he'd found a kinder approach. Wasn't I shutting out Mom and Summer the exact same way now, for the exact same reasons?

He shook his head. "It doesn't matter. The point is that you should have everything you want that you *can* have. Assuming you'd want this."

The question in those words hung in the air. A fresh tingle raced over every inch of my skin. I looked from Logan to Beckett, who was gazing back at me with his normally cool gray eyes smoldering. The last fragments of the wall I'd been holding up against my feelings for him cracked open and fell away. A swell of longing swept through me.

And how better to welcome Beckett all the way back into my life than with the man who'd once raised the most objections to his presence paving the way? We were a unified force now, no secrets or hostility left between us.

"I do," I murmured.

The instant the words left my mouth, Beckett swooped in to scoop me up in his arms. A squeal of surprise tumbled out of me as he hefted me up and around, my legs dangling.

Logan's smile grew. He motioned toward his bedroom, setting the pop bottle on a side table undrunk.

As Logan pushed open the door, Beckett carried me inside. Their scents mingled together, Beckett's crisp cologne rising from his neck and Logan's muskier smell laced throughout the room. Beckett lay me down on the bed, kneeling beside me, and Logan clambered after us to crouch at my other side.

They were a study in opposites, brown hair vs. blond, bulky brawn vs. leaner muscle. But they had so much in common, more than Logan had wanted to admit at first. And right now the most important of those things was me.

After all the arguments and the continuing power struggle

between them, I wanted them both. I *needed* them both, making a precious moment with me together.

My eagerness must have shown on my face. Beckett leaned over me, his lips an inch from mine when he whispered, "Do you like the thought of being fucked by both of us, Maddie?"

A bolt of heat shot straight to my pussy. A strangled sound of agreement escaped me, and then Beckett was claiming my mouth.

But his searing kiss only lasted a moment before those damn lips made their way past the corner of my mouth. He charted a path across my cheek to my ear. His breath tickled the lobe before he nipped it between his teeth just hard enough to draw a gasp out of me.

Logan simply watched for the first minute like he had the foot massage. Then he bent down and kissed my other shoulder. His hand slid up under my shirt, his fingers teasing over my belly and tracing the base of my bra.

My nipples pebbled in anticipation. I couldn't help squirming at another delicate nip of Beckett's teeth, and Logan chuckled.

"I think our girl needs a little more attention," he said.

Beckett eased back as if instinctively understanding him, and they both reached for the hem of my shirt together. I sat up a little and raised my arms so they could peel it off, and Beckett took the opportunity to unhook my bra as well.

"Good thinking," Logan said with warm amusement, and tugged the garment right off me.

Beckett matched his tone. "We can't let any part of her be neglected."

He rolled his thumb over my nipple, and Logan dipped his head to suck the other into his mouth. My back arched at the dual jolts of pleasure, a whimper I couldn't restrain leaving my lips.

Beckett went back to kissing my jaw and the side of my neck as he teased the peak of my breast to a harder nub. Logan applied his tongue and teeth as well as his lips, every swipe and graze making me tremble harder. My panties were soaked now. My nerves quivered with increasing bliss.

"You smell so good," Beckett muttered into my hair.

Logan raised his head and grinned, a spark lighting in his eyes. "I know where she'll smell even more delicious."

His fingers hooked around the waist of my jeans, one hand moving to quickly flick open the fly. My heart thumping faster, I lifted my hips to let him tug them off me. But then I couldn't help eyeing their shirts and pants while I lay there almost completely exposed between them. "I shouldn't be the only one getting naked around here."

Beckett arched an eyebrow at Logan. "I guess she does have a point."

They both reached for their shirts, Beckett needing to unbutton his partway down, Logan simply peeling off his fitted tee. As my stepbrother slid his jeans down his thighs, I couldn't stop my gaze from roaming over the sculpted body I'd never seen on full display before.

He had his Vigil tattoo, a hawk that matched the ones I'd seen on both Slade and Dexter, imprinted on his right hip. Several inches higher, a pale scar across his abdomen reminded me of the surgery that had saved his life and given him his second chance all those years ago.

I yanked my gaze farther up, knowing how little Logan liked to think about or be reminded about his transplant. But he didn't appear concerned right now. He was toying with the waist of my panties. As my eyes met his, he yanked them down after my pants.

He trailed his hand back up my inner thigh and circled his fingers around the spot where I was aching most. I swayed toward him, and he traced his thumb right down my seam.

At my moan, his pleased laugh carried through the room. "Good girl."

He thrust a finger right inside me while pressing his thumb down on my clit. As I rocked into his touch, Beckett focused his attention on my chest, palming one breast and slicking his tongue over the peak of the other.

Bliss radiated through every part of my body. Beckett sucked on my nipple at the same moment as Logan plunged a second finger into me, and I cried out. Need condensed low in my belly, a burning ache for release.

Logan pumped his fingers faster, but he seemed to have decided he wouldn't be satisfied with propelling me over the edge that way. He pulled farther to the side with a few more strokes and glanced at Beckett.

"Why don't you bring her the rest of the way there? Take her from behind. She deserves it good and deep."

Beckett held his gaze for a moment, a silent understanding appearing to form between them. Logan was proving just how far he'd go to accept Beckett into every part of my life. A lump filled my throat even as hunger seared through my veins.

As Beckett reached me, I flipped myself over. He pressed kisses down my spine, his hand caressing my ass. I pressed into his touch, but my attention settled on Logan's cock jutting rigidly from between his thighs. My mouth watered.

"This isn't supposed to be only about me," I said, shooting him a wicked smile, and leaned over to lap my tongue around his shaft.

The noise that left him made the gesture so worth it. I wrapped my mouth right around his erection as foil ripped behind me.

Beckett delved his hand between my legs and sucked in a breath at my wetness. "You're good with this, Maddie?" he said, one final acknowledgment of the fissure that'd opened between us.

I never wanted us to be at odds like that again. I hummed

encouragingly, and he pressed one more kiss to my back before rubbing his cock over my slit. Then he pushed right in.

There was nothing quite like the sensation of taking two men into me at the same time. Logan was rocking into my mouth, his breath coming short, and Beckett groaned as he sank all the way into my pussy. My channel stretched to encompass him with a heady rush of pleasure.

"Tug on her hair," Beckett suggested in a rough voice.

Logan grunted and wound his fingers through several strands. He applied pressure at a rhythm that matched the bobbing of my mouth and Beckett's quickening strokes inside me. Little sparks of sensation lit up across my scalp, only heightening the bliss of the moment.

"Fuck her hard," Logan said to Beckett, his voice breaking over a few of the words. "That's how she likes it."

To my immense delight, Beckett didn't hesitate to obey. He thrust deeper and faster at the same time, filling me so well that I panted around Logan's erection before sucking harder in turn. The wave of pleasure rising inside me surged higher with each stroke.

Beckett leaned over my back and tucked his hand around me to finger my clit. My moan reverberated over Logan's cock, and his hips jerked.

"I'm going to come," he rasped, tensing as if to pull back, but I clutched his thigh to hold him in place. With a groan, he spilled himself into my mouth. I swallowed until every drop of his salty release had coursed down my throat.

Beckett pounded into me harder still, and my lips popped from around Logan's cock with a cry. More gasps spilled out of me as he plunged into me again and again, circling my clit at the same time, sending me spiraling so high—

I exploded with a shudder, my channel clamping around his shaft. My face dropped into the bedspread as I keened my release.

Beckett swore under his breath and followed me with one final thrust.

He slumped over me with a happy sigh and then rolled us onto our sides so I faced Logan. My stepbrother sprawled out next to me and slipped his arm around my waist, not appearing to care if he brushed against the other man.

A different sort of joy bloomed in my chest and spread through every limb. We'd come so far to make it to this moment where these two men could accept each other and shower me with affection side by side, and no one could take that away from us.

CHAPTER 18

Slade

Striding out of the campus gym, I was dogged by an ache in my chest that wouldn't fade. I'd pushed myself hard enough in my workout that I'd needed to sit in the locker room for ten minutes recovering before I could confidently make it in and out of the showers with my prosthetic off, but despite wearing myself ragged, I hadn't managed to burn away as much of my emotions as I'd hoped.

The urge to go dancing itched at me. I hadn't hit the clubs in weeks, and I missed letting loose to the beats in an anonymous mass of people.

But it wasn't just me and a bunch of strangers on my favorite dance floor anymore. It was me, the dance floor, and Beckett. Knowing he owned the club, I couldn't see it the same way. It was his place, not mine. But at the same time, some part of me balked at the idea of being forced to go someplace else.

Heading along the paths across campus, I managed to keep my strides steady even though my muscles were wobbly from the workout. My gaze automatically scanned the other people passing by for anyone who looked suspicious, but how would I know anyway?

A painfully familiar voice called out from behind me. "Slade! Wait up."

I turned to see Maddie jogging over across the lawn, her backpack dangling from one shoulder. With her pale hair windblown and a flush of exertion turning her cheeks rosy, she was an even prettier sight than usual.

My spirits should have lifted, but instead they sank. A sense of wariness swept over me, more to do with myself than her.

She was one more reminder of all the ways I'd fallen short.

I couldn't take my frustration out on her, though. I plastered a smile onto my face and fell into step with her when she caught up with me. Her open smile in return sent a jab of guilt through my stomach.

"What have you been up to?" she asked, tucking her hand around my elbow as easy as anything.

God, I wanted her. Why did this have to be so hard?

I summoned my usual breezy tone. "Oh, you know, classes, working out, the usual."

"Off to anyplace interesting now?"

"I figured I'd grab dinner at the pub by the fine arts building. You know those creative types, they've got good taste in food too."

She laughed and squeezed my arm. "Would you like some company? I barely even had lunch—I could definitely go for a good burger."

Hell, I wanted her around me every moment of every day. But I had to be realistic. And there was no point in indulging my whims right now—I was in too shitty a mood for her to miss it if she spent much more time with me. If she hadn't *already* picked up on it.

I groped for an excuse. "I actually have some reading for one of my classes that I need to get done while I'm eating. But I'll see you back at the apartment later."

Maddie slowed, pulling me to a stop with her. My heart plummeted even farther as I took in her expression, her eyes clouded, her forehead furrowing. She studied me through several uncomfortable thumps of my heart.

"Are you avoiding me?" she said finally, her voice rough. "It's been feeling kind of like you've been pulling back from the other guys and from me lately. Is something wrong?"

I forced a chuckle and made a dismissive wave of my hand. "Of course not. I do have to get serious about my schoolwork every now and then to make sure they don't kick me out of this place. I love having you with me, but I won't be able to concentrate with those lips so close, Piccolina."

I reached out and brushed my finger over her mouth, provoking a twitch of a smile.

"I can see how hard you're *trying* to be convincing, Slade," she said.

Fuck. "Convincing? I'm just speaking the truth."

She grasped my hand and tugged me away from the path, over to the shelter of a tree where we were away from the students passing by. Her gaze stayed fixed on my face. "Tell me what's going on."

I couldn't. I couldn't explain it all to her. Not until I could come to terms with my feelings myself. "It's really nothing," I told her. "Nothing worth talking about."

"You know, you never have to talk to me if you don't want to. I'm not going to force you to stick around, but I don't want you to pretend either. You should never feel like you need to fake anything with me."

Her words cracked something within me. Faking. That was all I'd been doing since starting the Vigil with the guys. Since the moment we began calling ourselves the Vigilante Kings, I'd been pretending. I was a total imposter in the job that I'd been doing for all these years.

"What's the point in sticking around?" I asked, shaking my head. "I want to be there for you and the guys, sure. But I used to feel like I actually contributed, and now that Beckett's in the mix, it's obvious that I'm just there on the sidelines. I was always the least useful one even when it was just the three of us. So, I'm dead weight. And that's fine. But why should you bother sticking around with *me* when you've got three other great guys?"

Maddie stared at me, confusion etched across her face. "Do you really feel that way?"

My head drooped. "I wasn't planning on telling you. I don't want to get *you* down about it. It is what it is."

"Hey." She grasped my hand tighter until I looked up and met her eyes. "Let's start with the most important thing. You're not dead weight. Not to me, not to the Vigil. Not to anybody. I don't think any of us could function properly without you, Slade."

When I made a scoffing sound, she frowned. "Is it the sharing that's bothering you? Is it too much—and you're trying to let me down easy or something?"

I sputtered for a second before I found my words. "Maddie, the last thing I'd want is to let go of you. All I *think* about is you, and that's the problem. It's going to be so hard if you leave, so it's easier if I put the distance there first."

The furrow in her forehead deepened. "Why would you think that it's better to assume things won't work out? What if I *don't* leave? Are you so sure that I will?"

I made a vague gesture with my hand, the ache expanding through my chest so intensely it was suffocating. "It just… doesn't make sense for you to stay."

Maddie let out a huff. "You just talked about how much you want me. Why can't you believe that I'd want you just as much—just as much as the other guys? You make me laugh; you taught me how to dance. You compliment me in a million different languages. You're there for the people you care about no matter what. Why *wouldn't* I want to be with you?"

A prickling sensation rose up through my gut. I knew the answer to that question instinctively, but I didn't want to say it. I didn't talk about that shit with anyone. It shouldn't affect anyone but me.

I was supposed to be the one making her laugh and tossing compliments at her, not the one dragging her down with the crap I kept buried deep inside.

"Slade," she said softly, searching my gaze. "Please talk to me. I want to understand where this is coming from."

My throat constricted. How could I deny her when she was practically begging me? It would be worse to leave her wondering, thinking maybe she'd done something wrong, wouldn't it?

My voice came out uncomfortably gruff. "My own *mother* thought I was too defective to be around. She couldn't stand to keep taking care of me—she left my dad, the love of her life, because of it."

Maddie's eyes widened. "You don't really think that's why, do you?"

"People don't stay," I said with a rasp. "I can entertain them and make them happy for a little while now because I work my ass off at it, but in the end… if even the person who's *most* supposed to be there can't be bothered…"

"Slade." Maddie wrapped me in a hug so sudden I stiffened up before I registered what she was doing. My arms came around her of their own accord, my eyes burning as I tipped my head next to hers. The sweet smell of her hair filled my nose.

"No offense," she murmured, her breath tickling my neck warmly, "but your mom was a total jerk. No one deserves to be abandoned by a parent. But she probably left for reasons that had nothing to do with your leg. And if your birth defect *did* have anything to do with it, then she's an even bigger jerk."

A strangled sort of laugh tumbled out of me. "I'd pay good money to find her just so I could watch you tell her off like that."

Maddie hummed dismissively and squeezed me tighter. "She's not important anymore. She made her choices, jerky as they were, and now she's gone. You're here, and you're amazing. I love you exactly the way you are. I love your sense of humor and how much energy you always bring to every conversation, I love the fact that you don't let your leg slow you down and even manage to turn it into something fun with your crazy stories."

As my mind whirled with her declaration, she pulled back just far enough to hold my gaze again. "I love *you*, Slade. Everything you are."

It was impossible not to believe her when she said the words so emphatically, her blue eyes piercing into mine as if they were going to claim my soul. I'd have let her if I could offer it up.

I blinked hard, grappling with the wave of emotion that was rushing through me, a lot more of it good than it'd been before but still a mess. My voice came out choked. "I love you too."

I tugged her back to me, winding my fingers in her soft hair, and pressed my mouth to hers as if I could brand the truth of that statement into her. She kissed me back just as hard. The impact of what we'd just said reverberated through me, and all my despondency fell away in its wake. Maddie's touch and the memory of her words ringing through my head banished the gnawing doubts.

She saw someone amazing in me, and I was going to be that amazing guy with every particle of my being.

When we finally eased apart, our breaths a little ragged, Maddie grinned at me. At the sparkle in her blue eyes, I found my usual optimism came to me without any hesitation at all.

I tweaked one of her blond locks and grinned right back at her. "What do you say we go and get that dinner we both need?"

CHAPTER 19

Madelyn

I leaned back in my chair and massaged my temples, restraining a groan. I'd been stuffing facts about genetics into my head for the past few hours in preparation for next week's exam, and my brain felt ready to explode.

Before I could really consider taking a break, though, my ringtone pealed from my purse. I dug it out. At the sight of Beckett's name on the screen, I yanked it to my ear.

"Hey," I said. "What's up?"

"Hey, Maddie. I just wanted to give you a heads up that I've got some things I'd like to send your way."

"What kind of things?"

He paused. "Is everything all right? You sound exhausted."

I let out a grunt of frustration. "Just studying woes. I could use a change of pace."

"Well, I can certainly give you that." He chuckled, but it sounded a bit strained. "My people have dug up a bunch of files related to both the warehouse and the seafood market. I haven't spotted anything useful in them, but I thought it'd be good to have you give them a glance too since you'd have a better idea how anything might connect to your dad."

I sat up a little straighter. "Of course. I'll go through them right away."

"Thanks, Maddie. I know if there's anything in there, you'll find it."

His voice had gone distant, as if his mind had already moved on to other considerations. I frowned. "Is everything okay with *you*? You seem kind of distracted."

Beckett paused again and then allowed himself a deep sigh. "It's nothing to do with the case or your dad—nothing for you to worry about. I've just had an issue within the family business come up out of left field. It appears that rumors have been going around that I've been off my game lately, not focused on the work or committed to overseeing our people."

I couldn't hold back a scoffing noise. "They have to know that's not really true."

"I'm not sure. A few of my employees have abandoned ship. Others might be on the fence. I'm about to address a bunch of my direct reports at a meeting to hopefully put an end to the unrest."

Why would the people under him believe he was anything less than the totally dedicated man I'd always observed him to be? "I just don't understand—" I started, and then the answer clicked in my head.

My throat tightened. "Oh. It's because of me, isn't it? All the stuff to do with the investigation and protecting me."

Beckett's voice firmed. "Maddie—there've definitely been some questions about some of the tasks I've set people on, but it isn't your fault. They need to trust me to handle my personal concerns and aspects of our business that they're not privy to at my discretion. I'm going to set them straight."

My stomach twisted. I didn't love what Beckett did for a living, but I knew how much it meant to him—and how important it was in the grand scheme of things that he *kept* doing it rather than someone else pushing their way into his spot. If he lost his standing with his underlings because he'd tried to help me…

"What if I came and helped you set them straight?" I blurted out before I could rethink the impulse.

"What?" Beckett said with obvious surprise.

"Let me come with you. If they already know you're dating someone, they might as well see who I am and hear right from my mouth what the real situation is."

He hesitated. "I don't know if that's the best idea."

"Why? You don't think they'd outright *attack* me if I'm there with you, do you?"

A chill shivered over my skin, but Beckett immediately answered. "No, definitely not. They aren't animals. But you know what kind of work I'm involved in. They aren't your typical office workers either—not most of them, anyway. They might make some harsh comments. They won't necessarily be polite."

A nervous laugh tumbled out of me. "I think I can handle some rudeness. It'll be a step up from psycho murderers threatening my family. Anyway, I'd like to see you at work. It'll help me totally come to terms with who you are and why."

Maybe it was the last part that convinced him. "All right. If you insist. Can you get to the coffee shop just past the north entrance to the university in fifteen minutes? I'll pick you up around back on my way over to the meeting."

I stood up, already reaching for my purse. "No problem at all."

I hustled down the stairs and out into the warm spring air. The lingering winter chill had completely faded, and I was starting to taste hints of summer on the breeze. I might have enjoyed it if my heart hadn't been thumping in anticipation of the meeting I was about to attend. What had I gotten myself into?

Beckett would be right beside me the whole time. He wouldn't have agreed to let me join him if he'd thought I'd be in any actual danger.

I'd only partly reassured myself when my phone rang again. I pulled it out of my purse as I hurried around the fitness center and saw it was Summer calling this time.

My first instinct was to ignore the call and avoid another awkward conversation with her. But the idea of treating my bestie that way made me wince inwardly.

I forced myself to answer. "Hey, Summer! How's it going?"

"Not great, Madds," Summer retorted in a dry tone that wasn't as spirited as usual. "My best friend's been icing me out of her life."

I winced outwardly that time. "I swear it isn't like that—"

"But it is, Maddie. I'm tired of the excuses and the vague explanations. You're obviously hiding something from me, something bad. I want you to tell me what's going on. We've always been honest with each other. You know you can count on me, no matter what's wrong. Don't shut me out."

My stomach knotted up. I didn't know what to say to her. "I'm telling you as much as I can," I said apologetically. "You have to believe me that it's better if you don't know more about what's going on right now. *I* don't even know exactly what's wrong."

Summer snorted. "Bullshit. You know a hell of a lot more than you've been telling me."

"I'm still sorting it all out."

"Then sort it out with *me*," Summer pleaded, so emphatically that tears pricked at my eyes. "I don't care how big or how stupid it is. I just need to know that you're okay—or that I'm helping you if you're not. Please."

Summer wasn't normally one to beg. My throat ached with the urge to spill the details about our investigation after all. But an image of Mom right after the car accident flashed through my mind —her body all bruised and broken in the hospital bed. Nausea swept through me.

"I'm sorry," I choked out. "I'll tell you everything when I can— I promised you that, and I mean it. But I've got to go now. I really am sorry."

I hung up without giving her a chance to argue more and turned off the phone. Guilt sat like a boulder in my gut, but there was nothing I could do about it. I'd have felt ten times as guilty if I'd dragged her into this mess and she got hurt.

Within a minute of my ambling behind the coffee shop, Beckett's familiar sedan pulled up. I hopped inside as quickly as possible and buckled my seatbelt as he took off again. When I glanced over at him, he shot me a smile, but it was tight, and his eyes were dark with obvious worry.

"You've never had anything like this happen before, have you?" I said. "Your people doubting you?"

How could he have when I found it so hard to imagine anyone doubting him even in the current situation. He'd always seemed like an impervious force.

Beckett shrugged. "The kind of career I have isn't meant to be easy or conflict-free. I'll deal with it. I just want you in the crossfire as little as possible."

I set my hand on his arm. "Hey. You've pulled out all the stops to protect me. I want to be able to do the same for you in whatever small ways I can. If we're together, then it isn't going to be one-sided."

The smile he aimed at me then was softer around the edges. "Duly noted. And thank you."

When he pulled up to the curb, I realized he was parking off to the side of the office building where we'd had our brief picnic lunch the other day, the one where he was setting up his pro bono clinic. He came around the side of the car as I got out and tucked his hand around my elbow. "Stay with me, all right?"

"Nowhere else I'd want to be."

We strode to the building together and ducked in through a side door. Beckett led me down a hall toward an open doorway. Muttering voices carried from inside.

We stepped into a room that must have been one of the unclaimed office spaces, empty of furniture and cubicles, just open space with a high ceiling. But that space was crowded with people.

There had to be at least fifty of them milling around the room. Several were dressed similarly to Beckett's usual business casual style in slacks and button-up shirts, as if they might work in this office once it was set up. The others, though, clearly came from other lines of work. I spotted multiple tattoos and glints of nose, lip, and eyebrow piercings, along with a rainbow of different hair colors, many clearly dyed. Leather jackets, faded tees, and scuffed jeans were more typical fashion choices for that part of the crowd.

It wasn't as if I'd never seen people with vivid hair dye and interesting piercings before. Hell, there were students like that in all of my college classes. But the less professional-looking employees who'd turned up for this meeting radiated the sort of menace that I'd never felt from any of my peers. Their postures and expressions gave off an aura of toughness and hostility.

My muscles tensed instinctively with apprehension. But next to me, Beckett had composed his face into calm confidence. He circumnavigated the crowd with me at his side like a king ready to address his subjects. There was no denying he was a natural leader.

I took his lead and kept my head high. I wouldn't let my nervousness show. I trusted him to keep me safe, and I had to prove that to them, or I couldn't ask *them* to trust him to look after them too.

Skeptical gazes raked over my body. Someone let out a mocking whistle, and a couple of cat calls echoed off the high ceiling. Beckett ignored them, so I did as well.

All that mattered was that these people were the ones Beckett could normally count on. They *wanted* to stand with him, to believe in him, just like I did. Which meant we had one important thing in common no matter how many other divides lay between us.

There was a small, raised platform at the far end of the room, about half a foot off the ground. Beckett stepped onto it and guided me up with him. Then he turned to face his people.

It said something about how much respect they still had for him that the muttering trailed off within a few seconds of him casting his gaze over the crowd. Everyone from the office workers to the toughs fixed their gazes on him and waited in silence to hear what he'd say first.

"Thank you for coming to speak with me today," Beckett said in a steady, assured voice. "I know there've been rumors buzzing around about my conduct recently, and I felt it was important to set the record straight and answer any questions you might have. First off, I can assure you that I'm fully on top of all things related to our business. My focus hasn't faltered, and I'm sure if you think about it, you won't be able to find any instances where important matters were neglected."

A hesitant murmur rippled through the crowd, sounding more like agreement than argument. That was a good start. My spirits started to lift.

"I *have* made some new social connections," Beckett went on, touching my elbow again. "But they haven't interfered with my ability to oversee everything we're working toward, and I hope none of you would fault me for having a life."

The corner of his lips quirked upward, a wry note entering his voice, and several people throughout the room chuckled. But others narrowed their eyes at me.

"Just how much time *are* you spending on your side-piece slut instead of on keeping things running smoothly?" someone demanded from the back of the crowd.

My nerves twitched, but I held myself still. Beside me, Beckett's expression tightened. I could tell from the flash in his eyes that he was about to speak in my defense, probably with anger, and I doubted that would reassure the people here who needed it most.

As much as I appreciated his protectiveness, I jumped in before he could speak. "Since you've obviously been misinformed, let me give you a few facts. Beckett and I have only gone on a few dates in the past month, and that's the only time he's dedicated to me. Even in the short times he has been able to spend with me, I know his business has never been far from his mind. He's cut dates short because he had meetings and other concerns to take care of."

My heart was racing now. A droplet of sweat rolled down my neck under my hair as I took in the skeptical gazes evaluating me. But I met those gazes without flinching.

I'd gone up against gangsters and thugs before. I wasn't going to let these people intimidate me.

"That's not all we've been hearing about," someone else hollered from the crowd. "Nice try, little girl."

I glowered in their general direction. "Any time Beckett has spent on matters other than business recently has been to tackle someone who's been threatening both me and the business you seem so concerned about him taking care of. He's working to protect all of your interests and his own as well as mine."

"For now," a woman grumbled.

I cut my gaze in her direction, my pulse still wobbly but my stance increasingly steady. "Frankly, I've never met anyone more committed to his work than the man beside me, and I wouldn't want him to slack off on it. You don't have to worry about me distracting him. And if you don't already know that he gives this business and the people working with him his all, then I don't think *you've* been paying enough attention."

Someone made a noise of protest, but Beckett intervened before they got any further than that. His hands were clenched but loosely, and his eyes shone for a moment as he looked at me. Then he turned to his employees.

"As you should be able to see, I have nothing to hide. The real distraction here are these rumors, which are purposefully designed to unsettle you. They're absolutely untrue. Someone is trying to undermine my leadership. But you know me and what I stand for. I've never let you down, and I don't intend to start."

A more animated murmur followed that declaration. The idea that their leader might be under attack seemed to rile up his underlings even though some had moments ago been criticizing him.

Beckett went on, motioning to the crowd. "We're all dedicated to keeping this empire working as it should. You can count on me, and I'd better be able to count on you. Go and find out who's stirring up trouble against the Storm, and let's deal with them together."

Voices rose in approval while several of the underlings ducked their heads with shamed grimaces. At Beckett's wave, they all hustled toward the door as if eager to prove themselves to their leader. Relief trickled through my chest, but a deeper tension stopped it from filling me.

I turned to Beckett as the last of his people slipped past the doorway. "Do you really think someone's still out to displace you? That someone from the outside started the rumors on purpose? I thought Doom's Seed and his lieutenant were backing off."

Beckett swiped his hand across his mouth. His shoulders had relaxed a little with the end of the meeting, but at my question, he only looked weary.

"That's what Doom's Seed promised, but I'm becoming increasingly sure he was lying. This has to be Lindell sowing doubts about me, and he couldn't do it now without his boss knowing about it."

"Why?" I had to ask.

Beckett was silent for a long moment. "There's only one logical reason I can think of. Doom's Seed is planning on making a grab for the Storm's territory here. For *my* territory. And soon."

CHAPTER 20

Madelyn

My eyes were starting to glaze over. I dragged them away from my laptop's screen, rubbed them, and gazed blearily across the main campus library where I'd been sitting for the past couple of hours. Beckett had sent me a lot of files yesterday, but so far nothing I'd seen in them seemed at all connected to my dad.

I wasn't alone in my search. Logan, Slade, and Dexter were all sitting amid the rows of computers at the other end of the first floor, searching the digitized database of old newspaper and magazine articles with local news that might give us some clue about whichever of Doom's Seed's illegal businesses Dad had gotten wrapped up in.

So far they hadn't turned up anything either, as far as I knew. Logan had been leaving his computer periodically and coming around to see how I was doing, as if I were straining anything other than my eyes sitting here in this upholstered chair. But there'd been something so intense in his eyes and his voice that I hadn't hassled him about his concern, just reassured him. Each time, he'd lingered for several more seconds before seeming to tear himself away.

So it wasn't a surprise to see him ambling over again now. He nodded toward my computer. "Still nothing?"

"Yeah," I said, and restrained a yawn. It wasn't even noon yet, but I hadn't been sleeping all that well these days. "I don't think I can stand to stare at this screen any more. Maybe I'll take a little walk around." I shut my laptop.

Logan's attention homed in on me again, so penetrating it made my skin tingle. "I could use that too. Come with me?" He extended his hand.

Why not? I tucked my computer under my arm and let him tug me out of my chair. "Where are we going?"

"Not far."

He kept his hand around mine and led me along the wall to one of the study rooms that lined it. This door didn't have a reserved sign on it.

Logan opened it with an air of purpose, escorted me inside, and switched the sign over to reserved. As the door thumped shut, he clicked over the lock, lifted the laptop from me to toss it onto the meeting table behind him, and pushed me up against the door.

His hands fell to my hips, pinning me in place. His gaze pinned me too, staring down at me as if he were memorizing my face, in awe of every angle. A heady tingle raced down my back at his passionate examination, his musky scent winding around me with his closeness.

"What are you doing?" I asked, my voice coming out breathless.

He bent so his forehead rested against mine. "I can't get enough of you, you know. The curve of your lips." He brushed a finger across them, provoking more tingles. "Your cute little nose." He tapped it. "This hair. It's so soft. And the way you react when I play with it…"

He twirled a few strands around his fingers and gave them a light tug. I couldn't stop my eyelids from fluttering at the sparks that shot through my scalp. Heat was pooling between my thighs.

Logan drew my head back farther, exposing my neck. He dropped his head and pressed a trail of kisses along my throat. I quivered against him, a gasp tumbling out of me.

"I was thinking," he muttered, pulling his lips away as if it was an effort to do so. He left his hand in my hair, but he released the tension there, allowing me to look up at him. "It hasn't been just the two of us since we cleared the air. Since that night two years ago, I haven't been with you the way I wanted to, and even then…"

He paused, shaking his head, regret etched in his features. "It wasn't how I wanted it to go. Not our first time. Not *any* time."

"I know," I said, an ache forming in my chest. I believed him, now more than ever.

He stroked his fingers over my hair, meeting my eyes again. "I don't mind that you're with the other guys too. I've made my peace with that—and honestly it's fucking *hot* watching how good we can make you feel when we're working together. But I want a little bit of you all to myself."

"Of course," I said quietly, curling my fingers into the front of his shirt. "You've got me. There'll always be pieces that are special to just the two of us."

"I want this too. I want what our first time should have been. Things are getting so dangerous, and I don't want to wait any longer. I love you. And it's not going to feel right until I've written over all that crap from the past."

My heart swelled at his admission. He loved me. Logan Brooks *loved* me.

Before the answering words that'd been true for longer than I could say spilled from my mouth, he claimed my lips again. His tongue flicked along my bottom lip, making me whimper. He molded his body against mine, pressing me into the door with his massive muscular frame.

The feel of him set me on fire. My nipples pebbled inside my bra without any further contact. I was pretty sure my panties had liquified. I kissed him back with everything I had in me, wrapping my arms around his shoulders and tugging him closer still.

Logan kissed me again and again until my lips felt swollen. He nipped them and moved to my jaw. I ran my fingers over his short-cropped hair, and he groaned.

"I always thought you were amazing," he murmured against my skin. "Seeing you stand up for people the way you did in high school, how you never let anyone intimidate you." He shook his head in bemusement, his mouth grazing my neck. "It was so fucking hard staying just friendly after my dad and your mom started dating. I didn't want to make things awkward, but you were right there, all the time, beautiful and bold and smart. I thought I was going to go crazy keeping my hands off of you."

I shivered in his embrace with the thrill his words sent through me. I couldn't hold back my own confession. "I started falling for you all the way back in junior high." My voice hitched when he nipped the crook of my shoulder. "*You* were always so cool and confident—you stood up for me back then, remember? But you always seemed out of reach."

Logan let out a scoffing sound, pulling back to meet my eyes. "Me, better than you? No fucking way. If anything, you're out of *my* league."

The corners of my mouth twitched. "Maybe we can just agree that we're very happy we finally made it to this moment."

"Hell, yes."

Without warning, Logan lifted me up and spun me toward the narrow couch along the study room's side wall. He laid me down on the cushions and braced himself over me with his hips resting against mine. The bulge between his thighs aligned with my core, and with just the slightest squirm I was pretty sure I'd be the one going crazy soon.

There was no denying where we were headed. I wanted to say one thing before I got totally swept up in the collision of our bodies.

I reached up and trailed my fingers down the side of Logan's face, gazing up into his eyes. "I love you too. So much. That's why I couldn't give up on you."

His mouth tightened. "I wish you hadn't needed to consider giving up, but I'm so fucking grateful you keep believing in me, Maddie."

I smiled. "Totally worth it."

Then I dragged him down to me, bringing our bodies flush together and pressing my lips against his. He met me without hesitation. His mouth parted against mine, a flick of his tongue setting my lips tingling again. I could only close my eyes and hang on for the ride.

Logan pulled away to lift my shirt up over my bra, exposing my breasts. He eased down the cups and rolled his thumb over one nipple before sucking it into his mouth. I swallowed a moan, distantly aware of the library activity on the other side of this room's door.

His other hand slid between us to the aching spot between my legs. He yanked open the fly of my jeans and tucked his fingers right inside my panties. When the tips brushed over my clit, I gasped at the jolt of bliss.

"How do you want me to fuck you, Maddie?" he murmured, stroking me as I started to rock into his touch.

"I don't care," I whispered. "I just want you."

"Fuck. I'm going to make you feel so good. Like no other time could possibly matter. You won't be able to remember anything but this."

My breath shuddered out of me, and then he was yanking my jeans and panties right off. Voices filtered through the wall from the library, and I bit my lip to try to hold back another moan.

Libraries were really not the best place for this kind of encounter, and yet knowing how close we were to being caught somehow made it twice as hot. As I'd found out with Slade to impressive effect weeks ago.

Logan tugged his jeans and boxers down too. His cock sprang free, thick and corded, so hard I ached even more just looking at it.

But he wasn't rushing things. He cupped his hand around my cunt again and dipped a finger right inside me.

"I'm going to take you so high," he promised, pulsing his hand as he added a second finger. I gasped as he swiveled them in a motion that had me bucking into his hand. "That's right. Ride my fingers, baby."

He fucked me with his hand until I was teetering on the edge, waves of pleasure washing over me. My teeth were digging a hole in my lip from holding back my eager noises. When one whimper slipped out anyway, Logan's breath hitched.

"I want to bury myself so deep inside of you that you won't forget this for years to come. God, I'm never letting you go."

He pumped his fingers inside me a few more times and then grabbed a condom from his pocket. What felt like an instant later, he'd rolled it over himself and was plunging into me.

He filled me so well I couldn't restrain my next moan. Logan clamped his mouth down over mine, swallowing the sound with a kiss.

Our bodies smacked together, both of us moving frantically as if we couldn't get close enough. Logan met my eyes, holding my gaze even as his hazed with pleasure. "Love you," he murmured again. "So fucking much."

"I love you too," I whispered back.

I gripped his shoulder and hugged him to me. He returned the embrace even though it momentarily slowed his thrusts. Then he adjusted our position, lifting my ass off the sofa, and drove into me even deeper than before.

A thready cry burst from my lips. I clamped them shut and clutched him tightly. He pounded into me again and again and then I was bursting apart with a white-hot blaze that really did feel as if it was searing away all the pain that had ever existed between us.

Logan groaned softly at the same time. His hips jerked as he followed me over the edge, both of us crashing into the final surge of ecstasy together.

Logan sagged over me but didn't let too much of his weight bear down. He pressed a kiss to my temple and then looked at me with so much tenderness my pulse stuttered.

"I'm never pushing you away again," he said like a vow. "Acting like a prick didn't keep you out of danger anyway, so I can admit it was an idiotic move."

"You were trying to scare me away from the danger, but I don't scare easily," I said with a breathless laugh, and halted. Several thoughts collided in my head with that statement, setting off a spark of inspiration.

I nudged Logan off me so I could sit up and grab my jeans. "I need my computer. I think I might have figured it out."

Logan raised his eyes with a chuckle. "I didn't expect the experience to be *quite* that enlightening."

I swatted his arm. "I'm serious. You want me out of danger—let's get this figured out."

"Not going to argue with you there."

He did insist on stealing one more kiss before snatching my laptop off the table where he'd left it. I flipped it open and hastily clicked through to a set of photographs Beckett had sent me from the seafood market.

Logan sat next to me on the sofa, peering at the screen alongside me. "What are we looking for?"

I flicked through several photos before my heart leapt. I stopped and jabbed my finger at the screen. "Those."

The photo showed one of the storerooms where the market received deliveries. It was stacked with coolers, a few of which were marked with the word WARNING and a picture of a spiny-looking fish.

"What about them?" Logan asked. "Those would be for the rare fish that are poisonous or something, right? I think there are some that are legal. And any that aren't, they wouldn't be advertising it."

"Exactly," I said. "You'd assume they're for transporting toxic fish for restaurants and other special buyers. And no one would want to open those boxes unless they have permission because they wouldn't want to mess with something dangerous and risk getting hurt."

Logan's eyes widened. "I think I see where you're going with this."

"I need to tell Beckett so he can check it out right away. We don't know how much evidence they've already gotten rid of."

I dug my phone out of my purse and dialed the number as fast as I could. Beckett picked up on the second ring. "Maddie. Is everything okay?"

"I think it might be *good*, actually," I said. "I think I might have figured out a key part of the scheme."

His voice perked up immediately. "Seriously? Give me all the details."

I studied the photograph as I spoke. "The seafood market does at least a little business in poisonous fish. They're transported in containers that warn people away from messing with them."

"Oh, I already looked into that. The market has a license for things like lionfish and stonefish. There's nothing illegal about that aspect, and they wouldn't need to smuggle or hide them. From what Anthea said, your dad's symptoms don't look like any fish toxin anyway."

"That's not what I'm thinking," I said. "What if it's not always fish in those containers? What if Doom's Seed's people are moving their illegal merchandise in those specific coolers, knowing that no one who isn't approved will risk opening them and digging around inside? No one wants to get hurt."

Beckett sucked in a breath. "You're right. That would be a perfect disguise."

"We need to figure out all the places the market was shipping those supposed poisonous fish to. If any of those places isn't somewhere that should be dealing in actual fish, we've got a lead."

"This could be everything we need." He let out an exhilarated laugh. "Good job, Maddie. Hold on." His voice became muffled briefly as he passed on instructions, I assumed to computer-savvy employees he was working with right now. What had he been busy with when I'd called?

Beckett's voice became clearer again. "I've got some other things to handle, but I'll talk to you again as soon as we have— Shit."

At the dark tone of his last word, my body tensed up. "What's wrong?"

Beckett barked a couple of muffled instructions before answering me, sounding abruptly harried. "I was afraid of this. It looks like Doom's Seed or his lieutenant are making a more aggressive move on my territory—right now. I've got to go. You and the guys keep an eye out for trouble and be careful."

"Of course," I said, my throat constricting. Before I could ask if there was any way I could help, the line had already gone dead.

My gaze shot to Logan. "Doom's Seed is attacking Beckett's people. He's worried about us. Maybe we should go back to the apartment rather than staying here?" That smaller space with only one door and windows too high to easily reach felt much more secure than the wide-open library.

Logan frowned at my statement and jerked his head in a nod. We sprang to our feet and rushed out of the study room.

"I'll meet you guys by the front doors," I said to Logan, and he loped over to alert Slade and Dexter.

I shoved my computer into my backpack and hefted that over my shoulders, adjusting my purse as I did. My feet carried me across the carpeted floor as fast as I dared to walk without risking getting yelled at by one of the librarians.

I was just a few steps away from the doors when my gaze snagged on an unexpected figure just outside the doors. Was that… *Summer*?

I hadn't been planning on going all the way out of the building without the guys, but the sight of my best friend had me pushing past the doors onto the campus sidewalk.

It was her. "Summer?" I said in disbelief as she turned toward me. Her lips were pursed, and her eyes seemed somehow sad. And then Mom and Holand moved into view behind her.

What the hell was going on? My gaze jerked from them back to Summer. "What are you doing here?"

I started to take a step back toward the doors, but Summer caught my wrist. "We need to talk, Madds. I told you this was getting out of hand. I came all the way out here for a reason."

I shook my head. "You shouldn't have. You know I can't—"

I was so distracted by the figures in front of me that I didn't notice the form approaching from behind until arms slammed around my waist and chest.

Someone heaved me up, and another man bent to snatch my ankles. A hand clapped over my mouth before I could let out more than a squeak of protest.

Without a second's hesitation, my captors hauled me to a van parked next to the curb and carried me straight through the open back doors.

CHAPTER 21

Dexter

"Let's get moving," Logan barked, as quietly as a person could bark in consideration of the space we were in. I'd already grabbed my book bag from where it'd been sitting near my feet while I dug through articles on the computer. Slinging the strap over my shoulder, I hurried after him and Slade, just a step behind them.

"What's happening?" I asked. "Is Madelyn okay?" He hadn't filled us in on any of the details yet, just announced that something was going down and we needed to get home.

Logan nodded curtly. "She went ahead to the front doors. We'll catch up with her there. Something bad's going down with Beckett, and I guess he's not sure if it'll affect us too. She also figured out something about the case—but we can get into that after we're home and—"

Both he and Slade stopped in their tracks so abruptly that I stepped on the heel of Slade's shoe. I pushed myself backward with a hurried apology and glanced past them to see four police officers in full uniform marching through the library toward us. A librarian was scurrying along beside them.

I only had a second to wonder what the cops might be here about when the librarian caught sight of us and pointed a finger directly at us.

Logan cursed under his breath and spun around, Slade following suit. As one being, we dashed in the opposite direction even as one of the cops let out a shout. "You three—stay where you are!"

"Fucking Doom's Seed must have sicced them on us," Logan groused, veering around a row of bookcases to hide us briefly from view. "Who knows what trumped up charges his people invented to pin us with."

Slade let out a rough chuckle. "That prick is really getting on my nerves."

My heart sank. It could be even worse than they were implying. We'd done a hell of a lot of illegal things in the past few years, not least of which was *murder*. It'd be a little hard to prove that the few deaths on our hands had been in self-defense now.

How much did our enemies know about our past crimes? Was this just a distraction, or had they found a potential way to destroy us without having to do any of the dirty work themselves?

We all knew that if we let ourselves be caught, it might be game over. Prison time, or at the very least trapped in a holding cell for who knew how long. We couldn't let that happen, not when the same psychos who'd arranged this were gunning for Madelyn.

Oh, hell, where was Madelyn? Had the assholes sent someone else after her?

There wasn't time to check. The thump of running footsteps

carried from behind us. All we could think about was avoiding capture if we wanted to be around to protect Madelyn after this.

We hustled around the end of the aisle, and I spotted an exit sign farther down the wall up ahead, its glow dimmed.

"There!" I said, pointing, and pushed myself faster. My pulse was thudding so hard I could practically feel it in my feet as they pounded against the carpeted floor.

The sign was over a secluded stairwell with a plaque that said MAINTENANCE ONLY. We ignored that and pushed past the door. As it banged shut in our wake, we rushed down the stairs we found on the other side.

"Any idea where we're going, Dex?" Slade asked in a tone that wasn't demanding, only curious.

"Away from the cops. That seemed like the right direction."

Logan let out a huff of agreement. "We can figure out the rest later."

The stairwell ended at a basement level with another door. We shoved that open and came out into a dreary gray hallway that looked like it stretched forever into the distance.

"Let's get more of a head start on them," Logan said, propelling himself forward. "They'll probably figure out which way we headed before too long."

A sickly smell of industrial cleaner hung in the air, and pipes groaned somewhere in the distance. The florescent lights overhead flickered. Slade glanced up at them and grimaced. "Feels like a scene out of a horror movie."

"There have to be other exits," I said. "We just have to find one and get out."

Several other halls branched off from the one we were in. Logan took the first left and then a right at the next branch. The walls and floors looked identical with every turn. Through a couple of doors that stood ajar, I spotted dusty plastic storage bins and cardboard boxes.

"Seems like everything the university doesn't have a use for anymore is stashed down here," Logan said.

It definitely didn't look as if anyone had come by in quite a while, though the smell suggested that the janitorial staff had supplies down here too. The halls themselves appeared clean enough though eerie in atmosphere.

The sameness of the halls made it hard to keep track of our turns. I kept my ears pricked, but I couldn't make out any sounds of pursuit behind us. That didn't mean the cops weren't on their way, though.

"What do you think happened to Madelyn?" I asked.

Logan checked his phone and growled. "No signal down here, so no way to ask her—or let her know what happened to *us.* I hope we can get out of this fucking maze soon so we can find out. *She* hasn't been involved in anything major. The cops can't have anything real on her."

She had been with us at the warehouse where we'd ended up killing the two thugs in self-defense, though. And she'd come with us into more than one building where I'd picked the lock so we could enter. He couldn't know for sure they didn't have evidence of that.

A sense of gloom descended over me, making my stomach clench. The seemingly endless halls only added to my growing uneasiness. What if there *wasn't* another exit after all?

Another doubt crept up so insistently that I couldn't help saying it out loud. "Maybe we shouldn't have run. If they catch us now, we'll end up in even more trouble than if we'd talked to them and tried to address whatever they were concerned about. We had no idea what they actually wanted to talk to us about."

Logan shook his head. "No way. Everyone knows you don't talk to cops unless you have to. Especially when they look like they're ready to break out the handcuffs already. They'll grab at any reason to pin something on you so they can call the case closed."

"And we have no idea what they have on us—or think they have," Slade put in. "Given what this Doom's Seed psycho has pulled off already, I wouldn't put much of anything past him." He paused. "Of course, we're screwed no matter what if we can't find another way out of here without getting caught."

What would happen if we ended up confronting the cops down here? Did Logan have that gun he'd gotten from the chop shop on him? Would we end up in some kind of shoot-out—become cop-killers on top of everything else?

I could feel my thoughts spiraling into a panic, but I couldn't seem to rein them in. A shiver ran down my back as visions of sprawled, bloody bodies flashed through my mind. Like that first one—that night at the abandoned strip mall when I'd—

"Hey." Slade came around in front of me where I couldn't avoid looking at him, his voice softening. "I was just kidding around. I know we'll figure this out. And even if the situation gets worse, we're in this together, right?"

My breath hitched. I couldn't stop myself from saying, "We're only in this because of me."

Logan knit his brow. "What are you talking about, Dex? You didn't have any idea those cops were coming after us, did you?"

"No. But—but everything leading up to that. All the things they could arrest us for. All the things we did…" I pressed the heel of my hand to my forehead, but the pressure barely took the edge off the emotions whirling through me.

If this was a puzzle, then I knew exactly which piece made the key part of the picture. And I'd put it there. Two and a half years ago, that guy had lunged at us out of nowhere with a switchblade and stabbed Slade in the shoulder, and I'd sliced into him so automatically with the first rush of protective adrenaline. In just a couple of seconds, it'd been like he wasn't even human anymore, just a collection of fleshy parts that my mind narrowed down to its most vulnerable points.

What kind of person was I if I could reduce any human being to an object to be broken and destroyed?

"I'm pretty sure we were all there for all the things we did," Slade said, but a thread of worry wove through his joking tone.

I folded my arms over my chest. "It was me. The first time we went from guys just unraveling mysteries and tripping up the criminals to actually *murdering* someone. Maybe I didn't need to kill him. I put all that blood on our hands, and then nothing was too much. We just kept heading farther down that path."

Logan sucked in a breath. "Dex, man, you can't blame yourself for that. You were fucking amazing that night. If you hadn't jumped in there so fast, that asshole might have murdered *Slade*. We've all had to make the same call."

"But I started it. I set it all in motion."

"Dex," Slade said firmly. I could feel him peering into my eyes even though I couldn't handle the direct eye contact right now, my gaze fixed on his shirt collar. "It was going to happen sometime. Logan and I know that, one hundred percent. We were getting into more dangerous stuff already, more aggressive crimes, more hardened criminals… If it hadn't been then, it would have happened a little later anyway. I swear to God, it's not on you."

I'd never heard Slade Galvezo sound that serious. My eyes twitched upward to briefly meet his. He looked serious too, serious and solemn and like he'd have killed for *me* right now if he needed to, no questions asked.

"Have you really been thinking that way all this time?" Logan asked. "Like it's your fault that we've gotten so far off the straight and narrow?"

"Of course," I mumbled. It'd seemed obvious.

A ragged laugh spilled out of him. "I've always thought it was *my* fault. Pushing us to go farther and take on more intense problems. Digging into the stuff with Maddie's dad."

My gaze slid to him, my forehead furrowing. "Of course it isn't your fault."

Slade gave me a brief, light clap on the shoulder, careful not to let it linger. "And that's exactly what we're telling you, dude. It sounds just as ridiculous to us as Logan blaming himself." He raised an eyebrow at Logan. "For the record, I do also think your theory is ridiculous."

Logan gave him a baleful look. "Thanks so much for weighing in."

Their easy banter brought me back to earth. I inhaled slowly, and my nerves seemed to settle.

Could they be right? It wasn't really my fault but just a natural consequence of the general path we'd all agreed to go down?

I'd never seen it that way before, but maybe I hadn't let myself. I couldn't deny that it made a certain amount of sense, especially the way the other guys talked about it.

A soft glow washed through my chest, soothing parts of my spirit that I hadn't known were so bruised. It was okay. I'd protected my friend, saved his life. We were where we'd already been heading.

Trying out those thoughts, they felt okay. Maybe even right.

I glanced around the hallways again. We *had* been in much direr situations than this before, and I'd helped us get out of plenty of them. If I got my head on straight, I could handle this too. The path we took now was what really mattered.

Logan had called the halls a maze. A maze was a kind of puzzle. I should be the perfect person to crack its visual code.

"Let's keep going," I said. "I haven't been paying enough attention. I need to take a closer look at everything down here."

My friends started walking without question, trusting my process. That was the trust I'd earned from them over the past several years. We walked straight for a few minutes, then took another turn with me in the lead, then another.

My attention narrowed down to the small labels I hadn't given much thought to at first. They were meaningless at first glance, combinations of letters and numbers like L4 and P2, but every corner was marked with them.

And the pipes we'd heard humming... I cocked my head, absorbing the sound, and moved toward it. After another couple of turns, we came to a section of hall where a few thick pipes stretched along one side of the ceiling.

Studying them, a mental map of the university campus unfolded in my mind. I pointed to the pipes. "I think those lead to the library bathrooms. All the L labels are that way, and they must stand for Library. Which means that must be the western end of the building." I swiveled on my heel and motioned in the other direction. "So, this is east. And P must stand for something else. The PhysEd facilities are just east of the library, aren't they?"

Slade let out an awed whistle. "I have no sense of direction, but if you say it is, I believe it."

"The basements for some of the campus buildings are connected," I said with growing excitement. "Which means they must all have access points. Let's get back to the nearest P hall and see where we can go from there."

A bang of a door somewhere in the distance had us striding forward faster, trying to keep our footsteps as quiet as possible. We hurried down the first hall with a P label, and I scanned all the side halls we passed. Where had I noticed stairwells in the PhysEd building? To the left of the main entrance, and near the back, which relative to the library, would be right around...

I turned at another hall and spotted a door at the end of it.

Slade let out a near-silent whoop of approval and saluted me. "That's our Dex. Couldn't make it through any of this shit without you."

We hustled down the hall and were relieved to find the door opened no problem. It was a matter of seconds before we were stepping out in the humid air of a first-floor hall near the swimming pool. Logan smiled, now knowing exactly where we were —and how to get out of here—just as I did.

"We've got to get off campus," he said, and pulled out his phone. His smile fell away. "No texts from Maddie. If she's okay, she'd be wondering where we are."

He tapped in a quick message as we hurried to the front doors. I listened for the ping of a text in reply, but nothing came. My stomach knotted all over again.

We eased out of the PhysEd building and peeked around the corner toward the front of the library. A few students were walking in and out, but none of them were Madelyn. I couldn't make out her blond hair beyond the windows in the doors. And a police car was parked a few spaces down. We couldn't go back into the library without being seen.

Logan sucked a breath through his teeth with a hiss. He looked at his phone again, but the screen had remained blank.

We'd gotten to relative safety—but what the hell did we do now?

CHAPTER 22

Madelyn

I landed on my ass inside the back of the van with an audible *oof.* The doors banged shut, and I whirled around to find myself staring at my mom, Summer, and…

"Lee?" I snapped in disbelief, my gaze jerking from one of the guys who'd grabbed me to the other. "Eric?"

As Holland climbed into the front of the van and started the engine, the two guys made nearly identical sheepish expressions. I hadn't seen my cousins—sons of Mom's older brother—since Christmas, which was pretty much the only time I ever saw them since they'd gotten old enough to move out on their own several years ago.

"What the hell is going on here?" I demanded, my gaze veering from them to Mom.

"I'm so sorry, sweetie," Mom said in a cajoling voice, her eyes clouded with concern. "I didn't know what else to do. We've gotten so worried about you, and you wouldn't talk to me or Summer. Having a full intervention was a last resort."

Oh my God. I glared at Eric, the slightly older of the two guys. "And you thought dragging me off the street into the back of a van was a good idea?"

He held up his hands in surrender. "Aunt Lindsay gave a convincing story. We were just doing what she asked."

A growl escaped me. I looked to Summer next. "I can't believe you went along with this. I *told* you I could handle everything."

Before she could answer, my phone pinged with an incoming text. I reached to answer it, but Summer plucked it right out of my hand and shoved it into her back pocket.

"No way," she said. "You shouldn't be talking to anyone but us right now. Especially not Logan."

"What are you talking about? Logan hasn't done anything wrong."

Her lips pursed. "I know what you've said, Maddie, but it's also been obvious that something big is going on, something that's freaked you out, and he's mixed up in it somehow. It seems like he's gotten inside your head and dragged you into something dangerous. Just come clean about what's going on, and we'll figure out how to help you."

The van shifted with a turn, and I had to brace my hand against the wall to stop myself from sliding on the carpeted floor. My stomach was tying itself into knots.

Had the text been from the Vigil guys, wondering why I'd disappeared? Or from Beckett with another update about the escalation in his conflict with Doom's Seed? I had no idea what might be happening to any of the guys I cared about right now, and they'd start panicking if they couldn't get a hold of me.

I needed to get out of this situation.

"There's nothing to come clean about," I said in as firm a voice as I could muster. "Nothing's going on. I have class in half an hour —you're going to force me to mess up my education now? Why don't we stop this and I'll meet you for a regular dinner or something tonight?"

I'd thought that leaning on the education thing was the right call since Mom knew what my dream career meant to me, but her expression didn't budge. "We're doing this now. The sooner you start opening up, the sooner we can resolve this."

"Who knows if you'd even show up for dinner or anything else if we let you go," Summer muttered.

The words stung even though they were completely true. I'd tossed out that offering only to escape the intervention—I doubted I'd be any more ready to spill my guts tonight than I was at the moment. I gritted my teeth.

"You know, kidnapping is illegal," I told them. "You could get arrested for this."

Summer gave me her best "bitch please" look, which I guessed was fair since I was totally bluffing. I wouldn't have called the cops on her or Mom and Holland—Lee and Eric, I didn't have as many qualms about—and even if I would have, I didn't have anything to call them *with*. I was stuck.

"It doesn't matter how bad it is," she said. "You've got to fess up. That's the only way this is ending."

"This is ridiculous," I told her, and then my mouth stayed clamped shut.

The van jolted over a pothole, turned, and rumbled to a stop. Mom nodded to my cousins, who stood up. I pushed to my feet too and peered through the windows on the back doors.

We were parked outside the room at the end of a motel, a tarnished brass number 9 mounted on the yellow door.

I wrinkled my nose. "You're kidding me."

"We can do this in there or stay in the van," Mom said firmly.

I weighed my options and decided I'd rather take my chances in the motel room. There might be an emergency exit of some sort. I'd at least have more room to maneuver. Here in the back of the van, I was completely trapped.

"Fine."

My cousins marched me into the motel room with the others following behind. When Holand had closed the door and turned the deadbolt, Lee and Eric positioned themselves in front of it like bouncers. I glowered at them again and dropped onto the edge of the bed.

The comforter was a mottled grey, the carpet patchy navy. A faint smell of mildew hung in the air. Delightful. The yellow door was the only cheerful thing in this place.

"I still don't know what you want me to say," I insisted. "There's nothing to confess. I've been busy with school and extracurricular stuff, and I didn't want to stress you out by complaining. And I just haven't had much time to talk in general."

Summer snorted. "I've known you since elementary school, Madds. I can tell when you're lying. But I think this is the first time you've ever lied this blatantly to my face. You've been dodging the truth for weeks now."

Holand stepped up beside her, his expression so solemn that guilt started gnawing at my gut. "Maddie, you know your mother and I have always tried to give you and Logan plenty of freedom to live your lives. But if something's gone wrong for one or both of you—and it definitely seems like it has—we need to know. You're still our children."

I swallowed thickly. "What exactly do *you* think Logan's done?"

His mouth pulled with a grimace. "I don't know. I don't want to believe anything negative about him, but he's been so withdrawn for years now… It's hard not to wonder what secrets he might have been keeping."

"He has a right to secrets, doesn't he? We both do. We're grown-ups now; we don't need to share every detail of our lives with you."

Holand winced. "Of course you don't. But if Logan's gotten into some kind of trouble and mixed you up in it too, I want to know—so I can help both of you. That's all I want to do: help, however you need it."

Mom nodded emphatically and reached for my hand, wincing when I scooted away from her. "Refusing to talk to us only makes me more sure that whatever you've gotten into, it's very serious. Please, Maddie. Don't keep shutting us out like this."

My stomach clenched even tighter. They didn't understand. They didn't realize that there was *nothing* they could do to help. Having them separate from this mess and safer because of their distance helped me more than anything they could have offered if they'd known the truth.

But then, that *was* exactly the way Logan had thought about me—his reason for keeping me in the dark for so long. He hadn't believed I'd be able to help all that much, but I had. We'd gotten so much closer to unraveling the mystery because of what I knew.

In some ways, that was different. I'd known Dad so well, and I'd been with him when he'd died. No one else in the motel room with me could have had any idea about what he'd gotten mixed up in before his death except for Mom, and I already knew how far our enemies would go to hurt her.

Next time it might be fatal, the text I'd gotten after her accident had said.

But how could I get out of this intervention without dragging them all into the line of fire? The motel room had given me a little breathing room, but I was still just as stuck as I'd been in the van.

"You know how stubborn I can be, Maddie," Summer said,

folding her arms over her chest. "You're not winning this—other than I think talking to us will be better for you in the long run anyway. I don't care how crazy things are; I just want to know what's happened to my best friend."

The guilt I'd felt earlier expanded through my chest. It was with Summer where I'd screwed up the most. Mom would have accepted me being a little distant, because I hadn't talked to her *that* much to begin with, and Holand had put up with Logan's anti-social behavior for years. But I'd almost completely frozen out the friend who'd always been there for me. No matter what excuses I gave, that'd been unfair.

And it'd come back to bite me in the ass. If I'd opened up to her, she wouldn't have gotten so worried she'd compared stories with my mom. No intervention, no sitting here in this dank motel room wondering what fresh hell might be descending on my boyfriends. Maybe she'd have understood without pushing herself into harm's way on my behalf. She'd at least have realized why I couldn't simply walk away.

"I really think this was taking the situation to a huge extreme," I had to say. "Going this far… How am I supposed to trust you if you'd grab me and haul me off like this?"

A liquid shimmer entered Mom's eyes. "You need to trust that we're only doing this because of how much we care about you, Madelyn. Because it matters this much to us to make sure that you're okay—or that you'll be okay, at least."

I did know that. But I also knew that telling her and Holand about Dad's murder wouldn't just paint targets on their backs—it could destroy our chances of getting real answers too. They'd insist on going straight to the police with what we already knew, the police would interfere with the investigation the Vigil guys and Beckett were already immersed with, who knew what would happen to Beckett's family if the spotlight was turned on them…

No. Too much was at stake.

But I could take a different gamble. It might be the only chance I had. And I owed it to her.

I glanced at Summer and then at my mom. "Can I just chat with Summer for a little while? It's a lot of pressure, having you all hanging over me. It might be easier to hash things out one on one."

Mom hesitated, but hope had lit in her eyes. "I think that might be a good first step."

She looked at Holand, who nodded slowly. "We could go and pick up some lunch for everyone while you two talk," he suggested.

Mom wagged a finger at me. "But you're staying in this room until we're all clear on what you've been hiding from us." She beckoned to my cousins. "You two can wait outside the door. Make sure Madelyn doesn't try to leave."

Lee and Eric dipped their heads obediently. Eric shot me an apologetic grimace before they all headed out.

Summer flopped onto the bed a couple of feet from me and grimaced as she examined the comforter. "I'm not sure it's really safe to be making surface contact with anything in this place. Ugh." Her attention homed in on me. "So are you actually going to talk, or was that just an attempt at tricking your way out of this?"

My throat tightened. "I'm sorry, Summer. I really am. I know I've said that before, but I meant it all those times too."

She raised her chin. "Sorry doesn't matter much if you're just going to pull the same bullshit as before."

"No. I'm going to talk to you properly now. I probably should have before." I rubbed my forehead. "I'm still worried that you'll get dragged into the danger too, but… but I guess that's your choice to make, like it was for me. I'm just asking that you listen the whole way through before you make any decisions. I still feel like I need to keep Mom and Holand out of this."

Summer's expression was skeptical, but she motioned for me to go on. "I'm listening."

God, how did I even start? I groped for the right words. "You know my car got stolen a couple of months ago, and that's how I ended up talking to Logan again."

She snapped her fingers. "I *knew* he was involved in this."

I gave her a pointed look, and she closed her mouth with a zipping gesture.

"Yeah," I said, "but I doubt it's in any way you could have guessed. It turned out my car getting stolen wasn't random. It also turns out… you know how Logan and his friends have been investigating all those petty crimes on campus? They've gotten into more serious situations too. And a few years ago, they started finding evidence that my dad didn't really get sick—he was murdered. Poisoned somehow."

Summer's jaw dropped. "You're serious?"

I exhaled in a rush. "Yeah. It took me ages to be sure of it myself, but I've seen enough now that I know it's true. But the evidence we've turned up, it's not solid enough that we could take it to the police and expect them to investigate a crime that's not even recorded as a crime and that happened over a decade ago. We've been trying to find enough proof to get to that point, and… the people responsible have realized we've been investigating. They caused my mom's accident, among other things."

"Holy shit." Summer's eyes looked ready to pop out of her head.

"So that's why I've been so hesitant to tell any of you about it," I went on in a rush. "I didn't want them to target anyone else I care about. We've been laying as low as we can in the hopes that they'll think *we* aren't even investigating any more… It's gotten pretty complicated."

"This—this is huge." Summer shook her head. "You should

have told me, Maddie. You know I'd want to have your back no matter what."

I hung my head. "Like I said, I'm sorry. You have no idea how much I mean that. Logan made the same mistake with me, you know. He ghosted me because he was afraid if we got closer, I'd find out about the investigation, and he was trying to keep *me* safe."

Summer sputtered a laugh. "That makes a very weird kind of sense." She pinched the bridge of her nose. "Don't you think your mom should know too, at least? He was her husband."

"They've already left her injured, maybe even permanently. And you know she'd say we have to let the police handle it. I might end up on total lockdown if she knew I want to keep digging myself. But I can't let this go, Summer. I need to get justice for my dad. His murderers have been walking free for years… He didn't deserve what they did to him. And the guys and I might be the only people who can fix it, as much as it can be fixed."

"Okay. I get that. I still wish you'd told me sooner, but I guess this is better than you being hooked on meth or something." She sighed. "So, now what?"

I gave her a beseeching look. "So, now's your chance to really help me. We were *so* close to putting the pieces together. We'd just figured out one major clue when you guys grabbed me. But I can't see it through while I'm stuck here in this 'intervention.' I need to get out of here. This is going to be my best chance to prove Dad was murdered—maybe my last chance."

Her jaw tightened, and I thought she was going to argue more. But instead she pushed closer on the bed and wrapped her arms around me in a hug.

"You're always taking so much on your shoulders, Madds. You need to let other people carry some of the burden."

"I'm trying to do that now," I said quietly.

She groaned and gave me another squeeze before letting me go.

"All right. I'll help you take off. I don't think you should be putting yourself in all that danger… but I get why you feel you need to, and if I'm going to ask you to trust me, then I've got to trust you to make your own decisions too."

Relief flooded me. I grinned at her, momentarily lost for words. "Thank you," I managed finally.

She pointed a finger at me. "I do have a condition. No more keeping me in the dark. If it seems like you're in danger and hiding things from me again, I'm going to tell your mom everything. No second chances."

I couldn't even say that was unfair. "Absolutely. It'll be my fault if you feel you have to go that far. But hopefully this will all be resolved in a few days, and then I can tell Mom everything anyway."

"I'll keep my fingers crossed." She studied me for a moment. "Are you sure there isn't anything else I can do right now?"

"I swear I'd tell you if there was," I said. "And if something comes up that I know you could pitch in on, I'll tell you. Either way, I'll be keeping you in the loop."

"Okay. Let's do this, then." She dug into her pockets and handed me my phone and a car key. "That's for my Mazda—it's parked opposite the van. Please be careful with her. I want to hear from you within a few hours so I know where to pick her up. Now, to deal with your cousins…"

She rubbed her hands together, and a familiar gleam came into her eyes. I couldn't help smiling. This was the Summer I loved.

"Got it," she announced, and motioned to the door. "Stand back there. I'll get them to rush in, and you duck out while I'm distracting them."

I got into position behind where the door would open. Summer walked over to close the bathroom and then marched past me to yank the front door open.

"Oh my God!" she babbled. "You guys have got to help me! Maddie went and locked herself in the bathroom, and the sounds coming from in there—I don't know what she's doing, but it can't be good."

The panic in her voice must have convinced my cousins. They came barreling into the room after her, rushing to the bathroom.

I whipped past the door and sprinted across the parking lot. The gold Mazda unlocked with a beep. Diving into the driver's seat, I started the engine. Then, with a silent thank you to my bestie and any other powers that might be, I turned the car back toward the center of the city and hit the gas.

CHAPTER 23

Madelyn

The hole-in-the-wall cafe on the other side of town smelled of strong coffee beans with an undertone of stale sweat. I stared down at the coffee I'd received from the overly perky teen at the counter and debated whether or not I should actually drink it.

Slade chugged his without any apparent concern about the cleanliness or burning his tongue, and followed it with one of his cinnamon candies. Dexter was eying his mug with a trepidation that looked similar to what I felt.

Logan hadn't even bothered to order. He sat down at the rickety table near the front window, got up again, paced a couple of steps, and then forced himself back into his chair, looking like he wanted to march out there and drag Beckett to the meeting we'd managed to arrange after I'd called the guys.

After I'd gotten away from my mom and best friend's intervention. Which Slade wasn't finished heckling me about yet.

He shook his head at me with a teasing tsk of his tongue. "Look at you. Such an addict. Keeping such bad company that your parents had to do an intervention from your own stepbrother, and you came running right back to us the first second you could."

I rolled my eyes at him. "They probably thought I was on drugs or something."

"Or that Logan was pimping you out." Slade cocked his head as if considering that possibility.

"Shut up," Logan grumbled. "It's ridiculous."

"It's hilarious."

Dexter made a face. "It does make sense that they'd have been suspicious. Madelyn's change in behavior must have seemed pretty extreme."

I sighed. "Well, now we'll just have to hope that Summer can hold them at bay long enough for us to get what we need." I'd texted her when I'd left her car to join the guys in an Uber, but I hadn't had anything else to report to her yet, and she hadn't replied.

Logan looked as if he might have groused more, but right then the door to the café chimed. Beckett walked in with a glance around the place, wearing his more incognito clothing of jeans and a hoodie. His hair looked unusually rumpled beneath the raised hood.

He was the one who'd suggested this place for the meetup, confident that no cops were likely to cruise by on their regular patrols. I wasn't sure I wanted to find out how he knew that information so well, but it'd worked out. I still couldn't believe that the Vigil guys had needed to go on the run from the police in the short time I'd been gone.

He walked over to us as steady as always, but I could see the tension in every movement. I couldn't help checking him over for injuries as well as I could, but there were no signs of blood on his clothes or pain in his expression.

"What happened?" I said in a hushed voice as soon as he reached our table. "Did you get Doom's Seed's people to back off?"

He shook his head with a frown. "The attack's still on-going. I can't stay for long. But I wasn't accomplishing much at the moment anyway, so at least I can make sure the four of you are safe."

"What do you mean, under attack?" Dexter asked before Beckett could go on, leaning forward.

Beckett exhaled sharply. "Armed men stormed several of the Storm-owned businesses in the city—including the dance club, the trucking company, and my new office complex. It's obvious that they were looking to get in quietly and simply slaughter everyone working for me, but thankfully my people are alert and noticed some odd behavior. They were able to get out a warning to the others just in time to be on the defense."

My stomach had sunk. "What's happening now?"

"Everyone barricaded themselves in the buildings. But it's hard on the ground levels that have storefronts with big windows. They've ended up holed up in back rooms or basements where they can't maneuver easily. I've been talking to people at each location, and it sounds like most of them have survived so far, but they're under siege. They can't leave without getting shot, and they can't get good shots in at the people who've invaded."

Logan's brow furrowed. "And you don't have enough people who aren't trapped to fight back from the outside?"

Beckett grimaced. "My family has a lot of resources and people, but they're spread out. This has severely limited who I can call on in the area. I'm rallying everyone I can who isn't stuck, but I'm not sure if there's much we can do other than wait it out. If we get into a full shoot-out at all of my businesses, it's going to draw so much unwanted police attention... That could destroy our holdings in the city in itself. It'd be a total bloodbath."

My eyebrows shot up, the guys' account of their escape from the police racing through my mind. "Couldn't you use the police to scare off Doom's Seed's people? If they're actively firing illegal weapons and making a commotion…"

"They *haven't* been able to do all that much shooting so far, not so much that the police have been called in. These aren't residential neighborhoods. Unless they see something they can't ignore, people in the city tend to stay out of any kind of conflict."

"*You* could call the cops in," Slade pointed out with a click of his candy against his teeth.

Beckett aimed a baleful look at him. "And that really wouldn't help my concerns about police interference with my businesses, would it? They could just as easily end up shooting *my* people as the assholes attacking us."

My mind worked through the problem. Doom's Seed wouldn't want his people detained and questioned any more than Beckett did. And the cops didn't have to go right at them for the criminals to get worried. From what they'd said, the Vigil guys had gone on the alert as soon as they'd spotted the cops in the library.

"What if… what if you didn't point them at your businesses at all," I said slowly. "As long as the attackers *think* the police are going to show up and arrest them, they won't stick around, right?"

Beckett raised his eyebrows. "How would we make them think that if it's not true?"

"Give them something else to investigate. Like… 'symptoms' of a problem nearby that'll draw a whole lot of police attention, close enough that it'll spook Doom's Seed's men but not focused on any property you own."

Slade tapped his hand on the table. "I like that. Maddie bringing her doctor training to the task in creative ways."

Beckett's eyes glazed for a few seconds as he contemplated my suggestion. He was just opening his mouth when his phone rang.

He jerked it to his ear. "Yes?" Then his expression lightened. He stood a little straighter, nodding. "Excellent. You have an address? Send me all the information."

My heart leapt. But as Beckett hung up, his expression got more serious again.

He looked around at us. "That was one of my tech guys. He's identified a location on the outskirts of the city where some of the 'toxic' fish were shipped regularly but that doesn't appear to be a restaurant or any other business you'd expect to be ordering raw fish. He isn't sure *what* it is."

Logan's eyes widened. "That's the lead we need. But—you need to deal with this gang war you've got on your hands first."

Beckett swiped his hand over his mouth. "I do. But you know what—I think Maddie's plan just might work if I put the right spin on it. It reminds me of some strategies that got us pretty far back in Paradise Bend."

I smiled. "Then let's do it."

"*I* am going to do most of it," Beckett said firmly, and paused. "But you four had better come with me. If the police are going to be racing around the city, I want to be sure you're out of their way. And as soon as this is dealt with, we'll investigate this place and its toxic fish."

As I pressed the dial button, my gaze stayed trained on the street beyond the van's tinted back window. Beckett had gone off in that direction after we'd parked not far from his office complex. He'd texted me seconds ago telling me to go ahead with my part in the plan. I just hoped this worked, since it'd technically been my idea.

The line on the other end rang, and then a crisp professional voice answered, telling me I'd reached the police department.

"I have a crime to report," I said quickly. "I was at the Lotus Blossom Spa a couple of days ago, and I saw them selling baggies of drugs out of a back room."

"Hold on a second." There was a rustling sound on the other end. "What exactly did you see?"

I improvised on the spot, wanting to make sure they took the accusation seriously. "A couple of people gave the staff money and were handed baggies of this white powder. I saw one of them snort some of it. It was obviously making them high."

"And this is the Lotus Blossom Spa at Trinity and Highland?"

"Yes."

"All right. Can I get your name for—"

I hung up, leaving the tip anonymous. A sweat had broken out over my back, but Slade patted my shoulder reassuringly. "Nice work."

We'd decided that sending the police to some of the businesses in Doom's Seed's empire would add to the chaos and make him more likely to pull all his men out of their siege. But that was only one small part of the plan.

As for the other part…

Beckett hurried back to the van just as I was pushing my phone into my pocket. He hopped inside, slightly windblown, yanked the door shut, and pushed a button on the small rectangular device he was holding.

I knew what was coming, but that didn't stop me from flinching at the boom that reverberated through the air. A surge of fire exploded through a car parked across the street from the office complex. The roof burst open; the windows shattered. My ears rang with the noise.

"Too bad for the owner of that car," I had to say.

Beckett glanced at me with a mild expression. "His insurance will cover it. And anyway, I've met the guy who owns it, and he's an asshole."

Logan barked a laugh. "All's well that ends well, huh?"

"It's not over yet."

We sat, tensed, as the fire roared inside the car. All across the city, Beckett's people had staged similar explosions near the businesses under siege. They were being timed so that the cops weren't stretched too thin, but close together enough to make it clear there was an urgent problem.

Within minutes, incoming sirens wailed. Three police cars sped onto the scene. They parked around the burning car and leapt out.

As they stalked around the car and then started checking the nearby stores for signs of the perpetrator, a couple of figures emerged from the side door of the office complex. We'd specifically parked where we could keep watch, because Beckett had said that was where the attackers had broken into the building.

The two men eyed the cops and jerked back when one of the officers started striding in the direction of the office complex. They ducked back inside. My pulse stuttered with the fear that they'd hide out inside and go unnoticed. But seconds later, about a dozen figures hustled out and rushed down the alley to make their getaway.

Beckett sucked in a breath. "Lindell's with them. I'm not letting him get away with this."

He sprang past us into the driver's seat and started the engine. The van roared around and swerved down a side street. Logan gripped my arm to help hold me in place in the back.

I had no idea where Beckett thought he was going until he roared around another bend—and slammed on the brakes just shy of hitting a car that'd been about to pull away from the curb.

A tall man with bushy eyebrows and a heavy layer of graying

stubble stared out the driver's side window at him. I guessed that was Lindell. He reached for his door, but it banged into the van's front bumper, too close for him to squeeze out.

By then, Beckett had already pushed out of the van, a pistol in his hand. Logan lunged out after him, yanking out his own gun. My stomach twisted, but we all followed.

The stubbled man froze as Beckett and Logan circled the car. Beckett waved the gun at him. "Get the fuck out, Lindell. I've got a lot of questions I need to ask you."

Lindell looked like he was attempting a smirk, but his expression was so tense it came out sour. "Nice to see you again, Storm's heir."

"What are we doing?" I hissed as Lindell eased out of the vehicle through the passenger side.

"He knows *all* about his boss's business," Beckett said, checking the man over for weapons. He pulled a gun out of a hidden holster and tossed it into the back of the car. "He might be able to give us some answers about where we're going next."

He tipped his head toward the other guys by the van without taking his eyes off his enemy. "There's rope in my glove compartment. Get it. We don't want to leave this prick mobile for our little trip."

CHAPTER 24

Madelyn

The address Beckett had gotten turned out to be an ordinary-looking storefront with plain beige walls, a shade drawn over the dingy front window, and a logo-less sign that simply proclaimed the place to be "Teresa's."

"Teresa's what?" Slade muttered, peering at it. "Convenience store? Shoe shop? Hat boutique?"

"No way of finding out without going in. All I know for sure is they don't receive any other food or animal related deliveries." Beckett got out of the driver's seat and walked around to the back doors. He untied Lindell from the bar he'd secured him to and removed the ropes around his ankles as well, leaving his hands tied behind his back.

"Come on," he said. "You can give us the tour and tell us all about what goes on in this place. And if there's anyone inside, you'll make a handy shield."

Lindell grimaced around the strip of fabric that gagged him, but he went with Beckett without any further struggle. He didn't appear to be too concerned about ending up in the middle of a gun fight here, but I followed cautiously.

Logan pushed ahead of me, taking out his gun again. The sight of it made my stomach turn, but I couldn't deny that it'd been useful. I wasn't going to tell him to put it away until we'd seen what was waiting for us in this place.

The guys had fallen into a more cohesive comradery over the past several days. Beckett kept one hand on Lindell's arm and tipped his head to Logan, who rapped on the door. When no one answered, he tried the doorknob. It didn't budge.

Dexter was already there with his lock picks. "I can handle that."

His deft fingers and the tools made quick work of the lock. He pushed the door open and poked his head inside. "No alarm system."

Slade smiled thinly. "Because whatever they're doing in here, they don't want any outside security company finding out about it, I bet."

Beckett and Logan entered first, nudging Doom's Seed's lieutenant in front of them. The room we walked into held nothing but a small metal desk at one end and a single chair at the other. The linoleum floor was covered with scuff marks, and a sour chemical smell laced the air that reminded me of the hospital.

Beckett hummed to himself. "My guy said they only get deliveries from the market once or twice a month. Maybe they don't bother to have anyone manning the place in between whatever it is they do with those."

He pushed Lindell onward through the doorway at the other

end of the entry room. This space was larger, with a few padded chairs along one wall and an exam table set up at the far end next to a couple of counters and cabinets. It looks like a combined waiting room and medical exam room. It was as empty and silent as the front area, the sour smell thickening.

Dexter walked to another door off to the side and peeked in there. "More medical stuff," he reported. "No one there, no other entrances. The place is empty."

"Good," Beckett said. "Then we can talk."

He shoved Lindell down onto one of the chairs and bent to attach his bound wrists to the back of the chair. He fixed both ankles to the legs with plastic ties as well.

Watching him move so confidently and efficiently sent a chilly tingle down my back. He knew exactly what he was doing. How many people had he interrogated before?

How far would he take that interrogation if this guy didn't tell us what we needed to know?

But then, I'd already watched my other three guys beating up a security guard while they questioned him. Beckett would have to go pretty far to get more violent than that. The guy in front of us was involved in so many deaths and so much violence himself. I couldn't say I totally objected to him being on the receiving end if it helped us get justice for Dad.

When Lindell was securely bound to the chair, Beckett removed the gag. Lindell spat in his general direction and then glowered at him.

Beckett folded his arms over his chest. "You know we could do a lot worse to you than this. I caught you in the middle of an attack on one of my properties; you're lucky you're even still *alive*. The man you work for couldn't blame me for ending your sorry existence. But I'm giving you a chance to be useful instead."

"You'll forgive me if I don't thank you," Lindell rasped back.

Beckett continued as if he hadn't spoken. "Why did Doom's Seed attack the Storm's holdings in this city today?"

Lindell's lips curled with a sneer. "*He* didn't attack them. I did. Give credit where it's due."

So, he was going with the story that he was responsible for everything, that his boss hadn't even been aware and hadn't approved? I frowned, unconvinced.

From Beckett's tone, I suspected he wasn't either. "And why would *you* attack me?"

"To impress Doom's Seed," Lindell said without hesitation. "To show him how much I can do for him, how valuable I am. If I took the city all for us without him having to lift a finger, he could benefit without needing to take responsibility for it. That's the kind of loyalty he deserves."

Slade snorted. Logan was watching the conversation with narrowed eyes, his mouth pressed tight.

Beckett tapped his pistol against his thigh. "It wasn't just gaining territory you were interested in, though. You also went after four college students." He motioned to us. "You—or someone else under Doom's Seed—arranged for Lindsay Silver to have a car accident, and you burned down an office these three guys were using in the university law library. How about you tell me more about that?"

Lindell scoffed at him. "What's there to tell? They were poking around in the boss's business. It's *my* business to make sure he goes undisturbed. So I did what it took to shut them down."

His story felt way too pat for me. Too convenient that he bore responsibility for everything. Beckett had told me he didn't think Doom's Seed would allow any further attacks once Beckett had alerted him… unless he approved of them. He and this guy must have talked after Beckett had confronted Doom's Seed. It didn't add up.

But the gang war was lower on my list of concerns, especially seeing the medical equipment in the room. I took a step forward, and Beckett eased to the side, glancing at me. He gave me a slight nod as if to say I could take the floor.

A nervous shiver tickled through me. *I'd* never interrogated anyone before. But I knew what I wanted to ask.

"You didn't shut us down," I said, glaring at Lindell. "And now we know so much more than we did before. What is your boss using this facility for? What was he having shipped here in the cold boxes from the seafood market? Viruses and bacteria? Experimental toxins?"

Lindell shook his head. His voice came out even harder than before. "I don't know anything about that. This isn't my part of the business."

Beckett made a skeptical noise. "You're his primary lieutenant in this metropolitan area, and you have no idea about major activities he was running here? Nice try. Why don't you take another stab at answering properly?"

"He keeps some things separate. It's his right to do that."

"And Evan Silver?" Dexter spoke up abruptly. "Why have you been so focused on covering up his death?"

"Who?" Lindell asked, blank-faced, but this time I was sure it was an act.

"You know who," I insisted. "The only thing we've been doing that could have pissed off your boss is trying to figure out why he was murdered. That's what you're covering up."

My show of temper only seemed to make the lieutenant more confident. He shrugged. "You broke into properties under his purview. You were hassling people under him. It doesn't matter to me why; it needed to stop."

He was lying, but I didn't know how to force him to cough up the truth. My hands balled at my sides.

He'd given us the story he wanted us to hear, and now he was shutting down, refusing to admit to anything else. He didn't want to compromise his boss's real decisions and secrets, after all.

Beckett flicked off the safety on his gun while leaving it pointed at the floor. "I'm going to need to hear a little more than that."

"Well, that's too bad, because that's all I have to say."

Lindell stared back at us as immovable as a statue, and my heart started to sink. He didn't look like a man who'd break under pressure. He obviously didn't shy away from the possibility of violence. What good did it do us if we battered him and broke his bones and still didn't get any answers?

He had way stronger motivation to stay quiet, didn't he? What would Doom's Seed do to him if he found out his lieutenant had confessed?

I touched Beckett's arm and caught his gaze. "Can I talk to you for a second?"

Beckett searched my eyes and motioned me toward the front room. He glanced at the Vigil guys. "Make sure he stays glued to that chair."

Slade saluted him, and Logan nodded grimly.

We walked into the smaller room, Beckett shutting the door firmly behind us. The faint growl of a car passing on the road outside filtered through the shaded window.

Beckett rested his hand on my shoulder. "What's going on, Maddie? Did you notice something you didn't want to mention in front of him?"

My mouth twisted. I spoke in a low voice to make sure it wouldn't travel to the other room. "I mean, I'm getting a strong impression that he's making a cover story for Doom's Seed and lying through his teeth, but that's not very helpful. It's starting to seem like he's not going to admit to anything. Even if you… hurt him, or whatever you'd normally do." I restrained a cringe.

A shadow crossed Beckett's expression. "I actually agree, Maddie," he said. "He wouldn't have risen to the level of responsibility he has under the boss he's got if he broke easily under pressure, and we don't have much time. Which is why I made sure I'd have an ace up my sleeve if I got a chance to hash things out with Lindell. I think it might be enough to crack him."

I raised my eyebrows. "What?"

"I'd rather—" He let out a rough breath. "I'm going to have to say some things that I would never actually act on. But he has to believe that I would. So I'm going to be convincing about it, and it isn't going to look pretty. I'm not going to tell you what you can handle, but I don't love the idea of you seeing me like that. Are you sure you're ready to witness how far I need to go sometimes to get the job done?"

My stomach lurched. "You want me to leave?"

"I'm not telling you to. I just want you to be prepared, if you do stay… and to know it might be better if you stepped outside and didn't have to hear it." He paused, holding my gaze, and something in his expression softened. "Hell, if you told me it isn't worth it, that you don't want me to even pretend to be a monster, I'd listen to you. But it could mean we lose our chance at getting the answers we need."

I dragged in a breath, struggling to pull my whirling thoughts into order. Part of me recoiled at the thought of watching Beckett bring out the cruelest side of his criminal persona… but I knew that wasn't really him, didn't I? If he said he'd never act on what he was going to say, then I believed him. I knew he walked a difficult line doing his best to avoid unnecessary pain.

Being scary was part of how he got important things done—and this was the most important situation I'd ever faced. I had to be able to face every side of him, or how could I be with him? With any of the guys, really, considering they'd all gone to extreme lengths to see justice done in the past?

"I can handle it," I whispered. "Do what you need to do, and I'll be right here with you. I know what you stand for."

A sheen of gratitude and relief flickered in Beckett's eyes. He leaned in just for a second to claim a quick kiss.

"All right," he said. "Let's get this done."

He walked back into the room ahead of me. Lindell was in his chair where we'd left him, the Vigil guys poised around him. They eased back as Beckett came to a stop in front of the lieutenant. His face had hardened, and his voice came out icy cold.

"I think we've had enough of a run-around. You don't want to talk. I can understand that. But let's be clear: you need to give us something real, or you aren't the only one who'll pay."

Lindell snorted. "What are you talking about? Big talk from a little kid."

The smile that curved Beckett's lips was so chilling I had to tense my arms to stop from hugging myself. He leaned over the chair, setting his hands on its arms and pinning Lindell in place with his stare with just half a foot between them.

"A little kid," he repeated. "Interesting that you'd say that. Did you really think you could keep them hidden? I know about your girlfriend, Angela. I know about those cute little kids who should be thanking God they didn't end up with your ugly mug."

For the first time since we'd confronted him by the office building, Lindell looked shaken. The color drained from his face. "Fuck you."

"I really don't think that's how you should be talking to me." Beckett got out his phone and tapped on the screen. "Especially when I have people watching that lovely family of yours right now."

He held up the phone. Video played on the screen: a suburban backyard, a woman watching two kids race around on the lawn. A childish shriek of excitement reached my ears. My gut started to churn.

He wouldn't really do this. He'd told me that. But watching him now, I could see why he'd warned me. He *was* putting on the face of a monster.

"See the time stamp?" Beckett said in the same cold, even tone. "That's live. My men are ready to move as soon as I say the word. How many will it take before you remember the real answers to my questions? Should I have them start with little Benny, or maybe you're more attached to Delia?"

"Fuck *you*!" Lindell spat out again, jerking at his bindings. "If you touch one hair on their heads—"

"You're going to do what? You're tied up here. All you'll be able to do is watch. You know who you're dealing with, don't you, Clarence? I sit at the table alongside the man you call your boss. Would *he* hesitate to off a couple of kids if it got him what he wanted?"

From Lindell's sickened expression, Doom's Seed wouldn't. But he managed to sputter one more bit of defiance. "If you go after them, he'll know. He'll get payback—you'll regret everything ten times over."

Beckett shut off the video feed. "I wouldn't be so sure about that. You have a choice to make now, and you need to make it fast. You can keep your mouth shut, and then I'll kill you *and* your family and make sure word is passed on to Doom's Seed that we found out about this place we're standing in from you. Everyone will believe you're a traitor and that you got what was coming to you."

I hadn't thought Lindell could get any paler, but now he looked like a ghost. He opened his mouth, but he couldn't seem to find another argument.

"Or," Beckett went on, "you can tell us what we want to know, and your kids and their mother will continue living their happy, carefree lives. It's up to you. Like I said, we can always start with a half measure. Kill one kid, see if that motivates you to save the other. I'll make sure to have my men tell them exactly why they've come before—"

"Okay," Lindell broke in raggedly. "Okay. Leave them alone."

Beckett folded his arms over his chest and waited in silence. My throat constricted as Lindell took a few shaky breaths. But at least this was almost over.

"There's nothing all that complicated about it," he said finally. "That Evan Silver guy was poking his nose where it didn't belong, digging into the boss's businesses. So we arranged to have him taken out."

"Doom's Seed gave that order himself?"

Lindell shook his head. "I did. That was right after I was put in charge of this part of his territory. I'm not sure if he even knew about it—I didn't bother him with details like that. Silver hadn't gotten far enough into anything to cause any major problems."

"What was he looking for?" I had to ask. "Why was he poking around in the first place?"

"I don't know," Lindell said with a hopeless grimace. "I have no idea what he was searching for. I was just protecting the empire like it's my job to do."

"You have no idea at all?" Logan said, taking a step forward. "How about telling us how the specific businesses he was digging into were connected? What is *this* place?"

Lindell sighed. "There is no big connection that I know about. We ship all kinds of stuff. This is one hand-off point to obscure the trail. All kinds of things have been moved through this space at different times."

Dexter frowned. "You came down on us awfully hard for someone who didn't think there was anything much to hide."

Lindell focused on him for a moment. "I came down hard on you kids because I thought you might have found something incriminating about any of our activities that I hadn't realized Silver had stumbled on. I was protecting my own. That's all there is to it."

My heart sank, leaving me feeling hollowed out inside. Could that really be it? There was no huge conspiracy—maybe even Dad had been wrong to imagine there was? He'd gone following a lead into the wrong place and been murdered because of it?

My voice came out thin. "You're telling me that you had my dad killed just for looking around a couple of buildings?"

Lindell just gave me a baleful look. "I don't know what else to tell you. That's just how things work in this business."

CHAPTER 25

Logan

As I watched Doom's Seed's lieutenant answer Beckett's questions, the uncomfortable sense crept over me that none of this was really adding up.

Why would Maddie's father have been investigating standard criminal activities? It wasn't as if he'd been some kind of law enforcement. What would even have drawn his attention to a random crime?

But if there was something more to it, something unusual that did connect to his medical work, Lindell should have known that. And he was refusing to admit it.

I didn't see why Lindell would have gone to such lengths to make Evan Silver's death look like an illness either. That would have been difficult to pull off. Why not just shoot him and make it look like a mugging?

And the most important question of all: was the guy in front of us really responsible for Evan's murder, the mastermind behind everything we'd uncovered and faced during our investigation? Or was he still protecting his boss by taking all the blame?

I shifted my weight from one foot to the other restlessly, itching to grab Lindell by the front of his shirt and shake real answers out of him. But I could already tell that wouldn't get us any farther than we'd already gotten.

Beckett had come up with real leverage, enough for Lindell to confess to the parts of the story it was hardest to brush off. But now that he'd given us a full explanation that addressed all of our questions, how could we push him harder? I didn't want to start killing the guy's kids to see if he'd spill something else, and I doubted that Beckett did either.

His threat wasn't going to work as leverage any more if we weren't willing to act on it.

"What about the Baldwin file?" Slade asked, crossing his arms over his chest. "How does that fit into your boss's business?"

Lindell gave him a blank look that despite myself, I believed. "I don't know anything about that. Honestly."

That was totally possible. We only knew about it because of Evan's notes. It might have been something he'd seen at the hospital, something that hadn't actually been connected to Doom's Seed after all.

As the others continued to toss more questions at the lieutenant, I moved away, prowling through the strange room. Lindell had made it sound as if this place was only used for passing around deliveries, but the medical equipment was an odd choice. Was that just part of selling the front, or did they actually use it for some purpose he hadn't wanted to mention?

I moved through the area around the exam table, opening the cabinets and scanning the counters. There wasn't much in the storage space other than basic supplies like latex gloves, gauze, and antiseptic cleaner. Nothing that hinted at any specific activities.

I moved onward to the door Dexter had peeked through earlier. Stepping over the threshold, I flicked on the light.

There on the threshold, I paused to take in the scene that had come into focus in front of me. This was more than an exam room. It was obviously set up as an operating theater, with big circular lights mounted over a sturdy medical table, a sink in the corner, monitors off to the side connected to computer equipment too specialized for me to know what to do with.

A full row of cabinets lined the far wall, and a few smaller storage units stood around the electronic equipment. Everything was starkly white. The smell of the cleaner itched at my nose, bringing me back to the many hospital exams I'd endured since my own operation.

My skin prickled with apprehension. Why the hell would this nondescript, empty facility have a full-out operating room in it? Why would they have gone to this much trouble to stage the place if it wasn't being used? There were easier fronts they could have picked.

I pulled open the drawers on the storage units. At first I only found more of the basics, as well as sets of tools like scalpels and medical scissors. Then a drawer at the bottom slid out with a rattle to reveal several resealable plastic baggies full of pills.

My apprehension crept deeper into me with a chill that touched my bones. I pawed through the bags. They were unlabeled, but… I recognized the color and shape of a couple of them, along with the letters etched in their surface.

One of those types was the same kind I gulped down every day. The other I recognized was one I'd had in my regimen for years until the doctors had let me taper off. I could remember seeing it in the pill container Dad had made me use for organization, morning after morning.

What the hell was going on here?

Those medications could be used for other things, of course. One of them was a pretty standard antibiotic. I didn't recognize the other types of medication in the drawer.

Taking a page out of Dexter's book, I shoved down my growing uneasiness and snapped pictures of the bags with my phone so we could look them up later.

The cabinets at the back held medical gowns and face masks, more operating tools, and, crumpled in a corner behind other supplies as if it'd been accidentally forgotten there instead of getting thrown out, an empty bag with a label on the front. I tugged it out and smoothed the surface so I could read it.

Kidney Perfusion Solution.

The bottom dropped out of my stomach. For a second, I thought I might vomit. I dropped the bag and stepped away, the sharply sour smell of the place flooding my lungs.

Too many pieces were fitting together. Too much adding up… and making me wonder what else might be part of that equation.

I needed to get out of here, to clear my head and make sure I wasn't freaking myself out over nothing. I switched off the light and walked out, past the others to the entry room, right outside into the fresh air.

As the breeze washed over me, not really all that fresh with the whiffs of asphalt and car exhaust but better than inside, I let out a shaky breath. Dragged another in. Let it out again.

The things I'd found might mean nothing at all. They could all have been part of the staging. There could be legit operations happening in that place that had nothing to do with Doom's Seed or his illegal shipments.

But...

Before I had to follow that thought to its conclusion, the door opened. Maddie eased out and looked me over, her face tight with concern.

"Hey, are you okay?"

I opened my mouth and closed it again. I didn't know how to answer that question.

"I'm not sure. I—some of the stuff here—"

As I grappled with my words, Maddie touched my arm, her eyes softening. "Whatever's the matter, you can tell me about it."

I knew *that*. I knew how strong the woman standing next to me was. The problem was how much I wanted to admit to myself.

"The other room," I said finally. "It's set up like an operating theater. There were a bunch of pills—some of them the same kind I've taken since my transplant. And there was a bag of the stuff they use to store organs..."

My gut clenched up again with another jab of nausea. Maddie gripped my arm more firmly even as her eyes widened. "That is strange, but they have set this place up to look like a medical facility. They could have chosen to have those around for any number of reasons. Anyway, it has nothing to do with *you*."

She sounded so certain that I almost believed her. Almost.

I rubbed my hand over my hair. "I'm just getting a bad feeling that there's something worse going on than we've even started to suspect." Worse than I wanted to imagine.

Maddie held my gaze. "Whatever it is, we'll figure it out like we have so far. I think that—"

She cut herself off when a SUV pulled into the narrow lot a few spots farther down than Beckett's. Its glossy black shell held tinted windows that hid all view of the people within—until the back door swung open and a slim, blond woman in a posh dress-suit and sunglasses stepped out.

A sense of recognition hit me in that first glimpse, ricocheting through my brain. My mind was already starting to resist the idea rising up from my memories when the woman took off her sunglasses, and I couldn't deny it.

I was staring at my mom—what I had to imagine my mom would have looked like if she'd been alive for the past decade. Or else some mysterious identical twin I'd never known about. There were more lines at the corners of her eyes and lips and a few strands of gray in that golden-blond hair, but those dark eyes, that gently sloped nose, that hint of amusement in her quiet smile…

My heart had stopped. When the woman stepped toward me, it started beating again in a heavy, erratic rhythm. My throat closed up. I couldn't speak.

Her smile widened as she reached me. "Logan," she said with so much familiar warmth that the back of my eyes started to burn. That was her voice too, smooth and crisp.

She reached out to pat my shoulder, and I registered as if from a great distance away that the hand she'd pressed against me wasn't real flesh. She had a prosthetic attached to her forearm, the false skin a slightly artificial peachy shade that didn't quite match the rest.

On her left arm. Her left hand—the hand we'd buried in Mom's coffin because it was the only part of her remains we'd been able to recover after the gas main explosion.

Maddie had gone still beside me—how much because she could recognize Mom too from the few pictures she'd seen and how much because of *my* reaction to this woman, I had no idea.

My voice came out in a croak. "Mom?" And Maddie stiffened even more.

My thoughts were spinning in circles. This couldn't be possible. None of this made sense. How could my mother be *alive*? Where had she been all this time?

"I'm so proud of you, Logan," Mom said, beaming at me.

"Seeing how determined and clever you've become has been amazing to watch. But this game needs to end here."

Before I could process those words, her expression darkened. Her prosthetic hand whipped from me to Maddie, the fingers closing hard around Maddie's wrist. She yanked Maddie toward her —and pulled out a pistol with her regular hand, pointing the muzzle right at Maddie's forehead.

A choked sound burst out of Maddie. "What are you—"

"Quiet," my mother said sharply, rapping the muzzle of the gun against Maddie's temple. My arm had been rising to reach for her, but both Maddie and I froze at that gesture.

"Mom," I rasped. "You can't—"

She gave me a firm look that was so familiar from my childhood I could have drowned in it. "Leave everything you've been digging into alone and go back to your normal life, starting now. Bring your friends with you. If you don't, *she's* the one who's going to regret it the most."

Without another word, she hauled Maddie back to the SUV and through the door she'd left open. Shock blanked my mind. Only as she yanked the door shut with a thud did I convince my body to spring into motion.

"Mom!" I yelled, lunging at the vehicle. It was already roaring out of the parking lot onto the road. My hand snatched at empty air.

No. *No.* This couldn't be happening.

But it was, and I couldn't stop it alone.

"Slade!" I screamed out as I dashed down to the road. "Dexter! Beckett! Get out here."

My world had just shattered into pieces, and I knew only one thing for sure. It wasn't going to be right again until the four of us got Maddie back from wherever the hell my mother meant to take her.

TWISTED EMPIRE

CHAPTER 1

Madelyn

I sat tensed in the backseat of an unfamiliar SUV, staring at the pistol trained directly between my eyes and trying to determine exactly how I'd gotten here. It had happened so quickly—and been so incomprehensible—that I was still having trouble wrapping my head around the apparent facts.

Logan's mother was alive.

Logan's mother was holding a gun to my head, after dragging me away from Logan and the rest of my guys at the strange medical facility we'd been investigating.

I'd only seen the woman next to me in photos from before her supposed death more than ten years ago, but I could recognize the matching curves of her features, the pale hair and dark eyes that were so like Logan's. And from his response, he'd had no doubt it was her either.

How could she be alive? Where had she been all this time—why had she stayed away?

Why had she appeared out of the blue *now* of all times?

And what did she want with *me*? We'd never even met before.

My gaze dropped to her prosthetic hand resting on the middle seat between us. Logan had told me that he and his father had been forced to bury only her hand. They'd assumed the rest of her body had burned up in the explosion.

But really she'd simply left it behind… to create a convincing story of her death? Why had she wanted to disappear at all?

My mouth opened and closed, but it was hard to summon the courage to ask any of those questions with the gun staring me down.

My phone, which I'd shoved into my hip pocket, chimed with an incoming text. Faster than I would have expected—which maybe was wrong of me, considering how nimble I'd seen Slade move with his mechanical leg—Logan's mom switched the pistol to her prosthetic hand and leaned forward to yank the phone from my pocket. She held down the button to turn it completely off and shoved it into her purse before swapping gun-hands again.

"You won't be talking with anyone else for a good long while," she said.

I glanced at the driver, but all I could see of him was the back of his head with its ruddy buzzcut as he kept the SUV in motion. No sign that he thought there was anything strange about what his passengers were getting up to.

My attention shifted to the window next to me. If I could keep track of where we were going—

But Logan's mom obviously guessed my intentions. She tsked her tongue at me and dug a strip of black fabric out of her purse. "Put this over your eyes," she said, tossing it to me.

When I balked, she waved the gun. "I could start shooting off fingers and see how many you'll be left to work with when you give in."

She sounded totally serious—and totally calm about the threat. A shudder ran down my spine.

My jaw clenching, I grabbed the blindfold and tied it over my eyes. I meant to leave it a little loose with a sliver of visibility at the bottom, but no such luck.

"Tighter," Logan's mom demanded.

I gritted my teeth and tugged the knot a little more. Only a faint glow of light remained at the edge of my vision. I wasn't figuring anything out from that.

"Why are you doing this?" I couldn't help asking, wincing inwardly at how pathetic my quavering voice sounded.

"Don't you worry about that."

Yeah, right. Don't worry about the fact that I was being kidnapped at gunpoint. If I hadn't been so on edge, I'd have rolled my eyes.

This was Logan's mother, the woman who'd raised him for the first ten years of his life. She couldn't be completely horrible, could she? She'd acted like she still cared about him in the few moments before she'd grabbed me.

"Logan thought you were dead," I said cautiously. "Where've you been all this time?"

"That's none of your business. Just sit there quietly and this'll be easier for all of us."

For her, anyway. My heart thumped louder, but I risked another question. "How did you find us at that building?"

Was *she* tangled up in the crimes we'd been investigating somehow?

"Keep *quiet*," Logan's mom snapped. "I'm doing what I need to do to keep my son safe. If he matters at all to you, you'll accept it."

How the hell did kidnapping me keep Logan safe? My mind

whirled with confusion, but before I could open my mouth again, the muzzle of the gun tapped my temple.

"Enough," she repeated with a hard edge in her voice, as if she'd predicted what I was thinking.

It wasn't as if she was telling me anything useful anyway. I pressed my lips flat and tried to track the turns and stops of the SUV as it rumbled onward. But at this point, I didn't even know if we were heading into the city or farther away from it.

There was a long, unbroken stretch while the engine roared, and I suspected we'd gotten on a highway. Apprehension prickled over my skin.

Just how far were we going? Where was she taking me?

And what was she going to do with me there?

I didn't like how much time seemed to pass before the car finally came to a full halt, followed by the click of the parking brake. Logan's mom shifted on the seat next to me with a rustle of her clothes. The door at my other side opened, presumably at the driver's hand, and she prodded me to go out ahead of her.

My feet thudded onto a concrete surface. The air was still and slightly damp around me, and the clang of the closing door echoed off a low ceiling. An underground parking garage?

That didn't really narrow my location down.

"Come along," Logan's mom said, grasping my arm with her prosthetic hand. I let her guide me, adrift in the darkness behind the blindfold.

Hinges squeaked. We stepped onto a carpeted surface and paused there. Then there was a whir like an elevator door opening.

My suspicion was confirmed when the floor beneath our feet started to rise. My stomach flipped over with the rush of its ascent.

From the time it took even without any stops in between, we must have gone up several floors. The car glided to a stop, the door opened with a ping, and Logan's mom hustled me out again.

I lost track of the space we moved through, past another door, around a corner, my foot bumping into the edge of a piece of furniture. I stumbled, and Logan's mom yanked me upright.

"This way," she snapped, and propelled me onward.

"If you'd let me take off the blindfold—"

"Forget about it."

Another door opened, and she escorted me into a space that felt tighter than the others. Fabric rustled all around us. Logan's mom yanked my arms behind my back.

My instinct was to shove away from her in self-defense, but I had no idea where the gun was now. I had no idea how many other armed people might be nearby. I wasn't in a position to get the upper hand, so I forced myself to remain still while she wrapped what felt like a silk scarf around my wrists, binding them together behind me.

Then she set one hand on my shoulder and pressed down. I sank to my knees, and she backed away.

"I don't want to be bothered by you, so if you scream, I'll knock you out," she said tightly. "Nobody else will hear you here, so it's pointless to even try, but it will be an annoyance."

Her footsteps tapped away, and a door smacked shut. Quiet settled around me.

I was alone.

After a minute of listening, confirming that Logan's mom wasn't immediately coming back, I scooted a little to one side and then another. Fabrics with different textures brushed my face and shoulders. My knee bumped into the pointed toe of a shoe. A picture started to form in my mind.

She'd locked me in a walk-in closet. It was probably about as effective as a prison could get in an ordinary apartment, all the clothing muffling sound from inside.

Had she been telling the truth about there being no one who'd hear me, or had she just been trying to take away my hope?

I needed a better idea of what I was dealing with. Experimenting too aggressively wouldn't be worth it if I ended up unconscious as she'd threatened.

I squirmed around as quietly as I could until I found a bare patch of solid wall. Tipping toward it, I rested the side of my face against the plaster. Then I jerked my head downward.

Again. And again. And again.

The blindfold gradually loosened and slid upward on my face. In a few minutes, I'd lifted it right off my eyes.

I squinted around me in the dark space. I couldn't see a whole lot more than before, but a slit of light showed beneath the door.

I'd been right about it being a walk-in closet. Shirts and pants and dresses hung on hangers on three walls around me. I'd been rubbing my face on the doorframe. Shoes stood in rows beneath the hanging clothes with more on the shelves overhead.

I hadn't heard Logan's mom lock the door, and it'd be pretty unusual for a closet to have a lock on it anyway. But that didn't mean that bursting out into the apartment was a good idea. Her footsteps filtered through the door, moving from one room to another. She was still out there, and who knew who else was with her.

And the gun. That was the biggest problem. I had to play this smart, not run out and get myself into an even worse predicament.

Swiveling around again, I leaned toward the door. If she walked right out of the place, I wanted to know. And it'd be good to figure out if anyone else was in the apartment with her, and if so, how many people there were.

A sudden, heavy thump from somewhere ahead and to my right made my nerves jump. That had sounded like an outer door. Had she left me completely alone already?

Before more than a tiny flicker of hope could light in my chest, a male voice boomed through the space, diffusing it. “What are you doing, Yvonne?”

There was no mistaking the irritation in the man’s tone. Footsteps hustled over to him, and Logan’s mom—Yvonne, I’d forgotten that was her first name—answered in a rush.

“I was just fixing our little problem, darling. We have leverage now—Logan won’t dig any deeper while he’s worried about the girl.”

The man snorted. “You’re creating a new problem, more like it.”

Her voice dropped too low for me to make out whatever she said next. She didn’t want me overhearing their conversation.

What I’d already heard had only bewildered me more. Who was she calling *darling* and why did either of them care what Logan had been digging into?

As the man responded in a similarly low voice, I pressed my ear right against the gap by the doorframe. The solid edge bit into my skin, but I could just piece together most of the words when I focused all my attention on them.

“—know my son. It will work.” That was Yvonne.

“I can’t afford to have a bunch of damn kids messing up my business,” the man muttered in return. “I don’t care if one of those kids is yours. There are consequences, and you know that.”

“They don’t have any idea what they’re really getting into.”

“They should by now. Digging into buried history, sticking their noses where they don’t belong—taking up my time when I’ve got more important things I should be dealing with. I can handle them once and for all, and this will be over.”

Yvonne’s next response had an almost frantic breathiness to it. “Darling, no. This is enough. I’ve watched Logan, and I’m positive he won’t risk the Silver girl’s life over his silly hobby. And she can’t do any more harm while we’ve got her either.”

My stomach sank as the pieces clicked together in my head. The only person's business we'd been digging into was the crime lord who'd framed Beckett, the one who was a fellow member of the powerful underground organization Beckett called the Devil's Dozen.

Doom's Seed.

Could that really be *him* out there—the man whose worst crimes we'd gradually been uncovering? The one whose men had tried to massacre Beckett's people just this afternoon?

My stomach knotted. I couldn't think of any other explanation. Who else would have been tracking us so closely and known enough about the situation to realize we'd be at that building today?

And Logan's mother was calling him "darling." Was she *dating* him—the man who'd orchestrated my dad's murder?

How the hell would they even have met?

The man I was increasingly sure was Doom's Seed let out a growl of frustration. "We should kill her and all the others and wash our hands of it. Simple and straight to the point."

A few footsteps rapped toward the closet, and my heart lurched. Yvonne hustled after him.

"No," she said. "You promised—you said once I left him behind, we could leave him alone to live his life."

"Not when the way he's living his life is fucking up my plans. You knew how my world worked when you signed up for this. He's already gotten the second chance you bought for him—it's not my fault he's throwing it away with this stupid quest."

I froze, my pulse skipping a beat. *The second chance you bought for him.*

He couldn't mean…

"He'll never put it all together," Yvonne said pleadingly. "You've covered up the organ routes and the hospital records so well. We'll just hold on to the girl until everyone's thinking straight and realizes just how much is on the line, and everything will be fine."

Doom's Seed let out a huff. "It sounds like you're having second thoughts about your choice to stick with me, Yvonne."

"No. Of course not. I'm doing this *for* you. Less blood on your hands means fewer crimes the police might investigate, doesn't it?"

He paused. "Fine. We'll try your way for a day or two. But if it isn't working out *perfectly*, we end this immediately. It's enough of a mess already."

"It'll work. I swear. Thank you, darling."

Yvonne's voice had turned so simpering it'd have turned my stomach if my gut wasn't already churning with queasiness. The footsteps moved away, and their voices faded again until I couldn't hear them at all.

I slumped down on the floor, my spirits sinking. The weight of what I'd just discovered pressed down on my shoulders.

Organ routes and hospital records. A second chance Logan's mom had bought for him. The operating table in the facility we'd discovered—the pills that corresponded with his transplant medication. We'd wondered what it all meant, the suspicion starting to emerge, but those comments brought the picture completely into focus.

Doom's Seed was harvesting body parts and arranging illegal transplants—and Logan's liver had been one of those illicit organs. I didn't know why his mom would have felt the need to turn to a criminal for help, but every other part of the scenario made far too much sense.

That was how she'd met Doom's Seed in the first place. And that was how my dad could have gotten involved. He'd seen something suspicious in those doctored records and started following the trail from there.

And that was why Doom's Seed had ordered Dad's death… just

like he was on the verge of ordering mine and those of the Vigil guys as well.

Had Yvonne faked her death to be with this murderous asshole? What the hell had she been thinking?

I stared at the closet door in a gloomy daze. It didn't really matter why she had. From what I'd heard, she didn't hold anywhere near as much influence over her lover as she wanted to, even when it came to her son. Definitely not when it came to me. She'd barely bought any time at all before he slaughtered us too.

Was I even going to make it out of this apartment to tell the guys what I'd learned?

CHAPTER 2

Beckett

"She grabbed her," Logan said, pacing unceasingly as he repeated that part of his story. He raked his hand back through his short chestnut-brown hair. "My mom… she just took her. Held a fucking gun on her and took her."

His voice echoed through the vacant guest house that my family hadn't used in years—a house that shouldn't have any obvious ties to the Storm. It'd been the closest nearby building where the Vigil guys and I could regroup without worrying about the police or Doom's Seed's people finding us.

We needed to find Maddie, and we couldn't worry about anything else in the meantime.

Slade had managed to sit down on one of the armchairs in the dusty living room, but his knee bounced incessantly, the bright metal ankle of his prosthetic showing when his pantleg swayed. "Your *dead* mom. What the hell is going on here?"

Logan shook his head. "I haven't seen the slightest reason to believe that she was still alive in the last eleven years. I never would have thought she'd leave us on purpose. I had no idea she was even capable of handling a gun. Damn it." He aimed a kick at the baseboard, hard enough that it probably hurt his toes.

Dexter had been staring off into space as if processing everything from a distance, his normally alert green eyes gone hazy. Now, he glanced Logan's way. "Are you sure it was your mom who came and grabbed Madelyn? It wasn't just someone who looked like your mother?"

"It was her. One hundred percent. The way she talked to me…" Logan let out a ragged breath. "She told me she was *proud* of me, for fuck's sake, and then she yanked Maddie away from me. She told me I had to stop digging—she's got to be involved with the people we're investigating somehow. It doesn't make sense!"

"We'll figure it out," I said, reaching for my phone. "Whatever else is going on, I'll get my best people tracking that car. We'll figure out where your mother took Maddie and get her back. Maybe Lindell will cough up some more information too."

I didn't have a lot of hope about that last possibility. We'd dropped off the local lieutenant who answered to Doom's Seed with a bunch of my people so they could interrogate him at length. He'd have been too much baggage to drag around with us while we searched for Maddie. And I had the feeling he'd already coughed up as much as he'd be willing to—he'd choose death before saying more.

"Maddie still had her phone on her, right?" I said to Logan as I tapped my phone's screen.

He nodded, and just a tiny bit of the tension wound tight inside me released. That was a reason to hope.

Of course, who knew what this woman who seemed to have risen from the dead had already done to Maddie? What her goals were? Why she'd intervened at all?

This whole situation had gotten far more complicated than I liked, and I had no idea how to untangle it when new snags rose up faster than we could work through the previous ones.

My jaw clenched, but I forced my voice to stay even when my main tech guy on staff picked up. "I have a phone number I need you to trace," I said. "And I also need you to check the traffic cams around that address you sent me to earlier today for a black SUV. Follow its route as well as you can and figure out where it's gone."

"No problem, boss," Luis replied without hesitation.

I set the phone on my lap, my fingers curling tight around it as I looked around at the other guys. Until recently, they'd seen my criminal connections as reason to distrust me. Would they blame me for how the violence we were facing had escalated—claim it was *my* fault that Maddie had ended up at the wrong end of a gun?

My stomach twisted at the thought. I didn't know how this would work if we ended up divided again, whether I could ensure her safety alone.

The best thing I could do was show that I was working as hard as possible to get Maddie out of danger right now.

I focused on Logan. "Do you know any places around here where your mom could have gone to hide out—old properties, family friends, favorite spots to visit…?"

Logan shook his head and then pressed the heels of his hands against his temples. "Not that I can think of. But, I mean, I obviously don't know anything about this woman at all."

"Did she have any close friends who faded out of your family's life after she supposedly died?"

He paused and then groaned. "I don't know. I didn't pay that much attention to my parents' social lives."

Dexter frowned, his dark curls tumbling across his forehead as he tilted his head. "We could try searching property and rental listings for her name—but she must have been using a fake name and IDs once her death was registered."

"Yeah, that won't get us anywhere." Slade swiped his hand across his mouth and then looked at me. "Can you talk to Doom's Seed? Take him to task for this war he—or Lindell—started against you and find out if he knows anything about Maddie getting kidnapped? Everything seems to lead back to him."

It did, which didn't reassure me at all. I gritted my teeth as I considered my options.

"There are specific channels of communication I have to use to reach out to him," I admitted. "I can't just call him up—I wouldn't know how. And he could take hours or even days to respond if he decides to. He wasn't very cooperative before. We don't have that kind of time. And even if we did, the chances that he'd tell me anything helpful are next to none." I paused. "I'm not sure it'd be a good thing for him to realize how much Maddie's disappearance matters to me."

"Okay, you have a point there." Slade sighed and sagged back in the chair. The color had leached from his normally warm brown skin.

I swallowed hard, my throat constricting with my expanding sense of failure, and my phone pinged with an incoming text from Luis. I lifted the device and immediately grimaced.

"My main tech guy can't trace Maddie's phone," I said. "At best, it's shut off. At worst, it's been destroyed. And there were no traffic cams near the medical facility. He's running a wider search for a black SUV in the right timeframe, but it's hard to pick up when we don't even have the license plate."

Logan swore. "My mom must know what she's doing—or

someone helping her does. How could she…?" He let out a strangled sound of frustration.

"Hold on," I said, flicking through my contacts. "My tech people are good, but they're not the absolute best out there. If there are any new tricks or techniques, I know at least one guy who might be a bit more in the know."

I dialed Gideon's number, but the call went straight to voicemail, not even ringing once. My muscles tensed further as I tried the rest of the Paradise Bend crew: Rowan and Wylder, Kaige and even Mercy. The result was the same.

They must have been in the middle of a deal or some other work where they couldn't be disturbed. There was no telling when they'd be available again either.

And it'd been a long shot anyway. Gideon was brilliant, but his actual experience was mainly on his home turf, not on the level of groups like the Devil's Dozen. I wasn't totally sure he'd have been able to outdo my own people when searching territory he wasn't familiar with.

As that thought passed through my mind, inspiration hit me with a jolt. The possibility felt even more tenuous than my connection to Gideon, but if it worked out…

I sat up straighter, and the other guys immediately focused on me even more intently.

"What?" Logan demanded.

I wet my lips. "There's another member of the Devil's Dozen I could reach out to who I think is more likely to get back to me quickly if I say it's urgent. Our newest member—she took out the man who used to hold the spot, and since then she's been disbanding a lot of his more unsavory business as if she doesn't agree with them. It seems like she has a more solid moral compass than most of my colleagues."

Slade perked up, flicking his dark brown hair away from his

eyes as he peered at me. "And she'd know how to track down Logan's mom and Maddie?"

"I'm not sure," I admitted. "But I've heard murmurs that her closest associates are highly skilled mercenaries, so *they* should be the kind of people who know how to locate a target… It's far from a guarantee, but I can't think of anyone else to call on."

I braced myself for them to hesitate or even berate me for suggesting this course of action—for wanting to draw another high-level criminal into our problems with unknown consequences. How much did they even trust my judgment about who we could rely on?

But in a matter of seconds, all three of the Vigil guys were nodding.

"We have to take every available option," Dexter said.

Logan motioned to my phone. "What are you waiting for? Make that call!"

In spite of everything, a tiny spark of warmth lit in the midst of the turmoil gripping my chest. They were counting on me, cooperating with me. Working with me rather than shutting me out like I was another enemy, the way they had before. They recognized that I knew how to navigate the dark underworld we'd entered better than the rest of them, and they accepted it.

We might have had our disagreements in the past, but we were united by the belief that we needed to protect Maddie at all costs.

I tapped Lana's name on my phone's screen. If anyone could find the fastest way to send a message to another Devil's Dozen member, it was the Storm's business manager.

"It looks like you got the immediate disaster under control," she said without preamble when she picked up. "Impressive work there."

"Thank you," I said automatically. It was hard to think about the assault my people had faced that Maddie had been so instrumental in overcoming when now Maddie's life was on the line. "I have another disaster in progress… and I'd like to speak to the Blood Hunter about it as soon as possible. Can you pull all the strings you have access to and see if you can make that happen?"

Lana hadn't gotten her position by questioning the people in charge. "On it," she said without missing a beat, and ended the call.

"I don't know how long it'll take," I told the guys as I set the phone aside again. "Let's see if we can make any more progress on our own in the meantime." My own people might still get us somewhere. I focused on Logan. "Can you remember any details about the SUV your mom was traveling in? Something that could help pick it out of all the other black SUVs out there?"

Logan made a face. "I was so fucking distracted. If I'd just reacted fast enough to check the license plate…" His brawny shoulders tensed with frustration. "Details… It looked very new. Totally clean, really shiny. Almost definitely a recent model. That's the only thing that stood out about it, at least that I noticed."

"That helps." I wrote out a text to Luis. "Did you see what model it was, or even the make?"

"No. God damn it."

I looked up from my phone, my mouth twisting into a pained but sympathetic smile. "It isn't your fault. The mom you believed was dead was standing right there in front of you. Of course you weren't worrying about the car."

"None of us would have paid much attention in a situation like that," Dexter put in.

Logan glanced at him. "I wish you'd been out there snapping your pictures." Then his head lifted higher. "You were taking pictures inside the place. We should go over those—maybe we'll see a clue that connects to my mom that we missed while we were there."

"It's worth a shot." Slade pulled out his phone. "Have you got them in the cloud yet, Dex?"

"Adding them now." Dexter paused and then caught my gaze in one of his fleeting moments of eye contact. "I can add you to the album too."

That offer brought a hint of a real smile to my face. "That'd be great. I want to do everything I can—and the more eyes the better, right?"

After a half hour of scanning the photos, zooming in and peering at every nook and cranny, my spirits were starting to sink. None of us had turned up anything so far, and there weren't many pictures left to study—and at least one of the other guys had already looked at anything I hadn't.

I was just sucking in my breath, trying to figure out what to suggest we do next, when my phone's ringtone pealed out.

I snatched up the phone and yanked it to my ear at the sight of the call display. "Lana, what have you got for me?"

Her professional satisfaction hummed through her voice. "The Blood Hunter is willing to speak to you immediately. Should I connect you now?"

My heart skipped a beat. I hit the speaker button and set my phone on the coffee table between the four of us so we could all be included in the conversation.

"Absolutely," I said. "I can't wait to speak to her."

CHAPTER 3

Madelyn

I shifted my arms up and down, stretching the silky material binding my wrists so it gradually loosened. I'd been working at it on and off for what felt like hours, and every time I felt a little more give.

The smooth fabric didn't hold a knot well. I got the impression Yvonne didn't have a whole lot of experience at restraining prisoners. Lucky for me.

She'd left me alone in the walk-in closet the entire time. After Doom's Seed had marched out again, I hadn't heard any voices, only a single set of footsteps occasionally pattering from one room to another. At this point, I was sure it was just the two of us in the apartment.

How long that would last, it was impossible to guess.

I squirmed my arms a little more and tested my compressed hand against the binding. This time, the loop of fabric finally slid over the base of my thumb.

My heart skipped a beat. If I wanted to, I could slide my bindings right off now. I'd be free.

Other than the closet door and the woman with the gun waiting between me and the outside world.

I sank onto my butt to rest for a moment and consider my options. I could have called Yvonne's bluff and yelled for help, but even if *she* would have risked someone hearing me, I couldn't believe a huge crime boss like Doom's Seed would have let her keep me here if there were people nearby who'd hear a loud shout.

I couldn't count on anyone coming to help me. My guys wouldn't have any idea where she'd taken me.

To get out of this mess, I could only count on myself.

I had two tools at my disposal: persuasion and force. I wasn't sure either would be enough, but starting with the one less likely to get me killed seemed like the best idea.

First I wanted to scope out as much of my surroundings as I could and see if I could add any tools to my limited arsenal.

I pressed my face against the doorframe and used the friction to tug the blindfold back over my eyes, so she wouldn't realize I'd been able to dislodge it. Leaving my hands in their silky restraint, I scooted a little back from the door.

"Hey!" I hollered. "Are you still there? I need to use the bathroom. Unless you want me to pee in here on your stuff."

Yvonne's footsteps quickly tapped across the floor to the closet. It'd obviously been long enough that she could believe I genuinely needed to go—and I did feel a real twinge in my bladder.

The door clicked open. "Come on, then," Yvonne said brusquely, grasping the side of my arm to tug me to my feet. "Let's be quick about it."

I couldn't make out anything other than the hardwood floor as she escorted me down a hall and into a tiled bathroom. The boards in the hall gleamed with polish, not a mark on them—like they'd recently been laid down. That didn't help me with my escape, though.

Yvonne followed me right into the bathroom. "Can I get a little privacy?" I protested as she loosened my jeans.

"I'm making sure you don't get up to anything you shouldn't. You don't have anything I haven't seen before."

I had to restrain a flinch as her cool hands dragged my jeans and panties down my thighs. She pushed me down on the toilet, an awkward fit with my arms bound behind me. I forced my pelvis to relax so I could actually go and keep up my story, my skin itching with mortification.

So much for searching the place. She wasn't giving me a second alone to take a peek at my surroundings or grab anything. What I wouldn't have given for something as simple as a pair of nail scissors…

But there was no point in moping about the impossible.

"I'm done," I said when I was sure nothing more would come out.

"Then stand up. I'm not wiping you."

I guessed I'd rather that than have her reach right between my legs. Even the thought made me shudder.

I got to my feet, and she yanked up my jeans. She was using two hands, I noted, which meant she wasn't holding her gun right now. But she probably had it in her pocket within easy reach. I didn't like my odds of getting out of my bindings and making it to the door before she was ready to shoot me.

Not while she was still so alert, anyway.

Time to give persuasion a try.

As Yvonne hustled me back to the closet, I couldn't help

wishing I'd managed to absorb more of Slade's easy charm. I was good with facts and problem-solving, not so much with cajoling people into getting my way.

Maybe I should start by getting some facts, then. See if I could understand how both of us had ended up in this awful situation.

"Why are you doing this to me?" I asked as she pushed me ahead of her into the closet. My shoulder brushed the hanging shirts and dresses. "You know that Logan cares about me. You know how upset he'll be if something happens to me. He'll never forgive you."

"Then you'd better behave so that it doesn't come to that."

"You're really going to let me go at some point? That's not how stories like this usually end, and I think you know that." I didn't want to let on that I'd overheard Doom's Seed's threats, but she had to realize the likely outcome was obvious.

Yvonne simply let out a huff but didn't answer. I pressed harder. "Don't you care about your son at all?"

Yvonne prodded me farther into the closet. My back hit the clothes along the far wall with a jangling of the hangers. I half expected her to storm off, but she stayed in place. I could sense her standing there a few feet away—not close enough for me to reach her, but not leaving either.

"You have no idea what you're talking about," she said with a rasp in her voice. "You're practically a kid still. I already gave up *everything* for Logan. You'd never comprehend what I've been through or the choices I've needed to make."

My stomach twisted at her tone. "Did you have to run off and fake your death? Whoever you're with now, that man who came in earlier—did he force you?"

Yvonne let out a cool laugh. "That was my one consolation prize after everything else fell apart. You don't know what real love is yet either, even if you imagine you do."

She figured she was in love with a murderous criminal overlord, then? I restrained a shiver. No, I definitely couldn't comprehend that at all. He obviously wasn't even trying to put on a show of having a conscience, talking about killing me and her own son for nothing more than trying to get at the truth.

"You could have stayed with Logan," I couldn't help pointing out. "You didn't *have* to leave him."

"I made the best choices I had with the hand I was dealt."

Her shoes squeaked against the floor as if she were turning to go. I wasn't getting anywhere by talking to her.

My pulse stuttered, but I knew what I had to do, even if the thought made me queasy. If I couldn't convince her to sympathize with me using my words, I'd have to turn to my fists.

And to accomplish that, I needed her on this side of the closet door. Preferably as close to me as possible.

"So you're a shitty mother, basically," I tossed out. "Putting your love life over being there for your son. Some sacrifice."

As I spoke, I flexed my arms and felt the give of the silk scarf. I could slip my hands out in an instant—as soon as it was the *right* instant.

Yvonne whirled back around with a rustle of her clothes. "Don't you *dare* make any judgments about my choices when you haven't got a clue what you're talking about."

"Oh, I think I have a pretty good idea," I said, putting on as caustic a tone as I could manage. A little honest anger bubbled up inside me at the memories of Logan mourning the woman in front of me. "You met this guy, and you had an inconvenient husband you weren't quite as head over heels for anymore, so you chucked your whole family in the trash to chase your new 'love.'"

"It wasn't like that," Yvonne snapped. "Shut up about things you don't understand."

"I understand how much it hurt both Holand and Logan,

losing you. I've seen the pain on their faces, over and over. You'd know how much losing you wrecked them if you'd bothered to pay any attention instead of only caring about yourself."

"I did what I had to do. Shut your mouth and mind your own business."

I forced a derisive snort. "You kidnapped me. I think it's one hundred percent my business that you're a selfish, conniving bitch who never gave a damn about anyone other than—"

My taunts jabbed deep enough that Yvonne didn't even let me finish my sentence. She strode forward and slapped me across the face hard enough that my head jerked to the side, my cheek stinging.

But that was exactly what I'd wanted.

Even as her palm collided with my cheekbone, I was shoving my wrists free from the scarf.

My hands whipped forward, one snatching off the blindfold, the other already aiming a punch where I'd been able to estimate her head was. My knuckles slammed into her temple, just a tad off course. I'd hoped to sock her in the nose.

Yvonne shrieked as she stumbled to the side. She groped at her hip, no doubt for the gun, but I rushed at her with all of my strength and every instinct my Krav Maga training had drilled into me.

I just had to keep hitting until I was sure I could get away.

I kept my fists flying and swiped out with my foot as well. Yvonne flailed at me, curling her fingers into claws and stabbing her elbow at me, but it was obvious she had no training at all. I managed to dodge her blows and then kicked at her ankles, making her stagger.

At the last second, she managed to head-butt me in the stomach. I let out a whoomph as the air left my lungs, but then I flung myself forward again.

When I rammed my heel into her knee, she buckled over. I grabbed her hair at the back of her head and smacked her face down into the floor with all my might.

Yvonne groaned, her body trembling with the impact. She sagged to the side in a daze, and I sprang past her out the closet door.

Yanking it shut behind me, I scanned the room for something to hold it closed. An oak desk stood against the wall right next to the closet. When I shoved it over, I found it was as heavy as I'd hoped.

I hefted it in front of the closet and then dashed out of the bedroom.

Yvonne's furious voice rang out behind me as she started to pummel the door from inside the closet. "Get back here, you bitch! Let me out, or you'll wish I *had* killed you in the first place."

Ignoring her threats, I dashed through the apartment's living room. My gaze caught on a purse I recognized as Yvonne's from the first moments in the car—the purse she'd stuffed my phone in. Without slowing down, I caught hold of the straps and yanked it off the sofa.

I spared a quick glance out the living room window, but I couldn't see anything in the dark except the glow of city lights through the night that had fallen while I was trapped. My stomach flipped over.

It'd definitely been hours. The guys would be frantic.

I darted out the front door. The second it slammed behind me, Yvonne's screeches faded away. I sprinted toward the elevator—and jerked to a stop when I saw the floor number on the digital display creeping upward.

Someone was riding up. Maybe to another floor—or maybe it was Doom's Seed's people or the man himself coming straight here.

Shit. I dove into the stairwell at the end of the hall instead. My shoes thundered over the stairs as I dashed down them as fast as my feet would fly.

I'd won my freedom, and I was not letting myself get caught again.

CHAPTER 4

Dexter

It was hard to feel hopeful about Madelyn's fate when all we had was a cell phone and a blank-screened laptop sitting next to each other on the coffee table. But the woman Beckett referred to as "the Blood Hunter" was talking on speakerphone while the voice of one of her associates carried from the laptop, and apparently he had significant technological skills.

He didn't appear to be all that keen on using those skills to help us, though. "Who exactly is this woman you're trying to track down?" he asked with a note of suspicion in his voice.

Beckett leaned toward the devices on the table, his pale hair drifting across his forehead as his gray eyes turned even more intense. "She's my girlfriend. Who was kidnapped, probably at least in part *because* she's my girlfriend."

"And I can assume you're telling the truth because...?"

There was a rustling sound, and I got the impression the Blood Hunter had swatted him. "This is the Storm's heir—the one I told you seems like he's open to changing some things in the Devil's Dozen. I wouldn't have suggested we do this if I didn't believe his story."

"All right, all right," the man said in a tone that had quickly turned teasing. "You're the boss. Why don't you have a tech genius of your own, Mr. Heir of the Storm?"

"I do," Beckett said dryly. "But it turns out he's not quite brilliant enough. Your 'boss' seems to think you might be able to top him."

"Oh, probably." The man on the other end tsked his tongue. "No phone signal to track, and no way to trace the kidnapping vehicle?"

"Exactly."

Logan leaned forward from where we were all poised around the coffee table, his broad hands flexing and clenching. I was sitting rigidly still, but his obvious edginess resonated with the tension winding through my body.

We *had* to find Madelyn. How could we have lost her—and like this? Logan's mom still alive, taking her hostage…

I wasn't sure how she *or* Logan were going to be okay after this.

"Are you going to show us what you're doing?" Logan demanded. "All we can see is a black screen so far."

"Don't worry, we're all linked up. There's just nothing to show yet."

"So, you *are* going to show us something at some point?" Slade asked, his casual tone a little more terse than usual. His dark brown eyes held a glint that looked more dangerous than amused. He was just as worried as the rest of us, even if he was better at hiding it.

"I'm getting to that," the hacker said. "All in good time. Give me her number."

As Beckett rattled it off, I frowned. "But there's no way to track her phone right now."

The man chuckled. "Ah, that's where you're mistaken—and where the Storm's tech guy failed. Someone *really* in the know would be aware that a lot of cellular companies have started adding a function to their firmware that allows you to turn a phone on remotely."

"It's not their fault they don't have access to all the same info you do," the Blood Hunter put in.

"I'm just stating facts."

"You could be a little less patronizing about it."

"All part of my charm." I could practically hear the grin in the man's voice, and my own hands clenched. I didn't want him to be joking around right now—I wanted him to find Madelyn already.

Logan obviously felt similarly. "Great," he said brusquely. "And you can activate this firmware function?"

"Yep! To be fair, very few people are aware this exists. It's high-level law enforcement agencies pushing for the option, but the privacy violation makes it a major legal gray area. Thankfully, I don't really give a shit about legalities."

"Comes with the territory," Beckett remarked.

A little curiosity had lit Logan's gaze despite his frustration. "How exactly does it work?"

If he could still wonder about the technological side even with everything going on, maybe he'd come out of this all right after all.

"I've got to keep a few secrets to myself," the man said as a faint tapping sound carried through the speakers. "Basically, I need to follow the data trail attached to your gal's phone number to track down the activation code that goes with it. Then it's like flicking a switch… except a lot more code-y."

I shifted on my chair with a restlessness I couldn't shake. "How long will you need for that?"

"As long as it takes," the man said, very unhelpfully.

As we waited in uneasy silence, Logan squeezed his knuckles. Beckett got up and poured us all glasses of water from the sink, whether because he was worried about us getting dehydrated or just for something to do with himself, I wasn't sure. Slade gave him a grateful nod. I took a sip from mine and set it down.

We still weren't getting anywhere. What if Madelyn's phone was outright broken, or—

"Got it!" the man crowed on the other end of the line. "Okay, now I need to home in on the signal, and when I've got a clear location, I'll send it to your screen." He paused. "You do realize that this kind of tracking via cell tower never gives an exact address, right? We're going to be looking at a range rather than a specific spot."

Logan had already scooted forward to peer at the laptop. "Of course."

Several more seconds slipped by with the thumping of my pulse, and then an image formed on the screen. A map, contracting to show a smaller area even as its lines became clearer. In less than a minute, we were looking at a square of four city blocks.

Logan tapped at something with the trackpad. "That's about an hour from here." He pushed to his feet.

"But there are a couple dozen buildings in that section of the city," Beckett said. "We can't go bursting into all of them hollering her name and hope that'll work out."

The man hummed to himself. "Unfortunately, that's the best I can narrow it down from the phone. If you can think of other factors that would come into play, I can do my best to account for those too. I'm assuming to hold a kidnapping victim, it'd probably be a place that's not very busy, ideally not open to the public."

My mind started to whirl with possibilities, the gnawing panic fading now that I had a concrete puzzle in front of me. I hadn't been able to help much before, but fitting pieces together—that was *my* expertise.

"The kidnapper wouldn't have wanted to walk her across a public sidewalk with a gun on her," I said. "It'll probably be a building with a secluded parking lot, out of view around back or underground."

"That makes sense." The man clicked something, and several of the buildings on the screen grayed out.

My thoughts raced on, exhilarated by our progress. "There'd need to be a lot of space between where they're holding Madelyn and anyplace bystanders would be nearby, to make sure if she shouted for help no one could hear her. So that would eliminate any of the smaller buildings that are open to the public, I think. At least those that don't have basements."

A few more buildings grayed out, but not enough. I drummed my fingers on the edge of the coffee table, and inspiration sparked.

"Are any of those buildings not open at *all* yet? Not quite finished construction or closed for renovations—someplace they could ensure there'd be no chance of anyone seeing or hearing her?" Our enemies didn't have to be going to those lengths, but if they *could* be that careful, why wouldn't they?

The man let out a low whistle. "You know what, I think you're on to something. There is one condo building here that's finished construction but not yet officially open—no one's moved in. At least not in the existing records."

Beckett stepped forward, his eyes lighting up. "I bet that's where she's been taken."

I didn't want us to go rushing in without total confirmation, though.

"That one building—if no one's living there yet, it wouldn't be drawing any utilities, right? Can you check whether electricity, water, and heating have been active today?"

"I absolutely can. Ah, ha! All three have been drawn on as recently as this evening. Sneaky, but not quite sneaky enough to defeat the great Blaze."

"You know you just gave them your name, don't you?" the Blood Hunter broke in with amusement lacing her voice.

"Hey, it's an alias anyway. And they do seem like okay people. What do you guys think? Ready to track down your woman?"

Beckett was tucking a pistol into a holster at his waist. "I'd say so. Thank you for your help—and Blood Hunter, don't hesitate to call on the Storm if you feel we can return the favor."

"Never hurts to have an extra ally in my back pocket," she said, and both of the lines cut out.

Slade and I stood up in unison. We hustled with Logan toward the door as Beckett followed behind us, already placing a new call on his phone. "Yeah, I need you at this spot as quickly as you can get there. I'm going to need reinforcements." He recited the address we'd learned as he pulled out his key fob to unlock the doors on his van.

Slade glanced over at me as we clambered into the back, a sense of urgency vibrating through the air. He let out a strained laugh. "Never thought I'd see the day when I'd be racing off with a criminal overlord to rescue the woman I love."

Neither did I, I thought, so automatically that the truth of that statement only fully hit me a second later, with the lurch of the van surging toward the road.

It *was* true, wasn't it? This wrenching pain in my chest, and the frantic need to know Madelyn was okay. The chill that stabbed through me at the thought that she might have been hurt—the rush of relief when I imagined pulling her away from whatever Logan's mom had dragged her into.

I'd never worried about anyone like this before. I'd never wanted to protect someone so badly. A thrill shivered through me with the recognition of how much Madelyn meant to me, but it came with a terrifying flipside.

For the first time in my life, I could say that I loved someone—and if we didn't act quickly enough, I might lose her before I ever got a chance to tell her that.

CHAPTER 5

Madelyn

The stairs rushed by beneath me so quickly that I knew if I tried to think about it too hard, I'd stumble. So I just let my feet fly on, focused only on reaching the bottom. On making it all the way to the door.

When I hit the bottom of the staircase, my breath coming short, I eased more carefully to the windowed door. The dark lobby beyond looked totally empty, no one in the security booth near the front entrance. A few pieces of paper were tacked to the walls, like the kinds of information sheets you'd find in a building under construction.

Was this building even really open yet?

No one arrived in the brief time I was watching, and I knew I couldn't afford to linger very long. If Doom's Seed's people had been going up to Yvonne's apartment in the elevator, they'd have found her trapped in the closet by now.

I pushed out into the lobby and darted across the thickly carpeted floor. At the main door, I glanced around quickly and, seeing only a few cars cruising by under the glow of the streetlamps, slipped out. I strode away from the building as quickly as I could while trying to give the appearance that I was simply in a hurry and not fleeing for my life.

My phone—where was my phone? I had to call the guys—I had to have it in my hand so I could dial 9-1-1 if a bunch of criminals came after me.

I groped inside Yvonne's purse, the contents rattling around my fumbling fingers. But just as I caught hold of what felt like my phone's case, a familiar white van roared around a corner just a couple blocks ahead and raced toward me.

In the first second, I froze, my legs tensing to propel me in the opposite direction in case this was some kind of threat. There was nothing to say Doom's Seed couldn't use white vans too. But before I could dash off, an even more familiar face appeared through the open passenger window.

"Maddie!" Logan called out, his voice ragged.

I bolted toward them rather than away. The van screeched to a halt by the curb with Beckett's face, unusually frantic, staring at me from behind the wheel. Slade and Dexter spilled out of the back, Slade grabbing my arm.

"I'm so glad we found you," he said, yanking me into a swift hug before dragging me toward the van. "Come on. I have the feeling we'd better get out of here fast, yeah?"

"Yeah," I said shakily. "I think that would be a good idea."

I clambered into the back after the guys and dropped into one of the benches against the wall. As Beckett gunned the engine again, Logan twisted in his seat to peer at me. His eyes narrowed.

"Your cheek is bruising. Who the fuck did that to you?"

The protective growl of his voice sent a welcome shiver through me, but the thought of answering him made my stomach clench up.

"Your mom," I admitted.

He winced, his mouth tightening.

"I take it you got away from her," Beckett said, shooting me a quick smile of relief over his shoulder. "You always manage to impress me even after I think I know what you're capable of."

"I had no idea if you guys would even be able to find me," I said. "It didn't seem like I had much choice if I wanted to get out of there. But I'm glad you'd already figured it out. You have no idea how happy I am to see all of you."

"Take a little while to rest and recover while we get you to someplace safe."

"Where can we go that *is* safe?" Dexter asked, shooting me a worried look before focusing on Beckett. "Doom's Seed is obviously still after you and out for blood, and the police are probably continuing to look for the three of us thanks to whatever tip he gave them."

Beckett paused for long enough that my stomach started to sink. Then he shook his head sharply as if arguing with himself.

"I can take you to my main family home," he said. "It's not far, and Doom's Seed wouldn't dare attack us there. We have plenty of security if he wants to try."

Slade's mouth slanted at an uneasy angle. "Are you sure that's a good idea?"

Beckett shrugged. "It's the best place I can offer. I think our lives are so entangled at this point that it won't make anything more difficult for any of us."

"It's fine," Logan said. "Let's just get there."

Beckett pressed on the gas, and the engine revved louder. He reached to tap on his phone. "Everyone can head back to their previous positions now," he said to whoever he'd contacted via speakerphone. "The situation we needed to tackle is resolved for the moment."

Dexter scooted closer to me and tucked his hand around my elbow as he looked me over. It was a small physical gesture, but one that meant a lot from the normally awkward guy. His gaze lingered on my sore cheek for a moment. "Are you hurt anywhere else?"

I touched my stomach cautiously and found it was only a little tender from when Yvonne had slammed her head into my gut. "Nothing serious. It was just… kind of terrifying."

Slade wrapped his arm around my back from my other side and tipped his head against mine. "No kidding. But you're out now. We're not letting *anyone* get their hands on you again."

Logan was still staring back at us, looking like he wanted to climb right between the seats to join the group embrace. "I don't care that she's my mother," he said with an air of menace I'd only heard him use when speaking to or about someone who'd hurt me. "She isn't getting away with this."

My head was spinning with everything I'd learned that I didn't know how to explain, but I knew I had to tell them all one thing before they made any more plans. "She's been working with Doom's Seed. At least, I'm pretty sure it was him, from the things I overheard. That's why she wanted to stop us from investigating."

Logan's forehead furrowed. "How the hell did she end up mixed up with him?"

Oh, God, how did I explain *that* to him? All the pieces that intersected with his life in far too painful ways.

My mouth opened and closed, my throat drying up. "I—I don't know all the details—"

"Hey," Slade interrupted, squeezing me to his side. "Let's give her a chance to recover before we start some kind of interrogation."

Dexter peered at me with his sharp green eyes. "You didn't find out anything that we'd need to deal with right away, did you?"

I shook my head. "No. None of it was urgent, except, well, the kidnapping. Doom's Seed wanted to kill me."

As I said the words, Beckett sucked a rough breath through his teeth. A chill swept through me, the knowledge sinking in even clearer than before of how close I'd come to dying in that apartment.

"That fucking bastard," Logan muttered ominously, his hands flexing.

The van turned down a private driveway, and a heavy wrought-iron gate opened to admit us. "He won't get anywhere near Maddie while she's in here," Beckett said firmly. "Welcome to my home."

I turned to peek out the window, and then I could only stare. We drove through a carefully landscaped yard to a massive three-story house that really could only be called a mansion, Victorian-style in light gray brick with a darker gray trim. It had to be at least four times the size of the house I'd grown up in, surrounded by sweeping lawns and stately trees.

Slade let out a low whistle. "Well, I can't claim that crime doesn't pay."

Beckett parked in a sprawling garage off to the side of the house. The second I eased out of the van, all four guys stepped close around me as if in an unspoken agreement to play bodyguards.

Beckett led the way through a door in the garage and into a hall that was all dark wood paneling and gilded wallpaper. Our feet padded across a thick rug that stretched the length of the space to an expansive staircase.

"We won't want to disturb my father, but he mostly keeps to his favorite rooms," Beckett said quietly as we headed up the stairs. "I have a few rooms devoted to my use—a sitting area, an office, and a bedroom—all connected kind of like an apartment within the house. There are a few guest bedrooms just down the hall from that as well, so you'll all be able to crash for the night in comfort."

"Comfort?" Slade murmured. "More like total luxury." He stroked his hand up and down my side where he still had his arm around me.

Dexter's grasp had slid from my elbow to my hand. His fingers twined with mine as we stepped through a doorway after Beckett and found ourselves in a room as big as their open concept living-dining room in their apartment, with two linen sofas and a few matching wing chairs in a broad semi-circle around a gas fireplace, an eight-seater mahogany table off to the side, and several bookcases with glass doors. At Beckett's flick of a switch, light beamed down from a crystal chandelier overhead.

He turned toward me, his gaze searching mine. But even as he stepped to meet me with his hand rising as if to run over my hair, Logan pushed in first.

My stepbrother cupped my jaw and pulled me straight into a kiss, heedless of the other guys around us.

His mouth crashed into mine, and all my senses sparked to life. He was kissing me as if his life depended on our embrace, and in that moment, I needed his passion just as much.

I was here. I was okay. I was with the men I loved, and they were going to do whatever they could to ensure I was never in that much danger again.

As much as I'd let them protect me, anyway.

My knees wobbled with the rush of giddying heat. Logan pulled back just an inch, his forehead grazing mine.

"I'm never letting anyone get their hands on you again," he swore. "I don't care who the assholes are who're trying. You belong with me. With *us.*"

He glanced around at the other three guys, and their combined attention seared over my skin with twice as much heat as Logan's kiss had generated.

Beckett reached past him to guide my lips toward his. He claimed my mouth with a similar passion but plenty of tenderness as well. It felt like a statement of ownership and an apology wrapped into one.

It was one of *his* enemies who'd threatened me. Even if my own actions had drawn that man's attention to me, I didn't think Beckett would ever absolve himself of blame. "Never again," he said hoarsely when he drew back.

Slade leaned in to press his lips to my temple, his fingers teasing up under the hem of my shirt now. "No one will take you away from us again. If Logan isn't in a position to make sure of that, I will."

"And if neither of them can, I'll be here." Dexter raised his other hand to trace his index finger along my jaw, the mix of anguish and desire in his normally calm expression making my heart stutter.

"Just as long as you're okay with me protecting you too, when I can," I had to say.

Beckett let out a dismissive huff. "If I have my way, it won't be required in either direction very soon. But for just a little while, I think we can focus on showing you just how much we missed you."

His mouth caught mine again, melding with my lips before flicking his tongue between them. As it tangled with my own tongue, one of Slade's hands wound in my hair to massage my scalp with his dexterous fingers. I leaned my weight into him while Beckett messed with the bottom of my shirt, slipping it barely past my lower stomach before pausing.

He gripped my bare skin with his warm hands and took a deep breath to control himself. Slade leaned forward, resting his lips at the place where my neck met my shoulders and planting warm kisses there. Dexter took the initiative to ease my face toward him so he could draw me into a kiss himself.

I kissed him back hard, wanting him to know he meant just as much to me as the other guys even if he wasn't as confident. When my hand clutched at his shirt, he made a breathless sound against my mouth and pushed even closer against me.

Logan towered over us all, caressing a slow path along the waist of my jeans. In a matter of seconds, my panties were soaked. I couldn't restrain a needy whimper.

Beckett gripped my waist and tugged me toward one of the room's other doorways. "I think we should take this to the bedroom. Now."

Logan reached for me, but to my surprise, Dexter slipped his arms around me first. In a gesture I'd have expected from any of the other guys before him, he swept me right off my feet to cradle me against his lean but toned chest.

Slade let out an approving chuckle, and a sly smile crossed Logan's face, seeing his friend's growing assurance. We moved together to the bedroom door, my panties fully drenched now as I tucked my head against Dexter's neck.

When we stepped into Beckett's bedroom, the crisply masculine scent of him flooded my nose, making my mouth water. The pale blue walls, impeccably tidy dresser and side tables, and massive four-poster bed all fit the man I knew perfectly.

Dexter strode straight to the bed. One of the other guys might have tossed me onto it, but he had his own approach. He stood over the mattress and bent carefully to set me on the soft comforter like I was a precious artifact.

Then he climbed over me and sought out my lips. The heat of his mouth capturing mine washed through my entire body, leaving my skin tingling as if he were touching me everywhere through that one point of contact.

The other guys were climbing onto the bed around us. Someone's hand teased up my inner thigh to stroke between my legs. Another set of fingers tugged up my shirt. I was burning up all over, squirming with need. How was I ever going to survive all four of these incredible men at once?

I wasn't sure, but I was absolutely looking forward to finding out.

As I fumbled with the button on Dexter's pants, Logan breathed by my ear. "I'm going to make you feel so good, Maddie. We *all* are, and I can't wait to watch you come, again and again."

The promise in his words brought a gasp to my lips. While Dexter eased back to shed his pants, Logan pulled my shirt up over my head. Then his hands were cupping my breasts, his thumbs swiveling over the peaks with enough force to send jolts of pleasure through my nipples even with the fabric of my bra in between us.

"Get her pants off too, Dex," Slade ordered in an unusually gruff voice.

As Beckett leaned in to steal another kiss for himself, the other guys peeled my jeans off me. A hand brushed over my panties. Then Slade chuckled. "There's a more fun way of removing those."

He must have motioned to Dexter, because two mouths pressed against my hips in unison. Their scorching breaths tingled over my thighs as they dragged my panties down by their teeth.

Then agile fingers delved right into the spot where I needed it most. I jerked into Dexter's eager hand, my eyes rolling back with the blissful sensation it conjured.

Logan groaned. "That's right, baby. We've got you."

Clothes were being shed all around me. The encounter was melding into a blur of passion and need. I could barely think, only move with the skillful touches stirring delight all through my body, arching to meet one kiss and then another.

Somewhere in there, my bra disappeared, baring my breasts to the warm air. Beckett's thumb and forefinger closed around one pert nipple. "Try this," he said to Logan, giving the slightest tug that drew a moan right out of my throat.

Logan smirked and repeated the gesture on the other side until I was writhing between the two of them, still bucking into Dexter's massaging fingers. My body shuddered, so close to release. Then my gaze caught on Slade, kneeling near me as he rubbed his hand over his stunningly erect shaft.

A different sort of desire reverberated through me. I parted my lips with a flick of my tongue.

"Come closer," I murmured. "I'm going to make you feel good too, Slade."

"Oh, Piccolina, you know I can't refuse an offer like that."

I flipped over onto my hands and knees between them and lowered my head to suck Slade's shaft into my mouth. His breath broke as I swirled my tongue around him, his hips pumping toward me instinctively. His fingers tangled in my hair with the gentle tugs I loved.

Dexter had moved with me, continuing his attentions between my legs. He hooked a finger right inside me and exhaled shakily at my muffled moan.

"Do you want more than this inside you, Madelyn?" he asked in the sexiest voice I'd ever heard from him.

I hummed in what I hoped was a clear enough answer. There was a crinkling as a condom packet changed hands, and then Dexter adjusted my position so he could slide under me, gripping my hips as I straddled him.

His cock rubbed over my clit and then plunged right into me. I cried out around Slade's erection and then lapped it even more enthusiastically.

Slade jerked with my attentions, his fingers tightening in my hair. I sucked him down hard, and his breath hitched. He mumbled a curse as he spilled himself into my mouth. Then he lifted my head to kiss me with his taste still on my lips while I rocked over his friend.

When my mouth tore away from Slade's, Dexter reached around me to squeeze my ass. He curled his fingers right between my cheeks and grazed my other opening. Maybe it was something in my face, or maybe he'd seen signs from me before, but his lips curled with a pleased smile.

"I think she'd like to be filled here too," he said. "Who's going to take that honor?"

"That ass is mine," Logan growled, and I trembled with anticipation.

Dexter kept thrusting up into me, and Logan's hand replaced his friend's against my back entrance. With a rustling, someone must have passed him some lube, because a slick gel smoothed over my opening. He worked one finger and then another into me until I was moaning so loud I wondered if I was breaking Beckett's rule about not disturbing his father.

But the mafia heir didn't look concerned. He claimed my mouth, drinking in my desperate sounds as Logan slid his thick shaft into me from behind.

I'd never felt so stretched or so full… or so complete. I bowed over Dexter, shaking as my first orgasm blazed through me just like that.

All of my men were working together, encouraging each other as they gave me the time of my life. We really had gotten past all the animosity and jealousy. It was the five of us together, one cohesive team.

I wasn't going to neglect any part of that team myself. As I caught my breath, I reached down Beckett's well-muscled torso to his rigid erection. With a tight grip, I pumped my hand up and down.

"Fuck, that feels good, Maddie," he rasped, nipping my earlobe.

Logan and Dexter moved inside me in unison, pumping in and out with Dexter's hands on my waist and Logan's steadying my hips. Their rhythmic strokes pushed me right back to the brink again, the wave of pleasure expanding from my core.

I kept moving—kept pace as Logan roared and stiffened behind me. Dexter moved a hand between my thighs, the pressure on my clit sending my bliss spiraling even faster. He panted, holding on as long as he could, but he didn't need to wait much longer.

This time, the orgasm didn't rise and fall on the way to my peak. It came all at once, slamming into me like a tidal wave of ecstasy. It would have knocked me off my feet if I'd been standing.

Dexter let out a groan as he came with me. I slumped over him, my hand still clenched around Beckett's shaft, and had just enough wherewithal left to bend to the side and take the head of his cock into my mouth.

Beckett rocked between my lips hard and fast. I sucked him down as far as I could, and he came with a spurt of salty liquid and a strangled sound.

I collapsed between the four of them, and they sank down around me. I lay there perfectly surrounded, and for the first time since Beckett's call in the library what felt like a million years ago, a sense of peace settled over me.

That was what I felt surrounded by all of my men. A sense of everlasting peace and certainty. Unity and loyalty. Family.

The long, chaotic day finally caught up with me, and my eyelids drifted shut.

When I opened my eyes again, I barely remembered having fallen asleep. I definitely hadn't meant to. I blinked, staring at the four guys sprawled around me in the early morning sunlight drifting through the window.

Now that my exhaustion and shock had faded, the thought of how much they still didn't know hit me like a smack of cold water. I needed to tell them everything, lay it all out, as painful as some of it might be. We couldn't deal with the huge problem still facing us until we all understood what we were dealing with.

I stretched my legs. Slade jerked upright as my cool feet pressed into his side.

"Jesus," he muttered. "Keep those icicles to yourself."

His dark brown eyes met mine, glazed with sleep, but despite the complaint, his expression showed nothing but contentment.

"Could you shut the fuck up?" Logan groaned, rolling over and then rubbing his face.

Beckett chuckled, though his eyes hadn't yet opened. "Good morning to all of you too."

With a sigh in anticipation of the conversation ahead, I sat up.

Dexter peered up at me and pushed up on his elbows. "What's the matter?"

"There's a lot we still need to talk about," I said, measuring out my words. "A lot that I found out yesterday, about Doom's Seed and about Logan's mom." I paused, studying Logan's reaction, but his mouth only tightened a little.

I forced myself to continue. "I think I know how they got involved, and what Doom's Seed is trying to cover up—as well as why he had my dad murdered."

CHAPTER 6

Madelyn

"... And then I shoved the dresser in front of the closet door and ran for it," I said, wrapping up my account of my kidnapping.

All four of my men were staring at me from their positions around the living room. Beckett and Logan had staked out the spots on either side of me on one of the sofas, and Slade and Dexter had each taken an armchair nearby.

For the first several seconds after I finished speaking, silence hung over the room. Logan's mouth had flattened into a tight line. Beckett's expression was stormy. Slade set his hands on his knees, balled into fists, and Dexter rubbed his hand across his frowning mouth.

"An illegal transplant service," he said, breaking the silence. "It does fit all the pieces. That must be what they were transporting in the poisonous fish coolers: the organs they got by some illegal means."

Beckett nodded grimly. "And the building we investigated yesterday will be where they performed at least some of the transplant operations in this area."

Slade shook his head in bemusement. "I guess people must be willing to pay a hell of a lot for a procedure that could make the difference between life and death."

The instant after he'd spoken, his gaze flicked to Logan. I hadn't spelled out the assumptions I'd made after hearing Yvonne's conversation with the man who must be Doom's Seed, but the implications were obvious.

Logan looked up at us. His voice came out strained and without his usual force. "And that has to be how my mom met Doom's Seed. She must have paid him to handle my liver transplant—there mustn't have been a match soon enough, and she got desperate."

"That would fit too," I said carefully, watching his expression. I had no idea how hard this must be for him. Not only had his mother totally abandoned him without him knowing, but it'd been to join a major criminal whose crimes she'd involved her nine-year-old son in too.

Logan bowed his head, and I reached over to grasp his hand. He squeezed it back, taking a moment to gather himself again.

"It even makes sense why things were so tense between her and my dad after the operation," he said. "I don't think Dad has any idea how she pushed the operation forward, but she had to get that money from somewhere. At least one time I heard him saying something about their savings, and he mentioned more than once that he wasn't sure he could trust her anymore. She must have taken a bunch out and refused to tell him what for."

I stroked my thumb up and down the back of his hand, remembering the doubts he'd expressed in the past about whether he'd even deserved his second chance at life. How much more would this revelation have shaken his sense of self-worth?

"It was her choice, not yours," I reminded him. "You didn't get any say in it. And maybe she was wrong, and there would have been a liver by legitimate channels in time, and you getting the liver you did only meant that someone else's life got saved too."

Logan grimaced. "Still. The people he's getting those organs from must also be desperate—desperate or murdered. And now I…" He couldn't seem to finish, resting his hand on his abdomen over his scar instead.

Slade spoke up, equally tentative. "From what you said, it sounds like Yvonne's connection with Doom's Seed has gone beyond, er, professional? They're romantically involved?"

I tipped my head in reluctant acknowledgment, still focused on Logan. "She was definitely talking to him as if they had a personal relationship, like they'd built a life together. He wasn't exactly affectionate, but he didn't dispute that idea either."

Dexter's hand skimmed upward to run through his rumpled black curls. "For her to fake her own death to run away with him, she would have needed pretty major motivation. Just feeling like she owed him for a service she paid for wouldn't cut it."

"No," Logan said with a ragged bark of a laugh that had no humor in it.

Beckett leaned forward, his hands clasped together on his lap. "Let's lay out what we know in the order it happened. Logan had his transplant operation—fourteen years ago?"

"Yeah."

"And I'm guessing your follow-up treatment was in the same hospital where Maddie's father worked, since that's the only one in your hometown."

"That's right," Logan said again, a little of his typical determined energy coming back into his voice. "That's how Evan could have stumbled on evidence. Maybe there was something in my post-op treatment that tipped him off that something wasn't quite right."

"That would make the most sense," I said. "If Doom's Seed has been running this scheme for a while, there've probably been other transplant patients of his at that hospital, but I wouldn't think there'd have been any others around the same time as you. It's not that big a town."

"So your dad started digging into Doom's Seed's dealings," Slade said slowly, "following whatever trail he'd gotten on, and once he got to the point of poking around those properties, Doom's Seed obviously caught on that something was up."

Dexter cocked his head. "If he was still in touch with Yvonne then, which seems likely, he'd have mentioned that this was someone from the same town she lived in. She'd have been worried that he was going to expose *her* as well as Doom's Seed."

Beckett raised his hands. "I don't think there's any need to pin the murder on her. Doom's Seed would have wanted to eliminate anyone trying to expose his illegal work without any extra factors in the mix."

"But she might have encouraged him to get on with it," Logan said, his jaw flexing. "She kidnapped Maddie at gunpoint. Brought her into a place where her lover could threaten to kill Maddie. She obviously doesn't have anywhere near as much of a conscience as I'd have wanted to believe."

"It doesn't really matter," I said. "Doom's Seed would have had his people set up the murder. But your mom hadn't left yet at that point."

"No. It was three years after my operation when she—when we *thought* she died." Logan sighed and sagged back against the sofa. "I guess she got sick of family life and found an escape so she could be with the psycho she'd fallen for permanently." His voice got hoarser.

"Other people really *did* die in that explosion. She ran away from her responsibilities—and she was selfish enough to not care that she screwed up dozens of other lives in the process."

A gloomy silence descended over all of us. I had no idea how Yvonne justified any of her actions to herself. Maybe she blocked out everything from before she'd run away to join Doom's Seed, like that'd all been some other woman who didn't count anymore.

"That's everything," Slade said, sitting a little straighter. "We've got the whole story pieced together."

Dexter knit his brow. "Not exactly. We still can't *prove* any of this. Even the conversation Maddie overheard, if she gave testimony, a lot of what we've determined is making deductions rather than anything outright stated."

My heart leapt with a sudden jolt of hope. "I might have something that can help with that."

I scrambled off the sofa and found the purse I'd dropped beside it last night. Brandishing it like a trophy, I returned to the guys. "This is Yvonne's. I took it because she stuck my phone in it, but she'll have her own things inside. Things important enough that she wanted them within reach when she left home. There's got to be *something* useful in there."

Logan let out a chuckle that sounded less pained this time and pulled the purse out of my hands into his lap. "Maddie the purse thief. You never cease to amaze me. God, I love you."

My cheeks flushed even though he'd confessed those feelings before. It made me a bit giddy just seeing more of his enthusiasm for the investigation returning now that he had something concrete to delve into.

He dug through the purse and pulled out a phone that was definitely not mine.

Beckett whistled approvingly. "I'm guessing you can get a lot of mileage out of that."

Logan smiled at him. "And anything I can't crack, your tech people should be able to." A fiercer light came into his dark eyes as he considered the possibilities. "I'll go through the contacts and messages—and I need to check the records at all the hospitals in this city and the area around it for someone named Baldwin who had an organ transplant. If his file was the one your dad thought was the most important, it could be the key to blowing this whole thing wide open."

Slade rubbed his hands together. "I don't know how to hack, but I can definitely run searches on the records we already have."

Logan paused. His gaze dropped to his torso again. "We also have evidence in me. My liver is proof of what happened, no matter how well Mom and Doom's Seed covered their tracks. If we can connect it to the businesses Doom's Seed is running, then we can be sure he doesn't get away with any of this."

Beckett stood up, his tone calmly authoritative. "We'll cross that bridge when we come to it. In the meantime, let me know what you need so you can start hacking into those other hospital systems. I'll have my people help in whatever—"

The ring of his phone cut him off. Frowning, Beckett dug it out of his pocket and raised it to his ear. "Beckett here."

A moment later, his stance went rigid, anger flaring in his normally cool gray eyes. "They *what*? Those pricks…" He sucked in a sharp breath. "Hang tight. I'll get you out of there—I just need to summon reinforcements."

My stomach had already knotted by the time he hung up and glanced around at us. "What's happening?" I asked, dreading the answer.

Beckett's fingers gripped the phone so hard his knuckles whitened. "He's not wasting any time showing his true intentions. Doom's Seed has launched another attack on my territory."

CHAPTER 7

Slade

Beckett paced the room, making one call and then another, delivering his orders in a taut but steady voice. Even when clearly upset, he carried himself with so much authoritative confidence that I couldn't help thinking I wanted to be him when I grew up, even though the guy was only a couple of years older than me.

As he finally lowered the phone to shove it into his pocket, he turned toward us.

"What's happening?" Maddie asked quickly, her pale face tight with concern. "Are your people okay?"

Of course that would be her first thought—the human lives on the line. A pang of affection ran through my chest alongside my jangling nerves.

Beckett shook his head. "Not all of them, and none of them

might be if I don't get out there quick. My family has a farm not far from here that we use for stashing goods when we need a temporary holding spot. Doom's Seed must have figured that out, and his people are trying to ransack the place."

Shit. "And some of your men were there?" I said.

"Yeah. A bunch of them were on the property handling a new shipment. Two are already down. The rest managed to get inside one of the buildings and barricade the entrance, but now they're stuck. It's a fucking siege. And even if we only lose the items in those buildings, they're valuable—it'll shatter the trust of the clients who were counting on getting their purchases."

He shoved a hand back through his blond hair, rumpling the normally sleek strands, and turned toward the door. "I've called as many reinforcements as I can to take on the attackers, but the men here at the house can get out there fastest—and I need to go with them. Keep their spirits up, show that we're in this together. I can't let my people face this kind of shit alone."

Those words only solidified the respect I'd come to feel for this guy, regardless of his criminal associations. Beckett was good at what he did—and he clearly tried to handle things in much better ways than assholes like this Doom's Seed prick. I didn't like the idea of him getting screwed over—especially when it was happening partly because he'd tried to help us out.

I sprang to my feet with a surge of conviction. "We'll help too—we'll do whatever we can."

I'd already known Logan and Dexter would agree with me on that. They both stood too, their expressions determined.

"Absolutely," Logan said.

"And even though you probably didn't mean me," Maddie said, getting up with a swish of her pale hair over her shoulders, "you aren't leaving me behind. There's got to be some way I can pitch in."

Beckett glanced back at us, a darker shadow crossing his face.

"This could get pretty bad. They're actively shooting at anyone they can, and we'll be the first ones on the scene."

Logan flexed his shoulders. "Then let's go show them that they can't mess with you without consequences. You didn't turn your back on us even when we were being jerks to you, so we're sure as hell not leaving you in the lurch."

Maddie nodded. "We're in this together," she said quietly. "All of this is our fight too. I want to see Doom's Seed taken down as much as anyone."

More, no doubt, given what we'd figured out about her dad's death. I shot her a tight but supportive smile.

Beckett searched our expressions as if looking for any sign of uncertainty. He didn't want to waste time on arguments, I could tell.

"All right," he said, marching toward the door. "Come on. We'll get equipped in the van. I already have the men downstairs prepping it."

We hustled down the stairs and out a back door, where we found a van larger than the one we'd taken before idling. One of Beckett's employees saluted him from the driver's seat, another poised next to him.

"This bunch is coming too?" the driver asked with obvious confusion.

"They're with me," Beckett said. "They're pretty handy in a fight. Let's get out there and defend what's ours."

We leapt into the back of the van where two more guys were crouched with a large canvas duffle bag at their feet. They must have heard Beckett's exchange with the driver, because they didn't question our arrival. One of them jerked open the zipper on the bag and put the contents on display.

"Grab whatever you want first, boss. We've got lots of extra ammo too."

"Perfect." Beckett motioned us over. "Pick out whatever weapons you'll be most comfortable with. We should all go in armed."

Logan pulled his pistol out from his pocket. "I think I'll stick with the firearm I'm already familiar with."

"Fair enough." Beckett turned to Dexter, who'd come up beside him, swaying with the swerving of the van down the driveway. "How about you?"

Dexter knelt down to catch his balance and studied the array of weaponry with typical precision. He pulled out a pair of long, deadly-looking knives and tested them in his hands.

I saw him hesitate and suspected he was thinking of the attacker years ago he'd needed to stab to save my life. But he didn't shy away from the blades. He eased away from the bags and set them on the floor of the van beside him.

I went over next with a twist of dread in my gut. Fighting wasn't really my thing. *Killing* wasn't my thing at all, even if I'd had to do it once. I wanted to beat these bastards down, but if I could manage that without slaughtering them left and right, it'd rest easier on my conscience.

My gaze fell on a steel shaft buried amid the guns and knives. I carefully dug out the baton, extended it to its full length, and swung it through the air. A little of the tension inside me released.

It was solid and heavy enough to crack a bone, but not the sort of automatic death a shot or a stab would ensure. It kind of reminded me of the bars built into my prosthetic leg. In a way, I was extending the reach of my arm with this weapon just like the prosthetic extended my malformed leg so I could get things done more easily.

Something about that thought felt right. I sank down next to Dexter with a sense of satisfaction that I hadn't been able to summon before.

Beckett had pulled a couple of guns and a knife from the bags, arming himself more thoroughly than the rest of us. When he looked at Maddie, she grimaced.

"My training is mostly in hand-to-hand combat—assuming I won't have a weapon or at best I'll have to make use of whatever random thing I can get hold of. I'd be afraid I'd shoot one of the people on our side if I tried to use a gun."

He handed her a switchblade, the knife edge folded in. "At least keep this in your pocket, just in case." Glancing back at the duffel bag, he hummed to himself. "I think we might be able to set this up so that you don't need to do much fighting at all."

Maddie bristled automatically. "I *can* fight."

Beckett held up his hands. "I know, believe me. But out of the five of us, I'm guessing that you have the least experience tangling with people who are more than happy to kill you if they get the chance."

Maddie hesitated and then sighed in resignation. "Okay, that's a fair assessment."

"You'll still play a crucial role," he assured her. "We'll just keep you out of the worst part of the fray as much as possible." He patted the bag beside him before zipping it up. "My men under siege need to replenish their weapons and ammo, and you can be the one to deliver the goods. The rest of us will cover you."

A smile crossed my lips despite myself. Not only was Beckett determined to keep Maddie as safe as possible, he'd figured out an argument even she had to accept. Something Logan had failed at more times than I could count.

Beckett got on his phone again, checking how close his reinforcements were and then how things were going on the farm. After the last call, his mouth had tightened.

"We're almost there," he said. "And we're going to go straight in.

Do exactly what I say, and I think we can all come out of this all right."

The van tore down the road and around another corner. Beckett moved to the door, bracing himself by the handle with one pistol already at the ready. He tipped his head to us, a signal to prepare ourselves to spring into action.

"We're going to barrel right through the middle of the Doom's Seed contingent, as close to the barn door as we can get. Someone's waiting at the door to let Maddie in the second she reaches it. Maddie, you jump out and run straight to the door—it'll be around the right side of the van. My men in the front of the van will hold off anyone who comes at us from that side, and the rest of us will defend the rear. We'll use the van for cover with the barn at our backs. Got it?"

We all nodded. A metallic clinking carried from the front of the van—the sound of a rifle being cocked, I realized. My stomach flipped over.

Maddie was slinging the straps of the duffel bag over her shoulder. She hefted it to make sure she could carry its weight and then set it down again. I couldn't stop myself from pushing off the floor to go join her.

I touched her cheek. "Never a dull day around here, huh, Piccolina?"

She laughed roughly. "I'm looking forward to some boredom when all this is over."

"Oh, I'm sure we'll find ways to spice up everyday life—ways much more enjoyable than this." I tipped her face to meet mine and claimed a quick but emphatic kiss that I hoped told her how far I intended to go to guarantee we got that future.

I stepped back, grasping my baton. The driver gave a brisk shout. Then the van screeched to a halt, and we all sprang into motion.

Beckett whipped open the back doors and used them as a shield, taking a few shots out the back and then around the side. At the swivel of his arm, the rest of us charged forward.

Logan leapt out first and fired a shot of his own. More booms rang out from the front of the van, along with the thuds of bullets drilling into the van's wall. A fine sweat broke out over my skin, but I sprang out alongside Maddie without letting my fear hold me back.

Maddie dashed around the side of the van with the duffel bags in tow. I shoved between her and a burly tattooed guy who lunged at her and smacked him across the side of the head with my baton.

He reeled to the side and yanked out a gun, but before he could take aim, I slammed the baton even harder into his wrist. At the crunch of breaking bone and a pained grunt, the pistol dropped from his hand.

Dexter was slicing out at another attacker who'd gotten close to the back of the van. Logan and Beckett were still firing, but the swarm of Doom's Seed people was all around us. I lashed out at another who charged in close and pushed farther out of our temporary shelter to crack the forearm of a prick with a revolver.

The bang of the closing door sounded behind me, making my nerves jump for a second before its meaning sank in.

Maddie had gotten inside the barn. Maddie was safe—well, as safe as she could be while these assholes still had the whole area under siege.

We had to make sure they didn't make it to the door to follow her.

I threw myself even more into the battle, the pound of my heart egging me on more than unnerving me now. Every swing of the baton and every body I struck down was one more act to keep Maddie safe and fend off the pricks who thought they could hurt all of us.

My leg didn't once wobble beneath me. I whacked and bashed alongside the other guys with rhythmic rasps of breath until more cars and vans roared into view beyond the fray.

Beckett's reinforcements had arrived.

A grin sprang to my face, and I shoved away a man who'd hurtled toward me. Spinning around, I clocked him right across the forehead. My grip tightened around my baton, exhilaration and renewed strength surging through my body.

It didn't matter that my limbs weren't quite as whole as the other guys' or that my prosthetic put me at a potential disadvantage. I was giving the fight my all and holding my own.

We weren't going to let the real bad guys win. Not today.

CHAPTER 8

Madelyn

Staring at the bodies sprawled across the terrain around the barn, I couldn't help trying to tell myself that they weren't dead. They were just unconscious. Knocked out or fainted from their injuries, but there was still a chance…

The attempt wasn't convincing even to myself. Blood splattered most of those bodies. A few within my view were gazing at nothing with eyes that never blinked.

Death was all around. I only hoped that most of them were Doom's Seed's people and not Beckett's.

"It's… it's a mess," Logan said roughly from where he was standing beside me.

I hugged myself. "At least the four of you made it through okay. And I'll try to make sure that as many other people do as I possibly can as well."

Beckett hustled over with a plastic first aid box brought in one of the cars of reinforcements. "Here," he said. "I can show you who we need to patch up. The doctor we have on staff is on his way, but you're the only person on site right now with significant medical experience."

I nodded stiffly and pushed myself into motion. I knew I wasn't a doctor or even a nurse, but I *had* been training for this kind of work for years. If I could save even one life or at least a limb, what better time to start putting my studies into real practice?

As Beckett motioned for me to follow him, two of his men walked past us, hauling one of those blankly staring corpses. They tossed it into the back of a van. My stomach lurched.

I tried to focus on Beckett, but my gaze veered to a man slumped on the ground whose entire skull had been blasted open down to his bearded jaw. A horrified squeak escaped me.

Then Beckett was there, gripping my chin to pull my gaze to him. I met his solemn gray eyes, my pulse rattling through my veins.

"This is how my line of work goes sometimes," he said. "Not very often, thankfully. And I never like it when it does. But I swear to you, we only kill when it's that or be killed ourselves. I'd rather you'd stayed back at the house and not had to see all this."

I squared my shoulders, willing down my nausea. "No, it's okay. I asked to be here—I wanted to help, and I still do." And I could do something no one else here right now could.

Beckett pressed a quick kiss to my forehead and led me the rest of the way to a man who was leaning against the tire of a pickup truck. He was clutching his arm in front of him, blood still seeping from wounds in his shoulder and forearm. I had the impression someone had sliced him open with a knife.

"He'll probably need stitches," I said, crouching next to him on the trampled grass. "And to have the wounds properly cleaned first. I don't think I can do a good enough job with this." I waved the kit.

"The doctor can handle the most serious parts," Beckett said. "Can you stop the bleeding for the time being?"

I pulled out a roll of gauze and a couple of thicker pads from the kit. "I think so." I focused on the man in front of me. "Can you lift up your arm a little so I can wrap it?"

The guy hesitated and then glanced up at Beckett. Beckett offered him a gentle smile. "She knows what she's doing. She's studying to be a doctor herself."

At his reassurance, the man visibly relaxed. What Beckett said meant that much to him—he trusted his boss without question.

That was the kind of man I'd fallen for: the kind who ruled through respect rather than fear. Who cared about everyone working under him rather than seeing them as game pieces on a board.

He was a good leader, and he didn't deserve to be in this situation. In this war that was brewing in a large part because of the way the Vigil guys and I had enraged Doom's Seed by investigating my dad's murder.

Grimacing at that thought, I swabbed the man's arm and shoulder with rubbing alcohol, apologizing when he hissed at the sting, and wrapped both wounds as tightly as I could. When no blood made it through to the outer layer of gauze, I let out my breath in relief.

"I think that should keep you stable well enough until the actual doctor gets here," I told him. "I'm sorry I couldn't do more."

His smile was tight, but I could see the gratitude in it. "Thank you for trying."

Beckett guided me on to another man who was bleeding from a wide but shallow gash on his head where he'd been clipped by a bullet, and then to a woman who I was pretty sure had fractured her ankle and who cursed a blue streak when I eased it into a makeshift splint to stabilize it.

I had no idea what the gang's foot soldiers made of me at first glance, this preppy college-aged girl carrying a basic first aid kit, but as soon as Beckett spoke of my expertise, they offered themselves up for treatment without hesitation. The next man I checked out, who had a stab wound in his thigh, even told me I should go ahead and stitch him up myself.

"I really think it's better if you wait for the doctor," I told him. "If I miss something and you get an infection, that could be just as deadly as the bleeding."

Beckett checked his phone. "He's just fifteen minutes away now. We'll get you good as new."

The man grinned shakily. "I know you will, boss."

After doing what I could for another man who'd taken a bullet to the calf, Beckett waved me over to the van we'd arrived in. "That's everyone who needs looking after. I've got a bunch of other things to take care of. You can take a breather in the back if you want to get away from all this at least a little."

As he hurried off, I glanced around, noting Logan and Slade helping haul another corpse into the other van. A brisk breeze blew over me, and the back of my arm stung.

Frowning, I twisted my arm at the shoulder and craned my neck, reaching toward the spot with my opposite hand at the same time. My fingers touched damp, severed fabric, provoking another jab of pain.

Sometime during the fight, I'd gotten a cut on the back of my arm. It was shallow—it looked like it'd only just bleed all the way through my torn shirt sleeve. The adrenaline must have numbed me to the pain before now.

I still had the first aid kit, now tucked under my arm, but it'd be hard to bandage up that spot when I could barely even get a look at it.

"What happened?" someone asked sharply from behind me.

I turned, recognizing the voice but not quite believing it until I saw Dexter taking the last couple of strides to reach me. His black curls were even messier than usual, his pale face tight with strain, but his green eyes caught mine with all the intensity he usually brought to bear.

"I'm okay," I reassured him, my pulse fluttering at the concern etched in his expression. "But I could use a little help patching myself up… if you don't mind."

I held my hand partway toward him, letting him decide how far to take the physical contact. Dexter gripped my fingers without hesitation and carefully rotated my arm to the side so he could examine the wound.

He sucked in a breath through clenched teeth with a hiss. "We were supposed to get you to the building without you getting hurt."

"It can't be that bad if I only just noticed it. There were a lot of people fighting—I'm lucky this is all that happened."

The frown didn't leave his face. "*You* weren't even fighting." His gaze darted up to briefly meet mine again. "Tell me what I need to do to bandage it properly."

I had no doubt he'd follow my every instruction to the letter. I wiggled the first aid kit out from under my other arm and moved to the back of the van where I could set it down. Once I'd popped it open, I handed him the bottle of rubbing alcohol and a patch of gauze. "We should roll up the sleeve to completely uncover it, and then you can swab it with the alcohol. That'll disinfect it."

He nodded and helped me tug the ragged sleeve of the T-shirt up to my shoulder. Then he splashed rubbing alcohol on the gauze. I braced myself as he raised it to my arm. He swiped it over the entire area swiftly but thoroughly while I gritted my teeth against the burning sensation.

Dexter's attention flicked to my face, and he jerked his hand back. "I'm hurting you."

I offered him a tight but genuine smile. "That's actually a good thing. It means all the things I *wouldn't* want lingering in the wound are dying. But I think it's clean enough now."

With a grim expression, he set down the pad. "Now what?"

I peered at the wound as well as I could. It was definitely shallow, like someone had raked a knife across my arm without managing to really dig it in. Only a few beads of blood were welling up along the cleaned skin.

"More gauze," I said. "That should be enough to stop the bleeding completely and keep it clean for the time being. Cut off a strip a couple of feet long and wrap it around my arm. I'll tell you how much pressure is good. And there's tape to fix the end once you're done."

He got to work with the same brisk efficiency he brought to almost every task, but his fingers brushed against my skin with so much gentleness that my heart swelled with affection. I couldn't imagine what it'd been like for him racing into this battle when he was most comfortable snapping photos and piecing together data.

But he'd done it for Beckett—and for me.

"Thank you," I said when he'd taped the bandage in place.

Dexter eased my sleeve down and stared at the bloody edges of fabric for a moment. His eyes hardened in a way I'd never seen from him before.

"Do you know who it was who cut you?" he asked abruptly.

I shook my head, puzzled. "Like I said, I didn't even notice it'd happened until just now."

Dexter's voice roughened. "I wish I knew. If I find out, I'll do so much worse to them."

The vehemence in his voice, full of so much dark promise, sent a shiver over my skin. It wasn't entirely unappealing, but it startled me.

"That doesn't sound like you," I couldn't help saying.

Dexter lifted his head. This time he let his gaze linger on mine, even though I suspected the eye contact wasn't entirely comfortable for him.

"I can't help feeling that way," he said. "Like I'd tear apart anyone who even tries to hurt you. I—I *love* you, and the idea of losing you… I'd rather face a million unsolvable puzzles than ever face that possibility again."

A lump rose in my throat. I turned to him and pulled him into a hug, squeezing him hard. He returned the embrace as if he never planned to let go of me. His warmth wrapped around me, making the emotion that'd already filled my chest expand through my whole body.

"I love you too," I said, hoping he could hear how much I meant that. "And I plan on staying right here with you no matter what those assholes try to do."

I just hoped we could figure out the puzzle we were in the middle of before anyone else got hurt.

CHAPTER 9

Madelyn

You wouldn't think watching a guy type on a laptop keyboard could be all that thrilling, but something about the intensity in Logan's expression and the urgency with which his fingers flew over the keys sent a tingle through me as I watched.

Of course, it didn't hurt that I also considered him to be one of the most gorgeous men on the planet.

My other favorite men were gathered around me in Beckett's usual white van: Beckett in the driver's seat up front, Slade sitting on one of the benches in the back next to me with a reassuring hand on my thigh, and Dexter perched on the opposite bench beside Logan, his eyes glued to a tablet.

Voices carried through the wall of the van from outside. We'd parked near one of the city's hospitals, as close as we dared to the building. The emergency ward wasn't far away, and cars and taxis were constantly roaring by, dropping off people who hustled or limped through the doors.

At the wail of an ambulance, I tensed. But just as the siren cut out, Logan's head jerked up. "I've got it! All the records they have digitized. We can get out of here."

He'd hacked into the hospital's database with the help of a few tips from Beckett's tech crew, meaning to download every file he could get his hands on. This was our second stop so far, but we weren't finished yet.

Beckett glanced back at me. "Where do you think we should go next, soon-to-be-Dr. Silver?"

I couldn't help smiling at the title despite the tension filling the van. "There's St. Joseph's out in the suburbs. That's the next closest hospital."

He nodded and put the van into drive.

As it pulled away from the curb, Logan kept tapping away at his computer. "I'm transferring a bunch more transplant patient files over to you," he told Dexter. "I think I was able to separate out most of them right away, but I'm going to do a more thorough scan to make sure I didn't miss anything."

Dexter nodded without looking up from the tablet. He'd been studying the records Logan had dug up, piecing together potential patterns that might indicate which ones had been falsified to cover up an illegal transplant.

He clicked his tongue against his teeth. "Here's another one. This is the fifth file I've found with a red blood cell count of 4.47 million per microliter. Other than that, I haven't seen the exact same number in any of the records."

I frowned. "So they could be using data from previous legit records, an example of what they know things should look like to make their fake ones look correct."

He nodded. "There are a couple of other markers, like kidney function, where I'm seeing some repetition, although not all in the same files. They were being cautious, using a few different examples to mix and match, I think. But once you start noticing the pattern, it's obvious."

Slade stretched out his prosthetic leg with a soft thump on the thinly carpeted floor. "And you said they all make it look like the actual transplant happened at some other hospital, right?"

Dexter nodded. "All the files I've collected with at least one repeated number were transfer patients. It makes sense—they wouldn't want to pretend the transplant happened at the same hospital where they received after care, which the staff could easily realize wasn't true."

Excitement jittered through my chest. We were getting so close, catching the key details of evidence that could expose Doom's Seed's illegal operations.

"It makes sense that the staff wouldn't have noticed the discrepancy like this," I said. "How many years were those patients spread across?"

"The oldest one I've found was from twenty-six years ago," Dexter said. "And I've set aside twelve records so far."

"So that's less than one case a year. Between that and the mixing and matching, and how many patients the doctors and nurses would typically be seeing, it's no wonder no one else noticed the repeated data. We never would have if we didn't know to look for it."

Beckett spoke up from behind the wheel. "Doom's Seed must have some kind of shell company set up to transfer the records over in a way that looks legit."

I nodded. "That could be another lead, if we can figure out where they're coming from."

Slade glanced toward Beckett. "How far do you think this

business extends? Obviously it's not just this city since it covers our hometown as well. Presumably he's active in the entire region in between too."

"Given the reach of the average Devil's Dozen member," Beckett said, "I'd expect he's organizing the transplants throughout the state, at the very least. It's more likely he has connections and facilities set up in various places across the country. It could extend overseas as well."

The immensity of the crime momentarily overwhelmed me. My stomach lurched, and I wrapped my arms around myself. "We have to stop him."

Slade squeezed my shoulder. "We will. No doubt about it."

Logan jerked straighter upright in his seat, sucking in a breath. "Holy shit."

All our gazes except Beckett's shot to him.

"What?" I demanded.

He lifted his head to stare at us with a stunned expression. "I found it. The Baldwin file. It's *here*, in the latest batch of records. This has got to be it."

I sprang across the van to squeeze next to him on the bench and peer at his screen. Slade hustled over as well, leaning to peek over the top, and Dexter set aside his tablet to give the momentous occasion his full attention.

Logan motioned to the top of the record he had open on his laptop. The patient's name was Christina Baldwin.

"She had a dual kidney transplant," he said. "Sixteen years ago —not too long before Maddie's dad was killed."

"Remind me what's important about this particular file?" Beckett said.

While I started scanning the record, Slade filled the other guy in. "Logan found a bunch of old notes that Evan Silver wrote. Notes that seemed to be related to his investigation. A few of them mentioned the Baldwin file in a way that made it sound like it was some kind of key to his findings. We never knew what was in it or why he fixated on it, though."

"This could be the thing that tipped him off that something was wrong," I said, still skimming over the data as quickly as I could while still absorbing it. "The file passed by him for one reason or another while he was doing his usual research work… Wait a second. Scroll back up to the basic physical data?"

Logan complied, watching me instead of the screen. "What did you notice?"

I checked the woman's height and weight and confirmed what I'd thought I remembered. "She was really petite. Only four-foot-ten, ninety pounds."

Dexter cocked his head. "What made you want to check that?"

"Because down here…" I motioned for Logan to scroll back down, and he did until I tapped the screen. "The dosage of medication it says she was given to slow her heart rate for the transplant procedure. I did a project that touched on that drug earlier this year. That's definitely too high a dose for a person that small. It could have *stopped* her heart."

Logan's eyebrows rose. "But obviously it didn't, since she has a bunch more post-transplant records."

"It's probably not what they gave her at all—I'd bet it's another one of those copied numbers, and whoever put together this falsified document wasn't quite careful enough."

"Let me see." Dexter peered closer and then started tapping on his tablet. He let out a triumphant sound. "There are three more records just in the ones I already have with the exact same dosage. That's another marker—I hadn't caught that one yet."

Slade smiled tightly down at me. "Something like that—you figure your dad might have noticed the error."

"Absolutely. If it stood out to me, it'd have been even more obvious to him." I sucked my lower lip under my teeth to worry at it.

"Wow," Dexter said abruptly. "I found a record with that dosage from all the way back in the 1980s. How old was Doom's Seed then?"

"It could be part of his family legacy, a business that his parents were running before him," Beckett reminded us. "A lot of the ventures *I'm* involved with go back as far as my grandparents or even earlier."

The size of this psychopath's horrific practices and their impact on my world just kept expanding. I rubbed my forehead, my thoughts spinning as I tried to absorb it all.

"And they've gotten away with it for all this time," Logan muttered. "For fuck's sake."

Beckett's voice lowered. "You don't get this high up in the criminal world without being very good at covering your tracks. We're incredibly lucky to even come across that one obvious slip in forty or more years of records."

It all made sense, in the most sickening sort of way. I gazed out the van window with a growing sense of melancholy, watching the buildings whip by.

Beckett turned the vehicle into another parking lot outside a big brick building. "Here's St. Joseph's." He turned in his seat to check with Logan. "Are you good to get started?"

Logan flexed his fingers. "I'm ready. Let's see what we can dig up here."

As he resumed his urgent typing, Slade grabbed my hand and tugged me back to the other bench. "He's not great company while he's at work, Piccolina," he said with a wink. "And you've already figured out the key the rest of us couldn't."

I didn't feel all that victorious, though. My stomach churned as

Logan dug into the hospital's network and siphoned out copies of their files.

"Transplants, transplants," he muttered to himself, and then to Dexter, "Sending more over." He wasn't even waiting to finish the download before passing some on now.

Dexter's fingers flicked across his tablet's screen. "Here's one. Two of the figures I've seen repeated." He paused, his eyes darting from side to side as he scanned the screen. "Another—this one has the same dosage of that medication as the Baldwin file."

I slumped back against the wall of the van. The participants in the awful scheme were everywhere. How many lives had Doom's Seed ruined or outright ended to get all those organs?

"How can we prove what's going on, even with these records?" I asked. "There's nothing clear enough in the files to get the cops to take notice, is there? They'd brush it off as coincidences or data error."

Slade's jaw clenched. "Then we find people with medical knowledge who'll understand it the same way you and your dad did."

"But I already had all this other evidence to convince me there was a problem, and my dad pieced it together on his own. Any doctor or researcher we try to tell is going to dismiss us as crazy before we even get far enough for them to pay attention to the data."

"Once we have enough pieces, they'll have to listen," Logan insisted, but I could tell from the grimness of his expression that he didn't totally believe that either.

We had a whole lot of records that claimed those operations had happened legitimately and only the smallest of signs that it was a lie. Doom's Seed obviously had actual doctors under his sway, because someone had performed those operations. I could already imagine that if we tracked down the facilities where the records said the transplants had taken place, he'd have all the proof in place to make it look legit, and the only people who'd know it wasn't true on his payroll.

We still needed something concrete and unarguable to tie our case together, and I had no idea where we were going to find that.

CHAPTER 10

Logan

"Hey," Beckett called from across the room. "I figured I'd grab takeout for dinner. Does Mexican sound okay to you?"

I glanced up from the screen I'd been peering at, taking a second to reorient myself to the room around me—the opulent sitting room of what Beckett called his "apartment" in his family's mansion. It was safe to say I'd never lived anyplace that looked remotely like this. I'd never even had a vacation this fancy.

Not that our stay here was any kind of leisure situation.

"Sure," I said. "I think we all like that."

"I'll get a bunch of different things so there's lots of variety and people can choose what they like. If Slade and Dexter come back before I do, let them know I won't be long." He tipped his head to me and headed out.

My friends had gone out to take a stroll around the grounds after Slade had suggested they needed fresh air and exercise to clear their heads. Maddie had vanished into her guest bedroom to catch up on schoolwork—as well as she could with everything that was going on.

But I'd had a different kind of work to occupy me, one I'd been able to tell couldn't wait any longer after what we'd seen at the hospitals.

I picked up Mom's phone again, the one we'd found in the purse Maddie had stolen, and flicked to the next number in her Contacts list. When I ran a search on it on my laptop, it brought up the same name as it showed in her Contacts list: Celena's Nail Salon.

The website for the salon looked legit. I dug a little farther to see if I could find any connections to Doom's Seed's holdings, but it appeared the woman who owned the business was leasing the space from a perfectly above-board retail rental company.

Mom simply went there to get her nails done, presumably.

I sighed and slumped deeper into the leather couch cushions. That was basically all I'd turned up so far: Mom's personal service people. She had a hairdresser and a personal shopper and a stylist within easy dialing, and various shops and eateries. It was almost as if she had no social life at all, at least not with anyone she didn't pay.

Well, no social life outside Doom's Seed himself. I'd found a text thread going back years with an unlisted number that had to be him, given the explicit nature of some of the conversations it contained. Just remembering some of their exchanges made my stomach lurch.

Not only had my mother run off on me and Dad, but she'd done it so she could go around fucking a criminal scumbag every which way.

More and more, I found I couldn't even really think of her as my mom now. My real mom had died eleven years ago.

This woman—this monster who fawned over murderous crime lords and kidnapped innocent people—wasn't any part of my family.

Somehow she'd managed to keep anything business-related, at least when it came to her new lover's business, out of her phone. None of the service providers and shops I'd looked up had any connection to him even with extra digging to confirm. And when I'd scrolled back through their direct conversations, skimming the worst bits with a wince, I hadn't come across anything but the vaguest mentions of his illicit activities.

Comments like, "I've got a few things to deal with before I make it back to the apartment" weren't going to justify a warrant, let alone convict the prick for his crimes.

Even though I'd tried it already, I ran his number through my various tracking methods. All of them made it clear that the digits belonged to a burner phone with no specific information tied to it other than the basic provider.

If he called Mom's phone, I'd have had the chance to trace his immediate location with the right equipment, but otherwise the information was useless. And the chances of him calling when Mom would have told him about the stolen purse by now were pretty much nil.

I scrolled farther back through her message history, searching for any numbers not in her Contacts. I'd gone back to almost a year ago when the ringtone pealed out, sudden and loud enough that I nearly dropped the phone.

Closing my fingers around it, I stared at the screen. *Unknown caller*, the notification said. The ringtone sounded again.

My heart was thudding. I had no idea who this was—but shouldn't I make use of the best piece of evidence we'd gotten in every possible way? Maybe the caller would give away something we could work with.

Not that anyone could possibly mistake my voice for my mom's. But what the hell.

Just as the third ring sounded, I hit the answer button and brought the phone to my ear. "Hello?"

On the other end, the caller sucked in a startled breath. Then a far-too-familiar voice slipped from the speaker into my ear. "Hello, Logan."

It was Mom, calling her own phone. Probably trying to find out what had happened to it. Her greeting sounded as hesitant as I felt, not the coolly confident persona she'd put on when she'd spoken to me outside the medical facility.

Maybe that should have reassured me. I should have played it cool and calm like she had before. But at the sound of my name from her deceitful mouth, a surge of rage flared inside me. I couldn't contain myself.

"What the hell, Mom?" I burst out.

The question encompassed so much of my anger and hurt—that she'd left, that she'd let us believe she was dead, that she'd made me party to a crime without me even realizing it. That she'd kidnapped the woman I loved and brought her to where the vilest man in existence might have killed her.

None if it made sense. All of it made me want to scream into the phone, but I managed to contain *that* impulse.

"I'm sorry, sweetheart," she said, in exactly the voice I remembered from when I'd been a kid. "I didn't want any of this to happen this way."

"What do you mean?" I demanded. "None of it happened by accident. You didn't just stumble and end up running off with a criminal overlord or faking your own death."

Her tone hardened a little in response to mine. "There's a lot you don't know or understand. How could you? You were only a child."

A scoffing sound burst out of me. "Yeah, exactly. I was a child—I was your *son*—and you left me. You let me believe that you'd died. So you could live it up with some rich asshole?"

"He's a lot more than that," Mom said sternly. "You have no idea what you're talking about. I did what I needed to for my own sanity."

Was she even hearing herself? She thought abandoning her normal family to hook up with a psychotic crime boss was the *sane* option?

"If you were that unhappy, you could have just asked for a divorce," I retorted. "Then at least I'd still have been able to see you. I wouldn't have mourned you and gone to visit a grave that didn't really mean anything."

"It wasn't that simple."

I knew that, actually. My stomach churned before I forced out the words. "Right. Because as long as you were with me and known to be alive, you could be prosecuted for your crime. You didn't get the liver for my transplant by any method the police would approve of, did you, Mom?"

Even as the question spilled bitterly from my lips, some tiny part of me held on to a shred of hope that she'd tell me I was wrong about that one thing, that her shitty decisions hadn't tainted even me.

Her resigned sigh snuffed out that hope in an instant.

"I'm not going to apologize for *that*," she said stiffly. "I did what I needed to do to keep you alive. That's what a mother *should* do."

"You couldn't have just waited and let me get a new liver the regular way?"

"No. It was becoming so clear that there wouldn't be a match from a legitimate source in time. Your other organs were starting to fail. I took the one option I came across that would save your life, and I don't regret that for a second."

I closed my eyes, willing down my nausea. I'd already known it had to be true, but hearing her admit to the crime sickened me all over again, even more than when the revelation had first hit me.

"You did all that, supposedly for me," I said. "And then you chucked me aside like I was nothing."

"Logan, I wasn't happy. I loved you more than anything, but with your father holding me back, I was trapped. I couldn't have continued being a good mother to you while I was stuck like that—I could already tell I was failing you. What I did—what I had to do—was the only way I could get out."

"Get out? You had a kid and a husband. A good mother shouldn't even *want* to get out of that situation. You should want to be with your family."

"I put you and Holand first for years, and I lost myself to it. I leapt at the first chance I'd had at real happiness in over a decade. I gave you as many years as I could, and then I made a clean break so you could get over it quickly."

Did she really think that was how it worked? Hadn't she ever missed *me*?

I couldn't bring myself to ask that question.

"*This* man makes you so happy?" I said instead. "He kills people—he had Maddie's father murdered! He doesn't care at all about who he destroys if they're in his way. How could a monster like that make you happy?"

"There's so much more to him than that," Mom insisted.

I shook my head. No, I'd given myself the answer already. The problem was that my mother was plenty monstrous too. I just hadn't realized it before.

She'd had moments in this conversation when she'd sounded a little sad. The slightest bit regretful. Was there any part of her that *wasn't* a monster?

There had to be, didn't there? How else could she have convinced me so well that she cared about me back when she'd been in my life for all those years?

"Mom," I said, my voice getting rough, "we could end this here. No matter how much more there is to him, he's causing dozens, probably hundreds of deaths. You can stop him. Turn him in to the police. Save all the people he's going to kill before it happens."

"Sweetheart, you know I can't do that."

"No, I don't know that! You're a witness—you know all kinds of things, I'm sure. You could say what happened with me and Maddie's dad. It's the only way you could make up for all the other things you've screwed up."

Mom's voice stiffened again. "I may have made mistakes, but I did the best with the options I had. I love this man. I'm happy with the life I've made for myself. You have no idea what I've been through or what the bigger picture looks like."

There was a click, and the line went dead. It took me a few seconds to process that she'd hung up on me.

I lowered the phone and set it down on the coffee table. My shoulders slumped, my entire body seeming to have been drained of energy.

I could tell myself that she wasn't really my mother over and over, but that didn't stop the knowledge of who she was from lacing through me like a knife to the gut.

The door to the sitting room swung open. I sat up straighter, expecting to see Beckett or my friends, but it was Maddie who poked her head in.

"Hey," she said softly. "I heard you talking when I came up on the door… You sounded pretty upset. Is everything okay?"

I swallowed thickly and pressed my hand to my forehead. "Yes. And no. It was—I was going through my mom's phone, and she called it, I guess to see where it'd ended up. And we talked. It wasn't a pleasant conversation."

Maddie grimaced and slipped inside. She hustled straight to the sofa and sat down beside me, wrapping her arm around my back.

"I can only imagine. Did she say anything that would help us with the case?"

I shook my head. "I even tried to convince her to help directly by turning on Doom's Seed, but she wouldn't consider it. She says she *loves* him." Acid filled my tone.

Maddie winced and hugged me tighter. "I guess it might be worse if she'd done all that without even caring that much about him."

She might have a point there, but it didn't make me feel much better. I sighed and nuzzled her hair, letting the citrusy scent of her shampoo fill my nose and soothe my nerves a little.

"That's not even the worst thing," I mumbled.

Maddie pressed a kiss to my cheek. "Do you want to talk about the worst thing or just forget about it?"

"I don't think I can forget." I heaved a breath. "I already hated that someone died while I got my second chance. And now it turns out it was probably at the expense of someone who didn't even *want* to donate their liver. Someone who was forced into it or maybe even killed so their organs could be taken and sold to save my life."

Maddie gazed up at me, her dark blue eyes full of perfect certainty. "But none of that is your fault. You didn't have any choice in it. Nothing you did then or now could have stopped it from happening. You know that, right?"

"I do," I said, but my shoulders sagged again. "It still feels like shit."

And as wrapped up as I was in Doom's Seed's crimes, the stolen organ inside me wasn't even much use as evidence after how well the bastard had covered his tracks.

How the hell were we going to bring him down?

CHAPTER 11

Madelyn

Summer shook her head dismissively before her smile shone from my phone's screen, lifting my spirits. "It's not like it matters where he got it from. I realize I've been hard on Logan, but even *I* know that no one could blame him for what his mom and that creepy crime boss did."

I sighed and leaned back in the chair across from the side table where I'd propped up my phone for our video chat. "But it matters to him anyway. Someone could have been killed for him to get that liver, so I get why it's hard for him to accept the situation. The really scary thing, though, is how far this reaches. We've found a few dozen recipients just in this city and the nearby areas. We think Doom's Seed has been running the business farther abroad than that."

"We're talking all over the state?" Summer asked, balling a

couple of socks together. I'd caught her in the middle of a laundry session.

"Possibly the entire country—or even outside it."

My bestie paused in her laundry folding to gape at me. "Okay, that's just crazy. How can you guys think you'll take on this asshole on your own? No offense, but you're not equipped for this, Madds. I don't want to see any of you getting hurt—or even killed. And that includes even Logan."

I wrinkled my nose at the fact that she'd added him as an aside. "I know," I said. "But we aren't on our own now. Beckett and his people are doing a lot of the legwork, and they're on the same level as Doom's Seed. They know what they're doing."

"If you say so." Summer's gaze slid from my face to what she could see of the room beyond me. "He definitely has nice digs. I guess I could see hooking up with a criminal overlord if it comes with perks like that."

I mock-glowered at her. "I'm not with him for the perks. He's honestly got one of the strongest moral codes out of anyone I know. It's just… a little different from what we're used to. And you can believe he's doing whatever he can to protect me, even when I'd rather he did *less*."

"Well, I approve of that side of him, anyway." Summer winked at me. Then her smile faltered. "You're sure you're not taking on too much?"

"I think I'm safer getting to the bottom of this mess and making sure the people behind it *can't* hurt us anymore than I am sticking my head in the sand and pretending it isn't happening."

"You might have a point there." Summer grimaced. "Which is why I still haven't told your parents what's up, no matter how pissed off they are with me. Your mom and Logan's dad pretty much hate me now, just so you know."

"I'm sure they don't hate you," I said. "They're just… frustrated. Which I get."

"And so do I. But they have to accept that I'm sticking with you, and if I trust you, they should too."

A weary smile crossed my face. Summer really was the best. A jab of guilt ran through my gut at the thought that I'd ever doubted her ability to handle the dangerous turn my life had taken.

"Has everything seemed normal on your end?" I had to ask.

My best friend nodded. "I've been keeping an eye out around school, but so far I haven't noticed anything or anyone sketchy. No sign that the boogie man is coming after me."

I restrained myself from rolling my eyes at her blasé tone. "And you've been taking extra precautions to keep safe?"

"Yeah, yeah. I never walk anywhere alone. I've got my mace, and I wear my whistle like a good girl."

"I'm not just being paranoid. They did go after my mom. It's not like it's a secret that you're my best friend."

Summer held up her hands. "I'm not complaining. It just feels a little weird, acting like I'm a target when nothing remotely abnormal has happened in this neck of the woods. How have you been handling *your* courses since you've been hiding away at your boyfriend's house?"

I rubbed my forehead, remembering the reading I'd been doing right before this call. "The guys and I all told our professors that we had family emergencies we had to go home for the week to deal with. I've been working through my assignments whenever I get the chance while I'm here."

"And if you need to be in hiding for more than a week?"

I shrugged. "I'm hoping it doesn't come to that, but if it does, we'll have to figure it out then. I don't like how this is interfering with my studies… but I'm definitely never becoming a doctor if I'm *dead.*"

"Very true. Keep remembering that." Summer shook a clothes hanger at the screen and then set it aside to pick up a tube of lipstick.

As she applied it, I raised my eyebrows. "What are you getting all dolled up for? Do you have a hot date you didn't tell me about?" The thought sent a twinge of panic through me—how well did she know the guy? Where would he take her?

Could she really trust him?

But Summer just laughed. "Oh, this is for a shift at the restaurant I said I'd cover tonight. The more makeup I wear, the better the tips. Some of us haven't found our rich sugar daddies yet, you know."

She grinned wide to show she was only joking, and I did let myself roll my eyes then.

At the same moment, Beckett pushed past the door to his rooms with an urgency that immediately set my nerves on edge. After one glance at his tensed posture and dark expression, I turned back to the phone. "It looks like I've got to get going. I'll update you when anything else comes up, like I promised. Be careful out there, all right."

"As you've only reminded me a gazillion times." She made an air kiss in my direction. "Don't worry about me, bestie."

As she ended the chat, I swiveled around to face Beckett. "What's wrong?"

The sound of my question was enough to draw the Vigil guys in from the small terrace off the sitting room, where they'd been taking a moment to relax while I talked with Summer.

Beckett's gaze swept over all of us. "Doom's Seed is at it again. Apparently he's taken the attitude that if he can't have something, no one can."

Logan had already been frowning, and the lines around his mouth deepened. "What do you mean?"

Beckett let out a ragged breath and started to pace across that end of the room. "Instead of attacking our properties, now he's outright destroying them. All across the city—so much of what we've worked for… What *I've* worked for…"

With a sound of frustration, he pulled out his phone and flipped to the photos. Walking over to us, he held it up.

A gasp broke from my lips as I recognized the dance club that he owned, the one where I'd gotten awfully up close and personal with the other guys more than once, now a blackened burned-out skeleton. The only reason I *could* recognize that charred frame as the club was because of the chunk of its sign that'd fallen to the ground with a few of the letters still visible.

"No," Slade muttered, his eyes flashing with anger.

Beckett swiped through to another picture and another. "The trucking company—with a bunch of the trucks still inside. An apartment building we own in the city. A department store we took on a few years ago."

Each of them was equally destroyed, wracked by fire and maybe even explosions to cause that level of damage. Nothing remained but broken walls and heaps of ash-covered rubble.

I winced even harder when he reached the last picture, full of shattered glass and scorched steel beams.

"The new office complex," Beckett said, his voice getting even rougher.

I knew what that place had meant to him, how much he'd been enjoying seeing his new venture come together—and all the good he'd meant to do with it too. Doom's Seed hadn't just destroyed the income Beckett's family would have made from it but also the pro bono medical clinic that'd been going to serve so many of the city's people in need.

"Fuck," Logan said hoarsely.

But then, maybe I shouldn't have been surprised. This was what Doom's Seed did, wasn't it? He took good things and ruined them.

"How did he manage to destroy so many locations so thoroughly?" Dexter asked, ever searching for details.

Beckett tucked his phone into his pocket. "All the fires were set overnight with copious amounts of gasoline to ensure they'd spread fast and be difficult to put out. And having so many large buildings go up in flames at the same time stretched the fire department thin, which made it even harder for them to deal with them all." His head drooped. "Most of the buildings were empty for the night, but the apartment building—not everyone made it out in time."

I swallowed thickly and stepped forward to grasp his arm. He leaned a little into my touch, so clearly anguished that I wished I knew how to erase all the horror that psychopath had dealt out.

How could Logan's mom believe she *loved* a man who'd do something like this?

Logan squared his shoulders, his tone hardening. "Should we go investigate the scenes? Try to turn up some evidence that could prove Doom's Seed was involved?"

Beckett shook his head. "My people are already checking for evidence of the perpetrators, but I doubt we'll find anything we could use. We've already seen how good Doom's Seed is at covering his tracks."

Dexter had perked up a bit at the prospect of taking action. "We might spot something they've missed. With a different perspective—"

Beckett held up his hand to stop the other guy. "I appreciate the sentiment, but I'm also concerned that this could be a trap. In the chaos, he could have people watching, looking for a chance to grab or kill any of you. It isn't worth the risk."

I winced. "You think he did all this just to set up a trap?"

"I don't know." Beckett pinched the bridge of his nose. "Mostly

I think he just wanted to hit me in a way that would hurt. To get back at me as effectively as possible. I can't say he did a bad job of that."

No, because Doom's Seed had plenty of practice with those sorts of tactics too. A rush of chilly fear washed over me with the memory of Mom's car accident: the strange text that had warned me it might be fatal next time, the worried phone call from Holand, and then seeing her battered and bruised in the hospital bed...

My heart lurched, and I turned toward Beckett. "He might not stop with you. He's got to be pissed off that I escaped from Yvonne—and that Logan probably knows how he's involved in the organ business now too. What's to stop him from coming after everything we care about next? The *people* we care about?"

Logan's face turned sallow. "He did warn you about your mom."

I nodded, my heart starting to race. "He's switched back to personal attacks, and it's hard to believe he's going to draw the line at burning down buildings." I turned back to Beckett. "We've got to get them out. My and Logan's family and Summer—we have to bring them to a safe place before Doom's Seed targets them too."

CHAPTER 12

Madelyn

"How do you think they're going to take this?" Summer asked from the seat beside me as I pulled the big seven-seater SUV that Beckett had lent us into the driveway of my family home. With so much going on between his forces and Doom's Seed's, and with him being a stranger to my mom and stepdad, it hadn't made sense for him to join us on this mission, but he was joining us in spirit.

I glanced over at my bestie, who had her arms folded tight over her chest. *She* hadn't exactly taken my insistence that she needed to lay low for at least a few days super well, but she had come along with only a little arguing. But then, she'd already been aware of the dangerous situation I'd found myself in.

"We'll just have to give it our best shot and see how it goes," I said, squaring my shoulders, and looked back at the guys in the row behind us. "Ready?"

Slade gave me a cheeky salute that was offset by his somber expression, and Logan nodded before yanking open the door.

Dexter caught my gaze for just an instant in his usual fleeting way. "We'll back you and Logan up, however much of the story you feel you need to tell them."

"Same," Summer said emphatically, clambering out. "If you think the situation is serious enough that you're willing to spill the beans to them now, then they'd *better* listen."

Mom's and Holand's cars were parked farther down the driveway ahead of the SUV, so I knew they were home. I used my key in the door and eased it open, raising my voice to call down the front hall. "Mom?"

As the others filed in behind me, it was Holand who appeared first at the far end of the hall. He took us all in with a puzzled expression that turned sterner than I was used to. "We weren't expecting all of you. Not that it isn't good to see you after… everything." His gaze paused on me before sliding to his son. "What's going on, Logan?"

I dragged in a breath, letting the familiar faded floral scent that always filled my childhood home settle my nerves as much as anything could. "This was my idea."

"But I agree with her," Logan said right away, just as my mom appeared at the top of the stairs.

She walked down to them to join us, looking as confused and concerned as Holand. "Agree about what?" she said, and then couldn't seem to restrain herself from moving straight to me.

She pulled me into a tight hug. Her voice came out both choked and chiding. "You shouldn't have run off on us like that before. I've been so worried." She stepped back and looked all of us over, lingering on me the longest. "You are okay, aren't you?"

My mouth twisted. "In the most immediate sense. But we're not here for us. We came because I'm—we're—worried about the two of you."

Holand's brow furrowed. "What are you talking about? We've been perfectly fine. It's you two who've gone so quiet, refusing calls…" He trailed off, sounding as if he'd reined in his temper before he let loose more frustration than he'd prefer.

An ache formed in my gut. I hadn't wanted to put the two of them through so much stress, and I doubted Logan had either. This situation had spiraled out of our control so quickly.

"I know," I said. "And you have no idea how sorry we are about that. But that's why we came—because it's time we started telling you what's going on and made sure it isn't going to affect you any more than it already has."

Now Mom was frowning. "I don't understand, honey. What does this have to do with us?"

My hands twisted in front of me. Part of me wished we could be sitting comfortably in the living room, easing into this conversation—but there was never going to be anything comfortable about what I had to say. It was better to get it over with as quickly as possible so we could get our parents to safety quickly too.

"The truth is that we've made some very dangerous people angry," I said, beginning with the vaguest possible version of the story. The fewer details we had to get into, the less room there'd be for doubt and argument. "And those people are out to punish us however they can, including targeting the people we care about."

Mom blanched. "What do you mean? Is this something to do with drugs?"

I could have laughed if it hadn't been so much worse. "No, Mom, nothing like that. We haven't done anything wrong, but we stumbled on something that people with a lot of power and bad intentions didn't want us to know about, and now they're trying to keep us quiet."

"Then you need to go to the police," Holand broke in.

"We don't have enough proof," Logan said. "Believe me, we wish we could."

I caught Mom's gaze. "They've already caused your car accident. They texted me to tell me the next time they might kill you. I was hoping we could get them to forget about us, but it's become obvious that's impossible."

"My accident," Mom said, staring at me. "But—that *was* an accident."

I shook my head. "It was set up as a warning to us—to me."

"This sounds ridiculous, Maddie. If it's something that serious, we need to go down to the police station—"

"There's nothing to tell them!" I interrupted. "Just like Logan said. We've been trying to put together the evidence, but these criminals are very good at what they do. Which is why they're so dangerous."

"They're telling the truth," Summer piped up. "That's why I let Maddie make a run for it during the whole intervention thing. She explained it to me—she knows what she's talking about, Ms. Silver."

My mom's eyes widened. "You knew all about this too?"

"Only since the intervention," I said.

Holand's gaze fixed on Slade and Dexter. "And you boys are part of this scenario as well?"

"Unfortunately," Slade said with a crooked smile. "We've been right in the middle of it from the start."

"And why exactly are you telling us now?"

I swallowed hard. "Because we're worried that the people we're dealing with are going to go on the attack again, and Logan and I want to make sure you're safe. We're going to bring the two of you and Summer to someplace they won't know where to find you until they've been arrested." Or whatever else we or Beckett ended up having to do to ensure Doom's Seed was no longer a threat.

"You want us to take off in the middle of the week, dropping everything, to go to some unknown location?" Mom burst out. "Maddie, this is beyond anything I could have imagined. None of this makes sense. Who's been feeding you these stories? How did you get these crazy ideas in your head?"

My throat tightened even more. "It's not crazy, Mom. It's—" God, I hadn't wanted to tell her like this, but I didn't know what else to try. She wasn't going to budge until she knew what was actually at stake.

I drew up my chin and fixed her and Holand with the firmest look I could. "You know I've been asking about Dad more lately, and stopping by the hospital where he worked. It wasn't just because of the accident. We found information that makes it clear that Dad didn't die because of some mysterious illness. He was *murdered* because he found out about these people and the crimes they're committing. And while we were trying to find enough evidence to get justice for him, we caught their attention too."

I hadn't thought Mom's face could get any paler, but I was wrong. Her legs wobbled, and Holand slipped an arm around her waist.

"Your father—honey—the doctors said—" she mumbled.

"I know what they said—they never figured out what the cause was. We know for sure that he was murdered. We've heard it directly from these people. That's why they're trying to silence us by any means necessary."

Yvonne had confirmed it on the phone with Logan. But I didn't bring up that part because her presence was Logan's part of the story to tell. I doubted he wanted to dump the revelation that his mom was still alive on his dad right now like this, especially when that would only make our story sound crazier. I'd let him decide when the time was right for that discussion.

"I never wanted to tell you like this," I said to Mom, stepping closer to grasp her hand. "I swear that it's true, though. I can talk you through what we've found out—but that'll take time, and I don't know if these people will have already noticed we've come by the house. We need to get you to safety, and then we can deal with the rest."

"It's absolutely true," Dexter put in with his usual matter-of-fact tone. "I wouldn't get caught up in a mystery if the pieces didn't add up."

"We've been building our case for years," Slade said. "But just in the last few months, everything's started to unravel so fast."

For several seconds, Mom and Holand just stared at us. Then Holand asked in a low voice, "Where exactly do you want us to go?"

"We've made a friend who has experience with criminals like this," I said. "There's a vacant condo in a building he owns just an hour's drive from here. It'll be like a little vacation. Hopefully a short one."

Mom inhaled raggedly. "This is all so—I don't know what to think."

I squeezed her hand. "Please. Just come with us. Take a look at the place. Listen to what we have to say. And if you're absolutely sure you can't believe us, you can always come back. But I really hope you won't do that, because these people won't stop at anything to cover their tracks. And for them, that means destroying everyone connected to their crimes, which includes us too."

That last statement seemed to finally sink in enough for my mom to shake herself into action. She swiped at her eyes. "All right. We can call in sick for the next couple of days if it seems necessary.

I want to hear the full story as soon as we get to this condo, though."

"Yes," Holand said firmly. "No more dodging around the truth. We can't trust you if you're not trusting us with all the details of what you claim is going on."

I nodded, gratitude rushing through me. "I understand. Why don't you pack a bag as fast as you can, and we'll get on to that part right after we get you settled in."

Mom turned toward the stairs as if in a daze, but not before she shot me one last look, as if she were staring at someone she no longer knew. My heart sank.

Please, let her understand eventually. I had no idea how I could have done things differently before that would have turned out better, but I didn't want to lose her.

The city lights glowed through the deepening night beyond the windows of the condo's main bedroom. The place was a penthouse, and the cars cruising by below looked no larger than fireflies.

Mom and I had come in here after the Vigil guys and I had laid out our entire case, other than the parts about Logan's mom. Logan had gone off to the side with his dad too. I'd thought Mom had wanted to talk, but for the first few minutes, she'd stayed silent, as if she were still absorbing everything.

I couldn't blame her for needing extra time to do that.

"We're definitely safe from this gang boss here?" she said finally.

The question reassured me a little—it told me she was taking the situation at least somewhat seriously.

"It's the safest place we can put you," I said. "There shouldn't be any way for his people to figure out you're here, as long as you stay inside and don't use your credit card for anything. Or place any calls on your usual phones. We'll leave you with the burner phone and credit card I showed you, and you can use those for anything you need while you're here."

The building was owned by Beckett's family through a few layers of shell companies, so it was unlikely Doom's Seed would even realize it was connected to him, let alone that we'd brought Mom, Holand, and Summer here. A few of Beckett's people had been watching when we'd driven off and checked out the area enough to confirm that no one malicious had followed us.

"And you're sure this friend of yours has our best interests at heart?"

I hadn't explained the full details of my relationship with Beckett to her either. I figured we could ease into that later. "Yes. He's gone above and beyond for all of us more than once."

Mom sighed. "I suppose I can understand now why you and Logan have been acting so strangely. It was all because of what you'd found out about your dad?"

"That's all of it," I said. "I hope you can see why I hesitated to tell you… It *does* sound crazy if you haven't been right in the middle of it."

She rubbed her forehead. "I still wish you'd tried. Hearing it all at once—it's hard to wrap my head around it."

I could still hear a hint of doubt in her voice. She wasn't totally convinced that we weren't exaggerating the situation, imagining a murder where there was only an accident, turning a minor criminal who'd threatened us into a much bigger monster.

"I know, Mom. But even if you're still not totally sure what to believe, I hope you can believe me that *I'll* feel so much better if you take this little vacation. For me and Logan, so we don't have to worry about you. If it turns out there's nothing *to* worry about, then we'll get whatever help we need to. But right now, all that matters is knowing you'll be okay." I paused. "I don't want them getting to you like they did to Dad."

"It sounds like something out of a movie, you know. Illegal organ transplants, covert investigations." Mom shook her head. "I suppose your father was acting a little secretive in those last few months before he died, now that I think about it. Not in a way that worried me at all, just like he was a bit busier at work than usual, and he hadn't told me what he was working on. But he often had confidential projects."

"He's a hero," I said gently. "If it wasn't for him, we'd never have stumbled on this either. Because he did, we might be able to stop so many more people from being hurt."

She leaned back with her hands on the mattress. "That does sound like him too. Always wanting to protect people in his own way. Usually he did it with his medical knowledge… but I could see him getting tangled up in a mystery like this."

"He was trying to protect us too by keeping us out of it," I had to point out.

"I know." Her gaze darted to me. "I'm not sure you aren't being a little overprotective. Nothing about my accident seemed unusual—to me or the doctors. But… it can't *hurt* to take a little time off and ease your worries. We'll figure this whole thing out together, honey. I know we will."

I beamed at her, tears prickling behind my eyes. Mom held out her arms, and I met her hug halfway.

This was the most I could have asked for. As long as she was out of harm's way, we could see the rest of our mission through.

I could keep fighting for both of us—for us and for Dad.

A wordless shout of shock from beyond the door had my head jerking up. A second later, Logan's voice called out. "Maddie, you'd better get in here."

Mom hurried behind me as I pushed out into the condo's living room. The guys were gathered on the sofa facing the TV, Holand standing behind the sofa, his jaw gone slack. Summer dashed out of the second bedroom where she'd been getting her stuff organized for the stay and stalled in her tracks when she caught sight of the scene.

I rushed over to the side of the sofa where I could see the TV too—and froze with a lurch of my stomach.

They'd brought up the local news channel from back home. On the screen, a news anchor motioned toward a house behind him, lit up by the flames that were raging all through the building while firefighters swung their hoses toward it. "No one is sure what started the fire, but so far it's defied the firefighters' attempts to douse it."

I missed the rest of what she said as horror seared through my thoughts.

I knew that house. I knew the tree out front and the design on the awning over the porch. I knew the stones forming the path up to the porch steps.

I'd been at that house just a couple of hours ago. It was my family home that was burning.

CHAPTER 13

Madelyn

I'd never walked so cautiously through the house where I'd lived almost my entire life.

The place was a blackened shell of what it'd once been. The foundation stood mostly intact, walls and floors where they should be, but even those surfaces were so charred that I tested each patch of floor before putting my weight on it.

Technically it wasn't safe for me to be exploring the ruin at all, but I hadn't been able to stand the thought of losing one last visit to my former home. To see exactly how much Doom's Seed had destroyed.

The answer was pretty much everything.

Nothing remained of the furniture except the barest of bones: a few chunks of the sofa's frame, the scorched appliances with melted dials. Everything smaller and flammable had transformed into indistinguishable heaps of coals and ashes.

It felt as if I'd stepped into some alternate dimension where my hometown was a warzone. This couldn't *really* be my house in the world I actually lived in, could it?

But I hadn't hopped across any dimensions. The war we were fighting was all too real and happening right here around me. As the other people in the house with me were a stark reminder of.

Beckett glanced over at me when I raised my head. He'd been staying within arm's reach the entire time, as if he thought he might need to yank me to safety at any moment. Also toward that purpose, he had a few men stationed outside the building, watching for any sign of enemy forces.

Logan stood several feet away in what remained of the dining room. He was staring at the place where the table had once been, his hands clenched at his sides, maybe remembering the family dinners we'd enjoyed there during the short time he and I had shared this home. Slade and Dexter waited nearby, tensed and apprehensive, their gazes flicking between their best friend and me.

When Slade caught my gaze now, I gave him a slight nod to say I was hanging in there. Logan needed support too.

"I can tell it was a beautiful house," Beckett said quietly, reaching out to rub my shoulder.

I nodded, fighting the burn of tears behind my eyes. "Yeah. I couldn't have asked for a better place to grow up."

"I'm so sorry. I got you dragged into a war between two immense syndicates… I never would have wanted you—or anyone else outside of my world—getting caught in the crossfire like this."

The guilt in his words tugged at my heart. "It's not your fault," I said without hesitation. "This might have happened even if we'd never met. It was me joining up with the Vigil's investigation into my dad's death that put me on Doom's Seed's radar and made him want to scare me off." A rough laugh caught in my throat. "Maybe I should be apologizing to you for dragging you into *our* war."

Beckett let out a dismissive sound. "Doom's Seed must have had plans to move on my territory regardless. He just happened to be able to combine two of his goals. And connecting you to me probably made him even more determined to hurt you."

I exhaled in a rush. "At least I got Mom and Holand out in time. The house is just a thing. The people are what's really important." The laugh finally worked its way out of my mouth, but it didn't have much humor in it. "And now Mom totally believes that the danger I was trying to convince her about is real."

"Always looking on the bright side." Beckett stepped close enough to press a gentle kiss to my temple.

I was trying to stay optimistic, anyway. I'd said the house was only a thing, but I knew it was more than that. It was memories. It was a sense of belonging.

It'd held so many of my lingering impressions of Dad, and those were now burned up along with the furnishings.

Here in the living room, he would spread out the props for a scientific experiment on the coffee table and help me arrange them so we could complete a test of magnetism or kinetic force. Anything biological or chemical, of course, had to be in the kitchen because of the potential for mess. I could remember Mom standing in the doorway, shaking her head with a bemused smile, as I sent a wooden car careening off the table to bang into the baseboard.

So many times, we'd curled up on the sofa that was now ashes to watch one of the animated flicks I'd loved at that age, which Dad had always acted completely absorbed in even though he must have gotten bored to tears. He'd make popcorn fresh in the pan and douse it with so much melted butter it'd leave a sheen on our fingers.

I could almost taste the salty flavor I'd lick off my fingertips when the popcorn was gone.

How long would it take before those memories started to fade without the surroundings to remind me?

I swallowed thickly and turned toward the staircase. It was intact too but badly burnt. I crept over to it and treaded up it with even more care than I'd approached the floor downstairs. Beckett followed a couple of steps behind.

The banister had mostly crumbled away. I stuck close to the wall, edging along it to the door to my bedroom. The room I'd expected to come back to during the summer if I didn't get a position in the city that kept me there.

My wrought-iron bedframe looked almost the same as it always had, just blacker. And everything else was burnt black too, drifts of cinders rolling across the floor like dusty hills. My throat closed up.

All the nights I'd lain on that bed daydreaming about boys… most often Logan. All the assignments I'd completed sitting at the desk that was now nothing but dead embers. The posters I'd left on the walls, a little childish—a band I'd loved in tenth grade, an inspirational poster I'd gotten in junior high that was maybe a little saccharine—but *mine.*

Gone. All of it gone.

I dragged my gaze away and ventured farther down the hall. The door at the end opened up to what had once been Dad's office.

Mom had started using it herself, but she'd kept the big oak desk and the bookshelves lining every possible inch of wall, most of them still packed with his old texts and reference manuals. "You'll want your pick of them someday when you get that medical degree," she'd used to say to me.

Now every scrap of paper had been eaten up in the flames.

In the back of my mind, I could see the desk where it had once stood, with the trinket box I'd held on to perched by the corner.

Dad leaning back in his chair behind it, smiling at me when I'd darted in to ask him a question. Motioning me over to show me some video or computer-generated model he'd brought up on his laptop. Hugging me close while he explained the concepts with perfect patience.

I blinked hard and pulled myself away. My fingers had turned black from touching the walls for balance. I couldn't even wipe at my eyes without smudging my face.

An ache filled my chest, but there wasn't anything I could do about it. No way to deny or reverse the damage in front of me.

I turned around and headed back to the staircase, Beckett following suit and glancing at me over his shoulder to make sure I kept coming.

My heart was so heavy that it seemed to drag me down the steps. I found the Vigil guys standing in the living room when I reached the front hall, all their expressions grim. Slade motioned me over and pulled me into an embrace.

"It was a big price to pay," he said in an unusually rough voice. "You shouldn't have been the one who had to pay it."

"It was Logan's house too," I said, turning my head against Slade's chest to study my stepbrother.

His mouth stayed tense and slanted, but he shrugged. "I lived here for less than two years. I liked the place, but I know I don't have anywhere near the same kind of connection to it that you do. I'm so sorry, Maddie."

Dexter held up his phone. "I took pictures in case there's anything we need for evidence—or for remembrance's sake—later."

I shot him a tight smile. "Thank you."

As I eased away from Slade and took in the devastation around me again, a stronger swell of grief and melancholy swept over me.

Had our quest to find Dad's killer really been worth it when I'd ended up losing all this? It'd been Mom and Holand's home as well.

All the trappings that'd propped up so many memories, all the security and comfort this home had offered... So much we could never get back. And even if we could see justice done and Doom's Seed punished for his crimes, that wouldn't bring the house or Dad back.

Those thoughts ran through my head, and a spurt of anger flared up inside my chest. This was all that asshole's fault. He'd stolen Dad from us, and then he'd hurt Mom, and now he'd destroyed our home as well.

How much more would he get away with if we *didn't* keep fighting him?

If it hadn't been my life he was messing up, it would have been someone else's. No doubt it already was hundreds of other people's at the same time, with all his malicious business practices. And lots of those people weren't in any position to fight back themselves.

We'd set out on this crusade because it was right and because we could. Neither of those facts had changed.

Backing down and giving up was exactly what Doom's Seed would have hoped would happen when I was faced with his latest vicious act.

My jaw set. I was never going to give him the satisfaction.

His reign of terror had to end, and we were the ones closest to doing it. So we had to see it through before he destroyed even more lives.

I looked around at each of the guys, squaring my shoulders. "It doesn't matter how much I lost. We aren't backing down. All this means is that we need to get on with stopping Doom's Seed once and for all."

CHAPTER 14

Madelyn

Dexter moved around the mansion's kitchen like a storm. He'd sent Slade on a shopping trip to gather all the ingredients he needed to make some kind of elaborate meal for us. I knew, though, that the meal was mainly for me—to get my spirits up after what I'd just witnessed.

I wanted the gesture to work, but I was so wiped out. Images from the burned house kept wavering through my mind.

I'd come over to the kitchen island to offer to help, but Dexter was too busy ordering Logan and Slade around to give me any instructions. After he'd gotten Logan chopping one thing and Slade grating another, he finally looked at me.

"This is going to take a while," he said. "Why don't you get some rest? We'll let you know when it's time to eat."

I wanted to protest, but it was hard to summon enough resolve.

It wasn't as if Dexter couldn't handle himself in a kitchen. I wasn't sure I'd actually contribute rather than ruining the ingredients.

Beckett, who'd been watching over the proceedings with a vaguely bemused expression, slipped his hand around my elbow. "I'll come with you. It's been a long day—you need a break."

"Fine," I muttered, but I couldn't deny I felt a little relief being escorted up the stairs and toward his private apartment. I didn't even want to sleep—just to lie down and take the weight off my feet even if I couldn't remove the heavy burden pressing down on my shoulders.

Beckett didn't bring me to the guestroom where I'd spent the previous night. Instead, he led me right into his part of the house to his own private bedroom.

I sank down on the bed, still upright, with the sense that he'd wanted to do more than make sure I got to a resting spot safely. Beckett sat at the edge of the mattress and turned to face me. His expression had turned so solemn that my heart lurched.

"What's wrong?" I asked.

Beckett shook his head. "Nothing—not like that. I just—you know what you said at your house, about stopping Doom's Seed?"

"Of course. I mean, obviously we have to."

"*I* have to." He reached out and grasped both my hands. "Maddie, I'm aware that you meant every word, but I want you to listen to me. You should walk away. This is my fight now, against people I was at least partly prepared to go up against. You've been through so much already—I don't want to see you lose anything more."

I frowned at him. "I'm okay. I can handle this. Seeing my house burned down was a shock, but that doesn't mean—"

He squeezed my hands to stop me. "I'm not saying this because I think you can't do enough. I just want you to let me handle the risks from here on out. I'm in a way better position to cope. I swear to you, I'll put everything I have toward crushing Doom's Seed. You won't need to worry about him hurting you or the people you care about again."

My voice softened. "I'll have to worry about him hurting *you.*"

"That's going to be the case either way." Beckett held my gaze, his cool gray eyes fiercely determined. "Please, Maddie. Let me do this for you."

My heart fluttered at the passionate devotion in his words. He really would do it—fight this entire battle on his own, on my behalf as well as his. The flare of protective furor in his eyes set off an answering heat low in my belly, stirring me out of my melancholy daze in a way nothing else had.

"Beckett, you know what I have to say," I said, gently but firmly. "I'm as committed as you are to seeing Doom's Seed fall. I *want* to have a hand in taking down the asshole who ripped so much away from me—I want to know I got justice for my family myself, not just sitting on the sidelines while someone else did the work."

Beckett's jaw tightened. "You've already done a lot to get us to this point. You've hardly been on the sidelines."

"And I'm not going there now. I'm not letting you take all the responsibility after we've come so far." I got up on my knees so I could look down at him rather than the other way around and rested my hand on his shoulder. "I'm strong enough to stand beside you while we fight this battle. That's the only place I want to be."

To emphasize those words, I gave him a push, and Beckett didn't resist. I shoved him right down on the bed and pressed my mouth to his.

This kiss wasn't gentle or sweet the way I might have kissed any of the guys before. I melded my lips to his with all the strength and desire I had in me.

He needed to remember that I was so much more than a victim, that I could take charge even with a man as powerful as him.

I ran my hands down his chest as I kissed him again. Beckett tangled one hand in my hair and trailed the other down my side to my hip, returning the kiss fervently but letting me stay in control.

I eased back just enough to peer down at him, pinning him with my gaze. "I'm capable of fighting my own battles when I need to. I'm strong enough to take on whatever enemies come my way. I don't *need* you to take the reins, as much as I appreciate your help."

He smiled up at me. "You already have that."

"Good."

I slammed my mouth into his again, need swelling through my body and condensing at my core. When Beckett squeezed my ass, I couldn't help grinding against him through our clothes. He groaned against my mouth, and I devoured the sound with a whimper of my own, feeling the bulge that had already hardened behind his fly.

I could take whatever the world threw at me—and I could take him. I curled my fingers into his hair, rumpling the neat strands, and yanked his head back so I could claim his neck with my mouth as well.

When I nipped him with the tips of my teeth, he let out another groan, massaging my ass. "I think I like this. I should try to take over more often, just to see what comes out of you."

"No, you definitely should not," I muttered against his throat, and flicked my tongue across it. The hitch of his breath made me giddy.

I slid my hand down his torso to the hem of his buttoned shirt and tugged it upward. When it caught on his chest, I fumbled with the buttons between increasingly wild kisses. Beckett leaned upward to let me pull the shirt right off him and then reached for my own. I swatted his hands away with a sly smile and peeled it off myself, swaying over him.

"You're so fucking sexy," Beckett murmured, brushing his fingertips up my bare sides. I shivered eagerly at the contact and dove back in for another kiss.

This time, I trailed my lips down his neck and over his chest. Beckett stroked his fingers over my shoulders and into my hair, across my scalp, his breaths turning more ragged by the second. I flicked my tongue across one of his nipples and then delved my hand between us to cup the hardness I'd enjoyed so much against my pussy.

Beckett mumbled a swear word, his hips arching up to meet my grasp. He pumped into my hand through his slacks. I'd swear I felt his cock twitch when I swiveled my thumb over the head.

There was something so intoxicating about seeing this powerful, controlled man unravel under me at my attentions.

I needed more. I popped open the button of his fly, but when I gripped the zipper, Beckett caught my hand. He pushed himself up on his elbows, blinking the haze of pleasure from his eyes so he could hold my gaze.

"Maddie," he said, his voice steady if a bit rough, "I just need to know. Why does it matter so much to you to keep fighting when you don't have to? Why is it worth the risk?"

I paused, letting the question sink in. My answer rose up in my mind without any effort at all.

Dad had believed in me so much—but I'd fallen apart when he'd died. It'd taken years to get that inner strength back, but once I had, I knew he'd have been proud of all the causes I'd championed.

It was who I'd always wanted to be. Who I was meant to be, and no one was taking that away from me.

"There are only so many people in the world who are in a position not just to look after their own needs but also to try to make the world better for other people too," I said, measuring out the words as they came to me to make sure they felt right. "And for now, one of those people is me, so I'm going to do everything I can. Saving people who can't save themselves was always my goal with my medical career. Taking down Doom's Seed and stopping him from hurting any more innocents isn't any different."

A soft smile curled Beckett's lips. He raised his hand to my cheek and stroked his thumb over my skin. Awe shone from his eyes.

"Every time I think I couldn't admire you more, you prove me wrong. You absolutely can hold your own alongside me, Maddie. And I want you there. I love you."

My pulse stuttered. He'd never said those three words before. Somehow I hadn't expected them, even though he'd made his devotion clear in so many other ways. I hadn't known if he'd want to admit a feeling that vulnerable.

But he was willing to offer up that much of himself to me. Only to me.

My throat tightened with a swell of affection before I propelled the words out. "I love you too. So much. For your strength, for how much *you* care, despite the kind of world you grew up in."

Beckett pulled me into a kiss, one that stretched on and on until my head was spinning. But I didn't plan on letting him take over this encounter, not like that.

I intended to demonstrate my love in all kinds of ways.

This time, when I yanked down the zipper on his slacks, he didn't move to stop me. I wiggled his pants and boxers down his hips so his rigid cock sprang free, thick and already beaded with precum. I licked my lips.

"That's right," Beckett said in a husky tone. "You can take all of that too. My fierce warrior."

An eager shiver passed through my body. I wrapped my hand around the base of his shaft and sucked him into my mouth.

Beckett's hips jerked. He gripped my hair again, pumping up to meet the movements of my mouth but holding himself back from ramming his cock right down my throat. I swiveled my tongue around him and teased my fingers over his balls, drawing a strained grunt out of him. His salty, musky flavor filled my senses.

"Fuck, Maddie," he rasped. "The things you can do with that mouth… But I want to be inside you properly. I want to hear you come apart around me with all that strength and fierceness."

Oh, God, I wanted that too. When he tugged at my hair, I allowed myself to lift off his cock and clamber over his body. Beckett yanked down my jeans and delved his hand between my legs. He inhaled sharply at the wetness already soaking my panties.

He twisted away from me for just a few seconds to grab a packet out of the drawer on the bedside table. I snatched it from him and ripped it open, wanting to be a part of every piece of this act.

His eyes rolled back as I slid the condom down over his length. He gripped my hips but gave me the room to sink down over him at my own speed.

"Take me however you want," he murmured. "It's always so fucking good with you."

I took him in one inch at a time, whimpering at the thrilling stretch of his girth. When our hips met, I eased upward and plunged down again twice as fast.

Beckett's fingers dug into my thighs. As I set the tempo, he bucked up into me, sweat beading across his forehead.

The stretching sensation expanded into a deep fullness, which swelled into an ache for more. I rode him with every ounce of strength I had in me, taking him deeper and deeper, gasping with the pleasure of it.

I tipped my head back toward the ceiling, a moan tumbling out of me as Beckett thrust up into me with even more force than before. One of his hands slipped across my hip to settle over my pussy. His fingers flicked across my clit, and I pumped him into me faster, faster, bliss spiraling up inside me until I burst.

My orgasm crashed through me, jerking a cry from my lips and leaving me shuddering over one of the four incredible men I loved. My channel clamped around Beckett's cock, and he held me tight as he followed me over the edge with a choked sound of release.

"So goddamn good," he muttered, wrapping his arms around me and pulling me down against him so our chests were perfectly aligned. "You're a fucking goddess, Maddie. Don't let anyone ever tell you differently, even me."

A soft chuckle escaped me. I nestled my head under his chin, drifting on the afterglow and soaking up the warmth of his naked body. In that moment, I never wanted to let him go.

A chilling thought prickled through me on the heels of my contentment. I pressed myself tighter against him, but I couldn't escape the icy edge of fear that had crept into my mind.

Beckett had talked about how much I'd already lost. What if Doom's Seed tried to take this happiness from me too?

How could I be sure he wouldn't succeed?

CHAPTER 15

Dexter

"I hate that we're always simply responding to his attacks, always on the defensive," Beckett muttered. "We need to get the upper hand—or at least take more control over the situation."

I glanced over at him where he was poised at the table in his sitting room with the others, digging into leftovers from last night's dinner. As much as I liked seeing them enjoying my food, I wanted to contribute more than that.

Which was why I'd moved over to the sofa on my own to concentrate on the data in front of me.

I yanked my gaze back to my list of the attacks Doom's Seed's people had made on us and Beckett so far. I'd noted down dates, time of day, locations, and the apparent motivation behind the assault: personal or strategic, aiming to claim or to destroy.

It all looked random at a glance, but I knew that people were rarely able to make their actions totally random unless they had complex computer systems involved. They might *think* they were mixing things up too much to be predictable, but a pattern would still emerge if you took in the big picture from the right angle.

Doom's Seed didn't want us to be able to predict where he'd strike next. He was trying to keep Beckett and the rest of us on our toes. But he wasn't impervious. No one was.

If I could make a good guess at where he'd launch his next attack, Beckett could focus his manpower there instead of waiting for his people to call in and scrambling to launch a defense.

It would be coming soon. Since the first full-out assault, Doom's Seed had rarely waited more than forty-eight hours before launching another of some sort, and usually it'd been closer to twenty-four.

I ran through the list again in my head, feeling out the rhythm of it. Inside the city and outside. Business-related or fear tactics. He kept looping around between all the different factors… and when I considered which he *hadn't* acted on recently, his next step suddenly seemed obvious.

A surge of hope raced through me, but I made myself examine the data again to double-check my instincts. If I sent us off on a wild goose chase, Beckett could end up worse off in the face of the next attack, not better.

When I was confident, I pushed myself to my feet. "I have an idea of where Doom's Seed will come at you next."

Beckett's head jerked up, and Madelyn and my friends focused on me as well, Madelyn offering me an encouraging smile.

"By all means, let's hear it," Beckett said, watching me with a thoughtful expression. I could hear the respect in his tone.

I'd better make sure I earned it.

"Making an educated guess," I said, "I believe that his next target will be a property of yours that has strategic value but is a little farther away from where most of the conflict has been—outside the city. Maybe pretty far outside. Something like the farm, where it was separate from your businesses around here but still could damage your family's reputation if you lost it."

Beckett's eyebrows rose. He rubbed his jaw as his gaze went distant with thought, and then his expression tightened. "If you're right, then I know exactly where he'll come gunning for us next. I don't have many men out there. I can call more in."

Logan pushed his plate away. "We should go out there too. It worked well when you rallied the troops at the farm. And the more hands on deck, the better."

Beckett hesitated for a second, his gaze sliding to Madelyn, but when she gave him a firm look, he nodded. "Let's go, then. If we get there before he has his people in place, he might even call off his plans."

We rushed out to the same van we'd taken out to the farm, although Beckett got in behind the wheel this time. He'd mentioned that his people in the area were being spread increasingly thin with so many casualties and injuries after the past attacks.

A sense of nervous exhilaration kept sweeping through me as the van roared out of the city along one of the freeways. Please, let me be right about this. If I was, then I'd given us a huge advantage.

If I wasn't, then I might have totally screwed our new friend over.

Maddie had taken the passenger seat next to Beckett. "Where exactly are we going?" she asked.

"My family owns an entertainment complex out here at the far edge of the suburbs," Beckett said. "We use it to launder most of our money from our less legitimate local activities. It's almost as far from the city proper as the farm, and it'd be a significant blow if something happened to it."

He turned the wheel to veer down an exit ramp. I twisted on the bench to peer out the side window.

"It's just up ahead," Beckett said, and his phone's ringtone started pealing. He fished it out of his pocket while holding on to the steering wheel with his other hand and glanced at the call display. A frown darkened his expression. "It's one of my men who was stationed out there—I talked to him less than an hour ago when we left."

He hit the speaker phone button and set the phone down in the cup holder slot. "What's going on, Matt?"

At the same moment, gunfire boomed through the air—fainter through the windows and louder as it crackled from the phone's speaker. My stomach plummeted. Before the man even spoke, I knew what'd happened.

I'd been right—but I'd figured it out too late.

"The pricks just swarmed us," the guy on the other end of the phone hollered. "How far away are those reinforcements? Fuck."

More shots reverberated through the speaker. Beckett spat out a curse and slammed his foot down on the gas. "We're just a couple of blocks away, and the others should be right on our tail!"

He blew through a stop sign without a hint of concern and careened into the huge parking lot around an expansive entertainment center. Movie posters lined the wall of the cinema that bulged from this corner of the building.

But the people who'd come to enjoy those movies and everything else the complex had to offer weren't getting much entertainment right now. Shrieks and cries carried through the air as we screeched to a halt at the edge of the parking lot. Only a little relief flashed through me at the sight of three more cars tearing around the bend to follow us.

We were going to need all the help we could get. Beckett leapt out, and we did the same, but we stayed braced behind the doors to use them as shields as we took in the scene before us.

At least twenty figures waving guns were spread out across the parking lot close to the complex. Several of them were taking shots at the outside of the building, shattering a window here, smashing a store sign there. Others yelled at patrons who were now fleeing toward their cars.

They weren't killing those innocents—not yet, anyway—but they were doing their best to terrify them.

"Don't let us see your faces around here again!" one shouted loud enough for me to hear over the gunfire. "And tell your friends to stay away too."

Beckett sucked in a ragged breath. "They want word to get around that this happened—that it'd be dangerous to come here. Dry up all our business. Fucking assholes."

"Not just that," Slade said with an anxious note in his voice. "I think those guys right by the building have gasoline cans."

I squinted through the dimming evening light and realized it was true. Three figures were splashing liquid from what looked like gas cans against the walls of the complex.

They were planning to burn down even more of Beckett's business. Scaring off his customers was just a side benefit. And it meant that even if we stopped the fire in time, they'd already caused plenty of damage.

The other cars skidded to a halt around us. Men poured out of them, and Beckett hollered to them with a wave of his hand.

The attackers around the building looked our way and fired several more shots at the building before swiveling around. But they didn't even try to take us down. They dashed toward the vehicles they must have arrived in.

All except two of the men with the gas cans, who paused just long enough to flick open lighters and toss them into two separate puddles of gasoline.

Flames hissed to life at the same time as our side opened fire. "Be careful of any pedestrians!" Beckett was urging, but as far as I could tell, all the ordinary people had already fled the scene. Thank God.

A couple of the attackers fell under the hail of bullets, but most dived into or between their cars in time. The fire roared up the two sides of the building like twin demons, ready to dig in their claws.

Beckett glanced between the retreating attackers and the building and appeared to decide that it wasn't worth going for revenge if his property went up in smoke in the meantime.

"Let them go!" he shouted. "Focus on putting out the fire!"

"With what?" one of his men hollered back.

A few of his people raced forward with bottles of water, but even I knew those weren't going to get very far. My mind spun with all the knowledge I'd accumulated across my life, and I whirled toward the spot where I could predict the water main would be located.

There'd be a hydrant somewhere along it… There!

"Over here!" I called out, running toward the yellow structure I'd caught sight of down the street. Several of Beckett's men followed me, but it must have only taken them a few seconds to figure out what I was after.

"Hold on! Get out of the way." One of them sprinted back toward his car.

The next thing I knew, the guy was speeding the car straight toward the hydrant. He slammed into it grill-first.

The hydrant burst, water spraying over the sidewalk as far as the edge of the parking lot. Well, I guessed that was one way to get it open.

A bunch of the men, as well as my friends and Madelyn,

charged over to the hydrant. Everyone carried some sort of container, from the duffel bags that'd once held an assortment of weapons to bins and bags that'd been used for purposes I could only guess at. They held them up to the spewing water in turn and then raced toward the fire to toss the contents on the flames.

In the distance, I heard the first faint strains of fire-truck sirens. If we could just tame the fire a little, drown it as much as possible before the professionals arrived, maybe the damage would only be superficial.

A few of Beckett's people had remained by the cars, covering their colleagues with their gazes fixed on the retreating enemy. A handful of the attackers had paused by their cars to take shots at us, and Beckett's men returned fire without hesitation, determined to take down anyone they could.

My gaze caught on a man in that cluster of cars who was ducked down by the trunk of a sedan, his phone pressed to his ear. Was he talking to Doom's Seed right now?

He had to be speaking to someone important if he figured it was worth staying in the middle of a gunfight to find out what they had to say rather than racing off first.

"Hey!" I shouted at the men on our side who were closest to me, and gestured toward the guy who was mostly out of view. "We need to get our hands on that phone. It could lead us straight to the asshole behind this attack."

One of Beckett's men nodded and darted around the van to get a clearer shot. Just as the guy I'd spotted started to lower the phone, the man I'd called over squeezed the trigger.

The bullet caught our target in the wrist. With a yelp of agony, he jerked his arm toward him, blood spurting and the phone dropping from his fingers.

It clattered on the pavement. Beckett's people went back to

firing at the last of the attackers, who were all scrambling into their cars now.

As they peeled away, I threw myself across the parking lot toward the fallen phone. I had to get to it before any of our enemies considered how valuable it could be and crushed it under a tire.

I kept my body low, hoping the men behind me could fend off anyone who tried to shoot at me. A bullet whizzed by over my head, and my heart lurched. But I snatched up the phone and hurtled back the way I'd come, my pulse hammering away with a mix of elation and terror.

The sirens were blaring louder. Just as I leapt back into the shelter of the van, three fire trucks swerved into the parking lot. The firemen charged out and rushed to the hydrant, where thankfully Beckett's men had pulled the car out of range. Other firefighters started spraying down the building with water from the trucks' on-board tanks.

The flames started to sputter under the larger deluge of liquid. Doom's Seed's people hadn't been able to splash the gasoline all the way up the walls, and most of the fire sizzled out under the spray from the hoses. Black streaks cut through the pastel paint, but as far as I could tell, the flames hadn't eaten through the building to its contents.

Beckett was going to have a reconstruction project on his hands, but a much smaller one than it might have been if we hadn't headed out here when we had. His people's efforts with the hydrant had slowed the fire quite a bit.

At the moment, Beckett was waving to his men. In a matter of seconds, they'd jumped back into their cars while Beckett, Madelyn, and my friends scrambled into the van.

"The police will be here too, any minute now," Beckett said in explanation as we peeled out of the lot.

He drove in tense silence for several blocks before pulling over into a different parking lot outside a bingo parlor that was closed for the night. His breath came out in a ragged whoosh.

"We were too late," I said, my throat tightening. "I'm sorry."

"It's not your fault. It's that prick Doom's Seed," Beckett muttered. He sat up straighter, swiping his hand back through his hair. "You were right about the pattern. And it would have been worse if we hadn't been here. But business is still going to suffer a lot after the spectacle those pricks made. And having the cops sniffing around isn't great for us either."

"We stopped them from doing everything they wanted to," Madelyn insisted. "That's a partial win, anyway."

It occurred to me that in the panic of our departure I'd almost forgotten the one other possible win we'd made. I fished the confiscated phone out of my pocket. A smear of blood marked the screen, but it was otherwise undamaged.

I held it up. "We have this too. One of Doom's Seed's men was making a call on it in the parking lot—maybe getting instructions from the boss himself? Or someone else important. If he's the one who was getting the orders from people higher up, there could be some interesting material on there that we could use against Doom's Seed, right?"

Logan's eyes lit up. He gave me a thumbs up and took the phone from me. "That's brilliant, Dex."

Slade laughed. "Leave it to Dexter to find a way to turn a disaster around."

Even Beckett had perked up a little. He smiled at me with a tip of his head. "I saw you running over there—I didn't realize what for. Thanks for that. You really stuck your neck out."

"Anything I can do to help, I'm on it," I said, a strange sense of satisfaction washing over me.

I might not be immersed in the criminal underworld like Beckett's people, but I was a real part of this new, joint team we'd formed with him. I'd contributed in ways his men hadn't thought to on their own. Maybe hadn't even been capable of, when it came to recognizing the patterns.

And with the eager vibe that hummed between us as Logan turned on the phone and the rest of us looked on, we were becoming even more of a cohesive unit than we'd been before. Maybe even a family, with Madelyn right there at the center of it.

She caught my eye with one of her soft smiles, and I had to smile back. The family we'd formed wasn't just cohesive. It was the best one I could imagine.

CHAPTER 16

Madelyn

We pulled over to the curb next to a stretch of modest suburban houses, a few yards down from the specific house we were interested in. I peered at its pastel blue walls through the dim light from the streetlamps that'd blinked on with the descending night. A second car carrying the people Beckett had brought for backup parked behind us.

I dragged my gaze away from the house to glance at Logan in the seat next to mine. "You're sure this guy is connected to the illegal organ transplants?"

My stepbrother nodded. "The trail from the data we grabbed off that phone was clear enough once we dug far enough. And the guy's a doctor—Doom's Seed will obviously have needed some medical experts on board to make this work."

"We don't know exactly how connected Dr. Evancho is," Dexter piped up from where he was sitting next to Beckett up front. "It's possible he doesn't know the full extent of the situation."

"We'll approach him cautiously rather than aggressively." Beckett leaned forward to peer at the house. "I don't see any signs of a significant security system on the house."

At my other side, Slade tapped his window. "There's a car in the driveway. Someone's home."

I rubbed my arms, a chill passing through me despite the whir of the car's heater, and Logan set a reassuring hand on my shoulder. "It'll just be him. His one kid is grown up and lives in a totally different city now, and his wife's out of town this week speaking at a conference on the other side of the country. No innocent bystanders."

"Unless *he's* innocent," I pointed out.

"We'll figure that out," Beckett said confidently. "Let's go see what Dr. Steve Evancho will tell us, Maddie."

We all got out of the car, Beckett's men emerging from theirs as well, but everyone except Beckett and me hung back on the front lawn while the two of us climbed the steps. When we'd been hashing out the plan, I'd pointed out that seeing a young woman at the door might put the doctor a little more at ease than if he were faced with a bunch of tough-looking men.

The guys had only agreed because Beckett would be right there next to me—and fully armed, if things took a bad turn.

As Beckett pressed the button for the doorbell, my stomach knotted. I squared my shoulders and willed my nerves to settle, though my heart kept thumping on.

It was one thing to rush in to help in the middle of a fight already happening, when I could see there was an obvious threat. In this situation, for all intents and purposes, *we* were the threat. It wasn't a feeling I enjoyed.

The door eased open, revealing a man I knew from Logan's

research was in his early sixties, with thin gray hair swept to the side of his broad forehead. At the sight of us, his eyes widened slightly while his jaw clenched.

He definitely didn't figure we were just canvasing for charity.

"Yes?" he said in a nervous tone.

"Dr. Evancho?" I said, and went on at the brief dip of his head, "We need to ask you about something important. I think you have information that could save a lot of lives."

His expression tightened even more, and he took a step back, his knuckles whitening where he gripped the door. "You must have the wrong person. I think you'd better leave."

"Please, Dr. Evancho," I started, but he cut me off.

"I have nothing to say to you—I don't know whatever you think it is I know. I'd appreciate it if you left my property right away."

He started to close the door, but Beckett caught it with a smack of his hand. He held the doctor's gaze with the cool fierceness I'd always admired in him, and lifted his shirt just enough to flash the gun in the concealed holster at his hip.

"We could get the police involved in this matter," he said firmly, "but we're willing to handle it privately, which I think is what you'd prefer. Especially considering who you're entangled with."

A flash of pure terror crossed Dr. Evancho's face, all but confirming our suspicions about his connection to Doom's Seed.

I held out my hand to him. "Please. We're not here to hurt you. We only want your help. I already—I lost my dad because of the people you've worked with. You've got to know that what's happening is wrong. Don't you want to see it stopped?"

"I don't know what you're talking about," the doctor muttered again, but he shifted his weight, not trying to force the door.

"You went through all that medical training," I tried again. "You dedicated your life to saving other people's lives. I can't believe you'd want to let innocents keep dying if you have the chance to end the suffering. What did you take that oath for?"

His mouth twisted. His gaze lifted to meet mine. We stared at each other in silence for a long moment.

"No one needs to find out you told us anything," Beckett put in. "We're not going to spread the word. And if we have our way, the only people who'd retaliate will be out of the picture soon regardless."

I wasn't sure which of us convinced him more, but after another several seconds of hesitation, Dr. Evancho sighed. He stepped back. "Fine. Come inside, but please, let's make this quick."

"Nothing would make me happier," Beckett said. "But I hope you'll understand that we have some company just to make sure we *all* stay safe."

A couple of his people lingered in the shadows around the house to keep watch. Three others trooped inside along with me, Beckett, and the Vigil guys. The doctor led us into the living room just beyond the front hall. As soon as he stopped, Beckett's three men gathered around him with menacing glowers.

Dr. Evancho cringed. "Don't hurt me. I'm cooperating. I—I never even wanted to be a part of this. I'm not some criminal mastermind."

Beckett eyed him, folding his arms over his chest. "Let's make sure we're talking about the same thing. What didn't you want to be a part of?"

The doctor's eyes flicked over all of us. "The—the organ transplants. That's what you're here about, isn't it? I can't imagine what else—"

He fell silent at Logan's nod.

"How did the man who brought you on make you get involved if you didn't want to be?" Dexter asked.

Dr. Evancho wrung his hands in front of him. "It was under

duress. I made a mistake when I was a lot younger than I am now, when I'd first started out at my practice. He took advantage of my lapse."

Slade raised his eyebrows. "What kind of mistake?"

The doctor looked away. "I skimmed some money out of the clinic. I didn't think anyone would realize, but the wrong people found out and used it to threaten me. If I hadn't done what they asked, they'd have exposed the crime, ruined me and my ability to provide for my family—my son was only a baby…"

I was torn between sympathy and revulsion that he'd let his initial weakness propel him into a much greater crime. "You helped with the transplant operations and—"

"No," Dr. Evancho broke in urgently. "No, I never touched a single patient, I swear it. I wouldn't have let it go that far. I only—they asked me to help them falsify records to cover for the patients they'd taken on. That's it. Just paperwork."

Just paperwork. Paperwork that'd helped cover up hundreds, maybe even thousands of organs illegally obtained and transplanted over the years. That'd allowed so many lives to be destroyed while Doom's Seed made his money. My teeth gritted.

"Do you know any of the other doctors who were involved?" Beckett asked.

Dr. Evancho shook his head. "I have no idea who else those people brought on. They kept every part of their system totally separate so that there wasn't much chance of any of us turning on them." He looked down at his hands. "That's why I'm not sure I can do anything for you. I hardly know anything."

Dexter glanced at us with a grimace. He was the best at reading people for lies, and he obviously believed this man was telling the truth—there wasn't anything more we could get out of him.

In terms of what he could tell us with his words, anyway. I

stepped ahead of the guys, waiting until the doctor met my gaze again.

"We're trying to take those people down for good. We've already put together a lot of the pieces, but we don't have as much concrete evidence as we need to prove our case where it matters. If you have anything you used back then when you were working for them—real records or other references that we could use to prove the ones that the hospitals have now were faked—that could make a huge difference."

His gaze darted briefly to the side. I was pretty sure he was thinking about something he did have that we could use. But he simply twisted his fingers together, a quiver passing through his stout body. "I'm not sure…"

"This is your chance to make up for the harm you helped carry out," I reminded him. "Even if you never hurt anyone directly, you contributed—you bear some of the responsibility. Don't you want to do *something* to fix that?"

Dr. Evancho exhaled shakily and then lifted his head. A trace of determination had come into his eyes.

"I've been holding on to that guilt for a long time. It's been years since I last did anything for those people, but… I believe I do have the original files that I based my falsified ones on. You could use the originals to prove that some of the other records copied data in patterns that are clearly artificial. You'd have to pull the fake records from a lot of different hospitals to prove the repetition, though."

"That's not a problem," Logan said. "Where are the original records?"

"Let me—let me see if I can dig them up."

"Thank you." Beckett motioned to his men. "You go with him in case he needs any assistance."

He said the last word with a little wryness. Mostly he wanted to make sure the doctor didn't betray us somehow, I was sure. We wouldn't want him slipping off and coming back with a weapon.

The doctor hustled out of the room with Beckett's people at his heels. As their footsteps creaked into the basement, Slade cocked his head.

"Do you think he has something that'll really be that useful? Isn't he screwing himself over if he gives it to us?"

"No," Logan said. "Once we have the records, there'll actually be *less* evidence that he was involved, since they won't be stashed here in his house any longer. He'll probably be glad to get rid of them. I doubt he'd have lifted files that were connected to him originally."

My spirits started to rise. "Then this could be something really good."

Beckett smiled at me. "I think it is. And you helped convince him to go along with us. You've been fantastic, Maddie."

Logan brushed his hand over my hair. "She always is."

I wished I could take more enjoyment from their compliments, but all my emotions were tangled up in anticipation. What if Dr. Evancho hadn't held on to the originals after all? What if they'd been damaged beyond use over time?

We waited in silence while thumps and rustling emanated from the floor below. Finally, the doctor and his guards marched back up the stairs and returned to the living room. Dr. Evancho was clutching a manila folder.

He held it out to me. "These are the base files I used for the forgery. They're each from a different hospital—each from a different state. I was trying to be careful."

I flipped open the folder and held it so the guys could scan the papers inside too. They were clearly photocopies, the signatures a little grainy, all from the 1980s.

Dexter got out his phone and snapped pictures of every page so we had a digital copy as well. I glanced at Logan in question after we'd skimmed over the last one, and he gave me a tight smile.

"I can pull it all together. This is everything we need."

I turned back to the doctor. "Thank you. You have no idea how much I appreciate this."

He dipped his head, his expression abruptly softening. "I'm sorry about your father," he said quietly. "I can only imagine he'd have been very proud of you."

A twinge of loss ran through my gut. I swallowed thickly. "I hope so."

In that moment, I could see that for all his waffling and hesitation, Dr. Evancho regretted being a party to this criminal enterprise.

One of Beckett's men pulled himself a little straighter, looming over the doctor, and shot Beckett a pointed look. "Should we do anything else to take care of him?" he asked.

A shiver passed down my spine. I could guess at the implications of that question.

"He knows he's safer from the real villains if he keeps quiet about what he gave us and that we were here," I said to Beckett. "I don't think we need to worry."

And I didn't want to see any more pain coming out of this situation.

Beckett studied me and then the doctor. Dr. Evancho drew up his chin, but it quivered a little.

"My lips are sealed," he insisted. "It'd be a hell of a lot worse for me than for you if those people ever found out. And… I hope you do manage to take them down. I'd like to see that—to know that it's over."

"All right," Beckett said. "Keep an eye on the news, and maybe you will get to see it. I'll remember this." He held up the manila folder.

As we strode out of the house, the tension that'd gripped me rippled out with a rush of breath. A tingle of excitement took its place. Looking at the folder gripped in Beckett's hand, I couldn't help grinning.

We'd done it. We'd gotten the proof we needed. And those records were going to change *everything*.

CHAPTER 17

Madelyn

I should have expected nothing less than my mom making the condo her own in three days. When I dropped by and found her in the kitchen, the place held the familiar childhood scent of sautéing garlic and onions. She was making one of her trademark stir-fries.

"I can see you're hanging in there all right," I said lightly.

I could tell Mom's stoic expression was a bit of a front, but she smiled warmly enough that I knew she really was doing okay.

"It's like a little vacation," she said with a laugh. "But I enjoy getting some cooking in. Working with the ingredients is strangely relaxing. And I think Summer is appreciating having a few home-cooked meals. I missed having someone other than Holand to take care of, you know."

"Hey," Holand spoke up from where he was lounging in the

living room, peeking over the back of the couch and giving my mom a playful scowl. “I don’t need *that* much taking care of.”

“Dear, if you could tell the difference between an onion and a potato, I’d be shocked.”

I snorted lightly and Holand chuckled, looking back to the television. They seemed like they’d managed to set aside most of the stress that must have been weighing on them after their hasty arrival here and the destruction of the house.

Mom had already started the wheels turning for the insurance. She and Holand had packed their most precious items to keep them close and brought them here anyway, so it hadn’t been quite as big of a blow as if the fire had started while they’d been at work… or asleep and unaware.

I updated her on the assignments I’d been squeezing in around the adventures I’d rather not tell her about, and she described the movie they’d all watched last night, but her gaze kept twitching to me as she added chicken and then veggies to the frying pan.

Finally, she sighed and leaned against the counter with her gaze fixed on me. “I have to admit, I keep thinking about your father and how he was mixed up in these criminal enterprises. Do you have any idea how that happened? Or how far this conspiracy you’ve stumbled on reaches?”

My stomach twisted, but I didn’t want to lie to her any more, not unless I absolutely had to. And she deserved to know the full extent of the danger.

“We’re pretty sure he came across a medical record from one of the patients who received an illegal transplant and noticed discrepancies in the data,” I said. “Somehow he pieced together enough to start tracking down more information at the source. And —it’s a big source. Really, really big. We know for sure now that this business extends across multiple states. It could even involve other countries as well.”

Mom's jaw tightened. "And you really can't turn to the police and let them handle it?"

"We'd like to. We've been trying to build up enough of a case so that they'll believe there *is* a crime." I let out my breath in a rush. "I think we're almost there. In just a couple more days, you might be able to leave here."

She shook her head, with a distant expression. "I wish your father had never gotten caught up in this mess. Then *you* wouldn't have either."

I swallowed thickly. "That's true, but he was trying to be a hero. He *would* have been a hero if he'd gotten far enough. I'm carrying out the work he wanted to do… just in a different way from what I always pictured. I kind of like that."

"I understand." Mom reached over to squeeze my hand. "But I still don't like the idea of you being involved in something so dangerous. It's *my* job to keep you safe."

I shot her a bittersweet smile. "Not anymore. I'm grown up now—that's my responsibility."

She let out a huff. "I just don't want to see the same thing happen to you that did to him."

"It won't," I said firmly, for both her benefit and my own. "It's different for me. He was trying to go it alone, but I have a bunch of other people standing with me."

No way did I want to admit to her how nervous I actually was, how my nerves shivered just remembering the gunfight at the entertainment complex two evenings ago. That would only make her worry more, and she had enough trauma hanging over her head because of me as it was.

Holand switched off the TV and ambled over to the kitchen to prop himself in the doorway. "Some of those people being Logan and his friends, obviously," he said, and paused. "How is he?"

The strain in his voice and the melancholy shadow that crossed his face brought a fresh lump of guilt into my gut. Logan hadn't come back to the condo since we'd first dropped everyone off here. I knew he still hadn't talked to his dad about Yvonne.

His dad had to be able to tell Logan was keeping things from him. I couldn't imagine how much that would be eating at him with all the things Holand *did* know about his son's activities now.

But it wasn't my place to reveal anything Logan wasn't ready to get into yet.

"He's doing well, all things considered," I said, which seemed both accurate and vague enough.

"I gather that he's been investigating this conspiracy for quite a bit longer than you have. Trying to figure out what happened. He never mentioned anything about it to me at the time."

My voice softened. "I know. He kept me totally in the dark too."

Holand pinched the bridge of his nose. "I wish he would turn to me more. I've tried to be here for him as much as I can."

I didn't know what to tell him, but all of me ached to give him some kind of reassurance.

"He's put a lot of distance between himself and, well, everyone because he's been trying to protect everyone he cares about from the fallout," I said. "Once the mastermind behind all this is arrested and we can breathe easier, I'm sure he'll open up more."

At least, looking into Holand's anguished eyes, I hoped he would. Ultimately, that would come down to Logan and what he felt comfortable with. He'd built a huge wall between him and his dad, and it was hard to say if he'd ever be able to tear it completely down.

Holand gave me a sad but genuine smile. "I'm glad he's been able to turn to you now, at least a little, along with the guys."

"Yeah." I hesitated, and decided that this was one subject I had just as much right to broach as Logan would have. "We've gotten pretty close, you know. Even before you and Mom started dating, there was something between us… I'm looking out for him as well as I can. He means an awful lot to me."

I hadn't been sure if Holand would be able to read between the lines, but a hint of fond amusement sparked in his eyes. "You know, I did wonder back then, watching the two of you together… It's not as if you were ever really raised as siblings."

Mom tsked her tongue behind me and gave my shoulder a squeeze. "As long as you two are being careful in *every* way… I suppose it's good you have each other. We're not going to get in the way of that."

I exhaled slowly, relief sweeping through me. I hadn't really expected them to get uptight about our relationship, but there'd always been a nagging worry in the back of my head. We weren't actually doing anything wrong, though. Holand had never officially adopted me or Mom Logan, so we weren't siblings even in a legal sense.

"I'll give Logan a nudge about coming by to visit," I told Holand. "He's just been so wrapped up in tracing information we've found as well as keeping up with his schoolwork, but soon he won't have the first excuse. Now I'd better go visit the other resident before she accuses me of abandoning her."

"I heard that!" Summer hollered teasingly from her bedroom. "I was just generously giving you some family time before I dragged my bestie away."

"Dinner should be ready in about ten minutes," Mom called after me. "As soon as the rice is done."

I found Summer flopped on her bed, but she sat up as soon as I came in and patted the mattress for me to join her. Glancing at the huge window that filled one wall of the bedroom, only partly obscured by the sheer curtain hanging over it, she grinned. "You know, this place sure beats my dorm room. I could totally get used to this."

I laughed. "I wouldn't have put you up in a dump. Well, not unless I really had to."

She arched her eyebrows at me. "The friend who owns the place —that's this Beckett of yours, isn't it? He has very good taste in real estate. When do I get to meet him? And does he have any single brothers?"

I couldn't restrain a snort of amusement. "As far as I know, he's an only child. But if I find out otherwise, you'll be the first one I tell."

"Fine." She tipped back over on the bed dramatically and twisted a strand of her hair around her finger. "So what other news have you got? Something must have happened in the past few days."

"Well, we finally got our hands on some evidence that could turn the whole case around," I told her. "We're just making sure we have all our bases covered before we turn it in."

Summer let out a whistle. "Seriously? That's awesome! Then I can stop having panic attacks every time my phone rings, thinking you've been shot or something."

"I'd like that too," I said dryly. "Hopefully we'll have the details settled soon. How's school going with the distance?"

She let out a huff. "One of my professors is being an ass about me taking emergency leave. It doesn't help that I can't explain it. She's a friend of my mom's and I *know* my mom told her that I was lying."

I gasped. "No way."

"You remember how my mom is." Summer groaned. "She loves to know everything, and if she doesn't, she has to act like she does for appearances."

That *was* her mother. I winced. "I don't know how you handle that."

"I don't. There's a reason I never go and see my mom, and that's it."

"So is your professor letting you do the work, or is she refusing?"

"She's letting me do it for appearance's sake, I think. If I took it to the dean that she was giving my mom information on me, she'd be fired in a heartbeat, and she knows it." Summer rolled her eyes. "I can play the game, too."

"I have no idea how my professors are going to take it if I don't end up coming back to classes next week," I admitted. "Another reason I'm grateful it seems like we've almost got this thing wrapped up. I'd love to let the cops handle the rest."

Summer waved a finger at me. "And you *should* let them handle it."

I swatted her. "I know. I just—"

The chime of my phone cut me off. I dug it out of my pocket. As soon as I saw Beckett's name on the screen, I yanked it to my ear.

"What's up?" I asked, and mouthed *Beckett* at Summer. He'd known I was coming to visit Mom and Summer—he wouldn't be interrupting that if it wasn't important.

"Are you still at the condo?" he asked in an urgent tone that set me twice as much on edge.

My heart thumped faster. "I'm sitting beside Summer right now. What happened?"

He took a deep breath, but he couldn't quite erase the raggedness from his voice that showed how unnerved he was. "Have you heard anything there? Has anything happened in or around the building to make you concerned?"

I got up and stepped to the window, but nothing in the view

below told me what he might be concerned about. "No, nothing. It's been quiet. No alarms or anything."

"Okay. Okay, good." I caught the thrum of a motor in the background on his end of the line. "I'm on my way to pick you up. Something's gone down—I want you back with me right away. I'm calling in more people to keep watch over the condo building, so everyone there should be safe too. Head down to the lobby now. I'll be there in five minutes."

He hung up abruptly, leaving my nerves on edge. I glanced at Summer, who looked back at me wide-eyed.

"I've got to go," I told her. "Sorry to cut the visit short, but it sounds like there's trouble."

"You go be with your guys," she told me, sitting up to grab me in a quick hug. "But call me when you can to fill me in."

"Of course."

I hustled out to the kitchen, made hasty apologies to Mom and Holand for missing dinner after all, and squeezed Mom tight before heading out.

The elevator whirred down the building painfully slow. By the time I was crossing the lobby, I spotted Beckett's usual sedan through the glass doors.

The second I came into view, he pushed open the passenger-side door of the car for me. I hopped in and yanked it shut, and he hit the gas before I'd even put on my seatbelt.

"What's going on?" I asked, taking in his tense expression. My heart lurched with panic. "Are the guys—?"

"The other guys are fine," Beckett said quickly. "But only because they haven't left my house since this morning. I—" He shook his head with a slight slump of his shoulders that my heart ached to see.

"What?" I murmured. "What happened?"

His jaw worked. When we had to stop at a red light, he glanced over at me, his normally cool grey eyes stormy with turmoil.

"Doom's Seed has sent his people on a total rampage. They're shooting anyone they can connect to my family's businesses on sight, no matter where they are at the time. Just picking them off in the middle of the street, in regular stores…"

My throat constricted. "Oh my God."

He dipped his head as he urged the car forward again. "It's a bold move, but it's working for him. I've lost over a dozen people in just the last few hours, and if I can't figure out how to end this soon, I'm going to lose even more."

CHAPTER 18

Slade

Thin sunlight seeped past the curtains on the guestroom window. I groaned and rolled over to bury my head in the pillow, but I already knew it was no use.

Normally I could have tuned out full daylight—not to mention blaring music, animated voices, and anything else going on around me—if I was tired enough. But the turmoil of the past several days had left my nerves on edge. I could barely relax even in total darkness and quiet.

I grimaced, wondering how much actual sleep I'd managed to get between bouts of tossing and turning. From the muggy feeling in my head, I doubted it'd been more than a few hours.

Oh well. I definitely wasn't getting any more now. Might as well chug some coffee and try to make the best of the day, whatever new horrors it might bring.

It was still early, only a little past sunrise. The house was still and silent around me as I swapped the boxers I'd slept in for fresh ones and a tee and sweats combo in case I decided to do a stint in the workout room Beckett had showed us, with an offer of full access. A little exercise might jolt me back into proper alertness.

But first, caffeine.

I padded down the hall and slipped into the sitting room, expecting to find it empty and not wanting to disturb any of the others who would still be sleeping. Just inside the room, I jarred to a halt.

Logan was sitting in the exact same armchair where he'd stationed himself last night, in the exact same clothes, with his laptop poised in front of him. Bags were starting to form under his weary eyes, and his mouth was set in a grim but tired line. Even his short hair looked like it was drooping.

He glanced up at me, his reaction time slowed to a zombie's pace, his gaze hazy as if it took him a few seconds to recognize me.

"Dude, what are you doing awake?" I demanded in a hushed voice, striding over.

"What are *you* doing awake?" he shot back without much vigor.

I eyed him, the wheels in my head turning with suspicion. "Did you even go to bed last night?"

He swiped his hand over his face and appeared to suppress a yawn. "I had to keep following the trail. Beckett's people farther out have gotten me access to all the hospitals where Dr. Evancho got his base records. I managed to confirm they're all in the system still."

I couldn't help perking up a little even though concern still gripped my gut. "Even though they're from back in the '80s?"

"A lot of older records get digitized over time, especially in fields where quick access could mean life or death. It's a good thing, because we can't be sure even the photocopies would have convinced the cops. Now we can cross-reference to the actual files right in the hospital databases."

"That's great," I had to admit.

Logan nodded in a sluggish motion. "Having the extra data has let me turn up a bunch of other transplant records from all the hospitals we have access to now that are suspect. I think Doom's Seed must have had a few different doctors helping with the forgeries, because there are some repetitions that aren't in any of Evancho's files, but it's still a huge step toward proving our case."

"We're almost there." I glanced from the screen to him again, taking in all the signs of exhaustion etched in his face and his posture. "You didn't answer me before."

"About what?" Logan said in a way that told me he knew exactly what I meant and was only dodging. We hadn't been best friends for years for nothing.

"Did you sleep last night?" I pressed.

He continued looking at his screen, but his eyes stopped moving for a moment, dropping to his keyboard before rising again. "I don't see why it matters."

I narrowed my eyes at him. "You need a break, Logan. This whole case isn't on your shoulders alone."

He sighed and tipped his head against the back of the chair. "There's too much that needs to be done. I need to pull these last pieces together so we can end this before someone else gets hurt. Beckett managed to call all his people to safety last night, but they can't lay low forever. They have lives. Some of them have partners, kids… And now they can't go anywhere without worrying about being shot."

The anguish running through his voice made my stomach knot. Logan put on a solid front of being impervious, but I knew that a lot of things got to him more than he typically let show. And the last few days in particular had been brutal.

"Like I said, it's not all on you." I extended my hand toward the computer. "Tell me what to type in for the searches, and I'll pull some more files while you crash. This isn't worth losing your sanity over. You can't help anyone if you burn yourself out."

Logan groaned. "If I teach you what to do, we'll only be losing more time." He closed his eyes for a few seconds, and his voice dropped even lower. "This whole situation has gotten so much more intense than I was ready for. Maddie's lost her house—our family is in hiding… It's like my worst nightmare coming true. The last thing I want to do is *sleep*."

What the hell could I say to him that would be any comfort? I knew exactly what he meant, even if it didn't hit me quite as hard because it wasn't my family or a house I'd actually lived in.

I rested my hand on his shoulder with a firm grip. "All of that is true. I'm not going to deny it. But Maddie decided to be a part of this as much as you did. Neither of you made these decisions without thinking them through. She has a right to take those risks if she wants to."

"It's my fucking fault for starting all of this in the first place. I have to end it."

I let out a soft snort. "If we're getting technical, it was Maddie's dad who got all of us wrapped up in this case to begin with. If he hadn't poked his nose into it, we'd never have realized. So if you want to blame someone, you might as well blame him, not yourself."

"I insisted on digging into it more instead of just letting it lie," Logan grumbled.

"And if you hadn't, Maddie would never have gotten closure. She'd have kept blaming herself for her dad's death, and more people would have died from this illegal organ transplant shit."

"But at least I wouldn't have to worry about someone gunning her down."

I squeezed his shoulder again. "You know she wouldn't have been any safer if you'd kept it from her. She wouldn't have known she needed to be wary or protect herself. Hell, for all we know, Doom's Seed would have gone after her no matter what we did as soon as he realized she was going into the same field as her father."

Logan let out a sigh, but I heard resigned acceptance in it now. "Everything has become such a clusterfuck."

"Yeah, but we're going to unfuck it." I gave him a crooked grin. "*You* are. I've seen time and time again how hard you work to make things okay for everyone around you. That crazy dedication is part of the reason we're best friends. But it also sometimes works against you. You can't be at your best, giving this your all, when you're running on fumes. It's my job as your friend to tell you when I can see you've hit your limit."

"Yeah," Logan muttered, but he sat straighter to close his laptop and set it on the coffee table. Then he glanced up at me.

"I appreciate the kick in the butt, you know, even when I'm grumbling about it. I know you've always got my back. I have no idea how I'd have made it through the last couple of months—hell, the last couple of *years*—without you and Dex at my side. But you in particular… No matter where my temper's at, highs and lows, you're always there to balance it out and help me get my head on straight."

My smile softened. "Right back at you. And hey, I'm pretty sure my main job around here is cheerleader. I take my duty seriously."

Logan rolled his eyes. "You're a lot more than that. Don't sell yourself short." He paused, his gaze drifting toward the door that led to the hall. "I appreciate that you're here for Maddie too, you know."

My chest tightened just for a second. It wasn't a secret that Logan had struggled with the idea of sharing her affections at first—he'd said some pretty awful things to me a couple of times out of obvious jealousy. But I hadn't let his harsh comments faze me, since I'd known the place they were coming from, and we'd seemed to find an arrangement we were all satisfied with.

I hadn't expected him to outright say he was happy with the situation, though.

"You never have to thank me for loving her," I said lightly. "It's awfully hard not to."

"I just mean…" He shook his head. "It was stupid of me to go all caveman, thinking I should have her to myself. More and more, I can see how we all offer her different things, make her life better in different ways, and that's really pretty amazing."

He stopped, his jaw working, and then added, "I don't think I'm in the right headspace to give her what she needs right now. She's got to be stressed out too, and I can tell I'd only amplify that. But…" He caught my gaze again. "Maybe you could help her work through the shit she's grappling with like you have for me."

The words felt almost like a command—or maybe that wasn't generous enough of me. An invitation, a gesture of mutual respect, making it totally clear that he not only accepted my role in Maddie's life but welcomed it. Encouraged it, even.

A warmth filled my chest, the brotherly love I held for the man next to me and the sweeter adoration for the woman we both cared about so much mingling together.

"I'll see what I can do," I said, and gave Logan a gentle shove. "Leave it to me, and try not to worry about that too. Dr. Slade orders you to get at least three hours of sleep before you open up that computer again. I don't think that's asking too much."

Logan muttered something inarticulate, but there was gratitude in his last glance before he hauled himself out of the chair and headed back to his own guest room.

My own restlessness had settled down after our conversation, seeing that I'd made a difference with him, knowing how confident he was in my ability to help both him and Maddie through the mess we'd found ourselves in. Why shouldn't I find out if I could work a little of that spirit-lifting magic on her right now? If she was still sleeping, I didn't think she'd mind starting with a snuggle.

My own spirits buoyed, I set off down the hall myself. I was still several steps from Maddie's guestroom door when it opened.

Maddie stepped out, rubbing her eyes, looking perfectly gorgeous even dressed in casual leggings and a loose tee with her pale hair sleep-rumpled. She shot me a tired-looking smile.

"Trouble sleeping?" I asked, ambling over to her.

"Yeah." She looked me over. "I'm guessing that's going around?"

"It seems to be." As I stood there in front of her, basking in her presence, inspiration sparked in my head. "Might as well make the most of it. Come out for breakfast with me?"

"*Out* for breakfast?" Maddie repeated, cocking her head in surprise.

I reached out to her. "You'll see."

She took my hand without hesitation, and I knew I'd better make the most of the opportunity while I had it.

CHAPTER 19

Madelyn

When I met Slade at the back door of the mansion after a quick change, I couldn't help raising my eyebrows. His hoodie and sweats combo wasn't particularly unusual, but his shoes…

"You know," I said, "I think this is the first time I've ever seen you in sneakers that aren't the flashiest possible color."

Slade looked down at the black shoes he was wearing and chuckled. "I had to borrow these from Logan. Good thing he's only one size bigger than my usual. I figured there wasn't much point in trying to be covert if my sneakers were acting like a neon sign." He slung his arm around my shoulders. "Come on."

"Are you sure this is a good idea?" I murmured as we slipped out into the backyard that seemed to stretch an entire city block, expanses of grass and beds of flowers broken by the occasional stately tree. I tugged my hood a little higher over my hair.

By the time we'd turned in for the night, Beckett had managed to contact all of his people who lived or worked anywhere near Doom's Seed's territory and make sure they were staying out of the public eye and keeping their homes secure. We didn't know if the previous attackers were still patrolling the city looking for targets, but if they happened to spot us, I doubted they'd hesitate to take aim.

"We can get away for a little bit and still stay safe." Slade leaned over to give me a quick peck to the side of my head. "I scoped out exit routes from the mansion a couple of days ago. There's a spot where we can leave without anyone being the wiser, even if Doom's Seed has eyes on the house."

A nervous quiver ran through my pulse, but there was a little excitement in it too. That was why I hadn't turned Slade down when he'd explained this part of his plan.

It felt good to be defying our enemy's reign of terror, to prove that he couldn't completely control us. And right now, proving that might be the only thing keeping me from being overwhelmed by a sense of hopelessness.

There wasn't anything else Slade or I could do to help solidify the final pieces of evidence for the cops now. And when was the last time I'd really let myself simply breathe and enjoy a moment for myself?

"Here we go," Slade said under his breath as we reached the stone wall that surrounded the property, a little taller than I was. He tipped his head to one of Beckett's men who was patrolling nearby, and the guy nodded back without a hint of concern.

It figured that Slade had already made friends with the guards.

A bench stood under a tree a few feet from the wall. Slade

grabbed it and dragged it over before clambering onto it. Then he motioned for me to join him. "We're going up and over."

I climbed after him and peeked over the top of the wall. Another yard lay beyond it.

"Are you sure we won't get arrested for trespassing?"

"Not if we're quick about it. Come on, Piccolina. This isn't even close to the most dangerous thing we've done in the past week."

I glowered at him, but my mouth twitched with a smile at the same time. "Fine." He was making this an adventure, maybe specifically to distract me from the much more frightening adventure we were already wrapped up in, and I couldn't say I minded that.

He lowered his hands to give me a boost, and I set my foot on his palm. At his heft, I scrambled over the top of the wall and landed with a thump on the other side.

Slade heaved himself after me with just a faint thunk when his prosthetic bumped the edge of one of the stones. He dropped down with a grin already in place. "Almost there."

To my relief, we veered straight across the lawn to a hedge that ran along one side of the yard and pushed through a gap between the bushes onto a narrow but apparently public laneway. No one shouted out anything about trespassers, so we were home free.

Slade took my hand and tugged me along to the end of the lane. He peered out into the quiet street on the other side, checking for suspicious activity. Then we jogged across the road and into a sprawling park I hadn't realized was here.

A line of trees stood along this edge of the park, and in less than a minute, I could no longer see the street behind us. My shoulders came down, my nerves soothed by the knowledge that no one would spot us unless they specifically came looking for us here. And there was no way Doom's Seed could guess we'd have taken this little side-trip.

"You planned a breakfast picnic in the park?" I asked, still keeping my voice low, although it might not have been necessary. This early in the morning, the park was empty other than a lone jogger who puffed past us on one of the paths.

"This is a step up even from that. You'll see."

Slade urged me around another glade of trees, and then I stopped in my tracks, gaping at the structure in front of us.

A large, old-fashioned carousel stood in the middle of the clearing next to the path. Beneath its peaked roof, an assortment of wooden horses gamboled and reared, a few drawing chariots and sleighs, most of them with saddles that had posts through the pommels. The paint was worn, but I could tell from the faded remains that it'd once been vibrant. Here and there, spots shone with gold detailing.

"Wow," I said, collecting my jaw. "What kind of city park has one of these just sitting here?"

Slade laughed. "The kind of park you'd find in a neighborhood for people this rich, I guess. How's that for a picnic spot?"

I beamed at him. "Perfect. But where's the breakfast?"

"All in good time, Piccolina. Why don't you pick your seat?"

I circled the carousel until I spotted a sleigh that looked large enough to allow us to sit next to each other without getting too cramped. As I settled into the seat, Slade glanced toward the path. He waved to someone and then loped over to meet a skinny man in a windbreaker who'd just emerged from the shelter of the trees, carrying a couple of paper delivery bags.

Slade took the bags from the man with a bright smile and a thank you and carried them back to the sleigh. "Breakfast is served! I had someone from one of those food apps pick it up from a café in the neighborhood so we didn't have to be seen out there."

I shook my head at him, but affection tingled through me at how much forethought he'd put into this plan. He'd made what could have been a simple breakfast date into something almost magical amid all the chaos we were facing.

I couldn't imagine any of the other guys being able to pull that off.

Slade tucked himself in next to me on the seat, propping one foot against the opposite bench, and retrieved the items from the bags with a flourish. "Coffee, yours with plenty of cream and some cinnamon along with the sugar. Breakfast sandwiches in croissants. Fresh cut fruit, and custard pastries for dessert."

The savory and sweet smells flooded my nose, making my mouth water. "This looks amazing," I said, taking in the spread he'd laid out on the narrow table between the seats.

"Here's hoping it tastes at least half as good," Slade said with a twinkle in his eye.

I leaned over to claim a swift kiss. "I'm sure it does. Thank you."

His expression softened, and he touched my cheek. "You deserve this. We haven't had much chance to spoil you—much chance to do anything except make sure no one's shooting you down, in a while. This is what our life should look like. What it will look like, when we've gotten through this rough patch. I wanted to give you a preview so you know what you have to look forward to."

I hadn't known my heart could swell with any more love than it already had, but right then, I felt close to bursting. I twined my fingers with his and squeezed them tightly before turning back to our food. "We'd better dig in while the sandwiches are still warm. I'm starving."

Slade unwrapped one sandwich and handed it to me, his fingers brushing mine, his shoulder resting companionably against me. When the buttery croissant melted on my tongue, mingling with the creaminess of the egg and cheese within and the tartness of the sliced tomato, I almost swooned. He'd chosen well.

"This is delicious," I told him, snuggling a little closer. "You get full points."

His eyes sparkled. "The only win I need is having you here with me."

We both made short work of our sandwiches and then discovered that the sliced fruit was all in the same container. Slade jabbed the plastic fork into a chunk of pineapple and held it toward me. "Allow me."

I gave him a playfully baleful look but opened my mouth. When he popped the fruit between my lips, the sweet-and-sour juice had my taste buds singing.

"My turn," I said, snatching the fork from him, and raised a slice of orange to his lips.

We devoured the entire container of fruit that way, going back and forth. More and more heat collected low in my belly with each glimpse of some tidbit disappearing into Slade's skilled mouth. When he licked his lips after the last morsel, a quiver shot straight to my pussy. For a second, I forgot that the point was to eat.

Slade hadn't. He retrieved the custard pastries from the second bag and offered one to me.

The custard flooded my mouth, the perfect mix of smooth and creamy, and I couldn't hold back a groan. Slade's gaze lingered on my face as I polished off the pastry in record time. Then he leaned toward me.

"You missed a little."

He dabbed his thumb at the corner of my mouth to wipe a little blob of custard and then held it out for me. Meeting his eyes, I sucked the tip of his thumb into my mouth. It was hard to say what I enjoyed more—the last bit of sweetness or the flare of desire in his dark gaze.

"And now I need to return the favor," he said, his voice getting husky, and caught my hand in his. He brought my fingers to his mouth and flicked out his tongue to lick the crumbs off each tip, one after the other. With each gentle but heated swipe, I could feel my panties dampening.

By the time he reached my little finger, I was holding myself back from squirming in my seat. My thighs pressed together against the ache between my legs.

But Slade had never been one to leave me hanging. He slid his fingers up my arm to my shoulder and then down my side before tugging me onto his lap. "I don't think I've quite had my fill yet."

His mouth descended on mine, the delectable flavors of the meal mingling together with the heat of desire that'd already kindled between us. I arched into the kiss, and his arms wrapped around me, holding me tight.

Slade's lips melded with mine, coaxing them open so his tongue could slip between them and tease over my own. He tilted his head to deepen the kiss, one hand stroking up and down my torso. His fingers caught on the hem of my hoodie and slipped beneath it to stroke the bare skin of my waist where my T-shirt had ridden up.

A whimper traveled up my throat. I wanted more, so much more of this gorgeous, playful, and devoted man who'd created one of the most romantic moments of my life in the middle of a maelstrom.

His fingers crept up my side toward my breasts and brushed over the cups of my bra. Another needy sound tumbled out of me, but when I opened my eyes to gaze into Slade's, my awareness of the world around us snapped back into sharper focus.

We were still sitting in the carousel sleigh, the wider park all around us. No one had come by so far, but that didn't mean they wouldn't.

I hesitated automatically, and Slade eased back a bit to study my expression. "Everything all right?"

I bit my lip. "Anyone could come by and see us. Maybe we should take this back to the house."

Slade let out a low chuckle and nuzzled my neck just below my ear, a spot that sent a giddy tingle rushing over my skin. "I'd have thought that was a benefit, not a problem, considering how we got started. You seem to enjoy a little risk. But I guess we did have a little more cover in the library. Let's see if I can find the right balance for you, Piccolina."

Without warning, he lifted me into the air and tucked me against his chest as he strode around the carousel. "Slade!" I protested half-heartedly.

"Hmm," he said, ignoring my chiding. "This should put us out of view from the path."

He set me down on one of the wooden horses that was poised on its pole close to the carousel floor. With me perched sideways on its saddle, facing Slade, I was just the right height for him to step between my splayed knees.

He tangled his fingers in my hair and dipped his head close to mine. "No one should notice us here unless they go out of their way to peek, in which case it's their fault—or if you make too much noise, in which case it's yours."

I trembled eagerly at the wicked amusement in his voice and couldn't resist tugging him to me for another kiss.

As our mouths collided again and again, I rocked against Slade's waist. He teased his fingers over my chest, delving right inside my bra to roll my nipples until I gasped. Swallowing the sound, he stroked me again and again until I was clutching at him, my lips searing against his with my desire to connect with him in every possible way.

Then his hand skimmed down my body to my sweatpants. He hooked his fingers around the waistband and hefted me up an inch with his other hand, managing to tug the fabric right off me. I only realized he'd taken my panties with them when he set me back down and I felt my bare ass against the aged wood.

"You taste so good, Maddie," he murmured. "But there's more of you I want to taste before we're through."

"Slade," I mumbled, picking up on his intention before he'd even sunk to his knees.

He leaned between my thighs and flicked his thumb over my clit and lower. "So wet for me already. That's my girl."

At my whimper, he pressed his mouth up against me. His tongue swept over and then into my slit, parting me with a bolt of pure bliss. His upper lip worked against my clit, massaging pulses of pleasure into it as his tongue consumed me.

I tried to hold back any louder sounds, but my breath broke into pants despite my best efforts. "Please," I gasped. "Please."

All at once, his tongue swiped upward to swivel around my clit. Two fingers plunged into me, curling to press against the neediest spot inside me. With just a few enthusiastic deep thrusts, sucking me down at the same time, I was shattering apart.

As the rush of pleasure crashed over me, I shuddered against his mouth. Slade hummed approvingly, the sound reverberating into my body, and kissed me there again.

Then he was moving up my body, his fingers keeping up their steady pumping rhythm inside me, his mouth branding my belly, my ribs, my sternum, my breast. As he let my shirt fall again, he captured my lips.

The faint taste of myself on him made me shiver. He paused in his fondling to grip my thigh in balance as he fumbled in his pocket with his other hand. The second he'd torn open the packet with his teeth and slicked the contents over himself, he caught me in his embrace again.

His fingers returned to my pussy, and his lips claimed all the whimpers and moans that I couldn't hold back. He teased me until

I was jerking my hips into his talented hand, and then he swapped it in an instant to thrust the entire, hard length of his cock into me.

I almost sobbed with the pleasure of it filling me. My legs tightened around his hips. Slade gave a soft groan and gripped my ass so he could slam into me even harder.

The fresh, cool morning breeze wove around us, tickling against my bare legs and rustling through the leaves of the nearby trees. I barely noticed our surroundings though, lost in the flood of bliss this man was conjuring in my body.

He pounded into me over and over, only his grasp keeping me from tumbling off my wooden mount in our passion. Our mouths pressed together wildly, our breaths shaking.

"Oh, Piccolina," Slade muttered in between kisses. "You're perfect. Only you've ever made me feel this good. I want all your sounds, all your sweetness."

Another gasp broke from my lips, and he thrust into me even faster. The force sent me spinning into ecstasy.

My orgasm blazed through me. Stars sparked behind my eyes. In that moment, it was only me and Slade in the whole world as he grunted out a choked sound with his own release.

We clung together for a minute, sweat-damp and sated. Slade brushed the hair back from my forehead and kissed me there, then my nose, then my mouth again.

"My girl and our girl," he said softly. "I'll always find a way to win that smile, no matter what else is going on around us."

An ache filled my heart, but I believed him.

I hugged him tightly until reality sank in a little too much. When I hopped down from the horse, he helped me reassemble my clothes and tugged his own pants up. A blush colored my cheeks as we gathered the remains of our breakfast, as if someone would appear now and accuse us of public indecency.

But no one crossed our path until we were heading back

through the park, having tossed the garbage in one of the public bins, and the woman walking her terrier didn't give us a second glance. I leaned against Slade, our hands entwined, adrift on a sense of peace.

It didn't last long, though. The moment we reached the road, needing to scan it carefully before crossing to the secluded ally, my worries started to creep back in again.

We pushed through the hedge and heaved ourselves over the stone wall without incident. With every step, though, I pushed myself a little faster.

What if something new had gone wrong while we were away? What if another catastrophe was just waiting to crash down on our heads?

Slade squeezed my hand. "It's going to be okay, Maddie. Whatever happens, whatever comes, we're going to get through it."

His words reassured me enough that I managed to walk at a less panicked pace up the stairs and down the hall to Beckett's rooms. We stepped inside to find all three of the other guys there, Logan sprawled on the sofa, Dexter perched in the neighboring armchair, and Beckett standing over them both.

Our host lifted an eyebrow at the sight of us. "Where have you two been?"

Slade moved his arm around my waist. "I was just making sure our woman got some much-needed R and R." He paused to glower down at Logan. "Weren't you supposed to be sleeping for at least another hour?"

"I tried," Logan muttered. "The room was too… empty. I might be able to nap in here." He glanced up at me and patted the cushion next to him. "Sit with me?"

How could I refuse him? I sank down onto the sofa and cuddled up to Logan's weary form. He sighed and tipped his head against my shoulder as if he'd been waiting just for me before he could relax.

Dexter pushed himself off his chair and settled onto the floor by my feet, curling his fingers around my calf in a gentle massage. He pressed a kiss to my knee that left my heart fluttering.

Beckett leaned over the back of the couch to caress his fingers over my hair. And Slade grinned at us all as he dropped into the other armchair, as if he'd orchestrated this moment for me too.

I *was* their woman—all of theirs—and I'd never felt it more than in this moment, surrounded by their shared affection.

We were so close to having this happiness without any threats looming over us. Please, let what we'd gotten be enough to see us through to the end.

CHAPTER 20

Madelyn

"Go through everything again with me," Slade said, holding up a list of all the compiled evidence we had. We'd organized it as well as we could, with an explanatory letter laying out all the connections and highlighting the important aspects, and gathered it both in a packet of printed materials and a flash drive.

Beckett had even set up a scheduled email—one that would send if we didn't return and refresh the settings within two days. The message would go directly to the police department, with all the digital files and a note that something must have happened to all of us related to the case.

It was a precaution, just in case we never made it all the way to the cops to begin with.

Dexter leafed through the packet of hard copies. "We've got the photocopies and printouts of all the relevant hospital records, our notes on the seafood market and the operating facility where it was sending 'poisonous fish' along with key photographs, business records showing what front company owns that business and others, and a statement about the possible drug exchange Madelyn witnessed at the spa. And printouts of my photos of Evan Silver's relevant notes with related documentation."

The original notes and some other concrete evidence had been lost in the fire in the Vigil office at the university, but Dexter's relentless commitment to documentation had filled most of that gap.

I bobbed restlessly on my feet, wanting to think everything was about to fall into place for us but hesitant to get my hopes all the way up. "And all of that is on the flash drive in digital form too?"

Logan nodded. "I double-checked. And it has the video files that we couldn't fully add to the printed packet too."

I let out my breath in a rush. "Okay. It seems like that should be everything. All of this stuff has got to be enough, right?"

The five of us studied the thick folder, packed with all our assembled proof. "I can't say I have a lot of faith in the police," Beckett said. "But I feel like this much evidence has to be enough to get them started on an investigation of their own, even if they can't make any arrests right off the bat. And they have more resources than we do to make even more connections."

Slade tapped his prosthetic foot on the floor. "It'd be better if we had a direct witness. Too bad Dr. Evancho barely wanted to give us as much as he did."

I hugged myself. "If the police don't take action, we can always push harder on him, I guess."

"Or go to the media," Dexter added. "There's some provocative material in here—if they print some stories on the situation, it'll put pressure on the cops to take a look."

"Right." I forced a smile. "I just hope they can arrest Doom's Seed—whatever his real name is—fast. Because he's *really* not going to be happy with us once he figures out we've exposed his businesses to the police."

Logan gripped my shoulder. "We won't let anything happen to you. We've made it this far okay, haven't we?"

"I'm not the only one I'm worried about," I reminded him. "You've all become targets too—and everyone working under Beckett."

"Once the cops are on the case, we'll have some protection from Doom's Seed and his people," Slade said. "He'll know how closely the police will scrutinize the situation if we're even hurt. It might piss him off, but exposing him protects us too."

He had a point. I tried to focus on that rather than my lingering anxiety. "Okay. So we're ready to go?"

"Hold on." Logan dropped onto the sofa and opened his laptop. "I want to reconfirm one last thing about the source records. Then we're good to go."

As he tapped at the keys to regain access to the hospital networks he'd been patched into, I gave the other guys a crooked smile. "It's going to be weird when this is over. The investigation has been scary, but it's also what brought us all together."

Slade smirked. "I'd like to think we'd have found each other even without the case, Piccolina. Once we crossed paths on campus, you wouldn't have been able to stay away from me."

As the corners of my lips twitched higher at his teasing, Beckett shook his head. "We met before I even knew there was an investigation. Although I'm awfully glad I ended up being here to help you navigate my part of the world."

Logan let out a grunt that had us all glancing toward him. His forehead had furrowed. "That's weird," he muttered.

My pulse hiccupped. "What?"

"I can't get the right files to load. Give me a second."

As Logan's fingers flew across the keyboard, the rest of us gathered behind the sofa to watch. The sense of unease that'd been prickling through my chest grew claws, sinking deeper in.

Logan's keystrokes grew more forceful with each iteration. Then his hands clenched into fists.

"It doesn't make sense. I just looked at the originals in the hospital systems last night. This record was here then, and now it's like it never existed."

"Check a file at one of the other hospitals," Beckett suggested, but the tightening of his face told me he didn't feel any better about this development than I did.

My heart sank as Logan repeated the process on a different server. And then another, and another, and another. His head drooped farther with each failure.

Finally, he sagged back against the sofa cushions. "They're all gone—all of the original records that Dr. Evancho photocopied and drew data from."

I swallowed thickly. "Does it matter? We still have the photocopies."

"Yeah, but without the proof that those are real hospital records themselves, it could look like we made *those* up to try to prove our case. Fuck!"

Slade looked sick. "Someone deleted them from the system?"

"They must have," Logan muttered. "And no prizes for guessing who that someone must have been."

"But—Doom's Seed left them there for so long," I protested. "The whole time we've been investigating. We didn't go anywhere near the hospitals the records came from ourselves—it was all through Beckett's connections. Why would Doom's Seed have suddenly—" My pulse stuttered. "Dr. Evancho. If someone was keeping an eye on him and realized we'd gotten to him…"

Logan was already tapping at the keyboard again. He brought up a list of search results and clicked on the top one. I'd already braced myself before my eyes caught on the text.

It was an obituary, posted just a couple of hours ago. *Dr. Steve Evancho, survived by his son, Jason Evancho, and his wife, Mary Evancho.*

Logan scowled as his gaze darted over the screen. "It claims he died of a heart attack in the middle of the night."

Slade made a scoffing sound. "Unlikely."

"Doom's Seed arranged his death like he did my dad's," I said with a shiver. Only a much faster health crisis. I had no doubt at all that the heart attack hadn't been provoked by natural causes.

Yet another death in the long list that should have been on Doom's Seed's conscience, not that I believed he cared the slightest bit.

"He must have found out the doctor had been compromised somehow," Beckett said in a rough voice. "Now he's launching an even broader cover-up than before."

A sense of hopelessness settled over me that I saw reflected on all of the guys' faces. Logan pushed away his laptop and raked his hand back through his hair.

"Those source records were the cornerstone of our evidence," Dexter said quietly. "Without the originals to prove they're real, they're worthless."

I groped for any possible solution. "The real originals were paper records—the ones Dr. Evancho photocopied. Could those still be at the hospitals?"

"I doubt it," Logan said. "They were almost definitely destroyed after being digitized—that's part of the point of digitization, to free up physical storage space. And if they weren't, what are the chances Doom's Seed *didn't* make sure those vanished too?"

He was right, of course. Slade looked at the floor and then around at the rest of us. "So what do we do now?"

That was the question, wasn't it? We could still try to approach the police, but it felt almost pointless when the veracity of our most key evidence would immediately be called into question.

Beckett's phone rang. He ignored it for a moment, lost in a pensive daze, before he pulled it from his pocket. My stance stiffened even more as he brought it to his ear. We couldn't take any more bad news.

"Beckett here," he said, and then paused. Whatever the person on the other end said, it brought a shadow across Beckett's face, his brow knitting. He sucked in a breath. "Okay. I'll be right there."

He hung up and turned to us. "I have to go. Hopefully it won't take long."

My eyebrows leapt up. "Go? Right now?"

"It's—it could be important. I can't just ignore it. But I'll be back as soon as I can."

With those words hanging in the air, he hurried out of the room.

CHAPTER 21

Beckett

I rushed across the house as fast as my feet could carry me without looking outright panicked in front of the guards stationed nearby. The door to my father's home office was closed, but he knew I was coming, so I pushed right inside without knocking.

He was the one who'd summoned me, after all.

I stopped just over the threshold with the door thumping shut behind me. Dad looked up at me from his office chair, his hands folded on top of the desk in front of him.

His face still looked weary, and his hair was more rumpled than he'd have allowed it to get in the old days when he was as strict about his appearance as he'd been about everything else. But there was a firmness to his expression that I hadn't seen in months… maybe years. A renewed alertness in his eyes.

He could almost have passed for the man he'd been before I'd betrayed him to my friends in Paradise Bend.

"What's going on?" I asked, drawing myself up a little straighter instinctively under his scrutiny. He wouldn't have called me in for a face-to-face meeting unless it was important.

If he'd found some of his old spirit, could I dare to hope that we didn't need the intervention of the police at all? That Dad and I could rain down hellfire on Doom's Seed together and obliterate him and his men from this city?

"I realized that we should talk about the current conflict between our forces and Doom's Seed," Dad said, adding fuel to my hopes. "I gather you've been taking the lead on dealing with his people's offensives against us."

My throat tightened. "Yes. I've been giving Lana regular reports to pass on to you, but the ongoing attacks have required so much of my attention—I've been doing my best to handle the situation without needing to interrupt your other work."

I hadn't believed he'd have anything useful to offer was more like it, but I wasn't going to admit that to his face.

Dad nodded. "I appreciate that. It sounds as though you've done a capable job of rising to the occasion, as difficult as it's been. But you've done enough."

My spirits leapt for just an instant before he spoke his next words. "It's time to back down."

Any elation I'd felt snuffed out. I stared at him, my jaw going slack. I had to gather myself before I could speak. "What are you talking about?"

"We're going to cut our losses and pull out of the city," Dad said, coolly and steadily. "Let him have our territory there if he wants it so much. We don't need the handful of businesses we've established there—they're just a drop in the bucket of our holdings. It's not worth continuing the conflict."

My stomach knotted. "Are you kidding me? You want to just lay down and let him steal from us? How's that going to look to the rest of the Devil's Dozen?"

Dad fixed me with an unexpectedly steely glare. "If you're going to really become the Storm one day and stand at the table as their equal, you need to know not every battle is worth fighting."

Was *he* seriously claiming some kind of higher wisdom on that subject? The man who just seven years ago had poured so many resources into a pointless takeover that'd stretched our manpower and resources thin—that we'd only emerged from mostly unscathed because *I'd* stepped in and forced an end to the war?

"I do know that," I said, unable to stop an edge from creeping into my voice. "I also know that ceding established ground to another power is one of the first things you told me we never do. It'll only invite more attacks from other quarters. Maybe we can afford to lose our properties in the city, but how much else are we going to lose next? This house is less than an hour away from the downtown core!"

"And there's no reason for Doom's Seed to be interested in our family home. You may have taken on a lot of responsibility in recent years, but you're not the head of the family yet. I call the shots. And I say that it's become clear that our attempts at holding our local business properties are coming at too high a cost."

I held back a snort of derision. Now of all times he'd decided to start thinking about practicalities, after years of barely paying attention to our profit sheets? The urge to bring up all the investments we'd recently made in the city itched at the base of my throat, but another, chilling thought shot through me before I could speak.

Yes, why *was* he suddenly interested in getting involved?

I narrowed my eyes at him. "Did Doom's Seed contact you—say something to you that made you come to this decision?" We hadn't lost any more people in the latest attack on us since last night, almost twenty-four hours ago. It seemed odd that Dad would be spurred into motion now by that or anything else I knew about.

Dad's mouth flattened. "I can make my own evaluations of our dealings. It's not your place to question me."

"I think it is," I shot back. "I've been the one in charge for the last four years, in all but name. I've been the one handling the day-to-day business and most of the big transactions as well. I've been on the front lines of this battle for weeks, and I have no idea how much you even know what's been going on. So I think I have a right to ask for answers. Did he talk to you or not?"

Dad stood up, slamming his hand against the desktop as he did. "You'll listen to me," he snapped, a hint of a tremor creeping into his words. "I practically lost you once. I'm not letting it happen again."

A stillness swept over me, my chest constricting even more than before. "He did talk to you, didn't he? He threatened *me*? You can't listen to him, Dad. I can look after myself. We have to—"

"We don't have to do anything," Dad cut in. "We're ending this now, with no more bloodshed on either side."

"It's not really you making that call if you're only doing it because he threatened you."

Dad's mouth twisted. "He has the power here. I know how many men we've lost. If he goes ahead and comes right at the home I've worked so hard to build, at you…"

His voice faltered, and his shoulders sagged.

My heart lurched. I stepped toward him. "He called you up and told you that if you didn't back down, he'd attack us right in our home? Kill me? That fucking asshole—"

"It doesn't matter," Dad muttered, all but confirming what I'd said. "I'm not risking it. I took too many gambles in the past, and they could have gone even more badly than they did… I'm not testing my luck again."

Anger flared up inside me. "No. I can't believe you're letting him bully you after everything— This is *my* legacy you're trying to throw away now. Everything I've been working for, everything I've built. It's not just yours anymore. You don't get to decide all of a sudden that you're going to protect me and ruin everything that I've made mine."

And how dare that smug bastard Doom's Seed go behind my back and make his brutal threats to a man he obviously realized no longer had as much backbone as I did.

But Doom's Seed wasn't here for me to aim my anger at, and my father was. Even now, Dad was setting his jaw, ready to fight with me when he should have been fighting our enemy.

"I'm doing this to protect our empire," he insisted.

"Bullshit. When was the last time you even attended one of the Devil's Dozen meetings? They can all smell blood in the water, and I've been able to hold it together—by doing things my way. By showing a strong front. You let this slide, and everything we own is going to fall down like dominos."

Dad shook his head. "I've had enough failures without losing my home and my son too. My decision is final."

"Please, Dad," I said, my voice breaking. "Really think about this. Listen to me."

"I've already done all the thinking I need to."

I dragged in a breath, an ache coiling in my gut. There was no getting through to him, was there? I'd already known that—it was why I hadn't gone to him for advice about the situation in the first place.

The man who'd been the Storm, who'd raised me to follow in his footsteps, had stumbled right off the path he'd always taught me to follow, and there was no way I could yank him back onto it when he'd let his spirit be crushed.

And maybe it was partly my fault that he'd become so diminished, but I couldn't see how it would have been better if I hadn't prevented the full catastrophe that Paradise Bend could have been. So really, he'd destroyed himself.

It was time I stopped blaming myself for that and put the responsibility where it belonged.

He'd had the chance to build our empire, and I wouldn't give him another opportunity to tear it down.

I squared my shoulders. "I'm not giving in, Dad. I've been taking your role as the Storm for years now. I've formed alliances and taken care of all the good, bad, and dirty business while you stayed holed up in here like a recluse. This final decision is mine, not yours. And I'm not giving up."

Dad glared at me, a look that might have shaken my nerves when I'd been a teenager. But I wasn't a kid anymore. I could hold my own now.

His jaw worked, but he could obviously tell I wasn't going to back down. A sigh escaped him.

"You won't get very far if you try to continue the crusade. I've told our local people not to participate any more in the conflict, no matter what you say. You can't take on Doom's Seed alone."

Shit. I hadn't believed he'd go that far. He'd underestimated our people—at this point, some of them would follow me no matter what he said—but others were still more loyal to him than to me. He was leaving me with even less manpower than I'd had after Doom's Seed's attacks.

"Don't do this," I said. "It's a mistake—just as big a mistake as trying to take Paradise Bend was."

Rage flashed across Dad's face. I'd poked an even sorer spot than I'd realized.

"I suppose we'll see who's right in the end, won't we?" he growled.

I'd gotten my stubbornness from him. He assumed I'd have to give in if I didn't have the resources to continue.

And maybe some part of him really did believe he was doing it to save me.

It was no good arguing with him anymore. "I suppose we will," I retorted, spinning on my heel, and stalked out of the room.

As I strode down the hall, my thoughts whirled in my head. I couldn't let Doom's Seed win. I might as well hand over our entire empire to the rest of the Devil's Dozen and whoever they'd appoint as the Storm in my place once they'd picked over the pieces. But how the fuck was I going to stop him when I'd already been struggling with the resources I had?

I couldn't even hope that going to the police would put an end to the conflict, not when Doom's Seed had undermined our evidence so thoroughly. Even if they took a look at what we did have, I couldn't imagine it'd be sooner than months from now when they might finally dig up enough to even arrest a few of his people.

I was on my own.

That thought stopped me in my tracks. I paused, thinking back over the argument with my dad—and the history at the center of the tension between us.

Seven years ago, I'd run to Paradise Bend when the ruling gangs there were in trouble so that I could help them turn the tide—at my own father's expense. Those gangs had survived because of my help and grown more powerful in the years since. They might not compete on a global scale like the Devil's Dozen members, but a local territory conflict? They were more than equipped for that.

And if I'd ever needed my friends to return the favor I'd done for them all those years ago, now was definitely the time.

CHAPTER 22

Madelyn

I couldn't help feeling a little nervous as the Vigil guys and I ventured out into the yard behind Beckett's mansion, where dozens of strangers were milling around.

I knew Beckett had plenty of criminal ties from high-level, white-collar types like himself all the way down to minor gangs. But the two crews he'd told us he'd called in were both powerful and yet not at all like him—the two gangs who jointly ruled an entire county called Paradise Bend, which Beckett had told me he'd helped save in defiance of his father years ago.

He'd spent a lot of time with the leaders of these gangs. He considered them his closest friends, and they were clearly ready to do anything for him, given that they'd shown up so quickly and with so many of their people for support. But I couldn't help wondering what they'd make of me and the Vigil guys with our limited experience with the criminal life.

Every man who prowled across the lawn past us looked hardened and dangerous. Several gazes slid over us with expressions that varied from puzzled to incredulous. I hugged myself, fighting the urge to duck back inside.

These were our allies, the people who'd stand with us against Doom's Seed. I couldn't let appearances scare me off now, not when we were hoping to end this war today.

Slade clicked the cinnamon candy he'd popped into his mouth against his teeth. "Whoa. Now this is an army."

Logan frowned. "We just need a target to point them at."

Beckett emerged from the crowd with five figures striding along behind him. He flashed his brilliant smile at us, and a little of the tension inside me melted.

He trusted these people—cared about these people—and *I* trusted his judgment. They might look frighteningly cold and vicious, but I'd seen Beckett bring out his savage side when he needed to too. I knew it didn't stop him or them from having a solid moral compass, one I might agree with a lot more often than not.

"I'd like you to meet my good friends, the leaders of the Claws and the Nobles from Paradise Bend," Beckett said with his smile still in place, and motioned the others to gather around him. "This is Mercy, who keeps the Claws in hand all by herself."

The woman he'd motioned to let out a husky chuckle with a swish of her dark brown ponytail. She was about the same height as me, but her body was sinewy with muscle, and she gave off a similar air of total confidence to what I'd always admired in Beckett.

"I do get a little help here and there," she said with apparent amusement, and dipped her head to us in acknowledgment. "Glad to meet you, but I wish it wasn't because one of these Devil's Dozen pricks is threatening Beckett."

Well, I could agree with that sentiment. I found myself smiling back at her.

Beckett motioned to the four guys next. "This bunch wrangles the Nobles. Wylder is the main man in charge, Kaige helps him lay down the law, Gideon covers the tech side, and Rowan can negotiate anyone under a table."

The affection in his voice was unmistakable. I looked over the four men—all of them tough and assured, but otherwise very different.

Kaige was the largest, a little bigger and broader even than Logan with a sheen of dark hair on his scalp and a twinkle in his eyes that suggested he wasn't actually that scary as long as you didn't piss him off. Wylder was almost as tall but not quite as brawny, looking slick in his collared shirt and dark jeans but with fiery auburn hair that I had a feeling from his fierce expression matched his temperament.

The tech expert, Gideon, was slim though toned, almost delicate-looking, but he offset that impression with the bold blue of his dyed hair and his sharply penetrating gaze. And Rowan—I never would have guessed he was part of a street gang with his business casual button-up and slacks, his blond hair combed neatly back. But at Mercy's mention of the threat to Beckett, his face had momentarily darkened with a hint of brutal protectiveness.

"We're here to take this asshole down," Wylder said without a trace of doubt. "Whatever it takes."

"Yep." Kaige cracked his knuckles—and then cracked a grin as well. "And then maybe we can get to know Beckett's new friends with a whole lot less explosions and gunfire going around. We know how to have fun—the not-so-bloody kind—too."

His gaze veered to Slade's lower leg, where the other guy had propped it at an angle that revealed a sliver of his prosthetic above his typical neon sneakers. "Looks like you've already been through a war or two."

"Oh, this?" Slade drawled. "Crazy story, actually. My grandma went on this insane rampage when I was a kid—"

"He was born like that," I cut him off, hitting him in the arm. "And he's fine, before anyone asks."

Slade clucked his tongue at me, but his eyes glittered with silent laughter. "You take the fun out of everything, Piccolina."

"I'm just trying to keep us on topic," I told him with an affectionate bump of my elbow. "We do have an actual war to fight, as soon as possible."

Dexter nodded, his gaze pensive as he took in our new allies, flitting from one to the next without holding eye contact for more than an instant. "We have the manpower now—how are we going to use it to stop Doom's Seed? So far we haven't managed to do much more than fend off and avoid his attacks."

Beckett's smile vanished, his mouth settling into a hard line. "We've been discussing that… and I think it's time to go straight to the source. We've tried to work around Doom's Seed's offensives while searching for evidence for long enough. We go at him in one big move and rip the evidence we need right from him."

"What exactly does that mean?" Logan asked.

Beckett folded his arms over his chest. "First, we need to identify his main base of operations in this state. That's where the key materials will be. And between my tech guys, Gideon's genius, and your skills, I'm hoping it won't take long at all tp track down that location. If you're up for a little collaboration."

Logan glanced at Gideon, and one corner of his lips curved upward in a crooked smirk. "I think I can handle that. Let's get down to work."

I hadn't realized how quickly the techies could work once they combined their skills. In the mid-afternoon, Logan and Gideon called us into Beckett's rooms to go over their findings. The room was big enough that even with my four guys, Mercy and her four, and me all clustered around the sitting area, it didn't feel crowded.

Gideon brought up a map on his tablet. "Here we are, and here's the building we've determined that Doom's Seed is running the majority of his local operations out of." He pointed to a pin marking a spot quite a distance away in a different city.

The same city where Yvonne had taken me when she'd kidnapped me, I recognized.

"It's not the condo Logan's mom brought me to, is it?" I said, startled. I hadn't noticed much activity while I was there, but then, I had been shut in a closet for most of that time.

Logan shook his head. "No, it's at the other end of the city, but the presence of the condo helped us narrow things down." He smiled tightly. "Her kidnapping attempt worked against Doom's Seed in more ways than one."

"We've found the place," Dexter said. "But if that location is important to Doom's Seed, he'll have a lot of his people guarding it, won't he? And they'll have the advantage of being on familiar ground. We can't just lay siege there in the middle of the city for days on end."

My mind leapt to the memory of how we'd tackled the enemy forces when they'd had Beckett's people under siege. "We create some kind of distraction nearby to draw as many of them away as possible. He doesn't know we've located his main base, and we've never gone directly after him unprovoked before. He might not even realize it has anything to do with us."

"Especially since there's new blood in the mix." Wylder grinned and rubbed his hands together. "His people aren't familiar with ours, and we've got the manpower to keep them busy for a while. You five have a better idea what you're looking for. I say we divide and conquer."

Mercy's eyes lit up in anticipation. "Perfect. I'll take the Claws to one part of the city, you take the Nobles to another, and Beckett can bring his people to the base once it's less guarded."

Gideon motioned to the tablet. "We also identified a few major businesses Doom's Seed is running in the same city. Those would make ideal targets. We pick two that are far apart and not very close to the base, and that should divide his force."

Beckett inhaled slowly. "All right. We don't want too big a commotion at the base, or Doom's Seed will catch wind of our plan and call his people back. I'll bring a small squad of Storm people who are loyal to me and…"

He looked at me and hesitated. "This is going to be the most dangerous mission we've carried out—riskier than anything you've been a part of before."

I could already see where he was going with this. I narrowed my eyes at him. "Don't you dare suggest that I lounge around here painting my toenails while you and the other guys go charging into danger."

Beckett held up his hands. "I have to try. It'll be easier for me not having to worry about you getting hurt."

I raised my eyebrows. "And you won't be worried if I'm back here with hardly anyone left guarding the house? Doom's Seed already threatened to attack you here too. At least this way you'll know I'm okay—I'll be right there grabbing the proof we need with you. You know I've put up a good fight before."

His mouth tightened, and Mercy rolled her eyes at him. "Come on, Beckett. I thought you knew better than to try to leave a woman out of the action. She's obviously made of strong stuff if she's stuck with you this far."

Beckett's gaze jerked to her, dark with stormy emotion. "She isn't just *a* woman. She's *my* woman." He paused and let out a sigh. "And that means I support her choices even when I don't totally like them." He caught my gaze. "I'm sorry. I had to say it."

I gave him a half-hearted glower. "Just don't say it again. You don't have to like it, but I'm not leaving you guys to do this alone."

"None of us are staying back," Logan said emphatically, for once not joining Beckett on the over-protective side of things. I guessed he'd learned his lesson. He rubbed his mouth, considering the map. "And if we can find my mom while we're there, I can use that to our advantage. With whatever influence I have left with her, I'll gather any information I can."

My pulse stuttered. I hadn't thought about him having to come face to face with Yvonne again. "Do you have any idea where she's been staying?"

His gaze was pained when he met my eyes. "No. As far as we can tell, she hasn't been back to the condo building since you escaped. We haven't been able to trace her movements since then."

She could be anywhere. There was no reason to assume we'd encounter her. But she was deeply entwined with Doom's Seed, and this was his primary center of operations in the area.

We might even have to face off with Doom's Seed himself.

A chill ran through me, but I willed it away. It didn't matter how much danger we were facing. This man had destroyed my family, attacked my mom and my men, and been ready to kill me at the drop of a hat. I wasn't letting him get away with any of that, no matter what I had to do.

"All right. We're agreed, then." Beckett drew himself straighter, looking around at all of us. "I hate that the situation has come to this—I hate that more people may die today. But all of us have been through the wringer with people who think they can control us and claim our territory. It doesn't matter what tactics our enemy has been willing to use or what threats he's made, I know we'll come out on top. All Doom's Seed cares about is his business, but we're fighting for something much more valuable."

His gaze flicked to me, and then around over the others again. "We're fighting for family."

Kaige let out a little whoop of approval, and Slade offered a brief round of applause. Tears pricked behind my eyes at the sentiment.

I couldn't help seeing how we all marched out of the room with an extra pep in our step, buoyed up by Beckett's words.

He'd come into his own as a leader in every possible way, no matter what his dad had to say about it. No matter how much the old Storm disapproved of his son's choices.

I couldn't say for sure that we'd come out of this final battle unscathed, but with Beckett at the helm, our chances couldn't have been better.

CHAPTER 23

Logan

The modest two-story brick building stood stark against the sinking evening sun. I stared up at it through the window of our car from where we were parked down the street. A heavy mix of trepidation and apprehension churned in my stomach.

This was it, our final gambit. If we couldn't find something that would destroy Doom's Seed in his base of operations, then he'd essentially won.

In the driver's seat, Beckett tapped at his phone's screen. "All right," he told the rest of us. "My people dealt with the guards who stayed back after most of the people stationed here took off to tackle the Claws and the Nobles. They haven't seen anyone else in or around the place, although they have a limited view of the interior. We still have to be very careful."

I nodded, touching the pistol tucked into the waistband of my jeans. "I'm ready. We go in now?"

"The faster we get in there, the more time we have before the men my friends diverted return."

Beckett shoved his phone into his pocket and pushed open his door, and the rest of us spilled out after him. Maddie's pale hair swished over her shoulders as she raised her chin defiantly.

A pang of love shot through my chest. She was here standing with us right until the end. She really was an incredible woman.

I had to make sure this asshole could never hurt her or anyone she cared about again.

Dexter strode ahead of us, checking the front door and then hustling around to the back. As we came down the lane beside the building to join him, he returned, frowning.

"He's got some high-tech locks on the doors. I can't open them with my typical tools."

"Let's see." Slade marched down the lane and spun to take in the rear of the building. He let out a chuckle. "They were so focused on the doors, they didn't think about the windows."

He pointed to a large window on the second floor which was standing open to let in the warm spring air. The windows on the first floor were barred, but not those above. And a dumpster stood against the back of the building just close enough that we could use it to get us most of the way there.

I eyeballed it. "I'll boost you all up and then I should be able to reach it on my own. Or you can give me a hand from above."

The others nodded without a word. We all knew there wasn't time for arguing if one of us came up with a solid enough plan. We just needed to get inside.

We scrambled onto the dumpster, me helping Dexter when he wobbled. Not wanting to send Maddie through first, I gave Beckett a leg up. He pushed on the screen, and it popped out with a faint clatter on the floor in the room above. He scrambled inside.

I hefted up Slade and Dexter and finally Maddie, giving her a quick kiss first. She touched my cheek. "I'll be fine."

"I'm going to make sure of that," I told her, and boosted her to where she could grip the window ledge.

Standing with my arms stretched as high as they could go, I couldn't quite touch the ledge by myself. But after bending my knees, I managed to spring high enough to hook my hands over it. Slade and Beckett leaned out to grab my arms, supporting my weight as I clambered farther inside and then backing up to give me room to ease in.

We'd come into a bedroom where a few of Doom's Seed's men must have slept, cots lining the walls with a mess of clothing draped across their frames.

"No sign of anyone so far," Beckett said under his breath. "We all know the drill."

"I'll start downstairs," I said, since it looked like the upstairs might be more living space than work area.

My job was to find a computer, any computer, and gain access so we could steal all the files these people were keeping on it. The others were searching out physical evidence—paper records or anything else that could contribute to a case or give us leverage.

Whether we got the cops involved after all or we forced Doom's Seed to back off on our own, I didn't care. I just wanted this mess over with.

Maddie and Slade followed me down the stairs while Beckett and Dexter split off to check the upstairs rooms. Knowing Slade would have Maddie's back, I let myself hurry ahead of them since I could scan the rooms more quickly for my target. My pistol stayed in my hand, ready in case we encountered anyone.

There was a living room of sorts with a mix of clashing

armchairs, a dining room with a big scratched up table, and a room that appeared to be used for storage with loads of cardboard boxes and crates. Slade and Maddie started digging through the containers there, but I hadn't seen a single computer yet.

At least we also hadn't run into any adversaries either.

I pushed into another room and found a couple of desks, a filing cabinet, a bookcase stacked with odds and ends… and a laptop sitting smack in the middle of one of the desks.

"Bingo," I murmured, and then raised my voice to carry across the hall. "There's an office room here that could have some useful records."

"We'll check it out as soon as we've gone through this crap," Slade called back.

I sat on the edge of the desk with my back to the wall where I could easily keep an eye on the door and popped open the laptop. A window came up asking for a password.

Okay, time to get to work. I set my gun on the desk next to the computer and dove in.

My fingers darted over the keyboard, opening up the functions that would let me bypass the protection. I was about halfway through the sequence when a thump carried from upstairs, followed by a shout.

A shout in a female voice. Not Maddie's, but one I recognized.

It was Mom's.

I froze for an instant with a lurch of my heart, and then I threw myself off the desk, tucking the laptop under my arm.

I hurtled up the stairs, racing as fast as my pulse, and only slowed to get my bearings when I reached the upper hall. Beckett's low, even voice was carrying from a doorway near the end. "I don't want to hurt you. We're here to *stop* anyone else from getting hurt."

A scoffing sound answered him, wordless but with enough of a voice to it that I knew it was my mother. I hurried down the hall.

When I reached the doorway, I stalled in my tracks, my heart stuttering all over again.

The large room was set up like a combination bedroom and study. A queen-sized bed with a sleigh bedframe and matching oak vanity stood at one end. A heavy bookcase full of tomes that looked like they belonged in the university library stood against the wall across from the door. A narrow desk squatted kitty-corner from it.

Mom was poised by the foot of the bed, her hands raised but her mouth twisted into a sneer. Beckett had only come a couple of steps into the room. He was pointing his gun straight at her.

It was impossible to fully describe the barrage of emotions that swept through me at the sight of my mom—in general and in that position. Part of me wanted to run to her protection, even now. Part of me wanted to yell at her that she deserved Beckett's hostility after everything she'd done. Horror and loss and anger and the slightest flicker of hope all whirled inside me.

Beckett's gaze never left her, but he'd obviously noted my arrival. "I won't shoot her as long as she doesn't force the issue, Logan."

From the stone-cold expression on Mom's face, it was possible she would. She might be considering leaping at him and wrestling him for the gun, and I doubted that would have ended well.

But then her gaze slid to me, and a little shiver ran through her. Her lips pulled back from their flat line into a pained frown.

She still cared, at least a little.

I had to use that sliver of concern, not let it win me over. Maybe there could be some kind of reconciliation down the line, but not anytime soon.

Her hands were empty, no sign of weapons protruding from her fitted slacks or silk blouse. If she had anything in her pockets, it couldn't be very large.

I took a gamble, set the laptop on the desk by the door, and approached her with slow, careful steps. Her eyes widened, a hint of moisture shimmering in them.

"Logan," Beckett said in a warning tone, but he didn't move to stop me. I was careful not to step into his line of fire. I didn't trust this woman anywhere near *that* much.

When I was close enough, Mom raised her hand to touch my cheek. I stopped, swallowing thickly as her fingertips grazed my skin.

"My boy," she murmured. "It is good to see you again, even like this."

She didn't want to hurt me. Maybe I was the only person that could be said about other than Doom's Seed.

I had to do this. I had to try. Even if it sent a jab of guilt through my gut in spite of everything.

I turned back toward Beckett, which also happened to angle me so that my hip pocket with my phone was blocked from Mom's view. I tugged it out surreptitiously, just far enough to tap the controls I needed, and tucked it back inside in the space of a few seconds.

"Leave us alone," I said at the same time. "I need to talk to my mom privately, just the two of us."

Beckett hesitated, even though I knew he'd caught my move with the phone and probably guessed what I was doing. "Logan, are you sure—?"

"Yes," I interrupted. "It's fine. There are some things we should keep between family."

His jaw clenched, but then he inclined his head. "All right. I'll keep searching the building." He cut his gaze toward Mom. "You'd better tell me now if there's anyone else I might run into here, because I won't be as careful with my gun around *his* people."

Mom shook her head. "It's just me and the guards who were

outside. I assume you're already aware of them, whatever happened to them."

Beckett narrowed his eyes like he wasn't sure he believed her, and I wasn't sure I did either. But he backed out of the room and shut the door behind him.

Perfect. The more private Mom thought this conversation was, the better.

My fingers itched for the pistol I'd left downstairs, but I didn't think it would have set the mood here very well anyway. I had to act like I had more faith in Mom than I actually did if this maneuver was going to work.

I pulled my gaze back to Mom, backing up half a step to give myself more room to breathe—and to take in any telling gestures. "Mom, you have to realize it's over now. We're coming down on Doom's Seed hard. He's not getting away with any of this."

Mom's shoulders stiffened. "You shouldn't be messing around in—"

"*You* shouldn't have gotten involved in his mess," I shot back. "I still don't get it. How could you have thought that going to a crime lord for an illegally obtained organ was the best thing for me? Do you even know how he got that liver?"

"No," Mom said defiantly. "I have no idea, and I don't care. It saved your life—*he* saved your life—and that matters more than the red tape."

"Someone could have been *murdered* for him to have it. Doesn't that matter to you? I don't understand how you could have not only done that, but also gotten so involved with him that you'd fake your death and leave me and Dad behind to be with him instead."

"I told you on the phone, you don't know what my life was like." She sounded more choked up than angry saying it now, though. Her gaze dropped to the floor and returned to my face. "I've wished I could see you, talk to you, for so long. I hated leaving you behind. But it was the only way I could protect everyone I cared about. If anyone had found out the truth about your operation, it could have ruined your life too."

"Don't pretend you ran away *for* me," I said. "You told me that you weren't happy with Dad. Fine. But hooking up with a vicious mafia boss—seriously?"

"You don't know him. There's so much about him that you don't know."

"I know enough." I folded my arms over my chest. "Have you been helping him now—going out there and arranging for these organs to come in, finding people desperate enough to pay him for them?"

"No!" she insisted. "*He* doesn't even get that involved. He just gives the orders, and his people look for the marks. He's barely a part of it at all."

"He threatened to kill Maddie. He *did* order his people to kill her dad."

Mom grimaces. "That was an unavoidable precaution, or everything would have fallen apart. It's not as if I wanted to see Evan Silver dead, but if it was him or you…"

"And Doom's Seed," I filled in.

She just stared at me, her expression tight but her body trembling just slightly.

I had everything I could have wanted now. Comments confirming that the man who called himself Doom's Seed had illegally supplied my liver, had an ongoing business for arranging transplants, and had orchestrated at least one specific murder, all recorded in my mom's voice on my phone. She had no idea, and prickles of guilt were still nagging at my insides, but I'd done what was necessary.

Now I had to give her a chance to get herself out of this mess before it imploded around her.

I lowered my voice. "It's all going to end now, Mom. We're going to bring justice down on him, and anyone standing with him will fall too. It's time to do the right thing. You probably wouldn't even face any jail time if you agreed to testify against him about the things you've seen."

Mom outright shuddered. "I couldn't do that. I *love* him, Logan. We're in this together, me and him, come hell or high water."

I held her gaze. "Shouldn't you be able to say that about your own son? Isn't it time that you were here for me again? Walk away from this with me, please. You can divorce Dad properly, live life however you want it, in a way that won't put everyone around you under threat."

"Logan…" Her voice broke with emotion.

I pushed my advantage. "I want you in my life. I want to get what we should have had. Do you have any idea how much I missed you all those years?"

Mom blinked hard. She swiped at her eyes and took a step toward me. "I've missed you so much too, sweetheart. When I think about all the time I've lost with you, it kills me. I don't know—"

Her words were cut off by the thump of the bookcase swinging from the wall. I only had an instant to register that the bookcase had been concealing a hidden doorway when a broad-shouldered, graying man in a vibrant peacock-blue suit burst from the opening into the room.

He was holding a pistol pointed straight at me. As I jerked backward, my pulse skittering, he barreled toward me, and it clicked in the back of my startled, panicked mind that this must be Doom's Seed.

"He's your weakness, Yvonne," he growled. "The only one you

have left, and I'm going to eliminate him. Then you'll really be free."

His finger closed around the trigger—and as I wrenched myself to the side, Mom dove in front of him.

"No!" she cried out just as the gun boomed. Her good hand had snatched something from her pocket and plunged it at him, but in the same moment pain tore across my shoulder.

The bullet had gone wide, but not wide enough. Doom's Seed and I stumbled in opposite directions, me toward the bed, him toward the bookcase. The gun slipped from his fingers.

He clapped a hand against his side, where he was bleeding… because of the blood streaked blade my mom was still clutching in her white-knuckled hand.

Mom had stabbed him. Mom had interrupted his shot and attacked the man she said she loved in her attempt to save me.

But as blood coursed down my sleeve from the burning wound that had my left arm sagging, I wasn't sure it'd been enough.

CHAPTER 24

Madelyn

I was just stepping out of the storage room ahead of Slade when a gunshot blared through the building. My nerves jumped with a jolt of panic.

Without a word, both me and Slade took off for the stairs. Thudding footsteps behind us told me that at least one other of my guys was hurtling after us.

Where had the shot come from? Who had been shooting at whom? Had any of my guys been injured?

The frantic thoughts propelled me up the stairs and into the upstairs hall. A thump from a room farther down told me where to go. I dashed toward the doorway with Slade at my heels.

We barged into the room and jerked to a halt. It took me a few seconds to take in the scene in front of me and make any kind of sense of it.

Yvonne was standing almost directly in front of me, a bloody knife clutched in her regular hand, her body braced in a defensive stance. At her left, a man with gray hair and a flashy suit had sagged back against a large bookcase—which was pulled away from the wall to reveal a hidden doorway. He was clutching his side, where blood streaked from a wound on his belly. Yvonne's gaze was fixed on him as if she was worried about what he'd do next.

At her left, Logan was slouched near the room's bed. He leaned against the footboard while his other hand pressed to his shoulder —where *his* blood was coursing down his arm.

I couldn't suppress a yelp of alarm. At the same moment, Beckett burst into the room. He slipped between me and Slade with his pistol raised. His aim swung toward the man in the flashy suit the second he set eyes on him.

"Doom's Seed," he bit out. "Seems like the tables have turned just a little, don't you think?"

This was Doom's Seed. And Yvonne had stabbed him? Who had hurt Logan?

What the hell was going on?

Before my whirling mind could figure it out, Yvonne ducked down. She dropped the knife and snatched something else off the floor—a gun that had fallen. And the pieces clicked together.

Doom's Seed must have shot at Logan, but Yvonne had tried to protect him.

Clearly she wasn't totally turning against her lover, though. She lifted the gun and stepped between him and Beckett, protecting the man she'd just stabbed. Her hands shook, the prosthetic one supporting the one gripping the gun, but her face hardened.

"I'm sorry, my love," she said to the man she was shielding. "I—you came at him so quickly—I had to protect him—"

"Fucking bitch," Doom's Seed muttered, and Yvonne winced. But she didn't waver from her position in front of him.

She motioned at Beckett with the gun, and Beckett backed up one step, his jaw tightening. "You made the right choice with your first response," he said. "Don't screw it up now."

"Leave him alone," she snapped back. "If you try to hurt him, I'll shoot all of you. I don't care what happens to me."

My heart thudded at an anxious pace. I eased toward Logan and, when Yvonne's attention didn't leave Beckett, hurried the rest of the way to my stepbrother. His startled gaze shifted from his mom to me.

"She saved me," he mumbled.

"Not completely. Let me see that."

Bracing himself, he lifted his hand from the wound. I sucked in a breath of dismay. The bullet had only clipped his shoulder, but deeply enough to leave a thick gouge through the muscle. Blood streamed down from it before my eyes.

Logan focused on me more steadily. "I'm okay."

"You *will* be okay once I get the bleeding stopped," I said, putting on my best medical professional voice and tuning out my panic. "It's deep, and it'll leave a scar, but it hasn't hit anything vital."

I groped around for something to bandage the wound and grabbed the two pillows from the head of the bed. Once I'd yanked both of the pillowcases off them, I folded one into a thick pad that I pressed against Logan's shoulder and tied it in place with the other as firmly as I could.

His head bowed toward mine, his mouth almost brushing my cheek. "I got everything we need. It's all good."

I had no idea what he was talking about, but I couldn't focus only on him. Doom's Seed had started chuckling as he pushed himself straighter against the doorframe.

"Do you really think I'm finished now, boy?" he spat at Beckett. "You're going to regret every second you spent challenging me."

"Me challenging *you*?" Beckett said incredulously. "You're the one who's rampaged through my territory and tried to destroy my reputation. I might be young, but I've been raised to become the Storm since the day I was born, and you'd better believe I won't stand back while my empire is threatened."

Doom's Seed snorted. "*Your* empire? I hardly think so, especially after the conversation I had with your father. Now, he's a man who knows what's good for him."

"Then it's a good thing he's not the one really in charge anymore, isn't it?" Beckett's eyes glinted with anger. "Withdraw now and give all your territory in this state over to me, and *maybe* I'll overlook all those transgressions. Otherwise, it'll be your empire in ashes."

"I'll believe it when I see it," the other man said disdainfully. He pointed a thick finger at Beckett from where he was still slumped against the bookcase, his arm steadier than I'd have expected. "You haven't mastered this business yet. You haven't earned the throne. I have all the power here."

Beckett gave a rough laugh, and my pulse hiccupped at the twitch of Yvonne's hands. She still had the gun aimed directly at Beckett's chest, but he didn't show the slightest sign of worry.

"Are you kidding me?" he said. "You haven't been fighting this battle with my dad. You've been fighting it with me, and you know it. *Everybody* knows it. But you've never been man enough to come directly to me to work out shit. You target my friends. My *dad.* That's not strong. It's pathetic."

Doom's Seed glowered at him. "It's a strategy. One you'll need to learn if you haven't already. Until you shed your weaknesses, you'll always be a weak little boy. Now get out of my sight before—"

A figure sprang through the doorway with a shout, gun brandished. I had only an instant to recognize him as one of the

Storm men Beckett had brought along before a bang split my eardrums.

But it wasn't from his gun. Yvonne swayed with the recoil of her shot, her pistol immediately jerking back toward Beckett, and the guy in the doorway crumpled. The top of his head was nothing more than a mash of flesh, blood, and shards of skull.

My stomach lurched. "Don't look," Logan gritted out, as if I could heed the warning now.

I dragged my gaze back to Yvonne, a sharper queasiness welling up inside me.

She wasn't just posturing with the gun. She was totally prepared to use it—and her aim was good.

"Mom," Logan said, his voice still strained, but it was Doom's Seed who answered him.

"Don't go guilting your mother," the older man snarled. "No fucking respect. Aren't you grateful that she arranged for me to save your life?"

Logan stared right back at him. "I'd rather have died than have someone else die in my place who didn't need to."

Yvonne's mouth twisted, and at the same moment, I noticed Slade creeping around the edge of the room. He looked like he was getting into position to lunge at Yvonne, maybe hoping to grab the gun. But he only got halfway there before she pulled out of her momentary distraction and caught the movement too.

"Get back by the door," she snapped at him with a wave of the gun.

Slade froze and slowly eased backward again. Then Yvonne's attention whipped to Dexter. "And you. Whatever you've got behind your back, toss it down the stairs."

Dexter froze where he'd been reaching behind himself. Frowning, he stepped backward and tossed something that clattered down the steps—some kind of weapon, I had to assume.

Doom's Seed pushed himself all the way onto his feet with only a brief grimace. Yvonne's gaze flicked back toward him, but not for long enough for any of us to take advantage. Seeing him mobile, her lips pursed.

Abruptly, she gestured with the gun at all of us. "Out of the room! Every one of you. Out of the goddamn building, as fast as you can go, *now*!"

When we stalled, gaping at her, she stomped her foot on the floor. "Now, or I'm going to start shooting." She glanced at Logan. "I don't feel any need to protect your friends, especially after all the trouble they've created for us."

Every muscle in my body balked at the idea of giving up, but I couldn't see how to get the upper hand.

Logan gripped my arm with a meaningful squeeze. "We'll go," he said. "No need to shoot anyone else."

He caught my gaze, and I remembered abruptly what he'd said about having everything we needed. Had he already dug up files that could end the conflict from Doom's Seed's computer or found some other evidence that would definitively turn the tide?

I had to trust him. He'd been part of the confrontation with his mom from the start—he knew what he was doing.

I nodded and started to walk with him.

Beckett stepped to the side of the door with a pained glance at his fallen employee. "You all go out ahead of me. I'll bring up the rear, just to make sure these two don't try anything stupid."

I smiled tightly at him with a wave of gratitude. Please, let this be enough. Please, let it be over.

Slade and Dexter, who were closest to the door, filed out first. I nudged Logan ahead of me, wanting to get him to safety as quickly as possible since he'd have trouble defending himself with his injury.

Doom's Seed shuffled a little forward. Beckett's gun bobbed

toward him and then back to point at Yvonne. I gripped his shirt for just a second as I moved to pass him, a gesture of thanks and affection.

Just as my foot hit the threshold, Doom's Seed threw himself forward.

I spun around at the scuff of his footsteps and saw the glint of a metal blade in his hand—a blade he was stabbing straight at Beckett. He must have been counting on surprise to reach Beckett before Beckett could react and shoot him.

He wanted to end this conflict too—with one of the men I loved dead at his feet.

And maybe he would have succeeded, but my instincts honed by my Krav Maga classes kicked in. Without thinking, I hurled myself between the two men.

My elbow shot out, catching Doom's Seed in the neck twice as hard with the force of his momentum. He let out a choking sound and stumbled backward but then slashed out with the knife—this time toward me.

I ducked and kicked out, and my gaze snagged on another blade, right within reach. The small, blood-stained one Yvonne had set down on the floor after picking up the gun.

"Stop!" she shrieked as I snatched it up, but Doom's Seed was lunging at us again, blocking any chance of a clear shot. She wouldn't risk hitting him.

I had no such qualms.

He was on top of me, the knife raking over my side as he fumbled for a better blow. One more second, and I was a goner. So I did what I had to do to save my life and possibly Beckett's too.

I couldn't reach his neck at this angle, but I knew from all my medical studies exactly where to plunge that blade into his chest to stop the beating of his heart. I slammed it home with all the strength I had in me.

If this man survived, he'd only hurt more people. Kill more people. I couldn't let that happen. He was a disease, and I was cutting him out of this world.

I shoved the blade in deeper, and Doom's Seed collapsed over me with a gush of blood.

"Maddie!" Beckett cried out, crouching with me, but I could already tell the body slumped over me was vacant of life.

As I squirmed out from under Doom's Seed's heavy corpse with a ragged breath, Yvonne dropped to her knees at his other side.

"No," she said between sobs, groping at his wound as if she could bring him back. "No, no, no."

But Doom's Seed didn't so much as twitch as I staggered to my feet. He was gone.

CHAPTER 25

Madelyn

Slade flopped down at one end of the sofa in Beckett's sitting room with an exaggerated sigh. "Well, I think I've talked to enough cops to last me for the next century or so."

Logan sat next to him, careful of his newly stitched-up shoulder. "No kidding."

"It was necessary," I pointed out, but I couldn't restrain a yawn as I sank down at the far end of the sofa, letting my legs sprawl across Logan's lap. My eyes felt heavy, my head muggy.

It'd been a long couple of days. After figuring out our story and calling the cops to the scene of Doom's Seed's death, we'd all been in and out of questioning since yesterday evening, other than a brief reprieve back here to get a little sleep. Not that any of us had felt all that inclined to relax.

Beckett had managed to stay mostly on the sidelines, presenting himself as a concerned friend. We'd offered up our evidence from across the Vigil's investigation, including Logan's recording of his mom confessing her knowledge of some of Doom's Seed's criminal activities. In her emotional state, Yvonne had ended up admitting more to the cops than probably would have been wise if she'd been thinking clearly.

I glanced over at Logan. "It seems like your mom will be going away for a while."

He shrugged, though I could tell from the tensing of his jaw that he still had complicated feelings about the woman who'd raised him for the first several years of his life. "It's what she deserves. Maybe she'll get herself sorted out while she's in there… or maybe she's a lost cause. Either way, at least the truth is out."

Beckett stopped by the side of the sofa and looked down at us. "Speaking of the truth, did you find out why the cops were after you guys the other day?"

Dexter perched on one of the armchairs as he answered. "Doom's Seed must have had the manager at the Fresh Catch Seafood Market call in a complaint that we'd broken in and stolen something. They were following up on that accusation, wanting to question us."

Beckett's eyebrows rose. "But the police aren't bringing charges?"

Slade snorted. "It was all hearsay. They didn't have any proof. We said we snooped around a bit while the market was open to explain the pics Dex had of the shipping containers, but there's nothing illegal about walking into a back room without even touching anything."

"And they were too excited about getting to take a huge criminal kingpin down to be very worried about a little petty larceny anyway," I added wryly, and tipped my head back against the arm of the sofa. "We are going to have to testify in court once the cases against Logan's mom and some of Doom's Seed's top dogs go to trial."

Slade dismissed my remark with a wave of his hand. "Not for a while. We'll be totally recovered by then and ready for it. Especially now that this crazy case is off our plates."

Beckett focused on me. "You're not in any trouble over stabbing Doom's Seed, are you?"

I shook my head. "It was clear self-defense. I have the bruises and scratches to show he attacked me, and he'd already shot Logan —Yvonne confirmed that even if they hadn't believed us. I guess the scene must have shown a pretty obvious struggle too."

"Well, a whole lot of Doom's Seed's empire is about to crash and burn, with the organ transplant trade going first," Beckett said. "From what I hear, some of his people that the cops rounded up are already cutting deals, turning over evidence and testimony that'll implicate even more people and shady businesses."

"Good," I muttered. That'd always been the most important goal to me—knowing that I'd finished what Dad had started and brought down the business that'd been exploiting so many people. Hopefully he could rest easier now, wherever his soul had departed to.

Logan ran his hand over my calf and started to massage my foot. I wanted to melt into his touch, but too many questions were still whirling through my mind.

I twisted at the waist to get a steadier look at Beckett. "Now that he's gone… who will the next Doom's Seed be? Do we have to worry about them picking up the pieces and starting over?"

"Or trying to get revenge for his death?" Dexter piped up.

Beckett rubbed his chin, his expression turning pensive. "I'm honestly not sure who'll step up. It's possible he had children, at least one of whom would have been raised to take over from him when necessary like my dad raised me. But even if it's someone with a personal stake, with the police so involved it'd be madness to try to attack any of you again. And I've shown that the Storm isn't anyone to be screwed over."

"What if he didn't have kids?" Logan asked.

"Then the Devil's Dozen will confer about who to offer the position to. It could be we'll decide an associate of his could fill his shoes the best. Or we might invite someone totally new to take his spot at the table. Either way, I'll have some say on the subject since I'm officially taking over as the Storm now. No matter how my dad feels about it."

His voice hardened a bit with that last sentence. I shot him a reassuring smile. "I know you'll be amazing at it."

He'd make sure to pick someone who wouldn't try to resurrect the worst parts of Doom's Seed's empire. Beckett had been with me every step of the way, and he'd seen the conflict through to the end, no matter how dangerous it'd gotten for his own family legacy.

A wave of emotion washed over me, and tears welled up in my eyes. "It's finally over," I said, swiping at them. "We can get back to our regular lives without this hanging over us." The cops had already escorted Mom, Holand, and Summer back to their homes —well, in Mom and Holand's case, to a more local hotel while they sorted out the insurance from the house and decided whether to rebuild or buy something new.

We were all going to get to rebuild now, in our own various ways. And the five of us could build something *together*, enjoying the trust and loyalty we'd found with each other.

I reached out to squeeze Logan's forearm and let my gaze travel over all four of my guys. "I'm so happy to be here with you. I can't wait to see how good life can be once we can focus on simply living it."

"Cheers to that," Slade said with a grin, and my guys closed in around me in a joint embrace.

CHAPTER 26

One year later

Madelyn

Somehow Summer always managed to have perfect timing. I was just walking into the house when my phone pinged with an incoming text.

Inhaling the lingering floral scent from the wax burner Mom had given me as a housewarming gift, I pulled my phone out of my purse.

You've got to be home by now, Summer had written. *How did the presentation go? I need all the deets!*

I grinned and started tapping my thumbs as I kicked off the low-heeled pumps I'd worn for this semi-formal occasion. *The presentation went amazing. I still can't believe I got the opportunity at all! I'll have to thank Prof. Fernandez again… especially because I may have scored the most awesome summer internship in existence!*

OMG, what? Summer wrote back an instant later. *Don't leave your bestie hanging.*

My grin only grew as I answered. *Jamie Harvey from Harvey Labs attended the talk—that's the medical research facility I was telling you about that just won an international award for innovation. Afterward, he came up to me, told me he was impressed by my talk, and gave me his card telling me he'd love to have me interning at the lab this summer.*

I was still high from that accomplishment. The thought of all the things I might learn and get to be a part of in just a couple of months had me giddy.

That's fantastic! We need to go out and celebrate ASAP. I have some good news too, but not as big as yours. My date last night with the new guy was pretty spectacular.

My eyebrows shot up. *Don't tell me you've actually found someone you want to go on a second date with. That's front-page news!*

Summer sent a laughing and a tongue-sticking-out emoji in response, and I laughed to myself.

I've got to get back to work—break's just about over—but I'll call you tonight and fill you in, she wrote back.

I tucked my phone away and set my shoes on the mat in the front hall next to Dexter's loafers and Slade's spare pair of sneakers—neon yellow, naturally. Looking at them together, breathing in the scent I was just starting to associate with home, a softer smile crossed my face.

Just having this place, which we'd only moved into a couple of months ago, was pretty amazing. We'd only been able to afford the five-bedroom because of Beckett's significant financial contribution, but he'd insisted on the investment, saying it was a drop in the bucket for him.

Living with all four of my guys was fantastic. There was nothing better than coming out of my bedroom in the morning and getting to steal a good morning kiss—or a few—within seconds. Sometimes before I even left the bedroom.

The clinking of pots and utensils drew me into the kitchen: modest-sized but decked out with high-end appliances that Dexter had practically swooned over. A spicy, savory scent tickled my nose before I'd even reached the doorway, setting my mouth watering.

I found my culinarily-inclined boyfriend standing by the stove, stirring something in a sauté pan while two other pots bubbled merrily and something sizzled faintly from within the oven.

"Looks like you've been busy," I said, walking over and judging his response before reaching out for physical contact. When he leaned a little toward me in welcome, I slipped my arm around his waist and pecked him on the cheek.

Dexter beamed at me. "I figured a feast was in order. You had that big presentation—and the internship offer to celebrate too—and Beckett's getting back from his trip to hash out that huge business deal."

"We could have just ordered in," I teased him, knowing exactly what response I'd get.

He let out a huff of mock offense and adjusted the heat dial for one of the burners. "You're never getting a meal as custom-tailored to everyone's tastes with takeout. And I needed the mental break from my final essay anyway."

I laughed lightly and gave him an affectionate squeeze before letting him go again. "I'm sure we can find other ways to distract you if the cooking isn't enough."

He shot me a sly glance before returning to his work, and I found myself remembering my first rehearsal of my presentation with the guys looking on. Slade had acted out the advice "picture the audience naked" to a literal extreme… with interesting results that had definitely loosened me up.

A blush tingled across my cheeks. I glanced across the counter and noticed a few tomatoes sitting on the cutting board. "Do you need these cut up? I can pitch in."

Dexter looked between me and the tomatoes hesitantly, likely weighing the risks of me cutting them incorrectly by his standards, before he nodded and passed me a knife. I positioned the tomato in front of me on the board and sliced it down the middle.

"Have you heard from Beckett today?" I asked. "I texted him about the internship but haven't gotten a reply."

"He texted about an hour ago saying he'd just gotten in at the airport. I'm sure he'd have let you know too, but he was probably worried he'd interrupt your presentation. Maybe he's waiting to congratulate you in person." Dexter's gaze tracked my motions with the knife, and his mouth twitched. "Here, let me show you a more effective approach."

I suppressed a giggle as he came behind me and placed a hand over each of mine. He really liked having all the control in the kitchen, and I wouldn't critique him for it. Instead, I leaned back into his warmth as he guided my hand through the motions of cutting the tomatoes in a completely different way that he considered more effective. Which, knowing how conscientious he was, was probably true.

When we were finished, he dipped his head to press a scorching kiss to the nape of my neck. Then he nudged me toward the two stools at the kitchen's small island. "That's enough help after all the work you did today. You can sit and watch."

I gave him a mock salute and hopped onto one of the stools. I was just settling onto it when a key clicked in the front door's lock.

"It's me," Logan called out, a faint note of weariness in his voice that I only heard on days like today.

"We're in the kitchen," I said.

Moments later, my stepbrother strode through the doorway and made a beeline straight for me. He wrapped his brawny arms around me and hugged me tight, his head dipped close to mine.

I hugged him back, my throat constricting. "How was it?"

Logan sighed and pulled back just enough to rest his forehead against mine. "She's doing well, all things considered. We managed not to get into any arguments this time."

He'd made a habit of visiting his mom in prison every other week, and it seemed to help him cope with the disastrous turn their relationship had taken. He hadn't forgiven her for the crimes she'd been a part of or for abandoning him, but his residual anger had simmered down, so now he was mostly just sad. I knew from our talks that he no longer felt at all guilty about his role in putting her in jail.

It's where she belongs, he'd told me a few months ago. *And I can tell she's accepted that too. I guess that's some kind of progress.*

Logan's lips sought out mine, and I returned the kiss eagerly, our mouths melding together for the better part of a minute. When he drew back, I touched his cheek.

"Are you still meeting your dad for lunch tomorrow?" I asked.

He nodded, and his face lightened just a little bit. Joy sparked in my chest at the sight.

He'd become so much more relaxed about hanging out with Holand since the air had been cleared between them—and his dad hadn't shunned him the way he'd feared. We'd even gone to a larger family gathering for Easter a few weekends ago, and it'd warmed my heart to see Logan ambling around chatting up all the relatives he'd spent most of the past few years avoiding.

I'd been able to tell from Holand's expression that he was even more pleased than I was.

Logan moved to the stove, snatching up a fork and spearing a mushroom out of the pan. He popped it into his mouth despite Dexter's disgruntled sound and then fanned his mouth to cool it off.

Dexter elbowed him. "What did you expect? I'm in the middle of cooking it—of course it's hot."

Logan smirked. "Delicious, though."

Dexter waved him off. "Why don't you make yourself useful and set the table?"

"I can do that."

I joined Logan in getting out the plates and glasses. We were just setting them out on the maple dining room table when Beckett appeared in the doorway.

"You're back! I didn't hear you come in." I hustled over to give him a hug and then a lingering kiss. I hadn't seen him in a few days—and his presence was always less consistent than my other men's. He still spent half his nights either at the Storm mansion or roving around to various other properties they owned looking after his empire.

"Glad to be here," Beckett said, nuzzling my hair. "Always my favorite place."

"You said the meeting went well?" Logan asked. "Exactly how well?"

Delight crinkled the corners of Beckett's eyes. "The investors actually agreed to contribute *more* funding than I'd asked for. Which means we can add an extra wing to the building that I didn't think would even be possible."

"I'm not surprised," I told him. "You're very persuasive."

He chuckled and gave me another kiss. "And I hear you're on your way to earning your Nobel prize with this research internship."

I snorted. "I've got a lot more work to do before *that*. But I can't wait to get started."

Logan's phone pinged with an incoming text. He glanced at it. "Slade just got out of class. He should be here in ten minutes."

Dexter clapped his hands together. "Perfect timing. Let's get everything on the table."

He scooped the various delicacies out onto serving plates, which the rest of us carried into the dining room. Beckett pulled out two bottles of wine from the small collection he was building and got the chef to decide which was the better pairing. He was just filling the last of our glasses when Slade strode in.

"All this for me?" he joked, and slung his arm around my shoulders to pull me into a quick but ardent kiss. "Missed you, Piccolina."

"You just saw me this morning," I reminded him with a laugh.

"Any time without you is too long. But it looks like we'd better dig into this feast."

We all took our seats and grabbed portions from each dish in the spread. There was chicken in a creamy sauce, rice mixed with various spices that turned it a vibrant shade of yellow, and three different types of vegetables with varied spicing.

I took one bite of the chicken and let out a moan at the sweet but tangy flavor. "You've outdone yourself again, Dex. I think this is my favorite yet."

He grinned. "I plan to keep topping myself as many times as I can."

"So…" Slade said, with a playful note in his voice that had us all turning toward him. "I was chatting with a couple of guys in one of my classes today and heard something interesting."

Now he had our undivided attention. "What's that?" I demanded before popping another bite of the incredible chicken into my mouth.

His dark eyes glinted with anticipation. "It seems like a couple of thugs have been trying to intimidate the one guy's parents at the art gallery they own. Trying to extort them with threats. And the cops have been totally useless at tracking the pricks down to make sure they don't follow through on those threats."

The hum of anticipation leapt from him to flow through all of us around the table. I sat up a little straighter, and Logan leaned forward. "I don't suppose they'd be happy to get a little outside help?"

Slade waggled his fork. "From what I gathered, they'd like nothing more."

Dexter's gaze had already gone distant as he started working through logistics in his head. "I'm sure we'd be able to tackle a situation like that."

Beckett inclined his head. "And you've always got extra manpower from me if you need it."

The guys all glanced my way. I could have laughed at the question on their faces, as if they thought *I* was ever going to back down from the chance to deal out a little more justice in the world when the opportunity fell into our laps.

We were pretty darn great at being the Vigilante Kings—and Queen—and it would have been an awful shame if we'd totally retired.

I smiled back at all of them, my nerves already buzzing. "It sounds like a perfect new case for the Vigil to tackle. Let's finish with dinner and dive right in."

ABOUT THE AUTHORS

Eva Chance is a pen name for contemporary romance written by Amazon top 100 bestselling author Eva Chase. If you love gritty romance, dominant men, and fierce women who never have to choose, look no further.

Eva lives in Canada with her family. She loves stories both swoony and supernatural, and strong women and the men who appreciate them.

Connect with Eva online:
www.evachase.com
eva@evachase.com

Harlow King is a long-time fan of all things dark, edgy, and steamy. She can't wait to share her contemporary reverse harem stories.

www.ingramcontent.com/pod-product-compliance
Lightning Source LLC
Chambersburg PA
CBHW020720310726
48979CB00004B/1003
* 9 7 8 1 9 9 8 7 5 2 6 0 7 *